The Mystics

The Mystics

Leyna Barill

Marble, NC USA
2015

Copyright © 2015 Word Branch Publishing

All rights reserved. This book or any portion thereof may not be reproduced or used in any manner whatsoever without the express written permission of the publisher except for the use of brief quotations in a book review.

This is a work of fiction. Names, characters, businesses, places, events and incidents are either the products of the author's imagination or used in a fictitious manner. Any resemblance to actual persons, living or dead, or actual events is purely coincidental.

First Edition 2015
Printed in the USA

Cover illustration © 2015 Julian Norwood

Permission can be obtained for re-use of portions of material by writing to the address below. Some permission requests can be granted free of charge, others carry a fee.

Word Branch Publishing
PO Box 41
Marble, NC 28905

http://wordbranch.com
sales@wordbranch.com

 Library of Congress Control Number: On file

ISBN-13: 978-0692420874
ISBN-10: 0692420878

Author's Note

This particular story is my first. I have many others and intend to keep writing for as long as I have ideas. Each story deals with massive adventure, fantasy, fun, family, and a little romance. I enjoy including plenty of animal friends in each story as they are a huge part of my life and important to our future here on this planet. Being an environmentalist and a spiritual person, nature is also a huge factor in each story. Humans have grown apart from nature and I only seek to try and reunite us in some small way. I am a huge supporter of women and that is the main reason why each of my main characters will always be a young woman. Boys are important too, don't worry, but often I find that, in today's world, there are not enough female heroes. I am also a feminist and an 'equalist', which means I do not see men and women as being different from one another so I don't treat them differently either.

For each of my stories I have what I call a patron song, a piece of music that I feel completely embodies the story as a whole. Music is the main source for a lot of my inspiration so it is a huge factor in how I write and the creation of my stories. I am not a music writer or a composer so none of the songs I choose are mine; however, they're the work of artists from every genre. They can range from rock, to classical, to folk depending on the mood of the story and the song. For this story, my debut series, I have chosen the song Human by Christina Perri because it adequately portrays the whole story and the struggle that Rosey will face in this series. I hope you enjoy this first installment in the Mystics series and remember the power of the elements is within you always!

Table of Contents

Chapter One: Legend 1
Chapter Two: Truth 13
Chapter Three: To the Well 38
Chapter Four: The New World 50
Chapter Five: The NCD 72
Chapter Six: The Protector and the Protected 86
Chapter Seven: The War 100
Chapter Eight: The Keepers 136
Chapter Nine: Esperanza 171
Chapter Ten: The Story Continues 199
Chapter Eleven: The Silver Goddess Calls 232
Chapter Twelve: The Crystal Caverns 265
Chapter Thirteen: In the Past and the Future 286
Chapter Fourteen: Walking Through the Caves 305
Chapter Fifteen: Doubts and Nagging Feelings 337
Chapter Sixteen: The First Element 362
Chapter Seventeen: The Crystal 385
Chapter Eighteen: The Silent Marine 410
Chapter Nineteen: Dreams on the Water 434
Chapter Twenty: Interrogation 461
and Inner Knowing 461
Chapter Twenty-One: Captain Marine 480
Chapter Twenty-Two: Lie of the Sea 490

Chapter Twenty-Three: Behind the 508
Fog and Mist 508
Chapter Twenty-Four: Attack..527
Chapter Twenty-Five: The Water Element 554
Chapter Twenty-Six: Water's Fury..571
Chapter Twenty-Eight: The Eye of the Enemy..584
Chapter Twenty-Eight: Explanations and Preparations 597
Chapter Twenty-Nine: We Go One 624
Epilogue...640

Chapter One: Legend

She blinked. Her eyes gleamed with the reflections of early morning light. Soft dew covered her large body, making her muscles twitch as if chasing away flies. She breathed deeply, taking in every scent. She stood stock still. Nothing moved except the rhythmic rise and fall of her chest. Reaching out with her senses she traced the vibrations in the ground from the deer that wondered the woods, eating the plentitude of spring growth, all the way across the world to the townsfolk in Neran, readying for winter. A slight variation near Neran's eastern border touched her hooves and she froze, mentally examining the disturbance. With a tremendous amount of effort she pulled out of her trance and sank back into her own body. She sighed wearily. The evil was spreading, like a disease it was eating them from the inside out. Quite suddenly she was aware of her surroundings and the slight accumulation of dew that had settled on her body. She had never been a fan of feeling wet and the drops did nothing but tickle her skin like soft kisses. She shook herself, sending the tiny drops of water flying in all directions. She paused to allow herself to relax into a long stretch before gazing at the clear sky above.

In the East the sun finished rising and cast its full golden splendor over the Valley. Valley Elathos looked beautiful during spring. Of course, any place could be made beautiful when spring decided to grace its surface. She smiled. Gracefully she made her way to a small spring and took a long drink, enjoying the flavor of rich valley water. Her eyes slid over her reflection, assessing the creature she saw. In essence she resembled a Percheron horse though she was no specific breed. Her body was the color of shimmering silver with a unique dappled patterning that was splashed randomly across her shoulders and hindquarters. Her long tail, strewn with golden light, gently dragged along the ground when she walked. Perfectly elliptical hooves and a crystalline horn on her forehead shone with brilliance. She was well over twenty six hands high and could bring the mightiest of warriors to their knees. For all her wonder, the most fabulous appendages that graced her body were her humongous wings. Each one stretched well over fifteen feet long, giving her a thirty foot wing span. The wings were covered in immaculate feathers that were silver with golden celestial designs painted across their surface in delicate patterns. Indeed she was celestial, a being as old as the very planet she walked on. A being that held the planet's power in her heart and could use it with an iron will. She was a sight to behold, and could make the mightiest of beings crumble at her feet. Despite her immense power, she was also the gentlest of all that lived. Those who showed her respect and love would have no fear of her, only a growing admiration. She was truly a spectacular creature and one of a kind, for no other like her existed. She was…unique.

Falling into a steady trot, Adina carried herself swiftly and efficiently on a path that she had taken all too many times through the densely packed forest of the beautiful Valley. Usually the valley was simply known as the Settled Valley. It was a place that was pretty normal and held nothing out of the ordinary, nothing but familiar sights and peaceful sounds. It was a fantastic home for the small wildlife that lived there and Adina had chosen it as her own safe haven for as long as she could remember. Being an Immortal, her life-span stretched far longer than any creature on her world and the valley had always been her home. Perhaps it's age was the reason why she liked it so much? As she rounded a bend she kicked up her hooves in pleasure, soaking up the warm rays of the sun peeking through the trees overhead. Memory washed over her as she went. She knew her path so well that she welcomed the distraction.

About thirty years ago, her safe and peaceful valley had taken on quite an unusual transformation. It had welcomed the famous Valley Elathos into its center. Valley Elathos was, literally, a giant valley that traveled the universe, appearing on a planet when it was needed and disappearing when it wasn't. The Valley was famous for its ability to go from planet to planet, helping where it was needed and giving advice. It had the strange ability to sense when a world was in desperate peril or in need of guidance. Once it decided to help a world, it wouldn't leave till it had accomplished its goal and brought the world to peace. Its presence here meant that her world was in danger and Adina, more than anyone, was well aware of this. It was the very thing that had been haunting her mind and her world for so long now. It was a nightmare that she could not escape from.

A sudden feeling of fear and anger shot through her chest as she ran through the undergrowth, following her own well-beaten path. She ignored it and let the memories take her away. The first day she had sensed Valley Elathos's coming was still sharp in her mind. It had been a normal everyday kind of day, and then it had happened. In a matter of seconds everything had changed, but the valley hadn't. Even though Valley Elathos had arrived, it was invisible to the eyes. Valley Elathos had hardly changed the original scenery for it always blended in with the area it took the place of perfectly, not drawing even the tiniest bit of attention. The only sign of the Valley's presence was the energy that Adina could feel running through the ground and the plants around her. It was energy that she had never before sensed in her land. Only someone of her power would be able to notice it. There were many places on her world that held strong energy but her Settled Valley had never been one of them. It was simply a quiet, protected place that Adina had chosen to make her home but Valley Elathos's arrival had infused the once quiet Settled Valley will all kinds of energy. That energy surge had been what had alerted Adina to the Valley's arrival on her world and she'd been communicating with it ever since.

At the thought of communicating with the Valley, Adina felt herself smile despite herself. Out of all the amazing things that the Valley had within it, the Great Oak was her favorite. When Valley Elathos arrived and changed itself to match the terrain of the Settled Valley the only difference it had made was to create the domain of the Great Oak. Hidden to all from the outside by a magical barrier and only accessible to Adina, it was a beautiful place filled with various blooming flowers that never seemed to wilt. Though it was not too far away, it was still a good walking distance of about a mile. Adina enjoyed walking and trotting there as she was doing now. Even though she was blessed enough to have wings she loved to walk and run amongst the woods and the small living creatures that had shared this valley with her, and continued to, even after Valley Elathos had come. And why wouldn't they? The valley looked no different than it did before except for the presence of the Great Oak. The rest had been left untouched. The creatures living here would have no fear of Valley Elathos, in fact, they were now more protected then they were before thanks to the Valley's power.

Her mind's eye imagined the Great Oak standing before her. She felt her memories flash back to her long days spent under that tree, enjoying its company and relaxing in the shade cast by its branches. The Great Oak was actually not a normal, everyday oak tree but a Mountain Tree. Mountain Trees could, literally, be as tall as mountains and were known for being more magical than most tree species. Like herself, this particular Mountain Tree was an ancient creature. Its twisted limbs and gnarled bark were all that remained of an exhaustingly long life. During this long life it had discovered a way to communicate with other creatures, and had been enchanted by the Valley itself where it made its home. This mighty tree had been given an intelligence of its own and had become a being that existed for the sole purpose of communicating the Valley's thoughts and wishes to the inhabitants of the worlds it visited. Though the tree did not have a mouth to speak, those with a trained ear could pick up the gentle rustling of its leaves and understand its every word. Adina had such trained ears and had often loved settling down under the immense foliage of its pale green leaves to talk. Today she was not coming to talk but to start the ceremony which only she and the tree could perform. She had come to the tree every day since it had arrived on her world so long ago and had enjoyed every moment with it. She wished she could once again lie there and seek its advice and understanding but both of them knew that the ceremony was far more important. Today was a day that both of them had been waiting for a very long time.

She charged ahead through a grove of trees as her mind whirled with all that she had learned while talking with the tree. Not once had it ever truly explained how it had come to be or why it was the way that it was. According to what the tree had told her during their long talks, it lived in the Valley and went wherever the Valley traveled. It had seen many worlds and helped many other creatures, enjoying the experience of it all. It also allowed for certain actions to be done, acting as a conduit for the Valley's power. It held many secrets that Adina knew stretched far beyond her own knowledge and understanding. She knew that not everything was meant for her ears and, to tell the truth, she preferred not knowing. She had too much to worry about here than what had happened or what would happen on other planets. She was fine with the small talk that the tree seemed to favor. Sometimes small talk was all that one needed to feel better about their predicaments and Adina was no exception. She always felt more reassured after a long rest under the tree's branches. She would miss it when the time came for it to finally leave their world. The sudden idea struck fear through Adina's chest. When Valley Elathos departed a world it meant one of two things: that the world was safe, or it was in mortal peril and beyond help. Adina hoped that it wouldn't be the later. One thing was for sure, her world was in danger and the Valley had come to help.

As Adina neared her destination she slowed her pace to a steady trot. She bobbed her head wearily as she trotted to her destination. This was their last chance. There were no back doors. This was it. She lowered her head. The Emerald Jewel she wore at all times, clanked against her chest on its gossamer thread. The Jewel was precious to her, a powerful relic that she could never replace. It alone was a part of the great web of power that would hopefully save her world. She stopped, silent and still for a moment. The metallic sound radiating from the Jewel sent shivers down her spine.

Her large wings gleamed in the sun, causing golden rays of dappled sunlight to dance across the path. The reflected light shot across her vision. The Prophecy said that this time, this Keeper would be successful and rid their world of evil. She had to have faith in its truth. She shifted slightly as a breeze caught her mane sending it flapping in the wind like a flag.

She breathed out, her nostrils flaring in the heat of the day. She was the only Unapeg in her world and was also its Immortal. An Immortal was a being that was responsible for protecting his or her planet. It was up to them to take care of the world and see it through its worst problems. Every world had an Immortal but, right now, she felt like anything but her world's caretaker. With all her great power she was a creature unlike any other, yet she felt so helpless. She had been unable to protect her world and now it was dying from the evil that was infecting it. The Keepers were the Valley's gift, its creation. The Keepers were the only hope the Valley could give to help Adina to guarantee her world's safety. This Keeper was the last, the sacred third. What if this last Keeper failed? What if she did not finish? What if she joined the very evil she was created to destroy? Adina's heart sank as these doubts came rushing into her mind. They had been plaguing her dreams for years since the child's birth. No, she could not doubt, she must have hope. Hope was the last thing keeping her world alive. If she, this world's Immortal, lost hope then her world wouldn't be too far behind. No, no worrying, the ceremony needed to be completed…one last time.

A sudden strong breeze unsettled the tall grasses and cattails of a nearby stream, sending up giant clouds of tiny grass insects and bees from clovers. Turning she continued on her way. After a few brief sprints through tall grasses and across small trickling creeks, she arrived. She stopped for a few moments to gather her thoughts. She glanced at the entrance which, to anyone else, would simply resemble a copse of trees but, to her, was a mirror. It was the Great Oak Domain's own safety system. Only those that were permitted to enter could see the mirror entrance and walk through it. She swallowed whatever doubts she had and passed right on through.

On the other side, Adina approached the Great Oak with slow steps. When the tree came into sight she gasped. She had seen the tree many times but was still awed by its sheer size and beauty. Its branches stretched into infinity and its roots were as thick as a house. Its limbs moved in the wind billowing out towards her like a willow's branches. Adina gently walked forward when she glimpsed the faint outline of a face in the leaves. A broad smile welcomed her. With dignity and pride she came forward and bowed low. A large branch bent down and touched her forehead right above her horn. This was the trees' way of bowing, every magical tree bowed this way and she had met many in her own world. Being so large and stolid it was hard for trees to actually bend at the trunk and bow as humans and other animals could, especially towering figures like the Mountain Trees, so a touch of the branch was easier.

She righted herself and bridged the gap between them with a few even steps and touched the tip of her horn to its shimmering, scared trunk. Slowly and with great effort, like an old man struggling to stand, the tree unwound its thick branches and leaves. There hidden in the folds of the trunk was a small compartment. Focusing her powers, Adina sent a blast of mental energy at the Emerald Jewel hanging from her neck. It was the very thing that would, hopefully, end the fight for her planet's survival against the evil threatening it. She sighed as the importance of the situation washed over her, and then she shook herself and focused. Slowly, the jewel lifted from around her neck and moved to float in midair before her. Raising her head to the sky she reared and let out a fearsome whinny, "Let the great Emerald Jewel break and the ceremony begin!"

The jewel began to glow with a bright green light. It cast a large shimmering beam around the clearing, brilliantly noticeable even in the morning light. Though the jewel was called the Emerald Jewel it was not an emerald, the term emerald was used to describe its green color. The jewel was actually a crystal. Adina had been startled the first time she had seen it, surprised that this small, seemingly normal jewel could be the key to her world's salvation. The light it cast was as familiar to her as the air she breathed but, at the same time, just as hard to understand. Not much was known about the Emerald Jewel, after all, the jewel had been pulled from her planet's earth were it had been found originally and then modified by the Valley Elathos. Her knowledge of the jewel extended to its creation and this ceremony but that was it. It had been given to her for safe keeping and she had protected it ever since. She had to admit that she had had doubts that such a small crystal could actually hold the key to their salvation, but that belief had changed when she had witnessed the extent of the jewel's powers with her own two eyes.

Adina stretched out her neck and, touching her horn to the hovering jewel, sent it floating into the tree's compartment. As soon as the jewel was safely in the compartment the tree twisted back into its knotted self and began to pulsate different colors, giving the Valley a multicolored rainbow effect.

Within the compartment the entire world's energy became focused on transforming the medium sized jewel. Adina could feel the power reverberating through her muscled body. Her connection to the planet's energy gave her a front row seat to the action taking place. The power plunged in and out of the material world all around her. She breathed in its sweet scent, her heart thudded against her chest in triumph. The evil presence had not tainted the entire world yet with its malevolent poison. There were still patches of light fighting against its venom.

While the tree worked Adina had her own job to do. She lowered her head and touched the tree with the tip of her horn. She closed her eyes and focused hard. The ground around her seemed to disappear, yet she could stand. Again the world seemed to moan with effort. It was a conditioning act that the world had gone through in the past.   She went over it in her mind; she would help the tree split the jewel into thirteen different pieces, one larger than the other twelve. In her mind the image of the jewel inside the Great Oak came into view. Adina focused her energy and felt as well as saw the jewel break into the thirteen pieces; their shimmering surfaces polished and unblemished. Their light warmed her body and made her soul soar. The jewel had split successfully and now consisted of one large crystal and twelve smaller crystal shards, glimmering brilliantly. She focused harder and connected her own power to the planet's energy. She searched long and hard, but found what she was looking for: the twelve elements of her world. These elements were the life blood of her planet and they were the source of its greatest energy. Their amazing power would inhabit the twelve smaller crystal shards. The twelve elements obeyed her command and came to her through the energy of the world. They came to rest before her mind's eye, twisting around themselves in a perfect figure eight. She separated them and, breaking apart their learned formation, sent them spiraling into the shards. Adina stood stock still. Not even the strongest gust of wind could knock her down or disrupt her concentration. She was completely focused and nothing could stop her. She no longer felt a part of herself. She was no longer an Immortal, she, instead, felt like a puddle of essence neither with a body or a spirit but something in between. She shuddered as suddenly dimension, time, and the material world settled back around her. She remembered who she was and straightened her composure. Breathing deeply she steadied herself. She had to continue. Slowly the compartment opened and the tree trembled as if releasing a sigh of relief. Adina's own body shuddered with the effort it had taken to perform this task. Floating from the compartment the thirteen pieces glowed brightly for a moment and then their light settled like super-heated metal cooling down. Adina extended her horn and mentally commanded them to follow. They complied and arranged themselves around her horn.

 Sending out a command the thirteenth and largest crystal floated out in front of her, waiting for her. Another command was sent and a small loophole formed at the top of the thirteenth crystal. She touched her horn to the loophole and strands from her shimmering golden mane detached and entwined themselves into a beautiful gossamer chain of golden silk, as strong as dragon scales and as soft as cashmere. In this way a little of me will always be with her, thought Adina, proud of her work. She weaved the silk necklace through the loophole. The two ends began to glow like frayed wires. Slowly they looped over top each other and welded together, smoothing out any imperfections and finishing the crystal necklace.

Adina was again at peace. To anyone else it would seem like nothing had ever happened, but the absence of the elements within the earth beneath her feet delivered the sharp reality. Now it had truly begun. She breathed in and out slowly, calming her rapidly beating heart. For a moment she thought it was all a dream and nothing more, that everything was an illusion. Only the shards and crystal floating in front of her let her know she had actually done something. The feelings she experienced were never harmful. They were powerful but it was just uncontrolled energy straight from the world, the same energy that made her an Immortal.

It had taken about thirty minutes for the splitting of the jewel to happen. In that amount of time twelve other creatures had joined her: six unicorns and six pegasi. Only for today would these twelve creatures be allowed to enter the Great Oak's Domain. They were called the Mothers of the Elements, the honored title they received for their important roles as protectors of the elements. They had been chosen a week ago and now they were there ready to receive their shards. Some were the same Mothers from previous ceremonies while others were brand new but they all took their roles seriously. The fate of their world was at stake, it was something they did not take lightly.

Adina's gaze traveled over the twelve serious and determined faces before her. This was the third time she had done this; hopefully it would be her last. Feeling her breath hot against her chest Adina spoke in a voice like silk. The vibrations of her voice echoed around the Mothers making even the smallest whisper easily heard. "Mothers, you have been chosen to keep and protect the shards. I have put my trust into each of you. Do not fail me. Now, do you, Mothers, promise and pledge to protect, care, and love the shards as if they were your children and do you pledge and promise to be loyal to the elements and me, to ensure the success of the Keeper? In this I ask, do you?"

Adina stared down at them, her horn beginning to glow. In that stare she commanded the Immortal powers to burrow deep into each of the Mother's proud eyes. Her power overcame them and they bowed to her. The group raised their heads in brilliant splendor. Horns gleamed, catching the sun, while wings flapped sending dust and stray insects flying. "We do!" shouted the Mothers, each just as loud as the other. "In the presence of the Jewel itself, we pledge!"

"With the pledges freely given let the shards choose their bearers," said Adina. Glancing at the twelve shards she nodded and they slowly took the color of their element. They then spread out and floated in front of their chosen Mother. Then, turning horizontally on their sides, the stones gently bore into the Mothers chests, embedding themselves deep into their hearts. The Mothers did not cry out in pain, they only bent their heads and allowed the blood from their wounds to leak out and float as a small circle in front of them. The wounds closed and relief flooded their faces. Clear bubbles surrounded the blood from the Mothers and all twelve floated back to Adina. In a flash each one entered into her chest.

"This blood is the proof that you will honor your oath. If something should befall you, I can find you and take matters into my own. Thank you for making this sacrifice. Go and await the Keeper," she finished nodding. The Mothers bowed to her on one knee. Then turned and walked out. Adina watched them leave. She felt overwhelming exhaustion push down on her shoulders. Each new ceremony seemed to leave her more drained than the last. The Great Oak softly rustled its leaves as if to give comfort. Adina lay down in the soft grass soaking in the rich rays of the sun on her back and the sound of rushing water from the spring. The Keeper would be awakened soon, only time would tell if she could handle it.

A fine mist settled over the small grove. The sun was sinking beyond the tree tops, night was coming. Had it been that long? It seemed like the sun was just rising only moments ago, but the splitting of the jewel had contorted her perception of time once again. What had been moments to her had actually been hours. Crickets began chirping, hiding within the labyrinth of grasses while lightening bugs cast a ghostly haze to accompany their sweet music. She watched them smiling. A small flash of light reminded her that she was not finished. The white crystal necklace appeared weaving slightly in front of her nose as if teasing her, its gossamer thread followed it, afloat in midair. Adina nickered happily; the crystal was so carefree and innocent, perfect for this Keeper. The crystal floated closer, it was impatient to be with its Keeper. She inhaled taking in the fresh scents of the earth, water, and air surrounding her. She twitched her muscles as the soft furry leaves from a sweet smelling weed gently kissed her shoulder. With a wave of her head the crystal disappeared flickering out of this world and into Earth on its way to its new home.   Soon all the hard work and horrors of the past would come clean and not be wasted. For so long Adina had heard her people's cries. For so long she had been angry at herself. She had the power of the Immortals but she remained ultimately powerless to defend her people from this alien evil. This was the last time a Keeper would rise to take the place of all others who had failed. She would save their world once and for all. Adina had faith that Rosey would be the perfect Keeper for the job.

Chapter Two: Truth

Rosey Mystic had been awake for an hour, a real bummer for anyone used to getting up at 7:00 a.m. She'd lain there, unable to shake the feeling that something was off today. She had run over everything in her mind looking for anything that could be the cause of her worry. Her homework was done, her Uncle wasn't mad at her, there were no problems with her friends, and her pets were healthy and happy. So, why did she feel this way?! What was it about today that made her feel a little light headed? What could possibly happen? Picture day at school wasn't until Monday and the field trip was next week. There was nothing that should make her feel strange. Yet, it was there, a stirring in the pit of her stomach like butterflies had moved in.

She hadn't felt like this since her uncle told her that her mother and father had disappeared. She had been five years old at the time. Until then she had taken life and everything in it as normal. There was nothing to worry about or to question the motives of, even the fact that she only had one parent. During those first four years she wasn't aware enough to ask about why there was only one adult in the house. But, as soon as she reached five, the 'why' questions started coming. Suddenly everything around her was 'Why this? Why that? Why did this happen at that time, at that moment, during that year?' Her uncle, whom at that time, she had considered her father, had humorously told her he had never worked a day in his life until she turned five because he often had to research many of the things she asked in order to give an educated answer.

One question she sometimes wished she had never asked was 'Where's my mother?' It had begun as an observation at first. She had friends like any normal five year old and, every now and then, she'd see a woman come to pick up one of her friends from school as she boarded the school bus.

When Rosey turned five she began to wonder who these women were. When she asked her friends about the women that came for them they had said 'those are our mothers,' as if it was obvious. Of course the term 'mother' was alien to Rosey at that time. That same day she asked her 'father' that same question, 'Where's my mother?' and there in the living room, home from school, looking into her 'father's' brown eyes, she could have sworn she saw his heart break. Sometimes, she wished she had never wanted to ask 'Why?' Because of that question he was forced to tell her that he was not her biological father. In fact, he was her uncle. Her mother had been his sister. After her parents died he had raised and loved her as if she were his own.

Apparently her uncle's mother and father had moved to Africa from America to study the wildlife and cultures there. He and his sister, Esperanza, were raised in the heat of the African wilderness. When they were old enough Esperanza continued in her parent's footsteps after they passed away studying wildlife. John, Rosey's uncle, decided to move back to America to study computer analysis and ended up working for the government. His sister married Mathew Kingsly and had Rosey not too long after. When John went to visit his sister and her husband in Africa he would babysit his little niece, Rosey, while her parents went out to study wildlife. One day they did not come back and were never seen or heard from again. In their will they left guardianship to John. He brought Rosey home to America and had been raising her ever since.

Rosey would never forget that day, she stayed in bed almost all day thinking about them and looking at a small spare picture that her uncle had given her. Her mother looked beautiful with long black hair and deep blue eyes like her own and her father was a handsome man with short brown hair and green eyes. She had stared at that picture for a long time. A sudden stirring interrupted her thoughts and made her peer down at the two sleeping figures on her bed. Noly, her female collie, was sleeping at her feet and Hazel, her dilute tortoiseshell cat, was curled up against her left arm. Hazel's soft purring and Noly's little gasps of air every once in a while were the only sound. Rosey welcomed the silence as if she were in heaven and the image of her snoozing animal friends was all too perfect. Noly was pretty normal for a collie, despite her often silly and rambunctious personality. Officially, however, she was a sable merle with rich black and dark mahogany patches of fur mixing with the tan fur along her back. She was one of the prettier designs that collies came in, alongside another of Rosey's favorites, the blue merle. Casting her gaze down at Hazel, she was reminded of the odd ball in Rosey's little pet group. Hazel was a dilute tortoiseshell cat. Essentially a dilute was the same as a tortoiseshell with the traditional black and orange markings only they had light grey and light orange markings instead. Dilutes weren't as striking as regular tortoiseshells but Hazel had pulled on Rosey's heart strings from day one, besides Hazel's coloration was much more brilliant than most others, with occasional darker orange and grey spots that made her coat stand out.

She smiled. It was so peaceful watching her pets sleep. They looked so perfect and carefree. Their soothing effect beckoned to her, temporarily quieting the butterflies in her stomach and lolling her back towards sleep. Just as she felt the world of dreams creeping in, the alarm sounded. She slowly got up, hugging Hazel close to her like a pillow. She stretched and accidentally kicked Noly off the bed. She heard a thump and gasped. Releasing Hazel she peered over the side of her bed and laughed. Noly lay on her back panting heavily with a doggy smile on her face. Rosey laughed harder as Noly suddenly jumped up and covered her face in doggy kisses. Pushing Noly away, she frowned as she gazed around her room. It would be a miracle if she could find the closet. She bit her lip with frustration at how messy it was. The curtains were drawn over her window in an unorderly fashion, clothes were thrown everywhere and papers and homework where strewn across her desk in clumped piles. There was an oasis of neatness in one corner, though, where her collection of Breyer horses, statues of other animals, and trophies from her various extracurricular activities stood. They were perfectly spaced and polished on countless shelves. Her room was a lot larger than most kid's rooms, a good fifteen by fifteen with a large walk-in closet. She didn't necessarily need the large closet, although it did make a great room to store her Breyer boxes in, but she wouldn't have traded her room for any other.   She glanced around the room and saw her reflection in her full length mirror. Her pale beautiful face stared back, her bright sapphire blue eyes just as piercing as ever. Her long thigh-length, slightly curly, coal black hair was just as smooth and shiny, even after sleeping on it. She always made sure to brush it carefully, trying hard not to pull on the delicate strands. She'd always kept her hair long. It was the way she'd always wanted it and had never gotten it cut since. It was the one thing about her that she truly took great pride in. It was her only vice, though her uncle had told her more than once that loving long hair was nothing to be ashamed of and could hardly be called a vice.

"Honey, are you up yet?" came a voice from downstairs.   "Uh..! What? Oh... ah... yeah. I'm up!" Rosey yelled, startled. Noly and Hazel pricked their ears as if listening and she smiled at them.   "Well, get dressed, come downstairs, and eat your breakfast before you miss the bus!" her uncle yelled back, teasingly.

"Ok!" she replied, yawning. She hadn't realized how long she had sat and stared around. Butterflies and weird feelings would have to wait if she didn't want to miss the bus.

She pulled on a black top and a pair of blue jeans. Shifting through a pile of clothes she located her sneakers and slipped them on. She grimaced as she noticed that they looked like she had rolled around in the mud with them. Regretfully, she had no time to clean them. She combed her long hair into submission, using a clip to hold back a stubborn strand. Rushing into the bathroom she quickly brushed her teeth. Her long eyelashes and perfectly smooth skin made the idea of makeup a sin so she never used it, much to her uncle's liking. Besides, she had never agreed with the idea of covering one's face in a mask of animal fats and other forsaken minerals. False beauty was not something she was interested in. Her seventeen year old body was as smooth and well-toned as always after years of extracurricular activities behind her belt. They had left her looking athletic and fit, though she'd never had an ounce of fat on her her whole life. She took one more glance at herself in the mirror before turning around abruptly and heading down the stairs.

As she made her way to the kitchen her eyes caught sight of her uncle's office door, locked and closed as always. The only time it was open was when he was in it and he needed to be sure he could hear her if she called. He was a government agent who worked specifically on their digital hard drives and computer analysis systems. That was the extent of her knowledge as she was strictly forbidden to be in his office without his permission for government secretive purposes. For this same reason she was never told anything about his work or what he did for them beyond the general explanation she already had. She paused outside the door and stared at it, as if it held all the secrets of her inner thoughts. She felt the butterflies in her stomach dance again and shook her head. She quickly stuck her tongue out at the door and then moved on. She felt childish and unsure of why she had just done what she'd done, but, maybe it was because she hated secrets.

The smell of eggs and toast hit Rosey when she arrived at the swinging doors that led to the kitchen. Her butterflies tried to come back again but hunger easily outweighed them. She sat down at the table where her uncle waited and eagerly took a drink of milk.   "Morning dad," she said in a sleepy voice. Though Rosey knew perfectly well that John was not her biological father but her uncle, she still viewed him as her father. The old habit of calling him dad was hard to break and, frankly, she didn't want to break it. After all he had always treated her as if she were his own.

"Morning honey, did you sleep well?" he asked in a distracted voice as if he wasn't paying attention. Rosey frowned but paid it no attention. "Yeah, I guess so," She said between bites.

They sat at the small table in the kitchen where they always ate together every morning. This morning he seemed…preoccupied. He wouldn't look at her. She had never seen him act like that toward her. Usually every morning he would hug her, give her a kiss, tell her he loved her and then make up jokes to get her laughing. But today he was very different.

She wished her uncle would really talk to her instead of pretending that nothing was wrong. They usually had a good time together despite his refusal to have an actual serious conversation, especially about her mother and father. It was around the age of ten that she had started asking for more details about her family and if she had any grandparents or other relatives, since she had never visited them or seen any pictures of them. That was when he had begun closing in and shutting down. He didn't want to tell her, but why? It had always been an awkward truth that hung between them and that had made Rosey's life more difficult despite her uncle's love and compassion towards her. The truth was something Rosey wanted to know, but it was the same thing getting in her way.

"Eat your breakfast and get outside before you miss the bus. Hurry now," her uncle urged. He got up and put his plate in the sink, a glazed look in his eyes. He returned with the day's newspaper and a cup of coffee. He always had milk with his breakfast and then coffee with his reading in the morning. At least that was normal.

Rosey shook her head and decided to talk about it later when she got home and finished her homework. Her mind would be clear then and not jumbling with the new school day activities. She looked down and ate what she could. While she ate a steady silence grew, then her uncle said, "When you get home I have something very important to speak with you about." He met her eyes for the first time and they stared at each other. The longest moment passed between them and Rosey had the most bizarre feeling that her parent's death may have been more than it seemed. What could have possibly happened and would her uncle have lied to her about it? An uneasy feeling began to grow in the pit of her stomach. Before he could say anything else she heard a screeching of breaks and knew that the bus was down the road at the stop before hers. She had no time to talk. She used the bus as her excuse to get away muttering a 'Goodbye' and a 'Love you' as she went out the door. She barely heard him respond as she flung her backpack on her back.

The bus was just arriving as she got outside. The bright Montana sun pierced her eyes with brilliance, but not even those powerful rays could overpower the frigidly cold winds that snatched at her jacket as she ran to catch the bus. Rosey had never been raised in any other place besides Montana. They lived in a small off-shoot town of Cooke City called Silver Gate. Silver Gate was just right near the entrance to Yellowstone National park and was one of the more beautiful places to live in Montana. The small, country lifestyle suited Rosey perfectly. It was a no hustle and bustle sort of living that made one happy for the smaller things in life, but the tourists that came through for Yellowstone always brought excitement. She and her uncle had visited Yellowstone many times before. It had always been a commodity that Rosey had almost taken for granted since she lived so close by, however, she was never disappointed when they saw the churned up and bubbly world of Yellowstone. It never failed to amaze her and her uncle never failed to notice how impressed she was, so they'd kept going back to do all sorts of new things. He was like that, always getting her to do stuff, even things she wasn't so certain she really wanted to do. He had always been there challenging her every step of the way. She was happy he did because it helped her become brave and willing to try new things; that was a quality she could never imagine living without. She was yanked out of her thoughts by the bus coming to an abrupt stop before her. Hurrying up the steps, happily, she fell into the seat next to her best friend Rochell Calling.

"Hey, how are you doing?" Rochell asked, looking at Rosey with her large brown eyes. Those eyes were only one of the many things about Rochell that was odd. She was often overly excitable and easily impressed, though those qualities made even the most unlikable character love her. Rosey shrugged her shoulders, unsure of how much to reveal, "Oh... Okay I suppose. The only weird thing is...my dad said he had something important to talk to me about. He was acting so strange this morning. I'm almost scared of what he has to say." It came as no surprise to Rochell to hear Rosey's uncle referred to as 'dad' by Rosey, Rochell was aware of Rosey's parent's deaths. Rosey expected Rochell to share in her shock but something wasn't quite right with the silly brunette. She seemed unsurprised by what Rosey said, as if she had already known. Rosey shook her head and figured she'd been mistaken. Looking back at Rochell, the smiling girl suddenly looked away. Her eyes widened and she turned her head downwards. A dead silence followed. It was a lot like the silence that had filled the room that morning with her uncle. Rosey could tell her friend was thinking hard which was unusual for Rochell. Rosey stared at her inquisitively. Rochell seemed to notice and looked back up with a smile, "Don't worry about it, I'm sure everything is going to be all right." The way that she said it reminded Rosey of a person pulling a child from an accident and soothing their fears. A small ember of apprehension blossomed in the pit of her stomach. First her uncle, now her friend, what was up with today? Did Rochell know something Rosey didn't and if so, what? She didn't want to give away anything so she simply smiled and laid her head back against the seat to think. Noticing this, Rochelle smirked evilly. She then laughed and quickly threw her arms around Rosey capturing her in one of her famous bear hugs. She released her prey, then gave Rosey a nudge and said, "If you think too much your head will grow too big!"

Rosey smiled. That was just like Rochell, silly and carefree. It was nice to see her acting normally again.

"Then Alex's head must be huge, you know he never stops thinking," said Rosey seeing their other friend Alex Crane getting in the seat before them.

Alex's expression changed to one of mock worry as he peeked over the seat, "What about my head!?"

"Nothing," the two girls chanted, teasingly.

Alex just scowled at them, playing along with their little game. He then smiled and fell into a conversation with Rochell. Out of all the boys at the school Rosey enjoyed Alex's company the most. He was a gentle and easy going guy with the smarts to match. He was no pushover though, he was tough, not only that but he was also rather handsome. He looked especially handsome today in his blue jeans, red t-shirt and black sneakers with his short black hair and deep green eyes. Though Alex caught the eye of many young girls he was just a friend to Rosey, a very good friend. Most boys weren't like Alex and most girls weren't like Rochell. Rochell was average with…acceptable grades. She was more silly and outgoing than most which sometimes made others a little nervous around her, but Rosey enjoyed it. It was because of Rochell that Rosey had found her inner child. She was lucky to have Alex and Rochell as her friends. No matter what, they always knew just what to say to make her feel better. In fact, the school had gotten into the habit of calling them the three musketeers because they always were seen with each other. Not only were they great together socially but also physically. They were very athletic, participating in a number of strenuous extracurricular activities which added to their allure, much to Rosey's amusement. Rosey watched them calmly then settled back into her seat, letting their silly banter wash away all her apprehension. Maybe all of this was just in her head after all.

Rosey walked up the parched and worn steps into her beautiful old brick house. She was glad that school was over for the weekend so she could stay up late and do nothing.

Pictures of her, her uncle, her friends, and her animals covered the walls. It was odd to see that there were no pictures of her parents or other relatives. The only one that she had of her parents was the one on her bedside dresser. She wondered, like some people after a traumatic experience, if her uncle was avoiding her mother's death. He had avoided speaking to her about her parents ever since he had told her about what happened. He had never mentioned any grandparents and whenever she tried to ask he would always suddenly become distracted by something and hurry off to attend to it. She had soon stopped trying to ask.

She didn't have much time to ponder this for a mix of scratching and clawing came hurrying towards her. Noly came running from her room with the spunky Hazel right behind her. The two were just as glad to see her as she was to see them. Reaching down she greeted the two fuzz balls and gave each of them a kiss on the head. Then she noticed that something was off. Hazel and Noly were usually already at the door when she came home. The entryway was not strewn with light as it usually was. Strangely enough a candle had been lit. It sat motionless on the small table that sat beside the door. The lights in the entryway were usually on but today they were black as night. The darkness of the room seemed to fill Rosey's conscious as she glanced around. Why was it so dark, it was only four in the afternoon? When she moved further into the living room she noticed that the heavy curtains were drawn and the lights were off too, except for a few scattered lamps that cast a low, dull light. She suddenly got the feeling that she was being watched. She glanced around but found nothing out of place.

With Noly and Hazel right behind her, she walked into the kitchen, peered into the hallway, and glimpsed shadows from the family room. She scrutinized the shadows and gave a sigh of relief when she recognized the silhouette of her uncle and her friends Alex and Rochell. It was then that apprehension started to creep into her chest. What were they doing here? The bus had dropped Rochell off before her. Alex had been a car rider that day, so it was possible that he had been dropped off here before the bus arrived and Rochell could have made her way over to Rosey's house through the back door before the bus stopped here. The real question was why. They hadn't talked about coming over or anything and it was no one's birthday so there'd be no reason for a surprise party. She gulped and stepped away. Her dog and cat, however, walked halfway down the hall then turned and waited for her. They did not seem to be worried about Rosey's friends or their reason for being there. And why should they? Alex and Rochell came over all the time.

She told herself she was being silly and made her way down the Hallway. Tentatively she stepped into the room. The trio, consisting of her two friends and her uncle, were locked in what sounded like an intense conversation. They spoke in hushed whispers and seemed a little nervous. They abruptly stopped when they saw her come in and gazed at her with mixed emotions. Rosey stared back for a few moments, unsure of what to say. Something was definitely wrong.

Suddenly, Rosey became light headed. Her heart beat soared and she stumbled clumsily. Her uncle realized this and rushed forward to help her. He caught her as she was about to fall. Something was in her! It was moving, something hard. For some obscure reason her mind jumped to the movie Aliens and immediately her hand flew to her chest as if to stop anything from getting out. The pain, however, wasn't in her chest but her right side. The intensity radiating from it was making her head spin. She tried hard to resist but it was happening way to fast. She was vaguely aware of her friends all around her and her uncle gently holding her. She vaguely heard the words, "to soon" and "why now" coming from the trio around her but they had no meaning to her. The pain was growing, sharpening. She could see a bright light and for a moment she thought an Angel was coming for her. *Okay, no u movies for me,* she thought vaguely. Then, a little white stone protruded from her side. As soon as it came out the pain subsided. There was not a drop of blood on the tiny crystal and neither was there any where it had exited her body. The skin seemed to just peel away around the stone. Her heart beat soared, but strangely she was not afraid. The image of a gold and silver, horse-like, creature flashed across her vision before everything went black.

When she came to she was on the couch buried under soft blankets. Her head was spinning and it took a few seconds for her eyes to adjust. The lamps were still the only light source. Noly was lying on the floor on her back with her feet up in the air, gently snoring. Hazel was curled up next to Rosey purring softly. Rosey had taken naps before on the comfortable couch where she had awakened to similar sights of her two furry friends, but something was wrong. Suddenly she remembered what had happened. She tried to sit up but a strong hand gently eased her back down. She looked up into the face of her uncle. Glancing behind him she spotted Alex and Rochell sitting in the armchairs across from the couch, worried expressions lighting their faces. She was aware of a warm substance around her neck and looked down to see a small crystal resting there, its polished surface smooth and unblemished. She touched it absently and then looked at the group around her. She was willing any of them to talk to her, do something to clear all this mess up, but no one spoke. They all seemed speechless.

She suddenly grew angry. She was about to yell at them but her uncle spoke before she could get anything out.

"Rosey we have much to tell you, and we have confessions to make. It won't be easy for you to accept and understand but you must try. Please?" Rosey was confused. She had no idea how to respond to that. She wasn't a priest. She was a young seventeen year old who wanted nothing more than to get past high school. She suddenly had the impulse to run away and hide but the longing look in her uncle's eyes and the crystal she held between her fingers like she had owned it all along made her listen as her uncle began to explain.

The Mystics

"Rosey, there is something I must tell you. I need you to listen and to keep your mind wide open. What we're about to tell you will sound crazy and completely farfetched, but it is the truth and I only wish we could have told you sooner. This is going to be hard for you to hear, but you need to be strong." His voice broke and he reached out and took her hand in his before continuing." Trust me, please." Rosey felt her heart beat soar. What was going on? She clutched the crystal tighter, instinctively. She'd always wanted truth but this wasn't what she had been talking about. It was too hard to think, her mind buzzed and she felt the crystal grow surprisingly warm in her hand. She sighed deeply as its warmth flowed through her body, soothing her racing heart. Strangely she thought nothing of it. She turned and propped herself up against the red pillows of their light brown couch. With her uncle's help she eased into a more comfortable sitting position. She nodded and said, "You know I trust you, go on."

"For over three hundred years a planet known as The World Within A World has made its home inside of Earth, a dimensional pocket occupying the same space as Earth to be specific. It has thrived there in peace, but now it is being threatened, attacked. The people who call it their home are dying and you are their new Keeper. You must fulfill the prophecy and destroy the evil that has tormented our world for so long. You were raised here, on Earth, for safekeeping, but now it is time for you to return and start your journey. I know…I know this is weird and doesn't sound at all truthful, but it is…please believe me."   Rosey's heartbeat went back to normal and she had to stop herself from bursting out laughing. She had always known her uncle to be a jokester and do similar things like this in the past though not so dramatic. If he was playing a joke it was an extra good one for he even had her friends in on it. This was way out of proportion for him. Rosey's smile disappeared.

It was way out of proportion. There was no way that the pain she had felt of the crystal coming out of her body was a joke. Unless it was some elaborate magic trick, there was no way what just happened had been fake.

Her uncle would never harm her on purpose and would never do anything to cause her pain. What happened happened of its own accord and that scared Rosey more than the look on her friend's faces or the words that had come from her uncle's mouths.

Her uncle sat there and stared at her, waiting for her reaction. Looking around at the group, Rosey slowly started to panic. Her friends had never looked so serious, especially Rochell, who couldn't keep a straight face if you paid her. Alex looked kind but equally as serious and stolid. *Come on, somebody laugh or something!* She thought, but no one did. Her brows furrowed and soon the serious look in her uncle's and friend's eyes became too overwhelming. Rosey's heart beat jumped once again as she realized they weren't kidding.

"What?" was the only thing she could think of saying. "Rosey, what I'm saying is true, you are the next Keeper. That's what you are…the Keeper. A savior to this world! You're the chosen one the Prophecy foretold would save us," her uncle said. "Me…what can I do? What are you saying?!" She pleaded with him, trying to make sense of it all. "You're really starting to sound crazy. Surely you're joking?!"

She could feel the blood pounding in her ears, making her face grow hot. The fact that the house was warm, despite the cold Montana nights, was not helping any. What was going on? How could this be happening. Another world inside of Earth, occupying a dimensional…whatever! The Keeper? Savior? Savior of what, this world? Thousands of thoughts flew through her mind and she found herself speechless. The impossibility of the moment had frozen her vocal cords.

"I'm sorry Rosey," her uncle said, though she didn't look at him, "I wish it was a bad joke but it's not and we don't have a lot of time. I'll explain as best as I can in the time we have. This place is called The World Within A World and twice it has been threatened by an evil enemy and twice a Keeper, like yourself, has risen up against it. You are the new

The Mystics

Keeper, Rosey. You are the one that will finally destroy the Evil One where the other Keepers have failed."

"What are you talking about?! You expect me to believe that there is a world below us! In the Earth's dimensional…pocket thingy?!"
"There is Rosey. You know what a dimensional pocket is, you've watched science shows before. It can occupy the same place as something else can, right?"

"Yes," Rosey said nodding, "but none of them had a planet inside of them."

"Listen," he said taking her hands, "We, and many more, have been put in charge of watching over you and keeping you safe. Your mother came from that world." At this Rosey gave him a confused look. "She was the Keeper before you. She was from that world. I am from that world. When she died you were put in my charge to be kept safe on Earth and to never be told of your true destiny until it was time. Your mother wanted you to grow up in a normal environment instead of the horrors of The World Within A World. I want you to know that I have always loved you as my own daughter and still do. I know that this is hard but it is all true. I wouldn't lie to you about something as serious as this Rosey. You know I wouldn't."   "How can this be?" she said perplexed. "And what do you mean, you wouldn't lie? If what you're saying is true then you've been lying to me my whole life."

"Well…I…uh," he stuttered, rubbing the back of his head in embarrassment. "There is…not enough time to explain all this, but there will be later. We'll explain everything about your mother, father, and this new world, but now is not the right time."

For the longest moment Rosey didn't say a thing. She was afraid of what might come out if she did. She stared at her uncle and hoped that any moment she would wake up and it would all turn out to be one horrible dream. That was so unlikely that Rosey almost let out a small chuckle but, given the circumstances, that might not be such a good idea so she resisted.

At first she had thought it was a joke but her uncle and her friends would never joke around about her parents. This was real, there was no way they would say something like that then try to pass it off as humor. Her uncle hadn't even spoken about her mother since she was five. No, this was not a joke.

She pulled back her thick black hair and looked at the large windows of her living room. She felt very small as if this revelation had come down to crush and shatter her world, leaving her in total chaos. Had her whole life been a lie? Even though the curtains were drawn she knew that Mrs. Gibly's winter dormant garden was just outside that window. It was beautiful in the spring. The thought made her calm, the crystal pulsated a deep warmth that spread through her hand, up her arm, to her heart, soothing its fast pace and returning her breathing to normal. She looked down at it and held her gaze. Rosey could feel the power within it slowly start to transform her. It swept away all fearful thoughts and cleared her mind. Looking up she took a deep breath, feeling the swirling powers leave her. She clenched her fists and breathed slowly. The crystal warmed in her hands.

Rosey knew that she had to go through with this. It might be the only way to find out more about her family. She wasn't going to pass this up, she had to go. She had to know the truth. "What does this all mean… for me? What am I supposed to do?" she asked slowly, but with confidence. "You're all right with all of this?" asked Rochell, a hint of surprise in her voice.

Rosey faced her, her panic turning into anger. "No, I'm not all right with all of this, but what am I supposed to do? How am I supposed to react? You know how crazy this sounds. Am I supposed to run away and ignore what you're telling me? Most people would run away, but something inside me tells me to trust you. I can't explain it. Somehow I know you're right. Besides you'd never speak of my parents like that…not unless it was true. Not to mention that, whatever this is, points the way to the truth about my family."

Rosey paused for a moment. She smiled and said in a kinder, softer voice, "You'd never be able to keep up a joke for this long anyway Rochell, you know that."

Rochell smiled knowingly at this and Rosey continued. "What can I do but listen and hope you're right!? I can't run away from something that's this big, I mean…according to what I've heard a whole world is depending on me. No, how could I ignore that? How can I…"Rochell and Alex got up and sat beside her on the couch. She felt like slouching into their arms and taking a nap. She wanted to roll into sleep and wake up in fifty years, but that was way out of the range of possibilities for the time being. This wasn't something she could leave behind in some dream, this was real. It was really happening.

"It's Ok, Rosey. We're here and we'll get through this together because that's what we're here to do. We've always looked out for each other and that's never going to change," said Alex taking her hand in his. Rosey looked at both her fiends before saying, "That's so cheesy."

They all laughed and the crystal in Rosey's hand pulsed, sending warmth up and down her body as if it too was laughing. Once again she felt herself calming. She looked down at it and then at her uncle for the first time realizing that the crystal was even there. Before, the intensity of the moment and its soothing abilities had distracted her away from the crystal's appearance. She gently removed it from around her neck. She assumed her uncle had placed it there. Now she stared at it with curiosity.

"Well, first off, where did this crystal come from? Did it really come from inside me?" she asked, pointing to the crystal. "Yes, it came from your body," her uncle said.

Rosey dropped the crystal with a horrified look on her face. Alex quickly grabbed it before it reached the floor and handed it back to Rosey who looked at it like it had a disease.

"How did *that* get into my body!?" She almost shouted. "It's like a gallstone gone wrong."

"We're not sure on that, it's just all a part of the process. A magical process, perhaps? Don't worry it didn't harm you," her uncle said with amusement.

"Was it in there for very long? Wait…what…magic?"

"No, it came to you as soon as you got home from school. We weren't sure when it would happen. And yes, magic," he said emphasizing the word, "You'll learn about that soon."

Rosey tentatively turned the crystal around in her hand, examining it. To her it looked like a normal, ordinary, white crystal. It had the same lines, angles, and curves of a crystal and shone brightly when put up to the light. Oddly, deep inside the pristine surface of the tiny crystal Rosey could hear something beating softly, encouragingly, as if it was trying to communicate with her somehow. Rosey was soothed right away and she put it back around her neck enjoying the feel of it against her skin. "So what is it for and what's this whole Keeper business that you mentioned earlier?" Rosey asked, calmer now.

"The Keeper is a human who is chosen to be the Keeper of the crystal. The crystal around your neck," he said pointing to it. She immediately looked down at the crystal and then back up as he continued. "We, meaning the ones watching over you, were to wait until now, the twenty third of October, to tell you of your destiny. That crystal is called The Shanobie Crystal. It's what will make you a true Keeper."

"What am I supposed to do with it?" Rosey asked, not sure she wanted to know.

"I'm afraid we don't have the time for such details right now, the time for that will come later. It is more important, now that the crystal has come to you, that you are safely taken to The World Within A World," he said hurriedly, glancing quickly over to the large windows. He walked over to one and peeked between the heavy curtains. Rosey saw that it was night time. She had been out longer than she'd thought, that or it had taken her uncle longer to explain than originally planned. He seemed nervous, almost on edge. What was wrong?

"Hey, what was with all the darkness when I got in the house?" she asked watching her uncle closely.

He turned around and smiled embarrassedly, "It was supposed to help with the whole process…you know…staying calm and all."

"Oh," said Rosey annoyed, "You know what it did help? It helped to freak me out!"

"There's a first for everything, I guess. Plus I was trying to be stealthy."

Rosey shook her head, he was the same old uncle she had been living with all her life. He was still just as awkward and unsure of himself as ever. It was also one of the things Rosey loved about him the most. Despite her uncle's wariness, that didn't stop her sudden surge of feelings at his unsatisfactory words. "So…why can't I know more now? What's the hurry?" she said throwing up her arms in aggravation. She was just getting interested and now he was killing her enthusiasm.

He faced her, his eyes bright and heavy. "Rosey, the sooner you're there the better, I can't explain now but everything is taken care of. It is just better that you go to The World Within A World." He glanced back around at Rochell, who nodded.

"Is something wrong?" asked Rosey a little concerned, gripping the crystal in her hand tightly not even trying to comprehend the fact that she would be going to another planet. His words came back to her from before. What was he being stealthy for?

"Let's just say we might not be the only ones that sensed the crystal's awakening."

Rosey's eyes widened, "Who--?!"

"There isn't enough time, later you will know more. You'll know everything," he said interrupting her gently. He turned this way and that checking all angles. His voice sounded worried and his face was once again the serious mask of forced calm. She cringed with fear. Suddenly she was perfectly happy to get to this other world.

She nodded and hurried over to him, "What happens now?" Her uncle turned to her and took her shoulders tightly in his grasp, "We're going to take the horses and ride to the portal that will take us to The World Within A World."

Besides being the proud owner of a collie and dilute tortoiseshell cat she also owned a large Friesian mare called Sarabie. Her uncle had his dappled grey gelding, and her friends boarded their horses at her stable. They were an amazing group of horses, large, proud, and majestic: all the things horses should be. Rosey took great pride in riding with them but the idea of riding them to a portal completely put a stopper on her mind's processing capabilities.

Rosey cocked her head, "We have a…portal?"

"Yes, you know…a portal. You jump in and it transports you to another place…that portal. It's located on the Old Well Trail inside Yellowstone. In fact, the energy that is powering that portal is coming from Yellowstone, many such portals are…it's the only area on Earth where its Energy Flows are almost touching the surface, that's why there's so much activity and the energy coming from it is so powerful that it could easily support a good number of portals…" he trailed off as he saw Rosey's face. She was staring at him in utter lost confusion. He chuckled and rubbed the back of his neck, "We're just taking the Old Well Trail, okay?"

Rosey nodded and turned away, still mind blown from what she's heard. Energy Flows? Portals…it was almost too much to think about so she thought about something more down to Earth. She remembered the trail, she and her friends had enjoyed riding down that way many times during their long summer days and spring afternoons. The trail was open to anyone who wanted to ride and it only extended into Yellowstone a little bit before coming back out again. It was one of her favorite memories, riding down that trail. At least, it had been until they had decided to watch

The Mystics

The Ring one Halloween night, then it had just been spooky. Rosey smiled, remembering how Rochelle and Alex had dared her to take the trail that night. She proudly did then turned her Friesian horse Sarabie around and galloped the whole way back. They had laughed at her, at least until she dared them to do the same thing. She had no idea that the well was a portal and wondered if her friends had known then. She gave Alex and Rochell a suspicious look. Alex saw her face and smiled awkwardly, knowing exactly what she was thinking.

"No, Rosey," he said, "We had no idea that the well was a portal to The World Within A World. It was the portal we came to Earth through, however, we were too young to remember then."

"Yeah, the first time that we heard it was a portal was today from your uncle John. You can't imagine how surprised we were. Whenever we went back to The World Within A World it was through another portal a few miles away," said Rochell with her usual high-energized voice.

"That portal, which is also located in Yellowstone, is open all the time. Rochell and I and our parents always used it to return to The World Within A World to practice and prepare for when the crystal would awaken. The Well Portal, however, is what is known as a Timed Portal, which means it is only open when its creator opens it and thus we could not use it since it has been closed ever since we first came here through it. It is controlled by someone in The World Within A World. You'll meet her soon enough. She's…"

"…She's going to explain everything to you. She's called the Golden Goddess!" shouted Rochell with extra emphasis on the woman's name.

Alex gave her an annoyed look. Rochell seemed unaware and oddly pleased with herself. Rosey smiled at the two, amused despite the current crisis.

"Please be quiet, Rochell. We're trying to keep a low profile, remember?" her uncle said, checking one of the windows.

"Oh, sorry."

"Why couldn't this Golden Goddess keep the Well Portal open?" said Rosey, trying to get back on track.

"Security reasons, arrive by one way, leave by another. Besides we didn't want to draw attention to that portal, because it's the one you are going to be using."

"Is the situation that dangerous?" Rosey felt herself shudder.

"Yes, it is," Alex quickly calmed her fears, "but we, Rochell and I, are here to help you plus an escort will be waiting for us on the other side of the portal. Don't worry we have security taken care of."

"What about Noly and Hazel, are they coming? I don't want to go without them..." Rosey asked, sudden fear racing through her. Her two fluff balls had been with her since she was little. They had soothed her when she was sad, protected her when she was afraid, and made her laugh when she felt confused. They were more than just pets, they were friends and family. She could never imagine leaving them behind, much less never seeing them again.

"Yes, there is no reason they can't come. Your horses will be going with you as well," her uncle said, still watching through the window.

"*Your* horses?" She gave him a sharp look. "Aren't you coming too?"

He looked back at her, his eyes slightly unfocused, as if what he had to say was something he knew she wouldn't like to hear. Without hearing it she knew he wasn't coming with her. Her body shook, but she remained in control, her eyes only slightly moist from sadness, fear, anger, and more. It wouldn't be the first time she had been disappointed after all.

"I'm sorry Rosey; I will not be going with you. I...I have something I need to do here, it is very important. I want to go with you very much, but I'm afraid that..." he paused as she lowered her head. He left the window and walked over to her. "What I'm doing on Earth needs to be completed. Okay?"

Rosey looked up and smiled, "I understand, whatever it is I'll leave it to you. Besides, if anyone can figure something out it's you, dad."

Before she had finished her sentence his arms were around her hugging her tightly. Rosey smiled and wrapped her arms around him. Behind her she could feel the eyes of Alex and Rochell watching them, a warmth threading through them all as they realized this might be the last time they would meet together like this in this house, the house they had grown up in, played in, ate in, slept in, and so much more. Her uncle reluctantly released Rosey from the hug. Noly came up and rubbed herself up against Rosey. She tilted her head back, looking up at her with her great greenish brown eyes just asking to be petted. Rosey laughed and rubbed the collie's head enthusiastically. Hazel came over and purred loudly, jealous that Noly was getting all the attention. Rosey petted her lovingly then remembered something.

"If they're going with us than they're going to need their coats."

At the word coat, Noly immediately started running back and forth in excitement. After all these years she knew it meant she would be going outside. Even though she was a collie, the cold Montana winters required her to have a little extra padding to fight the freezing weather. Looking at Hazel, Rosey laughed, Hazel's ears were flat against her head. She hated the little coat Rosey had bought for her but Hazel, being a short haired cat, was more susceptible to cold than Noly and, seeing as how Hazel loved to go on rides with Rosey, even during the winter, a little winter coat was required. Rosey quickly retrieved them and put them on the two. Hazel meowed in protest but obediently let Rosey put it on her.

"So, should I pack a backpack or something?" said Rosey, once she was satisfied that the two pets were warm and secure.

Her uncle shook his head, "No, no, everything that you will need will be provided for. We've been planning this day for…" he shared a glance with Alex and Rochell… "for a long time. We are very much prepared, besides, we try not to mix the two worlds."

"Wait, there's something I don't want to leave without," Rosey left Noly and Hazel staring after her, their ears pricked as they wondered where their master was going in such a hurry. Rosey ran up the stairs and to her room. She grabbed the picture of her mother and father. As she turned to leave she stopped and surveyed the room that she had grown up in, a sudden longing washing over her. Would she ever see it again? Her gaze scanned the shelves of animal figurines, her desk where she had done her homework so many nights, and the bed where she, Hazel, and Noly had played and slept on for so many years. What would become of it all? In that moment there was no one around to see her or tell her that what she had known all her life had been a fake conjured idea and not the real thing. For a few moments she was back to being Rosey Mystic the seventeen year old high school student with her life ahead of her. Then she heard Noly bark downstairs and the noise awakened her from her vision as if she had been slapped in the face. Quickly she ran out of her room and down the stairs not stopping to look back and walked briskly into the living room. Holding the picture up in front of her she squared her shoulders and asked in as calm as a voice as she could muster, "Is this a lie too?"

Her uncle's eyes glistened over and she could tell he was trying hard not to cry. He walked over to her and gripped her shoulders gently, his gaze kind and happy. Rosey knew the answer before he even said it.

"No, Rosey, that is a true picture of your mother and father. It's the only one I have of her, at least, here on Earth. You can take that with you if you like." He bowed his head then. "Please know," he said slowly, "that we fabricated all of this," he swept his arms out around the room, "so that you could live a normal and happy childhood. When you get to The World Within A World, you will understand."

Rosey nodded, feeling her body tremble and her eyes grow wet with tears that she would never let fall. She smiled then and held the picture close to her, happy that she would be taking something with her. She gently stuffed it into her pocket, it was small enough to fit, though snuggly. She looked up and said, "Well, is it time to go?"

Her uncle checked all the windows then turned back to them, and nodded, "Yes."

Chapter Three: To the Well

Under the darkness of night, the six made their way to the barn at the back of the house. Her uncle had not allowed for any flashlights for the same reason he had been checking all the windows in the house. He was worried about there being someone or something that wanted to get to her. The idea that there might be some sort of assassin lying around was horrifying. Shaking her head, Rosey focused on placing her footing as she stumbled over the uneven terrain with only the light of the moon to guide her. She and her friends had traveled this small path many times to the stables, so, despite the dark, she was able to find her way rather easily. The stables were located directly behind the house and the tack room was attached to the back of the barn. She hoped they would make it there without any unexpected delays.

Rosey zipped up her coat a little farther and pulled down her cap over her ears. The cold of October was biting at their backs as the six figures quickly made their way to the large red barn. The looming structure was nothing but a silhouette in the night but Rosey knew every surface and inch of the place. It had been her first official play area growing up so she knew every nook and cranny. Alex and Rochell had asked to board their own horses here, or rather, their parents had asked. She had been thrilled to be having more horseflesh to take care of and her relationship with the two people that owned them had only grown stronger since that day. That was how the three of them had become friends in the first place, or so she had thought. Since hearing that even her friends were in charge of watching her she wondered whether they had really ever been her friends. There was nothing about them that had ever seemed fake to her or out of place. They had always been sincere and treated her like one of them, not like some savior. They had played with her, laughed with her, and even cried with her.

There was no way that they had been faking it. They were her friends through and through, and nothing would convince her otherwise. Smiling she picked up her pace, a sudden surge of excitement giving strength to her legs. The others hastened to keep up with her.

Finally they arrived at the barn door. As silently as possible her uncle gently eased the large wooden door open. Alex entered first, stopped, glanced around then went through, beckoning for Rosey and Rochell to follow. They entered with Noly and Hazel right behind them. Rosey's uncle came last, closing the door behind him. The horses all had their heads sticking out over their stall doors as if they had been expecting them. Softly greeting each horse, Rosey and her friends began saddling them. Rosey had done this so many times that it was easy to do in the dark. It helped that her eyes had adjusted to the light of the moon, allowing her to see most of everything with little trouble.

When she finished with Sarabie, her giant Friesian mare, she noticed her uncle saddling his quarter horse Dusty. The dappled grey's face was the only part of him visible in a sliver of moonlight coming through the windows. He watched the others excitedly. Rosey came over and cooed to him softly hoping she would see him again. Rosey looked up at her uncle and he smiled at her as he led Dusty out of his stall. The suspense of the moment was driving her crazy. Hugging the big gelding's neck close she slowly relaxed.

When they were ready, Rosey picked up Hazel and placed her on her shoulders, one of her favorite spots to lie when Rosey rode. Feeling the cold of Hazel's paws on her neck, she noticed, happily, that the little cat was now more than happy to be wearing a coat. Turning to Sarabie she gathered her reins and moved toward the large barn doors. Her two friends flanked her on each side as they prepared to leave the barn, Dusty and her uncle took the lead. Alex's Bronzo was a beautiful bay mustang stallion and Rochell's palomino Phana was a gorgeous Thoroughbred mare. Rosey's Sarabie was a giant in comparison. The pure, coal black mare was the largest Friesian Rosey had ever seen. She was a good seventeen hands high, and still growing. Because of the horse's height, Rosey towered over her friends in the saddle. Looking around her she noticed how focused everyone was. For a moment Rosey no longer felt annoyed about being left in the dark about all that was going on. *Oh*, Rosey thought, *we are in the dark.* She stifled a giggle to avoid startling her friends, whose faces were like statues; prepared and alert.

Rosey's uncle gently cracked open the large barn door. He peeked out, searching through the dark with an intensity that brought home to Rosey just how worried he was about an attack. Evidently satisfied he opened the door wide so that Rosey and the others could get through. Rochell led her horse out first, then Rosey with Alex close behind. Her uncle came out last, leading Dusty close behind.

Outside, they mounted their horses then Rosey's uncle led the way farther from the barn to the forested area that eventually lead into Yellowstone. Trails had been created for the horse riders, dog walkers, and runners who frequently used them and for all the tourists to enjoy when they came to Silver Gate. This particular trail hadn't been around for a very long time, less than twenty years. Rosey couldn't help but think that that had something to do with all this. Had it been only created for her? Noly skipped excitedly next to her uncle but she never yipped or whined, seemingly aware that silence was essential. They moved onto the familiar Well Trail. About four yards into the trail she heard a rustling behind her as if something had moved the foliage. Rosey glanced behind her, startled, but all she saw was darkness. Rochell and Alex hardly moved a muscle; once again she faced forward knowing it was too dangerous to talk.

Rosey's mind was working furiously. Everything was different now. Her life had been a lie from the very beginning. She felt as if she was being reborn and was taking her first steps into a new world. She wasn't too far from the truth. If everything went well, she would be in a whole new world.

After a while the evening fog became so thick she could no longer see except by the mysterious haze of deep moonlight. Sarabie, however, didn't seem to care. She was simply following the familiar trail she had walked so many times before. Slowly it began to snow, the small flakes drifted down wordlessly around them in a dance of flashing white. Rosey flicked her long hair back and opened her mouth to catch the snow on her tongue, if she was going to leave Earth and embark on a powerful and magical journey than she wanted to have a little taste of Earth to remember it by. The action comforted her, reminding her of her carefree days as a child. The bright moonlight was highlighting the tree tops giving her enough light to vaguely make out shapes in front of her. The many winter surviving plants that surrounded them made the trail scenic and soothing but also gave a sense of safety. High, strong maples and oaks stood together in clumps and large stones covered in years of growing moss covered the sides of the trail and interior of the forest. She would miss this old forest.

The trail widened enough for the horses to ride abreast. Alex and Rochell moved up next to Rosey on either side of her. Her uncle rode Dusty ahead of them, glancing back every few moments to make sure they were okay.

In a very low voice, Alex suddenly interrupted her thoughts. "When you enter The World Within A World, don't be surprised when your animals start talking. On our world animals can talk and have the ability to be intelligent." As soon as the words 'animals' and 'talk' had come out of his mouth he had her wrapped around his finger. Her attention had snapped and she immediately stared down at Noly walking beside her uncle ahead of them. Her interest sparked, she looked at Alex in delight and whispered, "How does that happen?!"

"The World Within a World has large tubes of energy running through it called Energy Flows. They are suspended in midair and are filled with a large amount of moving energy. They are what allows the animals to talk and be intelligent. It's also what allows humans and animals to use elemental and magical powers." She twisted her hair around a finger, contemplating what it would be like to talk to her animals. The concept of powers and talking animals was mind-boggling enough but no more impossible than a crystal melting out of her skin and into her hands. The word Energy Flows caught her special attention. Her uncle had used it before when talking about Earth. Does this new world have these flows too? Apparently so.

"Wait," she whispered, just now comprehending Alex's last words, "You mentioned elements and magic? What do you mean?" Silence fell as Alex hung his head, deciding how best to answer this. On Rosey's right, Rochell rearranged herself in her seat and patted Phana's neck absentmindedly. It was the only noise in the silence, besides the sound of the horse's hooves in the smooth grass.

After a few moments Alex looked up, exchanged looks with Rochell, who nodded, then turned to Rosey.

"There are twelve different elements in all. The twelve elements can be used by humans and animals thanks to the Energy Flows. Rochell here is an air elemental." Rosey glanced at her in awe. Rochell smiled and nodded in confirmation. Alex went on, "There are three levels of Elementals; Apparition, the lowest; God or Goddess, the middle level; and Queen or King, the highest. Rochell is a Queen level. People also have the ability to use magic. A human or animal must be born with a talent for working magic; if they don't then they can't work it. I am a magikin, a person who uses magic. Like elementals magikins have levels: a Wizard or Witch is the lowest, a Goddess or God level is the middle level, and a Mage is the highest. I am a God level magikin." "Wait, wait, wait, you guys…have powers?!" whispered Rosey startled by what she'd heard. By now she had moved beyond startled to just plain shock…that's it. She was now in a state of do-whatever-they-tell-you-to shock mode.

"We sure do, you'll get to see us use these powers first hand on The World Within A World, that is, if we run into any trouble of course."

"Trouble…ah…what kind of trouble," she said, seeing an opportunity to gleam more from them and, thanks to the levels of Freudian psychology, threats to her life took precedent over magic and elements.

"That's a little more complicated to explain. In fact it may be better for you to hold off those kinds of questions until later."

Rosey winced. Later. *There's that darn word again*, she thought, clenching her fists around the reins. *They better explain things soon or I'm gonna lose it!* If they could tell her no more, than there was one last question she wanted answered.

"I have one more question before we start this whole journey thing," Rosey said softly. "There will be no later on this one, I want this answered now."

Alex and Rochell waited patiently, they seemed a little edgy but did not refuse.

"Did you guys know all about this from the day you became my friends? Was it all just a hoax until I was ready to come here?" she asked looking down.

Rochell and Alex hung their heads, this time Rochell answered.

"Yes and no. When we first moved here we were too young to understand what was going on. Our parents were supposed to watch you, not us. We were always citizens of The World Within A World. We always knew about the Keeper, but we became your friends out of our own interest and were only told about whom you were when we were both fourteen, about five years after we met you. For five years we knew you like any normal friend, and then suddenly we were given responsibility over watching you just like our parents. They took advantage of the situation, but only to keep you safe. The important thing is we met you like any regular person, though our parents did go to great links to have play-dates together, it's still the same thing. You are our true friend."

Rosey smiled, happier than she'd ever been before. Somehow, that one answer made everything right again. No matter what she was going to face, she felt that it wouldn't be nearly as monumental as it had been. These three people, her uncle, Alex, and Rochell, had always been her rock in society. They had been her safety net and her greatest supporters, they were everything to her…and, hopefully, they always would be. If they had been false, then Rosey knew that it would have been too deep of a scar for her to ignore. Just another scar, deep down within. Their words meant more than they could even know.

"Thanks guys," she said.

She opened her mouth to say something more but stopped when her uncle cleared his throat. He had stopped and was turned around staring at them with an annoyed expression. Without saying a word he put his hand to his mouth and made a zipper motion across his lips. Rosey smiled at him like a kid who got caught with her hand in the cookie jar. Rochell stifled a laugh and Alex smiled knowingly. They continued on in silence.

The Well Trail was a good three miles long with one trail leading to the well and a separate trail leading away from it. It was five miles there and five miles back. It was the longest horse trail the forest had and the most beautiful during the spring time. All sorts of wild flowers bloomed along it and in the fall the trees were the loveliest shades of brown, yellow, red, and orange. The whole forest supported all kinds of wildlife, the most numerous being deer, birds, and other various critters. During the winter the place had a C.S. Lewis feel to it, as if the well was the lamp post and somewhere in the trees was a hidden wardrobe. Rosey breathed in the rich winter air and smelled something strange, something that shouldn't be there. It was a flowery lavender scent she had never smelled before. It was such an intense lavender that it almost tasted sweet. Before she could turn to Alex to ask what it was, her uncle drew their attention ahead of them.

"Look," he said, as they entered the well's clearing, "We're here," Rosey gasped in awe. She had made the trip to the well many times before but this time was different. It had a small, but spacious enough clearing to allow room for their horses with two picnic benches placed on either side of the well about ten feet away from one another. A small hitching post was stuck in the ground for people with horses who wanted to stop and rest. Nothing was out of the ordinary, except for one thing. Staring dead ahead she laid eyes on the most unusual sight she had ever seen. Surrounding the brick well and occupying every spare inch of grass were hundreds of shining, silver flowers that cast a bright glow, illuminating the entire clearing. Despite the intensity of the light it did not seem to penetrate any further than the clearing. It was as if light began and ended suddenly. There were no casted shadows or dimming light extending into the path like normal lighting would do. It was beautiful, but unnatural.

Then something occurred to her.

"Those flowers are blooming during the winter?"

"They're enchanted. They only bloom…ah…when the well portal is activated," said Alex shakily, as if he was drowsy.

Rosey pulled Sarabie to a stop and examined the flowers closely. They were of a different species, one she had never seen before. They almost resembled a snap dragon and a rose combined. Their rich aroma made her a little woozy, reminding her of soft pillows and down feathers. The sense of sleeping while flying on a cool comforting breeze seemed to overtake her. *These must have been what I smelled before*, she thought, barely getting her mind to cooperate with all the mucky feelings.

"Feel that?" Alex asked softly, his voice bringing her back from her daze. "It's called Aroma Dust…a powerful overwhelming fragrance…ooh, ah…that relaxes animals so that they don't comprehend what's happening and become…agitated or frightened." He shook his head, obviously affected by the flowers. At least she wasn't the only one feeling this. "Unfortunately it also causes great lethargy in humans. Hum…either way it makes the transition from world… to world a little easier to handle for animals and humans alike."

Through all of this Rosey was imaging how, if these flowers were used in horse shows, no horse would ever act up again, although the hospital would have a field day because everyone who was riding them would be falling off of the horse dead asleep. She laughed at her own silly humor and the group took that as a sign to get going.

"So where's the portal?" Rosey said, looking around halfheartedly. "The well is the portal," Rochell whispered, her eyes glazed and happy as she leaned over to Rosey, sloping over her saddle tediously. She snapped back into the saddle before falling completely out of it, looking not the least bit fazed.

Rosey took no notice of Rochell's giddiness. Such actions were usually normal for the brunette. "Doesn't look like a portal," Rosey said, squinting at the brick hole in the ground as if doing so would help her see something unseen.

"That's the point," Alex said almost absentmindedly, as if he was unsure of what else to say.

She was happy to see that she wasn't the only one affected by the flowers but it was a bit unnerving to see her friends so out of whack. They were keeping their sentences short and to the point, which was not at all like them. Looking at them she noticed Rochell shaking her head every now and then and Alex was busy pinching himself. If she wasn't so woozy she'd probably be laughing hysterically.

Looking down at Sarabie, Rosey could see that the horse's eyes seemed glazed over and under the smooth saddle blanket Rosey hardly felt a muscle twitch in the bulging frame of her beautiful black horse. Sarabie wasn't pretending, so all this stuff must be real. Even Hazel swayed on Rosey's shoulders with the swagger of a drunken man. Her eyes were slightly crossed and she stared at one paw as if there were two of it. Noly looked, amazingly enough, perfectly fine. Rosey guessed it didn't work on creatures that were already crazy and laid back. Rosey had no way of knowing if that was true and she was too woozy to care to find out.

Rosey saw that her uncle had dismounted and tied Dusty to one of the hitching posts. He walked towards them, slowly. Rosey could tell he was a little off balance. Dusty, who was known for his enthusiasm, hung his head, as if he were sleeping. Rosey smiled, if only they could get the flowers to grow near the barn, they'd never have problems with his high-spiritedness anymore. Rochell suddenly moved her horse forward about ten yards away from the well. Rosey gazed at her, unsure of what she was doing.

"Well, see ya on the other side!" Rochell said cheerfully, waving her hand lazily.

Then, lightly kicking her horse, they surged forward, galloping straight toward the well. Phana, under the spell of the flowers, did not bolt away from the well or stop and refuse the jump but, instead, obediently jumped up into the air at Rochell's command and dropped into the well. Rosey was horrified, thinking they were plunging to their deaths, but instead of a terrible scream, a flurry of bright blue lights and flashes crossed Rosey's view. She and her other companions covered their faces as the blue light became a small tornado that swallowed Rochell and Phana whole.

When Rosey looked back up Rochell was gone, the lights had died down and the clearing was silent. She turned to Alex, his face showed no surprise at seeing her disappear like that, though he rubbed his eyes vigorously at the intensity of the light. Obviously this was not anything out of the ordinary for him. She sighed and tried not to let herself sink back into the flower's trap. The sudden adrenaline that had coursed through her at Rochell's jump had awakened her senses. It was all so strange and unreal, like a dream. She stared down at Sarabie and saw that her eyes were now half closed. Her breathing was slow, coming softly and gently as if she was in a deep comforting sleep. If she didn't leave soon she worried she would have to gently shake Sarabie awake and that could take a while. When Sarabie slept, she slept deeply. Once again she felt the drowsiness taking over her senses. Quickly she bit her lip and the feeling subsided. She looked back at the well as if the blue lights were going to appear and swallow her whole in that one instant. Alex must have read her thoughts;

he moved Bronzo next to Sarabie and reached for her shoulder, he missed but corrected it and laid it there comfortingly.

"It's your turn Rosey and don't worry, it's perfectly safe. I'll be right behind you, okay?" he said groggily but soothingly.

She nodded then closed her eyes and focused. This was the only way she could learn the truth about her past. It was her only chance to find out who she really was. She wasn't about to be put off by a blue light show. Leaning forward she urged Sarabie into a fast walk toward the well. Before she could go much farther, her uncle stepped in front of Sarabie. Sarabie stood and waited; apparently she wasn't very sleepy after all. He came around to stand next to her, never taking his eyes from her face as if to memorize it.

Hazel seemed to wave at him, though that could have just been the effects of the flowers. He looked at Rosey with the saddest eyes she'd ever seen.

"Rosey, be a good Keeper. I know you can do it…just like your mother did." He said this last quietly so only she could hear.

She nodded, and then said, "Why can't you come with me?"

"I can't. My job here won't let me."

"Job? What, the government…"

"Not the government. Something …else…"

"Huh?" There were a million things she wanted to shout in her head but the effect of the flowers had her too relaxed to get anything intelligible out.

He shook his head, whether it was from the flowers or his own sadness she couldn't say. "I can't discuss it now. Maybe someday I will."

She looked into his eyes long and hard then, smiling, she lurched forward and embraced him. Sarabie shifted her weight a little, but otherwise held still. Hazel purred softly from between Rosey's hair. She heard Noly softly whine somewhere in the background and held back a stray tear. She pulled away and then turned and worked the small picture of her parents out of her pocket. She handed it to him. "Here, you keep this. This is the only picture you have of them on Earth, right?" He nodded slowly, unable to speak. "Then you need it more than I do, I'm sure I can find another. Just...take care of it for me, Okay?"

    He smiled and they embraced again. Rosey's heart almost split in two, she didn't want to leave it behind, but she knew she couldn't leave her uncle here without an image of his beloved sister. She pulled away and facing the well, said, "I promise you. I will be a good Keeper." With that she called to Noly to follow and urged Sarabie forward. Noly barked in response and joined Sarabie's side as they ran. Rosey squeezed her legs tightly against Sarabie's sides, anticipating the whirlwind that would come. She felt Sarabie's muscles flex underneath her legs for the first time since the flowers started their sleep spell. As they approached the well, Rosey leaned forward into the familiar launch of Sarabie's powerful jump. She was no longer Rosey Mystic the school girl but Rosey Mystic the Keeper.

Chapter Four: The New World

At first it felt as if she had jumped into clear plastic wrap, stretching tightly until finally breaking through to the other side. Rosey's body felt stiff, as if both she and Sarabie had been pushing against the surface for a long time. The light had been blindingly bright and dizzying. How she was able to stay on Sarabie's back she had no idea. Just as soon as it had begun it ended. She and Sarabie came to a complete stop as they landed on solid ground. Rosey's head swam. Cursing she held her head as pain shot through her nerves like electric pulses. She felt nauseous and everything was out of focus. Shifting slightly, she sighed with relief as her vision and nausea began to slowly clear. Hazel's tail wrapped around under her neck and tickled her ear. At least she knew Hazel was still there.

Suddenly all around her soft excited yips filled the air. Rosey's head immediately exploded in pain as the sounds grew. Rosey held her head and rubbed the throbbing area, trying to release whatever pressure she could. Something was off about the yips. Suddenly they started taking shape into words. The yips belonged to Noly. That much she was sure of, but words? They were so fast she couldn't make them out; they weren't complex enough to be words but they weren't barks either. As her hearing cleared she heard them more clearly, they weren't words but laughter, actual human-like laughter coming from her dog! A movement at her shoulder startled her as Hazel lowered herself into Rosey's lap from her perch on her shoulders.

"Would you stop that infernal laughing! Can't you see Rosey has no head for it right now!?"

The laughter stopped suddenly but Rosey was still unsure of who had told Noly to stop. Hazel moved on Sarabie's withers and rubbed her head against Rosey's hand. Rosey's eyes were still closed as the pain slowly subsided.

"Rosey...Rosey...R..o..s..e..y?"came the same voice that had quieted Noly. It sounded as if it was coming from her cat, in front of her.

"Hazel stop, my head is already throbbing enough."

"Oh sorry, are you all right?"

"I think so, I..." suddenly Rosey stopped and stared at Hazel, gripping the saddle horn of Sarabie's tack in disbelief.

"Hazel?"

"Yeah?"

"Are you talking?"

"Uh, duh," she snickered. Looking around at Noly she said irritably in a voice that sounded much too old for a cat so young. "I'm the only loyal pet who's actually got enough brain to answer you. Miss I'm-gonna-catch-my-tail-eventually is too busy running around in circles to talk sensibly, not that there's much sense involved with her in the first place."

The little cat looked back at Rosey whose mouth hung so low she could have easily tied it in a knot.

"What?" said Hazel with a confused look, she shrugged her little shoulders as if she had been doing it her whole life.

'It's just that...you're exactly the way I thought you'd be."

Hazel purred and rubbed herself against Rosey's arm. Rosey hugged her close, breathing in the warm honey scent of the precious cat she'd grown up with.

"I know this is a bit of a shock, but we are still the same companions your uncle bought for you all those years ago. It's just that now we can communicate, unlike her who seems to be unaffected by sudden intelligence," said Hazel, casting a disapproving glance at Noly. Noly stopped pursuing her tail and stared back, not the least bit fazed.

Hazel looked back at Rosey and said, "Dogs really have no dignity." Rosey laughed as Noly ran forward and jumped up to nip playfully at

Hazel. Hazel danced out of the way on perfectly poised paws mewing with amusement.

Rosey remembered what Alex had said about the Energy Flows making it possible for animals to talk. She laughed again at her small companions and cursed under her breath when it caused another sudden jolt of pain to slice through her brain. After a few moments it went away. She watched amused as Hazel expertly dodged Noly's nips with skill and precision. *I'm so glad I never teased or abused my pets*, she thought with a smile.

Out of all the things Rosey was sure to face in this new world, so far, this was the best part. These were her best pals beside Alex and Rochell, family really. Rosey's eyes softened as she watched them, a warmth beginning to spread throughout her body. *They're perfect, just the way I imagined them.* Looking up she spotted Alex a little ways ahead. When he saw her he turned Bronzo around and urged the buckskin gently over to her side.

"Hey, how are you?" he asked kindly.

"Oh I'm...good. Just add a migraine and I'll have the most perfect case of brain damage you've ever seen," she said, almost sarcastically.

Alex laughed despite the bitterness in her tone and said, "Don't worry; it's like that for all first timers. The nausea wears off the more you use portals.

Rosey nodded, happy to see that he too had made it through the portal and that nothing had gone mysteriously wrong.

Suddenly Sarabie nickered loudly, setting off, once again, racing pains through her head. "Rosey?" said Sarabie turning her head slightly to look at Rosey with one giant black eye, "Could you please tell these two to play on somebody else for a bit before I decide to accidently run over them."

Rosey was taken aback for a moment by the horse's voice. It was a loud yet sing-song voice, almost like silk. It was beautiful and sounded like...exactly what a Frisian might sound like. She tilted her head ever so slightly, her eye never leaving Rosey's. Rosey glanced at Hazel and Noly and the game they were still playing.

"All right you two, leave Sarabie in peace and go play somewhere else." She said smiling at Alex who shook his head knowingly.

Hazel immediately complied and jumped off Sarabie right onto Noly's back using her as an off ramp to the ground. As soon as her paws hit the ground she took off running with Noly right behind her.

'You think they'll ever grow up?" said Alex watching the two fuzz balls playing.

"Probably not," Rosey said smiling.

With her rambunctious pets distracted Rosey was finally able to inspect her surroundings. Looking around her she noticed that they were not far from a high cliff wall. The jagged rocks jutted precariously out blocking most of the sun. She could see nothing more beyond that because a gentle fog had settled over the land, thick enough to hide the sun that looked to be still new on the horizon. It must be morning. She felt a cold breeze swipe across her face and she shivered, hugging her arms to her sides. "Awwwww, its cold here too?" she said disappointed. "Yup, sorry. It's almost winter here as well," said Alex nonchalantly. Rosey pouted at him and they both smiled. Rosey's headache cleared a little but she still felt a buzz in the back of her head. She zipped her coat all the way up and felt her shivering disperse as her body adjusted. She took her cap off and smoothed out her rumpled hair then replaced the cap over her ears which had begun to go numb. She reached into her coat pockets and pulled out her gloves. She put them on and rubbed her hands together vigorously to warm them up. Rosey wasn't sure but it felt colder here than it had been at the well. It was then that she was reminded of her uncle and the strange way he had acted. "Alex, why were we being so stealthy on Earth?" "I don't know, your uncle told us to be on alert. We didn't ask questions." "Why?"

"Things are taking place on Earth that may be a little more complicated than anticipated and he's involved. Apparently something on Earth may have had the power to sense the crystal…or something like that. That's all I and Rochell know and that is the only explanation that he gave us," he said, looking at her apologetically. Rosey had wanted to ask her uncle why he seemed so nervous but things had happened too fast for her to do so. Even if she had had the time she doubted he'd have told her. He worked for the government which meant he was not allowed to talk about his work. Whatever it was that had put him on edge she hoped he could handle it and that he would stay safe. "Rosey, please try not to worry too much. Your uncle can take care of himself. For now, focus on what's happening on this world."

Alex gave her a soft smile, a smile he was well known for. Rosey was immediately comforted. Alex could calm a storm with that smile. She nodded and he relaxed, pleased to see that she trusted him and Rochell even after discovering all that she had, Rosey knew that there was nothing she could do about her Uncle now. Earth was no longer her concern, this world was. She needed to trust her Uncle and know that he'd do the right thing.

Suddenly the fog began thickening. Looking about her she could hardly see farther than ten feet in either direction. Rosey turned her head this way and that searching her surroundings as best she could through the fog but to not avail.

"Why is it so foggy?" "It's like this in the morning, it'll clear soon when the sun rises over the hills," said Alex.

"Wait a second, where's Rochell?" she said with sudden realization, glancing at Alex earnestly. She couldn't believe she had almost forgotten Rochell.

"Oh, yeah, sorry. She came through all right. I was just waiting until you felt well enough. The nausea can be a little overwhelming. She's over this way, follow me."

He turned Bronzo around and headed into the fog at a soft walk.

"Noly, Hazel, come on," Rosey called out over her shoulder.

The two come running. Hazel jumped up onto Rosey's saddle purring in laughter at Noly who pouted at Sarabie's side; apparently the two of them had raced each other to see who would get to Rosey first. Rosey rolled her eyes but enjoyed the warmth that rose inside of her at the familiarity of the act. *Nothing has changed; they are just as crazy as ever,* she thought happily.

A few yards away Rosey made out a mounted woman and a larger indistinct figure. Drawing closer the figures came into focus. One was Rochell and the other was a...Rosey gasped in surprise, she pulled Sarabie to a stop and stared, rather rudely, at a larger than life black, armored wolf. The thing that caught Rosey's attention the most wasn't so much the wolf but the armor it was wearing. The armor's style reminded her of medieval style costumes that she had seen at a renaissance fair once, but this golden armor was more than a stage prop. The metal clinked slightly as the colossal wolf moved its labyrinth of massive muscles. The muzzle of the wolf moved up and down like Hazel and Noly's had in obvious speech and its eyes were a deep bloody crimson. She noticed it wasn't the only one; other armored wolves were stationed close by, hardly detectable in the fog. Even with the thick fog she could still make out their armor and how it shone with a golden color.

Rosey noticed one of the wolves stood out from all the others. Her coat was a beautiful white and her armor was brilliant silver in contrast to the others' gold. Rosey eyed the beautiful creature with awe. Who was she? She felt Hazel stiffen and press closer to her as she gazed at the wolves; but then the feisty tortoiseshell puffed up her chest, her tail whipping from side to side. Noly stood next to Sarabie seemingly unconcerned about the wolves. Rosey patted Hazel affectionately and felt her relax. Rosey looked back at the black wolf talking with Rochell. She spotted Alex waiting patiently a few yards away and urged Sarabie over to stand next to Bronzo.

"Alex, who is that and why is he…they so big?" said Rosey motioning to the large black wolf and the others that surrounded them.

"That's Wolvereen, Commander of the Golden Goddess's Guards; they'll be escorting us."

"Escorting us where?" Rosey asked, remembering that Alex had mentioned an escort before when they were at her house.

"To the Golden Goddess's Castle, she'll explain everything to you then. The reason they are so big is because they are what's known as Dominants. Dominants are animals that are larger than normal animals. It's another power associated with the Energy Flows." He looked away at one of the wolves then back at her. "Sorry, I have to go check on something. I'll tell you more later, okay." He smiled apologetically then turned Bronzo around and trotted over to the wolf he had looked at before.

Rosey watched him in mild annoyance; she was really beginning to hate that word, later. That's the second time I've heard of her. *The Golden Goddess,* she thought, *I wonder who she is?* Looking back at Rochell she thought about going to talk with her but didn't want to interrupt her talk with the wolf. However, in all actuality, she just wasn't too keen about entering into a conversation with the black beast, so she stayed where she was feeling like a pawn in a game waiting to be moved to her next position.

Suddenly the black wolf turned away from Rochell. It looked like they had made an agreement. Rosey watched Rochell turn Phana around and trot over to Alex and Bronzo saying something as she approached him. After a few moments Alex broke away from Rochell. As Rosey watched, in a flash, like a ghost appearing out of thin air, the giant black wolf was there in front of her, about ten feet away. His large head was about level with hers. She was eye to eye with the black wolf. For a moment they studied each other. Rosey almost shrank away at the fierceness in the powerful red eyes glowering into her own blue ones. It was like fire and water fighting for dominance. A burst of sudden pride washed over her. She was determined not to lose this silent battle. She held her head high and stared back at him defiantly. Suddenly, nodding, as if he liked what he saw, he smiled at her and looked away. She watched him as he turned and called the other wolves to him with a quick low howl. She sighed with relief, feeling as if she had passed an important test with flying colors. Smiling with pride, she urged Sarabie forward to join Rochell. Phana whinnied a greeting to Sarabie and Rosey called out to Rochell in her own greeting.

"Hey Rochell, I thought I told you not to get involved with wolves."

Rochell laughed. As Rosey drew near Rochell gave her a playful shove, "You big pain, he's not a wolf, he's a wooooooolf," she said drawing out the 'o' to sound like a howl. Wolvereen glanced at the girls with one eyebrow tilted upward, his red eyes studying them. This only made them laugh harder. The black beast huffed in annoyance then turned back to his wolf guards.

"Oh, Rosey, I'm glad to see you're still your playful self, despite all this," said Rochell becoming serious all of a sudden.

"And you're the one telling me this?" said Rosey, giving her a skeptical glance.

Rochell laughed again, "I know, quite the shocker."

"So, what was that all about?"

"I assume that Alex has informed you about Wolvereen?"

"He has."

"Well Wolvereen was just filling me in on all the 'guard stuff' for the escort, nothing big, but he always takes things to the ultimate extreme. We're ready to move out once Wolvereen's wolves get into position. What about you?"

"Sure, the sooner the better," Gazing at the large wolf as he walked about his wolves a thought occurred to Rosey. It was such a small thing but Rosey was amazed that she hadn't thought of it before.

"Rochell, what language do you speak here? It's too much for me to say they all know English, right?" she said with a sheepish smile, already knowing the answer.

Rochell smiled back and said, "No, not everyone here knows English. Our language is called Angensile, it is a little bit like French and English smashed together except without all the strange sounds," she said wrinkling her nose as she tried to find a way to describe it.

Rosey almost groaned in her seat, "Am I going to have to learn this language?"

Rochell smiled and said, "It's better if Alex tells you about this. It always makes my brain ache whenever he gets all magiky." Turning in her seat, Rochell called out to Alex, who stood a little ways away speaking to one of the wolves.

When he heard her, he excused himself from the wolf and turned Bronzo towards them, gently urging the buckskin into a fast trot. He pulled up short before Phana and Sarabie. "What can I do for ya," he said kindly. Rosey repeated her question and Alex nodded, understanding. He then smiled, making Rosey stare at him suspiciously. "No," he said simply, "You already know the language. Why would we make you learn something you already know?" His eyes gleamed mischievously in understanding while she was left flabbergasted.

"What?" seemed to be the only word she could force through her mouth.

"This might not make much sense, but just bear with me. Before you were brought to Earth, a magikin transferred their knowledge of the language into your mind as an infant. There it remains, waiting to be used. Any magikin could have done so. It is fairly easy to transfer information from a magikin to someone else. They just cast the spell and link their minds together…" he trailed off when he saw Rosey's face twisting into one of confusion. "Don't worry about the details, it was easier to do this since we knew you would be returning to The World Within A World at some point and we didn't want you to have to worry about language barriers. Your uncle could have taught it to you, but there would be no

The Mystics

guarantee that you would take to the language well or remember it, this was just easier to ensure the transition was less stressful."

Rosey shook her head in disbelief, amazed that someone could have transferred information like that so quickly and that she had had it all this time without knowing. "Hold on, I don't have any knowledge of another language besides Spanish from school but…" her eyes brightened, "now I know why my uncle was so adamant about me taking French, you should have seen his face when I said I wanted to take Spanish…but anyway…I don't have any…I don't know how to say it…"

Bronzo seemed to smile as Rosey flapped her hands around her head gesturing wildly to pull in the right words. Sarabie snorted and Bronzo averted his gaze. Phana pawed the ground as if keeping the peace between them. Alex jumped in to help Rosey as she stumbled, "You wouldn't Rosey; the knowledge will simply come to you when you need it. On this world, you will not be speaking English, but Angensilian. You will be aware that you are not speaking English, but it will be natural to you. You can even write it and read it too."

Rosey gazed at him amazed and at a loss for words. What was she to say to that? Thanks? She huffed and felt Sarabie paw at the ground, tired of standing in one place. Bronzo shifted his weight off his back right leg and nosed Sarabie's face kindly. She nuzzled him back and Phana joined in. Somewhere in the distance, Rosey heard Noly and Hazel playing, their excited yaps and meows filling the empty space of air around her and Alex. A sudden memory occurred to Rosey and she swallowed, consumed by it. Almost as if she was unaware that she was speaking she said, "My uncle used to speak a strange language…he told me it was an African dialect that he and my mother would speak when they were in Africa. I didn't like it, but I wanted to know it…it was the language my mother spoke…." Rosey stopped herself, feeling a surge of grief grip her like iron. The sadness wasn't so much from the memory as it was from the realization that it was a lie, her mother wasn't and had never been from Africa and neither had the language, but it was still the language her mother had spoken. The thought gave Rosey strength and she pulled on that. Lifting her head she said, "He always said what it meant before he said it, in that way, I guess, he was hiding the fact that I would already know what he was saying? It would be a little strange, to know what a word or phrase meant without anyone teaching it to me…" Rosey trailed off and nodded to Alex, "Thanks, it's good to know I won't have to be learning a whole new system of conjugations and other stuff. That drove me crazy in Spanish."

Alex nodded, pretending not to have noticed Rosey's show of emotion before. He and Rochell had taken those classes with Rosey as well. They knew just how much trouble it had been. Rochell patted her shoulder and Rosey smiled.

Turning to them she said, "Who was the magikin that gave me the language?" She was no longer sad, just curious.

Alex and Rochell exchanged glances, uncertainty passed between them. After a few moments Alex said, "Your uncle, he is the one that did it. He's a God level magikin."

Rosey felt a sliver of shock run through her mind. She had not known that her uncle was a magikin, the idea unnerved her. It did, however, make her feel better. She was much happier with the idea that the person who had given her the language was someone she knew and not some stranger even though she knew the stranger would have meant her any harm. Still the idea that her uncle was a magikin was…strange. In a way, even though he was her uncle and had raised her, he seemed, now, more of a stranger than he did before. Rosey shook her head. She refused to think badly of her uncle, who had loved her like a father which had earned him her love back as a daughter.

Glancing at Noly and Hazel where they still chased each other around the clearing, Rosey said, "What about my cat, dog, and the horses? They're originally from Earth?"

Alex was quick to answer, "A magikin is going to transfer the knowledge in the same way your uncle did when we get to the Golden Goddess. Doing it right now would be too dangerous. Our first priority is to get you and everyone else to safety."

Rosey nodded, she didn't want to have to translate for the two fluff balls, not when half the stuff that came out of Noly's mouth was ridiculous and the stuff that came out of Hazel's was usually in retaliation to whatever Noly had just said. In this way they could annoy people with their own voices. Rosey frowned. Maybe it would be better to leave them without the knowledge of the language so she could regulate what they said. Rosey considered it then shook her head. Nah, I won't do that to them. The ability to communicate would be crucial in an emergency; still, the idea was tempting.

Before she had time to think of anything else, out of the corner of her eye, she saw a flicker of white. Startled, she turned to see the large white wolf she had seen earlier sitting not too far away, gazing at her. Compared to Wolvereen this wolf was bigger with a skinnier body, more muscle, and shorter fur. Alex turned his attention to Rochell, leaving Rosey to her peace. As they talked the wolf lifted herself up on long, powerful legs and walked towards Rosey. Rosey couldn't help but clench up, every instinct telling her to run. The wolf came to an abrupt stop before her at a respectful distance. Rochell and Alex looked at her, their eyes curious but not alarmed. The wolf studied Rosey for a moment with calm, piercing, blue eyes, then she spoke, her voice like icy silk. Rosey was dumbfounded as the words that flowed out of the wolf's mouth were noticeably not English but she understood them anyway. It took all of her self-control not to grin in surprise and childish joy which was made easier by the immense bulk of the wolf. She knew the creature was not there to harm her, nevertheless, Rosey felt herself stiffen from head to toe.

"Hello Keeper, I am Nagura, Commander of the Silver Goddess's Guards. Here, these are gifts to you and your friends from the Silver Goddess."

Nagura reached into a compartment on the side of her armor with her muzzle and lifted out five cloaks, a red, yellow, green, blue, and orange one. Nagura extended her muzzle towards Rosey and for a few moments Rosey stood stock still, unsure of what to do. Her brain screamed at her to accept the gift but her muscles wouldn't move. Reason and some innate sense of danger stopped her. Finally Rosey mustered up the strength to move herself forward and grasp the cloaks.

'Thanks," she managed to say, startled that the word that came from her mouth wasn't English, but, as Alex had promised, sounded normal and natural to her. She shook her head, astonished by how easily the words flowed through her mind as if they had been there all along. To distract herself from the on flow of words she examined what Nagura had given her. Looking at the cloaks Rosey saw that there were three different sizes, three where human sized, one was very small, and the other was medium sized. Rosey handed the yellow one to Rochelle and the blue one to Alex, they quickly put them on over their jackets. A little unsure, Rosey put on the red one over her jacket. The two smaller ones had extra straps attached and were very odd looking, causing Rosey to draw a blank as to what to do with them. Then realization hit her. She called to Hazel and Noly to come to her and they came racing over obediently. Hazel jumped expertly onto Sarabie's saddle and Noly came up behind her and nipped playfully at her tail but Hazel was out of reach. Noly stared at her with annoyance but said nothing. Gently grabbing Hazel, Rosey secured the smallest green cloak onto her slender body. The extra straps held the cloak securely around her tiny frame. For once, Hazel did not squirm; it was obvious that her intelligence had made her understand that she needed the device to stay warm. That was one good thing the intelligence had done. She then called to Noly who jumped up and placed her paws on the saddle. Leaning down Rosey secured the orange cloak around the fuzzy dog's body. Noly gave her a doggy kiss as she secured the straps. Rosey laughed and patted her head lovingly. Smiling, Rosey watched as Noly pranced away, showing off her new orange cloak, her tail was high and wagging a mile a minute. Hazel huffed in annoyance and flicked her tail at Noly before climbing up onto Rosey's shoulders, apparently done playing. Rosey sighed as her own cloaks took effect for the biting cold was suddenly replaced with pleasant warmth. Whatever the cloaks were made out of, it was doing the trick, far better than her jacket had been.

"Do you like them?" asked Nagura, looking at Rosey expectantly.

"Yes, I love them, thank you."

"Good to hear, it's the finest weather proof material in the world. I hope you enjoy it but before I go I have one more gift to give."

Rosey nodded. The excitement behind the understanding that she knew a language that she had never learned was starting to fade. Because it seemed natural to her, it was like trying to stay excited about breathing.

Rosey watched Nagura closely as she once again turned her head around and retrieved something from the small compartment. Turning she held in her jaws a long silver dagger sheathed in a scabbard crafted in ornate, delicate patterns and shining details. Diamonds were inlaid into the scabbard, both small and large. Each diamond was surrounded by a blue outline that resembled a snow flake. Nagura extended it to Rosey. Rosey gasped and gently retrieved it from the jaws of the white beast, careful of the sharp canines. Studying it, she found herself transfixed by the beauty of the craftsmanship and the intense metalworking. The blade was emblazoned with a strange language that she could not read. It wasn't recognizable in either English or Angensilian. They seemed to resemble something close to the hieroglyphics. Delicate subtle patterns decorated the spaces in between the strange letters, like old time calligraphy. The hilt was made of what looked like crystal and the end formed the head of a strange looking creature she'd never seen before. On the creature's forehead was a sapphire crystal as blue as her eyes. Golden flecks shimmered on the hilt adding to the decoration. Rosey looked up at Nagura and smiled, bowing her head.

"Thank you, I humbly accept this gift. Please, tell me…"

"Yes," said the wolf, expectantly.

"What is its name?"

Rochell and Alex gave her a strange look, one of disbelief and surprise.

"Well done, Rosey, it is called Silver Knight. Good day to you." With that the large white wolf turned around and was gone as quickly as she had come, disappearing into the mist.

Rosey watched after her then realized something, "Wait a second." She turned to her friends, curiously. "She said the Silver Goddess. Who's that?"

It took Rochell a few moments to answer. She was still startled by the way Rosey had acted before, especially knowing that the dagger had a name. Rosey wasn't sure why such a thing would startle Rochell, in a lot of books and legends most swords had a name to go by. Finally, Rochell blinked and said, "She is the Golden Goddess's sister."

"There are two Goddesses?!"

"Sure are."

"Uh-huh," said Rosey lost in thought, "So…is that why Nagura is wearing silver armor instead of gold?"

"Exactly, she's the leader of the Silver Goddess's Guards after all. Hopefully you'll meet the Silver Goddess one day. I have never had that privilege but you might."

Rosey shook her head, "If she's with the Silver Goddess, then why is she here?" She pointed down to the ground with a hand.

Rochell pondered the question for a moment then said, "Not sure, you'll have to ask her that yourself."

"So…who exactly are these Goddesses?" She said as she put on Silver Knight, buckling the silver buckles expertly as if she had done it her whole life. The belt itself was white with blue snowflake designs etched into it.

The Mystics

"They are powerful, Goddess level, magikins. The Golden Goddess is the protector of the city of Neran, a city that is just outside this forest, not too far from here. The path we are going to be taking out of here leads right to her castle's main gate. It passes through the city then out through the other side to the Golden Goddesses Castle." Rosey knew that a Goddess level was a middle level power in both elemental and magical abilities. She could only imagine just how powerful a God/Goddess level could be but it must be strong in order to allow someone to rise to such a rank as leader of a whole city. Rosey cast her glance down the path, "This path also leads to the portal. Do others know about it? Do they go to Earth?"

"Some do, but the portal is mostly used by those sent to keep an eye on you, to make sure you are okay," she said.

"What about the Silver Goddess, who's she? Since she has the name Goddess I would assume that she is also a magikin?"

"Yes, but beyond the fact that she is the Golden Goddess's sister and a God level magikin not much else is known about her. I'd wait to ask the Golden Goddess herself when we arrive."

Before Rosey could say anything more, a sharp howl from Wolvereen echoed across the walls of the cliff face making her shudder. Turning in her saddle, she watched him and the other wolves break apart from their meeting and begin heading her way. She studied him as he moved in front of her once again. Rosey admired him in awe. He was the only wolf in the escort with a coal-black coat. Up-close his shoulders were about six feet high off the ground. Rosey was considered tall at five foot, ten inches, but this wolf's shoulders would have towered over her head if she was standing next to him! On horseback his head was level with hers. Earlier when he was talking with Rochell, Rosey had easily seen that the wolf was tall compared to Rochell mounted, but up close and personal his size took on a whole new revelation. She managed to smile at him, and met his red eyes once again. His face was hard-set and small scars lined his right eye and one sliced through his lower lip. Regardless of how fierce he looked, as his and Rosey's eyes held, somewhere, in their bloody pools, she sensed a deep calming kindness. Caught off guard, Rosey flinched when he spoke. His voice came out in a heavy growl, "Welcome Keeper, I am Wolvereen, Captain of the guards under the Golden Goddess and these wolves make up a small portion of my elite pack. We are to escort you to the Golden Goddess as soon as possible. Everyone please follow me."

Alex and Rochell formed around Rosey, with her in the middle like always. The other wolves started gathering quickly around them. Yipping excitedly Noly barged her way in to stand in front of Sarabie. The collie looked tiny compared to the wolves but, though she kept a respectful distance from them, as before, she didn't seem to be bothered by them. She huffed in excitement and parked herself in front of the horses waiting patiently. The black wolf, Wolvereen, eyed the dog with what looked like annoyance before turning and walking in front of the circle. Two other wolves, a light grey and a brown, joined him on either side at an angle forming a triangular elliptical shape that curved around the horses. Two wolves in single file formed the sides of the elliptical circle. Following the pattern Rosey looked around and saw the sleek white she-wolf she had seen earlier forming the point of the triangle at the back of the horses. From above it would look like a pointed elliptical circle of wolves surrounding three horses side by side with a dog in front of the horses. There was no mistaking; this was not just an escort but a protective circle of guards. Rosey swallowed, not sure what to think. What could be so bad that she needed a wall of six foot wolves for protection?

Now that the wolves were closer Rosey could make out small ornate patterns etched within their silver and gold armor. It covered their foreheads and ran down to the tip of the snout ending in a V shape. The tail armor was spiked at the end like a dragon's might be. The spikes gave an unwelcome feeling: some had blood stains, others were broken off, and some had large claw marks on the surface. She expected the armor to clank as they moved but instead it was very quiet. The wolves seemed to know just how to move so that their armor was as silent as they needed it to be.

Leaning over to Alex, Rosey asked, "Are all the guards under the Golden Goddess wolves?"

Alex shook his head, "No, there are humans and other animals as well, it's just that dominant wolves have been found to be the most effective fighters against…our enemy."

The way he said the last word made Rosey start, was he hiding something from her? What enemy? Was it that Evil One her uncle had mentioned earlier? That was probably something they were going to discuss later. She shook her head in annoyance but didn't ask anything else.

Together the whole group started forward at a slow walk. The fog and mist had been so thick that most of the scenery had been blocked except for a few yards or so in front of them. With the rising sun the heat began to dissipate the gathered grey blanket to reveal their surroundings. Large evergreen trees outlined the small area and large cliff faces of rock circled them. The ground they had stood on was covered in what looked like fine mulch with a few patches of grass here and there. The mulch covered a large circular area before continuing down a trail about eight yards wide. The entire place was a large clearing against the cliff face where travelers from the other world could rest and recuperate after crossing through before continuing on their journey. Other trees stood amongst the evergreens at the edges of the mulch, leafless for winter. The mulch trail curved along a large lake and then continued downhill. Rosey expertly turned in her saddle. Through the last remnants of some rebellious fog she eyed a big black expanse stretching for at least six yards long creating an elliptical opening in the long cliff wall behind them. At first the large black expanse confused her but then she understood, although the explanation was just as unusual. They had entered this world through…a cave?   Seeming to read the question in her look Alex said, "Yes, that is the entrance to the portal. There are a fair number of portals on this planet. We will probably find more later on." She nodded, and then slunk down in her seat. Later! There was that word again! She shook her head then turned back around to stare at the portal entrance. The mist and fog cleared completely and the cliff walls towered high. Sure enough the black opening formed a large cave entrance. The water that flowed out from its interior traveled down a smooth slopping creek bed into the lake. The cave itself was the entrance for not only a portal but also an exit for water. There, just barely visible was the beginning of a tiny dirt trail leading into the interior of the cave running along beside the water. *That's where we must have come out*, she thought. *Strange, I don't remember hearing any running water.* She studied the water and noticed that it wasn't moving very fast, a trickle at most.

Motioning toward the creek as if he could read her thoughts, Alex said, "The water is slow because it helps with transporting people from world to world. The water is actually groundwater from Earth. The well we passed through, accesses the groundwater and the magic teleports us, through the water, to this world, though, we're not really in the water. When we came out of the portal we were on that small dirt trail there leading into the cave. That trail separates from the side of the wall and cuts a diagonal trail right across the water ending in an island platform. However, facing the interior of the cave the water flows deeper into it then shoots upwards. If you want to get back to Earth, than all you have to do is jump in the flow leading deeper into the interior of the cave. The water shoots you upward and to Earth. It's not fast, but once you jump in, it speeds you up till you reach the portal then slows back down, acting like a sling shot." She nodded trying to imagine a gigantic sling shot hurling her to Earth. Trying hard not to laugh she then said, "You know, you've been doing that for years and it's still scary."

For a moment he seemed confused and then a smile stretched across his face knowingly. He tilted his head up a bit in mock pride, pretending as if he didn't understand what she meant. "It's simple really, I had the same questions when I first came through that portal, at least, when I was old enough to remember."

His face returned to its usual calm composure. She smiled, happy to have her own Alex-library even while in this world, with the added bonus of his friendship. She hated to admit it but she was afraid her friends would be different after crossing over into this world. She feared they would become her guards and not her friends; she was pleased to see that they were both. The lake they were walking beside narrowed into a creek and then dipped back down into the earth, back into the caves. Reaching the slope of the mulch trail she gasped. They weren't just going down a hill but a mountain side. The large cliff walls suddenly dropped down on the left and the evergreen trees dropped off with it continuing down the gradually slopping mountain. Down below a whole forest of evergreen and leafless trees could be seen in the distance looking as small as the hairs on her arms. The fog was still covering the valley below. That's why it is so foggy, we're in the mountains! She smiled, she had never been on a mountain before, but she was already starting to like it.

She took one last look at the cave. As they got farther away the determined fog and mist filled back in around the cool cave entrance hiding all from view.

Suddenly she was hit with a wave of homesickness. That portal was her only way home. Leaving it felt like she was leaving everything behind, especially her uncle. Swallowing the sudden sadness that licked at her empty stomach Rosey distracted herself by admiring the scenery. It still felt so surreal. A few moments ago she would have never thought this was all real, but here it was. It wasn't some strange dream, it was truly here. There was actually a world inside of Earth!

Taking a deep breath, she inhaled pure un-polluted air. Lifting her right arm and combing her fingers through a nearby conifer branch she sighed watching the tendrils of morning dew race down her hand. Early moisture settled on her lips and she licked it, tasting a sweet watery texture, so different from Earth's slightly acidic rain. Fog rolled lazily across the path again obscuring vision to no farther than ten feet. As they slowly started down the mountain side, mist settled in the trees giving off an eerie yet soothing calm.

 Suddenly the trees thinned to one side and Rosey almost shrieked with fear when the gradually slopping mountain side turned into a sheer drop all the way down the mountain to a small river below. The trail they were on was about eight yards across. Freezing up Rosey turned her head away from the scene and kept her eyes on Sarabie's neck. Hazel stiffened beside her, her claws slightly unsheathing with anxiety. Sarabie seemed perfectly calm under Rosey's legs. The rhythmic clopping of her huge hooves stayed the same and her long legs kept their slow yet graceful gait. Shifting in her seat and taking deep breaths Rosey calmed her ferociously beating heart. It helped knowing that Alex and a large wolf were between her and the side of the cliff, not that she wanted any of them to fall, but that it would keep her from looking down. She had never had any problems with heights, but being on a tall horse, only five yards away from the ledge, could make you rethink that assumption. Rosey was vaguely reminded of the mule rides alongside the Grand Canyon, but those trails were much narrower. At least this trail was thick and sturdy so she wouldn't be tittering on the edge of certain death. To take her mind off the sudden drop she looked around her admiring the forest's mountain landscape. She had never laid eyes upon anything so vast and changing. The plants seemed to be moving, the water seemed to be talking, and the air seemed to be breathing. Everything felt so alive around her. There was so much beauty as if nothing could ever hurt this moment, this world, or its promising life. She took a deep breath and felt the crystal grow warm against her chest. Reaching up she gently grasped it, then sighed as the warmth spread through her body. There was something so familiar about this world. True, it wasn't much different from Earth except for the occasional strange looking plant, but it was the feel of the planet that was familiar not the exterior. Rosey felt as if she had found something she had been missing for a long time, the joy of finally finding it and celebrating in its return. She was so surprised by her feelings, so taken aback by how at home she felt. Shouldn't she be

missing Earth or feel like a stranger in a new land, no, to her this was home. The idea troubled her but not in a bad way. Rosey was pulled out of her thoughts by Rochell's sudden shout.

"We're here finally! Off the Mountain!" she exclaimed pointing dead ahead.

Looking closely Rosey saw that the path started widening and the ground became more level. The path was then bordered by large trees all a variety of deciduous and evergreen. They had made it to the bottom. For a few miles they walked through nothing but thick tree lined forests with piles of fallen leaves littering the ground and covering the trail in yellow and orange. The evergreens were the only thing that stood green and tall against the ever bare branches of the deciduous. Because it was winter, the normally thick foliage was nowhere in sight making it easy for the wolves to see beyond them and spot any potential danger. Soon they came to a stop before a large wooden gate that Rochell had mentioned, the gate into the city of Neran. Large wooden walls ran along either side of the gate and were lost in the tree line. Standing on either side of the gate were guards. Four women and four men in gold armor, each carrying large weapons, stood at attention. When they saw Wolvereen the woman closest to the door called out a shrill command so fast that Rosey was unable to make out what she said. After a few moments Rosey heard grinding, like old iron wheels turning against time and rust. The doors slowly opened. As they passed through Rosey made eye contact with one of the soldiers, seeing her he smiled and bowed to her. Rosey blushed in embarrassment, unsure of what to do, then she smiled back and bent her head to him in return, feeling that she had shifted from girl to savior in one nod of the head.

Chapter Five: The NCD

Riding into the town Rosey couldn't believe her eyes. Market stalls lined the streets and people and animals of every kind filled them to the brim with their talk and camaraderie. People wore a variety of clothing very different from Earth's style but also very similar. A plethora of colored and ornate looking pants, shirts, and belts were a favorite and many were wearing symbols and crests representing something they did or excelled in. Rosey thought It could also be the sign of their element of magical power. The symbols ranged from the images of fire to the images of shoes and metalworking, and some even looked like they might have been family crests. Studying the people, Rosey noted that they looked to be a mostly white skinned community with a variety of hair colors, some that weren't even natural like green or orange. Rosey could only guess it was dye or they were really born like that. To Rosey, the people reminded her of quiet mountain folk. Most of the people were dressed in long winter cloaks resembling the ones that the Silver Goddess had given to her, though brown and grey tended to be the more favored color instead of their red, blue, and yellow.

For the most part the people were…people. They looked like everyday individuals just going about their business, except that they were all living in an olden day's era. The only thing that really amazed Rosey about them was that everyone was smiling and laughing, and though it was a pretty large city, she saw no evidence of poverty or maltreatment. Looking ahead, thirty feet wide cobblestone streets served as their walkways. A good two yards of flat stone made for alleyways in between the houses. The houses stood side by side along the streets. Small street signs in gold with red lettering named the different twists and turns of the city. People and animals alike flooded out into the streets and stores. Men, women, and children hung out of windows and yelled down at one another with instructions, occasional curses, and affectionate words. Farmers strolled here and there with livestock, vegetables, and fruits. Some people put pies out to cool while others herded chickens or cooked succulent meats over large roaring fires. Rosey sensed a feeling of community mixed up in all the hustle and bustle, something that one got when she or he went to a family reunion. It was as if everyone wasn't just walking around with a destination in mind, but surveying everyone around them and taking note of their condition, asking after their relatives or friends and passing on the occasional good natured greeting here and there. It made her feel welcomed and cherished, as if she wasn't just another face in a crowd.

Looking up, Rosey studied the immaculate housing that occupied the city. There were all manner of sizes of buildings bordering the streets and not a single one of them looked run down or forlorn. Most were made from wood and decorated in splendid colors some, however, were constructed from hard mud, solid stone, and brick like Adobe houses. Scents of fresh bread flowed out on warm tufts of morning air from what must be a bakery. Cinnamon, ginger, pepper, and more itched Rosey's nose as they passed a small market booth displaying herbs and spices. Dried flowers, butchered meats, precious jewels, and intricate clothing littered the open stalls on either side. Billowing tufts of smoke from small contained fires was the only air pollutant Rosey could see. However, she didn't smell any smoke. Scrunching her nose she leaned over to Alex. "Alex, why don't I smell smoke? I can see the fires and even see the smoke, but I don't smell anything," she asked, fearful that something might be wrong with her nose. "The smoke is a non-pollutant; a spell is placed on the wood so when it burns it releases not smoke but a black steam-like cloud. It just looks like smoke." "You're kidding me, that's amazing. If only Earth could do that." "I hear ya," he said rather vehemently, knowing full well that Earth was not the best when it came to non-pollutants. Rosey couldn't blame him for his reaction, she'd often found herself flabbergasted with Earth's disrespect towards nature.

Looking back at the markets Rosey was amazed that the people were not afraid of the larger-than-life wolves that were walking through them now, making a path for the trio. No sooner had she thought this than she started to notice the strange creatures that lurked in the middle of it all. They had different or various animal parts mixed into one figure as if someone had broken off parts of animals and stuck them together. They were also talking and some were sitting at tables and entering buildings as if they were people. Then again, if they can talk and are intelligent than maybe they are people. No wonder the people weren't afraid of the wolves, not when there were other creatures around that were just as big and scary if not more so.

Much to Rosey's discomfort, some of these odd looking animals and people turned to stare or wave at her. Alex had insisted that she wear the Shanobie crystal around her neck outside of her shirt for everyone to see. Rosey wasn't sure this was such a good idea since they were trying to be subtle and protect her but Alex assured her that the wolf guards were not only more than adequate to protect her but were also a testament to who she was. Seeing her would give the people hope. Reluctantly she agreed, but she wasn't too thrilled to have so much attention drawn to her. She was normally used to being a loner with only her two best friends to guide her. Now, however, she felt like at any moment Alex would be accepting admission just to let people see her. She giggled slightly imaging the crowd lining up to get Rosey Tickets. She waved back awkwardly trying to look calm and collected. After a while she began to relax, the smiles of joy and the glimmer of hope she saw in these people made her feel more comfortable as she rode on. She leaned back and breathed in deeply, taking in the city. She had never really liked big cities, they were too crowded and there wasn't enough green, but this place was an exception. What was most unusual was how familiar the place was to her, it was like a memory from a

The Mystics

dream. Once again Rosey felt that feeling of joy swim through her body that she had felt before. She fingered the crystal absentmindedly.

After about twenty minutes of walking they neared the other side of the city. Ahead, another wooden gate, consisting of large oak logs, stood thick and strong along with the taller wooden walls. Unlike the other gate this gate's surface was scratched by wear and the remnants of battles. Squinting, she examined three long claw marks in the wood as they drew closer. It reminded her of the claw marks made by the raptors in the movie Jurassic Park. Suddenly she let out a shallow gasp as she saw blood smeared were the claw marks were. What she had mistaken as natural tints of red in the brown bark was actually smeared blood from...something, a battle maybe? Had something gotten inside at one time? She didn't remember seeing any destruction or construction. Was this normal or was it new? Was it happening because of her? This last made her shudder. Rosey hated knowing nothing, but no one seemed willing to explain, at least not at that moment. Eight guards, three men and five women, like the ones before, stood stock still on both sides of the gate, their mouths set firmly and their eyes focused. Rosey was reminded of the British guards in long, fluffy black hats. The guards wore the same thick form-fitting golden armor. As before, one of the women called out an inaudible command. The gates opened the same way as before with a grinding sound that made Rosey's jaw clench, it was like hearing nails scratched on a chalk board. Wolvereen shook his head from side to side as if to shake off the noise. Though she wasn't a judge of wolf character, he seemed to be worried about something. Thinking back to the claw marks she wondered if it had anything to do with whom they belonged to? Wolvereen huffed, sending the dust in front of him spinning and lurched forward at a fast paced trot.

Alex leaned over and tapped her shoulder. She nodded and put the crystal under her shirt, safely hidden. The city was okay to show it off but now, it was back to hiding. The simple act made her edgy as she peered into the distant forest.

The other wolves seemed tense while two of the wolves searched the undergrowth before them. A few moments later a low howl came and the two wolves returned. Rosey gently urged Sarabie forward with Bronzo and Phana on either side as Wolvereen took the lead. The wolves abandoned their elliptical formation and fanned out making a wider more sphere shaped circle. Some wolves' switched places and some stayed where they were. Wolvereen continued to lead the group. They hurriedly passed through the large doors and towards the wilderness beyond. As soon as the last wolf's tail had passed through the doors closed more quickly than they had opened with a loud thud. Rosey jumped and gazed back around. The three claw marks that had been present on the inside of the door were nothing compared to the hundreds of three toed claw marks on the outside. From what she could see they continued all the way around the city walls. *What in the world did that?* Rosey thought.

She leaned over to Alex on her right and gathering her courage, for she was not sure she wanted to know the answer, asked, "What made those claw marks and what were those strange creatures that I saw in the city?" "To answer both of those questions I'll have to tell you about the NCD," said Alex.

"Though this is information that can wait, I believe it would be beneficial to tell you about it now, seeing as how you'll be seeing a lot of it soon."

Who's it? Rosey thought, studying Alex. She said nothing, he'd tell her about it soon. She nodded and he continued, "About one hundred years ago a scientist called Dr. Leron said he'd found the ingredients that could be combined to create a serum that would solve a large problem at that time. Our animals were having problems conceiving and the reproduction rates were getting lower each year. This serum would, supposedly, increase the conceivability between animals thus increasing the population of the ones that were almost extinct or endangered. "We now know he actually found these ingredients in an ancient document from an unknown date. He decided to try and recreate it and ended up messing it up. It's known as the

NCD, the New Copy Disease. At first the solution worked fine when injected into the test subjects. New babies were born and the conceivability became normal, so it was injected into every animal species experiencing issues. In time it was used on a few humans who had trouble getting pregnant. It was only after the NCD had been released and had been widely dispersed through later generations that the flaws of the formula began to show. You see, the formula, though messed up, worked and did what it was supposed to, allowing animals to reproduce, however, around the third or so generation a mistake in the formula started to cause mutations. Although it did heighten the creature's ability to conceive, what came out wasn't always the same species. You see, the NCD was a biological list of all the species that needed help conceiving. When entered into a species the NCD catalyst that activates the serum reads the DNA of the creature it is inside so it knows what creature on the list it is helping to conceive. If a lion or a tiger were having trouble the catalyst would need to know which species it was so that it could help that species' particular breeding process. Every species has its own way of mating and conceiving after all. In other words, there are different biological processes that must be accessed depending on the particular species and if they're not followed mutations can occur. The fluke in the formula caused the catalyst to choose the wrong species or more than one species thus messing up the biological process associated with that species. That's why some animals look like they are three different species combined in one, because...they are." "So it's like fertility drugs but with a nasty twist," said Rosey, horrified. "Right-o my friend," said Rochell sadly, cutting in as she listened to them. "What happened then?" said Rosey, turning back to Alex.

"Well, apparently, he used human blood as the solute to mix the other ingredients in. That was where he went wrong. The text he got the ingredients from was written in an early language that was only mildly known. He made an error while translating the text and misread the solute as human blood. When we realized his mistake it was too late, the mutations of the babies had already started, and it wasn't, to our horror, just affecting animals.

"There are two kinds of mutations: animal and human. Animal mutations are classified as Leron, which resulted in the mixture of species that you saw in the town and can have any number of different mutations in one family group. They can have one mutation the first time they have a child and then, the second time, they can have another, completely different mutation. Human mutations result in what we call Falosaraptors. Humans only have a Falosaraptor mutation, no other. Around the third generation, instead of giving birth to a mutation, the human child actually mutates in their fifth year of life. They turn into what we call a Falosaraptor."

Rosey tried not to laugh, "Falosaraptor? Isn't that a dinosaur?"

Rochell leaned over to her, "We adopted the name but changed the spelling, miss smarty pants."

Rosey stuck her tongue out at Rochell and Rochell rolled her eyes. Alex didn't notice and kept talking, "Yes, Falosaraptors. Now, at first, they were no different than their original human selves. They still had their voices, their intelligence, and all their memories. For them it's more like a metamorphosis instead of a mutation. Basically they are humans, they just look different. The only problem is their aging. Once they become Falosaraptors, they can live for hundreds of years, often outliving their families and friends. It didn't take long for them to group together into small communities where they could find solace in the knowledge that they were surrounded by individuals that would last as long as they would."

He was silent for a moment, casting his eyes down as he rode. Rosey watched him, unsure of what to do. She sensed he was searching for the right words or maybe reliving some distant memory. If Rochell noticed, she said nothing. Before Rosey could ask he continued.

"We believe it was the Human Blood solute that resulted in transforming human victims instead of them giving birth to a mutation. The two

The Mystics

bloods mutated with each other messing up the biology of the human itself then mixed in biological makeup surrounding the animals from the list, but we are still unsure.

"When people found out what was happening they were enraged, but, by then, the NCD had its grip in many of the species. They could do nothing but ban Dr. Leron and any other scientists from the ancient text to keep them from using anymore of its formulas. It was taken from him and locked away in the largest library in the world, Sheorie's Library, where it would be well protected. Sheorie, and the Master Healers Cascade and Nornell set to work on trying to find a way to, hopefully, slow down the mutations before all humans were turned to Drakes and all the original animal species were extinct. They, thankfully, succeeded in altering the NCD so now it causes those who are infected, both humans and animals, to give birth to the mutated species as well as one of their own species. The mutated species, thankfully, are all sterile so they can't pass on their alterations. Of course, we named the animal mutations after their creator Dr. Leron."

He paused and considered something for a moment then said, "You know, it wasn't the mutations that worried us. The creatures weren't savage or anything; they were just new forms of life. What worried us was the blow to the natural genetics and, you could say, Mother Nature's own regular flow of life. We had created an artificial way for new, mutated life to be born into the world. So far, nothing terrible has happened and the genes and blood work have continued to be monitored by the Master Healer, Cascade. But concerns are still circulating. We are now starting to look into Earth's in vitro fertilization to see if there is a more scientific way to solve these issues. I believe it is called Magical Artificial Insemination?" "Not all mixed creatures are Leron though," said Rochell, startling Rosey with her sudden input, "there are many natural creatures that look like they are but actually are not Leron. Needless to say we're used to seeing animals that look like parts of other animals put together. Centaurs, Eglagors,

Dragnagors, those are all creatures that are original to our world, despite the drawbacks of the disease. In fact, it may be that because we have mixed animals here that the mutations were always possible and the NCD just enabled them to happen."

Rochell shrugged her shoulders, unsure, and then giggled under her breath as a pink butterfly flew by in a lazy arc. Rosey watched it half mindedly. She had little time to get excited about the idea of Centaurs much less the fact that Rochell had come up with such a deep thought before Alex said something that stole her attention.

"Yeah it would have been amazing if the Evil One hadn't gotten a hold of it too," he hissed under his breath in obvious anger, turning his head to the undergrowth and watching carefully. His finger tapped his saddle horn impatiently, seemingly bothered by something.

"The Evil One? My Uncle said something about him…before we left. Who is he?" asked Rosey, a horrible feeling of dread seeping into her heart; the word alone was enough to make her cringe. *How evil must something be to receive a name that so clearly defines them?* she thought.

"The Evil One is our enemy, the creature that threatens our world," said Rochell with the most serious look on her face Rosey had ever seen her make. Frowning, the brunette then turned her head to the undergrowth, searching as Alex was for…something. It made her nervous and a little unsettled to see her care free friend act in such a way. She was happy when Alex took over, his voice showing no signs of its anger from before. "We don't know how, but the Evil One has created its own formula from the old one and has used it to alter the NCD making it so its captive humans give birth to Raptors instead of Falosaraptors. Raptors are the complete opposite of Falosaraptors. They are evil, cruel, and ugly. People are taken by the Evil One to be used as breeders to grow its army of these monsters, so many have disappeared. Thankfully, the mutated NCD the Evil One made did not include the fix that Cascade and Nornell made, so

The Mystics

no human babies are born with the Raptor. I would hate to think of what would happen if they were."

Alex shuddered with the thought and Rosey found herself growing sick at the idea.

Carefully Rosey asked, "Are people still being taken today?"

Alex's face grew hard and emotionless, "Yes."

"But why? Shouldn't this Evil thing have enough…people?" She stopped herself from saying breeders.

"We don't know what happens to these people. There are all sorts of rumors. The mothers are torn apart by the birth, they are unable to have children after birthing once and so become useless…the theories go on and on. There is one thing for sure though."

His eyes met hers and Rosey was shocked by the anger she saw in them, Alex was not known for anger, he was known for his intellect and kindness but something like this was deserving of such obvious rage.

"The bodies of these people are never found."

A shudder passed over her and Rosey felt tears sting her eyes, she looked away quickly. With a furious strength the tears turned to anger. She shook in her saddle and for some reason she thought that Silver Knight, hanging at her waist, was shaking with hate. Alex turned back to the foliage his jaw tight as if it was hinged against speech. Without needing to look at him, Rochell took up the conversation in his stead.

"We are trying to figure out what the Evil One did to accomplish this and how it got its hands on the ingredients in the first place, but we are still clueless. Even Sheorie is at a blank, and that's supposed to be impossible for a prophet."

"A prophet…I thought she was a librarian?" For some reason Rosey's mind filled with the images of gypsies and people in tents with crystal balls. Shaking her head she pushed the ridiculous visions away.   "She is both. A prophet on our world is a person who knows everything in the universe. On Earth a prophet is a person who tells the future through visions; our prophet does see visions but differently; through a vast library that contains all the information on the universe in its archives. Any question you have can be answered. But there are rules; a prophet does not have to tell you anything, they will only tell you what you need to know."

Rosey leaned in her saddle, "Does Earth have a...prophet? Do all planets have them?"

"Sometimes...well..."Rochell stumbled for the right words. "It depends really. There are always people with vast knowledge but that doesn't make them prophets. Really there is only one true prophet and that's the great Sheorie. No one could ever manage to live up to her."

Rosey noticed that again Rochell and Alex were watching the foliage as if expecting at any moment for something to attack.

"Okay, what are you guys looking for!" Rosey exclaimed in frustration. Both of her friends stared at her this time, they looked at one another and Alex nodded. Rosey waited expectantly. Rochell answered, "We're watching for Raptors, Rosey."

"What!" Rosey almost screamed, the wolves flinched and she smiled apologetically at them. "Oh, no, I have no way of protecting myself except for a giant horse, a small dagger, and a cat whose claws are as big as an ant. No offense Hazel."

The little tortoiseshell only snickered in amusement and flicked her tail along Rosey's chin.

"I know I took Kendo and Iaido lessons but I don't have a sword and based on what you told me a few punches ain't gonna do much against a Raptor!"

Rochell opened her mouth but Rosey quickly beat her to it.

"And Silver Knight does not count as a sword," she said pointing at Rochell almost accusingly.

"That's what we and the wolves are here for, until you learn how to handle your elements and receive your sword we are here to guard you," said Alex, soothingly.

"Sword! Sword! What about a gun or a bazooka!" "We're not allowed to transfer weapons from planet to planet, nor do we want to. We much prefer our own weaponry thanks," said Rochell with such happiness that it made Rosey want to slap her. *How am I supposed to know that!* She thought acidly, *I know, maybe they'll tell me later! Urg!* Rosey kept her thoughts to herself for she knew her friend was just being her flamboyant self, "Well, you all are flinging around magic and wind, don't I have something? An element maybe? Or magic, could I use magic?" "Everyone is born with the ability to be an elemental, but not all of them become elementals. Not everyone, however, is born with the ability to work magic, like me. So, yes, you do have an element, but only you can discover what your element is, and that might be hard for you to do since you were raised on Earth and are almost an adult. If it wasn't for the fact that you're the Keeper, you probably wouldn't be able to find out what your element is at all. As for magic, the Keepers are never Magikins. Still unsatisfied she was about to give her friends what not for not telling her sooner when Alex spoke. "Earlier you asked about what made those claw marks on the gates?"

Rosey nodded in mild annoyance, hating how he was skillfully maneuvering her back into a listening mood by appealing to her curiosity. For some reason the term 'curiosity killed the cat' flashed through her head making her even more annoyed and rather fearful, making her cast a glance at the foliage herself.

"Well, the Goddess constructed the city to keep Raptor attacks away from the citizens; however they have become more and more desperate. They have recently begun attacking the wooden gate in small groups, trying to lure the Goddess out by threatening her people. She is one of the Leaders of the World and the Evil One wants to get rid of them, hoping to weaken the last defenses of this world. The Queen, the Goddesses, and more are all in danger. Do not think that your time on Earth has hidden your arrival to this world Rosey. As soon as you stepped through that portal the Evil One sensed you. It knows you are here. It is very possible that it will send a Raptor group to kill you. We, your friends, and Wolvereen are here to make sure that doesn't happen." Rosey stared at him wide eyed, her heart beating up a storm. His words hit her like a bucket of ice cold water. There was no threat in his words, simply truth. The fact that this truth was common knowledge to him but alien to her scared her more than any daredevil sport she had ever attempted. Her life was on the line and there was someone who wanted it crushed and destroyed. She suddenly got the feeling that someone was watching her and there was nothing she could do to hide herself. Her hand sought the hilt of Silver Knight; the long dagger glittered slightly at her touch. It was her only source of protection besides the ring of wolves and the two mounted bodyguards at her side. Alex saw this and began rubbing the back of his head in embarrassment, suddenly realizing what he had done.

"Great job wizzy, now she's really ready for the journey ahead," said Rochell sarcastically.

"Wizzy, seriously?" said Alex

Rochell gave him the look and he backed down. Meeting Rosey eye to eye she said, "Rosey don't worry, we've been planning this for years now and this is the safest way to take you. We've scouted the forests, there are guards everywhere in the surrounding area, and nothing is going to get to us before we know about it, okay?"

Rosey nodded. She felt a little better but said nothing else, unable to think of anything else to say. Her mind was suddenly a whirl with the details about her enemy, that unknown creature that was unspoken in the air and had everyone on edge. By the sounds of it, this wasn't some ruler in a far off land or a sister seeking a lost throne, this was something else, something so evil it deserved that very name. She could only imagine what it could be. Her lips drew tight drawing into a frown. This wasn't a game. She had known that all along, but only now did she realize just how much danger she was in. She shook in her seat and clamped her hand over the crystal hanging from her neck. Instantly warmth flooded through her and calmed her. A sudden dogged determination and flare of anger came upon her. She straightened in her seat and raised her chin high. Her brows furrowed and she sighed heavily, no matter what would try and come after her she wasn't going down without a fight. Rochell and Alex didn't say a word; though Rosey could have sworn that she saw them both smile.

Her hand, throughout the trip, never left the hilt of Silver Knight and Silver Knight never slipped from her grasp. Her own friends were warriors, by her side, ready to fight. Looking down at the pale skin of her hands and her own muscular arms she felt she could be as strong as Rochell and Alex. What had all those lessons and extracurricular activities that she had participated in been for if not to make her stronger? Her friends were ready and willing to face anything for her. She would need to prepare herself as well because once she started, there was no going back.

Chapter Six: The Protector and the Protected

The next thirty minutes of travel was filled with silence and quick glances into dark maple and oak foliage. The trail steadily made its way back up into the mountains. Every once in a while they would come to a break in the undergrowth showing off a beautiful pond or overlook and they would stop to admire the view. However, Rosey suspected that they only stopped so that they could get a birds-eye-view of the surrounding foothills and really weren't doing it for the scenery. She knew they were protecting her but, sheesh, couldn't they relax a little and enjoy the sights?! Or, maybe, at the moment, they could not let their guard down long enough to enjoy it. Rosey swallowed, and was painfully reminded of how vulnerable she was. They never stayed for long either. The wolves sniffed around and her friends watched the hills with prying eyes leaving Rosey with nothing to do but enjoy the fall display of colorful leaves all the while grasping Silver Knight's hilt. Despite all its differences, Rosey was surprised by how alike this world was to Earth. Oddly enough the idea comforted her and made her feel more at home. There was no denying, this world was beautiful.

At one of the stops overlooking a vast valley of red, yellow, and...spotted leaves, Rosey stared out into space wondering what to do. After thirty minutes of traveling in dead silence she was about to burst from boredom. Looking to her right she spied the ever graceful Nagura and remembered what Rochell had told her before. She gently urged Sarabie closer and said in the most welcoming voice she could muster, "Excuse me Nagura, but Rochell told me that you're the leader of the Silver Goddess's guards, do you mind if I ask why you're here with the Golden Goddess's guards?" The white wolf did not take her eyes from the overlook but said, "No I don't mind, I'm here to see my mate,

Wolvereen. When I heard about your arrival today I decided to tag along. I was curious, like everyone else, about the new Keeper. I wanted to see what kind of young woman she was. I like what I see."

Only then did the wolf turn to Rosey. If a wolf had the ability to smile, Nagura was definitely smiling. It wasn't a toothy grin, just a slight rise of the lips into a delicate almost artistic curl at the corners of her mouth. Coupled with her glossy blue eyes Nagura made for the gentlest looking wolf that Rosey had ever laid eyes on. Rosey tried not to look too embarrassed, she was surprised by how irresistibly charming the wolf was especially after meeting Wolvereen's rough around the edges demeanor. The fact that she was his mate was mindboggling as much as it was interesting. As far as Rosey could tell from their first encounters, Wolvereen was very harsh and brisk while Nagura was like a ghost dancing on a perfectly posed, muscled frame. They seemed so different, yet both led the guards of the Goddesses. *Well, they do say opposites attract, I guess*, Rosey thought. She dared say none of this out loud as she was still quite unfamiliar with either wolf and so was nowhere near the ability of offering compliments and comments on the subject. As she was becoming painfully aware, she was here to learn and to hopefully, become a savior, not judge relationships like some reality show. Nonetheless, she hoped that, in time, she would become familiar enough with the wolves to call them friends. The idea struck her as odd, wolves as friends, but the thought hardly lingered more than a second in her mind as they moved on down the road.

As they left the overlook and came back onto the trail she quickly changed the subject and launched herself into a conversation with Nagura about her life on Earth. Nagura looked very interested and soon Alex joined in to tell a little about the buildings and technology, though he continued to remain alert. The talk seemed to take the stress away from the moment and made everything seem more relaxed. Finally Wolvereen spoke up. "I've never heard of such things before. They certainly seem advanced. Earth must be very technical." "It is, but that may be its demise if it continues on its environmentally destructive path. Adina, our Immortal, hopes to one day give Earth a gift for supporting our world all this time. Who knows she might give them the gift of common sense," Alex said heatedly with sarcasm.

Rosey frowned. "Who's Adina and what do you mean you're Immortal? Is an Immortal any different than a creature with a never ending life?" She asked tentatively afraid she'd sound dumb. She knew what an immortal was but, like the prophet, it could mean something different here.

"They do have eternal life but they are also put in charge of looking after a planet and its people, like planetary caretakers. All planets have an Immortal. You should know that there are different types of immortals, those that can live for a long time but can still be killed and those that can't be killed. Adina is the kind that cannot be destroyed, neither in body or soul. If you were to destroy her physical body, she'd simply be reborn. She is eternal. As long as the planet lasts, she lasts. She is this planet's Immortal, she watches over us and has immense power, though, she cannot combat the Evil One herself, that is a job for the Keeper alone. Her power is the planet's power, and her strength is its strength. She is directly connected to the planet and it to her."

"What would happen if the planet were destroyed?"

Alex seemed to hesitate at this but then continued, "Then she'd die, but her soul would not. It would probably be reused as another Immortal for a new world somewhere in the universe or perhaps put on hold, stored for another time. Although, I'm not certain, that kind of information isn't really known to us." "So what exactly is Adina?

"She's a Unapeg, a unicorn with wings."

"Oh, I bet she's a sight for sore eyes," Rosey said, imagining what such a creature would look like.

"Only a few have ever seen her and they would probably all agree with you; but don't be fooled, Adina is not someone to be trifled with."

The Mystics

Rosey bowed her head in understanding. Alex turned to peer once again into the woods and Nagura paced ahead to talk with another wolf. They continued on in silence after that leaving Rosey to ponder all she'd learned. The silence, however, didn't last long. In the distance a sudden but powerful howl split through the air, making Rosey start in her seat. Every one of them came to an abrupt halt as every wolf pricked their ears and listened carefully. Several other howls joined the first, but some seemed weaker, or damaged in a way. Rosey suddenly saw the wolves begin to fidget. Their hackles rose on end and their eyes grew wide. They began to take on threatening stances, showing their teeth and growling deep throated threats. Sarabie and the others stayed stock still, waiting. Suddenly Rosey heard a powerful blast like thunder coiling through the undergrowth. It snaked its way through them and blasted over them like a shock wave of power. Rosey had almost expected to be shoved off of Sarabie's back but the blast swept through her like a cold bath of air washing over her. Next to her Alex's eyes grew wide and Rochell let out a tiny squeak. Alex turned to Rochell, "That was a warning blast from a magikin!"

She nodded, bouncing her brown hair, "I know, this isn't good." She glanced at Rosey and then met Alex's gaze again who nodded back. Rosey felt her heart sink, they were worried about her but they were too kind to say anything. She gulped and the image of the Raptors that they had told her about before entered her mind. She touched the crystal through her shirt and it grew warm in her hands. Her other hand tightened around Silver Knight's hilt. She knew she wasn't anywhere near the level she should be to adequately defending herself. Suddenly she felt all too helpless. Rosey gripped the dagger in anger and then carefully pulled it from its sheath. She might not be trained very well but she wasn't going down without a fight!

Wolvereen, his black fluffy pelt fluffed up and his lips drawn back turned to them quickly and was about to shout out some orders when his command was cut short by a deafening shriek. The shriek was so powerful that Rosey had to grip her ears in pain and fear. She recoiled immediately and Hazel backed up farther into her hair, pawing at her own ears. The wolves stayed in formation but they looked shocked and scared, gazing into the foliage with quick glances. The shrieking continued and Rosey wasn't sure if it would ever stop. Other shrieks began to join in but they were a long ways off, all hidden by the trees and the greenery. The wolves looked to Nagura and Wolvereen but Wolvereen was the one who spoke first.

"Everyone stay where you are, magikin!" Wolvereen's giant fanged snout pointed to Alex, "put a shield around you and the Keeper immediately!"

Alex nodded and began to chant, the horses stayed still, but Rosey could tell that they were nervous. Sarabie bowed her head and pawed the ground and Rosey heard Noly whine near Sarabie's feet. Alex's spell started working and Rosey could do nothing more than gaze in disbelief as a pink and yellow covering suddenly materialized over their heads and then draped down around her, Rochell, Alex, and Noly. The material looked like a thick shroud of some kind with sparks of light rippling through its surface. As usual, Rosey found she wanted to touch it, but the fear of the situation made her stay still. Her eyes focused on Wolvereen, ready for a sign. Ready for anything, she felt trapped and oddly alone despite her friends beside her.

She then felt something odd, a swishing of air near her arm. Glancing at Rochell she saw that the young woman had swirling masses of wind circling around her fists. Rosey was transfixed and for a few moments she was spell bound by them. Rochell had said she was an elemental, hadn't she? An air elemental…that's right. Rosey wouldn't have been able to tell that the air was even there if it hadn't been for the wind coming from the rotation and the slight debris of dust that had been caught in it. Rosey, once again, wanted to touch it, but she held back not wanting to interfere with the swirling action. Was she going to be able to do that someday? Was that what they meant when they said she, too had an element, something

The Mystics

like that?! Rosey couldn't be sure, but her heart thudded in her chest like a drum as adrenaline coursed through her. Barely even a few hours on this world and she'd already seen magic, her gaze flickered to the shield surrounding them, and elemental power, she once again examined Rochell's arms. The wind was now moving up along her forearm. She stared out at the forest, not noticing Rosey's attention. Rosey was happy about that, she didn't want Rochell to see her so off balance.

"Wolvereen!" Nagura shouted from the rear guard. The sudden noise made Rosey jump as she was reminded of their current danger. "Where are they at!?" The White Wolf flicked her tail in anger and annoyance, but she remained at the rear.

Wolvereen shook his massive head, calling back to her, "The call was too muddled, they're fighting nearby but they haven't yet got our scent!" he lowered his voice suddenly, his gaze flickering. Nagura nodded to him, her fur on edge, "They could be anywhere in these woods!"

Rosey's eyes grew wide, "Who?!" she said quickly, causing Rochell and Alex to cast glances her way in quick succession, it was obvious they weren't too happy about Rosey's current situation.

Wolvereen met her gaze and said plainly without pause, "Raptors, Keeper. Raptors."

Rosey felt her grip tighten on Silver Knight. She breathed a silent cry of fear, but tried not to show it. She nodded to hide her apprehension and Wolvereen turned away. Alex and Rochell exchanged glances and the horses whinnied to each other quietly. Hazel curled into Rosey's neck and then licked it with her rough tongue to try and comfort her. Rosey patted her head in thanks, but remained silent.

"Commander Sir, we need to get going!" one of the wolves, a pretty and sleek auburn and black furred youngling said, glancing at Wolvereen. He bowed down slightly when Wolvereen fixed his gaze on him. With a snarl Wolvereen snapped at the young male wolf, making him bark a plea of apology. Rosey winced, but knew that wolves were just like that and Wolvereen wasn't trying to hurt him.

"You fool!" Wolvereen barked, showing his long white fangs. "If we try and leave we could run right into the Raptors! They could be anywhere right now! Get back in line, show some pride as a wolf guard!"

The smaller armored wolf was pushed back into formation, "Of course sir, sorry sir."

Rosey gulped, could they really be anywhere?! She gazed into the undergrowth, but of course she couldn't see anything and the pink and yellow shield was blocking some of her vision. Rosey had no experience with shields and so she had no idea if they were all they were cracked up to be. She'd certainly read about shields in science fiction books but she'd never actually been behind one before.

Suddenly a rustling in the leaves to their left caught their attention and every wolf jumped in front of Rosey and her friends, ready to block the way if the need arose. Rosey barely felt herself breathe as they waited, the rustling continued and Wolvereen stood at the front of the group, baring his large fangs. A loud crash of foliage and a shriek of pain passed through the woods and met their ears, causing the wolves to pound the earth with their oversized paws and whip their tails from side to side. Whatever was going on was coming right towards them.

Rosey had no idea what was going to happen. Everything seemed to move in slow motion as time swept by. She felt the ground shake beneath their feet. Rosey stared down at it, amazed that she could feel it even when she was on Sarabie. The horses eyes shot forward towards the tree lining and their ears flattened against their skulls, eyes ablaze and teeth dripping with saliva. Sarabie hopped from foot to foot nervously but refused to budge from where she stood, the other horses followed her example.

They all watched the undergrowth with apprehension. The tension was strung between them so tightly that Rosey could almost feel it draping over them. Then it happened. The leaves began to shake and Rosey could see, just beyond the undergrowth, two giant figures wrestling with one another. The wolves yipped almost excitedly, saliva falling from their mouths. It was evident that some struggle was taking place but Rosey couldn't make out what or who was fighting, but she knew one of them had to be a Raptor. All the two figures had to do was advance a few extra feet and Rosey would see the fight. She could certainly hear it. She could almost feel the anger and the power, the snapping of teeth, the grinding of paws into the ground, the ripping and tearing of flesh and trees alike, the snarling and, finally, the shrieking. It was so blood curdling that Rosey was frozen in fear, she could hear the anger, the hatred, and the sorrow being exchanged through every sizzling moment of the fight taking place right before her but just out of her sight and she was very happy that it was. She tensed up, as a piercing scream exploded through the undergrowth. It was loud enough to hurt Rosey's ears but she couldn't move even to cover them.

Suddenly the forest was quiet, deadly quiet. The rustling had ceased and the noise was no more. What had once been loud enough to stretch across the world was now silent enough to make Rosey believe that it had never happened. It was apparent that someone had won the fight, but the question was who? Rosey felt her body shake, her muscles were so tense that she feared if she tried to move they would snap and break in response to her command. Her grip was so hard on Silver Knight's hilt that she felt the material rubbing her hand raw, yet she dared not loosen her grip, not for one moment.

Then a nose appeared from the foliage, the nose of a wolf. In that one second everyone relaxed, the wolves kept their protective circle before Rosey, almost blocking her view, but they let their fur lie flat. The wolf pulled herself out of the tree line and the whole world seemed to stop. The golden armored wolf was dragging one back leg behind her body, it was glistening with fresh blood, and it was so badly twisted that Rosey couldn't tell in which direction it was supposed to go. She wasn't even certain it was still a foot anymore. The armored beast slowly, carefully hobbled to

Wolvereen, who met her half way to save her pain. A sizzling sound could suddenly be heard and everyone backed away from the wolf in a hurry, all except Wolvereen who stood before her, his eyes glistening. The armor on the wolf's back was melting and smoking, being eaten away as if an acid had been poured over it. It had already broken through the wolf's back and her spine was starting to show through as the acid, or whatever it was, ate away her flesh. Rosey's eyes were glued to the wolf, for some reason she couldn't pry them away from her.

The wolf sputtered and coughed up a bout of blood, it spilled onto the ground, mixing with the dirt like some dark, black stain on the earth. She raised her head slowly, weakly. Rosey could barely make out the light grey and black patches of her once beautiful fur, drenched with blood but the acid that was now eating away her midsection was as clear as day. She spit out some blood dripping from her mouth and said, "Perimeter…ugh…secure…sir…ahh!" she then fell before him as her back legs gave out as the acid bit through her backbone and the tender spinal column. Rosey didn't hear any crack or split, just the terrible whine of pain, coming from the dying wolf. The other wolves watched on in solemn silence, their breath coming out in slow puffs. Their tails were down to the ground, their ears parallel to the earth. Rosey continued to stare, she refused to look away. Alex and Rochell followed her example. The horses bent their heads and Hazel made a sad muffled sound near Rosey's head. Noly, for once, was silent where she stood, eyes wide.

Wolvereen bent down to the barely breathing wolf and gazed into her eyes, "Well done Lyesal. Rest now." With one powerful bite, so fast that Rosey barely saw it, Wolvereen broke her neck, killing her instantly. She was no longer in pain, no longer suffering. Rosey gulped once again. She gazed at the tree line where the wolf had, just moments before, been fighting against a Raptor. Was the body of the beast she'd killed still there? Rosey knew it was, it would be silly if it weren't and yet, for some odd reason she felt that it wasn't there. Here she had seen the danger, seen that

The Mystics

sadness, and yet her enemy remained cloaked in mystery, it was like she needed to see that dead body to prove that it had actually existed.

Rosey's head turned slowly back towards the dead wolf, she had a slight smile on her face. It was strange for an animal to be smiling, and yet, there it was, a smiling face, right before her. The face of death and pain, death served for Rosey's own safety. It was enough to make Rosey sick, but she turned away instead. What had Wolvereen called her? Lyesal? Yes, Lyesal, that was a good name. Rosey knew she'd never forget it. Before anything else could happen, the foliage rustled again but not a single wolf jumped to attention, including Wolvereen, they all seemed to know that whatever had happened was over. A giant golden, orange, and black furred wolf walked into view. She was a splendid looking wolf, with an air of power and grace that might have rivaled even Nagara's. She held her head high and tail even, she was not a wolf to be messed with. She was so beautiful and striking that Rosey almost thought she was imagining her. To top it all off she was, to Rosey's amazement, much bigger than even Nagura or Wolvereen. She had blood spattered all over her armor, but looked otherwise unharmed. *It must not be her blood then,* Rosey thought, still peering through the shield. Despite its pinkish coloration the shield didn't seem to make anything else outside of it appear to be pink. It was a strange thing that, up till now, Rosey hadn't really noticed.

Wolvereen pricked his ears when he saw the beautiful wolf, his voice was steady but a little shaken, "Calra, I trust everything is safe now?"

The giant wolf called Calra was also wearing Silver Armor, just like Nagura's. She must be in the service of the Silver Goddess as well. So it wasn't just the Golden Goddess's warriors that were out protecting Rosey it was the Silver Goddess's too.

Calra bowed her head, "Yes Commander Wolvereen, the perimeter is now secure. A Raptor group managed to break through our barrier when they joined forces with another group, thankfully we were ready." Her voice was smooth and silky when she spoke, but held a demanding and powerful tone to it. Calra's gaze lowered down to the dead wolf called Lyesal at their feet. Her face twisted into one of pain and horror, "Damn," she spat out the word with malice, "Another good wolf…she went after it all on her own."

"It's a good thing too," Wolvereen said quickly. "Give her the greatest of honors. Let her family and pack know that she gave her life defending the Keeper. If it hadn't been for her, one of us might be in her place now and the Keeper might have been in danger."

Calra's eyes flicked to Rosey and then she brightened, "I see, well, she will be celebrated tonight with the greatest song that any wolf can howl. Her name shall be known far and wide. Someone will be by soon to pick her up and ferry her home, I will wait here for them, you continue on. The road should be safe now. We will be watching."

Wolvereen bowed his head in return. Obviously Calra wasn't just any wolf in the guard, she demanded respect. Calra then turned to Nagura and bowed low, "Commander," she said simply.

Nagura bowed as well, "Lieutenant."

This struck Rosey, she knew that Nagura lead the Silver Goddess's guards and that Wolvereen lead the Golden Goddess's guards, she had been there herself when they had been introduced as commanders, but she wasn't so sure about what lieutenant might mean, but maybe it was equivalent to the second in command? If that was true, then it meant that Calra was Nagura's second. Rosey shook her head, why would she care about that at a time like this? Perhaps it was because it was so effective against the memory of Wolvereen snapping Lyesal's neck or the way that the acid had dissolved her spinal column. Whatever it was, Rosey was grateful for it.

Wolvereen howled a low command and the wolves formed back into their formation around them. The shield suddenly dissolved as it was no longer needed. They turned ready to go and the horses and the wolves started walking once again. Noly trudged along after them, no longer trying to jump in front of the group, her tail hung low and she whimpered as she passed the dead body. As the horses passed Lyesal, Rosey took one last glance at her mutilated body. She shuddered in her seat but before she could turn away she met Calra's eyes. She bowed her head and Rosey nodded in return, that was all she managed to do.

Rosey turned back before her, unable to say anything. Hazel shuddered on her shoulder her tiny shaking body making Rosey feel protective all of a sudden. Her eyes darted to the trees and to the undergrowth, imagining something horrible jumping down at any minute. She felt the world closing in around her and the air leaving her lungs. What was happening? Was she panicking? She had to be, she didn't want to be here. She wanted to be home, back home. Dear home, she could almost feel it. Back with her uncle. She found herself wishing it was just a dream, just a nightmare that she'd wake up from. Please, oh please…she thought desperately. Please what?! She couldn't go home. She wanted to run, but the feet that were carrying her weren't her own they were Sarabie's. She…she…

Alex's hand rested gently on Rosey's shoulder and she turned to him. Rochell rested a hand on Rosey's hand, the one still gripping Silver Knight. It was trembling, trembling so much that Rosey probably would have dropped it. A bead of sweat raced down her face and fell onto her saddle. It was so silent that she heard it fall. Rochell rubbed her back as she slowly removed the dagger from Rosey's hand. She handed it to Alex, who was to Rosey's right. He carefully slid the dagger back into its sheath and then took the raw hand in his. He chanted something under his breath and her another hand suddenly felt a lot better. They didn't say anything, they didn't need to. They were just there for her.

After another ten minutes, Rosey felt much better, calmer, and ready to talk. This time she didn't direct her question at anyone in particular. She just continued to stare straight ahead, afraid of what she'd do if she met anyone's eyes. Carefully she said, "What happened to Lyesal?"

Alex didn't need any explaining to know what it was she was talking about, "Raptors have acid glands in their mouths. A fire elemental can counteract it but, anything less than that and well…"

He didn't have to finish for Rosey to know what he meant. The image of Lyesal flashed through her mind, so fresh and new. It would always be that way.

Rosey swallowed a lump in her throat. She'd just witnessed a death. If she'd still been on Earth, many would have related it to the death of a deer on the side of the road, after all, their bodies were usually left there to be collected by any wild animals that chose to feast on it, but here the story was different. That wolf hadn't just been an animal. The image of Calra standing by the dead body was proof of that. Lyesal's body wouldn't be left to rot, no; it would be carefully recovered and given the highest honors. That wolf had had a family, and a pack…she was a person. She was a person that had sacrificed herself for Rosey! What for?! Rosey screamed it in her head. Why, why was she so important! What did she mean to these people?! The questions zoomed through Rosey's mind, but, for the first time since coming here, she didn't want any answers.

Rosey turned her gaze to Sarabie's neck, fixating on it. "That's the first time anyone has ever given their life for me," she breathed the words out slowly, gently.

Rochell smiled at her, and then rubbed her back like a mother comforting her child, "Unfortunately Rosey, it won't be the last."

Rosey couldn't meet her gaze, for she knew the words were true. What exactly had she gotten herself into?! What had she signed up for? Was this something she could leave behind, something she could forget about? She had the strangest feeling that she never would, that no matter what she learned this was now her life. A powerful hatred crept into her heart and seemed to ignite her on fire. She'd never let anyone sacrifice themselves for her ever again. She would be the one taking on all the risk. But what risk was she taking on? What was it she was here to do? Lyesal flashed through her mind once again. Rosey closed her eyes and shook her head. What was so important that someone would give their life for her? Rosey then felt a sudden urge to become stronger creep into her chest. She needed to become powerful enough to face anything and take on anyone. Where the feeling came from, she didn't know. For some reason the idea felt right to Rosey, as if it had always been what she wanted to do. Had she always felt that way? She couldn't decide, but the need to protect was so strong within her that she could almost taste it. She had to become stronger.

"Let's pick up the pace a bit, we're almost to the Castle," Wolvereen said, calling over his shoulder.

Rosey and her friends urged the horses to a trot while the wolves kept up a comfortable lope. Noly padded along beside them, jumping every now and then in a brilliant leap of power. Hazel purred against Rosey's shoulder making her feel much better. She couldn't deny that something strange had just happened to her. She seemed to sense it in the world, and in the air, and in the trees all around her. She wasn't alone. She had Alex, Rochell, Sarabie, Noly, and her precious little Hazel. This wasn't a journey she was supposed to make alone. The wolves weren't there for their own sake, they were there for her, she was supposed to work with them and help them somehow. That much she knew, she had to help and they needed her help.

Turning around a small bend in the road they suddenly came into a huge clearing. The trees thinned out and turned into sparse bushes and small plant life. There, dead ahead, where the golden gates of the Golden Goddess's Castle. Alex and Rochell both stared at the place with equal interest. *This must be their first time seeing it too*, she thought. The wolves seemed unmoved by such grandeur, but Rosey was unsurprised, after all, they should be used to it since they worked for the Golden Goddess. The doors were set into a golden wall that stretched out and around on either side. It wasn't as long as the cities walls but it was still pretty lengthy. Taking a deep breath she urged Sarabie forward falling into step behind Wolvereen. They had arrived at the Golden Goddess's Castle.

Chapter Seven: The War

Rosey shifted in the saddle and tried to mimic Rochell and Alex's laid back appearance. Who was she kidding? She was absolutely terrified. There weren't any castles in Montana and she had certainly never been invited to any. A thousand questions zoomed through her head that, surprisingly, didn't have anything to do with The World Within A World. Did she know the correct etiquette? How was she supposed to act? Was she dressed properly? Looking down at herself, she scowled. Jeans and a black top didn't exactly scream 'castle worthy." Was the Goddess nice, short, tall, miniature… human? This last made her stop and think. She'd never considered the Goddess as not being human, but, after everything she'd seen, it was definitely possible. Images of the animals she had seen and the possible Leron swept through her brain making her shudder. Then there was the name of the Goddess herself. Why was she called Goddess? Why Golden? Did the term Goddess refer to her powers? According to Alex both magikins and elementals of medium power were called Gods and Goddesses. This person could be a powerful elemental or magikin, and not really a God at all. It might just be a title. Looking at the castle Rosey hoped she was right. She felt a fluttering of butterflies in her stomach and felt her heart beat race. She had never met someone of royalty or importance before. Here she was faced with terrible danger and peril and she was more scared of meeting a person that was supposed to be helping her. *Oh, what's wrong with me*, Rosey thought touching her hand to her temple and shaking her head. She raised her head and breathed deeply, calming her racing heart. She was Rosey Mystic and she and her friends would face this…person with pride and dignity. As soon as the thought entered her mind, Noly took off and plowed her way between Wolvereen and the slender grey wolf next to him. The large black beast cursed under his breath and watched with obvious annoyance as the dog ran around the outside of the wolf circle barking with excitement, evidently no longer traumatized by the incident that had just occurred. Rosey looked on horrified. *Okay, I will face this person with pride and dignity.*

From her perch on Rosey's shoulder, Hazel snorted and mumbled something about dogs before settling her head on her small paws. Rosey smiled, despite the dog's lack of restraint she found that Noly's silly antics helped to ease her worry and she wondered, in the back of her mind, if that had been Noly's purpose all along. Rosey called Noly to her side. She yipped excitedly and obediently came trotting over with her tongue lolling out in a huge doggy grin. Rosey smiled at her. Reassured, she raised her head high in confidence and gazed upon the large armored wolves that guarded them. They had never faltered in step the entire way here even when they had stopped and almost been attacked. They had remained loyal and strong and dedicated. Their backs were straight, their tails were held high, and their ears were pricked forward and alert for anything out of the ordinary. Rosey had never seen soldiers in action before but this was what she imagined they would do if on guard. If the situation before hadn't been proof enough then the wolves themselves were a constant reminder of just how much danger she was in. Rosey shuddered; she didn't want to remember the dead wolf, not now.

To distract herself, Rosey looked past the protective wolves and glanced ahead at the large double doors set in the twenty foot high golden walls about two hundred feet away. As they drew closer she examined them with awe. Ornate patterns adorned them with images of animals she knew and some that she didn't. The carvings formed unique floral patterns and symbols that danced in between the animals making it look as if they really moved. Rosey gazed at each door on which a carving of a tall woman stood: eyes direct and focused, chin raised, wand at the ready. She was so focused on the woman that she hardly noticed the screeching sound of grinding wheels from within the wall as they hoisted the large doors apart.

On either side of the door and all along the walls were groups of human soldiers, wolf guards, and other various animals all dressed in golden armor. Rosey's escort did not stop walking but continued on right through the doors.

The path curved slightly through a small collection of trees of all different species and several winter dormant gardens before entering into an orchard. There, just beyond the orchard she saw it. The castle was a golden beacon against the blue sky and the green, fog laden forests that surrounded it. Dew that had settled on its brilliant surface gave it a unique sheen in the sun, making her squint.   Swallowing, Rosey tried to contain her fear and excitement. Her earlier fears filled her mind once again. She clenched the reins turning her knuckles white. Sarabie seemed to sense her distress which was common in horses, especially now that she had intelligence. She tossed her head and snorted then raised her head high as if to show Rosey that she wasn't afraid. Rosey smiled, patted her neck affectionately, and tried to relax. This time she did not grip the crystal as she had done many times before but rested her palm on the hilt of Silver Knight, tracing the lines of the ornate daggers scabbard. The motion soothed her.

The path turned into a cobblestone walkway leading out of the orchard and around a hill up to the castle courtyard. Large trees of all species and ages lined the roadway giving the illusion of soldiers standing guard. Suddenly she tensed up, for all she knew, they could be. She eyed a maple tree as they passed, half expecting it to move at any moment. Hazel saw her and meowed with amusement, then gently rubbed her cheek up against Rosey's. Smiling, Rosey patted her head thankfully.

As they neared the entrance the path split into two making a loop around a small island of grass in which a large fountain sat gushing water onto the marble statues of unicorns that danced at its center. All around the loop were rows and rows of gardens stocked full with various types of plants and flowers. Rosey was amazed to see that some of them were in bloom while others were winter dormant. Rosey knew it wasn't so unlikely that some flowers bloomed in the winter months, but seeing them and their vibrancy delivered home to her just how alien this place was.

She placed a hand on Hazel's head as the cat peered out curiously from under her thick hair. Rosey leaned forward onto Sarabie's neck as they passed under the lower limbs of a towering conifer. She breathed deeply, taking in the warm fragrance of pine. Surrounded by so much beauty, she felt oddly at home. It was so relaxing, reminding her of the back woods near her house during the spring. She would take long rides with Sarabie, Noly, and Hazel, passing the world by.

Drawing close to the castle entrance, Rosey gawked in awe. Eloquent carvings and powerful gargoyles rested upon the fringed, golden surface of the castle giving it an almost medieval look.

On either side of the large castle doors was a guard. One was a black wolf and the other was a human woman of large build carrying a golden ax. Looking around Rosey spotted a few other armored humans, wolves, and other creatures stationed at various areas around the yard and castle just like they were outside the walls. Wolvereen turned to his own guard of armored wolves and dismissed them to rest and then return to their posts. The wolves bowed their heads and left, all except Nagura, who came up to wait beside Wolvereen. Turning back to the entrance Rosey spotted an officer coming towards them. He was a blonde man in his twenties with a pleasant smile and a rounded face. His eyes where a bright green and his shoulder-length golden hair was well groomed and pulled back in a loose ponytail. His outfit reminded Rosey of a police officer but instead of a badge and a tie, he wore a long blue sash over a simple black top and black pants. His boots were blue with golden clasps. His long sleeves had blue cuffs with golden clasps like his boot's clasps, and at his waist hung a simple saber with a golden hilt and belt.

"Welcome Rosey Mystic to the Golden Palace of the Golden Goddess," he said with a quick bow. "I will be escorting you to the Golden Goddess's study momentarily. She has important business that she needs to discuss with you, for now, make yourself at home." Rosey started for a moment, unable to respond. Either he did not know they had almost been attacked, or he wasn't worried enough about it to be concerned. Neither of which made Rosey very happy, how horrid must it be here for someone to be used to attacks happening all the time? Either way the man was polite and kind. He sounded just like a butler would on an old movie talking to a lady or a lord who had arrived at the ball. She squirmed under the sudden attention. Feeling stupid for being silent she forced herself to mutter, "Th…Thank you." Alex and Rochell nodded encouragingly and she smiled at them. While Rosey and the others dismounted, the young officer walked up to the large armored wolves, Wolvereen and Nagura, and bowed. What must have been stable hands came and asked the Horses to follow them after first bowing to Rosey. She wasn't exactly sure if they were stable hands or not because, for all she knew, even though they looked like stable hands, they could have easily been something else. She nodded awkwardly and the horses flicked their tails and nodded before following them. She watched the horses go with some level of panic, fear for Sarabie filling her heart. She knew it was ridiculous but, after what happened, she wanted the ones she loved close to her at all times. She couldn't help but see the image of Lyesal's dead body flash before her eyes. Rochell touched her shoulder and Rosey gazed at her carefree face. In that moment, everything was right again. She smiled her thanks and then followed the wolves and the officer into the castle's great foyer, her friends bringing up the rear.

    Wolvereen and Nagura pulled the blonde officer away for a moment and spoke to him softly. Rosey took the time to look around, her friends gawking right alongside her at the palace's grandeur. Rosey had never seen the inside of a castle before. She was sure they looked something like what she was seeing but she had never imagined them being so…gold. The floors were decorated with large, polished, golden tiles placed in a specific pattern to create the illusion of a larger space. The ceiling was bordered with silver etchings and large works of art hung from the gold painted walls. A crystal chandelier hung from the ceiling casting bright luminescent light from each individual shard, like a constantly shining firefly was caught within. In the middle of the foyer was a huge balcony with a clock at its base. At each side of the balcony there were two long staircases that led up to the second floor. The second floor extended back beyond her eyesight, disappearing into the endless expanse of castle. On the first floor where she stood, she could look to either side and see that the castle continued on in decorative long hallways. Long mirrors, images, and mosaics decorated the inner walls, while windows occupied the other wall and looked out over the gardens and hills. Along both hallways there were doors opposite where the windows were. Every door was a deep rich mahogany with golden designs, silver frames and doorknobs. Each of them was closed, giving Rosey the impression that they were little if ever used.

Ahead of her, below the staircases were two arches that led into what was probably a ball room. It was a large expanse of polished golden marble floors with flower designs and silver statues at the corners. Rosey was too far away to see what the statues were but she was sure they resembled a horse. She squinted and thought that she could see furniture and books but was unsure. Distracted by the beauty of the house Rosey hardly noticed when another officer, this one with short brown hair and calming green eyes came to her and extended his hands.

"Can I take your coat and cape?"

"Oh, yes, of course…thank you," she said surprised out of her observation. That was something that butlers said to rich people in movies not to ordinary her, but, then again, she wasn't ordinary and she was in a castle. She quickly unfastened the beautiful cape and her heavy winter coat. The room was toasty warm, but not hot, just perfect.

After taking her coat and cape the officer moved on to collect them from her friends, then from Noly and Hazel. After handing them to another officer, a young woman, he addressed Rosey. "On behalf of the Golden Goddess, I welcome you to the Golden Palace."

Rosey smiled, "Thanks for having me."

He then turned to Noly and Hazel, "Will you be staying in a separate room or with the Keeper, young companions?" Rosey frowned, the words sounded different somehow. It reminded her of when the stable hands, or whatever they were, had addressed the horses. Gasping she suddenly realized that he had spoken in English to accommodate Noly and Hazel. Suddenly she wondered if the two of them had even understood what had been going on before when they were attacked. Most likely not. Her cat and dog had not yet received the language knowledge since arriving so all they'd recognize so far was English. Rosey was amazed, had she truly been speaking and listening in a different language just moments ago? She hadn't even noticed until the officer had addressed her animals. She smiled, speechless.

"Sure, I've been sleeping with Rosey since I can remember, why stop now?" Noly happily replied, her tongue lolling out rather rudely. Rosey would need to speak to her about manners. Her words sounded just as odd, hinting that she was speaking English too.

The officer turned to Hazel.

"Ditto," she said purring.

"Wonderful, follow me please. I'll show you to the Keeper's room."

The cat and dog nodded. Hazel jumped down from Rosey's shoulders then promptly jumped onto Noly's back, flicking her tail in amusement when Noly growled at her.

Rosey watched Hazel, sudden fear running through her, her mind tracing the cold spot along the back of her neck where the little cat usually sat. Her eyes followed them as they followed the brunette officer, longing filling her heart. Once again her animals, those precious creatures she loved, were leaving her. Seeing her hesitation, Alex came over and gripped her hands in his reassuringly. Rosey squeezed back, finding new strength and confidence.

"Rosey, we're not coming with you to see the Goddess. Don't worry," she said quickly, seeing Rosey's nervous face. "It's better if you hear this alone, we'll see you later, okay?" Rosey reluctantly nodded and Rochell hugged her and then gave her one of her big, warming smiles. Rosey nodded, reassured. If her friends weren't worried than she shouldn't be either. She watched as Alex and Rochelle followed another officer, the woman who had taken their coats earlier, up the staircase and down the hallway out of sight. Seeing her friends leave her, Rosey suddenly felt all alone, but she knew that she needed answers and she couldn't keep pretending like this was some dream. She knew it wasn't, the death she had seen before was all too real. Still, the wall that had been built up around her, supported by her friends and animals, was now left bare. Everything that had been familiar was now replaced with the surrounding palace covered in gold and ornate decoration. She wanted to run away, but she couldn't. No, she wouldn't, she was not a coward and she refused to run. She had come here to learn the truth, if there was any truth to learn, and she wasn't going to back down now, not ever. Her sudden burst of confidence made her feel much better and she smiled encouraged.

The blonde officer she'd spoken with before rejoined her, having finished talking with Wolvereen. "I hear that you encountered a scare today on your way here, I'm glad to see that you and your friends are unharmed but I'm also saddened by the loss of a warrior. Please don't worry yourself my Keeper, we are here to protect you and to help you in any way we can. I believe that the sooner you talk to the Goddess the better."

Rosey nodded, she couldn't agree more.

"This way please," he said kindly, heading for the left staircase. Before following, Rosey faced Wolvereen and Nagura. They said nothing. They didn't have to. Rosey bowed her head in thanks, they both returned the gesture, then walked away to attend to whatever guard duties were required of them, their armor clinking metallically as they walked.

Quickly she hurried after the officer. Rosey was not too pleased about being alone but she trusted her friends and had no reason to doubt their sincerity. Suddenly the butterflies entered her stomach again. This was it. She was going to meet the Golden Goddess. They reached the top of the stairs and the officer turned left, into a hallway that much resembled the ones downstairs, except these did not have any windows on one side only more doors. At the end of it there were two huge golden doors. Not bothering to knock, the officer pushed open the doors and extended his hand in welcome. Rosey entered after a few hesitant moments and the officer closed the doors behind her.

Glancing around, Rosey spotted a slender, well-muscled, beautiful woman sitting at a desk at the far back of the room dressed in a golden, silver-trimmed, midriff top and pants. On one side of her body stretching from underneath her right breast down her waist and ending at her hip was a thick golden plate of armor. A silver belt attached to the metal plate looped around her midsection drawing the plate tight against her skin. Down her back a long flowing protective cape covered the woman's six foot height. Her feet sported gold, silver crested boots and her sleeveless arms were covered by long golden gloves with silver gantlets protecting the forearm. A silver breastplate covered the woman's chest and neck in links of plated armor. Long silky black hair, like Rosey's, fell down past the woman's waist ending just below her buttocks. It was decorated with golden and silver strands making it look like she had golden highlights. Silver beads were entwined in long braids down the front and part of her hair was pulled back at the top and tied in back in a braid with two silver ties. The woman's body was so magnificent that Rosey was afraid to study her face but she did anyway, unable to turn her eyes away. Gold colored skin tinted the lids of the Goddess's startling golden eyes, ending at the eyebrow in an elegant point. At first Rosey thought it was makeup, but upon closer inspection she realized it was a part of her natural skin. Her lips were the color of gold, not pink. She had high cheekbones and a slender face with a perfectly pointed chin. Upon her head sat a crown with a silver jewel at its center. To Rosey's surprise the crown was ordinary, more like a headband than a crown, but Rosey had no doubts that it was made of real gold. When they said The Golden Goddess they meant it. Her face, however, held a hard expression that clashed with her elegant exterior. Rosey stiffened, was something wrong? Looking at the Goddess you would think she was mad at seeing the Keeper, for a moment she hesitated, but Rosey was not going to be scared away, not now. She raised her head and kept walking. At that moment Rosey thought she saw the Goddess smile ever so slightly.

As Rosey got closer she began to see the long scars from ageless battles stretching across the Goddess's body and knew that her beauty was a clever disguise. Underneath that elegance was a firm, hardened warrior that was to be respected more than adored. Yet, there was a slight trace of kindness etching the Goddess's features: the slight wrinkle of a grin or the smooth encouragement of her golden eyes. Rosey smiled, this would be interesting. "Hello, welcome to my castle, Rosey," the golden woman said. Her voice didn't match her hard face, it was soft and inviting. Not the slightest bit of reproach or annoyance could be detected coming from her golden vocal cords. She stepped from around the desk and walked over to Rosey. As she drew near Rosey noticed that a silver scabbard containing a golden hilted saber was strapped to her side on an elegant silver belt. A similar scabbard hung on her left hip but was much smaller and looked as if it would hold a long skinny stick. *It's probably the compartment that holds her wand*, she thought with realization. She remembered how, on their way here, she had finally asked Alex why he had his hand in his jacket and he had promptly showed her the long scabbard. It was his own little compartment for his wand, kept tucked safely into the inside pocket of his jacket. Up until that moment, she had still been unsure about her friend's powers, now she had no choice but to accept them as real. Apparently his whole family had their jackets from Earth custom made to hold a wand out of sight so they'd always have it with them even though they couldn't use it on Earth. The idea had been surreal enough to quiet Rosey down for the rest of their trip.

Meeting the Goddess's eyes, she straightened her posture and smiled, trying to project a confident air. She had to admit, she was very happy to see that the Goddess was a human and not some weird looking creature. It would make talking to her much easier.

"Hello...and thank you for the escort," replied Rosey nervously, trying to remember her manners and hoping that there wasn't some special etiquette she should be using or something, if there was she was sure her friends would have told her about it. Eyeing the tall figure of the Goddess, she could think of nothing more to say and the constant hammering of her heartbeat was becoming a distraction. The Goddess's eyes swept over her. Her face revealed nothing. It was a solid block of emotionless observation. She seemed to be studying Rosey, but for what Rosey was unsure. She stood there shyly, hoping that the Goddess would see whatever it was she was looking for. After a few moments, Rosey began to fidget but did not dare take her eyes away from the Goddess's, like with Wolvereen she was determined not to be overpowered by the will of another. Finally the Goddess smiled, "I heard about the incident that took place today on your way here. It is but one of the many things you'll be facing on this world my child. The wolf who gave her life for you is now forever a hero as hopefully you will be one day."

Rosey felt herself sink at the memory and the Goddess's words didn't help any. They confirmed what Rosey had already assumed.

"But, before that can happen there are things you need to know before you begin your journey. I am here to help you with that. Your friends could have told you, but I know more. I will answer anything you have to throw at me...most of the things," said the golden woman with a smile. She made no reference to her little assessment a moment ago and Rosey sure wasn't going to bring it up herself. "Come, make yourself comfortable and we will talk," the Goddess continued, indicating a golden armchair as she moved back behind the desk and sat down.

"I can ask anything...?" stuttered Rosey surprised. She stepped forward, highly interested, and took a seat in the offered chair. It was amazing how quickly she could adjust.

"Oh yes dear, don't be afraid to ask. But before you begin...," she said, stopping Rosey as she opened her mouth, "...I need to first explain to you our history and how we came to be here in Earth, which might answer some of your questions ahead of time. Don't worry. It will all be answered soon." she said as if she had read Rosey's thoughts. For all Rosey knew she could have.   The Goddess turned her attention to a young woman who had come from a nearby room concealed behind specially made doors. Seeing Rosey's astonishment that the doors were made of three-inch-thick lead like lockdown doors, the Goddess explained almost bitterly, "Evil runs all over our world these days, they take great precautions for my safety." Rosey blinked, They? What did she mean by they? She decided to tuck the question away until later, besides the Goddess might explain it herself.

"Nashi, would you bring some refreshments for the Keeper please?" said the Goddess kindly.

Rosey couldn't help but think that she had waited long enough. Feeling betrayed somehow, the sudden urge to scream came to her and only with a huge amount of effort did she manage to hold her tongue. The Goddess was royalty, after all, and it wouldn't be right to push her. *Besides I am pretty thirsty and I wouldn't mind a little snack*, she thought, reasoning with herself. "Yes ma'am," said Nashi bowing. She turned and left quickly back through the doors she had come through.

Rosey noticed that Nashi was not wearing what you might expect a maid to wear. She had on a knee-length golden shirt, long loose silver pants, and golden slippers. Around her sleeveless arms she wore silver plates of metal that formed a point on the back of each hand. Around her left bicep there was a golden ring and her black hair was pinned up by an elegant, silver, metal tie. She was young, at least nineteen, but looked fitted for her job.

While they waited Rosey occupied her time by marveling at the ornate decorations of the room and doors. Looking at the desk she saw it was oak as were the picture frames. The pictures were mostly renaissance looking but some were of large powerful dragons, Leron, and various animals while others were of humans. The images had no name tags or anything of which to offer identification. The people in them could be family members or friends. They could be strangers, people that were fit only for the artist's eye and had no connection to the Goddess herself. Strangely enough they reminded Rosey of the pictures at her house, pictures of people she didn't recognize and who her uncle had identified as friends of his. Nashi soon returned with a cart carrying refreshments and various foods.

"Please take as much as you like, we have plenty," said the Goddess sweeping her arm out invitingly towards the delicious smelling food. Rosey reluctantly pulled her mind away from her memories and eyed the assortment of fruits, meats, grains, and drinks with awe. She wasted no time in grabbing some fruit and a cool glass of water. The Goddess poured herself some herbal tea and Rosey took some warm apple cider after gulping down the water. Finally the Goddess addressed Rosey.

"Are you ready?"

"Oh, I've been ready for some time now," said Rosey trying hard not to sound rude.

The Goddess smiled with amusement and nodded, sensing Rosey's annoyance despite her best efforts to hide it, "Yes, I know. I'm sorry about the lack of explanation. There is just so much to tell and so little time, but you deserve to know. Now it is time," she said. Taking a deep breath she began, "The best place to start is at the beginning, and for this story I mean the very beginning. About four hundred years ago our sun went supernova and ripped our planet apart."

The statement was so simple and yet in one sentence the Goddess had managed to make Rosey stare at her in utter awe. She'd watched some television shows on the Discovery channel about supernovas and had learned about them in her science classes but she had not expected to ever encounter a situation where one was relevant.

The Goddess continued, "We never saw it coming. We were never interested in outer space like Earth is. We were content with our life on our planet and that was all we needed. Because of that we had no way of knowing that our sun was reaching its end. Before I go on, do you know about Adina?"

Rosey nodded, a bit unsettled by what the Goddess had just said, "My friends told me. She's an Immortal." The Goddess nodded happily, "Good, that'll make this easier then. Immortals are caretakers of a planet. All planets have one, even Earth. They know a lot of things, and their knowledge is usually deeply rooted in the planet they care for. You would think then that Adina, being an Immortal, would have been aware of the coming disaster, but that is not so. An Immortal's purpose is to watch over their planet. They are to make sure that everything runs the way that it is supposed to, the sun and moon are not always included in this particular package apparently." The Goddess paused for a moment and tilted her head slightly, as if contemplating whether to say something or not. What it was Rosey could only imagine. She sat at the edge of her seat, waiting. Finally the Goddess spoke, "I'm not sure whether I should be saying this but…the particular circumstances surrounding the planets destruction are a little odd to me. Though, Adina told us that it was not her job to be sure as to the sun's state of being, I still find it strange that she did not know… something," the Goddess's eyes grew distant, as if peering back on a past memory. She straightened and her eyes cleared. "It doesn't matter, what's done is done and there is no reason for you to burden yourself with it.

"When the supernova destroyed our planet, Adina managed to form a barrier around a chunk of it in the form of an asteroid. Any buildings, houses, or people trapped within the barrier were saved, the rest, unfortunately, were not. She stuck this small collection of inhabitants in a suspended animation while she devised a plan to save us. We weren't chosen, we were simply all she had time to save. For years we wandered through the universe as that asteroid. Adina, being an Immortal, is quite powerful. She can't travel faster than light, nothing can, but she can bend time and space around her, almost like creating a portal from one place to another, but slower. I would say that we spent about," she trailed off, thinking, "…eighty years in that asteroid, but to us it was seconds, minutes. We knew nothing in our suspended state."

Rosey gaped at her, "Eighty years?"

The Goddess just nodded, "For awhile we stayed in suspended animation, floating along in space awaiting Adina's plan to unfold. We were unaware of anything at that time, our lives were in Adina's hands. Her plan to remove us from the asteroid involved connecting us to the energy of one of the nearest galaxy's planets. It was the only way we could survive. It was the only way she could help us. The nearest galaxy just so happened to be the Milky Way and Earth was the chosen planet.

"Using what powers she had left, Adina was able to create a physical planet within the same place as Earth, occupying a dimensional space. She did this without disrupting Earth itself or its natural laws. Because we occupy the same space we use the same sun and the same moon to operate. Don't really think of it as a planet existing inside of another, it's more like we are mirror worlds, parallel worlds living side by side but in different dimensions of time and space, yet, occupying the same area. Basically, Adina created a dimension that feeds off of Earth's energy and that has allowed us to stay in the same area as the Earth itself. Do you know what a dimension is?"

Rosey had some idea but she shook her head nonetheless, just to be sure. Suddenly, her uncle's strange words before weren't so strange anymore.

"It's a pocket of space located in another space, but this 'pocket' is unable to be seen, touched, or heard in the space that it occupies. It might as well not exist. That is what we are. We exist in an artificial dimension, held and maintained by the Earth itself. It's very strange, I know, but that's the best way I can describe it. Dimensions, believe it or not, are not that uncommon in the universe. Some planets are full of them. Ours is not natural, Earth certainly never had a dimension placed on it before. We put it there, but that was the only way to access Earth's power. However, do not be fooled, this is no planet we live on, it is simply a home. Things that exist in dimensions can take any form, but they are not real planets. This world works and is functional, for now, however, without Earth's power holding us up we would not exist. We live off another planet. It is for this very reason that we call our world The World Within A World, because it is not really a planet. One day we hope that will change." She said this with hope in her eyes and a smile on her lips.

Rosey said nothing, her mind racing. The idea that a world could exist within another was mindboggling enough without the idea of dimensions jumping into the picture. Just how powerful was this Adina? If she was so powerful than what could she, Rosey, do? She was just a seventeen year old girl, and, as far as she knew, she didn't' have any special abilities beyond some killer Kendo and Iaido techniques. What was stopping this Adina from destroying the evil creature herself? She certainly sounded like she had the power. All Rosey could do right now was listen and pray that she would understand what it was she needed to do.

The Goddess continued, "Do you need me to clarify, I know it's a bit difficult to understand?"

Rosey shook her head, "No, you did really well, I understand. I've watched enough science shows to have a basic knowledge."

The Goddess continued, "I'm glad to hear it. As I was saying, what Adina did saved what little of our world was left, but there were consequences to her actions."

Rosey's brows furrowed and the Goddess's voice thickened.

"Our time in the asteroid caused us to lose a lot of our memories so that when we awoke on this new world we had but bits and pieces of what was once our beautiful planet. When the supernova occurred it destroyed our civilization taking all that we had learned with it and killing many. All that we had of our once great planet was what was contained in that asteroid. What buildings, houses, and forests still remained on that chunk of rock and earth was all that was left. Along with our vast civilization, we also lost a ton of information about our animals, medications, history, and much more. Back then we had to face a future on a strange new world with only a portion of our memories to guide us. Today, we are saddened by the amount of information we lost."

The Goddess shook her head with apparent sadness. Rosey could understand. If Earth were destroyed and only a small portion was saved, those survivors would end up starting from scratch, especially if their memories were affected. A whole new world surrounded by unknowns and little knowledge of their history. If that chunk of survivors were from Africa, then their lives and their memories would vastly differ from that of Europe's or America's. Rosey wondered, what had The World Within A World been like before it was destroyed?

"You can imagine how surprised we were when we awoke on a new world after experiencing the supernova. It didn't help any that our memories were very limited, some people didn't even know who they were or what had happened. Nevertheless, it was better than being dead and we immediately got to work on rebuilding our civilization." The Goddess paused for a moment; her eyes seemed to glaze over as if she was seeing memories flash before her golden eyes, "We were such a small group of people when we emerged from the asteroid. We suddenly had a whole new planet to discover, a world started from the scraps of an asteroid torn from our old planet. That's how Adina made this world. She took the asteroid and used its own biological makeup to replicate what we once had. We'll never know if she got the right match." She seemed to snap out of her daydream and back into reality. "At first everything went very well. Because of our lost memories, we started anew from what we did remember and created what we have now. Books were written to begin recording our new history. The buildings that had survived on the asteroid were studied and the memories that we did have were compared and contrasted to help develop the future. Nations were created and villages and towns were built and established. We began learning and expanding across our world, discovering all its mysteries and truths. We were a new people, learning about our new world.

"Over three hundred and fifty years passed without incident, we were happy and growing in strength and power each day. While we would never be able to regain our lost civilization and memories we could still start anew and build a better one. We were so full of hope."

The Goddess's eyes glistened and Rosey could almost feel the loss coming from the golden woman's memories. "Rosey," she said suddenly, with force, making her jump. "I need to make sure you understand something before we go on. This might be hard to hear but Earth is a planet of war and destruction. Rarely does love and understanding triumph amongst Earth's kind. However, most planets are not like Earth."

At this Rosey frowned, surprised.

"I know that, to your ears, this may sound very unusual and it might be hard for you to understand but our world is peaceful. Its people are caring towards each other and this planet and most other planets are the same. It is abnormal to find a planet so riddled with hate, suspicion, and violence. Earth came to us as a huge surprise, their ways were very different than what we were used to, but in a way Earth's strangeness also helped us to prepare. We had no army, no soldiers, and no warriors. We lived simple lives with nothing but peace in mind and the well-being of our community. We had no idea how to fight, but we would soon have to learn how to."

She fixed Rosey with her sharp, golden gaze. "I have no doubt that you have already heard its name. We call it the Evil One, and it is the very reason why we were forced to become warriors on this world."

Rosey felt herself grow stiff in her seat. This was the enemy that her friends had spoken of, now she'd finally understand what it was that had everyone at the edge of their seats.

"We are not really sure exactly what this being is. What we have gleamed so far is that it is an entity that loves to wreak havoc where it can for no apparent reason. Its powers are limited depending on the planet and that planet's particular natural laws. Our world was weak and dependent on Earth which, you can imagine, made us perfect prey for the Evil One. This being attacked without mercy, sending its most ferocious beasts upon us, and we were utterly defenseless," the Goddess said vehemently, spitting out the words with hatred.

Rosey gulped, as she had suspected, this Evil One was no jealous citizen or power crazy idiot looking for a few countries to burn. This was something different, intelligent and evil. There was no other way to describe it, it was a being that lived and preyed on whatever it could without mercy or remorse. Rosey shook in her seat and gripped the crystal around her neck. Her hands were so numb she could hardly feel the warmth that spread from its small surface.

"When the Evil One found us hiding within Earth," the Goddess continued, "it established itself a temporary home floating in outer space. We have no idea how it was able to do this, it is simply one of its powers. It has never set foot on this land, so we have no idea what kind of power it has. We do know, however, that it is neither alive nor dead."

At this, Rosey looked at the Goddess with confusion written across her face but the proud woman kept speaking, taking no notice of Rosey's reaction.

"It is an entity of hatred and evil. Think of it as a ghost or…demon. It does what it wants and does it without mercy. We're not even sure how it knew we were in Earth but it did, and it wanted us. However, it found getting to us to be a difficult task. Thanks to Earth, we are very well protected from outside forces. Though she's never said so, we believe Adina may have done this on purpose. She knew we were quite weak; we were nothing but an asteroid after all. She knew that only a planet's energy could bring us back, one whose Energy Flows were well established, and powerful enough to help support another planet. That's why she chose Earth.

"In order to explain to you just how important Earth was to us I must first tell you about the Energy Flows. I am sure your friends have made you familiar with them and their various attributes. What do you know so far?"
"Well…" Rosey stuttered for a moment, surprised and a little caught off guard by the sudden focus on her. "I know that Energy Flows allow people to control magic and elements, and that they can give animals intelligence and increase the size of some animals into Dominants."

"Exactly, but that's not all the Energy Flow's do," the Goddess leaned back in her chair. "They act as a list of rules, natural rules, which govern all the life and biology on a planet. Every planet has Energy Flows, even Earth, and every one of them is different depending on the planet. Some are visible to its people, others are more subtle. On Earth we believe the Energy Flows are underground. Some of the electronic devices on Earth may sometimes pick up magnetic disturbances or energy fluxes; they are all the result of underlying Energy Flows. The information held within these flows ranges from the seasons, climates, and the weather, to the genetic codes of the people, animals, and plant life. They are like the genetic codes of the planet, its own DNA strand with all the planets vital information."

Hearing this Rosey couldn't help but remember what her uncle had said about Yellowstone. About how Earth's Energy Flows gathered there and so much energy was there that it could support many different portals. Things were making more sense now than they had before and it was scaring Rosey, as if all the secrets of the world were opening up for her.

"When Adina put us inside Earth she had to connect our Energy Flows to each other so that they could live off of one another. The supernova did some damage to our Energy Flows, so they really needed the extra support. By doing this it aligned our two worlds together so that they mimicked each other, that's why we follow the same seasons as Earth does, rotate like it, are tilted like it, and so on. We are definitely different biologically but that area of the Energy Flows is not as strict. We share basic things but not all things. It is in this way that Adina saved us in the first place. By connecting our weak and almost lifeless Energy Flows to Earth's, she restored them in some small way. They are stronger now than they were before, but they still depend on Earth's energy and Earth's power. We cannot stand on our own."

She looked away, unable to meet Rosey's eyes. "When we first heard of the Evil One's presence we were worried for Earth's safety, we could only imagine what the Evil One would do to Earth to get to us but Adina assured us that Earth was protected. Earth, as I said, is very different from other planets. Its Energy Flows are very technological, more so than any other planet, or most of them anyway. We considered the possible threats facing Earth. The Evil One would not be able to drive us out of Earth in any way except to destroy Earth and destroying a planet is no easy matter, so we ruled out that scenario. We even considered that it might try to attack Earth, but once again, we ruled that out. The Evil One doesn't have the kind of power needed to take on a technologically advanced world like Earth nor did we think it would waste time and effort to do so. We knew what Earth was capable of and we knew what powers it held in technology. The Evil One might attack but it would be fighting years and years of war, and even then could be defeated. We didn't even know if it had the power to attack Earth. It just didn't make sense for it to go after Earth.

"The Evil One only cares about our world, that particular reason is it's alone. That doesn't necessarily mean that it cares about what happens to Earth but it is not going to waste its time and energy on such a highly technologically advanced planet. We determined that Earth is safe for now, simply because it is very powerful in its own right, and it would take too much effort. The Evil One would not have the energy needed to take on Earth as well as our own forces. Whatever the reason, Earth would not be harmed by the Evil One; its powers would be little to nothing there. At least that is how Adina explained it to us. We are still a little fuzzy on the details but we trust Adina. At that time, that was all we needed to know."

Rosey found herself relieved. She couldn't help but be worried about Earth. It had been her home for her whole life, a place where she had been raised and cared for. Despite all its mishaps and less than satisfactory development it had still been her place, a place she'd called her own. She was happy to hear it would be safe. The Goddess carried on.

"As I said before, the Evil One created for itself a home where it could operate in outer space. We called this floating home the Hell Ship, a fitting name for the home of one so evil. We called it that because it looks very ship-like. It is a large floating fortress commanded by a sinister master. When Adina informed us of the Evil One's little home," she said sarcastically with menace, "we were devastated. We knew we were in for a long, drawn out war. With Earth in the way, the Evil One would have to work around it. The only way to do that was to create its own portals on the Hell Ship and connect them to ours. In this way it could send through anything it desired. It did just that, we assume. It could be very possible that it had some other way, but evidence so far has pointed to it using portals."

She looked up at Rosey, knowingly. "You yourself have experienced portal travel. You came here through the artificial portal that I made."

Flashing images of the portal located in the cave on the mountain came to mind and Rosey nodded. Her friends had told her it was the Goddess's portal.

"We were not going to put it past this creature to create its own portal, nor did we think that it couldn't connect it to ours. Anything was possible. We just had to be ready."

She shook her head, her eyes suddenly glazed with hate, "The Evil One changed all that we had ever known and forced us to defend ourselves. It…somehow created its own army of evil creatures that we call Blood Gorons and sent them to mercilessly attack us. It not only was able to create and connect portals but it was also able to create its own beasts. Since it had created its own home that didn't seem like a complete impossibility, but it was still quite a surprise. We were very much taken aback by the sudden appearance of these living creatures. It's one thing to create an artificial portal; it's another to create a live beast. We could do nothing but face this new challenge.

"Blood Gorons are small and have no elemental or magical ability; despite their size they are vicious and strong with a heightened intelligence that many find unnerving. As untrained as we were with no weapons to defend ourselves, it was a massacre. True we had elemental and magical power but we lacked the knowledge of how to use them in battle. We had never had to before, leaving us very vulnerable. We soon developed ways to defend ourselves, mostly with Adina's help, but the loss in numbers was staggering. The Blood Gorons were nasty fighters and very strong." The Goddess's eyes softened. "Adina had done so much for us, two hundred years of rest had restored her, but Immortals watch over their planet's life. Keeping the Energy Flows connected to Earth without causing any repercussions was difficult on her…is difficult on her. What power she had she used on us and still does."

Rosey was amazed at how much trust and joy she saw in those golden eyes. Adina was truly something special to inspire such respect and love from this powerful woman of which, in only a few moments, Rosey had come to revere with the highest respect.

The Goddess's eyes then hardened as she continued, "The Evil One did a very unusual thing by designing these Blood Gorons. Usually a creature like the Evil One would formulate its own creatures, mutations created from energy coming from its own body. Doing this is usually much easier, but for some reason the Evil One chose to create something living. We believe it chose this route because of its inability to enter our planet and so it needed something that had a much larger chance of surviving on its own and already had a somewhat established connection to our world. But to create something living you have to abide by the rules. If the Evil One was going to make something that would live normally then it had to model them after a pre-existing creature or something like it; otherwise it wouldn't be alive. It would be a projection. You see, the Energy Flows act as a sort of biological defense mechanism. They can't and won't allow something living that doesn't exist in the universe or reality. It must be fundamentally based on some sort of recognizable figure, even if it's not native to the planet..." she scrunched her nose, trying to find the right words. "Let me say it this way, on Earth you can create synthetic things, right?"

Rosey nodded

"Well, it's the same concept. These beings can be synthetically created, but they come from something, something that was already there. That's what I mean. Besides, working with a creature native to the planet is far easier to synthetically create than a whole new creature. The Evil One, for whatever reason, chose the Spine Backed Draconian," she said reaching with perfectly poised hands into a drawer in her desk and pulling out two pictures. She presented one to Rosey. It looked like a purple lizard with long pink tipped spikes running from its head to the end of its tail with a dog's body. Two dragon-like wings extended from its back with sharp talons at the end. The head was long and angular with sharp pointed teeth and bright blue eyes. Its front feet were that of an eagle with one of its talons slightly larger and more curved, resembling a raptor's claw. Its tail was heavily spiked with red and blue feathers and in between the long spikes it had the same feathers running down its silver scaled body. It was actually, for all its alien appearance, a very beautiful, intelligent looking creature. Rosey could tell why the Evil One would choose this creature to model on. The talons looked sharp, the teeth were long and perfectly curved, the spikes were numerous and the tail and body were heavily armored with tightly packed scales. Something puzzled her though, the creature, according to the description, was only four feet tall. The Goddess had said that the Blood Gorons were small, but that seemed too small.

"I see you've noticed that the height of this creature doesn't quite match up," said the Goddess studying Rosey's face carefully. "We were also quite surprised as to why the Evil One would choose to model its Blood Gorons after this small animal, but we soon realized that the Evil One has to make these creatures from scratch, which we venture to believe is probably a very difficult task. A smaller animal takes less time to recreate than a larger one."

Rosey nodded, understanding, "That makes sense. So the Evil One chose not to create these projections of itself, instead it created living creatures, the Blood Gorons, because of its location in space? Did it make it easier on the Evil One?"

"We believe so," the Goddess nodded, sitting back in her chair, "By creating a creature that was already close to the planet's biology it avoided having to try and send its own projections down to the surface world, through another planet no less. If the Evil One were already on our world, here with us now, it would find it much more convenient to create the projections."

"What are projections?"

"They are creatures that are fake, essentially. They can be anything, or anyone, any being or mutation that the Evil One fancies. They can even be copies of itself, like clones. Projections are a type of conjure, creatures that are raised into existence just to follow orders and normally don't have a will of their own. The only difference between projections and other conjures is that the projections draw their energy and power from the one that created them. Blood Gorons follow one will, the Evil One's, however they have a massive intelligence, fitting for a creature of life such as they. Having a

The Mystics

creature that is real and can exist on its own without the Evil One's help, being that it is in space, makes it possible for the Evil One to keep massive groups of Blood Gorons on the surface world and command them at will without having to use its own energy to sustain them." Her eyes rested on the image in her hand. "This is the Blood Goron that was created based off of the Draconian," she said, extending the second picture to Rosey.

Rosey handed the first one back and accepted the second. When she looked at the image she almost gagged. The beautiful, prideful, creature was replaced with a hideous beast. For the most part it looked exactly like the Spine Backed Draconian, except that where before there was beauty and humility there was now only ugliness and evil. It was colored in red, orange, and brown, with eyes so black that Rosey thought they must make black holes jealous. The spikes, horns, teeth, and talons were extended to twice their size with extra teeth and spikes along the sides of the tail, not just along the top. The feathers had been replaced with more spikes and the armored scales on the body had been extended to cover the whole body including the underbelly. The scales of the creature were not the flawless sheen of decorative designs and patterns but the stretched and wrinkled, dried brown flecks of a monster. Rosey shuddered and gladly handed the image back to the Goddess.

"The Evil One created these creatures to be purely evil killing machines, to terrorize and destroy all the life they saw," the Goddess said as she put the two pictures away. "They are highly intelligent but because they are artificially made, they have no will of their own so are forced to take orders and obey the Evil One. Also, and most importantly, because their DNA is very close to that of the existing Spine Backed Draconians, they are accepted on this world by the Energy Flows and allowed to live."

"Wait," Rosey said, thinking, "If Earth's Energy Flows and this world's Energy Flows are connected then why didn't Earth's Energy Flows attack it? We certainly don't have spine backed…whatever's on Earth."

"Good point, but..." said the Goddess raising her index finger, "just because the two are connected does not mean that they act upon each other. If that were true, our whole world would have never been allowed to merge with Earth." She paused for a moment and looked away considering. "We...are researching the possibility that the two may be affecting each other, but we are fairly certain that they are not. However placing a world within another has never been done before and things, not foreseen, could be happening. Some of the more...mysterious happenings on Earth may have been a result of our joining, but that has not been proven."

"Mysterious?" Rosey tilted her head, curious.

The Goddess rolled her head, searching for the right words, "Oh...like that Bermuda Triangle thing I've heard about. Really fascinating...but that's not important, you just need to know that the two planets don't fight with one another."

Rosey nodded, though she couldn't help but run through all the UFO stories and greatest mysteries in her head, relating them in some way to The World Within A World. Was it possible? Could their connection have caused that to happen? Rosey had no time to ponder, the Goddess's words were far more important.

"Seeing that the Evil One, this invader, was creating its own army, we had no choice but to act. The Leaders of the World met in the Stone Circle, a circle of stones on a distant continent about a two week journey from here. We wanted to stay in contact with each other when we began settling our new world, so every month or so the leaders would meet at this location. In this way we could be certain of each other's advancements, developments, and general morality. We wanted to be certain that we could help one another if the need came but we had no idea that one of those needs was going to be war. The leaders were not limited to kings, queens, or nobles, but also influential families. These were individuals that were trusted amongst the people and who had obvious leadership skills. So it seemed right that when discussing the protection of our newly acquired world, we should meet at the Stone Circle where we always had.

"It was at this place that we devised the war plans concerning the Evil One, the responsibilities to be taken by what nation, and the other important aspects of a war. This was the first time we had ever had to do something like this. It was alien to us, and very unsettling. After everything was sorted out at the Stone Circle, we began our counter attack. We were ignorant and naive of what battle was and we would pay for that in time, for the Evil One was not new to this fighting. Its purpose is to destroy," she said angrily, "and it knew all sorts of ways to do just that. Soon, we would become the warriors we had to be to defend ourselves, but not before many lives were lost.

"Thanks to the Evil One's Blood Goron monstrosities, we paid a heavy toll on the battlefield. Many of our people did not survive the ordeal and some were captured. We have never yet uncovered them since they were taken, and we fear we never will. Though these creatures are small, they make powerful adversaries in the air and on land, though they're not as affective in water. The Evil One pretty much chose where we would be fighting. It would send the masses of Gorons to one location through underground cave systems or cleverly disguised caravans that looked like our own, launching guerrilla tactics on our warriors. We were so unfamiliar with warfare that we were utterly helpless to do much but fight back. Over time we got better, we learned from our mistakes and were able to put up a good fight. Our research on Earth also helped, especially when it came to our weapon designs."

She paused and looked at Rosey almost shamefully, as if what she was about to say was a horrible crime, "You see when we came to Earth and our Energy Flows connected with it, some of our portals connected to Earth. We were very interested in Earth so we had many of our humans go to Earth to study and learn from it. That's how we were able to learn of Earth's Energy Flows, and it's also how we've been making sure that Earth is not being too overly affected by our connection. Of course Earth did not have all that it has now, that was about two hundred years ago after all, but we took what we considered to be acceptable and converged it with our own technologies and understanding. Some of the weaponry was especially helpful in our fighting. We were observers, watching and learning," she raised her head, proud but still a little ashamed as if taking something from anyone else other than themselves was a dishonor. "We even adopted some of your word choices and such. Some things may seem familiar to you here, some will seem very different. We were starting from scratch and many of Earth's developments were…attractive, despite their often violent behavior and even that had its purpose. When the Evil One attacked we at least had some knowledge of violence and terror than we originally had, enough to respond and to act accordingly. Everything that we had learned was all a part of our growing up and rebuilding. We have Earth to thank for that, though I would have liked to see what we would have come up with if Earth had not been involved, but there is no sense in dwelling on what cannot be changed."

Rosey tried not to laugh, this was definitely a woman of pride. She did not like that their world had taken inspiration from Earth, though, considering Earth's history of violence and suffering, perhaps the Goddess was right in being ashamed. However, Earth's achievements were great indeed, and did not merit being overlooked simply because of its people's pride. There was a lot of good that such technological advancements could provide when they weren't being used to destroy other people.

The Goddess quickly moved on, noticeably happy to leave such talk behind. "As I said, one of the most important things we adopted from Earth was their weaponry. Not their guns and tanks, of course, but their swords, shields, and other such medieval devices. They fit our world and our style very well. Earth taught us how to fight and how to protect ourselves, a skill that we could not live without now that we were fighting for our lives and our world. We also worked on adapting our elemental and magical techniques. The battle raged on for a whole year with neither side giving in. After a while it became apparent that we were slowly being beaten back. Even though Earth had helped us become warriors the Blood Gorons had cunning, lots of it. They could not be defeated by us or Adina and our troops were tiring. We needed help, we needed to attack the Evil One at its heart, but nothing was strong enough to do that."

The Goddess looked at Rosey, her face unreadable, but her eyes were as hard as rocks. Her gaze was so strong Rosey found it impossible to look away.

"You may be wondering why this beast never took its portal and came to our world, in that way it would not have to send Blood Gorons through the portals after us nor would it have to do things from so far away…in space, no less." She paused, watching Rosey closely. "You may also be wondering why Adina, with as much power as she has, is unable to defeat this creature. I can see from the look on your face that you want to know why you are necessary in all this."

Rosey was shocked into silence. She felt her body shiver, whether it was from cold or apprehension she did not know. She gulped, unsure of what to do.

"Rosey," the woman said, her golden lips moved slowly, "I need to be certain you understand the nature of this creature. Earth has taught you that things are scientific, but it is a very different story here. This Evil One, as I said before, is not a creature of either life or death. It is a demon, stuck between realities. One reality is life the other is death. That is a fundamental rule of all existence. You, on Earth, know this in-between existence as purgatory. That is an adequate description of where this beast lies. It is for this very reason that Earth's scientific knowledge would never be able to 'see' the Hell Ship floating out in space. It is also the reason why coming to our world would do nothing to help it. You see, when entering a world such as ours it would have to pull itself from purgatory and enter the world of life. To do that it would need to manifest itself into some form, a form that would be acceptable to the Energy Flows and thus be allowed to exist just as the Evil One had to do when it created the Blood Gorons. In this form it would be very weak, with none of its original powers for the same reason: the Energy Flows may not allow it. On Earth, or any planet, it would be the same."

Rosey sat in shock, it was such an alien idea but it made sense. She'd heard of how ghosts or things like it could manifest themselves. How they drew energy from the world around them to manifest into reality. The very idea made Rosey shudder in her seat. This being couldn't enter the world of life, the physical world, unless it took a different form but just the idea that it was so ghostly was enough to make Rosey start. The Goddess's voice held Rosey captive as she spoke.

"If they manifest themselves, these beings, these demons, use their powers to manipulate, control, and sway the existing population to their will. They enjoy destroying people slowly, usually using those projections I spoke of before to create mayhem. They want to ruin the people and make them do things they'd never think of doing. They are the ultimate deceivers and they will stop at nothing to achieve their goal. Trying to brainwash people, however, can take time. A long time. By staying in the Hell Ship, the Evil One is at its full power, and thus its power is unlimited. The only time that power is limited is when it interacts with our world. I'm sure it would have created something far more menacing than the Blood Gorons if the constraints of living in space hadn't of stopped it. This is also one of the reasons it does not, nor probably ever will, try anything with Earth. It doesn't want to waste the time or the effort to attack a strong planet. Not to mention that Earth's Energy Flows are far more restrictive than ours are," Rosey tilted her head with a questioning gaze, but the Goddess went on, "We, on the other hand, have only just begun our regrowth, and we have to deal with this..." she said vehemently. Her eyes held such sadness, but also a deep burning hatred and a desire like no other. "We've been through so much," she said under her breath.

The Mystics

The Goddess sat there for a few minutes then snapped back to attention as if nothing had happened, "As for Adina, she has no power against this creature. She is, essentially, much like the Evil One, except that she's not evil. An Immortal is created at the very early stages of a planet's development. They grow with the planet, and are one with it. They know everything about it, and govern all life that thrives there. It is their job to protect the citizens and the life that grows on their planet. As the citizens grow, so too does the Immortal. Her power directly comes from the planet and it's life force. The weaker the planet, the weaker the Immortal. They are linked."

"What would happen if Adina died?" Rosey asked, fidgeting with the end of her shirt.

The Goddess considered for a moment, "An Immortal can be killed, because they are born, just like you, me, anybody. However, because an Immortal is linked to the planet its soul doesn't have to move on if they are killed or die. If you or I were to be killed, our souls would move on into death. Her soul would simply remain here on the planet and wait for her new body to be formed or made."

"What makes the new body?" Rosey said, picturing a laboratory tube in her mind's eye.

"Immortals are linked to the planet and their powers are upheld by their planet, so it is the planet that makes them new bodies. It's a lot like the phoenix idea, only the new body is grown and born again...not risen."

"Would she look the same if that happened?"

"Possibly, an Immortal's form can be absolutely anything...even mist. It doesn't have to be a physical living form. Normally it is...but...look don't be too concerned about Adina. If anything were to happen to her, she would just return. That about sums it up in the best possible sense." The Goddess shrugged and Rosey nodded, though she felt as if she was given the kiddy versions of things to help move things along. She couldn't exactly complain.

The Goddess saw Rosey's expression and said in a kind voice, "Don't worry about this or Adina. It's ultimately not important to your overall goal. I just don't want you to think that the Evil One is a physical being. It's Hell Ship is a physical manifestation, but it itself is more like energy or a soul without a body. Either way, this creature is unlike any enemy you will ever face."

She was silent for a while and Rosey nodded slowly, taking it all in. She had no way to respond to that. Death had never been a subject she'd looked at too often with her parent's deaths hanging over her head. She had tried to stay away from it, but here it was haunting her. Of course, it sounded silly: trying to avoid death when it was the main subject of her life. Now it seemed the rules were being bent again. Her whole understanding flipped on its head. Yet, it still made sense, in some crazy way. People were born, and then died. That was the way the world worked, so it made sense that something that was dead, like the Evil One, would find it difficult to be born. In movies, bringing the dead back to life almost never worked out the way it was supposed to or what came back was never the same thing. This must be a lot like that. The Evil One was trying to come back, but the rules were hindering its return. She nodded, letting the Goddess know to continue.

"Are you sure?" the golden woman said, leaning forward, "I can explain more."

"No, I understand for the most part. Please continue."

She nodded solemnly and went on, "Adina is one with the planet and her power comes from the planet. Her abilities are almost unlimited because of this but they're only unlimited when used on the planet itself. She can't use any power that doesn't affect or include the planet specifically. The planet is her domain, but creating an ultimate power against evil is not. Her power is made to watch over the planet and that is the reason why she was able to connect us to Earth by creating a dimension, and why she was able to connect the Energy Flows to each other.

"Of course she wasn't alone when she merged us with Earth. Earth's Immortal had a hand in that as well. Before you ask," she said as Rosey opened her mouth, "I know nothing about Earth's Immortal. Adina is the one who contacted the Immortal and thus allowed for our two planets to merge. All I know is that Earth's Immortal is some sort of intelligent technological being. Beyond that I know nothing. Other planets inhabitants are not supposed to know another planet's Immortals. Only Earth's citizens can see Earth's Immortal and only people of The World Within A World can see Adina. Immortals can see and work with each other though, which is why Adina was able to contact Earth's Immortal."

Rosey's head swam with the possibilities. What was Earth's Immortal: a computer, a bear, a human...science...nah, probably not, she thought shaking her head. Rosey remembered when Alex told her that all planets had immortals, obviously, that meant Earth had to have one too, but for some reason she just never considered Earth having an immortal. *Probably because it is such a fanciful idea and so unlike Earth in so many ways*, she thought, glancing at the image of a dragon in one of the Goddess's pictures.

"Hold on," Rosey said as an idea struck her, "I'm an Earth citizen aren't I? Shouldn't I be able to know who the Immortal is?"

The Goddess was already shaking her head, "Rosey...you're not an Earth citizen. You may have grown up there, but you were born here."

Rosey frowned in disbelief, "I was... I mean I just figured...really?"

The Goddess nodded, her face was solemn and unchanged. Rosey felt her heart skip a beat, she had never really considered the idea that she wasn't from Earth. Her uncle hadn't really had the time to tell her anything, but the idea that she was from The World Within A World was a little staggering. She should have expected it; after all, her mother had come from this world, however, it had never entered her mind that she might not have been born on Earth. It was such a small notion and yet, it changed everything. She gripped her seat, suddenly unstable. She was born here, in this world. Still, Earth had been the place she'd been raised and loved.

Didn't that mean anything? Then again, she had always felt a little out of place, as if she didn't belong there. Was this why?

The Goddess went on, unaware of Rosey's thoughts. "As I was saying, Adina was only able to accomplish combining the two worlds by getting the help of Earth's Immortal. All Immortal's abilities are made for their planet's needs and it's because of that that Adina was able to save whom she could when the supernova occurred." The Goddess turned away; a look of sad joy crossed her face. "She altered the very rules of reality on our planet to lock us away in an asteroid so we could survive. Such is the power of an Immortal. However-" The Goddesses eyes became hard, suddenly fixing Rosey with their golden power, "-this power is limited to the planet. She is powerless against this Evil One because she does not have the kind of power to defeat it. If the two were to fight, their powers would balance each other out. They would be like two magnets with the same ends, constantly pushing against each other, but unable to meet. Neither can destroy nor really affect the other. For this reason alone, Adina can do nothing, but it also means that neither can the Evil One do much to Adina. Even if her manifested form were destroyed or killed, she would simply be remade, reborn in another body."

Rosey looked up, Alex's words came flooding back to her when they were on their way here. How Adina would simply be reborn if she were to die. It was unbelievable on one end but after all she'd seen Rosey knew it was anything but impossible.

"Creating a body is easy," the Goddess said, "but creating a soul is not and, in fact, it's impossible for a being to create a soul. Bodies are a collection of chemicals and cells, while a soul is eternal and sacred, especially an Immortal's soul. That's why they are called Immortals, they can't really be killed, only their bodies can. The same is true for the Evil One, its manifested form could be remade if it were destroyed, another reason why it doesn't waste time manifesting. To truly get rid of it, you have to attack its soul or...at least that is what we believe."

"Of course we already knew all this when the battles began," The Goddess said, leaning back in her chair. Her voice suddenly took on one of great pain, her words were filled with an angry frustration that a leader had when they faced the death of their people. "We fought so long and hard to survive, but we were hunted down by this thing…this…Evil One. It wanted us dead for some reason and we knew that we were powerless to stop it. It could send as many Blood Gorons down as it wanted. Granted it had to level out the number it sent because the portals can only transport so much at a time, but still, while our numbers take time to grow, the Blood Gorons take only months. We were outnumbered and outmaneuvered. We needed hope, we needed help, and we needed someone that would lead us, defend us and offer a way to get rid of the Evil One. We did not have that answer at the time. There was no way to reach the Evil One, no way to get onto its ship. The only way was if Adina were to transfer us there. None of us stood a chance against a demon in its true form and at its true power so that was out of the picture. We were at a loss. We were defeated before the war even began."

Rosey bowed her head, her mind reeling with the words the Goddess spoke. They were so simple and true. Nothing she said had been sugar coated. It was all there, laid out for Rosey to see, hear, and understand. It was up to her to listen and to learn, but, thankfully, that tale wasn't over yet.

"When we were sure that we were lost," The Goddess said, raising her head high, "that's when Adina called us, the leaders, back to the Stone Circle and told us something that changed everything."

Chapter Eight: The Keepers

"Adina told us that the famous Valley Elathos had come to our world. Though much of our memory was lost there were some things that remained and the legend of Valley Elathos was one of them. Not much is known about it. That could, of course, be because of our faulty memories but many believe it is just the way the Valley works. It's bathed in mystery and sustained on many different types of energy. Some think it even has its own separate Energy Flows, though much speculation surrounding the place is usually just false superstition. What we do know about it is very limited. It moves from world to world, placing itself were needed, when needed, at exactly the right moment. It always appears when a planet is in dire need, supplying it with whatever is necessary in order to survive. It alone has saved the lives of countless planets." The Goddess paused and cast her gaze downward, her voice lowered to a soft hiss of irritation, "Why it did not appear to us before the supernova, we do not know." She raised her head, her face as calm as ever, "It is not our place to question it, but its arrival meant that we might finally get some help in defeating this Evil One."

Rosey felt her head spin, now a whole Valley was getting involved. Just how different was this planet? She shouldn't be surprised though, it is another world after all.

"Adina told us that Valley Elathos had arrived in her home valley where she lives, the Settled Valley, about three days before notifying us. She told us that it had merged itself with the topography of the Settled Valley, resembling it in every way, shape, and form. Basically, it *was* the Settled Valley. More importantly, its arrival meant that our prayers had been answered and we began to hope for our world's future. With the Valley there was a chance we could win. Adina told us that she had yet to

The Mystics

learn of what the Valley intended to do but we were all eager to hear about it, after all, it was a place of legend. We were fascinated by it, like a scientist discovering something new. Many wanted to travel there but Adina warned us to be respectful of the Valley, so, reluctantly, we left it alone. Besides I doubt that the Valley would give us anything tangible to work with, knowing how secretive it is. Thus Adina was our only insight to what the Valley was like."

The Goddess went on to explain about the Great Oak that lives in the Valley and its purpose for communication as well as a gateway for the Valley to manifest its power.

"Apparently, all of the Valley's actions are performed through the tree for that is the only way that it can manifest its power in The World Within A World or any world, for that matter," she said, taking a sip from her tea. "Whether the tree is always an Oak or changes depending on the particular planet, I don't know. We're lucky to have learned what we did about the tree. Most don't get as far as we have."

Rosey thought for a moment then said, "So...the Valley only communicates with a planet's immortal?" The Goddess rubbed her temple unsure, "Possibly, but once again that is debatable. I guess it depends on the situation and the planet."

Rosey scowled; frustrated that she wasn't getting a better explanation, however she couldn't be completely annoyed with them. They were a huge civilization that had had to start anew after losing their planet and then almost all of their memories. She could only imagine how hard it would be for the people of Earth to rebuild from the scraps of their world with little to no understanding of what was around them. For all that the people of this world had been through, at least they had been able to comprehend their society and piece it back together again. She could imagine that Earth wouldn't have been so successful if put in the same situation.

"This Valley," Rosey said, "has it ever been to Earth?"

The Goddess shook her head, "As far as we know, no, but Earth is not our responsibility so it could have been there at some point. When it comes and goes it leaves no trace of itself behind so there's really no way to tell. There are even rumors that it can change its shape and that of the tree to look like every possible biome that exists in the universe, even ones that aren't valleys. The only thing we're certain of is that when it appears it usually means that the planet has done all it can against an enemy and needs help. There was no doubt that we definitely needed help." She was silent for a while.

Rosey bent her head, then said, "What happened next?"

The golden woman looked up sharply and launched back into her tale. "What happened next was one of the longest waiting games I think I've ever had to endure. Adina returned to the Valley and stayed there for a full year. She told us before leaving that she and the Valley had work to do and not to go looking for her until they were finished. She anticipated that it would be some time before they reached a conclusion so she helped us devise more battle tactics and war strategies before she left. The most important thing she did was instruct us to pull together the outlying villages and towns into large cities. In this way our citizens could benefit from the protection of their larger numbers and our remaining warriors would have something far easier to protect. We also had them start building high surrounding walls around the cities for protection. We were at the point where we were no longer worried about fighting but simply surviving and keeping as many alive as possible. We were worried about what we would do if things went wrong but Adina assured us that she would return, hopefully sooner than later. With hope in our hearts we settled to waiting for a miracle and in the meantime followed Adina's command to better prepare our citizens and protect them from harm.

"During Adina's absence the Evil One continued to attack, however, we were getting smarter. Our people started attacking long distance, because they were huddled together in towns they could rely on each other for safety. In numbers we were much better protected. The young were well looked after and some cities devised overhead protection with spells from magikins and barriers grown by elementals. It was great work," she said, noticeably impressed. "Even our farms and production of food was safe, earth elementals can usually grow food in a matter of seconds and well maintained greenhouses, something we learned from Earth, helped to destroy some of the need for huge plots of farmland, plus the food could be grown throughout the winter. When we did need large areas of farmland, the walls were simply extended around them. Overall we did very well," the Goddess said proudly, "But surviving is no way to live. We were living in fear, fear of what would happen next. Blood Gorons did occasionally find their way inside the city walls or found other ways to attack and destroy. While they kept us busy, the Evil One took the opportunity to learn and research. It was trying as much as we were to look for a solution to its problem. Remember, time does not matter. A demon like the Evil One will torment a planet for hundreds of years if it has too. It may even prefer to do so. Its purpose is to spread terror and sorrow. It doesn't want to just destroy life; it wants to do so slowly and with as much pain as possible. So it, too, was taking its time. The Blood Gorons attacked less and we started hunting them down. After years of fighting them, we started to get better. We were slowly making a comeback and that didn't make the Evil One happy.

"For a short time there was a lull in Blood Goron activity. We originally believed that Blood Gorons took months to make or maybe even less than that, but we soon realized that we were mistaken. Once we started becoming successful killers of these monstrous beasts, their numbers began declining quickly, faster than the Evil One could replace them. We soon realized that it did take the Evil One a fair amount of time to construct a Blood Goron. If it was farm mere seconds or a few months, we would have been outmatched in our fight, but it didn't. We're not one hundred percent certain how long it takes but we are pretty sure it takes about four months to make three Gorons at once. It was obvious that if the Evil One wanted to continue harassing us it would need to find something else to use, and so, being the smart ass that it is, the Evil One began searching for something that could take the place of the Blood Gorons. It needed something that could reproduce on its own without the Evil One's help or energy. Somehow it got a hold of the NCD."

The Goddess paused and gave her a curious look, "You are aware of the NCD, are you not?"

Rosey nodded and the poor wolf Lyesal suddenly snapped back into her head once again, "I saw the scratches on Neran's walls when we were leaving so I asked and my friends told me about the Raptors. And then, there was the ah…attack." Rosey couldn't manage to say anything more about it, it had been the first time she'd been attacked here in this world. The first time she'd ever been attacked at all and she hadn't even seen the beast that was attacking, only its killer who then died herself. Rosey shook her head to clear the image, feeling sick.

The Goddess nodded knowingly, "I assumed that, given this morning's…unfortunate encounter, you would have been informed." She sighed sadly but then looked noticeably relieved, "the only good that came out of that, if we can even say there was any good, is that it saves me some more explaining. You are, of course, aware then that the Raptors are the Evil One's doing, correct?"

"Yes, the Evil One altered the NCD so that humans would give birth to Raptors instead of Falosaraptors. Fortunately, the alteration it made stopped them from giving birth to a human infant as well as the Raptor," Rosey said, trying to remember all that Alex and Rochell had told her and desperately trying not to remember the dead wolf. "I'm sorry, but those names are really…weird and um…familiar. They're ah…why did you chose them?" Rosey was trying hard not to laugh at the dinosaur names that had been applied to these two. When she had first heard it she'd assumed they'd taken the names from Earth but she wanted to be sure.

The Mystics

The Goddess, despite Rosey's best efforts, sensed her humor and cracked a small smile at the corner of her lips, "As you may have guessed, the Falosaraptors and Raptors are names that we did adopt from Earth. We had seen images from Earth of the dinosaurs and thought they matched the descriptions so we adopted them. We just changed some of the spelling. I'm sure you'll come across more terms the longer you're here. We adopted other things as well, not only technology."

Rosey couldn't help but smile, it had been a little surprising to find such familiar names in such a strange place but she could understand perfectly. Why wouldn't they adapt names from Earth? Being a whole new world with a whole new beginning they'd be desperate for guidance. "I thought you didn't mix the two worlds?"

The Goddess smiled slyly. "Well...we don't bring specific technology from world to world but there's nothing against adapting and improving upon certain ideas and techniques. Anyway," the Goddess said, "the fix that Cascade created ensures that every species, including humans, with the NCD can give birth to one of their own as well as the Leron or Falosaraptor. On its own, without the human fetus, the Falosaraptor or Raptor can grow inside a human much faster. Whether the Evil One altered it knowingly or if it was simply fate is unknown, however, I would think that if the Evil One took it out willingly then it did so for time purposes instead of concern for the human children. If the alteration had not been made than I shudder to think of what would have become of those infants, nothing good I can assure you." She clenched the arms of her chair as if shaken by fits of rage, her face, however, remained calm. She smiled up at Rosey saying, "We learned all this from examining the bodies of the Raptors when they first arrived. Cascade also helped to verify our findings. She didn't even have to touch a Raptor to know what the Evil One had done. She assured us that no human children were being born. Thankfully, we don't have to worry about that. However, the NCD provided the perfect opportunity for the Evil One to create a new self-sustaining army, one that did not require the Evil One's energy to create, unfortunately to produce Raptors the Evil One needed humans."

Rosey squirmed in her seat, knowing what was coming next.

"It was able to create a few more Blood Gorons, not an army, just enough to send them on kidnapping missions. The Gorons that had managed to survive our hunting parties joined them. Some continued to harass us, but they did so more to distract us from the abductions than to actually do damage. All across the world people were disappearing, snatched away by Blood Gorons using guerilla tactics. They were very fast. Most of the people they sought out were travelers, far from the safety of friends or home, and all of them were powerless," the Goddess said, emphasizing the last word. "Not a single person who has been taken has had any magical or elemental powers. They were all normal humans. We speculate this serves two purposes: to keep their abductees from posing a threat to the Evil One and its creations as well as keeping the Raptors from inheriting any powers beyond strength and capability."

Rosey nodded, that made sense. You didn't make your army more powerful than yourself. From what Rosey had heard the Raptors were horrible and nasty beasts that attacked with tooth and claw not magic or elements, and what she'd seen done to Lyesal didn't look particularly magical or elemental. The same went for the Gorons but they had intelligence on their side which made them deadly. This Evil One was smart. Rosey looked to the Goddess as she kept on with the story.

"The remaining warriors from the war were helpless to defend the people and even more helpless to get them back. After a few months the kidnappings got worse, sometimes a whole village would be desecrated."

Rosey could hear the anger in the woman's voice. Her hands clenched the arms of her chair so hard Rosey thought they would shatter into a million splinters. Despite her obvious anger, her face was calm and controlled. Rosey was in awe of her restraint, however unstable it might appear.

The Mystics

"We think that during those first few months the Evil One was experimenting with the NCD until it found something that worked. We didn't fully know what was being done with captured humans until the Raptors first appeared and we captured one for study. By the time we realized it had human DNA it was too late. The Evil One had an ample amount of humans to produce its army of Raptors. Raptors mature in two months and have a gestation period of only three months instead of nine. Falosaraptors take nine months because the human baby must develop as well, but without a human fetus the Raptor can develop quickly. Though the time is still quite long, this new army required no help from the Evil One and any number can be born at one time, depending on the number of people captured."

The Goddess paused for a moment. She rubbed her arms as if she was cold, and then quickly took a sip of her tea. "So now," she said launching back into the tale, "the Evil One had a new army, however it wasn't all that bad. The Raptors may be big, mean, and powerful but they are as dumb as a Watserba."

Rosey cocked her head in confusion and gave the Goddess a blank stare.

The Goddess smiled, "It's a really big, dumb creature…the Raptors are just as mentally challenged. Evidently the Evil One sacrificed intelligence to gain as much brute strength and power as possible. They are mindless beasts that exist to follow their master's orders, the perfect creature to use in a war and much easier to control. Blood Gorons may have to obey their master but they still have a massive amount of intelligence that can make them sly and unpredictable. The Raptors eliminated that problem because they obey without question and love to kill. They're nothing but animalistic beasts of evil. Even though they are more ideal, that's not to say that the Evil One stopped making Blood Gorons, it just didn't use them like it originally had. Their job of terrorizing and killing was now taken by the Raptors, and the Evil One didn't waste any time using them. As soon as it could the Evil One sent the Raptors down in hoards to kill and conquer. The remaining Blood Gorons were commanded to capture people for breeding purposes. Raptors were too brutal and unintelligent to capture humans alive, it would be like asking a lion on Earth to not kill a gazelle because it is needed for study. The Evil One did not want to waste any precious cargo so it made sure that the Blood Gorons did all the kidnapping," she said spitting out the words with venom.

Rosey understood perfectly, the wounds inflicted to Lyesal were beyond any torture she could image, and the acid had been beyond tolerable. The image would haunt Rosey for a long time to come.

"Thanks to this new self-sustaining army, we were more threatened than we ever had been before. The number of attacks were higher and the amount of enemies was greater, too great for many of our warriors who were still too small in number after all our years of fighting. We switched from offense to defense. People began constructing more powerful and taller fortifying walls around the newly combined cities and towns. Smaller villages combined with others to share strength, warriors, and food and many relocated so that they would be in the vicinity of nearby towns and cities. No one wanted to be stranded or isolated, not anymore. With the Blood Gorons, it was maintainable but with the Raptors it was impossible. We were forced into a corner."

She cast her gaze downward. Deep shadows buried her features as sadness covered her eyes. Rosey thought that she could almost see the memories passing through them like a recording.

"We hated building all those walls..." the Goddess said mournfully, her eyes unfocused. "We are a free people that go and do whatever we want. Building walls was like proclaiming just how scared we were. It was humiliating as well as horrifying. We were, essentially, preparing for a different war, a continuation of the one that had never stopped. We were at a stalemate and were scared for our lives and our future. The kidnappings only made things worse, though banding together made it harder for kidnappings to occur, they still happened. They were a constant reminder of our vulnerability and that our only hope laid with Adina and Valley Elathos…"

"Wait a second," Rosey said swiftly before the Goddess could continue.

"Yes?" she said, startled out of her long monologue.

Rosey squirmed in her seat but said, "Why would the Evil One continue to kidnap people? Wouldn't it, after a while, have enough of them to birth Raptors? It can't have every citizen on its ship."

The Goddess sat in solemn silence, her eyes cast downward in thought, "That is one thing that bothers many of us today, Rosey. It is true that the kidnappings have lessened but even now, they continue. We are not sure why but we can only assume that something happens to the other breeders that, perhaps, requires replacing. We don't know what happens but the kidnappings still take place which means there's a reason for it. Childbirth is known for being a very unpredictable killer, and most of the kidnapped are women but some have also been men." The Goddess sighed in agitation, "There are just so many things we do not know, it is tiresome and annoying, but most of all, it is horrifying. This has to stop…"

She said nothing else for a few moments, Rosey wanted to say something but she didn't know what. The Goddess's eyes glistened with sadness but her face, as always, was a stone block of calm. The reason struck Rosey in the chest and startled her. *It's because it is old knowledge now*, she thought. It's still sad but it is still old knowledge. Just like telling someone after years that your loved one is dead, it may bring tears to your eyes but the shock of it is gone…worn away. *Just like when I learned about my mother and father being dead years ago.*

Rosey turned her head away from the Goddess. What could she say? What could she do? She felt almost helpless, caught up in the story that she knew she had to hear. "What happened next?" she said gently.

The golden woman gave no indication that she had been silent for so long. She launched back into the conversation as if she had never even stopped. "When the Raptors came the remaining warriors, including the leaders and I, joined the fight to keep them at bay. They caused us a load of problems. They attacked our walls and our defenses with a tremendous show of strength. Species all across the world banded together to help fight them as best as possible. The larger animals like the wolves in my guard were very effective against them but smaller animals, including the humans, found them very difficult to stand up to. We, the leaders, found ourselves sending massive groups of large animals and Leron all over the world just to support the smaller villages."

The Goddess shook her head, troubled by her own words. It was almost as if she was still there, reliving all the orders she had given to her people, all the commands, and all the heartaches that she had seen. Rosey gulped, but said nothing.

"Just as the Raptors were starting to become an extensive threat Adina once again called the Leaders of the World to the Stone Circle and told us what had conspired while in Valley Elathos. I can't begin to describe to you how relieved we were to have some news. It had been a whole year and Adina's absence weighed heavily on many who looked to her for strength and hope. Now she was back and she came with a plan.

"The tree had given her something she called the Emerald Jewel. In actuality it's not even emerald, it's really a crystal. It is called the Emerald Jewel because it is such a dark color of green. It was a gift from the tree, the means by which we would end the Evil One. The Great Oak told Adina that the Emerald Jewel had lain dormant inside the planet for many years." The Goddess stopped and thought for a moment, then nodded as she came to a conclusion. "Now, you remember what I told you about the Energy Flows right?" she said reaching for her tea.

Rosey nodded, happy to be back on topic.

"Are you also aware that the Flows gather in energy or spiritual hot spots all around the world?"   "Yeah, Alex told me along the way that they gather at major areas of influential or spiritual energy, something like that." Her uncle had also said something along the same lines when they had been preparing to leave, something about the Energy Flows of Earth gathering at Yellowstone and supplying it with a lot of energy. "Indeed, every planet has such energy hot spots. They can be as simple as major areas in history or as complex as plate boundaries. Each planet is different so they each experience their own unique energy spots. It was in such an energy spot near the Balon Mountains that the Emerald Jewel was created. It came about in much the same way as normal crystals do: pressure, years spent underneath the earth; nothing unusual. The difference here was that after a while the Energy Flows that gathered over top of this particular crystal began to be absorbed into it. The Emerald Jewel, being a crystal, is even better because crystal is able to contain vast amounts of information."

Rosey had heard this concept before, she remembered seeing it in a movie once and then had gone home to look it up and see if it was possible. She had been pleasantly surprised to learn that it was. Her uncle, however, had not. He had spent the next week trying to convince her not to try anything rash in order to copy the effects. Thankfully she had listened.

"The Energy Flows," the Goddess said, drawing Rosey from her memory, "gather in the form of whirlpools that sling new energy to different areas of the planet, like the circulatory system delivers blood all over the body. The Energy Flows 'scraped' against the Jewel embedding information into it which the crystal was able to easily record. Over time that information gained the jewel an amazing amount of stored power and energy. The main information stored in the jewel was concerning the twelve elements that exist in our world and are the main forces driving the Energy Flows. The elements themselves are within our planet and are a part of its life and biology. The Energy Flows were able to transfer what knowledge they had of those elements onto the jewel.

"Remember, the Energy Flows govern all life and, above all, they monitor the levels of the elemental and magical powers. Being an object of nature and not magic the information concerning the elements combined with the jewel more readily which is why there is absolutely no magical information stored on the jewel. Magic is its own separate entity here. It does not exist naturally within our world, here, it just exists. On some planets magic does occur naturally, our planet, however, is purely and naturally elemental. You might be wondering, then, how we can use magic, well, just because it is not a natural part of this world does not mean that we cannot access it. It is still here, it's just not a natural part of our life. Like the technology on earth, it's made by human hands but it still exists.

"The Energy Flows govern all the rules of a planet, even the parts that are not naturally occurring like magic…but more on magic later, let's get back to where we left off," she said waving her hand, "We were not surprised when we heard that this jewel held within it a vast amount of knowledge and power concerning the elements. Most of the energy coming from the jewel came from the planet itself.

"For a long time this jewel went unnoticed, undetectable under the whirlpool of energy. Many such powerful objects probably exist all over our world containing powers we couldn't begin to understand. However, we are not treasure hunters and we leave such powerful creations alone, even when we are aware of their location. When Valley Elathos arrived it detected the tremendous elemental power of the jewel and was able to find it. Upon studying it, the Valley decided it was the perfect means by which to save our world. We would never have dared to try and use the crystal on our own, but the Valley is a being of mystery. If anyone could figure out how to use it the Valley would.

"Adina told us that after some tinkering on the Great Oaks part, that lasted a whole year, the Jewel was ready. The tree explained to Adina everything that she would need to know to save our world. The day she

The Mystics

called us together she passed onto us what it had told her. The jewel would go through a complicated ceremony in Valley Elathos.

"The first part of the ceremony requires the Emerald Jewel to be split into thirteen different pieces or shards without releasing the stored energy kept inside. This is only possible through magic, specifically unicorn magic. Unicorns are known for their abilities to transform different metals and stones into others without a fire or a difference in extreme temperatures and pressures. They can also shape and mold them into any form they desire. It has something to do with the fact that their horns are made up of every metal and stone formation that has ever existed, even ones that do not belong to their own planet. Adina is, in essence, half unicorn, half Pegasus, and so has this ability. The energy that the Emerald Jewel has within it is essential to allowing the elements to connect to the thirteen shards. It was in twelve of these shards that the twelve elements would be placed."

The Goddess paused, "Before I go any farther do you know of the Elemental levels of power; Apparition, God or Goddess, and King or Queen?" Rosey nodded quickly, "Alex and Rochell told me…although…I am a little curious as to why the God and Goddess levels are called the same thing for both magikins and elementals?"

"We don't know either, when our planet went supernova that was some of the information we lost. It may indeed be that at one point they had different names, but everything that we were able to dredge up points towards this, so we follow it," she sighed heavily and leaned her head against the back of her chair in elegant defeat. "If only we could remember more of our past, but Adina didn't have time or energy to waste on saving books, besides the few building and houses she saved, she had to protect her citizens. She grabbed the only piece of our world that she could salvage and whatever buildings that were on it were what we got. It doesn't matter now, we're content with the way things are."

Rosey nodded. She'd long ago finished her cider, so she settled for another glass of water. She took a long sip, enjoying the cool moisture running down her throat. She listened closely as the Goddess went on to explain how after Adina had split the Emerald Jewel she placed its segmented parts within the Great Oak's compartment and allowed them to be infused with their particular elements. "The elements are: Fire, Water, Lightning, Earth, Light, Darkness, Air, Atmosphere, Ice, Gravity, Gold; a fancy name for sand, and Silver; a fancy name for clay," the Goddess said counting out each element on her fingers. "These elements are each embedded into one of the twelve shards, just like what happened with the Emerald Jewel and the Energy Flows, the elements are sort of 'scratched' onto the shard. The energy that the jewel has is used like glue, or a bonding agent to keep the elements intact in the shard. This whole process, or what Adina calls the Bonding Process, takes place inside the Great Oak's compartment. The information on how to obtain the elements is embedded on the Emerald Jewel. After all, the Energy Flows are associated with the elements. Such direct contact with the Flows unraveled a few secrets. The tree read those secrets and managed to discover how to obtain the elements and 'scratch' them into the crystal shards. Once the elements are firmly infused into the shards, they are given to six unicorns and six pegasi to look after them and protect them. These honorable twelve are called the Mothers of the Elements. The reasoning for the name is not completely known for the unicorn and pegasi kind rarely ever leave the outskirts of the Settled Valley and don't spread their secrets often. Adina is their Queen and they are her loyal servants and friends. Thus, many of their customs are unknown to us so the term Mother could have a different meaning for them. However, I suspect it is because once these twelve hold the shards they are forever changed and will protect the shards like a mother protects a child. But I could be wrong. In any case these twelve Mothers are sent away to wait for the Keeper to seek them out. The thirteenth, remaining shard is called the Shanobie Crystal and is sent to the Keeper directly."

Rosey looked down at her chest where the crystal hung, innocent and unmoving. Her heart thudded in her chest. The Goddess saw her and nodded, "Yes that is the Shanobie Crystal and you are the Keeper. I'll go a little more in depth about the Keeper in just a moment, for now listen closely because this is the most important thing I am going to tell you yet. The Keeper's job is to embark on a journey to collect these twelve elements from the Mothers and use them against the Evil One. She must collect them in the order I stated before. The reason is unknown but those are the rules. The Keeper must find and absorb the elements into the Shanobie Crystal thus enabling her to control all twelve elements. When we heard about this, it surprised us the most because, as you know, there is only one element per creature. There is never two or three and certainly not twelve, it is impossible to have all of them in one body at one time. Adina assured us that it was impossible to be stored in one body but not in the crystal. Through the crystal the Keeper can access whatever element she needs as soon as she has collected it of course. If the Keeper needs water, the crystal will give her water, if she needs fire, it'll give her fire. In this way the elements will not interfere with one another, after all, some elements are natural enemies like Fire and Water. The crystal allows them to have their own areas within it, sort of like having dorm rooms." She paused to take a sip of her tea before continuing. Rosey couldn't help but imagine tiny minute versions of the elements jostling around inside dorm rooms. She stifled a giggle as the Goddess continued. "I mentioned before how everyone has an element, right? Well, you may be wondering if the Keeper has to collect her own element. Yes. The Keeper must collect her own element. For example, your friend Rochell is an air elemental. If she were the Keeper she would still need to collect the element of Air despite the fact that she already has it naturally. The reason for this was very simple. The elements that the Keeper collects are not the elements that you would find in regular elementals like Rochell."

"They're not?" Rosey asked, tilting her head.

"Not in the least. The Keeper's elements are pure, raw, and potent, directly from the planet itself and that is why the keeper must collect her own element. The element within a person is not the same as the potent element from the planet. The ones inside of people are tamed in a way. That is another reason why the elements must be contained within the Shanobie Crystal. The human body, or any physical body, for that matter, could not handle their potency. The Shanobie Crystal is imbued with these potent elements and can easily sustain them, allowing their human user to channel the power through the crystal while avoiding the fatal strength of the elements' power. The crystal was created by the Energy Flows in the first place, and embedded with their elemental power and knowledge. The exact and full power of the elements is on that crystal, all twelve of them. It can handle anything, your human body: not so much.   "The next thing Adina told us was that the Keeper had to be a human. The Great Oak told her that only a human could be the Keeper because no other creature would be able to connect to the elements directly through the Shanobie Crystal as well as a human would. At least…that is how Adina explained it. There is nothing that makes a human special. There is no particular reason why humans would be able to control the elements better than any other creature would. We are certainly not as strong as dragons, nor as proud as griffons, but for whatever reason, a human is the only one that can be the Keeper. Also the Keeper must have no other power but elemental power. They cannot have any magical talent whatsoever, which is why your uncle could have never been the Keeper since he chose to be a magikin…"

"My uncle was in the running to be a Keeper?" Rosey said startled, she had a hard time imagining her happy-go-lucky geeky uncle as a Keeper.

"More on that later, it'll make sense soon, I promise," The Goddess said, smiling. Rosey huffed in silence but nodded, the tale wasn't over yet. Rosey had to remain patient and wait, but that 'later' word was really starting to get to her.

"The tree told Adina that the crystal wouldn't work for anyone but the Keeper because the crystal will only work for the person it chooses to obey. This person..." the Goddess paused for a moment, deep in thought. She stared at Rosey for so long that Rosey began to fidget nervously.

Is there something on my face or what? Rosey thought, irritably as the Goddess continued to stare. Finally getting up the courage Rosey said, "Um, is something wrong?"   The Goddess came out of her trance and blinked embarrassedly. "Sorry Rosey, a thought crossed my mind, nothing's wrong." "What were you going to say before…about the Keeper?" Rosey leaned forward expectantly, watching the Goddess's every move.

Her brows furrowed and she rubbed her temples undecidedly, "Hum, oh nothing, it doesn't matter. Now where was I?"

Rosey had the suspicious feeling that the Goddess had chosen to keep something secret from her, but she didn't feel comfortable trying to push the woman, especially since they had only just met. She would have told Rosey if it was really important, at least, she hoped she would have.

The Goddess thought for a few moments. One finger lightly tapped the arm of her chair as she tried to remember what she had been saying before, making Rosey slightly agitated. What could have distracted her so much? It was obvious to Rosey that though the Goddess had so much to tell her she was hiding things. This couldn't be a good sign. Although Rosey had been transported to a whole new world living inside another world, maybe she should just be grateful that the Goddess was telling her anything at all. From what Rosey had already heard, this world was extremely different from Earth, not only scientifically, but biologically as well. The Goddess might only be giving Rosey the bare minimum that was needed to get the job done.

Rosey didn't have any more time to ponder the thought for the Goddess had regained her composure, "Aw yes, no one could be the Keeper besides the crystal's chosen. Not even Adina could be the Keeper. As the planet's Immortal she could use the power of the crystal but not the elements from the crystal. Remember I told you that Adina is connected to the planet, and has all its powers. She can influence the planet and that includes it elemental capacity. However the crystal is out of her reach. She can use its power but not the elements within. Actually, the fact that the crystal could not be used by any other was a good thing for it meant that the Raptors could not take it from the Keeper and neither could anyone else, though no citizen of The World Within A World would ever think of stealing the Shanobie Crystal.

"The tree also told Adina that the crystal cannot be touched by evil hands, nor can it be used for evil intentions, which means the Evil One would find it useless. Adina also thought ahead so that in the rare case that the crystal was ever separated from the Keeper, whether it be by a battle, storm, or something else, it would immediately return to the Keeper's neck. The only way for it to do that is for it to be locked onto the Keeper's DNA and identity. Do you remember how the crystal came to you?" Rosey nodded, she did remember. How could she forget? The crystal's coming had been the first thing to happen to her before she had been thrust into this adventure. It was the strangest sensation Rosey had ever felt. Still, the sight of the crystal coming from her own body was at the top of her list of creepy and weird happenings. "It came from my body," she said, voicing her thoughts, "It didn't hurt and there wasn't any blood but there was a tingling feeling like when your foot falls asleep."

The Goddess smiled knowingly, "Well, appearing to you through your body provides the perfect way for the crystal to obtain your DNA thus bonding with you personally."

Despite the strangeness of a crystal melting through your body, Rosey couldn't help but be relieved. It had been a strange way for the crystal to come to her but she could just see herself losing it. At least, in this way, that was impossible. For some odd reason she suddenly imagined her messy, unkempt room on Earth and cringed slightly. Organization wasn't her strongest suit. She would have hated to make it to the end and then fail

The Mystics

because she lost the crystal. Rosey didn't have a habit of losing things but she would bet that the one time it was truly important she would start to lose everything that her hands came into contact with.

"Adina assured us that the Keeper's powers were special," the Goddess's words snatched Rosey's attention. "They were specifically made to target the Evil One and take it down. It's kind of like how bug spray is specifically meant to target bugs, not anything else. We were not exactly sure how this would work. This was elemental power that would be used against a creature of neither life nor death, a creature existing in Purgatory. But…we didn't care." She smiled slightly, "We were so happy just to have something to grab onto, something to look forward to.

"When Adina came to us at the Stone Circle, after all our time of uncertainty, there was finally a ray of hope. We quickly inquired after who this Keeper was going to be. Adina told us that she had spent most of her time looking for the perfect human. The Tree may have told her about the Keeper and the crystal but not who the Keeper was. The Tree told her to take the Shanobie Crystal to the person that she thought would be the Keeper and if the crystal reacted than he or she was the chosen one. Adina presented the crystal to a very special someone by the name of Maharen," the Goddess paused, and studied Rosey. She seemed to be contemplating something. Leaning forward she said, "Now, Rosey, this is the part where the first Keeper comes into play. What I say next will be very important to the part you play in all this, so listen carefully."

Rosey nodded, holding back the balloon of excitement that blossomed in her chest. She had been listening attentively, hanging onto any stray piece of information but now she perked up as a maelstrom of excitement and apprehension coursed through her. She straightened her back and leaned forward as if lessening the distance between them would help to catch whatever was going to be said. This was the moment she had been waiting for and she was not going to miss a single syllable.

"Before I go on I must introduce Maharen and her family to you. I know I mentioned once before that influential families are also counted as Leaders of the World. Well, Maharen's family was counted as one of the most powerful. They were what you would call activists. They were a very influential elemental family. They did many good things for many great and powerful people, including Adina. They were mostly known for creating war ships used to battle against the Evil One's Gorons and Raptors. Without those ships we would have been at a huge loss. Unfortunately, almost all of the family was killed in battle. The only survivors were a woman in her late thirties called Maharen and her two young children.

"Maharen was a very powerful, hard set woman. Sadly," she said, her voice becoming strained, "no matter how powerful someone is, nothing can compare to the realization that you and your children are the last of your family. It was a devastating blow, but, despite her heartache and because her children depended on her, she continued to push on and helped us rebuild what we could and protect as many as possible. She eventually became a commander in the field armies around Hayral, her home continent. She joined us in fighting off the Raptors that the Evil One rained down on us. She was the best of the best and the bravest warrior I have ever known..." The Goddess trailed off, her eyes glinting with unseen memories.

"You knew her?" Rosey asked, more as a way to draw the Goddess back then to get a confirmation.

It worked, the Goddess looked up, "Yes, I was much younger then, but yes, I did know her. Long ago..." the Goddess shook her head and continued, "The world was scared and she really stepped up to lead the new developments. The various rebuilding projects in the towns and cities only took a few months, quicker than it would on your planet, because, here, we have an unlimited amount of elementals with all of them willing to lend a hand. Most of our buildings are made of wood which any Earth elemental can make grow in a matter of seconds. A flick of the wrist is all it takes for a tree to grow then be cut into pieces and placed in the correct order for a house. Don't get me wrong, we do have to make some things by hand, like the piping and such, but making aqueducts, wells, and building materials is easy for any water and earth elemental. Besides, as I said before, most of the dwellings that were attacked were small collections of villages and animal habitats, the bulk of the rebuilding was done in cities to help the inflow of refugees escaping their small establishments. The large cities and towns had no limit to the amount of elementals and magikins living there, so casting a simple shield long enough for the elementals to set in place a wall to protect them was no problem. The smaller villages and habitats, however, had little if any elementals and magikins, mostly because they had come to the cities to learn from Masters, so they had even less protection, another reason for why they moved. The rebuilding and construction of residences is an easy and effortless task in this world. It takes up far less time than it does on your world, plus we have the added advantage of no currency."

"Wait...what? No currency, as in...no money?" Rosey asked, thoroughly shocked. At this the Goddess smiled slyly and Rosey couldn't help but smile back. *A world with no money!* she thought. It was almost too good to be true. She suddenly realized that, earlier, when they had passed through the city, the people weren't selling things but just setting them out. She never did remember any exchange of money, coin, or barter except for in words. The thought left Rosey speechless and...a little envious.

"Indeed my dear." said the Goddess unaware of Rosey's inner struggle. "As I have said, this world is built upon peace. The people of this world are united and love each other. That may be a laughable aspect for people of Earth, but for us, it is reality. There never used to be walls around our cities. They are the direct result of Raptor attacks not impending..." the Goddess paused for a moment tilting her head slightly to the left as she searched her vocabulary for the correct word, "...invasions, I think is what you call them. Also we have studied Earth closely and have seen that money is often the root of many of Earth's evils. We are determined, now, more than ever, to never accept any other forms of currency beyond a simple barter."

Rosey was still a little skeptical. "What about land rights, struggle for power, jealousy, envy, or greed?" After all, money wasn't all a person could be greedy for. "We do have levels of those emotions but not to the extreme experienced on Earth. Usually the people who have problems with one another work out the differences or find another peaceful way to deal with it and there is never a lack of mediators willing to help. Whatever it is, it usually never ends in violence. This society is what you might call a utopian society. No one murders or steals, we live our lives for each other. A farmer farms because if she doesn't then part of the city goes hungry. The textile industry makes clothes because if it doesn't then people will be cold."

"You never had guards, warriors, or weapons before all this?"

The Golden woman shook her head, "No. The guards and wolf patrols are new, in response to the Raptors. We didn't have warriors until the Evil One came forcing us to become proficient in the art of killing. Maharen was one of the first to become a warrior. If it hadn't been for the Evil One we would have never known war or even needed warriors."

"Well then, why do people do what they do, if not…for the sake of money? There must be some other reason why besides the knowledge that something bad might happen if they don't. What motivates them? Do you understand…what I mean?" Rosey said, shrugging.

"Yes, I believe I do, you want to know why someone would provide certain services like blacksmithing, or farming for a whole community. If not for money, then what do they do it for? Let me give you this scenario. People on Earth work and provide services for money to earn a living, right? Well, on The World Within A World, we don't have to pay for anything. Do you think that if you had the opportunity to not have to get a job but just stay in one place and do nothing, do you really think that you would be happy? I know that on Earth there are certain technological amenities that may keep you entertained but would you be happy doing nothing?"

Rosey thought about it for a moment, would she really want to just sit in her house all day and watch T.V. or play on the internet? For a while it would be fun but, it would get really boring. Imagine how it would be on The World Within A World where they didn't have those technologies. Suddenly the answer was clear as day to her.

The Goddess seemed to understand that she had discovered the answer for she smiled and said, "We provide services here because it gives us a purpose, something to do, to look forward to, and to take pride in. It's a psychological stimulation that gives us a reason to live. Those that don't have anything to offer usually live for their families or relatives, possibly helping out or volunteering. Either way, we find our place. Imagine if Earth operated in the same way. The idea of peace is not as unrealistic as you might think. In fact, it's more realistic than you could ever imagine."

The Goddess smiled and her whole frame seemed to be uplifted by her words. She then paused. A slight frown crossed her golden lips. She shook her head as if to clear away a stray thought then said, "I've strayed from my story. Let us return to how the Keeper came about. As I've told you, while we were rebuilding, constructing, and Maharen was making a name for herself the Evil One got a hold of the NCD and began sending down Raptors, making it a lot harder on us to replenish our strained supplies. Adina called us back to the Stone Circle and informed us about the Emerald Jewel and the Keeper. She told us that she had considered all the options and had found out who the Keeper was.

"Adina had considered what she had learned and decided that the keeper had to be someone with a strong mental and physical connection to their element, which is why none other than Maharen seemed the perfect choice. Her family valued and excelled at that special mental as well as physical connection. Adina knew that a regular person wouldn't work because of the particular nature of the elements themselves being raw and potent so she needed to find someone who could 'take the heat', so to speak. And who better to choose than the survivor of a very elementally influential family. Because of all this, Maharen seemed to be the right choice.

"She told us that when she had presented the crystal to Maharen, it burst into multicolored flames and encircled her, thus choosing her as its first Keeper. We all agreed that Maharen had experienced the sign of the Keeper which the Great Oak had foretold. Adina conducted the Ceremony for the first time and Maharen received the Crystal through her own flesh just as you did."

The Goddess paused and took a sip of her tea. Rosey took a sip of her water and was surprised to notice that although it had been a while her water tasted just as cool as it had been when she had poured it, as if it was enchanted to never get warm, which it probably was. Rosey drank from it deeply enjoying its soothing coolness on her throat. The Goddess sighed, placed her cup on a tray, and then straightened in her seat. She then slipped back into the story.

"After a few days of preparation Maharen set out on her journey. It was after she left that something very strange happened, the family mansion disappeared and has never been found since she left. No one knows what happened to it. We have tried and failed many times to find it to no avail," said the Goddess, sadly as if a precious artifact or piece of artwork had been lost. "Why have you been searching for it?" Rosey asked curiously. "If not for the simple fact that it was the home of the first Keeper and thus a historic building, then for its secrets rumored to hold heaven's bounty itself. I believe the bounty is just a rumor," She said, shaking off the words with a laugh. "My people are more interested in the castle for its heritage than its value. Others, however, see more in its sacred walls. Thus it is a highly sought after mystery."

She squinted, and leaned back in her chair, "I have a hunch that Adina is protecting the mansion and hiding it from the Evil One. Possibly because of the information it may hold, but I'm not sure. It could just be that the family placed a spell on it to make it disappear when there was no one occupying it, or something. When it happened, I asked Maharen about the disappearance. She said that she knew of no reason why it would be protected, or of any spells on it, or why it would disappear right after her departure, but with her family she said anything was possible and with no other surviving family members to ask besides her and her children, it remained a mystery."

She laughed and then leaned forward, "It's a good thing her children had moved in with me while their mother was away or they might have disappeared along with the mansion. Thankfully, I had volunteered to watch them for her while she was away to keep them safe and occupied. We were especially afraid that the Evil One would try to hurt them and use them for blackmail against Maharen."

Rosey nodded, after all she'd heard she wouldn't put it past this evil maniac to do just that and use the children to get to Maharen.

"Plus, it was easier to get in contact with Maharen from my location than it was from the Mansion," the Goddess said. "The Mansion used to dwell in the Coron Mountains. Of course it's not there now, but when it was there the mountains would often interfere with communications. My Castle is one of the safest, most secure, places in The World Within A World so her children could safely stay in contact. I wonder that if her children had not moved out of the mansion if it would still be there?" the Goddess pondered. She ran a lithe hand through her hair and then shook her head. "Unfortunately, all information about the family was kept in the Mansion, so, without it, there are no records of family lines or anything. However, there are some journals and reports written by people who worked with some of the family during the war. None of the journals were written by the family, and if there were any, they were sent to the mansion.

You may read what we have if you like and don't worry about the whole mansion business, if we find anything, you'll be the first to know."
"Why me? I mean I know I'm the Keeper and all but still."

The Goddess smiled knowingly, as if she had been waiting for Rosey to catch on to something she knew about. Rosey scowled. Again with their games!

"Because Rosey," the Goddess said, "Maharen, the first Keeper, was your grandmother, thus the place is your birthright as well as the information contained in those journals. You and your uncle are the last of Maharen's family line," she said with a smile. "The first Keeper was my grandmother! I knew that my mother was the Keeper before me but I didn't know that extended to my grandmother. So…Maharen's children, the ones you watched, they were my mother and uncle?!" Rosey almost shouted in awe. That amazing and powerful influential family that the Goddess had mentioned was hers! Her family! That was the family she had been bred from. The idea startled Rosey. Her very mother, the woman she wanted to know so much about, had walked in this very castle and possibly had even sat in the very chair she sat in. Rosey gulped and had the sudden urge to jump up out of her seat as if it might burn her. She breathed deeply, but her mind wouldn't stop reeling. It was one thing to talk about her mother; it was another to know she had been there, in that very room, not too long ago and her uncle too for that matter.

"But…wait," she said shaking her head, "If Maharen's family is my family, you said that they were elementally powerful. How then did my uncle become a magikin?"

The Goddess smiled slyly, "Nothing gets past you does it, young Keeper. Indeed Maharen's family was very elemental. In fact, your uncle is the only one to be born into the family with an ability to work magic. You see, Maharen was the only one of her family who ever married a Magikin. Until that union most of your family had remained matched up with elementals.

In fact, I think that every single one of the elements was seen in your family line, except for the rarest elements of Gold and Silver."

Rosey's mouth dropped open, all of the elements except for two?! That alone described to Rosey just how elemental her family had been.

"So," the Goddess said, pulling her out of her shock, "would you like to read some of those journals, I can have them delivered to your room if you like?"

The Goddess's words seemed to flow through Rosey slowly. Rosey looked up and focused on the Goddess. She thought for a moment then said, "No thanks. I don't think I'm ready to read them…yet. Maybe once I've fallen into the role of Keeper, I'll be more prepared." The Goddess nodded in understanding, "Of course, they are free for you to use whenever you wish, simply ask." Her kind smile warmed Rosey and put her mind at ease.

"Thanks."

"Let's get back to the story, shall we? The leaders and I were a little at a loss as to why Maharen had to collect the elements instead of receiving them. Why did there have to be twelve Mothers and their shards? Adina reminded us of the special relationship that can be forged with the elements. Adina said that because of the raw potency of the elements a person had to prove themselves worthy. You see these elements are not dead. They are…alive. These elements are sort of like spirits, alive yet without physical needs like food or water. They can completely overpower someone if the person is not ready for them. The journey must be taken to better prepare the Keeper to face the elements. The Keeper must triumph over every challenge, for collecting the elements would not be easy. Maharen would have to fight large ferocious beasts; monsters only found in legends, and take responsibility into her own hands. Maharen didn't have any problem with responsibility but some said that she needed a lesson in humility and there was a challenge for that as well.

"The need to conquer individual and difficult challenges is also the reason that Adina does not join the Keeper on her journey. She is an overwhelming force and the Keeper needs to focus on nothing but her mission. However, Adina does watch over the Keeper through scrying. Scrying is when a spell is spoken and the magically enchanted waters, mirrors, or other reflective surfaces show you images of the person you ask for. It only shows you an image of the person you are scrying, not their location, so there's no chance that the Evil One can scry you and find out where you are, that is, if the Evil One even has magic," she said quickly, at the look on Rosey's face. "Most scrying devices follow the same rules, so even if the Evil One had a different way of scrying, it shouldn't be able to find you. All it would get is an image of you. Scrying pools can also be used for communication. You just have to open up the ability to talk through them. It's sort of like a TV, except in water."

"You know what a TV is?!" Rosey gasped before she could stop herself.

The Goddess laughed. "I've been to Earth before. Those TV's are quite fascinating."

Rosey smiled, imagining a whole group of World Within A World citizens taking a tour through Earth with things on display like a computer, a TV, an iPod, and a cell phone. She giggled a little under her breath and then hushed herself as the Goddess began to speak. "Maharen tackled every challenge given to her by the Mothers with great courage and perseverance until she had collected every element. During her journey, which lasted a good two years, her children, Esperanza and John Mystic, grew up to be ten and eleven, John being the oldest. We all waited here at the castle while she faced the perils ahead. There was no set time for when the journey needed to be completed. She did many things besides just collecting the elements, for there were the Raptors to contend with. She would sometimes help a local village with a Raptor problem, or solve some travesty somewhere or other." The Goddess stopped. She looked down, her brows furrowed in thought. Her voice took on a frustrated, happy, surprised tone like a mother taken aback by her children's actions. "She could never leave a person in need behind. She never turned her back on anyone. That was why she took so long to collect the elements, but none of us would have had it any other way. She had become a hero of the people even before she was known as the Keeper.

"She continued to be just as good throughout her journey. Finally, the day came, she completed her journey and was ready to face the Evil One. After Maharen returned to say her farewells Adina opened a portal to the Hell Ship and we watched as she proudly strode ahead. We all wanted to go with her, but the Great Oak was clear, no one was to accompany her to fight the Evil One. We waited. Our scrying pools don't go beyond the planet so we depended completely on Adina for any news. Her scrying pools are more sophisticated than ours, some say she can even use them to find someone's location, but don't worry those pools are limited to her and her alone. Anxiously we waited for word and, after what seemed like days, Adina called us to the Stone Circle. Sadly, Maharen wasn't there. Without words, I knew that she had lost to the Evil One. Strangely, the only thing I could think about wasn't Maharen but how I wished I could keep her children from learning the truth. They had become so dear to me. I would have given anything to spare them."

The Goddess paused for a moment, her eyes glassed over and Rosey saw a look of pain spark in the Goddess's eyes. Lines of worry and suffering that hadn't been there before marred her beautiful face. In a matter of seconds, the Goddess suddenly looked much older. With painful clarity and realization, the Goddess continued. Rosey was surprised to hear not a flaw in her voice or a waver in c golden syllables. She was obviously skilled in the art of vocal deception. Rosey studied the Goddess's face. Probably, the only reason she could see the Goddess's pain was because she wasn't afraid to show it in front of her, after all she was as much a part of this suffering as she was.

"We were all shocked when Adina told us that Maharen had been defeated. For some reason she did not win the battle against the Evil One. We were devastated. It proved that the elements alone were simply tools. They had no power if the one that wielded them…was lacking. For two years Maharen won her battles and challenges and we had no doubt that victory was upon us. We had such hope she'd make it but she was defeated. There are no words to describe John and Esperanza's grief.

"Adina said that your grandmother, Maharen, faced the Evil One with the courage and power she was known for, but something went wrong and the Evil One managed to kill her. When Maharen died the Shanobie Crystal automatically transported itself back to Adina in Valley Elathos. Adina was devastated, for the crystal's return to her confirmed what she had seen in her scrying pools. She had witnessed the devastating blow that had killed Maharen. I can only imagine what it must have been like to witness that. Adina told us that she would spend as much time as she could figuring out what had gone wrong but she would need time. Time neither we nor the planet had."

Rosey could see the scene playing out in her head. Everyone gathered and talking, crying, and left utterly helpless after their only hope had been crushed. The Goddess continued and Rosey listened.

"At first the Evil One had no idea about the power of the Keeper or the threat she posed, but it did now and Adina was worried it would double its efforts to gain strength so that it could begin sending its Raptors down to the surface to hunt down the next Keeper to be, your mother Esperanza, or finish off The World Within A World while we were still vulnerable. At that time we were unsure of who would be the next Keeper, but Maharen's child seemed a likely choice. John, your uncle, we knew could not be the Keeper as he was a magikin but it was still quite possible that his beloved sister could be.

"Our world had never needed a vast army before the War, and now we hardly had any army left to defend the people. If it hadn't been for

Maharen's elemental help to fight off the Raptor attacks I don't know if we would have made it, even with Adina's help. Maharen's fighting prowess as the Keeper was magnificent," she said, her voice taking on a rich tone as she spoke of the fallen woman, "The power of just one raw element is so great that the Keeper can take the place of a whole army even without all of the elements. We had already exhausted what little defenses we had left when Maharen was alive, we couldn't afford to give the Evil One time to grow more in power and continue sending down its Raptors. Fighting Maharen may have weakened the Evil One pretty well but not enough to slow down the Raptor production, or the

amount it was sending down to our surface. When we lost Maharen there was only one thing we could do. We had to find a way to gain some time."

The Goddess shook her head, as if she was making the decision right then and there about what was to be done instead of simply telling a story. She straightened, her eyes trained on Rosey in her seat, "Adina knew that this time the Raptors would only have one target: Esperanza. As I said before, we were unaware if she was the next Keeper, but, being Maharen's child, she would be the most likely choice, and the Evil One knew that too. There was no doubt that she would be the prime target. Even though John could never be the Keeper we also feared for him. The Evil One could use him against his sister if she did turn out to be the Keeper. We also feared that the Evil One would be so determined to see the children dead, just to spite us and Maharen, that it would send Blood Gorons instead. Raptors are an annoyance, but Blood Gorons are a true threat," she said taking a sip of her tea before continuing.

"Adina decided that the best way to protect our world and give the next Keeper more time to prepare was to place a temporary seal on the Evil One's portals. As I have said Adina and the Keeper are the only ones that can use the crystal. Adina can use it, but only the power it has. The crystal is not a battery; it didn't lose any of its juice from the battle with the

Evil One, so it was still fully powered and ready to go. Adina knew she could use that power to create a seal. This seal would be unbreakable for a good ten years. Adina would have never been able to make such a seal on her own. Her power is exactly the same amount she would need to make a seal like that. If she were to attempt to make one without help she would essentially kill herself by draining all of her power. The crystal provided the extra power she needed to create the seal without hurting herself and gave us the time we needed. That precious time, was everything.

"Despite the fact that the crystal was still fully powered, the Evil One was not, it was weakened by the ferocious fight your grandmother gave it. It was weak enough not to be able to detect or interfere with the seal that Adina would make, at least, that was what she hoped. We really had no complete guarantee," the Goddess shrugged," but we were willing to try anything. We had a window of opportunity so we took it.

"Placing the seal was the best thing that had happened to us since the Evil One arrived and the Keeper was chosen. For the first time in a long time, we were at peace. The seal blocked any and all portals to and from the Hell Ship, even new ones. Thus the Evil One couldn't just make a new one to try and avoid the seal because the seal would act on all portals, new or old. It would be wasting time and energy, since any new portals would also be sealed.

"Once a seal is enacted it is unbreakable. No amount of power can undo a seal that strong, the Evil One would have to use something equal to that of the seal's strength to cancel it. Because of the Evil One's location it was now, essentially, trapped in its own home, unable to access anything, including its army. What Raptors and Blood Gorons that were left behind were now left without a leader and without a plan. The Blood Gorons had smarts on their side, so they hid themselves, awaiting their master's return. The Raptors, however, were not so smart and became wild, ravenous, beasts that were simple prey to hunt down and kill.

"Oh...Rosey..." the Goddess said, her voice filling with happiness, "for ten long years we were happy. We kicked into overdrive, determined to be ready and prepared. We hunted down as many Raptors as we could, rebuilt as many new homes, establishments, and walls as possible, reinstated and relocated many elementals and magikins across the world so every place had a powerful leader to protect it, and started making underground storage facilities for food, supplies, and weaponry. We even relocated whole cities and towns to more protected areas, areas that the enemy would find almost impossible to infiltrate. In ten years we accomplished so much, and so did your mother. Those ten years gave Esperanza time to grow, learn, and prepare. Remember she was only ten at the time and nowhere near ready to be the Keeper. It also allowed Adina time to review what happened with Maharen and, hopefully, discover what went wrong.

"Now Rosey," she said leaning back and clasping her hands on her desk, "I have just bombarded you with a huge amount of information. It you need me to elaborate, ask now because this is the moment I know you have been waiting for. This is the part where your mother comes in and I don't want to get into that until I'm sure you understand everything. Maybe you should take a few moments to-"

Just then Nashi came in with another woman following close on her heels. She was dressed exactly like Nashi and had long black hair and bright green eyes. She looked younger than Nashi but just as enthusiastic and cheerful. Both Rosey and the Goddess turned to see the young maids walk briskly to the desk and present the Goddess with a bow. The Goddess returned the bow with a small incline of her head. They then turned and bowed to Rosey. Rosey imitated the Goddess and bowed her head. She wasn't used to servants and the bowing felt odd, like she was in some fairytale.

"My lady and My Keeper, dinner is almost ready," Nashi said, smiling happily.

"Good, thank you Nashi, you couldn't have planned your timing any better. We will freshen up and be there shortly."

Nashi bowed slightly again, then signaled to the other woman to wheel away the cart that she had left behind earlier with all the refreshments on it. Rosey noted that they were still steaming hot or ice cold depending on what they were. Despite that miracle, Rosey was utterly horrified to see the Goddess getting up from her chair.

"Wait, what about my mother!?"

"After dinner, child. It is late and you must be hungry and in need of some time to think things over. This is the perfect opportunity for you to consider all I have said and to comprehend in case you have further questions and...quite frankly my voice needs a break," she said rubbing her neck slightly. She smiled at Rosey when she saw her face, "Come, you will not leave this castle before you learn of your mother, I promise. Be patient and we will talk later. Nashi will show you to your room so you can freshen up," she said indicating Nashi who stood patiently a few feet away.

Rosey sighed and fell back in her chair. *Later?* she thought. Suddenly her fists clenched and her anger began to boil up from the depths of her toes to the top of her head. *STUPID WORD!* she shouted in her head over and over again. It's always getting in the way, later this, later that. *Why! Why did she have to be stuck with everything being later!? Why not now? I have been waiting all this time and now I have to wait because of later. I'm gonna blah blah blah blah blah blah blah blah blah blah......*

"What an amazing child," said the Goddess to herself as she left the room, a broad smile on her face. "So very...patient."

Chapter Nine: Esperanza

Rosey was escorted to her room by Nashi. The young maid took her to the lower level and then passed under one of the arches that led to what Rosey had considered before to be a ball room. Rosey gasped when she saw what it really was. A giant family room stretched out before her where shelves of books upon books sat against the walls in perfect harmony. Several couches of fine golden cotton with blue and silver stitchery were laid about the room in seemingly sporadic arrangements. She weaved her way amongst them imagining what it would be like to sit there and dream the day away reading an exciting book. Some of the furniture was very odd looking and Rosey realized that they were made for animals just as much as they were made for humans.

On either side of her the bookshelves ended and large full-length, sliding glass doors let in the light of the day from two courtyards. Small blue pads set into the ground before the doors made Rosey start for a moment. Looking closer Rosey saw that they had an animal's paw design on it. Rosey gasped, it was a device for opening the door for animals. Thinking back she remembered the doors in the first two hallways near the foyer having similar blue pads as well. She smiled. Noly and Hazel are going to have a ball with this.

She cast her glance into the courtyards and stared at them in awe, from what she could see they were filled with lavish gardens, all of which were in full bloom, unaffected by the winter. Looking closer Rosey saw that there was a thin sheet of orange material over the small courtyards held up by a latticework of steel bars. *It must be like a greenhouse*, she thought happily. In each courtyard there was a fountain with mermaids surrounding a proud looking unipeg at its top. I wonder if that is supposed to be Adina. Surrounding the fountains were trails made of fresh layers of brown mulch with smooth gray stepping stones inlaid with blue designs. Small silver and golden benches surrounded the fountains, facing them.

As she walked her feet made soft rhythmic tapping noises on the polished marble floors and above her a great chandelier hung like a beacon on the raised ceiling that was painted a calming light blue. Rosey looked back and saw the arch she had come through. Most of the furniture was hidden behind the wall in between the arches, that's why she had been unsure before. Looking back at Nashi who strode before her she saw that they were heading for another arch that, like the furniture, was hidden from view in the foyer. *I wonder if this is where my friends are?* she thought, glancing down the hallway. As she neared the hallway she caught a closer look at the silver statues in the corners that she had seen before. They were each as tall as the ceiling and acted as columns. They were, as Rosey had thought, images of horses but not just any horses. Standing proud and tall was the image of a rearing unipeg at each corner. *Another image of Adina, probably,* Rosey thought, *I wonder if that's how she really looks?*

Nashi suddenly turned and indicated the room, "This is the family room or the sitting area. Guests and the Goddess herself use this room to rest, relax, and talk. You and your friends are welcome in it at any time. I'm sure you've already noticed," she said, walking over to one of the sliding doors and indicating the blue pads, "but these are for animal access. All manner of animals that don't have hands to open doors do so with these pads. A great magikin developed them long ago and it has made life much easier with our animal friends." She smiled and Rosey smiled back. Then she turned and continued on, "Right this way, your room is very close."

As they passed into the hallway under the large arch Rosey gasped as the marble was replaced by a rich crimson carpet inlaid with black flora designs. Golden walls stood proud and tall on either side with sporadic furnishings placed along their lengths. High vaulted ceilings were painted white while crystal chandeliers hung down in regular intervals casting bright light along the walls. Pictures hung from the walls: images of animals,

The Mystics

people, Leron, and great majestic landscapes. On either side of the hallway there were doors. They seemed to be the same mahogany doors with the silver frames and doorknobs that she had seen before. A blue pad reflected the light in front of each one.

"These are where most guests stay. We don't get a lot of them these days so you and your friends are the first to occupy these rooms in a while," Nashi said sadly, she hung her head but did not look back at Rosey. "Here is your room." Nashi stopped before a regular mahogany door that looked no different than the others. She had no look of sadness about her pretty face when she turned to face Rosey. "Your friend's rooms are on either side of yours. They, I believe, are roaming the castle grounds at the moment." She squinted trying to remember. "They're taking a tour."

Rosey nodded and was happy to know her friends were close by. Sighing she stepped inside and was immediately blown away by the beauty of her room. It was furnished in the finest linens and draperies with exotic colors and designs. An ornate raised ceiling painted to resemble the blue sky and surrounded by golden leaves made Rosey feel as if she was looking towards the real sky. The bed was huge, with fine blue linens and a comforter embroidered with golden images. A golden couch occupied a corner with a small mahogany table at its side. Shelves of books lined the walls, their crisp bindings reminding Rosey of old manuscripts and documents. A small desk and dresser set against one wall. Full-length sliding glass doors led out onto a balcony. The balcony overlooked the courtyards she had seen before. They must dip down and continue along the side of the building where the rooms are. *I wonder what is under these rooms then?* Rosey hardly paid it any attention as she cast her glance back inside the room. Last, but not least, was the bathroom. To Rosey's delight the bathroom was as modern as they were on Earth with a separate shower and tub. She ran into it and almost squealed with happiness, she could finally get clean after hours of riding.

Nashi came in behind her," Do you like your room?"

Rosey turned on her with alarming speed, her eyes glistening with happiness, "Oh yes indeed, I love it."

Nashi must have seen the joy in her eyes for she smiled, "Wonderful, the Goddess will be very pleased."

"Do I have time to take a shower, I'm a little dirty," Rosey said embarrassed. It had been bad enough sitting and talking with the Goddess while smelling all horsey but sitting down at a table to eat would be really pushing Rosey's moral boundaries.

Nashi smiled, knowingly, "Of course, you have plenty of time to get cleaned up. I will return in a half hour to show you to the dining room. New clothes are in the dresser. Leave your old ones in the bathroom and we will wash them for you."

With that she bowed, which Rosey returned with a head bow, then left the room, closing the door behind her. As Rosey turned to the bathroom she heard a rustling under her bed. She stopped and stared at it worriedly, then smiled evilly. Tiptoeing around the bed she bent down silently, reaching her hand underneath the white bed skirt she grabbed a furry tail. Noly and Hazel zipped out from under the bed, laughing as they went.

"Did we scare you?" they said in unison.

Rosey smiled, "Yes you did…but you know…" She said smiling wickedly, "I was going to take a shower, maybe I should, oh, I don't know, bathe you too?"

Rosey had to keep herself from laughing as Noly and Hazel's faces fell to ones of utter horror. Their ears went flat against their heads and their eyes grew wide in terror. Rosey was still amazed by the level of emotion she was able to see on their faces now that the two had gained intelligence. It was like looking at two other people, and, in a way, she was. Since they entered this world, they were considered people and had their own ambitions and attitudes, but Rosey knew them pretty well and, despite their newly found intelligence, they were still her precious pets.

Quickly they both started talking at the same time, "No, Rosey, please! They wiped my paws really well before coming in here, I swear!" Noly said, lifting each paw to show it to Rosey.

"I licked myself clean as I always do. You know I am a perfect, most dignified cat that always takes care of her pelt!" Hazel said, turning in a circle where she stood and showing off her glossy pelt.

Rosey burst out laughing. "It's okay, you guys, I'm not going to give you a bath," Rosey said, walking towards the bathroom. Hazel and Noly relaxed and gave each other reassuring looks. "Yet," Rosey finished. As she entered the bathroom she heard them groan. Rosey just smiled.

Rosey showered quickly, enjoying the fragrance of the shampoo. It was a rich lavender and lilac smell that made her feel all fluffy inside. She found towels and washcloths in the small cabinet in the bathroom and a long blue robe all of which were silky smooth and cotton soft. Rosey dried herself then combed her long hair. Looking in the small dresser she found blue cotton pants and a short sleeved shirt embroidered with silver lace. She changed into the fine clothes and then folded her other clothes neatly placing them in the bathroom as Nashi had instructed. All the while Noly and Hazel watched, completely unfazed by Rosey's naked body. At first, Rosey had been a little nervous about it but realized that they had seen her naked before when they weren't intelligent so why would they care now? Besides, they were both female.

They also informed her that they now knew the whole Angensilian language and told her in great length of how a magikin had come and transferred the knowledge to them earlier that day. Rosey listened intently, simply enjoying the sound of her pet's voices, something she would have never, in a million years, imagined she'd hear. Surprisingly, when they were done, she was just happy to know that she wouldn't have to be translating for the two. Rosey briefly wondered why a magikin hadn't just transferred the knowledge of this world to her mind as they had the language instead of this long conversation with the Goddess, but she believed she wouldn't have liked learning everything in one solid moment like that. In this way things were more personal and she had the ability to ask questions.

Once dressed, Rosey patted her two friends happily and grabbing a grooming kit she had found, oh so conveniently in the bathroom, she quickly brushed both Noly and Hazel then cleaned their feet more thoroughly along with their teeth hoping to make them as presentable as possible, having no doubt that they would also attend the dinner. Once that was done and her two fluff balls were as presentable as they were going to get she exited the room with them close on her heels. As promised Nashi stood there waiting, her smile as bright and welcoming as ever.

"This way to the dining hall miss, you'll be dining here every day for each meal," Nashi said leading Rosey, Noly, and Hazel down the hall in the opposite direction of the sitting area. For once Hazel walked on her own, refusing when Rosey offered her her shoulder. Rosey just smiled and walked on, aware of how Hazel made sure to never fall behind Noly.

Nashi lead them down the hallway for about 100 yards before coming to another hallway that intersected their own. Rosey stopped at the crossroad and looked down the two new hallways. There were rooms on either side as there where down the hallway behind her but dead ahead the doors stopped and were replaced with a shorter hallway about only ten yards long. Through it was another smaller sitting room but this one did not have the courtyards on either side. This sitting room resembled the first with its marble floors and silver statue columns of the unipeg in each corner. Beyond this sitting room where two arches just as before except that this time there was no foyer beyond them but a number of hallways leading in different directions. Rosey could only guess where they all led. In total she counted eight different hallways, Nashi lead her to the middle of the small room and stopped. The room they were in was, like the hallways, decorated with the same red carpet with black flora designs and golden walls. The ceiling had one small chandelier and was circular and painted a common white. The carpet continued down all the hallways.

Indicating the numerous hallways she said, "The first hallway leads to the training grounds, the third leads to the dining hall, the fourth leads to the kitchens, the fifth leads to the garden, and the seventh leads to the infirmary. The others I have not mentioned are, unfortunately, off limits to everyone but a select few of the staff and the Goddess herself. They are spelled to prevent anyone from entering who does not have permission." She said this last with a little contempt in her voice, but not much. Rosey could understand. She did not like having secrets kept from her either.

Rosey nodded silently, admiring the continued detail of the beautiful craftsmanship. Noly sniffed around, taking in all the smells. Hazel tried her best not to join Noly but Rosey could see her nose twitching irresistibly at all the new smells. Nashi then turned and led them down the third hallway.

The dinner provided for Rosey and her friends was nothing short of royal. All sorts of foods ranging from seafood to what looked like Chinese food decorated the table with its scrumptious flavors and savory sauces. Rosey had no problem stuffing her face and stomach full to the brim with fish, rotisserie meats, and vegetables, many she had never heard of before. Everything was absolutely perfect.

The Goddess sat eloquently throughout the meal at the head of the table while servants went around filling glasses with a special juice known as Lendosa, made from the fruit of the Lendosa Tree. It tasted like apple cider and apple pie with a twist of cinnamon. Nashi, surprisingly, had eaten at the Goddess's right hand side. Rosey was still unsure of how things worked in this world but obviously the lack of currency meant that servants, like Nashi, offered their services and loyalty willingly with no payment. They were doing it because they wanted to, and so were considered equals and given respect and kindness. It was an honor to serve the Goddess and many were probably proud to do so. People here weren't measured by their status but by their actions and services. *I'm missing Earth less and less,* Rosey thought.

The part she had loved most about the wondrous feast was meeting back up with her friends. Alex and Rochell sat, as always, on either side of Rosey asking her about all she had learned so far and helping to clarify anything she may have misunderstood or had questions about that she had not thought to ask at the time. The Goddess helped when necessary but for the most part she let Rosey's friends do all the talking, watching contently. They seemed very relieved to hear that she had yet to learn about her mother Esperanza, which worried Rosey, however, she didn't let it show, she just kept smiling.

Hazel and Noly sat across from them. They were the only animals at the table and Rosey was relieved to see that they had pretty good table manners. She was quite shocked, it may have been the only elegant thing she had ever seen the two trouble makers do, or, at least, attempt to do. They didn't use silverware, of course; instead, two human attendants had stood at their side and gathered whatever food they were asked to collect. Their waters were also brought in bowls, not glasses, like the human's drinks were. Looking at the two, Rosey knew she better enjoy the miracle now or she would never see it again. *Those two would never be so modest and quiet if they weren't in a gigantic castle with her golden majesty over there sitting at the head of the table with her sharp wand,* Rosey thought, trying hard not to laugh. She shouldn't have been too surprised, with their added intelligence it only made sense that they would know when to behave.

The dinner went on for two hours, filled with talk, laughter and jokes. Rosey, for the first time since coming here, felt comfortable and at home, caught up in the familiar babbling of friends. Even the towering ceilings of the dining room and the ornately decorated, golden walls and murals hadn't unsettled her with subtle messages of intimidation. Even the Golden Goddess was less scary, but, nevertheless, impressive. Rosey was also quite amazed by the level of familiarity everyone had with the Goddess. They were all respectful, of course, but their manner and way of speaking was really no different than the way Rosey would have conversed with her friends. Despite the Goddess's power and influence she never looked down on Rochell or Alex and never demanded their obedience. Rosey found it very liberating and calming.

When the dinner ended, Rosey and her friends separated once again. Noly and Hazel went with Rochell and Alex, though they wanted to stay with her. Rosey appreciated their loyalty but she needed to hear her mother's story alone. Once she saw them off, Rosey was then led back to the Goddess's office where she promptly hurried to take her seat in the comfortable chair she had sat in before. Rosey was filled with anticipation, now that the dinner was over she was eager to learn about her mother. Nashi brought in water to drink and some small mints to help settle the stomach after such a large meal.

"Did you enjoy yourself Rosey?" the Goddess asked, smiling broadly as she took her seat at her long desk.

"Yes, thank you, it was marvelous. That was beautiful food. Tell your cooks I am very grateful. Thank you Nashi," she said as Nashi poured her a glass of water.

"I will definitely make sure they hear the good news, they wanted to impress you, you know," said the Goddess taking her glass from Nashi and giving her a small bow of the head in thanks. Nashi reciprocated with the customary bow at the waist. She bowed to Rosey who returned with a head bow and then the good natured servant left through the second double doors that she had come in from.

Rosey turned back to the Goddess expectantly and said, "I haven't forgotten where we left off."

"Ah yes, your mother, the most important part of this whole story. First, do you have anything you want me to elaborate on before we start again? I know your friends helped a little at dinner, but that was a lot to take in."

"No," Rosey said a little too quickly. She straightened and said calmly, "No, thank you. Alex and Rochell gave me a few helpful hints at dinner and such. I know what I need to know, for now at least."

The Goddess studied her but nodded, satisfied, "Let us continue then."

Rosey's heartbeat soared. Finally! She would learn about her mother. The dinner had been so pleasant and such a blessing but through it all Rosey was still remembering the Goddess's last words, "this is the part where your mother comes in." Those words had haunted her all throughout dinner. The truth was her excitement was only halfhearted because, no matter what the Goddess said, nothing would change the fact that her mother was dead. Whatever the Goddess's story was, it would ultimately end in her mother's death.

The Goddess looked at Rosey and for a moment she saw, not the black haired young woman sitting before her, but the beautiful tall woman, Esperanza, who many times had looked at her with the same, deep sapphire blue eyes that Rosey had. The Goddess blinked and Rosey leaned back in her chair. The Goddess finally began talking. She was unsteady, but calm. Always calm. "Esperanza was, in my opinion, one of the best warriors I ever met. As a young woman, she was very loving and caring, not as hard as Maharen, but just as strong, brave, and courageous. Thanks to the seal Adina enacted, she had the time to grow into her adult self and she had the opportunity to have fun. We had been so war torn for so long that it was a welcome relief to be spared more bloodshed and pain. She grew up to be a fine woman surrounded by love and hope. She and her brother stayed with me after their mother's death, this became their new home," she said sweeping her arm over the castle.

Rosey cast her glance around her. Her whole body seemed to shake. Her mother had grown up here, she may have even sat in the very chair Rosey sat in now. Rosey closed her eyes and could almost imagine her mother sitting there possibly being rewarded, maybe scolded. Rosey smiled slightly, the idea warmed her more than ever before.

The Goddess continued, "Esperanza and her brother were very powerful individuals. She was a Queen level Earth elemental and he was a powerful God level Magikin. Esperanza had an uncanny understanding of her element. She grew even stronger in this understanding when she turned seventeen, an age that is considered by most to be the moment when an elemental fully matures in their elemental capacity."

"Is that why you came for me now?" Rosey asked, intrigued, "Because I'm seventeen?"

The Goddess tilted her head in agreement, "It's part of the reason, but for the most part yes. It is a very good age to learn elemental powers and techniques, though we're not sure why. Esperanza excelled very well at that age. While she was growing in power and learning about her element Adina was busy trying to find out what went wrong with Maharen. For a while she was completely confused but then Esperanza's unusual connection to her element gave Adina the idea for what might have happened. Adina believed that for some reason the connection between Maharen and the elements was flawed or not complete, something was missing between them."

Rosey's brows furrowed, intrigued.

"She saw how easily Maharen commanded them and how powerful she was with them, but, therein lay the problem," the Goddess tilted back in her chair. "Maharen was commanding, not asking. All elements are alive, the raw elements especially so, they are not dead things that can be claimed, and, although Maharen was aware of that, the potency of the raw elements demanded more respect and care than a normal element would. Maharen was just a very headstrong person, very powerful, very brute and not as kind or as merciful. She was always fighting and trying to stop the Raptors. The things she had seen and did made her even harder than she was before. The raw elements needed a balance between hardness, kindness, and mercy. Maharen, out of all of us, lost the most, all her family and her husband, and then she had to contend with the Raptors and the stench of the Evil One. She was a hardened warrior and the elements didn't respond well to being commanded. That is how Adina explained it to us. Esperanza and her brother were in their teens by the time she made the connection. Esperanza was determined not to make the same mistake her mother did, whatever that mistake was. She vowed to be better and to listen more closely to the elements. She started training harder than I've ever seen her train before. She was monstrously wonderful and strong."

Rosey felt pride blossom in her chest for her mother, it made Rosey feel complete inside for some reason just to know how brave her mother had been. It was hard to explain, having such feelings for someone she had never even known, yet Rosey couldn't help it. It was like some unspoken rule.

The Goddess leaned in her chair, making it creak. The sound was almost defining in the silent room but it didn't deter the golden woman's storytelling finesse in the least. "While Adina was making her discoveries and Esperanza was training, John was sent to Earth, not only for security but because he was interested in Earth. He had always been a nerdy scientist who loved to study and research. To John, at that time Earth was the most interesting subject. John wanted to be here during his sister's journey, but in the meantime he wanted to make use of himself. In some ways I believe it may have been his way of dealing with his mother's death..." the Goddess looked away for a few moments, but, just as quickly, recovered. "We obliged John's wishes but we still wanted to be sure he was safe. John was Maharen's son, and although the crystal would never chose him since he was a magikin, he could still be used against Esperanza when she started her journey. Even though the Evil One was trapped, we weren't taking any chances, so protecting him was a high priority.

"We created an organization that was specifically placed on Earth, not only to look after John but to also continue studying Earth. We'd already been studying Earth for some time, and to help integrate ourselves into Earth's society we had enlisted the help of Earth's Immortal through

Adina. All the necessary documents and such had been created and placed in the right place without anyone suspecting anything. Earth's Immortal knew what it was doing and it did it well. There, on Earth, John became the government's computer analyzer and you know the rest.

"The previous research teams had learned much about Earth during their time there, but John helped to spur on the love of Earth research. One of the things they studied was Earth's Energy Flows for obvious reasons. We wanted to make sure our connection wasn't causing too much trouble. What we found was very interesting. If stepping onto the planet itself wasn't enough to tell us, we soon learned that Earth has the strictest rules ever. Most planets' Energy Flows do not take away or regulate alien powers and abilities. We expected, when we first came to Earth, to still be able to use our abilities with elements. Magic, not so much because Earth doesn't have any magic; but the elements were a part of us, so we naturally assumed they'd still work. You can imagine how surprised we were when we were reduced to normal humans with no abilities. The second thing we noticed was a difference in communication. We discovered that the ability for animals to talk or communicate and be highly intelligent was also not allowed by Earth's Energy Flows. Coming from a planet where almost all of our animals have high intelligence and can speak plainly to a place where they couldn't, left us well…at a loss for words, but we went on.

"I wouldn't say that it's completely abnormal for a planet to actually deny and regulate what outside beings, or aliens, have in terms of their abilities, but to take away even our ability to work elements told us a lot about Earth itself. Most likely it was highly technological, so much so that it would change the very nature of any alien species and we were right. Still, most planets don't regulate alien specie's powers and abilities, most don't care. Just because Earth took away our abilities doesn't mean that it would do the same for another alien species, there's really no knowing what Energy Flows are going to do until something happens. They're very unpredictable, but we studied Earth's closely, especially now that we knew we were working with a planet so very different from our own.

"Earth *was* so very different. I've never heard of or seen a planet quite like it." She laughed and Rosey titled her head confused. The Goddess waved her hand dismissively, "It was hilarious the first time we came there. You can imagine what it was like, Rosey. We have little technological advancements because most everything we do is associated closely with the natural world so Earth was very strange. It was like people from the 1800s stepping out into the new age, it was fascinating. But," she fixed Rosey with a hard gaze, sadness in her eyes, "it was also eye opening. Earth was very violent, so much so that we were flabbergasted, taken aback by what we saw and heard. We don't have terrorist here on this planet, or murderers and assassins. Those were all new words to us and their meanings were more horrid than any nightmare. After only a few days on Earth's destructive surface, it became quite clear why Earth was so limited in power. Imagine what Earth would be like if it had the power we have, the elemental power, the magical power. Huh..." she smiled half-heartedly, bending her head. Rosey could say nothing, for it was all true. "One good thing came out of it though; we were a little more prepared for what the Evil One was to bring to our front door. What evils it had in store for us…Earth was an example."

Rosey found her throat tight with shame, though she wasn't born on Earth, she had been raised there and she knew all too well how evil Earth could be. She quickly took a sip of water, suddenly finding a bitter taste in her mouth. The Goddess carried on.

"That being said, Earth gave us a lot to cherish as well. It gave us some advancements we did not have as well as prepared us for a future in war. Not all of it was that bad." Rosey smiled, and the Goddess winked at her, continuing. "Later on in our research we discovered that if we were to bring an animal from Earth to our world it would gain the intelligence and ability to speak that, on Earth, it lacked. That is exactly why your cat, dog and horses were only able to talk once they crossed into our world. An Energy Flow cannot add something that was never naturally there. You see if someone from Earth were to come to our world then they would still have no magical or elemental powers, because, naturally, the ability was never there. The Energy Flows can't activate something that isn't natural to that person's particular biology."

"What about the animals?" Rosey asked thinking of Noly, Hazel, and Sarabie. "They didn't have intelligence until they came here. Does that mean that all animals, even the ones on Earth, have a natural ability to be intelligent no matter their origins?"

"Intelligence is a trickier area of the Energy Flows," the Goddess said, tilting her head, "because, naturally, all living creatures are born with some level of intelligence. Even a microorganism has some type of 'brain' that controls its purpose and function. You see, the intelligence is already there, it's just heightened or depleted depending on the planet and its rules. So they're not adding anything, just affecting it."

"I never thought of it like that."

"Neither did we, your uncle and our research team discovered all of this while they were on Earth," her eyes were steady on Rosey, their golden hue as powerful as ever. "We were perfectly fine with John's obsession with Earth and very much supported it but we were slightly worried about what being on Earth would do to a person's connection to their own element as well as John's ability to work magic."

At this Rosey looked at the Goddess with concern etching her features. The Goddess continued slowly and carefully, obviously aware of Rosey's fears.

"In some studies our research team, upon returning home, would experience a lack of elemental and magical power. For a short time it seemed blocked, but then would slowly return. By this time however," she said quickly seeing Rosey's continued worried expression, "we were assured by Adina that the effects were not permanent so we had no problem with

John living on Earth, though we did make him return every few months just to be sure. It also means that even if your element, Rosey, has become complacent from living on Earth, once returned to The World Within A World it will soon come back and awaken. Plus, even if you wound up not having access to your own natural element for some reason it would not hinder your ability to be the Keeper seeing as how the elements you'll be dealing with are not the same as the elements that normal elementals have anyway. So don't worry."

Rosey still looked a little unsettled, but she said nothing.

"While on Earth, John became a government employee as a computer science major and operator. He is considered a genius at what he does. The whole thing fascinates him. It doesn't surprise me seeing as how many things from Earth would be considered amazing just as I'm sure it is for you seeing our world having come from Earth. John loves it there and all that he has learned.

"Unlike John, Esperanza continued her training on The World Within A World but would, every now and then, go visit him. John's story on Earth was that his parents had studied in Africa and he and his sister, Esperanza, had grown up there. Then, when he was old enough, he moved back to the United States to train in the government while she continued their parent's work. Esperanza was simply his sister visiting from Africa whenever she came to Earth..."

Rosey's heart skipped a beat, this was the exact story her uncle had told her when he was explaining to her about what happened to her mother when she had first asked. It seemed like a lifetime ago.

"...Esperanza's little visits to Earth were like vacations, a chance for her to get away and relax. It was refreshing for Esperanza and a bonding experience for her and her brother. One day on one of these particular visits she brought someone with her. She introduced him as Mathew Kingsley. They had known each other for a while and had decided to marry. It was wondrous news and they were all very excited, by this time

Esperanza was nineteen and the seal was getting close to breaking. Remember, Esperanza was ten years old when it was first enacted. At her twentieth birthday, the seal would break. At that time however, Esperanza was just happy to be with the man she loved."

Rosey felt her heart break when she heard her father's name. She fidgeted in her seat awkwardly realizing that she must visibly look shaken. The Goddess didn't seem to mind, she just continued talking as if she saw nothing.

"Mathew was a trainee water elemental getting ready to join my guards. He trained at my castle with all the other trainees where Esperanza also trained and lived. They met and fell in love. Esperanza hadn't been looking for a husband but love doesn't wait just because you wish it to and on this world we only believe in marrying for love, not for that rubbish that the people of Earth seem to think is reason enough. Love, here, is a sacred and blessed thing between two people, and is never taken lightly. Esperanza honored her feelings and married him anyway despite the danger that would face them. Maybe they married because of the dangers. They knew there was a possibility that Esperanza might not come out alive, just as her mother did. They may have wanted to spend as much time together as they could. I can't say I would have done differently in their situation."

Rosey bowed her head, happy that her parents had been so in love, but feeling a hollowness creep into her heart nonetheless.

"Not too long after they married Esperanza felt she was prepared to take on the challenge and become the Keeper. She had trained hard enough and believed that she was ready and incapable of making the same mistake her mother had. Adina believed her and thought that her various times on Earth with her brother may have saved her from living the heart-hardening life that had caused Maharen's connection with the elements to be strained. Marriage was also a key factor in keeping Esperanza happy and laid back. Adina noted that Esperanza also seemed to have a deeper connection with her element. Spending time with her brother on Earth had probably increased that connection because she could not use her element there and thus had to search a little deeper inside herself to find that connection upon her return. Hearing Adina's approval, Esperanza felt much better about her journey, hoping beyond hope that she was balanced enough to make the right connection with the raw elements. Adina believed she was ready and Esperanza took comfort knowing that.

"Hold on," Rosey said, a thought crossing her mind, "My mother chose when she was to begin her journey?"

"Ah…" the Goddess said, understanding perfectly, "I can see how that would be confusing to you, however that's not completely right. The Shanobie Crystal appears to the Keeper when she is ready. For Maharen, it was a bit different because it was her first time and the first time the crystal had been used. For Esperanza, the crystal knew when she was ready to begin: when she had trained till she had honed herself body and soul for what was to come. She felt ready and the crystal agreed with her."

"Is that also the same for me?" Rosey said, her tone slightly unbalanced. She fingered the crystal at her neck.

"The crystal came to you when it felt you were ready, we were going to bring you to this world at seventeen whether the crystal came to you or not."

The Goddess's confession took Rosey by surprise. It had never occurred to her that her uncle and friends had not known that the crystal would come to her. On Earth, they had probably been just as surprised as she had been when it happened. Rosey swallowed and gave a silent thanks to her friends. *That was why they were so jittery.* They never believed the crystal would come to her then! And they managed to keep their cool and act like it was nothing out of the ordinary. She felt a smile touch her lips. She would have to remember to thank them later.

"Your time on Earth was necessary; we'll get to that soon," the Goddess promised.

Rosey nodded, determined now more than ever to learn the truth.

"A little while later the crystal appeared to Esperanza and she began her journey. John quickly left Earth and returned to The World Within A World as planned. He had constructed a plan on explaining his absence. John sent notices to his work that he was going back to Africa to visit his sister and his brother-in-law for a year or so. He had documents and such ready for any necessary paperwork that would be needed. John's bodyguard that had been assigned to him when he went to Earth took over his work while he was gone. She had done much of the same studies and research with him and they had become quite…close…"

For some reason the way she said the word 'close' made Rosey think that more had been going on than just friendly research. Rosey didn't ponder this for too long because the mention of Africa suddenly awakened memories within her. That was the same place her uncle said that her parents had lived while studying the wildlife and the culture. He had told her that they had left on a trip and never returned leaving her in his care. Obviously that tale was wrong, and Rosey felt in her heart the lie that her uncle had told in order to keep her safe. It weighed down on her but she was not angry at him, he had only been doing his best to protect her.

"When we first placed the seal we knew the Evil One would waste no time planning its revenge. I'm positive that we angered it quite a bit when we placed that seal. We could only imagine what carnage the Evil One had planned. The broken seal would mean that new Raptors and Blood Gorons created over that long time frame could start coming through and the ones left behind would then begin reorganizing and regrouping. Obviously the number of the creatures the Evil One could create on its ship is limited, given its size, but we knew there'd be many. We knew all this, and we feared what it would mean for us and the Keeper in the future to come.

"I thought this over and found that I was more worried than ever before, mostly because the Evil One knew about and would probably be expecting a new Keeper. I feared that it would send mass amounts of Raptors, not at the people of The World Within A World, but at the

Keeper herself once the seal broke. I voiced my fears and Adina agreed that further action needed to be taken beyond the normal organized army. I told her that I had come up with a way to stop most, if not all, of the Raptor attacks and hopefully help the Keeper when her time came to go on her journey.

"I offered to create an organization known as the Resistance. It would be a group of warriors led by the Leaders of the World that had the specific job of hunting down the remaining Raptors and Gorons. They would be made up of many of the warriors that had been used before to cut down the masses of Raptors, almost every warrior you see guarding a town or holding a toned weapon would become a member of the Resistance. Adina and the other leaders agreed to this and the Resistance was formed. We took advantage of our ten year lull. We built up defenses, retrained our warriors, and studied new ways to kill, trap, and destroy the enemy. Remember, when we placed the seal the connection between the Evil One and its army was severed so its left over Gorons and Raptors were left to wander without a leader. We hunted them down and killed them, as many as we could. It was a brilliant campaign and we were very good at what we did."

Rosey detected a hint of satisfaction in the woman's voice, clearly she was very happy with her organization. Rosey could only imagine what it would be like to be in charge of what were essentially assassins, trained in the art of killing monstrosities. Since they were monsters it must be more acceptable to kill them considering all they had taken from them. Still the idea of the Goddess, this calm and powerful woman, on the battlefield chopping off heads unsettled Rosey, no matter how much the enemy deserved it. Perhaps she too would find herself doing that one day? Rosey shuddered.

"By the end of those ten years we were seasoned warriors, ready to protect and defend our new Keeper," the Goddess's words rang clear and strong, her pride still audible as she spoke. "We would lie in wait at known portals then strike as the first Raptors came through. In this way we hoped to, at least, lower their numbers and distract them from the Keeper as she journeyed. Everything would be ready and in place to defend our Keeper when the seal broke. My Resistance is more than ready no matter the challenge. Even today they are the top warriors of their class. They are very good at what they do, although they sometimes can go overboard with their leader's protection," she said with annoyance. *That explains what she meant before when she said they take extra precautions to keep her safe,* thought Rosey. "They" were the Resistance. Before she could start up again, Rosey asked, "Are Wolvereen and Nagura a part of the Resistance?"

The Goddess looked up, startled by her sudden question, "Yes, anyone serving under me or my sister and any other Leader of the World are a part of the resistance. They may be my guards but they are also Resistance members. Oh," she said suddenly leaning forward, "do you know of my sister, the Silver Goddess?"

Rosey nodded, "I know that you have a sister and that that's what she is called, but I know no more than that."

The Goddess leaned back, "I hope you have the chance to meet her, she is a feat in her own right. I'm sure the chance will present itself soon, but back to that story!" she said throwing up her arms. "About a year before the seal was to break Esperanza started her journey. She did well in that year and with the Resistance in place our mighty Keeper found herself surrounded by a whole civilization of warriors dedicated to her survival. We no longer looked at her as the commander to lead our armies as we did with Maharen but as a savior, whom we were willing to give our lives to protect. Esperanza fought long and hard to rise to the occasion, inspired by our dedication. She battled various challenges and grew a little more every day. She wasted no time.

"A few trusted friends, her husband, and brother made up their fellowship. Within that first year, before the seal broke, she collected six of the elements before the Evil One sent its first new Raptors through the portals, we were all very proud of her and her strength. She had a fantastic head start and we were all confident she'd succeed. We were on top of the world. Then things became complicated. When your mother was collecting the eighth element, she became pregnant."

At this Rosey suddenly became self-conscious, she knew it was ridiculous but she couldn't help it. It was like eavesdropping on a private conversation about yourself.

"It was unplanned and unexpected. The two lovers had agreed to practice preventive measures against pregnancy until the journey was over but they were very much in love. Accidents happen and they let their guard down. They were overjoyed to be having a baby but also fearful for its life. This was simply more incentive to hurry and collect the rest of the elements. Esperanza quickly collected the last few and then returned back to my castle where she would stay until you were born. During this time security was very tight. We were trying our best to hide the fact that Esperanza was pregnant from the Evil One. We made sure that she didn't leave the castle while she was showing, not just to hide the pregnancy but also for protection. You were precious, to your parents and everyone that heard of you. You were an unexpected gift and a ray of light in all this darkness bringing your mother more happiness than you could ever imagine."

The sincerity and passion in the Goddess's voice was starting to make Rosey tear up. A small blossom of heat exploded in her chest and moved up her throat threatening to tighten and suffocate her. She breathed deeply and calmly, like the Goddess, she showed no outward sign of her struggle, but the Goddess seemed to see it anyway. She said nothing about it though, just continued on.

"It was also an added bonus because, even though we had no desire to think or talk about it, you were a potential Keeper if your mother…failed. You were very important to us."

The Mystics

Rosey could tell the Goddess struggled with her words, after all, the golden woman had known her mother personally. She had raised her and that kind of connection didn't just fade away with time.

"When you were born, you were healthy and lively, everything that a baby was supposed to be. Your Uncle was so happy to hold you and your father couldn't have been prouder... "

Rosey's eyes watered, her breath drawing short as realization struck her.

"I was born...here?" she stammered, pointing down to the ground.

"Well, not in this room, in the infirmary, but yes, I witnessed your birth. I was one of your mother's closest friends, I basically raised her after her mother's death. It was the best that I could do for them. I took them on as my own."

Rosey gasped in utter awe. She had had no idea that the Goddess witnessed her birth or had been so involved in her life and not just her mother's. Out of all that, the only thing that Rosey said was, "Oh...I'm not African after all."

The Goddess stared at her for a few moments then burst out laughing. Now it was Rosey's turn to stare.

"Is something wrong?" Rosey asked, a bit thrown off.

"No, no, you just remind me so much of your mother. You are just like her, so unpredictable, yet amusing."

Rosey lowered her head but continued smiling. Immediately, the Goddess sobered from her laughing. Rosey's heart beat was slow and cumbersome; her smile was weak and low. I may have been able to know what that meant if...if...she was still here. And my father, am I anything like him? For a few moments Rosey was lost in thought. Her mind continued to race back to all those times she had stared at the picture of her mother and father sitting on her bed stand. She remembered how she would daydream long into the night about what it would be like if they had gone to the park or to the movies or to dinner. It was only now that Rosey wondered if that picture was taken on The World Within A World or on Earth. It doesn't matter, or does it?

"Rosey," the Goddess asked gently.

Rosey looked up. The Goddess's face was stretched with worry. Rosey smiled and said, "I'm okay, just pining for what could have been. Please continue."

The Goddess looked at her for a little longer trying to find a weakness in her defenses but Rosey had learned long ago about how to school her features just right when needed. Being raised by an uncle and not your parents was a curious subject and everyone at her school had always wanted to know the story behind it. Most were very nice, but it was still hard. Rosey didn't want to let them see her cry. Over time she had become an expert at hiding her feelings. After telling the story for so long it had begun to become mundane to Rosey. A task that had been completed over and over again for another's curiosity. The Goddess looked away, and then did as Rosey asked, and continued.

"About a week after your birth Esperanza told us what she and Mathew had decided was the best course of action. She wanted to get you to safety and try to get you there as silently as possible. She gave you to John and told him to take you to Earth. If she and Mathew were killed in the fighting, John was to raise you there as an Earthling. She was also very insistent that you not be told anything about your true background until the crystal appeared. We all agreed that if the crystal did not appear to you by the time you were seventeen, we would bring you here, no matter what, for training. To this day I can't fathom why she wanted you to be raised on Earth so adamantly…I mean" she said, raising a hand, "I understand of course, for your protection." She gestured to Rosey wildly as if the fact that she didn't know something bothered her.

I can only image what that feels like, Rosey thought sarcastically.

"Still, it was the way she said it," the Goddess continued, taking Rosey by surprise, "It was as if… she knew something that we didn't but she couldn't explain it..." She trailed off and Rosey felt suddenly like she was in the spot light. The Goddess's eyes lingered for a bit on a spot on her desk and then she pulled out of it. "You know, it doesn't really matter. Perhaps it was desperation on her part. The simple need for a mother to know that her child grows up happy, at least for some amount of time. Of course, we never assumed that she wouldn't make it." She shook her head, her eyes glistening with memories. "That was always the strange thing about Esperanza; she always acted as if she knew things. Things…that people shouldn't know. That's what made us all believe so thoroughly in her, even me…Wolvereen promised to get you safely to Earth no matter what." The Goddess smiled, "We all did."

Rosey stared blankly at the Goddess, complete surprise registering on her face. Even Wolvereen had been there at her birth and had protected her as a baby. In a way, these people were her family. They had no blood relation to her, yet they loved her with all their heart, enough to risk their lives for her. Rosey suddenly felt an overwhelming feeling of gratitude.

"John would return to Earth explaining that you were the daughter of his sister and that she and her husband had disappeared in Africa when they had not returned from their last research trip. A legal document would be given that noted him as the only guardian. Since he was your only known relative and perfectly capable of taking care of you there would be no objections to him keeping you. This is the story your uncle no doubt told you about your parents, right?"

Rosey only nodded.

"Esperanza and Mathew pleaded with John to agree to take you and flee to Earth even though he wanted desperately to be by his sister's side. He knew that only the Keeper could face the Evil One and no one could accompany her, but still he wanted to be there for support. He knew, however, that taking care of you was just as important. You would be safe because on Earth the Evil One would definitely never find you or even know about you while you were there. Taking you there would also prevent

Esperanza and Mathew from worrying and allow them to focus on the battle at hand, so John reluctantly agreed. It was terribly hard on your parents to let you go but they were afraid for your safety and put that above all else. They knew that they could depend on John to love and protect you just as they would have here. While you were here, you would never be completely safe. John did what his sister wanted. He left not too long after your birth with a group of my finest guards including Wolvereen's pack."

"Before your mother set off to challenge the Evil One she called everyone to an emergency meeting with her and Adina. We were all surprised but okay with the idea, we thought that maybe Esperanza was going to discuss a plan of action for something concerning the Raptors. We were wrong. Esperanza told us that she had noticed her elemental powers were very weak. She told Adina that apparently, since you were born her elemental powers had seemed deprived and slow, even after months of recuperation."

Rosey stared at the Goddess at a loss for words; horrified that somehow she had caused a problem with her mother.

"Adina was dumbfounded and had no explanation for this. Once again something was going wrong with the Keeper. Adina told her not to attack the Evil One until she could consult the Great Oak in Valley Elathos, maybe she just required more recuperation time. Adina left immediately that day. The next day..."

Suddenly the Goddess looked at her with a dismal face. She stared down for a moment, lost in thought, then looked back up at Rosey with sadness in her eyes. The pain in her voice broke Rosey's heart. For once the Goddess's normally calm demeanor was broken.

"Now Rosey, what I'm about to say, is not going to be pretty. I want to warn you that your mother's story is not a happy one. I want you to know that if you need me to stop or wait, just let me know. This is the reason I wanted to talk to you alone, it may be easier, but we can call for your friends if you wish it." Rosey nodded unable to speak. She was too excited, no matter what the news was, to learn the truth. She was scared, happy, anxious, sad, and overjoyed to finally be learning the truth. She breathed deeply and sat down her drink. She focused on the Goddess and nodded for her to continue. "I can't wait any longer, I need to know." The Goddess nodded and went on, "The next day, one of your mother's fellowship members was taken over by something. She was completely unaware of what she was doing. Whatever was controlling her made her attack Esperanza, Mathew, and all the others. She went for your father first and killed him. All of the fellowship threw themselves in front of your mother to protect her, but it wasn't enough. This control over her was too powerful. Somehow she knew just what to do to stop even my attacks. She cut through them like butter. With all her enhanced strength...she mortally wounded your mother, whose elemental powers were too weak to provide protection. Even if Esperanza's elemental powers had been at full force, I doubt that she would have used them on a friend, possessed or not. Esperanza just wasn't that kind of person. It all happened too fast..."

The Goddess's words flew out of her mouth. Rosey had the feeling that if she stopped she wouldn't be able to continue.

"...Your mother lay dying. She knew her time was short. She knew she wouldn't make it. With her dying breath she took up the crystal and used all the elemental powers she had collected to place an ultimate guard on all portals to Earth against evil creatures and a shield around Earth to keep all evil at bay. She ensured that you would be safe on Earth; no creature of evil could cross to Earth through our portals and none could get to you through Earth's atmosphere. Now the Evil One was guaranteed not to attack Earth because it couldn't. It would not be able to manifest itself. In this way you could grow up and have a somewhat normal life, until it was time to return and take your rightful place here. Even if the Evil One found where you were, it would be powerless to hurt you.

"As soon as your mother cast that lock on the portals, whatever it was that had had a hold on the fellowship member was cast out. I can't begin to describe her despair at what she had done….even now, we still have no idea what it was that controlled her. There's nothing on this world Adina knows of that could exert that kind of control on another person. Whatever it was, your mother's lock on the portals stopped it dead in its tracks and we are hoping beyond hope that what she did keeps it away. It's either that or it was a onetime trick by the Evil One that can't be used again. I don't know."

She lowered her head, and her voice cracked slightly.

"John was devastated. He told me that the only thing he could think of doing was to hold you close. 'You were all that remained of her', he told me. Even now I think to myself, what could I have done? What didn't I do to protect my friend... my Keeper. I failed her that day, and I can never take that back. I failed you." She paused again, looking down in a long stare as if the memories still haunted her. Her eyes glazed over and Rosey sensed, somewhere deep inside, the Goddess's heart crying out in pain.

Rosey's heartbeat quickened and for a long moment she sat in silence, completely shocked. She heard nothing, felt nothing, and saw nothing. Slowly tears started falling down her cheeks and she buried her face in her hands.

Chapter Ten: The Story Continues

Rosey hardly remembered what happened after she lowered her head to cry. What she did remember was blurred. She knew she had stopped crying after a few moments and said that she needed to be alone for a while. She also knew that the Goddess had taken her by the hand and led her to her room. Once there, Rosey only remembered flopping onto the bed and falling into a deep sleep. She awoke the next morning feeling much better. She had always known that her mother was dead but she had no idea that one of her mother's friends had been the one to deliver the deathblow. Rosey thought about what the Goddess had said, she went over it again and again in her mind, sorting through the information. She knew that the Goddess's story was not complete yet, there was still much to tell. Now that the initial shock was over and Rosey could think about her mother without crying, she waited patiently, running through everything she had learned in her head. Normally she would have eaten with her friends as they had at dinner the night before but Rosey decided to remain in her room to think things through. Nashi did not speak to her about it and Rosey managed to whisper some polite words in response to the woman's kindness. Even Noly and Hazel, usually bouncing around all day making a ruckus everywhere they went, seemed to sense Rosey's distress and acted perfectly calm and collected to give Rosey the animal companionship that was so valued during an especially difficult time. Like herself, the animals had also been told the story that she had been told. Rosey had, at first, been unsure about being separated from the others while the story was taking place but now, later, Rosey was grateful for it. To try and distract her from her sadness Hazel and Noly went on and on about the new language and how amazing it was to be the only animals from Earth, along with the horses, who knew any kind of speech. They then would try to create different weird words from what they knew of the language just by combining words. Some of their accomplishments went along the lines of 'baggywrinkles' and 'skitterbrain'. Rosey appreciated their effort and found herself amused, but it didn't stop her mind from thinking over everything she had heard.

Amazingly, she wasn't as sad as she thought she'd be. She was more angry than sad. She was angry at the Evil One, angry at her uncle, her friends, her family, and everyone else who had watched her from afar. All those people who had always known about who she was and what she was meant to do while she, all along, was kept in the dark, ignorant of what was awaiting her. People who had never bothered to tell her, but had let her grow up in a lie knowing only shadows of truth. She was just angry at everything…and yet…she blamed no one. They had only done what her mother had wanted. They had risked everything to ensure that she thought she was from Earth, that she knew nothing but Earth. They had loved, guided, and protected her, all the while knowing what she would become. They had done what they could to ensure her future. The death of her parents wasn't what worried her or filled her with such rage and doubt, no, it was that apparent weakness that Esperanza had after giving birth to Rosey. She couldn't help but wonder if it was her that caused it. Had her birth robbed her mother of the strength she needed to fight? What had happened? She needed to know more.

Rosey patted Noly absently and watched as Hazel played with a small toy mouse filled with catnip. The two of them knew what to do to make her happy. Noly was fast asleep next to her, her head in Rosey's lap. She and Noly were positioned on the bed, with Noly's back to the door and her head lying on Rosey's right leg. Rosey rubbed under her ears in soft circular patterns. Noly was so relaxed that her tail lay perfectly still on the bed. Hazel suddenly quit playing with her mouse toy and jumped onto the bed next to Rosey as Nashi came in carrying a tray filled with an assortment of different miniature sandwiches, tea, and some ice cream. Noly lifted her head and gazed over her left shoulder at Nashi with a doggy smile on her face.

"Good day ma'am. How are you feeling?" Nashi asked politely. "Very well, thank you Nashi." Nashi placed the tray on the small desk in the corner of the room and took up Rosey's uneaten breakfast, or what was left of it after Rosey had given the okay for Noly and Hazel to have at it. Nashi then went back out to the hallway and placed the tray on a small cart. She picked up two bowls from the bottom level of the cart and placed them on the floor. Noly stood up carefully and jumped down off the bed, Hazel right behind her. Nashi lifted the covering from the bowls revealing what looked like dog and cat food. The two quickly began devouring the food after giving Nashi a quick 'thank you'. Nashi brought them two other bowls filled with water and took the old bowls of water back to the cart, along with their dinner bowls from last night. Rosey quickly called after Nashi before she could leave. "Nashi."

"Yes Keeper?" She paused at the door, staring at Rosey expectantly. "I'm ready to see the Golden Goddess again, when she is available of course."

Nashi brightened at this.

"Of course Keeper, I will inform her right away. I'll come for you when she is ready." During their talk Rosey had walked over to the tray of food. "Thank you, this looks delicious," she said taking a sip of the tea. It had a warm cinnamon taste that wasn't overly spicy. It was delicious enough to satisfy the taste buds but leave you wanting more afterwards. Rosey felt her cheeks grow warm from the heat. After such a dreary day and night, it was like a fresh awakening.

She nodded her praise and took another sip.

Nashi beamed happily from the praise.

"I made it myself. Enjoy Keeper, and if you need anything else simply ring the service bell. Remember the castle is open to you, nowhere is off limits, feel free to explore."

"Thanks."

Nashi gave a quick bow then left.

Nashi came back a few minutes later and told her that the Goddess would not be able to get with her for an hour or so. After Rosey and her two goofy, lovable pets had finished eating she decided to take them out on a little walk around the castle. Rosey quickly showered and got dressed into her newly washed clothes, enjoying the scents and feel of the soft fabric, even her jeans were softer. She couldn't help but wonder what kind of detergent they used, and then wondered if they even used detergent. Rosey brushed Noly's long cream and brown colored coat into submission and then gave Hazel a quick brushing as well. Afterwards they left Rosey's spacious and ornate room to explore. Along the way Rosey ran into Rochell and Alex. The two of them at first had smothered Rosey with worried questions:

"How are you?"

"Are you feeling well?"

"Is there anything you wish us to elaborate on?"

She had kindly declined, telling them that she wanted to wait until after the Goddess had finished her story to ask any questions. She told them that she was exploring the castle and they gladly joined her. The three of them walked around enjoying the castle and its many wonders.

After about an hour, Nashi arrived and told Rosey that the Goddess was prepared to see her. Rosey left Noly and Hazel with Alex and Rochell and followed Nashi. She led her down to the small room where the eight hallways loomed before her and led her down the fifth one. It eventually opened up into a huge indoor garden area. Above them Rosey could see natural light pouring down through a clear see-through substance. It was not too unlike the stuff covering the courtyards by her room. A slight breeze sent the substance into a slow flapping dance, like a fan blowing on fabric. *Fabric, that's interesting*, she thought. Although the temperature outside was frigid, thanks to the coming winter, the garden was warm with a slight but comfortable humidity. *The fabric must let in light but not the cold,* she thought. *I wonder what else it lets in or keeps out.* Despite the amazing fabric, nothing compared to the glorious display of the gardens.

Flowers of all types bloomed everywhere irises, roses, snapdragons, hyacinths, daisies, violets, orchids, lilies, and some she had never seen or heard of graced the garden with splendor. Rosey stood for a few moments shocked and in awe of everything around her. She had never seen such a luscious and well-tended garden. Rosey was so enthralled by the beauty that she hardly noticed Nashi waiting patiently for her. She quickly hurried after her. Nashi smiled at her and turned around. She led Rosey down a pathway shielded overhead by arches made of woven trees and hanging vines. Rosey reached out her hand and let her hand graze the vines as she walked past. "It's beautiful isn't it?" asked Nashi while still walking.   Rosey nodded, and then she realized that Nashi couldn't see her from behind and said, "Yes, they are comforting and relaxing."

"The Golden Goddess thinks so as well. She often comes here to rest and to think."

Before coming to this world Rosey had never had to take time to rest and to think. Her life had been one of relative leisure and carefree abandon but now, all in the course of one day, she had been jostled around into another planet and then to a golden castle right out of a storybook. The experience had given her a feeling of jet lag that had nothing to do with a jet. But if an entire war was going on and an evil psycho maniac was on the loose than, yeah, she was probably going to need some quiet and peaceful place for serious thought. Rosey had no time to contemplate this further for they entered a small clearing with a large ornate fountain in the middle. The entire area was finished in cobblestone and several other paths broke off from the circular clearing continuing to other parts of the garden. The path Rosey came from was the only one with arches overhead. Nashi bowed to Rosey and lifted her left hand to indicate the seated Goddess not ten feet away. She was wearing the same thing as the day before except that her hair was pinned back into a neat bob held together by a long golden twine. She smiled at Rosey and repositioned herself on the small stone bench that she sat on. Nashi bowed to the Goddess then turned and left. Rosey approached the Goddess at a fast walk, eager to learn more. The Goddess patted the seat beside her and Rosey gladly took it. "So, Rosey, how are you?" asked the Goddess in her sing song voice. Her bright golden eyes searched Rosey's sharp blue ones with kindness.

"I'm ready to go on now, thank you. And you?"

"Very well, thank you. Now, I hate to get right into business, but there is more of the story to be told." "Yes I know. But first, let me thank you for being patient with me yesterday," Rosey said rather awkwardly. She had later, when her grief had worn away, felt rather foolish for breaking down in front of a stranger, and one as powerful as the Goddess for that matter. No. Rosey thought, looking at the Goddess. *She's not a stranger, not any more.* "Don't you worry about it," The Goddess waved her hand, dismissing the idea. "I wasn't expecting you to be all hard faced and serious about it. I knew that you would probably need to resume our conversation the next day." "Well, thanks anyway. Please start where you left off. What happened after my mother was…killed?" She said this last part awkwardly, pain still visible in her voice. If the Goddess noticed Rosey's hesitation she didn't say anything. Rosey found she was very grateful that she didn't. The Goddess started up carefully, "As I said before, we all wanted to help your mother, but everything happened so fast. We were speechless. We were shocked. To this day we still don't know what happened to the Fellowship member or how she was possessed. As you may expect she was very shocked and on the verge of suicide for what she had done. It took all our strength to keep her from hurting herself. Once she was stable enough she was sent home to her parents to, hopefully, live in as much peace as she could find. A few weeks later we got word that she had run away. In the letter she left behind she explained that she was very grateful to all of us for still loving and caring for her even after what she had done, but she needed to be alone for a while. We haven't heard from her since. We have no idea whether she is alive or dead. I can only hope she finds peace."

"What about…scrying…I believe that's what you called it. Alex mentioned it once and I remember you said something about it…?"

"Some people know how to block their own signatures."

Rosey looked at her skeptically. The Goddess frowned.

"Basically she found a way to stop us from scrying her. We're not certain how, but whenever we try the image comes up black. Even if the person was dead we would see a gravesite or body or…something, not black. She's the only one that's ever produced that response from a scrying pool before. Somehow, she's found a way to stay hidden. We can only hope that she's all right."

Rosey nodded, knowing that she wanted nothing less for the woman. She didn't blame her whatsoever for her mother's death. It was all the fault of that horrible bastard, the Evil One.

"After the battle John continued to raise you on Earth, saddened but his hope for you strengthened. He had every faith and hope in his sister's plan for you and wanted to honor her memory no matter what."

For a few moments the Goddess was silent, the memories of Esperanza playing through her mind. Rosey could almost see images of her mother flashing through the Goddess's head in remembrance. She must've been like a daughter to her. The idea bewildered Rosey because it meant that she was more than just a savior to this woman, she was family. The woman's beautiful face contorted in deep sorrow so quickly that at first Rosey thought she had imagined it. Rosey herself felt her own sudden pain well up but pushed it down as the Goddess doggedly continued. "On Earth, your uncle was well aware of who you were to become and what you would have to face, so he took advantage of all the activities Earth had to offer: soccer, track, tennis, horseback riding, any sport that got you moving and in shape. I even believe he had you scuba diving on vacations and put you in karate, Tae Bo, Kendo, and Iaido lessons, which are Japanese sword techniques, if I am correct?"

Rosey nodded vigorously, she had never gone through very tough training but she was a considerable black belt in karate and pretty good at kendo. *So that's why Dad always encouraged me to do all sorts of sports.* A lot of times she'd thought it was annoying, but he was preparing her! A deep admiration blossomed in her chest for her uncle.   Rochell and Alex had also been in many of those classes. Before, she had thought it just coincidence, but now she wondered if they had been purposefully placed there to help encourage their budding friendship and to also keep them in shape. If it was, Rosey didn't mind so much, she had enjoyed those classes together with them and wouldn't have wanted it any other way. Besides, Alex and Rochell's parents were also well aware of where their children were to be heading and what they would be facing, they probably wanted to keep them just as fit and prepared as her uncle had done for her. Aloud she said, "Yes I know Kendo and Iaido and some pretty good Tae Bo."   "Well, I would expect nothing less from the future Keeper. Your uncle did well; he wanted you to be prepared even if he couldn't tell you everything. How good are you at Kendo? I believe that is a sword art, is it not? "Good, not a novice, but not a master and yes it is a sword technique like Iaido."

The Goddess nodded eagerly, "That should make it easier to teach you in our ways of the sword."   "You're going to teach me how to use a sword, a real sword, like..."   Rosey held up her hands and slashed through the air as if she was wielding a sword and made "swishing" sounds each time she brought down the imaginary blade.

The Goddess chuckled a bit at Rosey's play, "Yes, real swords. The sword is a temporary form of protection until you acquire the elements and become more accustomed to using them in combat. Your friend Rochell is a very powerful air elemental and will probably be teaching you the most about how to use your elements. If your muscles weren't well toned before, they will be soon." Rosey nodded, she was sure that the techniques she would be learning would help her with the sword techniques she already knew. During her Iaido lessons she had used a real sword, so she had some practice. This would be more like the sword fighting in movies, fast-paced and hard, nothing like the slow deliberateness of Kendo and Iaido, but at least she wasn't going in blind. "In the meantime, I want you to remain strong and proud," said the Goddess, snapping Rosey out of her thoughts. "We all wish we could have done something, but we can't change the past and what happened did so for a reason. Your mother wanted you to be raised on Earth so you could have a normal and carefree childhood. She didn't get the chance to face the Evil One. We have hope that you, the third Keeper, will have what it takes to make that special connection between the elements and take down the Evil One." The Goddess's voice had steadily become higher with pride as she spoke. Now, she looked down at Rosey sitting next to her with a confident smile on her face. Rosey tried to smile back but she couldn't. Something gnawed at her hungrily, but she was afraid to ask. Still, she had to know.

"Why did my...mother..." the word seemed to stick in Rosey's throat, "I mean, if she was able to block the Evil One from entering Earth through the portals then why not just block it from ever entering The World Within A World...problem solved?"

The Goddess's brows furrowed, as if Rosey has stumbled upon something that she had yet to see in all her infinite wisdom. "You know...I don't know," she confessed with a look of shock. "Perhaps she was afraid that the Evil One would go to Earth if it couldn't get to us. She was so kind...even though you'd be safe, the people of Earth wouldn't be? Maybe she simply didn't think things through...perhaps you were all that was on her mind in her...final moments? It might be that her protection won't last forever?" She gave Rosey a small smile, "That's a good question, but one that, I'm afraid, has no answer."

Rosey looked away. Despite her sadness the night before, she had been unable to shake the
feeling that her mother had defended Earth for some other reason besides just the fact that she had been there. She looked at the Goddess with steady eyes. "Why do you have so much hope in me?" she shook her head in disbelief. Her shoulders suddenly slumped in defeat. "I'm just a seventeen year old girl, I'm not thirty or twenty, but seventeen. I haven't even gotten all the way past all of puberty yet."   The Goddess laughed. Rosey just scowled at her.

"Rosey," the Goddess said between laughs, "being the keeper has nothing to do with age." "Then why didn't you wait until I was older?" Rosey fixed her with a questioning stare.

"Honestly, time," she said, quieting her laughter, her voice becoming very serious. "There isn't enough time to wait around until you're in your twenties to send you on your journey. Every day the Evil One grows stronger so we can't afford to waste time. Despite that, Adina wouldn't allow you to begin your journey until you were at least seventeen. As for your other inquiry about why we have so much hope that you will succeed, well, there's no doubt that we are more prepared now than we were before when the Keeper was new to us. This time we will take extra precautions to make sure that you are successful. Of course, there is the threat of the Raptors but the Resistance has plenty of trained warriors ready to fight for you. However, I do not want you to think that this means you're safe from the clutches of harm." The Goddess's eyes narrowed as she spoke, "This brings me to a pressing matter that I need to warn you of."

Rosey wasn't sure she liked the sound of that

The woman turned to Rosey and fixed her with her gaze, "There are various reports of Minions, warriors of various species that work for the Evil One. They are identified by a black crystal embedded in their chest. These may be exaggerated reports but we must be careful and you need to be warned. This is new, the Evil One has never used any creature but the

Raptors and Blood Gorons until now and for that reason we are not sure of what powers these Minions hold. We are constantly tracking them down, but because of our lack of knowledge it is hard to gain an upper hand. At the least we can keep them busy enough to distract them from you and your goals."

Rosey's brows furrowed as she heard the Minion's name. She almost laughed at it but managed to ask with a straight face, "Why do you call them Minions?"

"We do," the Goddess said, sensing her amusement, "because we don't know what they are or who they are. What we do know is that they seem to be working for the Evil One and thus we address them as such: it's Minions."

The seriousness of the Goddess's voice silenced Rosey and drove away any humorous thoughts. Obviously, this wasn't a laughing matter and the Goddess wanted to be sure she knew it. Rosey gulped but said nothing as the woman continued.

"They are indeed a true threat, Rosey. We cannot always be successful and we cannot be everywhere at once. Your fellowship, however, has been well trained and is committed to protecting you with their lives if necessary. Our existence depends solely on you being able to complete your mission. The fellowship is made up of your closest friends and protectors; they are not just bodyguards, but guides, companions, and family." She fixed Rosey with a hard gaze, "There is...one specific reason why we are confident of your success. There is something more, something we place great trust in."

Rosey nodded, feeling herself pulled by the tale.

"It was during your time on Earth, not too long ago if I remember correctly, that the Prophet Sheorie, also a librarian, keeper of all the knowledge of the worlds, set down a Prophecy. A Prophet is a person who has all knowledge of the Universe. They receive visions called Prophecies every once in a while, usually when the world is in danger. Sheorie's Prophecy told that the third Keeper would be the last and final Keeper that The

World Within A World would ever see. She would save the world from the Hell Ship once and for all. You Rosey are that Keeper and that is why we have such high hopes." Rosey remembered her friends mentioning the Prophet Sheorie earlier when they were telling her about the NCD. Was a prophecy all it took to make her journey successful? No, there had to be more too it. She couldn't just be willed to win the fight. Was she really capable?

Breathing deeply she lowered her head in thought. Her whole life she had dreamed of her mother and her future. Here it was, she could uphold the hope her mother had died for or run away and hide. Hiding was not an option. Eventually the Evil One she let takeover would find her and most likely kill her because of her potential threat. Whether she liked it or not, it was now her responsibility. *Besides, what would stop it from turning on Earth once it was through with this world?* she thought, reasoning with herself. She clenched her teeth and felt her muscles tense, she couldn't let what happened to her mother happen to anyone else. There was one thing she needed to know before she said yes. "What, besides the Prophecy, makes you so sure I can pull this off?" she said lifting her head and gazing directly into the deep golden eyes of the Goddess, feeling, for once, since walking through the portal into this world, not at all intimidated. What made her so special? What made her different? What made her a better Keeper than the fierce Maharen or the gentle Esperanza? How would she, someone who had no prior practice with elements or any knowledge of them, much less more potent elements like the ones in the crystal, be better than two highly intelligent war heroes who gave life and limb to fight for their world's freedom?

"Because," said the Goddess simply, "it is in your blood and your mother died for it. Your family understood more about the elements than any elemental has ever dreamed of. Something about them, about you, makes you special. What it is, we may never know. I can give you nothing else except the assurance that you were made for this, whatever 'this' turns out to be."

"It wasn't for my mother and grandmother," said Rosey sadly, averting her eyes and feeling as if she was a child searching for any available excuses to get her out of a bad situation.   The Goddess gently placed her hand on Rosey's back, "That's not true. Your grandmother, Maharen, discovered many secrets of the planet while on her journey, much of which is in Sheorie's library. Your mother did something that was considered impossible when she sealed all the portals leading to Earth preventing evil from passing between. On your journey, I have no doubt that you will discover more."

Nodding, Rosey played with the end of her shirt, still a little unsure of herself. Looking up she said, "I need to know one last thing. This whole prophecy you mentioned…Sheorie foretold it. Who exactly is this woman? What is it about her that would make you trust her and her word so adamantly?"   The Goddess nodded in understanding, "What you ask is understandable but to really explain to you why we trust her so, I must first tell you about what she is. I was going to hold this off until later but you will be meeting these people pretty soon so why wait? Sheorie is an Elf, a species that is considered to be shrouded in mystery and myth. They are the wisest and the strongest. An Elf is one of what we call the Five Species of Elemental Humans."   Rosey looked up sharply in surprise. She had read about elves in fantasy books and fairytales on Earth but she doubted that these elves were anything like those. They had certainly never been referred to as species of humans on Earth.

"There are…species of humans?" she asked, bewildered.

"Elemental Humans," the Goddess nodded, "There are Elves, Atlantians, Enerjons, Daymons, and Warfs. The Five Species of Elemental Humans are identified by which one of the elements they have been claimed by. Now, before I go on, I want to make it clear to you that an Elemental Human is not the same as a regular human elemental or magikin.

Each Elemental Human species has been joined with a specific element. The Elves have earth, the Atlantians have water, the Enerjons have lightning, the Daymons have fire, and the Warfs have air.

"And before you ask," she said with a smile as Rosey began to open her mouth, "the Atlantians have nothing to do with your lost city of Atlantis. I must confess that we adopted the name for them when John, your uncle, told us about them in one of the books he was reading from Earth. Our Atlantians used to be called the Water Walkers but they decided that the Earth name Altantian sounded much better. If you remember we did the same thing with the Falosaraptors and Raptors. Anyway back to where we left off. Each of the species is recognized by a different physical type. The Elves have pointed ears, green eyes, brunette hair, and green markings around their eyes. The Atlantians have blonde hair and blue eyes. The Enerjons have long black hair and pure golden eyes. The Daymons have red hair and purple eyes. The Warfs have blue-black hair or silver hair, silver or grey eyes, and their elders develop wings." "Interesting, I take it you aren't an Enerjon then?" said Rosey, a little disappointed that she hadn't discovered the sunken civilization of Atlantis.

"No, I am human," the Goddess said, laughing slightly. "A Goddess level Magikin, but a very powerful one."

"Shouldn't you be a Mage level instead?" Rosey asked, the sudden idea making her turn to the Goddess in surprise. After hearing about how powerful the woman was, she found it odd that she wasn't a higher level than Goddess. It fit for her namesake but still, why was she only a middle level?

The Goddess explained, looking exhausted all of a sudden, as if the information she was going to share weighed on her heavily, "Magikins...are a little different. You see, their power is not always limited by their level. Unlike elementals, in time, a magikin can actually raise their level because magic is not a natural part of this world and thus not a biologically sustained entity as an element is. A magikin is only limited by how much they

The Mystics

know. Despite my power I am stuck at this level. Unfortunately, no one has ever achieved the Mage level. We know it exists from stories and old books but no one has ever reached it. We think that it might have been lost to us when the planet was destroyed and the level of magic existing here was severely weakened, but we are unsure. The lower the magic levels the lower the capacity to perform magic and use it as we will, that is why my sister and I are considered the most powerful magikins of them all even though we are only at Goddess level. We are on the higher end, but not enough to achieve a Mage level. Elementals are very different since their level cannot be changed. It is the way it will be at birth until death."

"So...how do you know what level you are in both magikins and elementals?"

"With magikins it depends on your knowledge and the power of your spells, with elementals it depends on the elemental capacity that you have. Take the water element for example. Its levels are determined by how many gallons of water you can control at a time. An apparition level can control 0.1 gallons to 100,000 gallons; a God or Goddess level can control 100,001 gallons to a million gallons; and a King or Queen level can control a million and one gallons to a billion gallons."

Rosey nodded then thought about the Elemental Humans. "So, what happens if two Elemental Human Species mix, which element does the offspring receive? What if they mix with a regular human elemental or magikin?"

The Goddess frowned but not in anger, she looked flustered and amused, "You are indeed very adept. This is a bit complicated but I'll see if I can explain it correctly. If two Elemental Human species mix then the child will either have one element or the other, in rare cases they are a mixture of both. Since the elemental and magical ability are carried on genes there is always a chance to receive either power, it just depends on what genes a person happens to get. Although, Elemental Humans do not have an ability to work magic, that only happens if they were to mix with a regular human that does have the ability, and the gene got transferred into the family line."

"Elements are carried on genes?" Rosey said, fascinated.

"Yes, just like all characteristics of living beings. Let's say that a regular human child, though this works for animals as well as humans, has a regular human mother and father with powers of water and earth. Either they get one or the other or, in rare cases, they combine. This is known as an Elemental Birthright. An Elemental Birthright states that the elements passed down in your gene pool are your right, you have a chance of receiving any one of the elements in your gene pool. However, it is by pure chance that you receive the element you do just as it is with all genes. These same genes also determine an elemental's power level: Apparition, God or Goddess, or Queen or King.

"Magic, on the other hand, is different. It is a separate entity that exists only outside of the body and is not a natural power that exists within a person like an element does so it is not located in a person's genes. What is in their genes is only their ability to work magic. Two elemental parents can have a child that is a magikin. As long as the gene for working magic is present, it doesn't matter. The gene also, in this case, does not determine their level. It only determines their ability to use magic. Now, if the child does turn out to be an elemental, it may not have the parent's elements. Because the elements are carried on genes sometimes an element that has been carried through the family will suddenly show up and not be either one of the child's parent's powers at all. It's kind of like having a black haired kid when you have brunette and blond parents. It's a part of your Elemental Birthright. You have the right to those elements. Even if your parents' didn't have them, someone in your family did. With purebred Elemental Humans of the same species there are no such chances for different elements to arise. An Elf with an Elf will always produce an earth elemental Elf. The only chance of there being another element is if the parents are two different Elemental Human Species or if an Elemental Human decides to be with a regular human.

"Now, if a regular human and an Elemental Human decided to have a child two things could happen. Either that child will look more like the Elemental Human or they'll look more like a regular human. An Elemental Human's genes are much more dominant than a regular human's genes thus if the child looks more like their Elemental Human parent, let's say an Elf, then they are more likely to have the Elf's element: Earth. If they resemble a regular human, whose genes are more recessive than an Elemental Human's, then they are more likely to have the regular human's element, or one that existed in the family line. In most cases the dominant gene of the Elemental Human is passed down, but genes are finicky and anything can happen."

"But...how do they keep themselves from becoming...no longer a purebred, if they can marry outside of their species?" Rosey asked, struggling for the right words.

The Goddess pursed her lips in thought, "Most Elemental Human species stay within their communities and do not live with regular humans. They grouped together when the Supernova destroyed our world and put into place strict breeding laws, desperate to preserve their species. Now they have built up their numbers and are a little more lenient about marrying outside the community. Once an Elemental Human does marry outside the community they will usually move out of the community and join the regular human's, not because they have been kicked out," she said hurriedly when Rosey looked shocked and angered, "but because it makes it easier for them to live with their human mate. Living with Elemental Humans can be very daunting, they are often bigger and more powerful than regular humans and their customs are strange and otherworldly at times. This also has the added benefit of keeping the bloodlines clean and the species going.

"Elemental Human's genes are very dominant and have an extreme bond with their element. They evolved to their element like when a creature evolves to a changing environment. We're not exactly sure what triggered the change, or why it has only happened for five elements, but we are still looking. We figure it is another one of those things that was lost in the supernova. We know that the Elemental Humans were around before the supernova, but that's about it. Even Sheorie is not sure how they came about."   "I thought she was supposed to know everything?" Rosey said, her brows furrowing teasingly.   "Only the things we are allowed to know," the Goddess said, returning her tease pleasantly, "For all we know she could know the answer and just not be allowed to tell us. There are limitations to all knowledge, remember that."   "So how are you so certain that this prophecy is true and that Sheorie's word is right? Is it just because she is an Elf?"

"Partly, but not completely. It's more about what comes with her being an Elf. Sheorie is a mystery in many cases. We know that she wasn't on our world to begin with but.."

At this Rosey's mouth dropped open, "What!?"

"Sheorie is much like Valley Elathos," the woman replied, not at all discouraged by Rosey's interjection, "she moves from planet to planet spreading wisdom and knowledge where needed. She's been here longer than the Valley; in fact, she may have arrived shortly after we entered Earth. I remember my father telling me about the great Sheorie who helped piece together our civilization and then continued to stay here. She's still here on this world, even now, though she and her library are only found if they wish to be."

"So this prophet is just like Valley Elathos...planet hopping to help wherever she can and whomever is in trouble?" Rosey murmured, thinking.

The Goddess gently nodded. "The most likely scenario is that, like Valley Elathos, Sheorie saw that our world was in peril and faced by evil, so she came to help guide us...and here she remains until we are back on our feet again. Think of her as a universal prophet, not limited to one planet, but able to choose where to add her insights."

Rosey stared at her curiously. This world just kept getting better and better. She was learning things about her universe that she knew would blow NASA's mind and everyone else's with it. "So" she said, focusing on the story, "how is a new prophet chosen if Sheorie were to die?"

The Goddess's face took on a look of embarrassed despair, "I was hoping you wouldn't ask that but here it goes. No one really knows Sheorie's origin or her birthday. There is speculation that she was made by the universe itself...much like the Valley. Thus, it would probably be the universe that would choose another if she were to perish. Though...I'm not sure she even can perish." The Goddess touched her chin, lost in thought.

"Huh?" was the only thing that Rosey managed to say.

"To someone who was raised on Earth, this might sound farfetched, but don't think of the planets and universe as a dead structures. Think of them as living beings that have consciousnesses of their own. It's kind of like the idea of Mother Nature or Mother Earth," the Goddess said as Rosey opened her mouth. Rosey shut it, a look of surprise spread across her

face. "Look, don't ask anything more about her, the best person to ask would be Sheorie

herself," The Goddess reasoned gently. "Many have tried already and have not succeeded. She's a very secretive person. However, because of all that she has done for us and her reputation, we trust her, just as we trust Valley Elathos to do its job and save us. It is for this reason that we have faith in Sheorie."

"Reputation?" The word stuck in her throat, as if lodged there.

"Though we have lost much of our memories, the knowledge of such unusual people like Sheorie and the Valley Elathos has stayed with us. We know that wherever they appear they only mean good will. It is this that inspires us to put our hope, trust, and the future of our world in their hands. You must remember we're not like Earth. Our world is not based on suspicion and distrust. We are not afraid to put our trust in another's hands."

Such a look of hope overcame the Goddess that Rosey forgot all of her doubts. After what she had just heard she understood how they could place so much faith in the prophecy. Slowly Rosey said, "Do you really think the prophecy could be right?"

"It may not come true," she said, startling Rosey, "but that is up to you. A prophecy can only do so much. You must grow and learn and commit to making it come true. Things can happen to change the direction of our future. An unknown variable such as you refusing to take on the quest and returning to Earth could happen to alter the coming events. Sheorie would have to relook at the possible future of our world without your help. From my own personal opinion, I believe we would have been destroyed long ago if Maharen hadn't stepped in. It must be your choice Rosey, no one else's."

Rosey thought for a moment. The inevitable truth was that she couldn't say no, not after everything she had learned. There was a whole world asking her for help, the possibility of finding out more about her mother plus going on one of the greatest journeys of her life. Rosey doubted she would even want to return to Earth, she couldn't live her life as a regular school girl anymore especially now that she knew that a maniac killer was out to get her and this world that had fought so hard to survive existed. Shaking her head, she knew she had lost the argument to return home before it had even begun. There was no turning back; this wasn't something she could walk away from, this was something that she had to do whether she liked it or not.

"All righty then…anything else I need to know before I begin?" said Rosey, wishing to God almighty that there wasn't.   The Goddess's eyes shone brightly with admiration and an overwhelming sense of relief washed over her face as if she had been tense all along as they spoke. The Goddess looked at her and smiled more warmly than she had ever done before in Rosey's time there, something Rosey hadn't expected. *She knew I could have said no.* She couldn't imagine what kind of stress that must have caused the woman, someone who had fought against this evil for all her life and even led armies against it. How selfish and naive Rosey was, sitting there and wandering about herself when everyone was desperately hoping for a miracle. Rosey closed her eyes and tried not to let her guilt show. Looking up she returned the Goddess's smile.

"I'm very pleased that you have chosen this path, especially now that you have been told about our unfortunate past. It's a lot of responsibility for one so young to take on but I have faith in you." Leaning forward she grasped Rosey's hands in her own. Rosey was expecting her hands to be soft and smooth but they were callused and cracked with wear and tear, a warrior's hands. She looked into Rosey's eyes and said with a kind voice, "Know this Rosey. The people of this world are all behind you. We will give our lives to protect you and help you to complete your mission. You can turn to anyone if you need help and you'll get it, no matter what. I give you my word. There isn't a single person on this world that doesn't know of the importance of your success. We will not fail our Keeper this time."

Rosey was stunned into silence. Her heart thudded in her chest as if she was running. She sighed deeply and managed to nod and say with a voice like steel, "Thank you, I won't rest until I make that prophecy come true."

The Goddess smiled and gave Rosey's hands a gentle squeeze. She then released them and straightened where she sat looking relieved and relaxed. "There are a few things I need to tell you now that you have accepted the task," she said, her voice had once again taken on its powerful authoritative tone. It must have been more stressful waiting for Rosey's answer than she had thought. Rosey nodded, if she was going to do this she needed to pay close attention. "First off you need to know how to locate the Mothers of the elements. There is a spirit inside the Shanobie Crystal known as the White Witch. She knows where the element's locations are. She will only inform you of one element at a time and will only give you the next location after you have collected that element. You will meet this woman in your Dream World, a place you go in your sleep. People often practice powers, study, or simply think in their Dream Worlds. It is in this place that you will find the White Witch."

"Dream Worlds?" Rosey said, her brows furrowed in thought. "How does that work?" She paused for a moment, "I mean, how does…" she stumbled for the right words but the Goddess beat her to it.

"I understand Rosey, it might seem a little unusual but here on The World Within A World dreams are a place where our consciousness meets our subconscious. The Dream World is the only part of our subconscious that we can control and enter. We do still dream every now and then. We don't always go to our Dream World in sleep, but it's an option that's available when we need it."

Rosey nodded, though she felt slightly apprehensive about having the ability to enter a place within her own mind, a place located in her subconscious no less. Nevertheless it was necessary.

"Now, the Witch will not always appear to you, which can simply mean that your job on that region is not complete or you do not need her help. You see, sometimes the Keeper will take a path that will automatically lead her to the next element, so the White Witch will not have to tell you where the next location is. Don't freak out if you don't see her. It just means you are already on the right course. She will let you know if you are not headed on the correct path."

Rosey nodded, jumbling the name White Witch around in her head as if looking it over. It was definitely an odd title, but no odder than the Golden Goddess.

"Secondly, I hope you will agree to have Wolvereen with you during your journey. He will not only serve as a guide but also as a protector. He knows much of this world and can help you find your way, not to mention that his status as the Golden Goddess's Commander of the Guard will permit you access to any Resistance Headquarters. Of course the Resistance knows of you and your identity but with the Minions around we are getting more and more careful. We still don't have full knowledge of them or how they work, however I'm sure we can at least keep them busy. Wolvereen will also guarantee your safety even amongst the most..," She stumbled over the right words for a moment then said, "…unusual of places."

Rosey nodded, remembering the huge black, red eyed wolf perfectly from the other day when he had led her so faithfully to the Golden Castle. She had seen the size of his long canines and the glint in his eyes was enough to make anyone stop and think twice about attacking. He would make a good asset to her Fellowship. "Rosey, there is one more thing. It is the main reason why I chose to talk with you today out in the garden rather than in my office."

Rosey raised an eyebrow in interest.

"One of the Resistances warriors and my loyal friend has asked to join you on your journey and I have gladly agreed. He's protected me many times and has proven himself through every challenge. His name is Eglen. He is an Eglagor: part dog, eagle, and horse. Eglagors are very loyal creatures, and, despite what you may think, he is not a Leron. There are many animals in our world that look like they are Leron but are, in fact, not. The main way to tell the difference is whether they are referred to by a species name. If they are not then it means they don't belong to a particular species because they are one of a kind. Leron are one of a kind creations. You never get the same looking Leron twice. They are all different. My companion is an Eglagor, thus, you know that he is not a Leron. He will make a good companion to you and a good member of your fellowship." Rosey nodded. "So…why do we need to be in the gardens?" she said reminding the Goddess of what she had said earlier.

"Well, every garden has a gardener and Eglagors do so love plant life. When he is not on duty, Eglen, and a few other warriors, prefer the more natural outdoors. However, it can take time to call them to the Castle to assign them to a mission, so I had this indoor garden built. It allows for a peaceful, natural environment, allowing many of my animal warriors to stay close by while remaining comfortable. Of course we couldn't allow the natural seasons to also take place in the palace so it is always spring here. The animal warriors don't mind too much since spring is a mutually loved season. Eglen was informed to meet me this afternoon. He should be here in a little while," she said glancing into the surrounding gardens.

While they waited Rosey glanced around and noticed that even though you could see the ceiling you couldn't see the walls or how far away they were. Large trees stood proud and strong amongst the budding flowers and extravagant fountains blocked much of the view. If Rosey couldn't see the long hole in the ceiling covered by the translucent fabric she never would have known she wasn't in a forest. The place could be huge for all she knew. Turning away from the ceiling and the surrounding gardens she got up from the bench and examined the fountain in the middle of the clearing they sat in. She noted the fine detail and craftsmanship. The image was that of various looking animals, some of which Rosey recognized. One was a griffon, another was what looked like a dragon, and there was possibly a chimera, the others were unfamiliar to her. All the figures were bursting out of the water in the pool as if they were about ready to land right in front of her. The leaping figures continued on around the fountain. As her eyes traced the lines of the proud heads and the magnificent level of detail that went into the artwork she hardly noticed the large creature that had joined her.

"Magnificent, isn't it?" the creature said in a kind male voice neither deep nor light.

"Yeah..," said Rosey still distracted. Then her eyes grew wide and she turned to her right to come face to face with a large eight foot tall animal that Rosey guessed was an Eglagor. He had the head of a dog but the body of a horse. Following the image of his massive body Rosey's eyes rested on his feet. Instead of four hooves he had eagle talons. Rosey gasped, he had a

The Mystics

brilliant blue roan body, with deep red stockings on his legs, and a gorgeous crimson mane and tail. Around his neck was what looked like a lion's mane that wrapped around the withers and shoulders and connected to the horse mane. It was the same red color.

He walked gracefully around till he was standing in front of her and bowed elegantly, "I am Eglen. Let me say it is an honor to be helping you Keeper."

He was so tall compared to her. He was even taller than the six foot tall wolves she had seen the other day. She forced her mouth to move and managed to say, "Thank you. I'm honored…to…to have you in my Fellowship."

Rosey looked upon the gorgeous creature glad that she had accepted his offer of assistance. Upon closer scrutiny she could see well sculpted muscles, sharp canines, and intimidating talons. He would be a fine addition indeed. "Hello Eglen, my old friend. How are you?" said the Goddess lifting herself effortlessly off the bench and gliding over to the huge creature to give him a big hug.

Eglen tilted his head downward and pushed her further toward him with his dog-like muzzle, the equivalent of a human returning a hug. Rosey smiled, warmed by their embrace. "Perfectly well, I came as soon as the irises would let me. They needed some extra tending." "Are they still giving you problems?" she said playfully not at all sounding surprised. "Oh it's nothing I can't handle," he winked at her, his withers quivering as she stroked his neck soothingly. The pair laughed for a few moments and Rosey felt oddly out of place. But once again she was doubting herself when she should have known she would never be forgotten, at least not on this world.

"Rosey do you accept Eglen's offer?" said the Goddess turning towards her. Rosey stared at Eglen, momentarily frozen, and then said, "How could I refuse, I'm going to need all the help I can get." The Goddess smiled and nodded, "Spoken like a true Keeper. Thank you Eglen, you may return to your irises."

Eglen bowed his large head and said, "Thank you my lady." Passing the Goddess he walked over to Rosey, "Young Keeper I look forward to our journey together next week." His eyes seemed to scrutinize her suddenly, but not as Wolvereen had done. It was almost as if he was searching for something, something that he had missed or expected. Rosey didn't know what to do, so she stood her ground. Finally he smiled with a slight rise of the lips then bowed quickly and took off at a steady trot down one of the paths. Rosey's eyes lingered where he had disappeared then she turned to the Goddess, "What does he mean 'next week'."

"I knew that your uncle had put you in Kendo classes and such because he kept in touch with me about your progress. Despite your apparent success at the practice I want to expand upon your knowledge of the art and teach you a little more, so I have planned extensive training sessions in the way of the sword for at least a week's time." Her gaze traveled down Rosey's small frame then rested on something at her hip. Smiling she said, "I noticed the other day that my sister had given you the dagger she made for you," she motioned to the long dagger at Rosey's side. "Do you like it?"

Rosey stared at it in surprise and realized that every time she had changed clothes she had always put the dagger back on, as if she had worn it her whole life. She felt strange without the dagger, and liked its constant company. It was strange to think that a dagger had that kind of effect on her but she couldn't deny that it had a special hold on her, though she wouldn't put it past that feeling to have originated from her current lack of defense. The dagger was her only way of fighting back besides some hand to hand combat, but she much preferred a sword or sharp pointy object to her blunt fists. She touched the hilt now, tracing the designs in the scabbard as she ran her hand along its surface.

"Yeah," she said, "I keep it with me all the time, it's like it's a part of me now..."

The Goddess smiled seemingly understanding what Rosey meant. Aloud she said, "I have a gift for you."

Turning she picked up a bundle that was lying hidden in some shrubs behind the bench. The bundle was long and thick looking, tied elegantly with blue leather and wrapped in golden and purple cloth. As soon as Rosey lay eyes on it a strange feeling crept into her chest making her feel a little wobbly. She steadied herself as the Goddess unwrapped the bundle, unaware of Rosey's imbalance. From the folds she pulled out a sword. Gently she drew the sword from its gold etched, light brown, leather scabbard. The sound was crisp, clear, and perfect. Rosey's heart hammered in her chest, a deep power surged from the sword, touching Rosey gently. All over, her body began to shake. Then the Goddess spoke.

"I'm not surprised to see the sword reacting to you. This, Rosey, was your mother's sword."

Rosey couldn't believe it, she knew her mother had been a great warrior, but she had never considered her a swordswoman. All she had heard about since coming here was the collection of the elements, training with a sword had been extra, an adage to the protection. It was never something that Rosey considered as being a main weapon, but looking upon her mother's gleaming sword, she was now no longer sure.

The sword was the most beautiful thing she had ever seen. It looked to her like a heavy bladed sword like the knights of the crusades would have carried except that the hilt was much more elaborate. At the center of the hilt right above the blade was the carving of a unipeg's head, with the wings making the cross guards, a small horn adorned the unipeg's head as if it was also a unicorn. Strange markings ran down the length of the blade in intricate patterns. The hilt had a golden sheen with the unipeg's wings having blue highlights. The sword's fuller was bright blue with a purple edge. The pommel formed a shooting star with an orange flame color at its middle, the long tail making the design down the golden grip and forming the mane of the unipeg's head. The point and edges of the blade were lightly dusted with golden flecks. Looking around at the back of the sword she saw the image of a woman decorating the hilt in the same place as the unipeg's head, her long black hair was lifted up, flowing to envelope the pummel. In the middle of the hair was the image of a white crystal. The woman's arms reached out to either side of her gripping the feathers of the wings of the unipeg that formed the cross guards. Once again, as in front, the sword's fuller was blue with the purple edge and at the sword's tip were golden flecks. The woman's head was lifted up as if in a deep sleep, her eyes gently closed. Rosey found herself utterly perplexed as she realized that the woman represented the Keepers, but who was the unipeg? As if she could read Rosey's thoughts the Goddess answered her.

"I'm sure you know that the woman is the Keeper, the unipeg, however, is Adina. She is a unipeg, both unicorn and pegasus, the only one of her kind as far as we know. Esperanza had this sword specifically made for her so as to represent who she was fighting for and the power that she held as the Keeper, although we're unsure of who made it. All we know is that she had it commissioned but that's the extent of our knowledge. I know it would be her wish to see you wield it and succeed where she did not. It is yours."

She held the sword out to Rosey who stared at it unsure of what to do. Then slowly she reached out and gripped the hilt. An electric shock ran through her body like lightning. She held the sword to her forehead and heard a name whispered on the wind around her.

"What was that…" she listened closer, "Ah, Andraste…is that your name." she said holding the sword at arm's length, studying its hilt.

The Goddess stared at her in wonder, amazed that she had heard the name of the sword, there was just no end to the power of the Keepers. Aloud she said, "Yes, that is its name, its Celtic for unconquerable. Your mother took a liking to the Celtic culture of Earth and named it that."

The Mystics

"Is it really…unconquerable?" said Rosey, still studying the blade.

"I believe so, your mother never lost a battle with that sword. Swords and other objects usually take to their names quite literally, Andraste is no exception. I only wish that your mother had drawn it when she was attacked by the fellowship member. She may still be alive, but she would never draw her sword against a friend."

The Goddess looked down, lost in thought.

"Andraste isn't meant for spilling innocent blood," said Rosey, matter-of factly.

The Goddess looked at her sharply in surprise, once again taken aback by the strange effect this sword was having on Rosey. Rosey herself seemed to realize what she had just said and looked at the Goddess in wonder.

"Sorry, don't know where that came from."

"Don't be sorry, your bond with Andraste will only make your swordsmanship better, faster, and stronger. The stronger the bond the better," she said giving Rosey a small smile, "Here is the scabbard, wear it proudly."

Rosey accepted the scabbard and sheathed Andraste, the sound of the metal against the brown leather made a clear ringing sound that reverberated in the silence. Rosey wanted to hum to the sound. She then noticed that the belt attached to the scabbard was longer and thicker than would be required for a belt. She wasn't supposed to wear Andraste at the belt but on her back. She quickly looped the belt around her and over her right shoulder, as she was right handed. She buckled it in place. A smaller buckle looped under her right arm at her waist and looped around to connect in the back, so that the belt wouldn't slip along her back but be held in place. She had never carried a sword this way but thought she liked the feel of it. Looking at the Goddess, she saw the hard face of the woman soften and knew that she was seeing Esperanza standing before her instead of Rosey. Rosey squirmed self-consciously under the Goddess's golden eyes, but understood that it must be just as hard for the Goddess as it was for her. She was Esperanza's daughter after all; she probably looked just like her.

The Goddess shook her head and broke free from whatever vision had distracted her. "All right then, you will stay here for the next week and reestablish those sword skills and, hopefully, add to them. At the same time I want you to learn as much as you can about this world. My library is open to you at all times and I advise that you go there to study for at least three hours each day, or whatever fits your fancy. I know this is a lot to expect in only a week, but a week is all we can afford to give at this moment." She paused and considered, "Well Rosey, that seems to be all I have for you right now, you will certainly have more questions later on and I'd be happy to answer them for you. Do you have any other questions at the moment?"

"Just one last one," Rosey said, "It was something my Uncle said before we left for…here."

The Goddess's brows furrowed, her golden eyes watched Rosey quietly.

"He said that there were others that had sensed the crystal's awakening. Did the Evil One ever know I was…on Earth? Did it ever know I even existed?"

The Goddess was silent for a few moments, her eyes seemed to be looking everywhere but at Rosey. Finally she spoke, "Originally, we believed that we had hid Esperanza's pregnancy well enough that it was unaware of your birth. However, after what happened…we are unsure. We can only assume that if it did know you were alive then why did it not go after you sooner? Perhaps it had planned on killing you right after it took your mother but hadn't expected whatever she did to stop it so well? Perhaps we may have moved you in just enough time to protect you or keep you hidden? Perhaps all this time it's been planning on what to do when you returned? I don't know." The Goddess closed her eyes for a moment, lost in thought.

Rosey said nothing. She was amazed by the Goddess's words but not surprised. Either the Evil One had always known she was there and had

The Mystics

been preparing for her, or it hadn't and had been preparing its final assault...but for seventeen years!? Would it have really taken it that long to come up with a conquering plan? Rosey could almost hear the Goddess's voice in her head going 'perhaps', after all, trapped in its home, the Hell Ship, and located in outer space the beast's options were probably quite limited. Rosey shook her head, the particulars didn't matter. What mattered now was destroying the Evil One before it could make any more plans.

The Goddess suddenly gasped, drawing Rosey's attention. "I almost forgot. I overheard during dinner last night that you had to leave behind the precious image of your mother and father with John, so..." she reached into her pocket and pulled out a long silver chain with a round clasp at the end, "I had this made for you." She held it out and Rosey took it.

Rosey flipped it over in her hands and found a small latch on one end. Gently pushing, it unhooked and opened up to reveal two images. One was of her mother on the inside clasp, while the other was of her father. It was an oval silver locket. Rosey felt her throat thicken with sadness and gratitude. Her eyes watered as she studied the happy face of her mother and the handsome features of her father. She held the necklace close and then placed it in her pocket. She looked at the Goddess and thanked her with a soft voice. The Goddess bowed her head, but said nothing of it.

The Goddess then straightened and said, "Now I hate to run, but I have business to attend to. You can continue exploring the palace if you like, but training starts tomorrow at noon. Nashi will come for you. To find your way out of these gardens simply follow the signs. Goodbye and have a splendid day." With a quick snap of her fingers and a wink she was gone, leaving behind a shimmering firework display of golden sparkles.

Rosey stared at the spot where the Goddess had been, surprised by her sudden departure. Then, just to be sure, she reached out and felt the air around the area where the Goddess had been standing. When her hand touched nothing, Rosey straightened in awe. Was there nothing they couldn't do on this world? Shaking her head Rosey shifted her weight to her right leg, her thoughts reeling. For some reason, she had the funniest feeling that the Goddess was running away from her and whatever memories she had stirred.

Rosey chose not to stay in the gardens. After everything the Goddess had told her she needed to take a walk. She had found that walking always worked best for clearing one's head of thoughts, doubts, and questions. The simple feeling of motion was an invaluable medicine to the body.

She followed the signs and found her way back easily enough. She made her way around the castle exploring it and letting her mind wander until she ran into Alex, Rochell, Noly, and Hazel. She quickly informed them of what the Goddess had told her about Wolvereen, Eglen, and the sword training and proudly introduced them to Andraste which sent Alex into an information overload. He immediately started explaining to her everything he knew about the sword and its legendary battles with her mother, this time Rosey was more than happy to let him carry on.

When Alex stopped long enough to replenish the oxygen supply that he was surely missing by now, Rochell chirped in, "We'll practice too, Rosey! Alex and I both! We'll show you how we use our powers and we'll help you when you get the elements," she said giving Rosey her large grin.

Alex nodded in agreement, "You can count me in."

Rochell grabbed a hold of Rosey's arm in mock horror, "Not being able to tell you everything all this time has been total torture. You can't image how hard it's been to keep my mouth shut. It's such a relief to have everything out in the open after all this time, especially for me."

"Yeah," Alex said, giving Rochell a hard stare, "I can't tell you how many times I had to kick her under the table whenever she was about to blurt something out. She's living proof that conditioning works, after some time all I had to do was twitch my leg and she'd stop."

Rochell almost hissed at him, "Say that again and I'll make you float off somewhere for three days."

The Mystics

Seeing her two friends start bickering again as they normally did made Rosey smile. It had been nice to see them on the same side when they'd brought her here, sticking together to help comfort her, but even now they still found time to pick at each other. It was their favorite pass time on Earth, like brother and sister. The familiarity of their squabbles was comforting and Rosey felt warmth spread throughout her body. She smiled at them. Suddenly finding her voice she said, "Thanks guys."

The two stopped immediately and their heated but friendly exchange melted away in a heartbeat. Alex put his hand on her shoulder comfortingly. Rochell once again gave her that large grin she was famous for, while Noly and Hazel rubbed up against her encouragingly. Rosey may not know what this new world had in store for her but she was sure she could do it as long as her friends were there with her.

Chapter Eleven: The Silver Goddess Calls

During the next week Rosey was schooled in the art of the sword. As she had told the Goddess, she had some training with a sword from her Kendo and Iaido classes, but nothing as lethal or vigorous as real life fighting. The Goddess did not take it easy on her and Rosey had the bruises to prove it, but she caught on quickly. The Goddess adapted Rosey's knowledge of Kendo and Iaido to the more brutal form of sword play that Rosey thought would have been practiced in the days of King Arthur. The lessons, though tough, were not too different from her classes so she soon began to get back into the feel of wielding a blade. It helped that her connection with Andraste was growing stronger; the magnificent sword was becoming more and more a part of her every day. By the end of the week it was no longer just an object but an extension of her, body and mind.

She had also done some work with Silver Knight. The Goddess had even shown her how to wield Andraste with one hand and then spring a surprise attack with Silver Knight in the other. Rosey's confidence was getting better, and soon she was matching the Goddess step for step as they dueled. Rosey thought that her quick learning may have been contributed more to Andraste than herself. The sword spoke to her in ways that Rosey alone seemed to understand. When she lifted, struck, or blocked with the blade some part of her mind was imagining her mother doing the same thing. This image made her stronger, more focused, and determined. Rosey felt confident she could be a formidable opponent to anyone willing to engage her.

During this time her friends had also taken the opportunity to show her what they were capable of. She had only needed to see their powers in action once to have a newfound respect for the power in Alex's wand and Rochell's fists. Though Alex was particularly impressive with his vast knowledge of words, signs, and spells she watched more carefully as Rochell moved her body while controlling her element: air. As Rosey saw it, it was like dancing with someone, except that someone was your element. It was fascinating to watch but Rosey didn't take it lightly, she saw the sweat on her friend's brow and the strain of her muscles. This was definitely hard work and she had every intention of practicing to perfect her own skills.

The whole week wasn't just spent practicing with her sword it was also spent on elemental techniques, lectures, lessons, and practice. Much of that practice centered on trying to awake Rosey's own element. Like everyone else, Rosey had an element, but to her surprise and worry she was unable to connect to it. No matter how hard she tried, how long she meditated, or how many different techniques Rochell and various others made her go through, Rosey was unable to find her element. She knew, from her talk with the Golden Goddess, that there was a chance that her time on Earth might have affected her own natural element but Rosey had been assured that that wouldn't be too much of a problem. Of course she hadn't been on The World Within A World for that long and it might just take a while for her element to awaken, still, it bothered Rosey. According to everyone around her, she should have at least started sensing something as soon as she had stepped into The World Within A World. So far, Rosey had felt nothing, not even the slightest twinge of the presence of an element and because of that it was hard for Rosey to know what to look for when Rochell was training her. It was like trying to teach mathematics to a baby, Rosey had no experiences or feelings to pull from so she couldn't understand what Rochell was talking about. Despite her fears she was still determined to try. However, it soon became apparent that Rosey's element was not going to show itself, at least not yet. The realization was disheartening and Rosey knew that it was also quite unusual, but what could she do? She couldn't use something that wasn't showing itself. Rochell had tried to reassure her that because she had been raised on Earth it was just going to take a while for her element to come forth, and, that in time, it would awaken. Rosey took her assurances with thanks but she couldn't shake the feeling of apprehension in her gut. Not having her own element to control meant that her only defense would be her fellowship and her own skill with her trusty sword and long dagger. It put Rosey in a more dangerous position until she received the first element in order to defend herself, before that she would have to rely on her skill alone and that scared her.

To distract Rosey from the fact that her element wasn't appearing, the Goddess had stepped up Rosey's training regimens, training her longer, harder, and faster so that her sword strengths would be spot on. Since it was the only form of defense she had at the moment, she would have to make do with it. She even had Rosey train with her non-dominant left arm. She'd do one technique and then have to repeat it back using the opposite hand and weapon, it was jarring work but Rosey had held in, determined to master it.

Just to be sure that Rosey was getting the best sword training the Goddess had brought in one of the finest swordsmen in the world called Durag. He had been a tall man with a strong upper body who hefted a sword that looked thicker than his arms. Rosey had thought the Goddess was crazy for matching him with her, but when they started to spar Rosey was amazed at how well she had been able to keep up with him. As the swordsmanship training continued, Rosey's connection with Andraste deepened. Over time she began to wonder if it was this connection she had with the sword that the Goddess had wanted to test and strengthen rather than Rosey's skill. Nevertheless she kept at it, every morning and every night.

The sword was not the only weapon Rosey was trained in, she also had some schooling in archery. It wasn't her favorite weapon, mostly because no matter what she did or how hard she tried aiming the tiny, arrow-shaped rock head at a target far away it never seemed to go very well. In fact she appeared to only be able to hit everything around the target and not the target itself. Archery, unlike the sword, was a much more difficult skill to learn and took years not days. Neither her archery teacher, Fania, nor the Golden Goddess had expected Rosey to become skilled in the bow and arrow in just a week. Rosey agreed to continue practicing but she knew with almost certainty that the light and airy bow and arrow was not her kind of weapon. Her uncle had tried once to get her into archery but it had been one extracurricular activity that she had adamantly said no too. It had just never been her thing. She found herself wishing that she'd agreed, maybe then, like the sword, she'd have been a little more prepared for the training. However, she did far better with a heavy sword made of finely sharpened metal, as robust as the fire it was forged from, than a tiny stick on a tightly drawn line. Besides, she was pretty certain, once she received the fire element, that if she continued trying to learn archery she might just accidentally set the bow on fire.

Much of the week passed by in training and learning but Rosey's elemental power wasn't the only thing that interested her. Magic was also a topic of high interest. She had been told plenty about the elements but magic was not of much importance since Rosey, being a Keeper, did not have the talent for magic. However, she wanted to know as much as she could about magic since she would be around not only elementals but magikins as well. Plus it gave her more distraction from the fact that she was unable to use her element.

On the third day of the week after a particularly hard sword lesson with both the Goddess and the master swordsman, Durag, she had showered then tracked down Alex and asked if he would tell her about magic. She didn't want the whole philosophy behind it, she just wanted to understand how it worked and its relationship with the elements. He had been only too happy to tell her about his abilities and so had sat her down in one of the common rooms where the four statues of Adina, for they *were* Adina, stood proud and tall in all four corners and books lined the wall with their treasure troves of knowledge. As they settled down in the room on a long red couch, a servant brought them a tray of refreshments and sandwiches which they had greedily consumed.

Alex had wasted no time. He told her that magic was indeed a separate entity from the planet, however, it was still governed by the Energy Flows. The Energy Flows of each planet governed everything that existed on that planet including the stuff that wasn't a natural part of the planet. If the Energy Flows of The World Within A World didn't include magic in their laws then they could just as easily attack magic and destroy it, vanquishing its existence from the world. Thankfully, the Energy Flows included magic in its laws and thus it could be used.

Magic, he had said, was controlled by using spells spoken in the Fracture Language which keeps the power of magic from taking a hold of its master or running amuck. The Golden Goddess had never mentioned this language but, then again, they hadn't talked extensively about magic. According to Alex the discovery of this language and how it was created was only thanks to the Book of Magic. Like many other books it was one of the few that had survived the supernova in a small library that had been on the asteroid that Adina had salvaged. It had been written by a magikin called Elorina Dorsava. From this book they had learned of how the fracture language was discovered. Apparently, the language was created long ago by a few people who had discovered that their world had magic running wild all over it. Magic, unlike what most people thought, was a form of mineral gas or energy. It floated around the atmosphere, invisible to the eye but capable of being used. It required no energy on the part of the magikin. It just needed a command to follow. The larger and more complex the spell the more magic would be needed to achieve the result. Having studied magic extensively and finding all its flaws they then started searching for ways to use it and soon discovered the Fracture Language. All one had to do was recite words where the alphabet was backwards. Z would stand for A and Y would stand in for B and so on. In this way alone, magic would react and do as it was told. The language was simply the alphabet backwards and because of this they called it the Fracture Language. Rosey didn't know why but she had thought this to be funny and laughed pretty hard. Alex told her it was the strangest thing they had ever discovered. Of course it was the Angensilian alphabet that was backwards not the English alphabet. Thanks to the information that had been given to Rosey when she was an infant she knew the Angensilian alphabet as well as the English one, they were basically the same except for a few letters.

Despite how well the fracture language worked, it was also what made controlling magic hard. You were basically speaking backwards where every letter you spoke was actually in relation to another. Alex had said that unlike elements, magic was much harder to control because it was a free power that wasn't a part of living things like the elements. A living creature was always born with an element but they were not always born with the ability to work magic. That was why Magikins needed spells to control their magic; otherwise the dangers could be unspeakable.

"There are four different types of elementals and magikins," he had said, holding up four fingers. "There is a person who is just an elemental and they have no other ability than their element. Then there is just a magikin, someone who is born with a magical ability but their element is potential. A potential element is an elemental ability that never activated and never will. Remember, everyone is born with an element but they are not always born with the ability to work magic. In this case, the person is born with their element like normal, but that element is unable to be used, leaving them with only one option: their magical ability..."

Before he had been able to go on, Rosey had jumped forward, sudden fear filling her heart, "Is that why I can't find my element? Am I potential?"

Alex had immediately consoled her, "No, it is impossible for the Keeper to be a potential elemental because if you were then the other elements, even if they are in the Shanobie Crystal, would have to abide by the rules of your body and be unusable. Basically, if you are a potential user, then you must stay a potential user no matter what and no special potent element is going to change that. Besides the Shanobie Crystal would never choose someone who was potential. It knows that if it did then its potent elements would also have to be potential and what good would that do?"

Rosey had been relieved to learn that her powers weren't potential but she had also been unbalanced by it. What was wrong with her then? At least if she was potential then she had a reason for why her powers weren't working. She was still unable to use them and did not know why. It was like being sick without knowing what you were sick with. Rosey had swallowed hard and listened as Alex continued.

"The next type is someone who is just a potential elemental, a person who is born with their element, like normal, but it is potential and they have no other power what so ever. The last and very rare type of person is someone who is born with both a working element, which just means that they are not potential, and the ability to use magic. I am one of those rare people, Rosey. When you have both the talent for magic as well as an element you must decide on which you wish to pursue for you cannot be both and I, of course, chose magic."

Rosey had been astonished to hear this and her respect for Alex's power grew even more. She had asked Alex why he had chosen to be a magikin and not an elemental. He told her that from the very beginning he had chosen to become a magikin mostly because his family was a magically influenced family just as Rosey's had been elementally influenced. It was in his blood. His parents had given him the option of course, for he had been one of the few in his family who had a working element as well as a magical talent, but in the end he chose magic. He had no idea what his element was, nor what level he was. Since he had chosen to abandon his elemental powers, he cared not for what they were. When he had told her this he hastily explained that once a magikin became a magikin there was no going back, the training was entirely different from that associated with the elements and the relationship was much more complicated than it was with elements. Simply put: a magikin could never become an elemental and an elemental could never become a magikin, the relationships were just too different. When he'd told her this, he then frowned, a look of curiosity touching his face. He went on to say that he had often wondered what his element was and what he would have been had he chosen differently but, in the case of most magikins, it was better not to know their element. The knowledge would tempt them to use their element and the magical ability they had learned would then fight against them.

"It's like you have entered into a contract. Once you make that decision there's no going back and if you try," he had said, shrugging, "you could end up losing your magical ability forever."

That had stopped Rosey in her tracks, "Does this work both ways?"

Alex had nodded, "If an elemental who has the talent for magic chooses their element over their magic and then tries to use magic, they could lose their elemental power and become a potential user instead."

Rosey had shaken her head, flabbergasted, "Why?"

"Because, the two powers are just too different, one cannot exist while the other is around. Your initial decision determines which one will be on the chopping block should you be tempted. So, I prefer not to know."

Rosey had continued, determined, "But…how can you protect an innocent child from making that mistake and accidentally cause themselves to lose one of their abilities? How do you know what power they have?"

Alex had leaned forward and taken a sip of his tea before answering, "When you are born here, your birth is overseen not by a midwife but by a healer. That healer will immediately assess the child and report on what powers they have and don't have, like the doctors at a hospital running a full checkup on a newborn baby, it's the same thing. The parents are then required to be sure to keep their child aware of their abilities as well as mentor them well. It also helps that for the first ten years of your life, your powers are useless,"

Rosey had looked at him startled, then her eyes had brightened with understanding, "By that time their parents have diligently explained to them what they need to know and they are old enough to make a decision."

Alex had nodded, "Just as my parents had done with me to insure I knew what decision I was making."

Rosey had thought about what he had told her, both amazed and unbalanced by it. She had felt sorry for the ones who were potential, they wouldn't have the chance to know their element, but Alex told her not to feel too bad for them. He told her that some potential people had heightened senses or talents not related to the elements or magic. These talents could be any number of things like psychic abilities, talking to and sensing spirits, and seeing visions. Earth was known for having a large amount of these gifted people, but it was more likely that their abilities stemmed from heightened brain activity due to years of technological innovations and adaptions rather than some secret potential elemental power, though, anything was possible.

He next told her how magic worked and how one started to use magic. A young magikin would be sent to a magikin school around the age of ten, when their powers would start to activate. They would then spend most of their first two years learning, studying, and reciting phrases and words of the fracture language under their instructor's watchful eye. They'd learn spells but they'd be unable to use those spells until they'd fashioned their own wands, and they wouldn't make a wand until they had earned a mentor. Their mentors would take over their training at the age of twelve or thirteen once their schooling was complete. During that time the mentor would train them until they pronounced them ready to create their wand. The creation of a wand was said to be the halfway point to becoming a full-fledged Magikin. Once the mentor determined that they were ready a young magikin would be given a branch from a tree or plant. They would then recite the spell and wait in intense meditation as the stick transformed into their wand. The process could take hours or minutes depending on the magikin. Alex's wand had taken him three hours to finish. The longest that a wand had ever taken to complete was by the writer of the Book of Magic herself, Elorina Dorsava. According to her author's note she had taken a day and a half to make her wand, a truly fascinating feat.

When a magikin took on a mentor none of the student's parents, guardians, or teachers were allowed to assist them or interact with them in any magical way except if their life, or other lives, were threatened. It was the student's duty, from the moment they met their mentor, to train on their own and figure out answers to their own problems. Each mentor was different and trained their student differently. Some required them to live away from home for a number of years. Others required them to take on various tasks or go to various places and solve problems. Each mentor was different because each student was different and learned differently. The apprentice magikin would contain their mentor within their bodies until the mentor determined that they were finished and had been taught everything they needed to know. Thera, Alex's mentor, was inside of him now and he was fast approaching his initiation as a true magikin. Alex, however, wouldn't know what level he was until his mentor Thera had deemed him worthy to be a fully-fledged magikin. It was only at the successful completion of his training that his mentor would tell him his level. Then his true powers would be revealed.

Alex had met Thera the way all the magikin apprentices did, one day she just appeared. Traditionally, there is no prior meeting for a magikin mentor and their apprentice. When the apprentice turns twelve or thirteen, depending on their power level, a mentor comes for them and that is all there is to it. No one really knows how these mentors are aware of when and where they are needed or even how the decision is made as to which apprentice gets which mentor but it always turns out to be the right pairing so no one questions it. Rosey had thought this to be fascinating. The idea that the relationship between a mentor and a student could be so powerful that it was enough to combine the two organisms together and leave behind no after effects was more mindboggling than finding out her animals could talk, and to think that your mentor would just come to you all of a sudden. In a way it had made Rosey a little jealous, being an elemental. Elementals could have mentors too to teach them, but usually their mentors where family members not an unusual creature specifically chosen to train you by a mysterious being. But she couldn't complain, she wasn't a normal elemental after all, she was the Keeper. And besides, she probably would have preferred being taught by a family member instead of some stranger.

A magikin's wand was everything. Without a wand a magikin was defenseless. Wands worked by drawing magic to their tip from around the area. Magic was everywhere, it was just like air, even though you couldn't see it, it was still there. The wand would draw the magic to it then release the magic when a spell was spoken. The magic would do the rest. As long as there was magic around a magikin could cast as many spells as they wanted. Rarely did a fight or battle last long enough to use up all the magic in one given area, but if it did, then the magikin would have to resort to physical attacks instead of their magical ones which was why most magikins also carried a sword or a dagger. Once the magic was used up in the area, it would eventually come back. It was a lot like a battery, once the battery was all used up, it would have to be recharged. Magic was the same. When all the magic was used up in a specific area, it would take some time for it to 'recharge' itself or replenish its supply. That could take anywhere from days to years depending on how much was used for a spell and how effective the area was at replenishing the magic. Magic, like all energy, is neither created nor destroyed, so the amount they had on their planet now would always be...unless another supernova happened or something dramatic like that.

Alex told her about his mentor, Thera. She was a tough teacher and a Leron, which meant that she had no particular species, so unless Rosey saw her there was no way for her to identify her. Thera was inside him now for he had long since passed her test and was in the final stages of his training. He told Rosey this with confidence and pride. Alex's pride wasn't of the boasting kind, it was far more humble and understanding, a feature that Rosey liked in Alex. If what he said was correct, and she had no doubt it was, then Thera had been in him for about three years now. The idea had shaken Rosey to the core with amazement.

"Learning magic can be a pain in the butt if you don't have patience," He had said. "It's like math, some people are good at it and some aren't which can also help to determine their level."

Rosey had remembered how the Goddess told her that magikins could raise their levels based on what they learned and the spells they knew. Someone who was better at it was a higher level and someone who wasn't as good was a lower level. Magic wasn't a part of the person like the elements were so not everyone had a chance to be a magikin. You had to be born with the talent to use it, but that didn't mean that you were going to be a strong magikin. It took a great amount of skill, time, and discipline to learn how to use it correctly and even then there was no guarantee.

Alex had then told her that most people who became magikins were potential elementals. They were people who had a magical talent but their element was unusable and so they went with magic. They didn't have to choose magic if they didn't want to. There were also many of them who decided not to pursue their magical ability despite the fact that they were potential, leaving them dependent on weaponry. The reason why was simple: magic was hard to control and there was no guarantee what kind of talent you might have. Magic was freer, wilder, and spirited, not as connected to mortal creatures, making it hard to control and unpredictable. For that reason many decided to ignore their magical talent, however some didn't and pursued it. In Alex's case, where he had to choose between his element and his magic, he had made the most uncommon choice of going with magic. Most people, if given the option between their magic and their element would always go for their element because it was the easiest to learn, control, and use. Because of this, elementals far outnumbered magikins. Alex had told her this with a noticeable look of sadness. Rosey could tell Alex had a lot of pride as a magikin, but it was like being a part of a dying fad or species. Rosey had understood, she had witnessed Alex's hard practice sessions many times and so respected the great power it took to control such unstable energy as magic. She was happy that she would never have to know what it was like.

"Another reason why some people chose not to be magikins is this whole Mage business." Alex said, shaking his head as if annoyed, "The Goddess told you about the fact that our world, since the supernova, has never had a Mage level, right?"

Rosey had nodded and he said, "Well, this often frightens some people away from magic. They think that it is a dying ability. We have plenty of elementals at all the three levels but not a Mage level in the magikin area. The Goddesses are the only ones considered anywhere near the Mage level and that's only because their power is so great, yet they are not Mages, they are more like upper level Goddess levels. The fact is that, they are Goddess levels when really they should be Mage levels. It's like there is some kind of…thing that is preventing magikins from getting any higher in their level than God or Goddess. The Goddesses think that the reason behind this is because our planet has a limited amount of magic on it, less than what it had before the supernova, and so is unable to support a Mage level magikin's power. They believe the supernova blasted a large chunk of our magic into space, scattered like leaves. We *were* only an asteroid, after all. I don't know…it seems logical…" he had faltered in his speech and looked down, lost in thought. Rosey had seen this happen many times when Alex thought about things, but never like this. He had seemed down and deeply saddened. It clearly pained him that the magikin power was so weak and that no one seemed to really know why. It broke Rosey's heart but there was nothing she could do for him but distract him with another question.

The Mystics

Hearing about the Fracture Language made Rosey come to another question. Did everyone on their world speak the same language? Since Rosey only had one different language in her noggin she had been pretty sure that the answer was yes, otherwise she would know them too. Of course, she could and she just didn't know it yet because she had only met people who spoke the Angensilian language, but she wanted to be sure.

Alex had shaken his head and said, "No other language is spoken here besides the Angensilian Language. When the supernova took our world it took a lot of our information and memories including a lot about our language but, if you remember, the asteroid also contained buildings and houses. One of those was a small library, the same library, in fact, where we found the Book of Magic. Using the library we were able to piece together the Angensilian language and the Book of Magic helped as well. We had different people from all over the world around us, and we couldn't rebuild and work together if we tried learning thirty different languages, so we agreed on one language and rebuilt our world with that language. Besides, most of the various people's memories were so bad with their original language that they opted for a new, simpler one. I do believe that, for a while, we all communicated by means of charades but we got by all right."

They had laughed over that for a few moments before Rosey had asked her last question, "Why do you call yourselves magikins instead of magicians?"

Alex had regarded her knowingly, "Aw, yes, well, as you may have guessed, that is one of the many words that we adopted from Earth. The name for magic wielders, like myself and others, was lost to us and the book's name for them was unknown in any language or pronounceable, strangely enough." His brows had furrowed in confusion at this as it often did when talking about things that they had lost. Rosey could only image what that was like. "When we heard the word on Earth we liked it, but," his gaze had hardened then with pride, "we did not like the notion of a magician being a trickster, so we changed the spelling a bit and the sound to make it our own, just as we did with the Falosaraptors."

Rosey had nodded. It made sense. After all, the magic here was real and did real things, on Earth, magic was a trick or sleight of hand played by a cunning man or woman with a flashy hand but goodness in their hearts for they certainly didn't mean to disappoint anyone. It didn't seem right to be named after someone that played harmless, entertaining tricks when the magic wielded on The World Within A World could never be called a trick. It was real, solid, and deadly.

Rosey had gone to bed that night pondering over all that she had heard, amazed and, at the same time, worried. The idea that her powers could be potential frightened her, despite Alex's assurances that they definitely weren't. She hadn't had much time to dwell over it though for she had soon found herself continuously at work. If it wasn't one practice move or study session concerning strategy then it was another that kept her mind geared and her body sharp. However, each day wasn't just spent in swordsmanship. Even though Rosey couldn't use her element it didn't mean that she would stop her training on how best to use them. Other elementals were brought in to perform before Rosey and show her what each element was capable of. During the first session she had seen, a thought had crossed Rosey's mind. She and the Golden Goddess had been sitting on the benches overlooking the practice arena where a water elemental and an earth elemental were sparring. Rochell was sitting next to Rosey pointing out various techniques as if she were critiquing a piece of art. When the elementals had taken a break from their demonstrations and the excited brunette had stopped in her long monologue, Rosey had turned to the Goddess and said, "Am I going to need a mentor for each of my elements?"

The Goddess had smiled almost with embarrassment, "You would think so wouldn't you, but no. Magikins must have a mentor because there is little room for error when working with magic. The wrong spell or the wrong word could end in disaster; however, an elemental does not require a mentor."

Rosey had stared at the tall woman in surprise, "They don't!?"

"No, since an element is a natural part of a person's biological makeup it is often times left up to them to discover the best techniques for their elemental powers. Just as different authors use different methods to create a storyline or different mathematicians use different formulas to reach the same outcome. That doesn't mean that some elementals don't acquire mentors, especially if they want to learn more advanced techniques at an earlier age. Most elementals are taught by their parents or a guardian of the same element but a mentor, no matter who they are, does not have to have the same element as their student, which is why it is okay for Rochell to be teaching you."

"Wouldn't it be easier though if they were the same element?"

"It can be, but like I said before, not all elementals use the same techniques to reach the same outcomes. What may be an alien concept to me may be music to your ears."

Seeing that Rosey still did not look convinced, the Goddess then said, "Consider a child that has a water element. Their mentor, no matter what element, will teach them the basics. Can they create a ball of water, levitate it, and then toss it at a target? Can they change the water into different states of matter: gas, liquid, solid? These are basic techniques for all elementals to learn. There's more but the list is too long to convey in one sitting. Any elemental, no matter what element, can teach you the basics. It is then up to you to discover what you can do with them. You'd be surprised how quickly you can catch on. Besides," she had said, glancing back towards the arena, "there is not a single mentor we could assign to the Keeper, Rosey. Your potent elements would easily overpower the mentor in minutes. Your elements are just too powerful." She had turned towards Rosey and stared at her with an eerie intensity. Rosey had squirmed in her seat. "The basics, Rosey, will not even be the slightest bit of a challenge for you. Rochell, though she is of air, will be more than adequate enough to teach you everything you need to know."

"I have one other question. You said that the Evil One had to create portals on the Hell Ship in order to send down its Raptors and then you said that my mother may have sealed the portals to Earth to protect me. I guess what I want to know is if portals are magically or elementally controlled or created?"

The Goddess had smiled, "That is a little more difficult. Portals are both. They can occur naturally in our world but they can also be created artificially by magikins. Your friends told you that the portal you came through to this world was created by me, did they not?" Rosey nodded and she continued, "Well, only a small portion of magikins can make a portal. To uphold an artificial portal takes energy. Once a magikin creates that portal they must either close it so that it doesn't kill them by drawing on their energy or feed it a constant supply of energy or magic to keep it going. Rarely does a magikin create a portal because of how risky it can be, but some do, as I did to insure your safety. When the portal I made isn't being used I close it, even now it is closed waiting till it will be useful. As far as anyone knows, and this is also confirmed in what little information we were able to dredge up from our remaining library after the supernova, no elemental can or has ever created a portal. However, it is said that earth elementals can communicate with existing portals, both magically created and naturally created. Some speculate that, if they are strong enough, an earth elemental can even close and open them at will. We think that this is how your mother affected all the portals when she died for she was an earth elemental, but we are still unsure."

"But, how did the Evil One create a portal then? Does it have a magical ability?"

The Goddess had grown very still upon hearing this, as if the question had weighed heavily on her shoulders. "We don't know, there are some creatures that can create portals naturally, and then there is another group

The Mystics

that can create what we call vortexes. Vortexes are basically portals except that they are…portable…sorry I couldn't help it," the Goddess had said snickering, her happiness returning in those brief seconds. Rosey had nodded and laughed despite herself, "Anyway, portals have one rule: they cannot be moved. Magically created portals are artificial and so can be moved and destroyed at will by whoever created them, but naturally occurring portals are there to stay, though there is speculation that an earth elemental can move them," she shook her head as she thought about it, "A vortex can be moved and is much easier to create and takes less energy but you have to have the ability to do it. Some magikins can conjure one up but some can't, and some can make both portals and vortexes, it all just depends. Since the Evil One has been able to connect with portals and create its own, we have assumed that it has the natural ability to do so, maybe more so than a magikin does, but that is not a definite answer. There could be any number of reasons as to why the Evil One was able to create its own portals but we just don't know enough about it to give a definitive answer."

The elementals had started their match again, refreshed and ready to perform some more demonstrations. Rosey had sat there for a long moment going over everything the Goddess had said in her mind. She had watched the match mesmerized by the dancing figures that dueled before her. She was taken aback by their power and tried to memorize each technique and movement. To Rosey, their duel had looked a lot like a dance. Every movement of their body was significant to making their element react in a certain way. Still, what the Goddess had said scared her, just how powerful was she and just what kind of power did this Evil One have?

Seeing the practice session had worried Rosey because it reminded her of her own missing elemental power. Rochell tried her best to console her but the longer the element eluded her, the more worried Rosey was.

"Being raised on Earth seems to have indeed affected your element as we feared, but every person is different. You may yet discover your element later on when you are surer of your elemental strengths," Rochell had said one day after a particularly hard practice run. Rosey had made it a habit to practice the fighting moves with Rochell so when she received the elements she would have some knowledge of how to use them, plus the training was helping her body in strength and stamina. "I wouldn't worry too much, just don't give up on it. Your element will show itself sooner or later."

Rosey was grateful for Rochell's assurances but remained unsure. How was she to be a good elemental if she couldn't even awaken her own element? She took comfort in knowing that she was at least skilled with Andraste and Silver Knight. The Goddess made a habit of telling her and so did her sword master Durag.

Sword play, magic, and elements were the more physical aspects of her training, the rest was mental. As the Goddess had advised her to do, she spent much of her time in the large library where she had been introduced to the head librarian, a rather large, beautiful jaguar-looking creature with blue spots and a white body called Jasira. Jasira showed Rosey specific books of the Goddess's choosing on camping, hunting, cooking, and other basic survival needs. Books on wildlife, geological regions and climate were also some that Rosey skimmed through. The Goddess understood completely that Rosey would not be able to memorize everything and had no expectations of Rosey doing so, but she thought it best that Rosey become a little familiar with this world before she began her journey. After all, there would be no telling how long it would take Rosey to complete that very journey.

To Rosey's delight Jasira also showed Rosey were the journals written about her various family members were being kept in case she ever wanted to look. Though Rosey was thrilled to know where to find them she still felt it best to wait until she had some more knowledge of her family line

The Mystics

and ties so these people she would read about wouldn't seem like strangers but…well… family.

Unlike most teenagers, Rosey enjoyed the trips to the library and the various books that she looked through. She loved studying animals and plant life and had always been a nature person so the topography articles and species documents that she read were a welcome, relaxing time for Rosey after a hard day of sword lessons and elemental skills with Rochell. Sometimes her friends would join her, mostly Alex, who had taken it upon himself to be her personal teacher much to Jasira's dislike, seeing as he was essentially taking her place. Rosey made sure, however, that Jasira was equally asked as many questions as Rosey asked Alex which seemed to appease the jaguar's jealousy. Nevertheless, she felt infinitely more prepared. She learned all sorts of things including how to find her location on a map, know which plants were edible and which were poisonous, what to do when faced with a dangerous species, or how to use a heavier, broader sword with more ease. Rosey had the bruises and headaches to show for all of her hard work and was left feeling mildly satisfied and ready for a new challenge.

There was only one thing besides her missing element that was still bothering Rosey: during the whole week she had heard nothing from the White Witch. According to the Goddess the Witch was the Keeper's only communication with the crystal and the only way to find out the location of the elements. Without her there was no way to find the Mothers. The Goddess assured her that the Witch's absence was a sure sign that Wolvereen's choice of direction for the beginning of their Journey was the right one. The first day that Rosey had stayed at the castle, Wolvereen had already been hard at work scouting, tracking, and mapping out the best possible routes away from the castle with the help of his wolves and the Goddess. Together they had determined that the Molt Volcano, a large volcano just a few days trip from the Castle, would be the most likely place for the first element and if not, the docks were not too far away from there.

The volcano was the closest destination and a famous volcano seeing as it was one of the major energy collection spots for Energy Flows, not to mention all kinds of magic and elemental power was rumored to be stored there. Magic was attracted to areas of energy, especially the Energy Flows, so the place had, over time, developed a large amount of magical buildup that had become a barrier of sorts to protect the volcano from evil beings. Not only was the place magical and elementally strong but evil creatures seemed to find it impossible to come within two miles of the volcano, thus the place was a good midway point between the castle and the docks for Rosey's safety. Even if the fire element was not there they could still make it unscathed to the docks where the Goddess planned on giving Rosey one of her favorite ships to travel in. There were no airplanes here and dragon flight was difficult and hardly stealthy. Going by sea was the fastest and safest route since Raptors couldn't swim. Rosey's head had spun at the thought of dragons and flying but she relaxed and decided to focus on one thing at a time, nevertheless, later in the library, she had looked up a book on dragons, finding it hard not to be fascinated by the beasts of legend. Finally, the end of the week came and Rosey still had not heard from the Witch. Frustrated, she made her way to the Goddess to discuss what she should do before she left the next day. Finding Nashi, she asked if the Goddess was available but was surprised to find that Nashi had been looking for her.

"What is it?" said Rosey, as Nashi bid her to follow her.

"Apparently someone important just arrived and the Goddess sent me to fetch you, I don't know who it is unfortunately," she said hastily, motioning for Rosey to hurry and follow her.

Rosey complied and fell in beside the flustered woman. "Where are they?" she asked.

"They're in the gardens."

Rosey couldn't help but be happy to be visiting the garden area where many a time during that week she had gone to rest, relax, and read a book or study some material she had found interesting in Jasira's library. She had already been there earlier that day relaxing in the sunlight as she rested after a hard day of morning exercises, where she had also chatted with Eglen. It would be nice to return there once more before she had to leave it all behind.

Coming around a corner they neared the familiar hallway leading to the massive indoor gardens. As they left the corridor behind and entered the maze of life, beauty, and greenery, Rosey felt herself immediately uplifted. She stretched in the bright sunlight filtering through the unusual fabric covering above then hurried to catch up with Nashi who was clearly impatient to deliver her to the Goddess as ordered.

Rounding a bin they left the cobblestone walkway and entered a mulch path. Nashi began leading her through a series of twists and turns that she was unfamiliar with. Finally they came into a small round courtyard with various human and animal looking statues placed at the edges of the soft mulch floor. Nashi waited by the entrance and gestured for Rosey to enter. There at its center was the Goddess in all her glory and standing next to her was a horse sized creature with the head, tail, and wings of a dragon and the body and legs of a horse. In between his horns was a long feather colored in crimson red with amber and mahogany highlights and tints. His body was long and slender, more like an Arabian's, with bright green eyes. He sported a fancy dappled grey coat with almost coal black stockings, the grey slowly formed into a red color on his head and tail. His horns were a striking silver color and his long dragon's tail ended in a tuft of silver fur. He was, in a word, beautiful.

Upon their arrival, both the creature and the Goddess turned to Rosey. Rosey eyed the dragon-horse with interest but with none of the fear and surprise she had experienced upon first coming to The World Within A World. After meeting Jasira, Eglen, and Wolvereen she was quite used to meeting large, unusual, and intelligent animals.

"Ah, Rosey," the Goddess straightened upon seeing her, "I have someone I want you to meet. This is Argno, Dragnagor Messenger to myself and the Silver Goddess, my sister," she said motioning to the Dragnagor with a small twist of her wrist.

It was the first time Rosey had seen the Goddess since their morning sparring and practice session and Rosey was aghast to find her looking so elegant since the whole week of practice she had been sporting old, worn, leather pants and a stained white blouse; her hair tied back in a neat, tight pony tail. Now, she stood tall and elegant in golden pants, a long sleeved, silver trimmed golden shirt, and elegant silver boots. Her wand and saber were worn at her waist and her long black hair was tied back in a casual, but decorative, braid. The head piece Rosey had seen her wear the first day she came to the palace rested on the Goddess's head, as usual. The only time Rosey had ever seen her not wearing it was during their practices. The Goddess wasn't as ornately dressed as she had been when Rosey first came but she was still a dashing beauty to behold, and just as intimidating. Though Rosey had been here for a week and even clashed swords with her, the Goddess remained a symbol of strength and power, which, many times, made Rosey feel as if she was small and insignificant. Rosey knew that in the Goddess's eyes she was nothing of the sort, as the Goddess made sure to remind her every day of how important she was to them all.

Rosey broke away from her thoughts and turned to the mighty beast standing next to the Goddess. He bowed low to Rosey, his wings forming an arch to either side, she was amazed to spy the intricate designs upon the backs of the dragon wings. They reminded her of the eye patterns found on some moth's wings to scare away predators. The eye was a red iris with mahogany and golden colors stretching throughout the rest of the wings. The other side of his wings was a silver color with black spots at the ends.

"Oh, my Keeper, I am honored to stand before you," he said rising. His voice reminded her of honey for some reason, soft and flowing but stuck together in an iridescent gel of sugar. She inevitably felt her stomach

The Mystics

growl and quickly made note to get herself something to eat afterwards, preferably with honey.

"The honor is mine, Argno. I'm Rosey, Rosey Mystic. It's nice to meet you too," said Rosey bowing to him in return.

"Argno has just delivered a message to me from my sister, the Silver Goddess, which you need to hear. Go ahead Argno." The Goddess extended her hand toward Rosey in invitation. Rosey turned her gaze to Argno and waited expectantly.

Looking a little nervous he said, "The Silver Goddess wishes to meet you and provide you with a safer means of transportation to the Molt Volcano. She is aware of your intended location and wishes to assist you in any way that she can."

"Oh…ah…sure, I'm all for that," said Rosey, giving him a brisk nod. Her mind raced with excitement, she was going to meet the Silver Goddess! With the week coming to an end and her training progressing nicely it would be nice to meet one of the Goddesses not as a novice but as a trained Keeper.

"So may I tell her that you are on your way?"

Argno's question jerked her back into reality. She quickly nodded, a proud smile lighting her face.

"You sure can, but…how are we going to find her?"

"Nagura will show you the way."

Of course, Rosey had almost forgotten that the large white wolf was the Head of the Silver Goddess's guards, just as Wolvereen, her mate, was the Head of the Golden Goddess's guards.

"Of course, thanks Argno, I very much appreciate this."

"You're welcome miss." He flashed her a kind smile, his bright eyes welcoming and kind.

"Now Rosey if you'll excuse us, Argno and I have some…catching up to do," said the Goddess kindly.

Rosey nodded but nevertheless felt disappointed, she just knew they were going to be talking about something secret or Resistance related. She hated being left out but she knew better than to try and argue. She turned to Argno, "It was nice to meet you Argno, see you later."

"You as well, my Keeper."

Rosey doubted their catching up had anything to do with familiar chatting but she had learned that the Goddess was subtle with her messages and this was not the time to seek to challenge her. Besides, she should probably speak to Wolvereen and let him know that their plans changed, then head to the kitchen to grab a quick bite to eat, she thought, remembering her rumbling stomach and the honey she had promised it. I can't wait to see how he reacts. Knowing how hard he has thought things through and planned for the next few days, he's sure to cause a fuss. Trying hard not to laugh she left the gardens following Nashi back to the corridor where she took off to find the grouchy wolf, her heart beating wildly at the thought of meeting the Golden Goddess's sister.

As promised, both Eglen and Wolvereen joined Rosey as they prepared to leave the following morning before the sun had peaked over the horizon. Before Rosey mounted she turned to Nagura who was making her way to the front of the group where Rosey stood. Her mate, Wolvereen followed her; disappointment clearly written on his face. His master plan for getting to the Molt Volcano had been discarded. Rosey tried not to laugh at his annoyed expression as he and Nagura came to meet her. Rosey smiled, overjoyed to be seeing the large white wolf again. In their short week together she and the massive wolf had developed quite a friendship. At first Rosey's instincts to run from a larger than life wolf had made their connection strained, but Rosey had slowly, but surely, warmed up to Nagura and Wolvereen. Nagura had the gentlest voice that made you feel as if everything was going to be all right. For such a large predator she carried a softness about her snowy white fur and luscious blue eyes that made the world around her seem at peace. She was patient and understanding. Some days, hidden amongst the ferns and willow trees of the indoor garden, Rosey had crawled up to the giant wolf and buried her head in that thick coat, telling the wolf her fears and her greatest pain. She had never told these secrets to anyone, not even to Hazel and Noly. Somehow, Nagura knew what to say. And yet…Nagura was tough. She was a hard fighter and a fierce competitor, but she struck at her opponents with mercy and forgiveness. Rosey had never known there could be so much kindness in a warrior like Nagura, especially seeing her mate Wolvereen. Rosey hoped that she too could earn such high esteem in society as well as in spirit. Looking at her now, Rosey found it hard not to run up and give her a great big bear hug, which always made Wolvereen angry. According to him being hugged was demeaning and would lower him down to the level of some common pet. Nagura would flick his nose with the end of her tail and he would role his eyes and give up, knowing perfectly well Nagura could care less about whether a hug made her look like a dog or not.

Rosey hated to admit it, but the reason she felt so close to Nagura was because, in some ways, Nagura was more like a mother than anything Rosey had ever had. Nagura's presence soothed Rosey and made her feel safe and warm like she was wrapped in her mother's arms. She had never told anyone about this, even Nagura or her friends. It was a small secret Rosey kept hidden in the depths of her heart and she intended to keep it there. Maybe one day she would say something, but right now she was content to keep it to herself.

"Morning Nagura," said Rosey as Nagura sat down in front of her, her ornate silver armor clicking to life along her slender muscled body. Wolvereen's golden armor was shined to perfection, but it was hard not to admire the way Nagura's silver armor made her look like some sort of white ghost. Her blue eyes were the only indication that she wasn't some apparition.

"Good morning child, I've checked with everyone and everything is accounted for, we are ready to move out on your signal."

"Then let's get to it," said Rosey, grabbing Sarabie's reins.

Nagura nodded, giving Rosey a broad wolf's smile. Turning to Wolvereen she said, "If you would dear, please spread the word, we are ready to leave."

Wolvereen nodded briskly, turned and walked amongst the group letting them know that they were about to move out. Rosey looked into Nagura's eyes and gave her a hug; softly she spoke into the wolf's fur.

"I'd be lying if I said I wasn't scared," she whispered, feeling herself shaking a little. Andraste, strapped to her back, shuddered in her scabbard as if she could relate to Rosey's fear.

"I would be surprised if you said you weren't. There is nothing wrong with being scared, what is wrong is giving into that fear. Keep fighting it and you win no matter what happens," said Nagura, giving Rosey's face a soft lick.

"Thanks Nagura."

"Anytime, now we best be going," Nagura said as two armored wolves slunk back through the entrance to join the group. They had been scouting ahead to see if the way was clear. With their return, it was time to go.

Rosey nodded then turned to mount Sarabie who nuzzled her gently in worry.

"Don't worry Sarabie, I'll be fine. After all, I have you here to protect me."

"You can be assured of that," Sarabie said, eyeing Rosey with a warm expression.

Rosey patted her thankfully, mounted, and then waited as Hazel jumped up onto the saddle, crawled up onto her shoulders, and then draped herself around Rosey's warm neck. Rosey gently moved Sarabie into position. Her friends took up their usual places on either side of her and Noly hung back behind them with Eglen, although Rosey was sure Noly would be wandering everywhere as they journeyed, that dog could never seem to stay in one place for more than a few minutes.

Nagura took the lead with Wolvereen right next to her. She cast one look behind her to make sure everyone was ready then, with a low bark, she led them through a large golden gate behind the castle and into the mist filled woods. Rosey breathed in the deep early morning aromas of the forest. At this time of day a thin layer of dew and mist was normal and it clung to everything, even their clothes. The frigid air was crisp and reminded Rosey of the smell that came after it rained. It was the smell of freshness like everything had been wiped clean by a new coating of fresh air. The chill was also a reminder that winter was coming. The cold was actually a good thing. Wolvereen had told them that Raptors were heavily affected by the intense cold. It slowed them down and made them easier to kill. Attacks on the Resistance and local towns were extremely rare during the fall and winter times. That was why Rosey's transfer to The World Within A World had been scheduled for this time of year, whether the crystal was with her or not. She was happy that it had come to her now, and figured that it was no coincidence that she started her 'scavenger hunt' at the beginning of a great freeze, and the Raptors knew it. Many would still be after her, despite the cold, so they were cautioned to keep their guard up.

Another consideration for starting the journey at this particular time was the weather. Some areas would get more dangerous for traveling the later they postponed. It certainly wasn't going to remain average out in the wooded lands for too much longer and, according to some strange magic-wielding Leron that lived in the indoor gardens and resembled an owl with four long eagle wings, it was going to start snowing in less than three days which meant that Rosey now had only two days until snow started to fall. If they were forced to wait till things cleared up, they would lose their opportunity of a virtually Raptor-free head start.

To help them on their cold trek the Goddess provided Rosey and her friends with new wardrobes, ones much more fit for this world and all its surprises, along with some anti-venom, small medical packs, and other gear for the trip. Rosey and her friends now wore hard, tough leather and cotton outfits designed to meet their personal styles as well as their various weapons and environmental needs. Not only did the Goddess give Rosey and her fellowship new clothes and various necessities she also gave them special gifts. They had each been given a green cape to hang over the cape/jackets that the Silver Goddess had given them earlier that was spelled to help hide them if enemies were around. The horses were given new tack and armor that matched in color. The handiwork on the tack was exquisite and beautiful. Rosey noticed right away the lightness of the bridle that was different from the one she usually used. They were definitely different from Earth's models; theses had no bit but instead rested lightly on top of the nose and then looped around the ears. The material used for the bridle was very soft but tough enough to handle hard use. The saddle was standard but contained a cup for Hazel to sleep in as well as a few saddlebags and an area to attach her quiver. Rosey regarded that area in shame, knowing full well that she would have to practice her archery at some point and dreaded the coming results. Her bow she kept strapped to her back with Andraste. It was a standard bow, neither overly special nor unimportant. It was just perfect for her area of expertise.

Hazel, Noly, Eglen, Wolvereen, and the horses had all been washed in a special formula that would make their skin and fur much stronger and help keep out the cold and deflect rain or snow. The animals had also all been given leather-like shoes and cotton stockings to keep their feet and legs warm and to protect them from rough terrain, even the wolves. Their armor had been polished and hardened for battle. A red cotton-like blanket was fashioned to be worn underneath their heavy and cold armor, helping to keep the giant wolves warm and their skin protected. Nagura's blanket was the only exception, instead of bright red, it was a soft blue. It fit the silver color better. Rosey had no doubt the other Silver Guards wore the same blue covering as Nagura did.

Because of all the new gear they did not need to wear their coats from Earth and were advised not to because they wanted to keep as much of

Earth separated from The World Within A World as they could. However, Rosey and her friends kept them just in case something were to happen to the new capes, then they would at least have something to wear to keep them warm. Rosey also kept her old clothing that she had worn when coming here. Alex and Rochell had opted to leave theirs at the Castle, but for some reason Rosey wanted to hang onto hers. It was all she had left of her life with her uncle on Earth, and that life was just as important to her as the one here was. She didn't want to lose those memories.

As the thought of her uncle and her life on Earth came to mind, she wondered how he was doing and how he had explained her disappearance. She had never thought to ask, it seemed so trivial compared to everything else, but what had her uncle told the schools? A thousand possibilities entered her mind but Rosey came to the conclusion that if they had planned for her return to The World Within A World then they would have also planned on her disappearance from Earth and prepared a story to explain it. She trusted her uncle, but made a mental note to inquire about it later, just for curiosity's sake.

A silver glint caught Rosey's eye, it was the chain of the locket the Goddess had given her. Since Rosey wore the Shanobie Crystal around her neck, she didn't want to wear another necklace on top of it, so the locket was safely attached to Rosey's belt and tucked away inside her pocket. Some of the chain hung out in a stylish manner. Even if she could wear it, she would have still had it hidden. She didn't want the pain of her parent's loss so visible for all to see. It was far too private for that.

After a good three hours of silence to help hide their departure from any prying eyes, Nagura gave them the all clear and Alex began to speak softly. "We have entered one of the three forests that grow on the borders of the city, Neran."

"What do you mean by three forests? Isn't the city surrounded by one?" Rosey asked, shifting in the saddle and trying to remember what she had read in the library. Hazel hung around her neck acting as a living scarf, her tail and paws draped around Rosey's neck protecting it from the chill and sharing Rosey's warmth. Her tiny head and tail were the only things visible under Rosey's thick hair and the hood of the green cape. "Well, yes and no," Alex answered. "You see a long time ago when unicorns and pegasi ruled the lands on which the city was built there were three forests, the Enchanted Forest, the Sacred Forest, and the Forest of Unknown. They were combined into one great forest but separated by the different animals that chose to live in each area of the forest." "What kind of animals lived in each?" asked Rosey, spying Alex's left hand tucked in his jacket. *Probably holding his wand,* she thought, trying hard not to grab for Andraste strapped to her back, instead she settled her arm on the hilt of Silver Knight. The action echoed through her mind reminding her of the danger she faced. Alex considered for a moment, then looked up and said, "The Forest of Unknown contains animals that are ancient and special, more intelligent than the other animals here. The Enchanted Forest contains animals that use and practice magical powers. The Sacred Forest contains animals that control unusual mixed abilities and animals that are rare." "Which forest are we in?"

"The Forest of Unknown, this place is the least likely to have any Raptors because the creatures here are less tolerant of evil and more able to combat them."

"Do these differences even extend to the plant life?"

"Yes but I'm not familiar with them all," he said irritably as if his confession to having any lack of knowledge was a sin.

It hadn't taken Rosey long to learn that Alex was the guy to go to for any information that she needed. He knew more than she could probably fit in a text book. Rosey knew that, as a magikin, he had had to study for long hours and memorize a multitude of spells, such knowledge as what Alex had was a rare gift in itself. He had told her that his mentor Thera was pushing him very hard in his studies making him memorize all sorts of things and forcing him to go way beyond what most magikins his age were required to do in order to test his limitations and his strengths. Thera was a tough master who was highly regarded and respected. Because of her reputation, she expected a lot from her students and Alex was the perfect candidate.

Rochell, on the other hand, was not so…blessed. Rochell was in no way, shape or form, unintelligent but she was much more optimistic in everything that she did while Alex would probably tell you the definition of optimist and pessimist rather than try and decide which one he was. Rochell, unlike Alex, had no other mentors than her parents; powerful air apparitions themselves at the God and Goddess level. Rosey didn't mind her friend's quirks. She had lived with them long enough to know what made them tick. She enjoyed and welcomed Alex's explanations while looking to Rochelle for fun and laughter. But over the years the three of them had meshed their personalities to fit each other perfectly, matching one another word for word and learning to delight in each other's vices and strengths. With them there was never a dull day.

As they drew farther into the heart of the Forest of Unknown Rosey and the others fell into respectful silence. Silence wasn't exactly a necessity but everyone seemed to be enjoying simply observing their surroundings. Winter might be a time when things died and laid dormant, but the transformation of the land in response to winter's coming was a spectacular and sometimes rare sight. Rosey found herself happy that everyone, including Alex had chosen to stay quiet. Rosey welcomed this silence in that it also gave her time to think about all she had learned. Thoughts about her mother, Nagura, Eglen, Wolvereen, her uncle, and everything she had left behind filled her mind up to the brim with more questions. Questions that the Goddess had assured her everyone wanted to know the answers to as much as she did. Rosey tried to make sense of the story in her head, especially the apparent possession of her mother's friend. She was well aware that the Goddess had not spoken the woman's name to keep Rosey from worrying or preoccupying herself with her, but Rosey couldn't help but feel sorry for the woman and imagined how she'd feel if she'd been forced to kill Alex or Rochell. The image frightened her and she quickly pushed it away, but the thought still lingered like a memory from a distant past. Though Rosey knew she was here to help this world and save it she had every intention of doing everything she could for this woman and hoped that one day she'd find her and somehow put her mind at ease. She shook her head and thought about something easier to process, like if she would meet any of the strange creatures she had read about in Jasira's library. As the day wore on, they paused only long enough to have a hurried lunch then were back on the trail again. The farther they got from the castle the more alert everyone seemed to become. Rosey hoped that they would be nearing the Silver Goddess's place soon. No one had ever mentioned anything about a Silver Castle or palace or whatnot, they only spoke of the Silver Goddess as the Silver Goddess. Rosey knew little to nothing about her except that she was the Golden Goddess's sister, and no one had tried to tell her anything about her. Rosey didn't think it was because they were hiding the information but that they did not know themselves. They were just as clueless as she was, heck, Wolvereen might not have even met her yet, though Rosey doubted that. She didn't know if the Silver Goddess was anything like her sister or completely different, but whoever she was Rosey could only present herself with confidence and show that she wasn't afraid of being the Keeper.

Chapter Twelve: The Crystal Caverns

Rosey leaned back and studied the sky. From the position of the sun she determined that it was around 6:00. Because the telling of time using the sun, moon, and stars was so accurate and second nature for most citizens, clocks from Earth hadn't been adopted by The World Within A World. Rosey, however, was used to the short and long hands of the Earth clock so Alex, while training at the Golden Goddess's castle, had taught her how to read the time in the same way the citizens did, although, she was having trouble telling time by using the stars. She drew a quick breath and reached up to pet Hazel perched around her shoulders, making sure to scratch behind her ears like she liked. Her instant purr was comforting in the silence surrounding the small fellowship.

Nagura hadn't said anything about where she would be taking them to get to the Silver Goddess, no one had asked, and Rosey felt that it would be useless to do so. From what Rosey could tell from how everyone acted, the Silver Goddess handled covert or some kind of stealth operation within the Resistance. It would make sense that everyone was "hush hush" about her. Even Alex seemed to be stumped and Rosey didn't remember reading anything about her or really finding anything out about her in the library. If everyone including Nagura, whom she was very close to, was willing to keep information about the Silver Goddess to themselves than she had no doubt that she would be turned down if she asked about her. Although, if they were being covert, then why was she being lead to the Silver Goddess in broad daylight? Rosey couldn't be sure, but she trusted Nagura and that was all she needed to know.

After about another half hour they came to a small clearing. Tall evergreen trees barely inches away from each other, bordered the edges of the clearing looking like silent soldiers on watch. It was a barrier of trees. Rosey relaxed, hoping that they would be stopping for a rest and to make dinner, but Nagura kept walking. She paced softly on silent paws up to a large evergreen tree, bigger than the rest. It looked to be hundreds of years old and was taller than anything Rosey had ever seen; it may have even been larger than the Sequoias of Earth. She stared at it in awe. She couldn't even see around it, it was so large. The roots stretched away from it in giant interwoven strands of harsh bark. A few areas remained bare and the wolves began to search every nook and cranny, though the forest remained silent around them. Eglen and Wolvereen began walking around the perimeter; the only sound was a slight clink from Wolvereen's armor before it fell into silence. Nagura jumped from giant root to root, shifting easily through the limbs. Her armor was silent as she was. Rosey and the others reined the horses to the side, a few wolf guards stood surrounding them.

Nagura came before the giant tree and bowed low. Rosey watched as the white ghost of a wolf leaned forward and whispered something into the bark of the great tree. Suddenly the ground under the evergreen began to shake and the earth fell away revealing a large hole. Rosey grasped the saddle in surprise as she watched the labyrinth of roots twisting in the ground and uprooting themselves. They formed a small but adequate path leading to the hole. The tree stayed aloft on top of the opening while the roots ran down the sides of the opening acting as supporting beams. Rosey stared wide-eyed into what was now an unusual cave entrance. It was nothing more than a tall hole about eight feet high and about two yards wide. The tunnel was slanted at an awkward but manageable hypotenuse. It was pitch black within except for the first few feet where the evening's sunlight vaguely shimmered. Evergreen vines hung from above the opening dropping down large tentacles of greenery across the entrance making it hard for her to see too far in. Water drops ran along the edges and streamed down the sides of the glassy smooth walls giving the illusion that the tunnel kept growing.

She gazed at the tunnel entrance in wonder, still a little shocked. The wolves and Eglen rejoined Rosey not in the least bit stunned, though they looked impressed. Rosey felt embarrassed for being so awestruck, things like this must be normal to them. Nagura glanced back at her with a smile on her face and Rosey immediately felt better. She dismounted and the others followed her example. The tunnel was way too small for them to ride on a horse but large enough for them to walk through comfortably."Why is the passage so small?" asked Rochell as she stepped up beside Rosey, Alex close behind with Phana and Bronzo at their sides. "Too small for Raptors but perfect for wolves and some other creatures like Eglen," said Nagura, "Now, I'll go first. Rosey, you and your friends come in right behind me. Noly, you stay behind them, and Wolvereen and Eglen will take up the rear." She then stepped forward and bowed to the rest of the wolf guards. "From here on out your services are no longer needed. Well done, and thank you for your help."

They bowed their heads to her, honorably. Wolvereen stepped forward and said in a gruff voice, "Exceptional work team, Dismissed!"

They nodded and bowed again, "Yes sir!" they chorused, before turning and disappearing silently into the forest. Rosey wished them well. They had protected her and served her team splendidly.

She turned to Nagura who said gently, "Follow me and don't be frightened of the dark, it will get light soon."

They all nodded, and Noly waited patiently, eyeing Wolvereen and Eglen as first Nagura then Rosey, Alex, and Rochell entered. As soon as Phana was fully in the entrance Noly fell in behind closely followed by Eglen then Wolvereen. Rosey faintly heard the sound of what must be the entrance closing up and the light dimmed. The ground did not shake or move an inch. There was no indication that anything had taken place, but the lack of light was proof enough. She gulped; there was no turning back, literally.

Rosey moved slowly through the cave's eerie darkness, trying not to slip on the wet rocky floor. The tunnel gradually angled downward but not so steep that it made walking difficult. After a few minutes Rosey found herself warming up as she got deeper into the cave just as she had expected with the constant temperature that caves were known for. As Nagura promised, after a few minutes of walking light filled the corridor. Torches were spread out about six yards from one another allowing for an ample amount of light as they followed the passage deeper underground. Looking closely at them, the torches didn't seem to be burning anything. It was like a small flame was held suspended in the torch, constantly lit, even though it wasn't burning anything. Rosey was sure she remembered reading about them but couldn't remember what it was they were 'burning'. She shrugged and couldn't help but think about how much good some of The World Within A World's technology or magic could help Earth, especially environmentally.

The corridor started to widen, and began looking less like a cavern and more like a natural cave. It didn't take long for Rosey to realize that they were leaving a magically made tunnel and entering into a naturally occurring cave system, conveniently used by the Silver Goddess. The constant color brown blended in with everything making Rosey's eyes seem comfortably out of focus like they normally were when she went to see caves back on Earth. Her sense of direction and space was a little messed up thanks to the constant color and cave designs but Rosey loved the feeling. Taking it all in, everywhere she looked she could see evidence of life; there were camel crickets, strange centipedes, and an occasional bat. She smiled. She had always loved the mysterious power of caves. Now that the passage was much wider, her friends wasted no time taking their usual places on either side of Rosey. Their horses hung back, walking in the same pattern as their riders were with Sarabie in the middle and the other two on either side.

They walked through the caverns for a few minutes enjoying the beauty of the natural cave system. Noly, ever so frisky, was racing back and forth occupying her time by seeing how fast she could run each circuit, to Rosey's delight and probably Noly's as well, it was driving Wolvereen up the wall. Nagura simply smiled at the playful dog and kept leading the way, her white fur and bright silver armor standing out in brilliant contrast to the brown barren walls. As they rounded a sharp corner, a bright light suddenly illuminated the cave. As they drew closer the light began to take on a bluish purple color. The trio gasped as the cave suddenly went from brown to an unbelievable shade of blue-violet covered in crystals ranging from as tall as buildings to as miniscule as microorganisms. It was like walking into a crystal palace. Large geode crystals hung from the ceiling like daggers of light shedding fragments of dazzling brilliance across the ice covered walkway. The floor was not slippery even though it was clearly...ice.

"What? Ice! Why isn't it melting," she asked, still dazzled by the room. "My dear, nothing is impossible with a little magic," said Nagura smiling. Cold was not a factor of this glittering world either. The fifty five degree temperature was replaced by comfortable warmth. She took off her coat and cloak and stuffed them in her saddlebags. Her friends followed her example. While Nagura waited for them to get their bearings Rosey removed Noly, Hazel, and the horses winter articles. Nagura and Wolvereen removed their winter gear as well, though how they did so so fluidly around their armor she'd never know. Together they admired their surroundings, taking time to study the designs the geode daggers made on the ceiling. A kaleidoscope of colors poured into the room from where large multicolored crystals hung or stood proud as guards watching over their king and queen. Rosey was happy that this time she wasn't the only one awestruck. Even Wolvereen had abandoned his haughty demeanor and was admiring the formations, a thoughtful look on his scared face.

Alex's voice broke the silence, "Where are the Silver Goddess's guards?"

"Oh, they're around, hidden and well out of sight I'd think," said Wolvereen with a deep growl, his eyes still taking in his surroundings. He cast his gaze almost reluctantly at Nagura for confirmation, she only nodded.

Rosey walked slowly through the corridor gazing intently at the crystal statues and carvings. Small fountains of water poured down the sides of some of the carvings and into springs on either side of the passage. Reds, blues, pinks, magentas and more bathed the walls in an iridescent light show, then faded back to violet and blue. Her fellowship whispered words of admiration behind her, yet Rosey hardly noticed. She was so completely transfixed by the height and beauty that the shards of crystal mannequins delivered in the heart of the underground oasis that she was hardly aware of the calm composure of Nagura in front of her or the fact that she was following her rather hypnotically. To her amusement everyone else seemed to be doing the same thing, including Eglen and even Wolvereen, though he now seemed to be more blinded by the dazzling light display than amazed.

After about twenty yards the corridor opened into a large chamber. It continued in either direction as if a fast flooding river had come in and carved it out within minutes instead of the centuries it normally took. The icy pathway they had been walking on suddenly rose into a slight incline bridging a huge chasm below. The railings of the bridge were made of bright, blue crystal. Translucent colors made twisting patterns within them giving the illusion that they were moving. They ran along on both sides of the bridge and for good reason; there was a straight plummet down if you fell. Looking over the railing she saw a large ravine below them. At the bottom she spied large crystals sticking straight out of the ground like white daggers. Some looked large enough to be the size of blue whales. The bridge was wide enough to ensure a safe passage of about twenty people standing shoulder to shoulder. It led up to a platform where the path continued along the wall into an opening that led deeper into the cave. Rosey tried her best not to be shocked by the intense décor but she was losing that attempt quickly. When she reached the platform she turned and peered down the side. She could see the bottom but only just. It was at least a good 300 foot drop. There was what seemed to be another bridge below. The image of the other bridge rippled and she realized she had been seeing a reflection of the bridge she was on. She had crossed a crystal clear lake that was about forty feet down. The large crystals she had seen were really there however, breaking the water only slightly. The lake was so clear that you couldn't see it unless you stared at it for a long time or something dropped into it that would disturb its surface. She cast her gaze upward and more spiked crystals jutted from the ceiling in menacing points of captivating beauty.

Rosey reluctantly left the railing and joined her friends once more as they followed Nagura along the wall, keeping as far away from the railing as possible. Finally they made it to their destination, a large circular room with a small oculus allowing light. It was just as glorious as the rest of the place, completely bathed in crystals and ice. Smooth walls and iridescent light played tricks on the eyes making the chamber seem bigger than it was. If all that wasn't impressive enough it got even more interesting. Not too far away was what looked to be a set up for a living room. Chairs and couches of various size and shape rested on silver and crystal frames carved in the shape of many mystical animals. A crystal table adorned a side wall. On it there was what looked to be an assortment of beverages and snacks held within an intricately carved crystal box like a refrigerator or a cabinet. A small, silver, rat-like creature sat next to the crystal box attentively. When it spotted them it jumped down and came to greet them. It did not seem to be a real animal. It looked like a piece of silver Jell-O that had been carved to resemble the shape of a rat.

Alex leaned forward and whispered into Rosey's ear, "Classic magic spell, a small charm on a jell known as flub and then carved with a wand. I used to make them all the time." Rosey smiled at him, grateful for his ever helpful knowledge. She was offered a seat by the little rat flub and she took it, grateful for the rest after the long walk. Her friends were all offered seats on the various assortments of chairs, some were made especially for horses and wolves like Wolvereen and Nagura just as some of the furniture had been in the Golden Goddess's palace. The tiny rat creature ran back to the cabinet/refrigerator and started serving refreshments. Water was the popular choice. Everyone thirstily gulped it down with gratitude.

After the fellowship had been rested and thirsts had been quenched, Rosey heard the 'tip tap' of footsteps. Getting up and turning to see who it was she was hardly surprised. It was the Silver Goddess and she, like her sister, was named well. She was dressed in the exact same style of clothes as the Golden Goddess except everything was silver instead of gold and the metal strip was under her left breast instead of the right. Her long black hair was woven with silver strands as opposed to her sister the Golden Goddess who wore golden strands. Silver coated her lips and highlighted the tops of her eyes making her seem more like a heavenly creature rather than the human she was. Once again, just as with the Golden Goddess, Rosey noticed that the markings weren't makeup but natural as if nature itself had declared her to be the Silver Goddess. Upon her forehead rested the same headpiece as the one the Golden Goddess wore except this one was silver. Around her waist hung a silver hilted saber in a golden scabbard, opposite to her sisters golden hilted saber and silver scabbard. She also wore a silver wand case at her side. The power she projected far surpassed any that Rosey knew, except the Golden Goddess.

"Welcome Keeper," said the woman, fanning her arms to include the whole room, "I am the Silver Goddess, the Golden Goddess's younger sister." She circled Rosey with a keen eye. Rosey noticed that the woman was much shorter than the Golden Goddess and not as heavily muscled.

She carried the same air of power but it seemed younger and not as mature. Either way Rosey intended to show her the same respect that she had shown her sister.

Rosey bowed her head slightly and smiled saying, "Thank you for inviting me and thank you for Silver Knight and the jacket capes, they are much appreciated."

The Goddess's eyes brightened, "You are very welcome. Silver Knight is not as amazing as Andraste I must admit, but I hated to have you come here without some sort of weapon." The Goddess returned her slight head bow and then began to bend down as if to be seated, the only problem was there was no chair there. Rosey was about to say something when a silver throne materialized underneath the Goddess just as she sat down. Rosey should have known: magic. She would have thought seeing the Golden Goddess would prepare her for this meeting, but the Silver Goddess had an over powering presence that was all her own, something Rosey never really remembered feeling when with the Golden Goddess except for her feelings of intimidation. It was almost as if the Silver Goddess's powers and abilities were running rampant while the Golden Goddess's had been restrained and organized. Rosey wasn't sure if that was what was happening or if the Silver Goddess just preferred more extravagance.

Smiling the Silver Goddess said, "Now Rosey, you understand that for some time now many Raptors have been seen in these areas. I heard that you were planning on journeying to the Molt Volcano, and though I agree with the destination and have no doubts about Wolvereen's skills as a scout, I would like to offer you a safer underground passage to the Molt Volcano. Through that tunnel...," the Goddess turned in her seat and extended her arm to indicate an entrance to a tunnel at the other end of the huge chamber," ... Nagura will lead you through a series of cave systems that will exit outside not too far from the Volcano." Rosey felt the heat rise within her, she hated being useless. She had proven at the Goddess's castle that she could fight but it still wasn't enough, they still insisted upon holding her hand. Could she really blame them? Their last two Keepers were killed, Maharen because she wasn't connected enough, and her mother by one of her own friends through a mysterious possession. *They can't afford to lose you too,* Rosey thought, hating the extent that everyone was going through to protect her but, inevitably, seeing their reasoning. However, just because she hadn't gotten into a fight yet didn't mean she couldn't defend herself. Andraste seemed to hum against her back, as if in agreement. She could almost feel the blade in her hands vibrating with excitement. She knew that to have a chance at succeeding she would need the elements, right now she was without any elements, only a blade at her back and her friends at her sides. Obviously she would need to be patient if she wanted to succeed and getting angry about it wasn't going to make a difference. She stifled her frustration and turned her attention back to the Goddess.

"Actually, I did not call you here just to tell you about the cave systems," the Silver Goddess continued. "Being the commander of the Resistance's Stealth Force I have access to information that could be of some help to you, mostly concerning the Raptors and the Blood Gorons. I have one of the largest archives of information on them and I think you will find it quite helpful. Everyone else except for the horses and your cat and dog are well aware of the information I am about to show you but you are not and thus I would like to offer you and anyone else this rare chance to see into my secret archives. Are you interested?" The woman cocked an eyebrow at her, awaiting her answer.

Rosey nodded, "More than interested, the Golden Goddess told me that you might offer to show me such information that you have kept here within the Resistance but she was unsure if you'd call on me."

"Yes, indeed. I almost did not, because we, the Resistance, I mean, have been so busy lately tracking down the Raptors that it would have been inconvenient for you to come visit at the moment. Those monsters are starting to reorganize and have become more focused and vicious since

The Mystics

your arrival, keeping us constantly on the alert. But when I heard about where you were heading I decided to offer you a safer passage through the cave systems."

"I'm very grateful, thank you," Rosey said, dipping her head.

"The pleasure is all mine. Now, before we go, there is just one other thing and I hope you don't mind but, there is someone you are going to meet here later on. She's an old friend that asked to meet you and I didn't want to turn her down. I hope it's all right?"

Rosey nodded, "Of course." She couldn't exactly say no.

"Good, I know it will benefit you deeply, though, I'm curious as to her interest in meeting you. Oh well, it can't be helped. Now, if you'll follow me, please," she said rising elegantly from her throne, which disappeared as soon as she stood, "I'll take you to the archives. If there is anyone else who wishes to come you are more than welcome." She extended her arms to the others in invitation. Slowly Noly, Hazel, and the horses got up from their seats with curiosity written across their faces. The others stared after them but stayed where they were.

Rosey jumped to her feet, though she had seen an image of the Blood Gorons she had learned little about them or the Raptors. The Golden Goddess had wanted to teach Rosey about them properly before they left but then the Silver Goddess had invited Rosey to her Caverns and she had decided that the information the Silver Goddess had would better prepare Rosey than anything she could say in words so she had left it up to her sister to teach her.

What really excited Rosey was the idea of meeting this old friend the Goddess spoke of. It seemed that ever since she had come here the only thing she had been doing was learning, reading, practicing, and meeting people. It was all exciting and there was so much to learn but it could get a little boring, not to mention annoying. She was determined, however, not to let that show, it would be a terrible injustice to everyone who was giving their lives and their safety for her sake. So she determinedly hurried over to the Goddess willing to learn as much as she could so that when her time came to fight, she would be prepared.

Once Rosey had joined her, the Goddess addressed her fellowship, "Please excuse us, we'll be right back." Rosey eyed her friends, who nodded, giving her smiles of encouragement, then she turned and followed the Silver Goddess, Noly, Hazel, and the horses at her heels. The Goddess went right up to the crystal wall a few yards away from where they had been sitting. Without hesitation she walked right through the wall. Rosey stopped midstride and stared at the wall as if it was some kind of disease. Noly made a "oooohhh" sound and yipped with excitement then plunged herself right through the wall after the Goddess. Rosey stood there stock still, staring at the wall. Snickering and hushed laughter reached her ears, no doubt coming from her fabulous and loyal fellowship. She began to sizzle inside with embarrassment when she felt a reassuring, gentle nudge from Sarabie on her back. The large horse whispered in her ear, "Go on Rosey, it's all right. We're right behind you." Her warm breath washed over Rosey smelling of hay. She nodded and patted the horses muzzle in thanks feeling comforted. Hazel purred against her leg and she automatically reached down to let the little cat jump onto her shoulders. Hazel would never admit it but Rosey knew she was probably just as surprised and unsure as Rosey was and this was the perfect way to escape walking through the wall on her own.

Taking a gulp of air and swallowing whatever fears that may have sought to stop her, she bolted right into the wall and came out the other side. She was so surprised that she stumbled and almost fell to her knees but a quick and strong arm pulled her up right before she could hit the floor. Amazed at the strength in that arm, she gazed up at the Silver Goddess in thanks and straightened herself. She turned back and examined the wall. Nothing seemed out of the ordinary, just a plain, smooth, crystal wall. The same wall she had walked through. Many would think that walking through a wall would give you goose bumps or a strange weightless feeling, like being in space, but not in this case. Rosey had felt...nothing. It was as if she had just taken a regular step forward. There was no weightlessness, no strange sensations, just a plain step forward and that was it. Noly raced up to her and licked her hand. Rosey smiled and patted her head, stroking the soft brown and white fur. Gently she moved them out of the way as the horses came in behind her. Looking back, Rosey couldn't help but be curious about the strange door but summed it up to the work of magic. The Goddess was a magikin after all. The horses filed in one by one, their massive bulk moving through the door easily. They stood patiently to the side, their heads turning to take in their surroundings.

"What..?" she began, but the Goddess beat her to it. "It's a magical illusion. They are fairly easy to cast and are mostly used by the Resistance to keep information hidden but close at hand. The door changes locations every now and then, only I and a select few know where it is at all times." "Aren't you worried about security?" The Goddess cast her gaze downward as if ashamed. Her voice was calm and kind but strong. "The Evil One does not care about the Resistance, Rosey. The only thing it cares about is killing you. It knows the information we have is not nearly enough to supply an advantage. You're the only advantage we have over the Evil One." She fixed her silver gaze on Rosey making her flinch inwardly. "The information we have is good for you to know to survive the Raptors but not to defeat our enemy. The Evil One would never waste time trying to destroy us. The changing door locations are enough in terms of security." "But...," Rosey said finding her voice, "at Neran there were scratches everywhere on the gates. Some looked fairly new. Why would they be attacking them?" "That's mostly in response to the Golden Goddess's presence in Neran. They're trying to challenge her to come out of her palace. Many leaders are having the same problems." The Goddess's voice suddenly took on a prideful tone. "But while those blood thirsty Raptors are dealing with my sister they completely overlook my own operations below grounds in these caverns." She swept her hand around her indicating the icy-looking room. "As you can imagine, we're pretty safe. Remember the Raptors are used to harass and kill while the Blood Gorons are used for other matters."

Rosey felt her heart sink. These people faced more horrors than she could even imagine, yet they held out for some hope. Rosey looked up at the Goddess.

The tall silver woman returned her gaze and smiled, "Rosey, don't worry about us, we've been facing the Raptors since your grandmother was the Keeper. It hasn't been as hard, nor as horrible as you may think, remember, my sister is the leader of Neran. We are tough and strong."

Rosey didn't need to be told the significance of this, her memories of the powerful golden woman flashed through her mind. Her powerful thrusts and parries with her saber in her hands, the quick zap of a magical blow, and the lightning speed of her hand to hand combat moves. It was enough to make any enemy think twice about attacking. The Golden Goddess alone was powerful enough to protect Neran, not to mention the guards and the armored wolves. Feeling much better she followed the Goddess as she led her down a long corridor of crystal. Every few intervals a shard of ice hung from the seven foot tall ceiling casting a thin beam of blue light. Rosey followed the Silver Goddess, listening to the pattern of sounds their feet made on the crystal and ice floor. Sighing deeply, she was suddenly aware of just how close the walls were. They were about two yards across making it so that the horses had to walk single file. She found herself getting claustrophobic the longer they walked. The 'clip clop' of the horse's hooves and the 'tat tat' of Noly's nails were the only sound throughout the chamber. The echo was enough to make Rosey's skin crawl. The Silver Goddess, however, was undeterred and did not waste time. They walked briskly through the long corridor until, suddenly, they reached a dead end. As before the Silver Goddess kept walking, never breaking her smooth stride, but once again Rosey's instincts got a hold of her and she paused before she too walked through the wall.   The room they stepped into was what Rosey could only describe as being like a science fiction refrigerator room where samples of DNA and other various forms of information were kept, except that there was a lack of frigid coolness. Instead, it was the same warm temperature as the crystal chambers. Long skinny tubes were filled to the brim with small compartments. They had a blue, purple, and turquoise glow about them, as if they had a long, round light bulb stuck down the middle of them.   "Now, do you know what a Raptor looks like?" said the Goddess suddenly. Rosey shook her head, "I know it's bigger than the armored wolves but that's all I know. The Golden Goddess was going to teach me about them and the Blood Gorons before then you called for me, so she left it up to you. I have seen a picture of what a Blood Goron looks like though."

"Ah yes, I have a real one here on display," she said, "They're not as large as the Raptors but they are very intelligent and vicious."

"What do you mean 'on display'?" Rosey asked hesitantly.

"In the Resistance we don't just hide and gather information and perform attacks on Raptors, we also study and research the Raptors and the Blood Gorons. It is that research that has allowed us to discover how the Raptors work, how Blood Gorons survive and other basic pieces of biological information. We are also, in a sense, scientists. It is here that I have a display set up about these monstrosities. You may know what a Blood Goron looks like, but you don't know the particulars about them." She raised a callused hand. "If you are, Almighty One forbid, separated from your fellowship, even with the elements, you will need to know a few things to keep yourself safe from Raptors and possibly Blood Gorons. We have been studying them to learn more about them and we have a few life size models."   The Goddess then went on to open some of the various compartments in the long tubes showing them the prints that the Raptors and Blood Gorons made, the Raptor's green saliva, their attack techniques, their natural instinctive ways, and how to outsmart, hide from, or confront and attack a Raptor and/or Blood Goron. The silver woman even showed the group the skeleton and body of a Raptor and Blood Goron all of which were contained in two large chunks of ice and crystal. These were the creatures she had on 'display'.

Rosey gulped as she studied the immobile bodies. The Golden Goddess had been very precise and careful when teaching Rosey how to kill a Raptor and a Blood Goron, however, Rosey found that she enjoyed the extra information and seeing the beasts upfront and in person gave her a better idea of how to fight them. Rosey felt Hazel stiffen and her fur rise up along her back where she sat under Rosey's long hair. Seems Rosey wasn't the only one spooked by the not-so-live images of the two monstrosities that inhabited this world. Rosey smiled and patted the cat's head comfortingly. The Horses joined her on either side. Rosey gripped Sarabie's long mane, twisting the fine hairs around her fingers as she looked upon the very real Blood Goron and Raptor.

Seeing it up close, Rosey could understand why this world had adopted Earth's name of Raptor for them. It resembled what Rosey had seen in books and movies about dinosaurs, except that this one was oddly colored in greens, blues, and other various colors. Its most distinguishable feature was the long line of spiky white hair that ran along its back from the forehead to the tip of the tail. The eyes, much to Rosey's dislike, were a milky violet, set against black markings making them look crazed and bloodshot. The Blood Goron looked exactly like the image the Golden Goddess had shown her at the Palace. It was indeed small, no more than four feet tall, but menacing. Its eyes held a powerful intelligence that made Rosey more afraid than its armored body or spiked tail did.

Last but not least the Silver Goddess told them about the number one danger when dealing with a Raptor. They had acid glands at the top and bottom of their mouth all along the teeth line just above the gums. When they bit down they always released a stream of acid. It wasn't a very strong acid but it was powerful enough to give most skin types a second degree burn. The acid was there to cause pain and to incapacitate their prey. Rosey didn't have any intentions of getting bit by a Raptor, much less getting near one, and after everything she had just learned she certainly wasn't going to now.

Rosey asked many questions concerning the Raptors and the Blood Gorons and she was pleased to hear Hazel and the horses voicing their own worries. After the horses had been so silent, it was nice to hear their voices. Noly, to Rosey's surprise, seemed to be paying close attention though she, oddly enough, looked like an elementary student on a field trip and only asked one question which was to inquire if there were any bones in the display cases that she could chew on. Rosey was embarrassed but the Goddess's only response was to reach into another compartment, pull out a bone, and toss it to Noly who thanked her appropriately and carried it with her throughout the rest of the tour. Rosey decided not to ask and just go with it. Only after Rosey had seen so much that she felt she could write a book about Raptors and Blood Gorons did they leave the un-cold refrigerator room behind and rejoin her fellowship.

After returning to the hall where her friends waited patiently Rosey turned to the Silver Goddess and said, "You said there was someone you wanted me to meet? Am I to meet them now?"

"Yes, she is a very powerful ally. She should be here by now but she has a habit of being…late," said the Silver Goddess with a hint of annoyance as well as amusement. Rosey thought that it sounded a lot like how she might sound if she were talking about one of Rochell's antics.

"I am never late, everyone else is simply early," came a voice from the darkness.

Rosey looked to the left, almost jumping out of her skin. There stood an unusual transparent figure that seemed to be walking towards them. As it drew closer its indistinguishable body slowly took on a more recognizable shape. The form began to transform into the image of a large blue and white horse. The creature stepped out of what looked to be a swirling vortex of some kind. Rosey gasped as she realized that it was one of the vortexes that the Goddess had told her about, a portable form of a small sized portal. She had little time to contemplate this as the figure inside the vortex was drawing ever closer. To Rosey's amazement it wasn't just any horse but a unicorn. Rosey knew that unicorns and pegasi lived on this world and many other worlds beside this one but she had never imagined she would be seeing one. It resembled a large Andalusian, more fantastic than any she'd ever seen. The beast was a vision of perfection with a silky smooth covering of skin over a vast array of muscles that stood out below the white fur so fluidly that they seemed to propel the unicorn through water in gentle strokes as she walked. She had a more Friesian style face and her legs were feathered but the rest of her seemed to be Andalusian and a big one at that. She was much larger than even Rosey's Sarabie. She had to be at least twenty five hands high if not larger, never had Rosey been so towered over by a horse before. But this isn't a horse, she reminded herself, this is a unicorn. She could only imagine how tall Adina was if this was a mere unicorn. The giant equine was the most beautiful color that Rosey had ever seen. Her body was white with light blue and dark blue highlights, but the highlights were…moving. They fluxed along her body in various waves of patterns, disappearing across her flank and withers in an array of designs as she walked almost as if her skin was a constantly moving image. Her horn was a spiral of crystalline perfection with a blue swirl running through it. Her hooves were perfectly elliptical with grey spots lining their edges. Her mane and tail were white with blue and turquoise highlights at their ends. The only thing that Rosey noticed about the huge horse was her large and intense sapphire blue eyes which matched her own so vividly. After a few seconds Rosey found it hard to keep eye contact with the large unicorn. She had no idea if this was due to the respect she had for her or the startling power of her eyes. Rosey couldn't help but wonder if that's how other people felt when they gazed at her own blue orbs. Trying hard not to look too shocked she walked up to the unicorn and bowed her head slightly as she had learned was the custom when amongst more eloquent company. She was happy to view the Goddess and everyone else following her example out of the corner of her eye. While the Goddess did as Rosey had, the others all bowed at the waist or on one leg. The large horse returned the gesture with a bow of her large head.

"Hello, I am Rosey Mystic, the Keeper," Rosey said just managing to get the words out, but her voice was steady and strong.

"Good to meet you, Rosey Mystic, daughter of Esperanza and Mathew Mystic. I am Ysandir, Adina's most trusted advisor and administrator. I am the one she sends to schedule meetings, file reports, and simply find out anything new that is taking place." The unicorn's voice wasn't harsh, but Rosey could tell she was someone who was used to being respected and expected it. Rosey didn't disagree. "However, she has recently assigned me to look after you. Though we completely respected your mother's decision to have you raised on Earth, I am afraid it has left you at a large disadvantage. You lack a sufficient amount of knowledge pertaining to this world, which leaves you very vulnerable. To make sure that you have every possible protection provided to you, I have been assigned to advise and guide you throughout your journey. Being a unicorn I hold much more knowledge than any library and can ensure that you remain safer than any Keeper could ever claim." She raised her head proudly, obviously uplifted by her proclamation of strength. "I will be joining you on your journey. However, I cannot always be around you. During the more… uneventful parts of your journey I will be attending to other duties. I hope this does not worry you. Even if I am not there I will still be keeping an eye on you no matter where you are."

Rosey couldn't help herself and asked, "Even in the shower?" She could hear Noly and Hazel snickering and tried her best not to herself.

"If I must!" Ysandir proudly proclaimed, though she held a hint of amusement in her silky smooth voice. For some reason it reminded Rosey of cream.

"That's oddly creepy," said Rosey under her breath.

"Rosey, we cannot afford to take any chances or let our guard down," Ysandir said, stressing her words for emphasis.

Rosey nodded, realizing that she had been extravagant in her outburst. She couldn't help it though. She just had to break the staidness of the unicorn's speech. It had frightened her a bit and unsettled her. "I understand. I appreciate Adina sending you, please thank her for me when you see her next?"

"I will. You will be traveling through the cave systems for a while and then you will be heading to the Molt Volcano, I will meet you there. But remember I'll be watching and will come immediately if you need me." She was so adamant in her declaration that Rosey found the promise to be very stabilizing. It was the kind of promise that one made to their confidant and their friend.

Noly peeked out from behind Rosey's legs and said under her breath in a deep male voice, "I'll be bacccckkkk." Rosey gently kicked her in amusement, if Ysandir heard she did not say anything.

Turning to the Silver Goddess the large horse bowed her head, "Good to see you Silver Goddess, as always."

The silver woman returned the head bow and said, "And to you, may I offer you some water or oats before you leave? Maybe a place to rest?"

"No thank you, Adina is expecting me. Good bye everyone, I will see you at the Molt Volcano."

With that the large horse vanished in the same way she appeared, slowly fading into a whirling tunnel that appeared out of nowhere right in front of her. As soon as she was gone, the tunnel closed up leaving the room as if it had never been there.

"Sorry about that, Ysandir is so busy lately that all she has time to do is work, work, and more work," the Goddess quickly explained, noticeably worried about her friend. "She's been dropping in and out of places more recently as we're busy with the Raptors, tracking their movements. She is kind of like the Resistance's look out really." She rested her hand gently on the hilt of her saber sighing gently. Seeing Rosey's worried expression, the Goddess hurriedly explained, "Don't worry Rosey, she's been doing this long enough to know how to stay out of trouble. She's not Adina's Chief Administrator for nothing. Now, I believe it is well past eight o'clock. Please, dine with me and stay here for the night. It is certainly much safer here than it is above ground and the food is cooked to perfection," she added with a smile.

"Thanks, that sounds great. What do ya' say guys?" Rosey said turning to survey her friends.

"Sounds good to me," said Alex, happily getting up to stand beside Rosey.

"I'll second that," said Rochell, her arm swung around the neck of her palomino Phana "I'm starved!"

The horses stomped their hooves and whinnied a series of 'yes's', Eglen bowed his head and said, "How could I refuse." Hazel purred her agreement against Rosey's neck. Wolvereen and Nagura nodded in amusement. Noly jumped up and down yipping, "Bring on the meat!"

"Oh no, you're in the dog house," Rosey said, putting her hands on her hips in mock disapproval.

Noly slumped to the floor and put on her best doggy suck-up face, "What? Why?" she pouted.

"You know why, you bad girl," said Rosey teasingly.

Everyone's laughter echoed throughout the large room making it sound like it was filled with the voices of a large gathering rather than a small group of cherished friends

Chapter Thirteen: In the Past and the Future

The Silver Goddess was awake and staring blankly at the ceiling. She did not particularly like living underground; she missed the Golden palace and the comfort of its thick walls that had surrounded her in memories of her father, Roderick the Red. She paused for a moment as the memories came flooding back to her. He had been a huge man with fiery red hair and a short, well-trimmed beard. When he had died early in their lives from a strange illness, she and her sister were left in heartbroken despair. They were in their early twenties and Maharen had only just been chosen as the first Keeper. They had then risen to power in magic like their father had and had named themselves in honor of his name, Roderick the Red. They became the Golden and Silver Goddess and had forever sworn to protect the Keeper and honor their father's spirit. He had been a man that always yearned to do well. He had died before he'd ever seen the image of hope, their Keeper, take her stand. His deeds in the fight against the Evil One had been so great that they were still known far and wide across the world years after his passing. He had been a good man and an even better father. The Silver Goddess hoped with all her heart that he was looking down upon them with pride.

Her heart ached in her chest, as the image of her mother flashed before her eyes. Their father had not been the only one to adopt a name of color, so too had their mother. She had been known as Castella the Purple, because she loved the color purple and wore it all the time. She had been the only one in their family to be an elemental. For centuries their family had been completely made up of magikins. Most everyone in their family had always married magikins, so their union was very unusual. However, Castella and Roderick had fallen in love. Castella had been a gentle woman with fine black hair and soft purple eyes. Her element, consequently, was

The Mystics

Ice and Ice's color was purple. The Silver Goddess trembled at the memory of her mother because it was her birth that had killed Castella. Having a second child so close to the first had been too hard on her, and, though no one had ever said anything, the Silver Goddess blamed herself.

Her mother had died nineteen years before the Evil one came. Their father had raised them after that, until he joined his wife in heaven. It had been their mother who had named them. The Silver Goddess was called Hroevi and her sister was Tlow. They had never told anyone their true names since their father's death and anyone who knew what they were kept the knowledge to themselves. The Goddesses cherished their names. Like sacred blossoms of memories flowering but never for all to see. People often asked why they kept them secret, the reason was simple and some might even say it was ridiculous. Hroevi, the Silver Goddess, had been the one to initiate the idea when she learned what had happened to her mother. She had asked her sister to keep their names secret from everyone else because they were the gifts their mother had given them, especially to Hroevi, before she died. Their mother, in honor of their magikin family and powers, had given them names in the fracture language. Hroevi actually was the word silver in the backwards alphabet, and Tlow was the word gold. The Goddesses had decided this together, to hold their names close to their hearts and never let another soul learn of them.

When they were older, they discovered that keeping their names a secret was a better idea than they could have ever imagined. Since their names were in the Fracture Language and magic responded to that language, calling them by their names had not only enhanced their powers but had caused their abilities to physically manifest within their bodies. The signs were subtle but there: their golden and silver eyes, their occasional natural golden and silver hair strands that Rosey had mistaken for decorative beads, their gold and silver eye shadow and lipstick that painted their faces, even the gold and silver plates of armor were molded into their bodies despite everyone's belief that they were worn armor. They had their clothes specially designed to make sure it looked that way too.

Without thinking she ran a hand down the line of armor attached to her skin beneath her pajamas. It felt so natural. The ridges of the armor were almost soft like skin, but harder than any armor known to their world. Closing her eyes the Goddess sighed. Though their names affected both of them, the Silver Goddess feared that her powers may have been more affected than her sisters causing explosions of leaking energy. Magikins did not have magic within them, it was their ability to use magic that acted like a magnet drawing magic to them and their wands so that when the time came they could use it. In the Silver Goddess's case, she was attracting so much magic that it was melding with her very being and then leaking back out. She and the Golden Goddess shared that problem, and their names, though now unspoken, often times helped to strengthen that magnetism, though why she was leaking this tampered form of magic and her sister wasn't was still a mystery.

Lying in a room underground, furnished and created by her own unnaturally rampant powers, the Silver Goddess wondered about herself compared to her sister. Her sister had always been able to control her massive amount of magical powers well, without pause, and yet she was unable to. The power she possessed slipped through her hands and slowly leaked out of her against her will. It was the Master Healer Cascade, who had shown her how to mold this power that leaked from her and use it to her advantage. It had taken her years to perfect the art, and those years had made her a master at it. Even during sleep she could control the energies that had shaped and molded the cave systems into the ice, geode, and crystal wonderland that had amazed and mesmerized Rosey so. Despite its beauty, the Silver Goddess would have given anything for it to have never been made.

Suddenly a light tapping at her door drew her away from her memories. Her door opened and Nagura peeked in. The Goddess sat up in bed.

Looking at the large wolf, standing in her doorway, she wondered if things would ever be different. If maybe, one day, she could control her powers enough to leave the cave systems, which were, at the moment, the only places large enough to contain her powers and strong enough to resist them.

Blinking to adjust her eyes to the sudden light, she beckoned Nagura forward. The white wolf floated in on silent paws and stopped before the Goddess lowering her body in the wolf's bow. The Goddess bowed her head in return. Nagura straightened and said in her silky voice, "There have been reports of some kind of disturbance near the cave exit, ma'am. Argno detected it and has contacted Ysandir to see if she can be spared long enough from what she is doing to lend her unicorn eyes."

"Is it Raptors?"

"We're not sure; whatever it is, it's hiding itself pretty well. Calra is waiting in your office, she came to me immediately when Argno reported the disturbance."

"Great, if that's the case then it is probably a Minion," she said with disgust, quickly throwing on her robe and leaving the comfort of her room behind, Nagura at her heels.

Minion sightings were hard to confirm and even harder to pin point. They were new, brand new. There had never been Minions around when Esperanza was Keeper. Their arrival had disturbed the Leaders of the World, including Adina, and had been the main cause behind creating a stealth unit led by the Silver Goddess to capture and gather information on them. To date the unit had been unsuccessful. The creatures, whatever they were, were elite, powerful, and experts at staying hidden. The Evil One intended them to stay that way. They deployed guerrilla tactics, used magical gas to escape, and only operated at night. More and more reports had been pouring in from her sister at the Golden Palace about someone or something that had attacked a traveler or citizen and taken something. The strangest thing was the reports of what they were taking, small, meaningless things that could easily be made or acquired. There was no end to the Evil One and its tricks, the small everyday items it was stealing were no doubt essential to some bigger plan, a plan that they had yet to understand. The worst part was that the Minions could be anyone and could appear anywhere. They could be hiding in broad daylight as some everyday citizen. The less the Resistance knew about them the more chances they had at causing mayhem.

If the Minions were spotted near the cave exit then they might be hiding in wait for Rosey. What the Silver Goddess really wanted to know was how they acquired the knowledge that Rosey was here, if, that was why they were here in the first place. *They probably found out in a way that is much better than the one my own stealth force is using*, she thought bitterly. Nevertheless, they could not take any risks.

Bursting into her office she turned to Calra who had brought the report from Argno pertaining to the incident. Calra bowed as Nagura had done then stood at attention to the right of the desk. Calra was the largest wolf ever to be recorded, standing at seven feet tall with a coat that was so red it looked like deep crimson blood. Her striking black and cream highlights gave her a fierce and intimidating stare which had the effect of making you look away from her rather cold golden eyes. Her silver armor fit her wonderfully and made her look mighty intimidating. She had been the first wolf Nagura had ever trained. Calra had been a fast learner and was far more muscular than Nagura herself, though the large red wolf had never bested Nagura in any fight. Because of her fierce loyalty and her fighting abilities she had been given the title of Lieutenant of the Silver Goddess Guards under Nagura, the commander.

"Calra," the Goddess spoke, her voice even but strong, "I want you to take your best guards and scan the whole perimeter. Leave no rock unturned, find whatever it is, even if you have to search all night!"

Before Calra even moved, Nagura growled deep in her throat her armor clinking to life as if in protest at the order as well. Calra cringed as

Nagura said, "Wait, I am the commander, not Calra. I am still in charge." The Goddess gave her a warning stare and Nagura immediately laid her ears flat against her head in apology, "Sorry, Goddess. I do not mean to challenge your authority."

The Goddess waved it away and said, "Are you sure you can fight, I thought you could not in your…condition." She hesitated, eyeing Nagura worriedly.

Nagura eyed her with her head held high. "I saw the Master Healer Cascade today and she told me that I have a good two weeks before I need to retire for the season, so yes, I am more than capable to do my part."

The Silver Goddess looked Nagura up and down, her silver orbs piercing into the large white ghost of a wolf's own blue eyes. The two of them stared each other down, but the Silver Goddess gave up. There was nothing she could do when Nagura had an idea in her head. She was as stubborn as could be, even more so than Wolvereen, who followed orders to the point. *Speaking of which, where was Wolvereen?* she thought, noticing that the large black beast was not with his mate. She knew he had been assigned for the time being to the Keeper but still he should have reported in.

Turning to Calra the Goddess was about to give her new orders when Eyasha came into the room, her wings creating a small whirlwind in the office. The Goddess sputtered out of the way flabbergasted, reaching wildly for papers that weren't strapped down. The Wolves in the office made room, but did not react beyond that for this creature was known to them. Eyasha was the Lieutenant of the Golden Goddess's Guards and had been away on a small mission for the Golden Goddess. She handled many long distance needs and errands that the Golden Goddess needed completed. She was the best of the best. She had been scheduled to return to the Golden Palace tonight and must have stopped by to see what all the commotion was about. At least, that was the only explanation the Silver Goddess could think of. She scowled as she rearranged the papers on her desk and righted a few overturned pencil holders. She cast her gaze to the great beast entering the room, her wings gently folded at her sides. She shook her head in wonder.

Eyasha was a Capricosi, able to take on human or bird form at will. In bird form she resembled an eight foot tall peregrine falcon, in human form she was a five foot six, dark skinned woman with black and cream colored hair. At present in her bird form she had blue, golden, and black designs on her feathers making them shimmer and dance in the light of the room. More fascinating than that, however, was the miniscule layer of scales covering her body. The Goddess couldn't see them where she stood, but she knew they were there. Like her own silver plate of armor growing from her body, the Capricosi carried its own armor. While in bird form its feathers grew in-between the scales making them look like any regular feathered bird when really they wore a secret set of armor. Because of this armor Eyahsa was the only one in the Guards that did not wear full body armor, however, the head and legs of a Capricosi were less scaled then the rest of their bodies so Eyasha wore a golden helmet with visor and golden gantlets for her long legs.

Turning into a human to better fit inside the office, she stood before them. The helmet and gauntlets still fit her perfectly even though she was no longer in bird form. The human form was a mystery in itself. As far as anyone knew, the Capricosi was the only creature that could transform back and forth between two forms: human and bird. Their bodies had the ability to change their scales into scaled clothing when in human form but for some reason they still kept their giant wings on their back when they transformed, making them look like large angels.

Eyasha turned her elegant magenta eyes to the Silver Goddess and bowed low. "Sorry to barge in here like this, but I have a new report," she said her voice flowing in and out soothingly like the wind on a clear autumn's day. Her stance betrayed nothing and her eyes were focused and clear. She had high cheekbones and full lips that were tinted a yellow color like that of a beak. She was one of the best warriors in the Guards.

The Mystics

"I see, please give your report," said the Goddess, leaning forward. She did not want to waste time asking after Eyasha's mission. Whatever the bird-woman had been doing was usually confidential or would be given to the Silver Goddess anyway at a later date, so it was of no consequence. Right now, this was more important.

"Ma'am!" Eyahsa said proudly, straightening, "I was on my way back to the Golden Palace when I noticed a disturbance in the forests. Upon further inspection I discovered that a large amount of the guards were looking for something so I decided to investigate. I found Calra and she informed me of what was happening. I quickly pitched in to help. I came upon Argno and saw that he was fighting with something."

At this the Goddess frowned, her brows furrowing. An immediate alarm went off in her head but she remained quiet to hear the rest of the tale.

"I couldn't tell what it was, unfortunately, but I jumped in and fought it off. It fled after it realized who I was. I don't think it expected to be so thoroughly challenged." She said this last with a small smile on her lips, obviously happy with herself.

"Argno was there?! He was supposed to contact Ysandir and then get out of there. Did he say what happened?" the Goddess said, feeling her heart beat rise in her throat. Argno was an important creature; he was one of the Goddesses' messengers and so carried a lot of information. His work was much like what Eyasha did only he was more short distance, limited to this continent and even then he was mostly concerned with the information gathered between the Goddesses. If a Minion got a hold of him then they could get information from him valuable to their cause, especially concerning Rosey. A knot twisted in the Silver Goddess's stomach thinking about it. Argno was a Dragnagor, not a very powerful creature, but renowned for its flying ability and stealth operations which is why he made a good messenger. Unfortunately, his flying abilities made him hard to protect and govern, so the Goddesses had crafted something for him to protect himself with. It was a small spell attached to a pendant that attracted magic to it. The spell was activated by words, when they were spoken Argno would be covered in a force field. What could have possibly been so powerful that it had been able to break through his barrier?

"He told me he was leaving ma'am but then was attacked from above."

"From above...then this enemy can fly. That's at least some information." The Goddess sighed, they hadn't the slightest clue about any of these so called Minions and now she had something. It wasn't a lot, but it was a start.

"Yes, according to Argno, he was forced to land and whoever it was that attacked him was strong enough to break through the protective spell you and the Golden Goddess made for him. I would've hated to know what would have happened if I had not been there." Eyasha hung her head, her eyes glistened with worry. Everyone in the Resistance, including the guards, were like family and when one was down or attacked the whole group felt that pain.

"Indeed, me, as well," the Goddess said slowly, "Argno is not the best of fighters, but, perhaps, that is my fault, not teaching him and preparing him adequately. Where is he now?"

"At the infirmary, he was wounded by the Minion, and so was I. But his was worse than mine."

"Are you all right?" the Goddess asked worriedly, scanning Eyasha for a wound. She found it on her shoulder.

"Yes, fine, just a scratch," the Capricosi waved off the concern, seemingly oblivious to her own wound.

Taking a closer look, the Silver Goddess wouldn't have called the three long claw marks on Eyasha's left shoulder a scratch, but she looked none the worse for having the wound. Her eyes were bright, alert, and clear and her face did not seem pale. *She's probably running on adrenaline, the poor thing,* she thought, eyeing the dried blood trail that had run down the entire left side of Eyasha's body. She had barely noticed the blood before in all the

The Mystics

confusion not to mention that it had always been hard to make out anything with Eyasha. Her clothes always seemed to be moving, which could make you very disoriented, so the Goddess preferred to look at her face as much as possible. Besides the red looked so much like her clothing that she had mistaken it to be a part of the design. The Goddess frowned worriedly. On her human body, the wound looked horrific, but on Eyasha's giant bird form it probably was nothing more than a scratch. Still she could not let Eyasha leave until the wound had been looked at.

"Thank you for your help and quick report, go to the infirmary and make sure that you get yourself properly taken care of before you report to my sister," said the Goddess with a kind but stern look.

Eyahsa smiled and bowed then turned and left through the door she had come through. The Silver Goddess then turned her attention to Calra. "Calra, Nagura will join you shortly I need to speak to her alone please."

"Yes Ma'am," she said briskly.

Calra's voice had always made Nagura squirm a little inside. Looking at Nagura, the Goddess saw her slightly cringe. Calra had a certain ring in her vocal cords that, oddly enough, reminded Nagura of her mother's voice. It had been long and flowing, almost musical: a soothing and calming sound. Calra's voice had that same long and flowing tone but was lacking in musical prowess. It was more like a rock band style than a classical eloquent style. Nagura had prided herself on emulating her mother's sweet voice, but Calra's voice was like an insult to her mothers and often made Nagura seethe inside. The Goddess knew that Nagura did not fault Calra for this, she couldn't help how her voice sounded but, nevertheless, it still irked Nagura. The large wolf had never done anything to deserve Nagura's ire.

When born, Calra had been the largest pup and had grown to be a giant. Because of her size she had usually been left out of activities so she wouldn't cause trouble with the other pups who were much smaller than her. Nagura had noticed this when she was still only a lieutenant before becoming commander and decided to take the red-coated wolf's training on herself. Calra, as suspected, became a great fighter and could take down anything. When Nagura became the commander she quickly made Calra the lieutenant. She had been nothing but loyal, kind and strong since those days and the Goddess had little to no doubt that Calra was trying to repay Nagura for showing her such kindness and interest. She had never said anything but it was something that Nagura could feel, the Goddess was sure of it, she certainly could feel it. The large wolf walked towards Nagura and nodded to her before passing her, Nagura returned the nod then turned her attention back to the Silver Goddess.

Eyeing Nagura almost accusingly, she said, "Why did Wolvereen not report in?"

"I was finishing up for the night and told him to retire without me," her voice softened as she spoke of her mate, "He was almost asleep on his feet from his trip the other day. I received the information shortly before I was about to join him for the night. I felt there was no reason to wake him up considering all that he's doing for the Keeper. He'll need his rest if he is to stay in top condition."

The Goddess pursed her lips, knowingly dragging out the conversation, she knew that the longer she kept Nagura talking the less danger there was to her. Nagura knew this; she had been her commander for far too long not to know when the Goddess was stalling. The look of frustration across the ghostly wolf's face was priceless but the Silver Goddess kept her composure, trying hard not to overly anger her dearest commander.

"Are you sure you just didn't want to wake him because you were sure he'd insist upon you not joining the fight?"

"Possibly," Nagura said. The slight sound of clicking could be heard as Nagura, in annoyance, struck one claw against the floor boards.

The Goddess continued, suddenly becoming dead serious. Nagura seemed to sense this and threw her ears forward, her blue eyes alert and focused. "Are you mad at him for continuing on with Rosey without you, considering the situation?"

Nagura gave her a strange look, then burst out laughing. The Goddess had seen the laughter of many animals but it always amazed her how similar the laughter was compared to human laughter. It was just as boisterous, loud, and silly.

"Are you kidding, I almost bit his head off when he told me he was going to stay with me and send Calra in our place. I didn't just train her, I trained him as well before he became my mate, and it was my moves that made him the commander of the Golden Goddess's Guards. There was no way I was letting anyone lower than a commander go with Rosey and if it couldn't be me than it was going to be him. Calra is good but Wolvereen is better. We can't afford to let anything happen to Rosey before she's had a chance to collect the elements. She's fairly defenseless without them, even with her exceptional sword skills."

"I see, well as long as you're sure..?" The Goddess fixed Nagura with her gaze questioningly.

"Completely," she said confidently, squaring her shoulders and standing straight up, her tail lifted high in the air and her ears thrust forward in anticipation. Just then, Calra reentered the room with a small, brown, silver-armored wolf at her heels. The brown wolf looked young but strong with lean muscles and a powerful build. The Goddess saw Nagura staring at him in confusion. She didn't recognize him, and she wouldn't. The Goddess had enlisted him while Nagura had been away visiting Wolvereen for the past few months and put him under Clara as his mentor.

"Sorry ma'am, but this young scout says that they have checked the perimeters and found it secure and quiet. What further orders do you have?" said Calra, making Nagura flinch slightly, Nagura hid it by lifting her paw and licking at an imaginary itch. *How did she ever train her properly without betraying herself?* the Goddess wondered. Aloud she said, "Continue the patrols throughout the night, and make absolutely sure nothing is there.

Argno was attacked on our turf. I don't want those no-good-for-nothings thinking that they can come this close and get away with it. It is unacceptable and will not happen again!" she said with force. Everyone in the room straightened and held their heads high as pride surged through them. Turning the Goddess said, "Nagura, lead them well."

Nagura nodded then turned to the young brown wolf as they left, "Well done, you'll make a fine wolf yet. What's your name young 'n."

The small wolf seemed to shrink in size as he gazed warily up at his commander in her striking silver armor that had a habit of making her look like a ghost. Shaking, the small creature raised its head and said, "It's Cocoa, ma'am, my mother l-loved the word and so n-named me after it. She said my fur looks like it too...ma'am."

"Cocoa," said Nagura, sounding out the name almost affectionately, "I like it. I am your commander Nagura. Welcome to the Silver Goddess's Guards. Now, let's get to work."

Walking back to her room the Silver Goddess couldn't help but be utterly frustrated. She was not now, nor ever had been, disappointed in her guards and warriors but she just couldn't shake the feeling that, despite all their best efforts, the Evil One had the upper hand. All of her best guards had performed splendidly: Nagura had tidied things up well with the patrols, and Eyahsa and Argno's wounds were healing well and responding to treatment...and yet, they, technically, had accomplished nothing. These strange beings that the Evil One was deploying were as mysterious to them as the dark side of the moon, more so. They always hid their faces, even their whole bodies in dark concealing clothing and masks. They never spoke or responded to any questions asked of them, and they usually always got what they came for, except this time, thank goodness. The Silver Goddess had hated dealing with the reports brought in from her sister from local citizens or the weary traveler about some unlikely attack because she knew she could do nothing about them. The only good thing out of all this was that these creatures hadn't attempted to kill anyone, at least not

The Mystics

until tonight with Argno, and even then their main objective may have been capture. She hated calling them Minions, it sounded so cliché and cheesy, but she knew nothing else to call them. Because of their high grade stealth operations there was no way to know if they were human, animal, male, female, tall, small, or even if there was more than one individual doing all the attacking. The small information they had collected consisted of the presence of a black stone on their chest and now, after tonight's attack, that one of them had the ability to fly. Also, this recent attack had provided them with the understanding that not only were these creatures stealthy but they were very powerful. Whatever had attacked Argno so easily had also blasted through the Goddesses personally constructed barrier. It had taken both her and her sister days to complete that spell and attach it to the necklace Argno wore. Before tonight, there had been no one besides Adina that could break a barrier like that. It was very frustrating for someone who handled stealth operations daily and prided herself on the work she did. She rolled her shoulders feeling exhausted and worn out, but such was her life as the head of the Stealth Division, one of the many divisions in the Resistance that she leads. That got her thinking about her Research Division, of which she was also the leader. It was the best of the best and the main reason they knew what they knew now. It seemed, however, that they had been discovering less and less as time had gone by.

In a way, facing her sister every month with nothing to report about these creatures was embarrassing and struck home to her pride in herself, though her sister never said anything. The Golden Goddess was well aware of the personal turmoil the Silver Goddess found herself in and sympathized with it. *She may even blame herself for not giving me enough information to work with*, the Goddess thought, remembering when, once, her sister had taken her hands in hers after she had become frustrated about something and had told her that she would figure it out sooner or later. The Silver Goddess had built herself up on those words alone, 'you'll figure it out sooner or later', and she wasn't going to let her sister down, not when she knew she could do better. But what could she do? She had already doubled the guards, sent out her best trackers, and even staked out some of the Evil One's most widely used portal locations, hoping to catch one of them, but to no avail. It was like they knew their every move. If that was so then, Keeper or no Keeper, they were in trouble. If she couldn't find a way to at least capture one of these 'Minions' then she didn't have many options left but simply to hold off, report the incident, investigate to the best of their abilities, then wait and see what happened next.

The Silver Goddess didn't like admitting defeat, but then she had never looked at it as being a defeat. She had once told her sister, "I'm not defeated, I'm just waiting out the ride until my next chance comes along." The Golden Goddess didn't quite understand, she being the sister who had adopted their father's hard and almost unfeeling belief that giving up was not acceptable and accepting anything less than success was preposterous. However, being isolated with nothing but her guards to keep her company in her caves while she learned how to capture her leaking powers had taught the Silver Goddess the power of patience. She had learned to balance out the relentless fire that burned deep within her, the last of their father's red haired spirit, and had come to realize that there was great wisdom in waiting and being patient. She wasn't defeated. She just needed to work harder to achieve victory no matter how long it took.

Her sister would have hated the chaos that happened today. The Silver Goddess hated it herself. Every time she would give an order another report would come flying in. New orders would have to be relayed and by the time those were delivered there would be another complication. And poor Calra never had time to leave her office for very long before having to rush back with another report, though that may have been out of respect towards her master and commander Nagura.

The Silver Goddess didn't want to admit it but the Minions knew what they were doing and the fact that she knew little to nothing was making her, not only frustrated in herself, but scared. Why were they doing this?

The Mystics

Who were they? What were they collecting? How many were there? All of these questions ran through her mind mocking her and her lack of knowledge, but what could she do? She couldn't make the information pop out of nowhere, although she would have gladly appreciated it. At least this time around she would be reporting to her sister with new information about the Minions. It wasn't much but it was better than nothing. Argno being attacked might have spelled disaster if Eyasha hadn't been there to help. The attack, however, had given them a little more information about the Minions: flight and power. Knowledge about both would be essential in how the stealth force and the Resistance would be operating and responding to future disturbances. Its ability to fly might have been the reason why it had always gotten away in the past. Now they knew to watch the skies. She couldn't wait to hear what her sister had to say, she would probably figure something out.

Something wasn't right though, with so much power why would these creatures turn tail and run whenever there was more than one entering a fight. Eyasha's report had been normal, like most of the other reports concerning these beasts: the creature kept itself covered so you couldn't tell what species it was and only used weapons while attacking, so they had no idea if they were elemental or magical. Also the creature had immediately retreated when Eyasha showed up to help Argno, leaving Eyahsa and Argno only slightly wounded. It used the same variety of weapons, or at least, carried the same variety of weapons that it had previously been recorded to have. The uniformity of the attacks was probably used in an attempt to confuse them about whether there was one or more of them. They were skilled and dangerous and that was really all they knew.

Taking a deep breath she pushed the thoughts out of her head, she was way too tired to be thinking about this right now. Nearing her room she spotted Eglen a little ways down walking towards her calmly, a walk that the Silver Goddess admired in the patient, gentle giant but also found somehow annoying. It was almost as if he was moving in slow motion and she was speeding through time. She greeted him with a smile knowing full well that he was aware of her irritated reaction to his walking style.

"Eglen, what are you doing up at this hour?" she said curiously.

"I heard some commotion and came to check on things, is everything all right?"

The Silver Goddess hesitated. Although Eglen was no longer in the guards, since he had resigned after Esperanza's death, he was still a valued member of the Golden Goddess's Resistance. These days, he wore no armor and served more as an advisor than a warrior. He was certainly not serving as an advisor on this trip though, and, given the circumstances, the Silver Goddess found no reason not to tell him, after all, it might help him in his attempt to protect Rosey. Quickly, she told him about Argno and Eyasha's encounter with the Minion.

Afterwards he regarded her carefully, knowing that she was frustrated in herself for their lack of information and for not making sure Argno was better trained.

"So, is Argno all right then?" Eglen asked, worry fringing the edges of his honey clear voice. The two of them had become good friends throughout their years together and had taken it upon themselves to watch after each other. It was no surprise to the Silver Goddess to find him so distraught and worried.

"Yes, he's fine, Eyasha too."

"I should visit him...and Eyasha," he quickly added, "Thank you and I hope you sleep well."

He was about to walk away but the Goddess quickly called to him, "Eglen?"

He stopped dead in his tracks and focused his attention on her.

"Yes ma'am?"

Taking a deep breath she phrased what she was about to say carefully. Eglen could be unpredictable when it came to Esperanza. Looking him straight in the eye, she held him in her gaze for a few moments trying to read his thoughts, but, once again, she found herself oddly thrust out of Eglen's mind. The woman who had killed Esperanza had been a dear friend, and, even though she had been possessed, the memory of what she had done weighed heavily on him. The Silver Goddess always knew that Eglen had suffered the most from Esperanza's death but she had no idea that the death had sliced so deeply into Eglen's heart. *Is that why he is with Rosey, to be sure to protect her since he couldn't do the same for her mother?* She pulled away from his solemn expression and said, "Are you going to tell Rosey about you and Esperanza?"

He tensed at the mention of Esperanza, his musculature suddenly becoming hard and tight across his flanks and shoulders. His eyes flashed angrily but he somehow managed to push it away. The small mane of hair surrounding his shoulders and neck bristled slightly but quickly lay back down. When he spoke he sounded normal, almost too normal.

"No, not yet."

"Why?" It was such a simple word and yet it carried so much weight. She leaned against the wall, watching him.

"Because she has enough to deal with, let her grasp the little stuff before she gets to the big stuff."

"I see, thank you. Argno is waiting."

"I know. Thanks." He nodded to her, his eyes bright and happy again as if nothing had ever happened. He stepped past her and began making his way to the infirmary then stopped and turned his head to look at her. She stood there watching him go, her room a little ways down the hall. A stray length of hair lay over her left shoulder.

"What are you going to do about those Minions?" He asked, amusement lighting his eyes and his muscles lying relaxed and calm.

He was once again the old Eglen she knew, loved, and had grown up with. He didn't mistrust her, in fact, he trusted her with all his heart. Never again would she doubt him. Smiling confidently she lifted herself away from the wall and flipped the stray length of hair behind her shoulder.

Placing both hands on her hips and twisting her body slightly to show the full beauty of her muscled and battle hardened body she proudly proclaimed, "Oh, I don't know, but I'll figure it out sooner or later."

Chapter Fourteen: Walking Through the Caves

The pervasiveness of darkness seemed to collide into her being. Rosey gulped and tried to remain calm, she had never been a fan of dark places. A dim, unseen, light source cast an eerie low light and shadows danced within every corner. She peered around, her breath coming in shallow gasps. Where was she? Her body felt stiff and unfocused, like she was some kind of ghost fading in and out of existence. She looked down at her bare arms but saw no difference, nothing to confirm the strange sensation. The last memory she had was of talking with Ysandir, eating dinner, going to bed, and then falling asleep. A small memory at the back of her mind came into focus. The Golden Goddess was talking about a place you go when you dream. Was she in her Dream World? She hadn't entered a place like this while she was at the palace so maybe it was. Though Rosey had had many interesting and unusual dreams like everyone else, she hadn't imagined her Dream World would look like this. Rosey had absolutely no indication or previous warning as to what her Dream World would be or how it would appear, that would be for her own consciousness to decide, however, when she envisioned a Dream World this was the farthest thing from it.

She knew this wasn't just another dream. In most dreams you are not aware of the strangeness of the situation, nor do you usually understand yourself to be yourself. Usually you are seeing things as if you're watching them, not even able to comprehend your own form or character. In this instance Rosey was definitely awake and definitely conscious of herself and her surroundings as if she were awake. There couldn't be any doubt. This had to be her Dream World. Right in front of her was a bed covered in dull white linens. Feeling cold and clammy, she effortlessly lifted herself onto it and grabbed a blanket folded at the foot of the bed. She pulled the blanket tight around her shoulders and watched as her breath came out in billowing fog. Not sure of what else to do she waited silently for something to happen. From what she could see she was in a medium sized room no larger than fifteen by fifteen. A desk sat against the adjacent wall and large cabinets lined the wall in front of the bed. Small nightstands stood solid and oddly plain on either side of the bed. She could see no arrangement of figurines on either one of them that could offer her clues as to her surroundings. Turning and looking to the wall to the right of the bed she saw nothing. Swinging back to face the left wall she saw the long outline of a plain wooden door, but Rosey dared not move to open it, something about it felt forbidden or taboo. Even in the dim light she could see that the walls were a white or light grey color. This place was like a scene out of an old black and white movie.

Suddenly she heard whispering. It grew louder as if being carried on the wind. The voices swirled around her and seemed to be coming from everywhere at once like she was in the middle of a tornado. Just as suddenly as it had started, the voices stopped, leaving a ringing feeling in her ears. Then the door opened inward right in front of where Rosey sat. She felt her heart beat quicken. Instinctively, she held her head high and slid off the bed silently, leaving the blanket behind. She reached her hand up and grasped Andraste tightly. She glanced at the sword in amazement; she hadn't realized she was wearing it. Knowing that dreams were notorious for not making any sense, she ignored it and focused back on the door. She tensed, her muscles bulging against the leather outfit she wore. Suddenly the room was filled with a brilliant light. Rosey let go of her sword and covered her eyes. She fell back against the side of the bed. Whatever was coming through was going to, unchallenged. When the light stopped she looked up to see, who could only be, the White Witch. Her beautiful face gave Rosey a plain but sincere smile. Rosey regarded her curiously. Slowly her curiosity turned to amazement. The White Witch walked over to her side. Her flowing white robes billowed out behind her as if she floated. Her hair was elegantly pulled back in an elaborate white head piece. Pearls hung loosely around her arms and hair. White outlined the lids of her eyes and her lips where lightly painted a pale cream. A thousand scents hit Rosey all at once in a burst of sensory overload making her feel dizzy. Cinnamon, violet, rosemary, and various other spices, came rushing at her in a wild display of scents. She gripped the edge of the bed to steady herself as the scents faded and became more subtle immersing the air around them with tiny bursts of fragrance.

Rosey looked the witch up and down in amazement, she hated to admit it, but she had assumed that the White Witch would…well…look like a witch with a pointed hat and a broomstick, except in white. The woman that stood before her was anything but that, with an elegance and charm that made Rosey's original image seem childish. *Does everyone in this world always look so distinguished?* she thought, sighing deeply. She leaned against the bed in irritation then straightened. She felt better now that she knew that this was no foe but a friend, a friend she had been waiting for the past week. This was it; the White Witch was going to give her the location of the first element, Fire. She sure took her time getting to me though! Rosey knew that it was not up to her as to what the Witch did or didn't do, but being a new Keeper and newly introduced to The World Within A World she would have thought that the Witch would have made it a first priority to meet with her as soon as possible. *Because of her timely manner, I almost had a heart attack thinking that something was wrong.* Rosey sighed, exasperated. There was nothing she could do about it and there was no sense in bringing it up.

"I was wondering when you were going to show up?" said Rosey teasingly, trying to lighten the mood and make a good first impression despite her inward irritation. It worked. The Witch laughed daintily as an amused mother would. "I'm sorry to have kept you waiting but the time was not right. I have the location for you now." Her voice could only be described as ethereal, as if many voices were speaking all at once and then not at all. It was a kind, powerful, and wise voice beyond the years of any that Rosey had ever heard. Even the Goddesses' voices paled in comparison. Rosey nodded, stunned by the complexity of the woman's speech but recovered to ask with determination, "Where is it?"

"The Molt Volcano is your destination. Any other time I would have let you continue on your own path since you were heading in the right direction but it is your first time and it's important you meet me." "I see," Rosey looked away. Once again she was meeting someone. She wondered how many others she would meet before she had finally met everyone important. Suddenly a painful realization gnawed at the back of her mind. One thing in particular had plagued her about the Witch. If she resided within the crystal then she must have known Rosey's mother.

Turning back to the woman she said abruptly, "Did you know my mother?"She held back tears as she continued, "You had to. You were her Witch too, weren't you? Please…could you…tell me…about her?"

Every word felt like lead in Rosey's mouth, she was surprised to find herself shaking. Andraste shuddered against her back as if it too was saddened by the memory of its former master. A slight tingling raced down Rosey's spine as she looked into the Witch's eyes to see an almost emotionless face. The Witch stared at her for the longest moment and the most heartbreaking silence filed the room making Rosey fidget slightly. The Witch turned her back and Rosey closed her eyes to hold back the tears. She wanted so badly to know about her mother, this brave Esperanza. She would have asked the Goddess but her entire time at the palace had been taken up by practicing, studying, and so forth. She had barely had time to talk to her friends much less reminisce about her mother with the Goddess.

Rosey had no idea why the emotions were spilling out of her now. Perhaps it was because this was a Dream World so no one could ever see her or hear her here. She was completely safe from prying eyes. It was only now that everything started piling on top of her. All of this would be so much easier if her mother, the Keeper before her, were here to help her learn. Mustering the strength and the will she slowly spoke, surprised but happy to hear her voice was calm. "All I want is to know her, to understand what she understood about being the Keeper." Rosey looked at the Witch but her back was still turned. Silence. The Witch remained turned. "I'm sorry, I cannot say," the woman finally said with what seemed like disappointment. "I am *your* Witch now." She turned around and said with a voice that reminded Rosey of a tough mentor, "Each Keeper is different and has her own dilemma to overcome. What happened left you to deal with a messed up situation." She paused and Rosey looked at her with confused pain written across her face. She did not have to ask to know that the Witch was talking about the peculiar circumstances surrounding the death of her mother. The woman's eyes glistened with an unseen power. Rosey, for a moment, glimpsed her own reflection in them but then it changed and she saw the face of a much older, more mature woman: her mother. She almost reached out to her but the Witch blinked and the image disappeared, "Rosey you have the power to change our world, to save it…don't waste it."

In that moment all time stopped and she felt herself jerked awake as she left the Dream World. Looking about she recognized the beautiful room she had been shown to the night before after a boisterous and happy meal provided by the Silver Goddess. The room was the complete opposite of the place she had just been to in her Dream World. Like everything else in the underground cave systems where the Silver Goddess lived, the entire bedroom was composed of bright multicolored varieties of geodes, crystals, and ice. As before, there was not one thing that wasn't bathed in color. Only the covers on her large bed where not crystal, but they might as well have been. The only thing Rosey could think of comparing them to was plastic wrap, but they felt like cotton with a silken texture. They weren't see-through, but had a cloudy, cream colored look about them. They were the most comfortable covers that Rosey had ever slept under and even her nightgown had been composed of the same material.

To Rosey's relief the room wasn't as extravagant and ornate as the one she'd had at the palace. It was plain with its own full bath that was just as modern as the ones at the palace had been. A simple dresser, mirror, and bedside tables occupied the room decorated with simple designs. The room was lightly lit by strange iridescent glowing tubes that ran the length of it. Their brightness was adjustable and right now they were on the lowest setting with only one side of the room lit. Usually Rosey slept in the dark but being underground with no windows made it a bit too dark, even for her, so she had kept a small portion on.

Rosey moved her right hand and brought the locket the Goddess made for her to her face. She'd been sleeping with it every night since it was given to her. It comforted her in some way and made her feel as if she was a bit closer to the parents she never knew. As if the locket was proof that she was with them. She opened it and gazed at her parents for a few moments before closing it and rubbing her face in exhaustion. She turned her head and looked at the small bedside clock that the Silver Goddess had been so kind to give her. Usually the people of The World Within A World told the time by the stars, moon, and sun but being underground the Resistance did not have access to them so they had made use of the Earth clock, much to Rosey's happiness. She was even more surprised to learn that it did not run on batteries but from a small stone that conducted electricity with the help of a spell. Gazing at the familiar clock hands she saw that it was too early to be getting up so she rolled over and went back to sleep, regular dreams filling her mind with the image of a woman with long black hair and the same startlingly blue eyes.

For the second time that night Rosey awoke. She felt oddly numb inside from the meeting with the Witch, as if it had left a dark hole in the pit of her stomach. Awkwardly she sat up in bed and rested herself against the plush soft pillows. She was drowsy and it was clearly still too early to be getting up but she just couldn't fall back to sleep. Since waking up after, what Rosey was now considering a nightmare, she had found it hard to sleep peacefully for the rest of the night. Now she felt groggy, but in a soothing way like that feeling you get when you are so warm and comfortable that you want to be lazy all day and just lie there and doze. Taking a deep breath, she figured that would be the best thing to do until she either dozed off or the time became reasonable to be up and about even for an early riser like herself.

Glancing down, she gazed at the sleeping images of Noly and Hazel curled up at the foot of her bed. Years of sleeping with them had made Rosey an expert at moving around in bed without disturbing them. For some reason watching them sleep made her feel tired. She snuggled into the pillows more, pulling her parent's locket close to her heart, and happily fell into a peaceful slumber.

When she next awoke it was 9:00 a.m. Rosey happily jumped out of bed feeling rejuvenated and filled with energy. She immediately ran a hot bath and soaked in the heated water loving that though, The World Within A World was more of an olden days style, it had updated and almost modern looking furnishings. Finishing with her bath she quickly got ready, packed her stuff in her travel bag and then made the bed. She knew that the sheets would probably be taken off and cleaned but she didn't care, she wanted to show her thanks in some way. She quickly gave Noly and Hazel a good brushing then all three of them tidied up making sure everything was exactly the way they'd found it when they first came.

Rosey shouldered her bag, strapped Silver Knight to her waist and fastened Andraste securely upon her back. The two weapons gleamed in the light cast by the strange lights lining the room. Part of training with her sword and dagger was learning how to take care of them. Last night before going to bed Rosey had spent a good amount of time carefully cleaning her swords and their sheaths. She admired them for a few minutes, taking great pride in the work she'd done. Then, turning, she, Noly and Hazel left the room behind and headed to breakfast.

Walking into the dining room Rosey spotted Alex, Rochell, Eglen, and the others already eating breakfast. The Silver Goddess wasn't present. Rosey was a little happy that she wasn't the last person to breakfast but couldn't help but wonder if the Silver Goddess was okay. After taking her seat in-between Alex and Rochell she inquired after the silver woman to Eglen.

"She was up late last night with some Resistance business so she might be sleeping in," he said, giving her a warm smile.

Rosey returned his smile but felt her curiosity poking at her sides. She had half a mind to ask about what the 'Resistance business' included but then thought better of it. If they had wanted to tell her then they would have. It was obviously something she didn't need to be worrying about, besides she wanted to tell them about her dream. Getting everyone's attention she told them about what the White Witch had said. They were all surprised but happy that the White Witch had visited her and even happier to hear that they were heading in the right direction.

"Good thing we were heading there already," Alex said after she had finished.

"Yeah, it saved us some time," Rosey said, aware of how Alex's eyes bore into her. He knew perfectly well that she had probably asked about her mother. She evaded his questioning eyes by striking up a conversation with Rochell. Out of the corner of her eye she saw Alex shaking his head knowingly. He had known her long enough to know when to quit.

To distract herself from him, she asked, "So this Molt Volcano…is it active? You know…is it a 'will destroy on contact' kind of volcano or is it extinct? I know the Golden Goddess said it is very magical but is it anything like a normal volcano?"

As suspected, Alex jumped on the question with eagerness as if he had been waiting to be asked something.

The Mystics

"To start, it's most definitely not a normal volcano. It has never erupted but it doesn't show the signs of a dormant volcano, either. For the most part you just need to be careful and treat it with respect."

"Has anyone died around it?"

"Only the ones who are stupid enough to go near it," said Wolvereen from down the table. He was eating a chunk of blood stained meat from what must have been a deer. She swallowed hard as she saw the blood soak into the tablecloth were a small drop had landed.

"That won't happen to us. You are the Keeper, I'm sure the Mother will shut down the Volcanoes defenses while you're on her turf," said Rochell, trying to reassure her.

"And if she doesn't shut them down, we'll make the right choice and do what we always do…kill her," said Alex, with a twinkle in his eyes as he casually took a bite of his eggs. The group was silent for a moment, staring at Alex in shock, then they all started laughing.

Wolvereen bit off another chunk of meat then rolled his eyes, "Children!" he breathed under his breath in annoyance. Eglen smiled knowingly.

An hour after Rosey arrived, the Goddess came in wearing a silver, gold trimmed, leather outfit similar to the brown ones given to Rosey and her friends. Rosey repeated what she had told everyone else. The Goddess looked pleased and congratulated Rosey on meeting the witch for the first time. Rosey thought she looked exhausted but didn't say anything. Whatever problem took place last night, it had taken its toll on the tall woman.

After the meal everyone gathered and made sure that they had everything packed and ready to go. The Goddess re-provisioned them and had had all their clothes washed the night before. Rosey felt bad that they were leaving so soon, but they had to get on their way and the Goddess was only too happy to be seeing them off on their journey. After they said their farewells to the Goddess and thanked her for everything she had done, they resumed following Nagura with Wolvereen at her heels, through the crystal and ice covered tunnel until it opened up into a regular cave system.

Rosey walked with Noly by her side through a series of spectacular caves that made Rosey wish she could stop and take pictures, but not having a camera or the time, she couldn't. Still the beauty of the caves was breathtaking. Patterns and hard rock surfaces made the maze of carvings a labyrinth of excitements. She had never seen a cave so big before and was glad she had been given the chance to travel through such an extraordinary one. This particular part of the caverns looked to be more natural, no crystal could be seen and water was still dripping in some places. The walls were barren scarred rock and layered limestone, not icy fluorescents. She was now sure, after seeing that this part of the caverns was regular looking with stalactites and stalagmites, that the crystal wonderland that the Goddess lived in was influenced by her power and hers alone, but whether that was intentional or not was unknown.

Alex had told her that the caves were made long ago by the magma flows from the Molt Volcano and various underground waterways from the sea line. The flows went downhill burrowing away from the city of Neran which sat partially on a hill. He also explained that though the Volcano was somewhat active, it was also surrounded by magic, magic that many Magikins would dare not try to use. This magic was very wild and unbalanced and so had often made the volcano unstable. Alex told her that sometimes magic would gather in places called energy spots, just like with the Energy Flows. These places, like Earth's Incan Empire in Peru, were said to hold intense spiritual energy. The volcano's activeness, however, was the reason why Rosey was continually seeing areas of smooth, black, silky-like rock everywhere inside the caves. Over time, leftover rainwater and the underground waterways from the sea had come in cooling and widening the magma-made tunnels, making them much more cave-like. Rosey used Alex's willingness to share his knowledge of The World Within A World to pass the time and was vaguely aware of Rochell listening just as carefully.

Rosey didn't like the fact that she would have to stay in the cave for another two days. She was hoping to be able to see the sun again before she laid eyes on the volcano but that was impossible. After the first day of walking, she was starting to hate caves and their dullness. And it just kept getting better. Rochell, of course, was loving every bit of it and just couldn't wait to tell Rosey about the strange new rock she'd found that always looked exactly like the last one. Alex was ... Alex, talking about the structure of the cave and how it was not good to make a fire in a place where the smoke could not escape as if she didn't know. Wolvereen was grumbling about not having any meat. Eglen was silent as ever. The horses were complaining about rocks in their shoes (all except Sarabie who seemed to only be praying for when they'd find their way out). Noly wouldn't stop asking if they were there yet, Hazel was sleeping in her little bed on Sarabie's saddle, and Nagura led them on, not stopping to look back at the group. The next day was exactly the same and Rosey was so irritated that she was sure she could take on any Raptor with her own two hands, all they would have to do was lead her to them. Rosey noticed that the caves were not lit by the strange smokeless torches that she has seen before, but by small round orbs containing a florescent light. When she hesitantly, for fear of another magic lecture, asked Alex about the orbs, he told her they were easy magic spells that allowed for light and nothing more. Before he could say anything else she pretended like Rochell needed her. By the end of the day, when they were supposed to leave the caves, they had to change their plans because there were reports of Raptors nearby. A smaller, brown wolf called Cocoa delivered the news, appearing seemingly out of nowhere just in time to scare the crap out of the group. Noly had laughed at the occurrence especially when she had seen Wolvereen's furry body fluff up like a cat's tail. Rosey had held back her laughter afraid of what the annoyed wolf might do, but embarrassment had silenced him.

Much to Rosey's disgust, her fellowship was not taking a chance with her life, so they stuck to the cave routes yet again. The Silver Goddess provided more provisions for them and Nagura and Wolvereen made trips outside to hunt for meat with other alternating armored wolves. While they were gone the others stayed as quiet as possible, waiting for their return. It was difficult waiting for them since they all wanted a chance to go outside, breathe in the sweet air, and feel the sun on their face.

Because the caves were safer, Nagura insisted on using them to go a little farther towards the volcano than was originally planned. Rosey had to agree with her, despite her annoyance. Even though she trusted the Silver Goddess and Nagura she had a feeling that it wasn't just Raptor reports that were keeping them in the caves. *I wonder if it had anything to do with that "Resistance business," Eglen spoke about the other day.* she thought. But not having the patience or the time she didn't bother asking.

That wasn't all she was annoyed about. She understood that while she didn't have an element she was pretty helpless against a large Raptor, sword or no sword. It made her angry anyway knowing that she was powerless to do anything, plus the constant scenery of nothing but rock and water wasn't helping any. Sure, the place was unbelievably amazing and warmer than the winter world outside, not to mention cooler for the heavier furred of their fellowship, but it became quite boring after a while and the constant lack of sunshine was depressing. On top of that, the ceilings were low enough to make Rosey feel constricted as if at any moment the walls would come crashing down on top of her and it meant that they couldn't safely ride, despite the rare large openings that they'd happen upon. She was beginning to appreciate more and more the weight that Sarabie usually bore as they traveled along on the dirt and rock packed floor.

The end of the caves and their third day inside them was approaching when Rosey and the others suddenly heard a strange rumbling above ground. They all stopped in wonder. Rosey looked to Alex and Rochell, but they all seemed startled beyond belief. The horses kicked up their hooves and Noly whined. Wolvereen's harsh growl sounded over them, "Hush now, and don't move. This is not right…" he put his scarred snout to the

The Mystics

air and began sniffing. His tail was raised and the fur on his back was sticking up. Nagura growled beside him then padded forward on silent paws. She zoomed past Rosey, her ears erect and pointed at the passage before them. Someone or something was coming.

Rochell and Alex were beside Rosey in a heartbeat. Hazel lashed her tail from her perch on Rosey's shoulders. Noly took a defensive stance in front of Rosey while the horses ringed them in, pawing at the ground. Nagura did not sound any alarm, only stood powerful and strong in her gleaming armor. All the while the ground kept rumbling, a few powerful blasts went off above their heads and dust fell from the ceiling. Rosey didn't know what to do, her heartbeat soared and sweat beaded her forehead as the ground above them seemed to tremble. What was going on!? The sudden urge to run leapt into Rosey's thoughts, but she held it back, knowing that running would do more harm than good. Noly shivered but leaned on Rosey protectively. Rosey bent down and hugged Noly close, Hazel buried her head in Rosey's hair. The small lights illuminating the path flickered as the rumbling got worse and more powerful, the elaborate shadows they cast on the walls and the pathway only helped to make things seem worse.

"What in the world is happening up there?!" Alex said, using a tone of voice Rosey had never heard him use before, probably because it sounded panicked. He stared at the ceiling in silent wonder. Rochell did the same. Something wasn't right, yet Wolvereen and Nagura remained calm, Eglen too, though he looked shaken.

Alex whipped out his wand and was about to utter a spell when Cocoa, the tiny brown armored wolf, came running from the passage before them screaming at the top of his lungs.

"RUN, NOW! RAPTORS ARE COLLAPSING THE CAVES!" He yipped at them to follow him before he took off. That was all it took and they were suddenly in hot pursuit of the brown wolf, right on his heels.

Rosey barely saw or comprehended anything after that. She was vaguely aware of Rochell and Alex grabbing each of her arms and pulling her along with them, staying on either side of her no matter what. Noly was in front of them beside Cocoa. Rosey saw flashes of white to her left so that must have been the looming, giant figure of Nagura with her white pelt and Wolvereen was to their right based on the flash of golden light she saw every now and then coming from his armor. She was aware of Rochell and Alex beside her every step of the way, but the others were lost amongst the rising chaos.

The world suddenly became a convulsed confusion of sounds and terrified screams from above. How she could be hearing screams was beyond Rosey and how the caves could be collapsing didn't seem to matter. The hard paced pounding of the horse's hooves and scrapping of Eglen's claws were powerful sounds behind, around, and in front of Rosey even though she was sure they remained behind them. The fact that they had chosen to stay behind Rosey, despite the fact that they were far faster than her any day, escaped Rosey's mind at the moment. Mounting them would have made for greater speed, but the caves were so unpredictable, it could have been what ended her life instead of saving it. It was the same reason why she had stayed walking for the past two days, and the other reason was to avoid Raptors. Now, it seemed they had found their way to her, but how? Rosey could hardly think then, suddenly, her hearing was blocked out by a roaring boom that seemed to resonate throughout the entire cave. She didn't look back, she couldn't look back! All she could see was the walkway in front of her and the backs of Cocoa and Noly. They were all that she could see and if they hadn't been there then she'd have never known where to go. The lights began flickering more and more as the cave began to collapse behind them. The resonating sound was so loud that Rosey's ears rang with a powerful drumming. Adrenaline surged her on and she and her friends rushed through the caves at break neck speeds. Alex wasn't even able to put up a shield or use any spell, if he tried he'd risk falling, messing it up, or worse. There was no time; any lapse in seconds could mean death. Not to mention that a shield spell wasn't always capable of holding up

The Mystics

against certain extreme weights and the gigantic rocks of the cave ceiling probably would have been in that weight range.

A sudden whoosh of cold air and a blast of dust billowed at the back of Rosey's feet, making her run faster. The dust cloud was starting to catch up with them and Rosey quickly covered her face as stray bits of grit tried to fly into her eyes. Hazel hung on for dear life and Rosey reached up and grabbed her leg to make sure she didn't lose her. She knew she was squeezing too tight, but it was better than losing her grip. Her friends had the same strong hold on her and Rosey sent prayers that the others were okay and safe.

Rosey had long ago lost the sounds of Eglen and the horses and she couldn't see Nagura or Wolvereen anymore. The flashes of white and the gold that she had seen earlier were now gone thanks to the cloud of dust. Noly and Cocoa were the only ones she could see. Tiny bits of debris hit Rosey's back and small pieces flung past her face, if one hit her leg or foot just right, she'd be done for. Hazel hissed and turned around, she yanked her leg free but presented Rosey with a back leg. Rosey gripped it and had little time to realize that the tiny cat was batting away falling rocks, small ones obviously, and keeping an eye out for any large sized ones. Rosey wanted to ask if she could see the others, but she was afraid to speak, afraid to stop her steady flow of breath. In and out. In and out. In and out. She said it over and over again in her head as she ran, determination drawing her on. The exit was almost there, just around the corner, maybe the next. Almost! Almost! Her muscles screamed at her, her ears rang with the sound. So much sound and dust all around her. Everywhere! It was almost unbearable, but sheer will power beat out blind panic and adrenaline forced her legs to work.

After what seemed like hours, Rosey saw light. Her hopes rose so powerfully that all the pain in her muscles and chest seemed to dissolve, that is, until she got outside. With no other possible rout of escape or time for strategic planning they burst out into the open and right into a full-on battle. Rosey was hit immediately with the freezing air of the winter world, but her heated body barely noticed. She tried to reach for her sword but her friends slammed her to the ground as a giant creature, Rosey wasn't sure what, flew over their heads screaming in pain. Alex's wand was out but he cast a powerful spell in another direction. Rosey could barely see what was happening, but she heard the spell make contact and a scream split the air. Alex muttered what she thought was a protection spell and felt just a bit safer as the pink, shimmering bubble started to surround her. Rosey was now safe, but everyone else wasn't and she couldn't do anything to help them. Shields were stationary and didn't move unless constructed to. If Rosey moved outside the shield, it wouldn't follow her and her friends weren't planning on letting her go anywhere any time soon. She was stuck and she was unable to help.

Rochell lifted her arm and air seemed to swish around the three of them as it plowed into the chest of a giant creature on two massive legs bearing down on them, jaws agape. Rosey gasped at the power in Rochell's attack. It was so strong that it immediately threw the giant beast backwards and into the winter thriving bushes it had emerged from so fast that she hadn't been able to recognize it. It was now nothing but a tangle of legs, arms, and screaming agony. Rosey had no doubt that it had been a Raptor. Rochell and Alex hovered over top of her, physically shielding her with their bodies. They were almost sitting on top of her and pushing her into the ground. Hazel managed to make it out from under her neck before she was crushed, she stood at Rosey's neck hissing in defiance and clawing the ground. Andraste was pushing into Rosey's back so there was no way she could unsheathe it. She fumbled for Silver Knight but she was so wedged against the ground that she couldn't get to it either. She fought the urge to shout out in anger and wounded pride at her helplessness. The only possible defense she could think of was to pull her legs in close to her, like she had been taught, to make sure nothing went for them.

She tried to locate Noly or the horses but couldn't see or hear any of them. Suddenly she saw a black mane and tail, it was Sarabie. Rosey watched in horror as something large slammed into the giant horse, knocking her back. Rosey almost screamed in pure terror and anger, but had no idea if it was a Raptor or a good guy. She heard Sarabie scream and give a giant huff but couldn't see what happened to her or what she was doing. Rosey felt rage flare up inside her heart, angry at whatever was threatening her horse. She could no longer stay silent. "DON'T TOUCH MY HORSE!" she screamed, trying to burst forth from Rochell and Alex's cocooned protection. Her adrenaline rush almost knocked them both off of her. She was so angry that she didn't know what to do. She just wanted to do something, even if it was useless. Her friends, however, had their wits about them. They grabbed Rosey in unison and slammed her between them once again and back down. Rosey's strength was zapped from her and she let her head fall in misery at her current state. Suddenly, a giant black figure soared over top of Rosey and she thought she recognized the golden armor of Wolvereen. He was over her in a heartbeat and went in the direction that Sarabie had been knocked. The wolf reminded her of her dog. Where was Noly! Where were Nagura and the others!? Where were they? Fear started to creep into her heart and her body trembled. Hazel stayed by her face, her tail lashing. Sounds clashed together all around her and the world began to slow as everything seemed to stop.

She desperately wished that she had never wanted to leave those caves. How clueless had they all been to think that walking through a cave was so terribly boring. How had that led to this! The one good thing about her outburst was that she had finally been able to draw Silver Knight from its sheath. She held it aloft before her, waiting, but with Alex and Rochell blocking her view Rosey could see nothing. She could only hear the fear, pain, and suffering coming from all around her. The screams, snarls, and scratching sounds were so loud that she actually felt them impacting her body. They came from every direction, surrounding her with the promise of death. The image of Lyesal's dying form came back to Rosey's mind. Her heart skipped a beat as the wolf was replaced by Noly, Rochell, Alex, everyone she'd ever loved. She wanted to scream, she wanted to act, she wanted…to fight! Suddenly, that wasn't going to be necessary. The dust from the collapsed cave behind them finally seemed to catch up with them in a blast of sudden and thankful coverage. Rosey knew that only seconds had passed since they left the cave, but it had felt like minutes.

The dark, dusty cloud covered them in a thick layer and Rosey coughed. She lifted her shirt over her face and her friends did the same. She grabbed Hazel who was also coughing and shoved her under her shirt. To Rosey's surprise Rochell and Alex almost dragged her into the thick dust cloud further, back to the collapsed cave exit. They were using the dust cloud to hide her which made perfect sense but made it very hard to see and breath. Suddenly the air around Rosey was clear and pure. She looked up to see Rochell twisting her arm. The air around them was swirling around and around, encasing them in the middle of a miniature dust tornado with a core of clean air. The dust joined the whirlwind and became a swirling mass. It was an extra personal shield of air to add to Alex's magical pink one.

Hazel poked her head out of Rosey's collar and gulped in some badly needed fresh air. Rosey held Hazel close, her tiny frame was shivering, but she was safe. Her beautiful and familiar eyes made Rosey feel warmth flow through her, it was the only solace in the whirlwind of emotions flowing through her. She sank to the ground and listened to the sounds, closing her eyes and hoping for the nightmare to stop. Without any element and only a sword and dagger to help her, she was essentially defenseless. All she had were her friends and they were protecting her diligently, she couldn't risk getting in their way. She had to stay low, stay quiet, and stay calm. She said those words in her mind again and again, trying to calm herself. She grasped the crystal around her neck and warmth spread throughout her whole body immediately. The screams, the pain, and all the chaos seemed

The Mystics

to disappear to be replaced with what Rosey was sure looked like a woman. Standing before her was the see-through shape of a tall woman with long, flowing black hair staring at her, a smile on her face. Rosey wasn't sure if she was hallucinating or if she was losing her mind, but the figure was there, hiding in the folds of the multiple wisps of wind. She didn't say or do anything, just smiled.

Rosey reached out for her, only to see her image disappear as a solid sheet of blue, pink, and purple icy crystal surrounded them. Turning to the cave exit, Rosey saw small tendrils of icy liquid leaking from the cracks and rocks of the collapsed cave. It formed around them in many patterns. She vaguely saw other strands of the tiny stuff branch off in other directions, where they were going was unknown to Rosey. She just barely saw a vortex suddenly appear and Ysandir come charging out, whinnying a war cry and embedding her horn into an advancing beast before the crystal covering extended over Rosey's head, encasing her, Alex, Rochell, and Hazel into a wide and very tall crystal dome. Rosey had no doubt as to where it was coming from, it was the same flawless design of the Silver Goddess's powers. She had sent the crystals to protect them and Ysandir had come as promised. Rosey's heart suddenly filled with happiness. She was certain that the other tendrils of icy crystal were going to find and protect the others! It had to be. Rochell quickly dropped the protective tornado and then fell to her knees next to Rosey in an utter release of absolute, pure, relief. Alex joined them on Rosey's other side, his hands resting gently on her back. Rosey saw their lips moving but could barely hear what they were saying. Her mind zoomed with everything that had happened and she was mute for a few moments before Alex and Rochell's voices started to make sense and Rosey was able to answer them. She breathed deeply, focusing on each breath carefully. Alex helped her, almost coaching her. Silver Knight was still clutched in Rosey's hand. She stared at it for a few minutes and then sheathed it. Alex took this as a good sign. It was then that Rosey noticed that the dome was soundproof. She could no longer hear the terrible sounds of battle that raged just outside the thick, crystal walls. Her voice, cracked and dry, finally came through, "What's going on?"

Alex shook his head, "I don't know. Seems to me that the Raptors either found out you were down in the caves or knew about them and wanted to destroy them anyway just in case. We're safe now, the Silver Goddess's crystal barriers are impenetrable by most regular means." He leaned up against the wall, turning his head upward revealing a small cut that lay just below his cheek where a stray rock must have cut him. He looked exhausted and his face was dirty. Dust coated his forehead and neck. He licked his lips and grimaced at the dust. He took some water from his pack and slapped it onto his face, washing it off. Rochell was doing the same. Rosey reached up to touch her own face, finding it just as thoroughly covered. She found her water and began cleaning the dust off. Even Hazel jumped down and started licking herself. The chaotic world just moments before had now been reduced to a completely quiet sanctuary. It was amazing how fast things could change, at least Rosey was still alive and kicking.

Once again Lyesal's image shot through her mind and Rosey shifted positions uncomfortably. She couldn't think about everyone that was dying or sacrificing themselves for her. Was one of them Noly? Maybe Sarabie was out there whinnying in the dirt as she bled to death. Rosey could barely think about anything. Her muscles ached, her back was surely bruised from Andraste poking into it, and her lungs felt as if they'd been run on a high rinse cycle. She could only image what was going through her friend's minds; probably how in the world the Raptors had learned about them, while all Rosey seemed capable of thinking about was how stupid she had been to agree to do this. This was the first real time her life had been in danger. She had known it could happen, she'd been warned and she'd been assured that danger would catch up to her but that had always seemed miles away, not as close as it was now. How could she have agreed to this? How could she have decided that she was some hero here to save the day?

The Mystics

She couldn't do this…or could she? She had to, didn't she? It was the only way to really find out the truth about everything and herself. Right now, all she wanted to find out was the best spot to take a nap. The chaotic mess outside was far away, the dome was sound proof and only she, Rochell, Hazel, and Alex's noises could be heard. Rosey could only image what was going on out there, the sounds, the terrible sounds. She found herself thanking the Silver Goddess deeply for thinking to block that all out. It didn't take away the image of Lyesal in her mind but it was close.

"So…" she said shakily, "we just stay here?"

"That's all we can do, Rosey dear," Rochell said, leaning towards her. She didn't seem in the least bit phased by what had just happened. Her now clean, but wet, face, beamed at Rosey happily. She flicked her hand and a gust of powerful wind blew across her face drying it immediately. She flung some at Rosey and her wet skin dried without drying out. Rosey nodded to her in thanks.

Alex jumped in, "Thank the Almighty One this place had adequate magic, I didn't want to have to dive into the magic I have stored up."

Rosey nodded, she knew what he was talking about. One of the things Alex had done at the Golden Goddess's Palace to prepare for their journey was to store up magic in his wand just in case they ever came upon a magical dead zone. It had taken him five hours each day of careful mediation the entire week they'd been at the Castle to completely fill his wand with the maximum amount of magic it could hold. Only higher level magikins could store magic in their wands and Alex had only just learned how to do it, so it had taken him a long time. Rosey could understand why he was happy not to have had to dive into that collection of magic he had just spent so much time gathering. To have to replace it so soon would have been frustrating.

Seeing her quiet demeanor, Rochell and Alex gave her a smile and Rochell blew air in Alex's direction to dry his own face. He nodded his thanks but then squinted his eyes in amazement at the crystal, icy-like structure surrounding them, "I'm surprised that the Silver Goddess can do this. She must have a lot of magic stored up for something like this...and when we're so far away from her." He rose and started to examine the gleaming walls and Rosey had to stop herself from laughing. That was Alex, finding something to analyze and examine even in the face of danger. It must be his way to calm down, a welcome distraction from reality.

"I want to apologize," Rosey said suddenly, drawing her friend's attention. "I shouldn't have done what I did."

They looked at her startled and Rochell placed her hand on Rosey's shoulder squeezing it tightly, "You've got nothing to apologize for Rosey. For your first time, that was well done. You stuck with us and you didn't scream hysterically or anything," she said, adding that last part just to make Rosey laugh and she did. "You did well."

"Was it...your first time?"

Rochell's smile vanished for a few moments but was quickly replaced by a goofy one, "Well, yes. It was our first real battle, but we are well trained and perfectly capable of getting the job done, right Al?" She shot Alex a look and he nodded.

"We're the best, there's nothing we can't handle."

Rosey smiled at them both, then leaned forward and hugged Rochell close. Rochell enfolded her in her arms gently as Rosey began to let silent tears fall down her cheeks. Hazel rubbed against her leg and Rosey gently pulled her close. Alex came over, flopped down next to her, and circled his arms around them in a great, big hug. They stayed like that, safe in each other's arms, till Rosey felt better, her fears far behind her, her eyes empty of tears, and her hand grasping her parent's locket.

When the crystal barrier came down, Rosey saw nothing. She had expected to see dead bodies, blood, even the evidence of a terrible struggle in the form of torn foliage, but nothing seemed to remain. The only traces of the horrible battle were the scuffle of mixed footprints and the dust and rocky debris from the collapsed cave behind them. Rosey didn't really care

The Mystics

about that so much as for the figures in front of her. Everyone was safe. Noly came running up to her yipping and barking happily, she was talking so fast that Rosey was barely able to make it out. Something about biting the leg of a giant, upright walking, mutated reptile which she took to be a Raptor and there was something else about being happy to see that the fur ball, Hazel, was all right and that Rosey was okay too. Beyond that Rosey wasn't sure what she was saying. She then saw Sarabie and Rosey held back tears as she rushed to the giant horse and threw her arms around her neck. Rochell and Alex did the same with Bronzo and Phana. Sarabie pushed her muzzle into Rosey's back, holding her close. All Rosey could say was "Thank God you're okay, thank God, thank you…" Sarabie didn't say anything. She didn't need to. Rosey then pulled away and rushed at Eglen and the other horses, exchanging hugs and sharing in the happy understanding that they were all okay. Rosey even managed to get a hold of Wolvereen, hugging his giant neck as he cringed but only slightly. Rosey especially hung onto Nagura. If the gentle white wolf had died it would have been like losing her mother all over again. She then turned to Ysandir last. The giant unicorn had blood spattered over her body, but it started to disappear, melting into Ysandir's flesh as if it had never been there. Ysandir's horn gave off a low light and then settled as the last of the blood disappeared. She removed it with magic. Rosey thanked her and the unicorn bowed to her.

"I only wish I had gotten here sooner, but it's a bit hard to compete with a collapsing cave system. I'm glad to see you and the others are all right," Ysandir said. "I will meet you at the volcano, good luck." She said her farewell's quickly and then turned and disappeared down another vortex so fast that Rosey didn't have time to say good bye.

Rosey rolled her eyes, at least the unicorn had kept her promise and assisted them as she said she would. It was nice knowing she could rely on her. The sudden image of the woman Rosey had seen before came rushing back at her. The strange see-through apparition…Rosey feared what it meant but knew it had probably been an image of her mother. What she didn't know was if it had been real, or just a product of her panic. She rubbed her face into Nagura's fur, she didn't want to think about it. She was just thankful that no one had suffered any horrible injuries beyond a small scratch or bruise. Even Sarabie, who had indeed been attacked by a Raptor, had escaped terrible injury when she nailed the beast in the head with a well-aimed kick before Wolvereen bit its head off. She would always be grateful to him for coming to the aid of her beloved horse.

They quickly got moving as Wolvereen so kindly reminded them that they needed to get going. Though Nagura assured them that the Goddesses had put extra effort into clearing the woods further of any Raptor menaces, the day was getting closer to night and they didn't want to be stuck out in the open. They needed to get to the halfway point to set up camp while they still had some light left. According to Wolvereen this halfway point was a safe location, a secure camping site about a mile up the path. Everyone agreed and quickly donned their winter gear before mounting up. After walking in the caves for three days a little walk outside was a blessing, even if it was winter. Nagura offered to stay with them until they reached the volcano the next morning which was a five hour ride away. Rosey gladly accepted. Wolvereen seemed happy to have his mate with him a little longer but at the same time looked to be a little on edge as if something about his beautiful mate was bothering him. He looked to be in a hurry, his eyes darting every which way, his tail erect. He kept constantly looking to Nagura as if he was a lost puppy sucking up to its mama. After the battle, she could understand if he'd be a little on edge but this had been happening even before the battle. Rosey decided not to worry about it. Whatever it was that was bothering him, it was clearly between him and Nagura. Unless it pertained to the Fellowship and their journey Rosey had no right to butt into their relationship.

Wolvereen and Nagura took the lead, assuring everyone that the way was clear and thoroughly checked. After what had happened, Rosey wasn't

The Mystics

sure any place was safe but she refused to argue or let her fear show. Without any more delays they got on their way. Only then did Wolvereen take the opportunity to explain what happened as they moved through the winter dormant forest. They weren't sure if the Raptors knew that Rosey was in the caves or not but a huge group of Raptors had shown up, most likely in response to the last Raptor group that was killed when Rosey had first arrived, the one where Lyesal died. They might have been following up on the first attack or something else, but they had been ready for a fight. They weren't really certain why or how but a Raptor had been carrying a Time Release Spell. When Wolvereen said this, Alex cursed and threw up his hands in exasperation. He quickly explained that it was, essentially, the same thing as a time bomb. Wolvereen nodded, then said that a Raptor had made its way to a spot and started digging, the others had surrounded it to protect it as it dug and then boom, the spell went off. It was a good thing that they had had Cocoa running back and forth with information just in case. Wolvereen assured Rosey that he and the Silver Goddess believed that the Raptors had not known for certain that she was in the caves, but they had had a hunch. As for where they got the Time Release Spell, that was unknown. It must have been one of the tricks the Evil One had up its sleeve.

That didn't sound too good to Rosey but she couldn't say or do anything to change it so she said instead, "Why are there no signs of the fight?"

Nagura turned her fluid body around and walked backwards, speaking to Rosey directly, "The Silver Goddess thought you'd seen enough fighting for one day, Rosey. She didn't think you needed to see its aftermath so everything was cleaned up."

The white ghost of a wolf turned back around and the group settled into silence as they rode and walked. Rosey felt herself shiver, Nagura was right. She had seen a lot in such a short little day, making sure that there was no evidence of the battle was not only a kind gesture but a wise decision. Getting rid of battle evidence could help avoid other battles later on and also avoid the chances of disease festering in dead bodies, not to mention the fact that family members would need to receive the bodies of the fallen. The fact that they had done it so fast though was what amazed Rosey, from what Wolvereen had told her, they'd only been protected in the crystal barriers for about an hour. She remembered specifically because he had been so angry about the fact that he had been included in the number of people protected by the barriers as if he'd needed the protection. She smiled and glanced at the passing foliage. The Silver Goddess must have even had earth elementals grow the few winter plants back into life. She felt her entire body suddenly relax, as if a great burden had been lifted. She felt surprisingly light and it hit her that it was the feeling of having survived something that she should and could have died from. This realization was grim and shockingly sobering, but it left her chest light and her head pounding with new worries. Instead she tried to focus on the occasional evergreen or wild winter vine as the forest flowed by.

After about an hour's slow walk they arrived at a round clearing surrounded by an impenetrable dome of a special plant called the Big Thorn Bristle Weed. It was a huge vine-like weed that produced the largest thorns ever to be recorded on The World Within A World. Along with its sharp edged leaves it proved to be, literally, a killer plant and the perfect specimen for a protective covering. Rosey remembered reading about it when she was studying in Jasira's library. Walking up to the large weed dome Wolvereen spoke into it and slowly the vines moved out of the way. Rosey tentatively followed the others into the dome. Nagura, the last of their group, took one final look around and then walked inside. As soon as she did the vines fell back into place perfectly as if the opening had never existed. Inside, the structure of woven vines was thick enough to make getting in impossible from the outside but unwound enough to let in light. Rosey also noticed, happily, that all the thorns were pointing outward away from the interior of the dome. She had been worried about those thorns, some of which could hold a deadly poison in them. Thankfully, it was obvious that getting poked by a deadly weed thorn was not going to happen. Eyeing one of the thorns, barely visible through a crack, Rosey remembered reading that not only was the plant poisonous but it also smelled absolutely horrible to Raptors and could mess up their sense of smell pretty bad. It was so strong to them that they could smell it from three miles away. To them it was disorienting, annoying, and itchy; the equivalent of having that sneezing feeling without sneezing.

The Resistance had apparently discovered this plant and its effects on Raptors and ever since they had constructed safe camp sites like the one they were in all over the world to help travelers. Rosey took a few deep breaths but didn't smell anything but regular plant smell: dirt mixed with rocks, clay, and the sharp tang of winter snow. Realizing that if she continued taking deep breaths she'd get a brain freeze she immediately started helping to set up camp and remove the necessary items from their saddlebags. After the battle, they were all just too exhausted to really do much but go through the motions.

Sarabie turned and rubbed her head against Rosey's shirt, seemingly understanding her sudden imbalance. Rosey stood there for a few minutes breathing in Sarabie's soft horse breath, memories of home flooding through her mind: her time in the stables brushing and bathing Sarabie, trail rides in the spring and summer, races across the fields, and the collection of apples from their various natural apple trees come harvest. Rosey was unsure as to why the swirling vortex had reminded her of such things. Perhaps it was the battle and the fact that she'd thought she'd lost Sarabie? Maybe this was her first taste of homesickness. Maybe she was just nostalgic, though nostalgia seemed a little early at her age. She was yearning for something lost, something she had been a part of but had been taken away from at birth: The World Within A World. She was from this land, yet she had been raised somewhere else. She found herself wondering sometimes if she would ever truly become one with this world and no longer think of it as alien, strange, and weird. But, at the same time, she loved her life on Earth, and there was nothing she could do about that.

Hugging the gentle black giant's neck Rosey continued removing the stuff from her saddlebags. She removed Sarabie's tack and put on her warm winter gear. Laying out her bed roll, she positioned herself close to the small fire that Alex had started. Alex took up a place beside her and Rochell took the other side. They too had tended to their horses. They all prepared lunch and ate in relative silence, weariness dragging them down. Wolvereen had gone out hunting and brought back two deer for him, Eglen, and Nagura to share. They ate outside the dome so as not to make a bloodied mess or to cause the others to lose their appetites. Although Wolvereen seemed hesitant to let Nagura leave the dome, a quick snap at his left ear reminded him to keep to himself. Rosey wondered at what was going on between the two. In the short time that she had known them, Nagura and Wolvereen had gotten along pretty well. *Are they fighting perhaps, and if they are, what are they fighting about?* she wondered. Rosey quickly put it out of her mind. It was none of her business just so long as they continued to do their job well.

Suddenly an idea occurred to her as she watched the three carnivore's silhouettes through the thick vines. "Alex," she said, gently patting his arm. He looked up expectantly ready to answer whatever it was she had to ask, "There are intelligent animals on this world and unintelligent animals right?" He nodded, "Well..," she said stumbling over her word choice, "...how do you know what's okay to eat and what's...not?"

Alex smiled understanding perfectly what she was saying, "You mean do we eat the meat of intelligent animals?" When Rosey nodded he continued, "We've always had intelligent animals on our planet, including before the supernova, so we apply the same rules as we did then, or what we hope are the same rules. Our rules are called the Rules of the Hunter. Rule One: you cannot hunt any being of intelligence. At the time people were mostly aware of what was intelligent and what wasn't. The books in the small library that I mentioned before also helped. Basically the rule is, if, during a hunt, you are unsure, then you don't hunt it. Rule Two: You are not allowed to hunt an animal that is pregnant or has young. This was a rule that was made mostly in response to the number of species that were endangered at that time. However, many species of intelligence didn't want to hunt and kill a child just as you would not want to hunt Bambi." Rosey nodded in understanding, Alex went on. "Rule Three: A creature, upon being killed, though they are not intelligent, is to be honored at their death. This could simply be an offering of the animals' preferred food choice, or a blessing, or even a burial, whatever it is, something must be done. Rule Four: Hunting will be done according to the seasons and the appropriate sex will be hunted at that time according to their species. During some seasons the males are the best for hunting because the females are pregnant or have young, during other seasons either sex is fair game. Rule Five: All manner of endangered or critically endangered species are never to be hunted until further notice is given. Finally we have Rule Six which was added when the Leron came. No Leron is to ever be hunted and consumed as they are a rare species and could potentially pass on the NCD to you and your young if they were eaten."

"That's it?" Rosey said, eying him teasingly.

"Well," Alex said, undeterred, "I could explain to you about each of the species and how, during what season, they are most likely to be hunted…"

"That's okay, I was just joking," she said hurriedly, smiling at him.

He smiled back, "Okay, but no, that deer that they are eating is a very common deer, no more intelligent than the one's on Earth," he said gesturing to the silhouettes.

"You know about every species?" she said amazed and a little skeptical.

"Being a magikin, that's not that unusual. It comes in handy if we learn about what we are casting spells against. However, magikin or elemental, there's not one child you'll come across that doesn't know how to take care of themselves. You see, here on The World Within A World children are taught from an early age how to clean, cook, make clothes, hunt, repair various things by hand, build their own house and so on. There's very little we can't do. On Earth, all that stuff is bought with money and schooling, we are home schooled and orphans are taught by their orphanages. When we turn sixteen we can go out into the world and build ourselves a house, travel, take up a profession or an interest, or simply stay at home, it's our choice. We don't have those responsibilities that Earth seems to pride itself on. To us, Earth is a beautiful place, but almost everything that its people have done is in the conquest of making other people's lives miserable. That is the one thing we will never understand. There is just too much 'me' and not enough 'we' on Earth," he said growing serious.

"Yeah," Rosey said, unable to say anything else.

After lunch they all sat and talked for hours. Rosey used this time to be updated on a few things that were common knowledge. She learned about certain jokes told about certain animals, plants, and humans. She listened to tales and legends about the ancient beasts that lived below the lands and seas. Eglen seemed to be the center of attention, his stories being the best and most eloquently told. Wolvereen, sitting side by side with his mate and showing none of the unrest Rosey had seen recently, told a ghost story about a sunken war ship, one of the ones designed by Rosey's family. Even the horses chimed in, telling horse tales that they had heard from the horses at the Golden Goddess's stables. Alex, of course, was talking a mile a minute about the various reasoning behind natural phenomenon, which many found interesting and helpful for solving some unexplained case or story that some local had told. Rochelle gave the others some of her best stories about the days when she was learning to become a wind elemental from her parents. One story was of how she had been trying to reach something placed high up and had lifted herself off the ground to reach it but didn't know how to get herself down. Her parents had let her float around the house for a whole day until she finally figured it out.

The Mystics

Rosey mostly sat and listened to everything, enjoying the jokes, the myths, legends, and fairytales. Whenever she didn't understand something, Alex would lean over and explain it to her so she didn't have to ask and then feel awkward because everyone else already knew what it was. Oddly enough, Rosey learned more in those few hours than she had in one of Jasira's books.

Occasionally, they would ask Rosey, Rochell, and Alex about Earth and they would tell stories about things they'd done there and about all the places they'd been. Their friends would listen to them in quiet wonder about this alien world that they depended on for protection. The stories and the laugher helped smooth out the jitteriness left behind by the battle and Rosey was grateful for it.

Once the storytelling was done, they all decide to play a local game centered on passing a ball of twine between one another. Whoever got the ball, would unravel a piece of twine and then draw a card from a deck with four sets of the alphabet written on them. Whatever letter they got they had to shape that letter with the twine then try and piece together a word with the letters they had. Whoever got the longest word within thirty minutes won. It was called Thirty Minute Wording. Rosey thought it was a lot like scrabble and she told them so, which made them immediately want to play it. Rochell, being the gamer that she was, had packed games for these occasions and brought out that very game. She, Alex, and Rosey laughed and showed them how to play. By the end of the day it was one of their favorite games, that is, until Rosey mentioned playing cards. With a twinkle in her eye, Rochell quickly pulled out a deck from her pack like she was pulling a rabbit from a magician's hat. All of the games had been spelled by Alex ahead of time to be miniature versions of themselves, perfect for travel occasions.

A few hours later, everyone began to settle down. Dinner was made and passed around, then people started to doze off. As night neared, Rosey still found herself wide awake despite the three days of cave travel, the battle still in her mind despite the day's distractions. It was at least midnight by the time Rosey was able to relax and fall into her bed roll. Looking up she gazed through the small oculus in the ceiling of the dome at the stars above. Her fellowship was back to normal, they were no longer annoying her or each other. It seemed the cave was responsible for their bad moods. Being cooped up in a depressingly dark, small place was not their thing. It definitely wasn't Rosey's and today's rest had been the perfect remedy to lift their moods.   She sighed and stared at the constellation that Alex had showed her a few hours ago. It formed a beautiful griffon. Staring at it she was aware of Alex lying down next to her, he had stayed up to wash the dishes from dinner. He was about to open his mouth but, afraid that he would launch into a long lecture and spoil the moment, she closed her hand over it before he could say anything.

"Don't..." she said with a smile.

He smiled back and said, "Wouldn't dream of it."

Chapter Fifteen: Doubts and Nagging Feelings

Rosey and the rest of her fellowship awoke at dawn and immediately got to work. While they packed up camp, Nagura and Wolvereen, once again, checked their surroundings for danger. Rosey, Alex, and Rochell prepared the horses and cleaned up camp. Their breakfast had been simple for they didn't want to take too long when the Volcano was within only hours of walking distance. When the two wolves had returned they didn't come alone. Calra, the lieutenant of the silver guards had come with them. She had bowed to Rosey and then delivered to her and the others an official apology for not stopping the raptors in time. Rosey told Calra that she was simply thankful that they had been there to help protect her and to not feel bad about it. Calra had bowed again before confirming that the coast was clear, and that the guards had taken extra precautions this time around. When the giant wolf left, they set out.

As they rode through the winter dormant forest, Rosey breathed in the sweet scents of the early morning, cool air. It was such a sharp scent that it made her smile with pleasure. It smelled so normal and so similar to Earth's winter air that Rosey believed, for a short time, that she was back on Earth again. She could see it now, her uncle and friends riding next to her on one of the many trails in the forest. If it hadn't been for the large wolves and Eglen beside her, walking on the same trail, she could have believed her own fantasy. She opened her mouth to let her tongue catch a snowflake, chasing the idea away in her head as nothing but short-lived homesickness. She had no time for thoughts like that. Earth was in the past now, this was her future.

To be perfectly honest, Rosey was more than excited to be making her way to the volcano. It meant that she would be drawing ever closer to her first element and that was far more exciting than all the training she'd done at the palace. The elementals and their wild variety of techniques that they had performed for her were still fresh in her mind and she found herself interested in what it would feel like to be in control of one of those elements herself. Maybe, soon, she'd have her answer.

A sudden deep sadness stirred in the pit of her stomach as her gaze settled on Nagura, the wolf's proud figure strong and tall ahead of them. Rosey seemed to wilt from all of her excitement. Getting to the volcano might mean getting her first element, but it would also mean saying goodbye to her beloved friend, Nagura. The white wolf had come to mean so much to her, it was hard to imagine letting her go or never seeing her again. Rosey swallowed hard and Hazel seemed to sense her unease. She meowed softly and rubbed Rosey's neck affectionately. Rosey patted her head. She couldn't think about that. Right now she had to enjoy Nagura's company while she could.

Five hours later they arrived at the volcano unscathed and in one piece. The group seemed to sigh with relief as they viewed the mountainous crater high above them. After days of walking, traveling, and time consuming scouting for enemies the team was noticeably exhausted and in need of a break. They deserved it too. They all seemed to relax; only now realizing just how tense they had all been. It was one thing to talk about travel through possible inhospitable lands, it was another to actually do it, and it had a lasting effect. The volcano was a welcome sight, like seeing an old friend after a long separation. It was a sure sign of safety and an inevitable sign of farewell.

Rosey tried not to think about it but Nagura was already turning to their group, a look of sadness on her face. Rosey dismounted and came to her as softly as she could. She, without pause, hugged the wolf's thick furred neck, feeling hot tears burning at her eyes. The sudden emotion surprised Rosey. She loved Nagura more than anyone else she had met so far, not that anyone had been inhospitable, for everyone had been nothing but kind and respectful to her since she had arrived, but no one had pulled

The Mystics

on Rosey's heart strings more than Nagura. She found herself deeply wishing that Nagura was staying with her instead of Wolvereen. As soon as the thought crossed her mind she regretted thinking it. Wolvereen had been nothing but loyal and attentive, protecting and assisting her where needed. It was just that Nagura was so comforting and warm. The image of her as the mother she never had made Rosey even more saddened to see her go, but Rosey knew that Nagura could not stay. For some reason she was completely devoted to returning to her duties as the Commander of the Silver Guards. Rosey almost laughed at herself, imaging this big wolf as her mother when she wasn't human. It was enough to make her giggle with annoyance. Yet, Rosey knew that physical appearances had nothing to do with the power of Nagura's soul which lifted Rosey aloft in sweet hugs and warming licks. She was going to miss her.

Rosey had a feeling, that her eminent departure might also have something to do with why Nagura had been so standoffish to Wolvereen recently. It wasn't easy to say goodbye to someone you loved. Rosey was finding that out all too well lately. Wolvereen wasn't bad, it was just that he was not as approachable as Nagura, but she had chosen him as a mate so there must be something in him that Rosey would come to love just as much as she loved Nagura. Rosey took this to heart and pushed away her doubts. Pulling out of the hug, she looked deeply into the blue eyes of the white wolf.

"Thanks for everything; I hope to see you again soon," Rosey said.

"You as well, Rosey. Be a good Keeper."

"I intend to."

Nagura smiled then licked her face lovingly, like a mother wolf licks its pups. Did she think of Rosey as her daughter just as much as she saw her as a mother?. She was far too afraid of the answer to ask. Rosey watched as Nagura said goodbye to Wolvereen. They rubbed faces affectionately, and then licked each other slowly and methodically as if memorizing each other's scents, look, and design. Now that Nagura was leaving, Wolvereen seemed much more relaxed and more like himself. Though it was obvious to everyone that something was going on between the two, once again, she ignored it; it was none of her business.

Once Nagura had left they got to work surveying the area. Though she had never seen a volcano, she was sure that it wasn't supposed to look like this. A normal volcano wouldn't be radiating an area of heat around itself to keep it at a warm tropical temperature when everything else was covered in snow. Of course Alex supplied the reason, saying that the volcano's magic always kept the place alive with life and that it was famous for keeping a good two mile radius of land warm all year long. This was the volcano's magic not the Mother's.

Rosey started as she felt something touch her consciousness. It was like a hand had passed over her. She touched her head, taken aback but found it okay and untouched. Suddenly she felt a warming in her chest, a nagging feeling that was calling to her. Rosey thought it was weird but also good. It was a good thing. It felt like heat and fire and lava all at once. Without a doubt in her mind she knew it was the element, calling to her. Her eyes settled on the volcano dead ahead, and she let the feelings roll over her consciousness. She wanted to tell the others what she felt but she just couldn't. What was going on felt…private. It was…something that only she should know about. Rosey didn't know how to describe it but she knew, in her heart, that it was supposed to be happening. She slowly pushed away the feelings and they obeyed. They left so quickly that Rosey almost felt as if they hadn't happened at all. The others waited and talked amongst themselves, planning, unaware of her feelings. She knew now that they were in the right place, the element waited for her in that volcano.

She felt unbalanced by what she had just experienced but her friends and the need to make camp were far more important. Rosey determinedly set her jaw and dismounted. She eyed the area with awe. You could draw a line where the snow ended and the warmth began. It was like being at the border of two states and having one foot on either side. One side was twenty degrees and the other was seventy. Noly and Hazel played with it, jumping in and out of the Volcano's warm radius to the cold area of the natural wintery world while the others looked on in laughter and Wolvereen with embarrassment. Once the two had had enough of freezing then warming, freezing then warming, they raced back to Rosey. She, Rochell, and Alex removed Noly, Hazel, and the horse's winter gear along with their own heavy winter cloaks and coats from the Golden and Silver Goddesses then folded them neatly into their saddlebags. From there they continued on foot to find a place to bed down. They took their time for the ground was uneven and treacherous in some areas, shaped over the years by the volcano's power. Large piles of fallen rocks from the volcano covered most of the land with small patches of long grasses dispersed here and there.

As they walked a feeling of relief washed over them. Wolvereen had assured them that the two mile radius of warmth around the volcano was impassable by evil creatures which meant that they were now Raptor free. No one really knew why the magic here was so strong or why it did not allow passage for creatures of evil, but Rosey wasn't going to question it, she was just thankful that for once she could be at peace. She could go to the Volcano and not have to worry about the potential danger of Raptors or her team falling into the hands of the enemy. For the first time since she came here, everyone was relaxed. Their normally tight grouped circle split apart to allow distance between them as they walked on. Noly and Hazel climbed rocks all around them and scurried about like happy young children. The Horses tossed their heads and cantered around their group inspecting new smells and grabbing mouthfuls of luscious grass before moving on. Eglen joined them, looking much like a horse himself amongst their ranks but leaving the grass untouched. Wolvereen was the only one amongst them that held his composure and continued to lead the way. Rosey, Rochell, and Alex stayed near each other content to watch the others play. They never strayed far, just enough to allow some personal distance.

In the end, no matter how much fun it was to be experiencing the tropical weather with a winter view, Rosey still had a job to do. They settled down as they got closer to the volcano and grouped back together as the large piles of rocks became more numerous. Rosey felt the nagging feeling come over her every now and then and would temporarily let it enter her mind. She'd then push it away, unsure of herself and her surroundings. It felt so strange to have something like that happening, but at the same time, she knew it was right.

After half an hour of walking they stopped to rest. Wolvereen then suggested that they disperse into small groups to help shorten the time looking for a good place to make camp. With the threat of evil attackers gone, there was no reason not to, so they readily agreed.

Rosey and Alex were one of the small groups. They scrambled over the sparse greenery and random rock falls. They walked for a few minutes then stopped to catch their breath. Rosey took the opportunity to take a good long look at the Volcano itself. No matter what she had been told nothing could prepare her for one of nature's toughest children; the volcano. She knew that the extent of its magic reached only two miles while the crater was said to be at least a half mile wide. Alex had readily informed her that it measured almost three miles high and the magma flows ran underground nourishing the soils. The vegetation slowly wore down and revealed a barren, brown, rock-covered landscape leading up to the jagged cliffs of the volcano's peak. She kept an eye out for any good place to camp as well as anything that might offer an entrance into the volcano.

After about an hour of finding neither an entrance nor a good camping area they returned to the place they had agreed to rendezvous at. Once there they discovered that Ysandir had rejoined them. She came trotting into the group with Wolvereen beside her. Rosey stared at them, surprised and happy to see Wolvereen's large height belittled by the even bigger unicorn. He had been the first one she ran into upon arriving. Hearing that they were searching for a good place to camp she flipped her mane about her with a knowing grin and told them she had spotted the perfect place upon her arrival. Traveling towards the base of the volcano and then veering around it for about half a mile she led them to a grassy place bordered by large rocks that would provide a perfect camp. There they began setting up camp and preparing lunch. Wolvereen and Eglen left to hunt. While Rochell got a small fire going Alex and Rosey took off the horse's tack and brushed them down. They whinnied their thanks then traveled a little ways away from the camp and began happily grazing on the thin meadow of grasses that surrounded them in small clumps. They rolled around in the dirt sending up clouds of dust. Ysandir joined the horses in grazing and even, to Rosey's amazement, rolled in the dirt. Once a horse, always a horse. Rosey watched them amused then got out some dried meat for Noly. Hazel left and returned triumphantly with two mice in her jaws followed soon by Wolvereen and Eglen who brought with them a boar. They offered Rosey, Rochell, and Alex a section of meat and they accepted. Rosey watched, amazed, as Alex prepared the meat, cutting it into neat square pieces. Rochell took two metal poles from her pack and placed them on either side of the fire, she then took another and skewered the cut pieces of meat, making it look like a meat kabob. She then laid it over the fire on the two poles, suspending it perfectly above the low flame. Rosey had learned about outdoor living, but she was still a little hesitant when it came to handling the bloody meat. Watching her friends proved what Alex had said before: people on this world were taught from an early age how to take care of themselves and that included preparing meat. They all ate in silence, enjoying one another's company and the peace and quiet after so much tense traveling.

Later, after everyone had eaten, Rosey stood up and paced away from the fire. She needed to stretch her legs, riding for that long on Sarabie wasn't the easiest thing to do and it left her feeling stiff. She stretched where she stood and cast her gaze at the vast side of the volcano. She was unsure of what to make of all this. She had no idea how she was going to find an entrance into this behemoth, much less a place fit for holding the mother of the element of Fire but that wasn't all that was eating at Rosey. Ever since she had sat down to eat she had felt something moving through the earth. The nagging feelings had returned and she had let them in. They had suddenly though, become more sporadic and hectic, unlike they had been before. They seemed to be out of control or amplified. Like tendrils of energy, they coursed through the soil, up through her legs, and into her heart. She had felt uncomfortable and itchy, as if there was something that she needed to do but couldn't remember what it was. And, though she hated to admit it, she could swear she heard something calling to her from deep within the volcano. Whether it was a voice or a tugging on her chest like a rope was tied to it and it was trying to pull her in, she was unsure. She had never felt anything like this before, it was annoying, yet it soothed her. It was like she had done something bad and had finally confessed. It was a great sense of relief hidden behind a nagging sharpness like needles in the pit of her stomach. A sudden feeling struck her, as she stared at the volcano. It poked at her consciousness again and again. She tried to ignore it but it was there like a headache that wasn't aching. It was a strong pressure, something that was calling to her. It was a nagging presence at the back of her mind. Rosey fidgeted where she stood, unable to get comfortable. She felt as if she was crawling with desire, a desire to do something. She wasn't sure why but it felt like it was coming from the volcano. This hadn't been what she'd felt before, this was different.

Alex came up and stood beside her, studying the cliffs, unaware of her conflict. She hadn't seen him come after her but she didn't mind. Perhaps he was just taking a walk like her or maybe he had wanted to discuss something with her. She felt grateful for his sudden presence, no matter what it may be.

"Alex," she said, hoping her voice sounded normal. "Yeah." "I know this is going to sound strange but…I want you and Ysandir to come with me into the volcano. I may need *your all's* knowledge. Just in case. I don't want all of us trying to scale a volcano so I think we should stick with a small group." He looked at her sharply, but his voice was calm. "You're going to try now?"

"Yeah, I have this…feeling that I need to get in there. There's something pulling me. The element, it's calling to me. At least that is what I believe is going on…I don't know…and …," Seeing his bewildered expression, she quickly said, "I mean… why wait?" She knew she sounded a little strange, but she couldn't shake the feeling that she needed to do this as quickly as possible.

Seeing she was perfectly serious, Alex nodded. Though he still looked a little surprised, all he said was, "Sure thing." He patted her on the shoulder and then left to collect Ysandir.

Rosey watched him leave, wondering if she had communicated her need to him in the right way. Was something wrong? Why did she have this feeling in her head? She didn't know, but it was strong and it wanted her badly.

Alex took a deep breath and let it out slowly. He had never seen Rosey acting that way; it couldn't be because she was on a new world. She had been here for over a week and had taken it better than he had expected. She was a citizen of The World Within A World after all but, citizen or not, being spirited away to a whole new world, much less learning you were the savior for that very world, couldn't be easy. *Especially after learning about her past and the death of her mother and father,* he thought. He tried imagining how he would feel if he learned his parents had been killed. An image of his brunette, blue eyed mother came to mind. His whole body shook as an image of a bloodied, tattered body, lay dead at his feet; her bright intelligent eyes, that had always been a source of comfort for him, dead and glass-like as her life drained from her. Then an image of his father flashed before his eyes with his stark red hair, a contrast to his mother's dark brown, caked with dried blood as his lifeless body lay over hers. He shuddered and pushed the images away. His parents were safe, deep within the city of Calback, a whole continent away, living in the safety of the palace of the Queen and her daughters. They were not in any danger and were doing fine. He fingered the letter they had written to him hidden in his pant leg pocket as if its physical presence was proof that his parents were all right. His mother was a Goddess level magikin who was known for her hobby of turning water into ice sculptures with magic. She had a quiet disposition, a kind smile, and a welcoming heart. His father was a Wizard level magikin, who made up for his low level by being one of the smartest men in the world. They were both taking it easy at the Queen's palace along with Rochell's surprisingly scholarly parents. Both of their families had been shipped there for protection while Alex and Rochell were with Rosey, along with any of their other acquaintances and loved ones so as not to provide the Evil One with any means of coercion.

Alex had always found Rochell and her family to be a mystery. Her mother was a short woman who had a vast amount of common sense and wore thin glasses. She always seemed to be regarding you through them as if looking through a mirror. Rochell's father, in broad contrast, was a hulk of a man with a musculature that would make Hercules jealous. It was no wonder since he was a Warf; they always prided themselves on their muscles, which was why Rochell was so physically well sculpted. No matter how hard Alex would try, his muscles never seemed to get as big as hers. Even though she didn't have a huge amount of Warf in her, having mostly inherited her mother's human genetics, she still carried her father's Warf blood, making her incredibly strong and flexible like the wind. He, on the other hand, was completely human.

Alex came from a Magikin family much like the Goddess's family, except his and Rochell's family were known best for their spectacular services to Esperanza. In fact, Rochell's mother and Alex's father were the only survivors from Esperanza's fellowship. They had been somewhere else and thus had not been around at the time when Esperanza's friend had been possessed. Alex was very grateful for that because, if they had been there, he would have grown up without one of his parents and Rochell wouldn't have been born. In fact, Rochell and Alex were the whole reason they had been away. Their births had retired their pregnant parents to their homes just as it had done for Esperanza, only their homes were located somewhere else and they hadn't wanted to give birth at the Golden Palace. Thus Alex and Rochell hadn't been at the palace. Who would have known that such a small decision would have saved them from such a huge life or death situation?

Rosey knew all of this, even the fact that Rochell was part Warf. It was one of the many things that he and Rochell had discussed and confessed to her when they were at the Golden Goddess's palace. They had spent long hours talking about everything they had gone through, pointing out important facts about themselves. The only thing Rosey did not know was that Alex's father and Rochell's mother had been in Esperanza's fellowship. Like the name of the woman that had been possessed and thus killed Esperanza, that information did not need to be around to tempt Rosey away from her journey. At least that was how the Golden and Silver Goddesses had put it. Alex and Rochell had disagreed with keeping anything from Rosey, but Adina and their parents had both told them to keep it secret so they did. It didn't make it any easier when Rosey asked them why their parents weren't joining them on the trip. She had been surprised as it was that they had come back to The World Within A World, seeing as how her uncle had stayed behind she had simply assumed that they would as well, but it had made her start when she realized that they wouldn't be joining them. She had assured Alex and Rochell that she would have had no problem with them being a part of her journey, and even preferred it. Alex and Rochell had already been asked to keep enough from Rosey about their parents so they were happy to report truthfully on this subject. Their parents had given them one answer to give to Rosey. They did not want to interrupt the special friendship that had grown between Rosey and their children. They had said that their presence might make things awkward or distract Alex and Rochell from keeping Rosey safe if they were worried about their parent's safety and vice versa on their part; after all, if one of them were to see Alex and Rochell in danger they would choose, instinctively, to save their child instead of their Keeper. Rosey had understood, but Alex could tell that she seemed unsure about it and he knew that if given the chance she would have still encouraged their parents to come with them.

Alex knew that that wasn't the only reason why they had chosen not to come. After years of watching Rosey he had become quite good at understanding how one really felt inside. Alex and Rochell's parents still felt responsible for not being there to help Esperanza, and seeing Rosey would only remind them of their failure. This way was best. They would be well protected with the Queen so Rochell and Alex could be left to help Rosey in every way possible.

Thinking about it made Alex wish his mother was here with him, looking at him with her bright blue eyes and chasing away all his fears like she used to when he was a child except this time it wasn't a ghost but the fear that something was happening to Rosey. Since they settled here at the volcano she had been fidgeting and acting weird, only in a way that a close friend would notice. He had known her long enough to have become familiar with her every move but also to know how good she was at hiding herself and her emotions.

Seeing Rochell he grabbed her arm gently and pulled her away from the others. She had been quietly brushing out Noly's long fur for Rosey. Upon seeing and recognizing his 'panic face' she quickly got up and left with him. Noly didn't seem to be startled by the sudden shift, if she was, she didn't say anything.

The Mystics

Pulling her out of the faint ring of light that was cast around them they ducked behind one of the large stones that were surrounding the clearing. Casting a glance around to be sure no one was around, he looked at Rochell his face a mask of confusion.

Rochell eyed him worriedly, "What is it? What's wrong?"

"It's Rosey," he said, almost coughing up the words. His throat was suddenly dry. He grabbed his water skin hanging from his belt. He took a long drink, savoring the clear crisp water running down his throat.

"What about her?" Rochell prompted, looking annoyed with him for taking so long.

"She's acting strange. It's as if the Volcano is calling to her. She has this odd look when she stares at it and she just asked me to come with her along with Ysandir to the volcano."

"She's starting tonight?" Rochell gasped, surprised.

Alex nodded. Rochell glanced at the slowly sinking sun, unsure of this idea.

Looking at him, she regarded him knowingly, "We knew this day was coming when our parents told us the truth. She's not just Rosey Mystic anymore. She's the Keeper now, too." She tried to comfort him but he could tell that she didn't seem to believe her own words.

"I know, it's just that…I wish our parents had prepared us more for this. I didn't…I didn't think it would make me feel this way. I'm…I'm afraid that…."

"…that she'll die just like Esperanza did?" Her voice was flat and clear. It was obvious she had had the same fears as he had.

Alex nodded, his eyes glossy. He had always been prepared for this, hadn't he? Alex wasn't so certain. Until just over a week ago she had been nothing more than his normal best friend. They shared the same planet, though she didn't know it at the time, and she was always so normal and carefree. He knew things were going to change, but it all seemed so surreal to him now. How could she just go from being the Rosey of Earth to the

Rosey of The World Within A World as their Keeper and savior? It was different, more different than Alex had realized it would be.

Rochell seeing his distress, hugged him, knowing that there was nothing else she could do. She felt the same way and Alex knew it. Then, she held him at arm's length and held his gaze with her big brown eyes. "We are here to make sure that what happened to Esperanza doesn't happen to Rosey. Are you with me?"

He was silent for a moment, shaken by his sudden emotion. He took another swig of water from the skin then hung it back on his belt. For a few seconds that felt like years his mind skipped through all the kindergarten classes, lunches in the cafeteria, school jokes, bus rides home, and those occasional summer and spring rides through the forests. All spent with Rosey. They had grown to love this girl and care for her not just as their Keeper but as their friend. He still remembered when his parents had told him the truth: told him about her and their world. When they had taken him back home for the first time and when he had returned to Earth to then face the rest of his years on Earth acting like nothing was different. He'd always felt like a traitor deep down inside, like a man getting ready to pull an elaborate kidnapping plan on a perfect stranger, only, she was his friend. He wanted to protect her and help her succeed, just as much as Rochell did.

"Bring it on," he said, suddenly finding strength in the brown depths of Rochell's eyes.

"Good, now go get Ysandir before Rosey comes looking for you."

The others were a little surprised that Rosey was going to go on ahead to the volcano that day. Rosey promptly told them about the feelings she had, the pull towards the volcano was strong. They all seemed a little surprised by Rosey's emotions, seeing as how she had lacked such obvious connections when she had been at the palace, but they did not question her. This was Keeper business and it was as strange as it was predictable, they could not ignore it. Wolvereen nodded and said that she needed to

The Mystics

answer the call. Noly and Hazel wanted to come, but Rosey was adamant in her decision. When they started to argue, Wolvereen growled deep in his throat and they reluctantly stopped. Rosey admired their bravery and dedication but the volcano was still… a volcano and she didn't want anyone going anywhere near it that didn't need to be there.

Alex and Ysandir joined Rosey and the fellowship wished them luck as they set off. Following the pull she felt still tugging at her, she led them around the volcano's base to its other side. What had before, been a land of mystery was laid out for Rosey on a silver platter as if she had been there her whole life. Without hesitation she found a long staircase leading up to a small hole in the side of the volcano and, wordlessly, began climbing it. Rosey took the lead but Alex and Ysandir looked uncertain, though they followed without hesitation. To Rosey it couldn't have been clearer: this was where she needed to go.

The stairs at the bottom of the volcano were formed by fallen rocks and magma layers. Jumping from rock to rock, Rosey, Ysandir, and Alex slowly made their way up the stairs. After a good ten minutes of climbing they reached the opening. Inside they rested from the long climb, though Ysandir seemed unfazed.

Alex told them it would probably get much hotter once they were further inside. Taking out his wand he cast a bright light around them that would protect them from any smoke and heat. Rosey felt the air clear around her and the temperature adjust as the spell took effect. She smiled. Magic sure did come in handy every now and then.

Glancing down she studied Alex's wand. It was the first time she had seen it up close. It didn't look too different from the wands seen in movies and television only this was the real deal. It resembled a dark mahogany stick with designs etched in it. She was surprised to see that his wand was much more ornate looking then the Goddess's wands. Their wands had been long sticks of smooth gold and silver with gold and silver twine wrapped around them. She remembered Alex telling her, when they were at the Golden Goddess's palace, that each wand was different according to its owner. Just because somebody was important or elegant didn't necessarily mean their wand would be too. Even the size of a wand differed. Alex's was shorter than the Silver and Golden Goddess's wands but his father, who was a wizard level magikin and, despite his studies, had achieved no level higher, had a wand that was almost long enough and thick enough to be considered a walking stick. It was said that wands like that would normally become Magikin staffs over time, but that, once again, depended on the owner. A staff wasn't much different than a wand but it was said to make it easier on their owner to cast spells. According to Alex it could make the casting time a lot quicker than normal.

After checking to make sure his protective fields covered them completely Alex returned his wand to its scabbard and motioned for Ysandir and Rosey to move forward. They entered the tunnel with caution. Ysandir went first, with Rosey behind her and Alex bringing up the rear. The walls were dry and made of patchy black earth. They were nothing special and Rosey couldn't see any source of light, yet the tunnel was bright enough to see in. Perhaps it was a lingering type of magic or something else, but Rosey wasn't going to stop to ask. The nagging feeling in her head was too intense, thrusting her forward along the path. They hurriedly followed the tunnel, taking turn after turn as if in a confusing collection of mazes. Whenever they came to a dead end with multiple tunnels to choose from, Rosey would carefully pace around them and listen to the nagging feeling in her head. When she passed before a tunnel that made the feeling more intense she would declare it the right direction and plunge in, down the corridor, the others in hot pursuit. They did not ask questions and did not doubt how Rosey knew which way to go. They trusted her and followed patiently, letting Rosey set the pace.

After a while the tunnel opened into a large magma crossing where a long and narrow, rock bridge stretched over a field of magma flowing down into the earth. Ysandir started across it as if magma crossings were a normal everyday thing, barely glancing down at the hot molten rock. Rosey halted, for the first time doubting the nagging feeling that had led her to this place. She glanced at Ysandir who walked across smoothly and felt a spark of pride blossom in her chest. Remembering her time back in the Silver Goddess's crystal caverns she haughtily started across. Going too fast she missed a step and fell back against Alex in surprise. He held her steady until she had regained her balance. She smiled her thanks and at his encouraging nod turned back to the bridge, walking carefully this time. She cursed herself in her mind, reminding herself that she was worth nothing to this world if she was dead. She trembled as she walked; imagining what it would feel like if the shields weren't protecting them. They'd probably be experiencing the extreme heat of the inner caverns. She steadied herself, this was not the time to think about that but still it was hard to forget. She was walking across a pit of magma on a five foot wide bridge that felt like it was melting underneath her. She steadied her racing heart and followed Ysandir. She dare not glance up from where her eyes watched her feet for fear of losing her balance again but she knew that Ysandir was probably snickering at how long it was taking her to cross. Thinking back to the bridge she had crossed at the Silver Goddess's, she knew she did not fear heights but she was deathly afraid of falling into magma, plus, the Goddess's bridge had railings and was significantly wider than this one.

 Finally reaching the other side she almost lunged for the platform that extended a few feet from the side of the wall. Sweat beaded her forehead and she wiped it away, feeling as if she'd been played. "Where is this Mother anyway, Ysandir? I want to slap her," said Rosey as she balanced herself evenly on the platform and slowed her racing heart. Ysandir chuckled before saying, "She will appear when she thinks it best."

 Rosey didn't like her answer. She wanted to get the element. She could hear it calling to her now, like a distant echo she was following, hoping to find its source. While on the bridge, all of her focus had been centered on not falling in, so the constant nagging of the element's call had taken a back seat. Now the noise in her head was so strong that she could feel her head throbbing. Rubbing her forehead she steadied herself. Realizing that Alex was giving her a strange look, she quickly straightened and smoothed out her long hair that she had tied back in a fancy braid that the Golden Goddess had shown her. Glancing up, Rosey realized that Ysandir had not waited, she was walking ahead and about to round a bend in the path. Rosey quickly ran to catch up, taking advantage of the opportunity to avoid Alex's questioning gaze. Alex watched after her then followed. Rounding the bend both were surprised to see that Ysandir had disappeared. "What! She better not jump out and scare me," Rosey said looking in every direction. She shot a warning glance at Alex.

He threw up his arms in surrender, but was noticeably amused. "I'm just as surprised as you are."

"Oh great, a double scare." Her head was throbbing way too much for this.

"It may have something to do with the Mother. I can't imagine Ysandir deliberately trying to trick us." Alex tried to reassure her, but his gaze seemed unsteady. "Maybe, well no sense in worrying about her. She's a full grown unicorn; I think she can handle herself," Rosey reasoned. "True, I'm sure she'll rejoin us soon," Alex said gripping Rosey's shoulder reassuringly. They followed the black tunnels swiftly. The patchy dirt suddenly turned into hard, black, rock tunnels as they got deeper and deeper. Or what they thought was deeper. They had made so many turns and twists that Rosey was completely disoriented. For all she knew they had followed a series of tunnels going in a circle. She couldn't imagine what she was feeling to be leading her on the wrong path, but it was sure annoying to believe that it could. The nagging feeling was so intense that she was certain she'd not made a mistake. She could only hope she was going in the right direction.

They plunged on ahead for what must have been an hour until the tunnel opened up into a large domed room. Here Rosey was surprised to see

The Mystics

magma falling down the walls on either side of the hard packed earth. The heat suddenly hit Rosey like an explosion of great power. She reeled back and Alex followed suit. They immediately backtracked back out into the hallway and stood catching their breath and fanning themselves. To Rosey's amazement, the protective spell surrounding them was now gone. Alex lifted his wand to put up the shield again but then cursed under his breath. Rosey gave him a surprised look and he confirmed her fears, "This area is magically dead and it just took out my protective shield!"

Rosey shook her head, "How can that be, this volcano is supposed to be very powerful, you know, magic central!?"

Alex nodded, "Yeah, but magic doesn't always spread evenly. This area is what you might call a Black Hole, it's an area that is magically void even though the rest of the area around it is magically charged. They do happen sometimes though no one knows why. We can't go that way, I can't protect us from the heat." He sheathed his wand looking defeated. "Rochell would have been able to keep you cool no matter what, sometimes magic is a pain." He wiped a bead of sweat from his forehead. Rosey shook her head and gently pushed him in quiet denial of his own self-doubt. He smiled at her and panted at the heat flying from the room.

Rosey swallowed and licked her dry lips, feeling the heat piercing her face from the room beyond. "That's just great! We have to go that way, that's where the feeling is leading me! I thought you said you stored extra magic in your wand for moments like this?"

"I did but it doesn't matter. It wouldn't work. Black Holes don't allow any magical action no matter what. That's why they're called Black Holes. They swallow all the magic that gets near them."

Rosey shook her head in anger at herself. There was no way she could have known that there'd be a Black Hole, obviously, but that didn't stop her from feeling partly responsible for not being fully prepared. She hadn't thought this through as much as she should have but that nagging had made it almost impossible for her to think. Even now it was still there. She tried to think. She put her hand to her head and said, "There's got to be a way to…maybe…oh!" Suddenly she twisted around and grabbed her water container hanging from her belt. "Let's pour our water over ourselves and make a run for it. We should be fine as long as we're fast. The heat's not that bad."

Alex nodded, "That could work. Let's do it." He grabbed his own water bottle and they wetted down their heads and clothes, leaving a little for consumption if they needed it. Rosey checked to make sure her hair was tightly held in place and that she was thoroughly wet, Alex did the same. Alex took a step behind her, "Keepers first," he said, indicating the door on the other side of the dome. Rosey shot him a bemused glance and then prepared herself. She set off across the floor and the heat came at her like a stifling cloud of ugly lung-filling gas. The air was so hot that Rosey coughed and sputtered, but she charged through, putting her wet hand to her mouth to try and act as a filter. The water on her body started to steam and the droplets started to fly off of her in a fast frenzy as they evaporated. They were only halfway across when Rosey started to feel almost completely dry. The running wasn't helping either but still she pushed on. To her utter horror, the doorway before them suddenly drew shut. Rosey and Alex both came to a halt, eyeing the doorway in confusion. Almost in unison, they turned back around to head for the door they'd come from, their instincts taking over. They were just about to make it when the door suddenly slammed shut, a wall of magma flowing over it. Alex grabbed Rosey and yanked her backwards to help stop her from running into it. She fell against him and then looked around. This was bad. They were now trapped, but why? For what purpose?

A sudden gurgling sound came from behind them. They turned to see a giant bubble of magma stretching out from the flowing stream of the magma waterfall against the walls. It condensed slowly, turning and falling over and over again forming a shape. Rosey drew Andraste, sweat beading her forehead. The room's heat was stifling but she'd just have to push through it. Alex wiped away sweat and reached for his long dagger, a weapon he only used when magic wasn't an option. He pulled it out, the golden hilt gleaming while the red jewel in the middle reflected the colors of the magma around them. It had been a gift from his mother but Rosey had never thought she'd see the magically empowered Alex have to use it. She held Andraste ready and fixed her gaze on the beast that was forming. It took on the shape of a human covered in hardened lava armor. As it finished forming, it turned its head and gave her a deadly stare. Its entire body was nothing but pulsating magma while the hardened armor set over top of it like floating islands. Rosey felt a bead of sweat trickle down her cheek and she gritted her teeth. What in the world was going on!?

The armored humanoid took a step towards them and raised its right arm, in it a sword began to form. With a sickening feeling, Rosey knew what the creature was here for. It wanted a battle. Was this her test? She felt her whole body shudder, she hadn't expected something this extreme for her first test but there was no turning back, literally. She was trapped, and the only way to move on was to go through the circling giant magma man before her. The humanoid had two glowing eyes that looked like golden holes in its head and its armor had multiple layers. It lifted its left arm and a giant hardened lava shield began to formulate. Rosey almost blanched as she saw it, a shield was a good idea in any fight, however, Rosey wasn't too worried. Shields could either slow you down or protect you depending on how you used them. Rosey suddenly had a thought, could this be one of the traps set by the Mother or could it be her test? Wolvereen had assured Rosey that the Mother wouldn't allow any traps to harm her but, what if the mother had decided to use one of the traps or had forgotten somehow. That seemed very unlikely, but Rosey's mind was in overdrive right now, her instincts to survive kicking in as the heat intensified. Rosey kept a firm stance as she began to circle the beast, Alex by her side. They were keeping a good distance from the magma creature but that didn't last for long. A sudden and powerful wave of magma reached up from the wall and slammed down in front of Alex, separating him from Rosey's side. Rosey gasped in shock and tried to reach him, but knew better than to approach the magma. That answered her question then. Alex was okay she was sure, but something had purposefully separated them from one another. It was also the reason she had been drawn to this spot that just so happened to be a Black Hole where Alex's magic would be useless. This *was* a test. It had to be. The nagging was humming in her head, telling her to move forward but Rosey had to block it out now and focus on the fight she knew was coming.

Rosey gritted her teeth and gave the magma warrior before her a glaring look. Alex was a good friend and if anything had happened to him, they'd have her to answer to. The creature stepped cautiously and Rosey mimicked it, carefully evaluating her opponent as the Goddess had taught her. She held her stance perfectly, knowing that she would wait for as long as necessary to allow the humanoid to attack first. Finally the giant made its move and came at her quickly with finesse. She dodged out of the way as it came at her and danced behind it, swinging her sword she knocked it off of its feet and used its forward momentum to send it flying head first. The creature flipped as it did so and landed on its feet, squatting. It turned and examined her with its deadly eyes. *That was a move to simply evaluate my skills*, Rosey thought, firmly moving back into a new stance. She waited patiently; sweat drenching her shirt near her chest and running down her forehead. She wiped it away carefully without breaking eye contact or stance. She wasn't going to be caught off guard. The thing came at her again in the same manner and Rosey once again dodged around it, but the humanoid placed its feet firmly and brought its sword around to her, thinking she wasn't able to block, but Rosey had seen this coming. Attacking in the same way could only mean that they wanted to give her a false sense of ability before attacking with a surprise. She blocked and used the momentum to gain some distance before neatly landing away from her attacker. The lava humanoid turned to face her again, its blank eyes narrowed. It cocked its head as if it was impressed at her display. Rosey simply took up another stance. She knew she could not remain on the defensive for long, but she had to wait for the opportune moment. She had to focus on conserving her energy against the searing heat of the room for she'd quickly tire if she strained herself too much. This fight was all about patience and careful observation.

The humanoid then did something she wasn't expecting. It lifted its arm with the shield towards the air. The shield began to become gelatinous as it reformed itself into the image of a bow. The bow wasn't just any bow, it was a crossbow, a one handed one and it was aiming right at her. Rosey felt her heartbeat sore, and she cursed as the creature released an arrow in her direction. *Great!* Rosey thought as she dodged the arrows. *The damn thing can change its weapons!* What next, could it conjure up some monster lava dogs to sick on her? *Nope, I better not tempt fate.* She quickly dodged again, doing her best to avoid the arrows finding their marks. Rosey's hatred of the bow and arrow extended to the crossbow too because it was far worse than the regular old bow and arrow. It could fire multiple rounds in a fast amount of time and it was pretty accurate too, as long as you knew how to shoot them. Rosey dodged each arrow perfectly for the Goddess had made sure that she was exemplary in dodging arrows if she didn't have any skill in using them and a long range weapon like that would be a big threat to her life if she wasn't careful. There was no cover here to think of so Rosey was reduced to running away and she was feeling pretty happy that Alex couldn't see her right now. Dodging arrows wasn't as graceful as a sword fight could be. A crossbow was going to be very difficult to take down and Rosey only had one weapon! No, wait, she had two. Her eyes settled on Silver Knight at her side and she smiled. She knew what to do. She switched Andraste to her left hand mid flip while avoiding an arrow to make it look like the only reason she did so was to help her flip be completed successfully when, in actuality, she needed her right hand free for Silver knight.

She took off, running around the warrior. Normally, she would do this until her attacker ran out of arrows or she found an opening but the giant seemed to have an endless supply of fire arrows mutating from its lava body. She'd have to wait for an opening and then launch her attack. Till then, she kept up her dodging, all the while keeping her left arm, holding Andraste, pointed at the humanoid so that it would think she was doing it so that she could deflect any arrows. In fact, she did just that as one zoomed at her close to her head. She lifted Andraste perfectly and the arrow was deflected. Rosey kept a close eye on the creature, waiting…waiting…finally there was a lull in time between the arrows firing. It was a small second of time, but it was all Rosey needed. She immediately acted. She lifted Silver knight from its sheath and sent the small dagger hurtling toward the lava creature with expert precision, ironic given her terrible aim with arrows. It was so distracted by the lull in its arrow's timing that it didn't notice the dagger before it was too late. The dagger, however, hadn't been for the humanoid, only for its crossbow. The dagger imbedded itself perfectly in the crossbow and had the desired effect. It not only tipped the humanoid off balance by the sudden change in weight, it also distracted it by making it look at the crossbow. As fast as lightning, Rosey jumped forward and kicked the warrior off its feet and onto its back. Rosey had the sword hovering at the creatures neck as it propped itself up. The battle was over, Rosey had won. The humanoid reabsorbed the crossbow and its sword back into its body. Silver Knight clattered to the ground and the humanoid picked it up. It bent on one knee and extended the dagger, hilt first, to her. Rosey reached out and took it, sheathing it. The creature then stepped backwards and the flowing magma-covered walls encircled the warrior, reabsorbing it back into its surface. The doorways were suddenly flung open and the way forward was once again clear. Rosey turned and saw the wall surrounding Alex disappear. He stepped toward her, his dagger still drawn. He was covered in sweat but looked none the worse for wear. He cast his gaze around but when he saw Rosey and her calm demeanor he sheathed his weapon and quickly joined her.

"What happened?" he said, extending his arms in confusion.

Rosey smiled, "I think I just won my first test," she said happily.

Alex smiled, "Really," then his face fell, "and I missed it, man…I would have liked to have cheered you on."

Rosey smiled, "Don't worry. I'm kinda happy you didn't see what happened." She wiped away the sweat beading her forehead. The heat was killing her and she quickly nodded towards the open door. "Let's get going, I've got an element to collect." The nagging feeling was back again with a vengeance. The fight had been a good distraction but now she could feel the need to keep going pulling at her even more. She ran on ahead, sheathing Andraste as she went. She'd have to thank the Golden Goddess one day for teaching her how to do the attack she used on the lava humanoid. Once they were outside the Black Hole, Alex put the shield back up. Magic was once again plentiful. There was no way she was going to let anything get in her way now, not when the element was closer than it had ever been before.

Chapter Sixteen: The First Element

To Rosey's utter horror, they spent almost another hour following her nagging feeling through other various passageways. Her head was spinning by this time and she was feeling especially fired up for some good butt whooping when she finally met the Mother. After a few more turns and bridges over flowing magma, they found themselves in a gigantic room. They were suspended in the air about twenty yards above the ground. A small platform with a railing extended out from the tunnel about three feet. Exhausted from their long trek, they both grabbed the railing and surveyed their surroundings. Looming about a mile above them was the gaping hole of the crater. The evening light poured in from above casting dim but sufficient light on the walls. Below them, instead of the magma Rosey had expected to see at the center of the volcano, there was a large brown and black circular floor. There, Ysandir stood, waiting for them.

Alex took out his wand and muttered a spell, suddenly, the protective circle flared out. It was no longer needed. To Rosey's amazement the air was cool and still like the inside of a cave. She looked to her left and saw stairs leading down to the ground. They were the same hard brown material that had made the precarious bridge before. She quickly pushed onward. She hated to rush but the throbbing in her head was starting to really get to her.

Looking at Ysandir, Rosey realized something that she had wanted to ask but had never gotten around to. This was the perfect thing to distract her from her throbbing head. She wasn't certain it would work, but she had to try something. "Hey Alex, how do animals focus magic? Humans use wands, but obviously animals can't carry around wands. I know that creatures like Ysandir use their horns to focus magical power, but what about others?"

Alex answered faithfully, as he followed her down the stairs. He seemed just as happy for the distraction as she was, though what would have him more worried or anxious than her was a mystery to Rosey and she was way too preoccupied with the nagging feeling to ask. "They use various stones that they hang from around their necks. They're created in the same way humans create their wands. The spell is slightly different and instead of a branch or stick they are given a piece of stone or precious gem to forge their stone from." He gestured to Ysandir, "In the Book of Magic, it mentions an old legend where long ago unicorns were believed to be the masters of magic and were the teachers to all others about how to use it. When humans were searching for a way to focus magic and draw it to them they copied the shape of the unicorn's horn and fashioned a wand. Animals, however, could not use wands so the unicorns showed them how to create stones that could be used in the same way."

Alex's explanation was a gratifying distraction from the distant ground that still looked so far away. In her head Rosey suddenly saw an image of Noly and Hazel, and the horses wearing stones around their necks throwing magic around. She giggled slightly then frowned in thought. Could they have magical and elemental powers? Rosey quickly dismissed the idea. Noly, Hazel, and the horses were all from Earth. They would have no magical or elemental powers. Their intelligence, as the Goddess had said, was simply heightened because the intelligence was already there. On Earth it was stifled, but here it was heightened. These thoughts helped to distract Rosey but not completely. She slowed down her pace as the stairs began getting steeper. She held onto the railing with one hand and used the other to balance herself. In her peripheral vision Rosey saw Alex doing the same. She'd rather get there safely then end up as an omelet on the ground because she couldn't slow down a little. Besides, she'd waited this long she could wait a little longer. But that was getting harder to do, the pounding of the element was horrendous and its call was almost like a scream in her head. It took all of her strength to stop herself from holding her head in pain. And, as if that wasn't enough, even her sword Andraste, faithfully strapped to her back, was beginning to vibrate in its sheath as if it was excited, or in rebellion, or…something. Rosey didn't dare draw her sword to discover what was ailing it on a small staircase and she definitely didn't want to offend the Mother by drawing her weapon so she decided to ignore it as best she could. Finally, they landed on the hard surface of the ground. Quickly they moved to join Ysandir, casting their gaze across the wide crater and its walls stretching up towards the sky.

She wanted to burst out in anger at the unicorn and chide her for making them worry but the throbbing in her head made her mute. It didn't matter right now for the nagging, throbbing…something was driving her crazy. She put a hand to her forehead but the pain seemed to come steadily. She knew she was in the right place for this certainly looked like where she was supposed to be. Ysandir probably wouldn't be here if she wasn't in the right place. She looked at the unicorn again with sharp daggers in her eyes but she just couldn't formulate the right words with her head in such a state. Instead she looked around, trying to distract herself.

Rosey could barely cast her gaze upward were the blinding light penetrated the darkness so far away. The towering walls of the volcano narrowed the light into a ball shape, almost like the sun at its brightest during the day. The light only hurt her eyes and put pressure on her already throbbing head, so, instead, she looked down. The circular black floor covered the entire circumference of the area. Rosey barely was able to make out grooves in the rich black rock, she bent down to better examine them and noticed that they corresponded to one another in equal lengths and consecutively designed patterns. These weren't normal grooves, these were designs knowingly etched into the black floor. What had made them was unknown to Rosey and Ysandir didn't seem to know either. She eyed them herself, examining them carefully, curiously. Alex was doing the same, reaching his hand down to touch them and feel its surface. Rosey did the same. It didn't feel any different than what she thought hardened lava would feel like, for that is what it looked to be: hardened lava.

Rosey barely had time to contemplate the designs for she suddenly felt a rush of pain enter her head again, different than it had been before. It was more intense but also more focused, as if something was coming. Suddenly the cracks in the floor lit up as if real lava was pulsing, flowing, in-between the grooves. Rosey stared down at the liquid and realized with certainty that it was lava, molten hot, lava that, for some reason, left them alone and not in the least bit affected. It was there but it did not harm them, which was both fascinating and scary at the same time. What would have the power to do that?

Suddenly in a fiery torrent of pure energy, the Mother finally appeared. She came in a gush of exploding fire that burst from the magma under the hardened lava floor forming an arch and landing in a swirling mass of crackling energy before them. Had the lava always been underneath it, and the grooves were just letting some leak into them? The question burned in Rosey's mind unanswered. The floor repaired itself behind her, and the red lava continued to swirl through the grooves in its cracked surface. Rosey barely noticed this for her eyes were focused on the Mother. Swathed in flames she formed into the image of a large horse. The pegasus stretched out beautiful red, yellow, and golden wings, their plumes blazing in flames. Her mane was nothing but fire suspended in midair. Her tail was a long, twisting, flowing mass of flames. A long line of fire connected the tail and mane like a dorsal fin on a fish. Long twisting feathers made of fire surrounded all four forelegs. Long tendrils of flame, like fire from a jet engine, were attached to her shoulders blowing back towards her flanks. Her orange and red streaked body gave the impression of glowing lava. Beautiful yellow eyes and muscled limbs made the Mother seem more powerful than the whole volcano itself. She was tall, a good twenty five hands high, as large as Ysandir was.

She approached Rosey cautiously, her body as beautiful as it was intimidating. Her wings were huge, massive even, and perfectly large enough to carry the horse's large bulk. They would have to be for the horse was easily much larger and heavier than anything Rosey could ever think to be. She paced on large hooves that looked big enough to crush Rosey's body easily, but she faced the Mother with not a single fear in her mind. In fact, she felt herself oddly relaxing in the presence of the Mother, she had none of the same feelings she had had before when facing something so much larger than her, so much more powerful. The nagging in her head was almost like a list of instructions, edging her forward and telling her what to do. In a heartbeat, Rosey had changed from her normal self to another. Something else had taken control. She was very much in a stupor, like a ghost. She simply walked forward; barely conscious of why she was doing what she was doing. Something else was driving her forward, forcing her to abandon all minor doubts and ideas. The only thing that mattered was the pegasus and what she bore inside her. Rosey could almost see it, there, turning inside. It was like she had x-ray vision and the pegasus was wide open for her to see through. The element was the thing she sought, the thing she cherished and needed. If Rosey had been fully aware of herself at that moment she would have found herself to be thoroughly scared by her actions. Perhaps it was because it was the first time she had collected an element, perhaps it was the lack of her own elemental power that was making her so drawn and act so strange…but she couldn't process that at the moment, it was a minor issue and not worth her time. She pushed it from her mind and continued walking.

    Rosey was no expert but she would guess that this beast of a pegasus was anything but normal, she was without a doubt a regal and supremely royal creature. Rosey was irresistibly drawn toward her. She continued forward on legs that felt numb as if her body was responding without her will. Alex and Ysandir stayed behind in silent wonder. The moment the Mother stepped toward her Rosey felt a startling power course through her

The Mystics

as the element inside of the Mother pulsed. It copied the Mother's pulse, beat for beat, and left Rosey dumbfounded as to why she could sense it so powerfully. The Mother smiled and then bent back her head as long tendrils of red energy began to pulse out from the Mother's form. She neighed slightly, but did not move, the element surged toward Rosey becoming a menacing fireball of flaming heat. It struck her straight on and consumed her in massive fiery torrents. The throbbing in Rosey's head began to burst forth and Rosey felt as if her whole head was on fire. Startled, she fought it at first, but then some deep instinct set in and she relaxed into its soft fiery grip. She was ready for this. Somewhere inside she had always been ready. Nothing was important at that moment. Not the rumbling of the volcano, not Alex's startled cry, not the shaking that she felt from the volcano as it reacted to the power of the Keeper and the Mother. There were no words necessary. She knew what she needed to do. She stepped closer, closing her eyes, allowing her body to relax and become limp so that all the power the Mother possessed was given to her. She was vaguely aware of the Shanobie Crystal around her neck beginning to shine a bright red as the element of fire sought her out. It was glowing with a power she had never felt before, a burning sensation that could only be described as the force of fire, the first element. This was a power that was one with her as well as completely different and separate from her.

    The heat overwhelmed her and she cried hot tears of…happiness. They felt so strange yet so perfect. Pure joy filled her heart, but it wasn't coming from her, it was coming from the element. It was singing with joy, burning with jubilation and crackling over her skin with excitement. Rosey had no other way to describe what she was feeling, the immense joy of the element coursed through her. It was so happy, so filled with purpose. It was like the element was welcoming her, talking to her, soothing her. Then Rosey heard it, a sound like distant thunder. It was calling something, her name, it was her name. Slowly she opened her eyes. At first the strange heat and exploding power of the emotion emanating from the element almost made

Rosey's head explode. The element sensed her pain and backed off, but she could feel it flickering before her as close to her as it could get without hurting her. Rosey focused her mind and tried to make out what it was saying. A strange form appeared before her swathed in flame. All she could make out were two yellow eyes burning with intense heat. Finally she could hear it, echoing all around her. The voice sounded like the crackling of a fire in a warm hearth. She could only assume it was coming from whatever was in front of her. She knew without a doubt that the voice could only be heard by her. Though the words echoed all around her they were also present in her mind, making Rosey start when the creature spoke. It gasped and wisped, drawing out the s's on its words.

"Oh Rosssssey, Rossssssey, Rosssssey! My chosen one, my master, my Keeper. It is so good to sssssee you again, sssssso good to be one with you after we have been sssssseparated for ssssso long. I love you with all my fiery passsssion. My Rosey, my child, my flower. Take me and do with me as you see fit."

Rosey could not answer or even cry out for at that moment the fire, that had been holding itself back, suddenly exploded all around her like a thousand fireworks. She wanted to scream, not in pain, but in jubilation. The stinging of the heat was exciting, exhilarating, racing across her body and setting her blood on fire. She leaned her head back as the power flowed through her. She did not see the Mother backing away from her, exhausted, as the power raced through Rosey's veins. She did not hear the rumbling of rocks as giant pieces tumbled away from the walls. All she heard was the gentle stirring of the power within the shard as it forged with her, its real master, its real mother. Not Adina, not Ysandir, not the Mother, but her. She was the one that it belonged to, the one the power hungered for. She let it come, welcoming a new part of herself. She felt a little more complete in that moment as if a small part of a void had been filled. She was the Keeper, this was her element.

As the element entered her crystal the last piece of the fiery power surged through her body and settled down into a simmering control. Suddenly the pain and the thundering thudding in her head faded away replaced by a new strength and power. Slowly she opened her eyes and cupped the power in her palms. Feeling the love that beat there she let the element encircle her and change her. Her hair and eyes changed to a deep orange color with red and yellow streaks. Her outfit burst into flames and a new orange one blossomed across her body. There was a powerful jerk as the fire encircled her again and she suddenly started falling. She felt a twisted pain as something powerful and hard grew near her shoulders. Wings! She had wings! She was startled at first to find them there and then overjoyed. Who wouldn't be ecstatic about two giant wings on their back? Not knowing that she had been lifted into the air in the first place she instinctively unfolded her fiery wings and flapped them proudly. She lifted into the air effortlessly and experimented with her new appendages. It took a while to get used to the movement of the wings and the new muscles in her back but finally she got the hang of it. The knowledge of how to use her wings somehow came naturally to her. Maybe it came with the element, at that moment she didn't care. She flew around the crater's circumference laughing with pure joy. She looped and soared, trailing miniature fires from her plumes in her wake.

Looking down she saw Alex jumping up and down in delight, whooping and cheering her on, a large grin on his face. Ysandir simply nodded her head but a strange look crossed her face. She was examining Rosey with something like surprise but Rosey didn't care, she was just so happy.

Landing, Rosey folded her wings neatly behind her back, the plumage trailing on the ground. Alex stared at her in wonder while Ysandir stood beside him, smiling brightly. Rosey stretched out one of her wings and saw that it was easily twelve feet long. It's shimmering feathers were beautiful, their perfectly rounded tips sprouted from her new wings in perfect order. She slowly reached a hand out towards them, afraid they'd burn if touched, but she just had to feel them for herself. They were as soft as air, like billowing cotton. Warm, but not scalding. They were so smooth that Rosey felt breathless where she stood, overcome with joy. She tested the muscles, feeling the way her second arm bent, moving the wing as if she needed to be certain that they really existed. She beat them and flapped them around her, loving the fiery tendrils that swirled off of their heavy plumage. This was the stuff of legends and it was happening to her, her! She had never imagined this in a million years, and yet it all felt so perfect and so…right. She couldn't quiet the raging storm inside her: the power, the strength. It was like drinking a fizzy drink and enjoying the feel of the carbonated liquid running down your throat. That feeling expanded through her chest, making her breathe deeply. It was then that she noticed that she wasn't dressed in her normal clothes. Looking down, she almost jumped where she stood in utter shock. She was now wearing a sleeveless, orange, midriff top. It was cut down the middle and the lose sides were tied in place across her stomach and through her belt by brown leather ties. A red, metal plate, decorated in golden designs, covered her breasts in an 'm' shape. Long red metal strips encircled her arms. Looking closely she saw they were shaped like dragon scales. A brown, leather belt held up long orange pants covered by crimson knee-high boots, once again designed to look like dragon scales. A gold head band with red rubies and orange ambers rested gently on her forehead. Gold tendrils of beads attached to the headband cascaded down her long orange and red colored hair. If the new outfit wasn't enough, it got even more elaborate. Rosey's shoulders sported two masses of fire, blowing outward, fiercely copying the Mother's own shoulder flames. They were not in the least bit hot near her face, nor did she seem to be able to determine if they were fed from her own body or just resting in place. She shrugged her shoulders and watched as the two billows responded, moving in rhythm. They were there to stay.

Glancing at her arms, she whistled in astonishment. Her muscles had doubled in size, increasing her strength. She flexed them admiringly, imagining what she could crush with them. She was also a lot bigger than she remembered. Her head was almost as tall as Ysandir's was and Alex's head only came up to her chest. She felt like a titan or a queen. She was bigger, badder, stronger, and a hell of a lot more powerful. She could feel the fire running through her veins and the heat falling off of her in waves. It was exhilarating and strange at the same time. Rosey felt complete, perfect, as if she had found something she had been missing. It was…the perfect feeling.

Seeing Alex she launched herself at him in excitement, "You didn't tell me I'd have wings. This is awesome!" she shouted making Alex cover his ears. She hugged him close and noticed that what fire touched him turned blue and left him unharmed. "I…didn't know! I don't think any other Keeper has had wings before! I've only been told about the Keeper before you, I've never seen her myself or I would have remembered. You look…stunning." He said admiring her new look. He seemed breathless and at a loss for words. She had been his friend for so long, just as herself, she could only imagine what it must be like to look upon her when she was different than anything he'd ever seen. "Thanks," she said turning a complete 360 to show off her fiery self.

Looking down at her crystal she saw that it was glowing bright orange. She had the element. She could feel its power stirring. The warmth that spread through her reminded her of life and home. She felt like an inferno but not in a painful way. She could hear faint whispers in the flickering flames. Patterns of orange, yellow and red colored her vision. She sighed and breathed deeply, as if she was feeding the oxygen to the fire instead of her lungs. Her whole body radiated. She was stronger, bigger, just…better.

Something else was also better. Her sword, Andraste, was humming a strange tune against Rosey's back. Grasping the hilt she expertly pulled the blade from its sheath. As soon as the first bit of the blade touched the air it exploded into flames. Alex and Ysandir stood back as they watched Rosey bring the burning blade around in front of her. It looked exactly the same except the blade had turned a bright orange, as if it had been heated in the fires of a forge. The entire blade was on fire, casting its own orange light around them. Rosey grasped the hilt tightly, amazed at the transformation that the sword had taken on. Studying it for a few moments longer, she finally sheathed it. As the blade entered the leather sheath it ceased being orange and the flames snuffed out. *So it is only like this when I'm in this form*, she thought eyeing her new look. She smiled, impressed by the sword's transformation. She glanced down at Silver Knight. With curiosity she pulled the dagger from her sheath, but it did not transform or even glow. Rosey sheathed the dagger, a little disappointed but not daunted. She held the Shanobie crystal in her hands and turned toward Alex. "This is amazing! I can't wait to see what the other elements feel like and what my Andraste will look like!" she said, almost bursting with energy. "In such a hurry to leave Mercury, Rosey?" said the Mother with an amused look. Rosey spun around, surprised. In all her excitement she'd almost forgotten that the pegasus was still there. She smiled sheepishly. The Mother's voice was distinctly feminine though not as sophisticated sounding as Ysandir's was. It had more of a homey feeling, like she'd known Rosey her whole life.

Rosey rubbed her head apologetically, "Sorry about that. Mercury...is that your name?"

"Yes it is," said Mercury drawing closer. Her hooves were silent on the dirt floor. Her fiery power had died down and she seemed calmer than she did before. Rosey noticed that the flames that had created the pegasus's, mane, tail, wings and legs, were gone, replaced instead with a regular orange and red color. Her mane and tail were bright red with golden flecks, her skin was a sharp orange with red designs at her flank looking much like an appaloosa, and her hooves were pure black like coal. Her large wings were red with yellow and black highlights. She was just as large as she was before but since Rosey was almost as large as she was now, she was not as intimidated.

The Mystics

"You Rosey, now have the power of Fire. Use it wisely for it can be very wild as well as tame. You must find the balance between them and use it to your advantage. This is your first element, thus your tests were very simple."

Rosey almost wanted to slap the pegasus for thinking that those tests had been simple, but the fact that she did think they were simple made Rosey go as still as a rock. If those tests were easy then what else would she have to face later on when she went after the other elements?

Mercury went on, "The first test, as usual, needs to be simple, but not too simple. Normally the first test consists of a physical as well as mental challenge because of your lack of an element, and, in your case, a definite lack."

At this Rosey felt herself go cold despite the heat, "You're talking about my inability to access my own natural element, the one I was born with."

Mercury simply nodded, her withers twitched in quiet embarrassment for having brought up a touchy subject but Rosey understood that she had meant no insult. "So…given the circumstances, I rearranged my test. It consisted of two parts: the first was for you to find me on your own. Which you did…rather quickly," she said under her breath as if surprised. She straightened and went on before Rosey could say anything, "Your test was easy, track the element and let it lead you to it. I admit I intensified things a bit, but not too much. The ability to sense the elements comes naturally to the Keeper, so don't be surprised when you next feel it, but what I did was far more powerful than what you should normally feel. It was a way for me to help establish and test the bond between you. There is no greater bond than the one forged between you and your element. It is that bond that led you to me. You did splendidly; better than I thought you'd do for your first time."

Rosey felt her cheeks flush with pride, but it could have also been heat for all she knew.

"The second part was a physical test. I wanted to see how well you'd do under harsh conditions, which is why it was fairly hot, and how you reacted to a one on one fight. You also passed this test with flying colors and far more skill than I expected for someone of your age. You've had training prior to this haven't you?"

Rosey assumed that the Mother knew that she had been raised on Earth and so knew that the pegasus was talking about her time on Earth before she was brought to The World Within A World to receive her training from the Golden Goddess. "Yes, I took Kendo and Ladoe lessons while I was on Earth. My uncle went out of his way to make sure I was…prepared." She turned her gaze away. The mention of her uncle opened up a can of worms she didn't like getting into. The fact that he had chosen to stay behind still, kind of, held a hard edge for Rosey, even though she trusted him completely.

Mercury tossed her now normal mane, "As he should have, he knew you were destined for this life. He did the best he could, and it shows. You were exquisite in your fight, that's the fastest anyone's ever won against my magma golem."

Rosey recognized the word golem. It had been one of the many things she learned about in Jasira's library. A golem was a creature that could be made of any material substance but had no mind or soul of its own. It was created simply for the purpose of carrying out its creator's will. It was a lot like a robot but where robots were led by hardwires and programs, golems were led by the will that created them. Most golems were made from earth or rocks but they could be formed using anything material except gases like air.

Rosey looked at her sharply, "Magma golem, you mean that magma creature I fought one on one? I was the fastest? Really?"

She nodded, "Yes, Maharen and Esperanza were great warriors but my golem is made to find your weaknesses and use them against you. Maharen focused way too much on power, while Esperanza was far too passive.

The Mystics

They did both make it, but Maharen was shot down at least three times by the arrows before she finally got smart." Mercury snickered and pawed the ground in laughter.

Rosey gave her a surprised look, "Wait, what do you mean Maharen was shot down three times by the arrows!? Are you telling me those arrows back there wouldn't have hurt me?" She gestured back in the direction of the stairs leading out the way they came, remembering the strange duel she'd had with the magma creature. Alex gave Mercury a questioning look. He was just as interested as she was.

Mercury laughed, once again pawing the ground, "Of course not dear! None of the Mothers would ever make a challenge that you could actually die from. If you'd been hit by an arrow or the sword, you'd just feel the pain as if it had hurt you. It wouldn't have actually done you any damage. We're not evil. If you fail a test, it won't end in your death, only the knowledge that…you know…you failed."

Rosey knew all too well what it meant. The Golden Goddess had been very specific. If she failed even one test, she would not earn the right to the element. That was as simple as it got. There were no redos and no second chances. Rosey had thought that this concept was a bit unfair; after all, everyone makes mistakes, but the Goddess had insisted that these mistakes weren't lessons to be learned, no, they were proof that you were worthy to gain the power that the element had to offer. Failing once meant that you weren't ready. It was as simple as that. To fail would mean that you weren't physically or mentally capable to be the Keeper and, though the Shanobie Crystal was very good at choosing the right person, it was ultimately up to the individual to prove their worth. The Keeper was a 'perfect being', she was meant to be the ultimate weapon against the ultimate evil and failure to collect an element wasn't an option. Rosey had to be very certain that she took every test seriously and considered not only physical attributes but mental and emotional ones as well. Still, it was nice to know her life would never be in danger during one of these tests.

Mercury spoke again, pulling Rosey from her thoughts, "But other tests will not be so kind, Keeper." Her voice became stiff and she eyed Rosey intensely. "These tests may be the worst of the creatures you fight or the best. They could challenge your beliefs, your understanding of life, and even your perception of reality. Always be brave."

"So you made me feel all those things before? That nagging feeling?" Rosey asked incredulously. It had felt so natural and yet so rampant. Maybe she had let some leak out but Rosey hadn't expected it to be so strong. Alex gave her a look that said 'you were feeling something else and didn't tell me!' Rosey ignored it.

"Yes and no, I simply intensified something that was already there. When you draw close to the element, you'll begin to sense it. It helps you to find it, otherwise you could be running around it and never know the difference and we don't want that."

Rosey shook her head in agreement, "No, I wouldn't think so." Turning to gaze up at the walls of the volcano, her brows furrowed and she said, "Um… What happened to the volcano, if you don't mind me asking?"

Casting one last gaze around, she shuddered at the scene. Everything had stopped and the volcano was no longer the same. The constant rumbling and shaking ground movements were gone. The chamber's charcoal black bottom with its odd grooves had been replaced by regular old dirt with small clumps of greenery here and there, signs of an extinct volcano. The fiery power that had flowed before was no longer there, she could feel the truth in this. She could sense the energy was simply…gone. It was as if it had never even existed. Rosey wondered as to why this would have happened or how. The Mother's hiding place was no longer needed, true, but there was more to it than that. Rosey got the feeling that the volcano had been zapped of its own fiery power by something or someone. According to Alex the volcano had been a gathering spot for magic and the energy flows but something had changed. She wondered if the exchanging of the element between herself and the Mother had caused it, but why would it? The element she had collected was different than the normal ones and the natural magma of the volcano wasn't fed by an element but the mantle, like any other. It had to have been an external source that caused it. That was the only explanation she could come up with.

She looked to the mother expectantly. She hoped that she had an explanation so that her earlier fear that she had caused it was not true. It was one thing to accept an element but it was an entirely different story to take all the fire from the surrounding area and pull it in like a vacuum cleaner. The idea that she had been strong enough to change the world around her sent a shiver up her spine.

The Mother regarded their surroundings. "I'm not sure," she said, tossing her mane. "I believe my elemental presence may have aggravated it, and then, for some reason, once you collected the element it…died. Almost as if the power keeping it going was sucked out of it." She stared at one spot on the wall, taken by her thoughts. Rosey wasn't sure what to say or do. Finally the mother huffed as if it was nothing, "Oh well, this volcano has a habit of doing whatever it wants. I believe that the magical barrier around the volcano is still in place, though, so you shouldn't have to fear any attacks."

"Could I have…" she asked hesitantly, "been the reason behind it? Did I…suck the elemental power from the volcano?" Fear filed her heart as she said the words. If she had been the reason why the magnificent volcano had died she wasn't sure what she would make of it.

"I'm not sure, could have been, but…," The large pegasus shook her head as she saw Rosey's face fall and become stricken with surprise, "it's not important. This volcano can handle itself. There is no reason to fear this situation. If it was you, then it was, and that's nothing to be afraid of. If my presence affected it than I'd hope that yours would too, since you are the Keeper and your power does far outweigh my own. Please Keeper, do not worry."

Her voice was reassuring but Rosey was not so sure she felt better about it. How powerful was she to be able to affect something as strong as a volcano? Still, she trusted the Mother and decided not to bother with it. She looked away, a bit embarrassed, twisting her hands around each other. Her gaze suddenly rested on the waiting Ysandir, Alex stood beside her, grinning from ear tip to ear tip. Rosey had some choice words for the unicorn. She took off walking briskly for her, excusing herself politely from the Mother's side. She opened her mouth but so many of the sentences swirling around in her head sounded so good that she couldn't decide which one to start out with so she ended up standing before Ysandir with a big 'o' on her mouth. She was flabbergasted and quite annoyed that the giant had abandoned her and Alex before. She was supposed to be her protector after all and provide her with advice. Why would she just disappear!? Rosey assumed it was because she knew Rosey was safe and so didn't find any reason to stick with her or maybe she had just grown tired of waiting. Rosey gritted her teeth, neither of these explanations was good enough for her.

Ysandir beat her to it, understanding her turmoil. "Sorry to have abandoned you Rosey, but I'm afraid the Mother didn't want me with you."

At this Rosey frowned, confused.

"She asked that I leave you to find your own way and that someone of my power," she lifted her head in pride, "would only serve as a distraction. So I left. Do forgive me. I would never have left if it was not of the utmost importance." She said this last with a deep bow of her head in apology.

Rosey felt the ground shake a bit as the giant frame of the Mother joined them. She looked up at her and regarded her as she spoke, "It's true Keeper. I did ask for such a thing, please do not be angry with Ysandir."

Rosey stared at Ysandir, unsure of what to say. She could hardly be mad at her now. If the Mother had demanded such an action, then it certainly wasn't right for Rosey to doubt the unicorn or challenge her choices. Still, would it have killed the unicorn to have at least told Rosey

The Mystics

that she couldn't be with her. That wouldn't have led her astray would it? Rosey shook her head and glanced up at Mercury, "I understand, don't worry." She faced Ysandir with a smile. "It's okay, I'm just glad nothing happened to you...we were a bit worried for a second, that's all." She looked to Alex for support and he nodded his agreement.

Ysandir looked shocked by her words. The Mother chuckled under her breath, "See there, Ysandir, looks like you've made some good friends." She tilted her head and gazed at Ysandir through knowing eyes, as if saying 'see, you old pain'.

Rosey cocked her head, confused, but decided that it was none of her business.

The Mother suddenly cleared her throat politely, drawing their attention, "I must take my leave, Keeper. Farewell, the sooner you are back on the road the better I'm afraid. In this world, you must be diligent, as time is drawing short for your journey. You may use this shortcut if you like." Mercury waved her head and a separate passageway revealed itself not too far away from where they stood, heading back the way they had come.

Rosey regarded her, surprised by her abrupt end to their meeting, but she understood. She didn't have time to waste here. She set her jaw firmly and nodded in agreement. She thanked her and then bowed, her wings folding out at the sides. When she rose her leather outfit was back and her wings and shoulder fires were gone. She hadn't really noticed the fire power receding but it felt almost natural as if she had been doing it her whole life and did not need to focus on it. She took it to be another Keeper thing and dismissed it. For a few moments Mercury stared at her with something like curiosity and intrigue in her bright eyes, but before Rosey could ask what was wrong, the pegasus returned Rosey's bow. Rosey watched in awe as the pegasus walked away and slowly started to disappear and then burn out in a blast of heat and sparks. A puff of smoke was all that was left of her and her great power.

Rosey blinked away the sight, and then turned and hugged Alex again as he approached her, her fear of causing the volcano to go dormant forgotten in the excitement of the completion of her first task. She had finally taken the first real step to destroying the Evil One and becoming the Keeper! She had gone through something unimaginable and didn't feel the slightest bit tired from her ordeal. If anything she felt powerful and strong. She felt like she could handle anything, even a whole group of Raptors.

Her heart beat hard in her chest as she thought about the fiery power within her. She wondered what it would feel like holding its power in her hands and using it in combat. She did not care how much power it would give her, what she cared about was the warmth that would flow into her while she used it. Combining with the element had melted away all those times she felt a stranger in this world, all those times she felt stupid and ill-informed, leaving her feeling much more confident and proud in her own skin. Rosey didn't want to lose that feeling: the feeling that she belonged. She shook her head. She was sounding so farfetched yet she knew it to be true. The elements needed her just as much as she needed them. It would have been something she would have never considered possible a week or so ago but now it was more normal than her daily bus rides had been to school and back. Now that was the distant memory that didn't belong. That was the feeling that was old and no longer had any place in her new world, in her new role as the Keeper. She had taken this responsibility on and it felt so good, better than she'd expected. Suddenly a thought occurred to her. Had her mother felt this way? What about her grandmother? Did every Keeper experience the same feelings for the elements? Did they hold the same need? And what about what the element had said to her, that it was happy to be joined with her again? What did it mean by again? She would never know. Sadness enveloped her as the thought of her mother and her grandmother took root in her mind. She shook herself. She could not let anything get in the way of her goal. She pulled away from Alex and then, with a sly smile, took off quickly down the hidden passageway.

The Mystics

"Race ya back!" she called over her shoulder with a laugh. "No fair, you always play dirty," Alex said taking off after her once he had recovered from his open mouthed shock.   Ysandir stared after them and laughed quietly to herself, amusement shining in her eyes. With a small, playful buck she galloped through the tunnel after them adding her own voice to Rosey and Alex's laughter. They laughed all the way out of the volcano and into the dying sunlight.

Rosey and her Fellowship where all around the fire talking, excitement ran through them as the realization that they had collected one element overcame them. She examined the night sky and determined that it was probably around nine o'clock. When she, Alex, and Ysandir had appeared and told them the good news, the rest of her fellowship had stood and started clapping. She had settled down and told them all about her encounter with Mercury and what it was like retrieving her first element. They all listened intently, wagging their tails stomping their hooves, or meowing with delight at the picture Rosey painted for them. After she was done, it was well into night and she lay down happy that they were back in camp and out of the volcano. They all agreed that they would stay there until word had been sent to them about the Goddess's ship. Even though the volcano now seemed lifeless and dead, the magic surrounding it was still providing a barrier from evil, the Mother herself had said so, thus there was no reason to leave the volcano, plus it had the added bonus of warmth.

Rosey still had no idea as to why the volcano had died, and no one had any other answers for her. She still had a nagging feeling that she had caused it but there was nothing she could do about it now. Rosey was happy, however, to spend a little more time with the volcano, she had never seen one up close and they were quite daunting as well as majestic.

Rochell had decided to take out a hidden bottle of a delicious smelling drink that tasted like apples to celebrate Rosey's collection of her first element. When asked, Rochell confessed to having kept the bottle in anticipation of this event. They each toasted to Rosey's success and then drank their fill. To Rosey's surprise the bottle never ran out of liquid, no matter how much they drank. Once again, magic was at work. As they sipped at the drink they told stories to pass the time. They sat for a while enjoying each other's company and the sound of their voices laughing though the cool night air. Wolvereen was even persuaded to tell them about one of the battles he and his pack had been in with the Golden Goddess. Eglen wasted no time and once again launched into storytelling mode, putting in details that Wolvereen left out. Finally, when the night beckoned to their tired and joyful hearts, they snuggled into their sleepwear and fell asleep.

Before they settled down to sleep Alex and Rochell took a few moments to sneak away. Alex needed to tell Rochell something important and the look he had given her let her know that it was something serious. They successfully managed to sneak off without inspiring any questions and once again found themselves behind one of the large boulders that surrounded the camp.

Taking a deep breath Alex said, "Remember when Rosey said she was flying around the volcano cavern after receiving the element?"

Rochell nodded, Alex saw that she was out of breath as if she had been running a far distance. The weight of their secret conversation was weighing heavily on her. Rochell had never liked being dishonest or secretive, especially with Rosey, and this meeting was indeed a secret they were keeping from their friend.

"Well," he said, framing his words carefully, "Ysandir and I were watching her and I asked Ysandir if this was anything like what Esperanza had gone through....she said...no."

Rochell stared at him dumbfounded. Slowly she crossed her arms, cast her eyes down, and shifted her weight to her right leg, extending the left leg slightly outward. Alex recognized it as the position she took whenever she was considering something important. It was the same thing her mother did when she was thinking. Alex stared at her for a few moments, allowing

The Mystics

her to consider what she had heard. She finally said, "What does this mean?"

"I asked Ysandir that same question, she told me not to worry about it. Rochell, I am worried. It wasn't just Ysandir who was surprised, the Mother was too. They were staring at Rosey like she was some kind of freak of nature. Ysandir had this look on her face as if she was seeing something she didn't quite believe was there. The Mother looked taken aback."

He considered for a few moments, running through everything that had happened in his mind before speaking again.

"But that's not the strangest part. When Rosey came to the Mother, she didn't even speak to her. The Mother burst into flames and these red tendrils of energy began to run off of her and into Rosey. It looked like Rosey was sucking the element right out of her! Rosey didn't look anything like her usual self. Her eyes were so blue they were shining and her hair looked like it was alive. I thought it was the way things were supposed to be. I mean, how would I know the difference? But then…the Mother looked…horrified, scared, and surprised as if something was wrong. I don't know what's happening but, whatever it is; Rosey is not doing what is expected of the Keeper. Something is different and I don't know if that's a good thing or a bad thing."

Neither of them spoke for a while after that, lost in their own thoughts. There was nothing more to say. Alex looked up and could see Rochell's worried expression. She looked at him, her face unreadable.

"That's not all. I don't understand why the volcano died," he said shaking his head. "That volcano has never been dormant. Do you think it's possible that Rosey zapped the elemental power from the volcano, so much so that she caused it to die?"

Rochell was unsure. She shrugged, not able to speak. It wasn't hard to notice that something, whether you were a magikin or elemental, had changed about the once lively volcano. It was now dormant and dead, as if someone had unplugged the life support and left it to suffocate. When Rosey told them what had happened they had all realized it was something big but no one had dared to comment about it and interrupt the celebration of Rosey's first elemental collection, so they had remained silent.

Taking a deep breath Rochell said, "That area is a hot spot for the Energy Flows, maybe once the elemental power was gone the Volcano died? Let's let Adina worry about that." She suddenly took his hand in hers. "We pledged ourselves to Rosey. Even if things are different we aren't going to turn our backs on her, right?"

"Never!" he said without a doubt in his heart.

"Then that is all we can do for her."

Slowly, together, they walked back to camp. What they did not know was that Wolvereen had heard them from the shadows and, solemnly, he too felt the weight of their burden.

Chapter Seventeen: The Crystal

Rosey hated this Dream World. It was so dull and lifeless that she could hardly think of it as a place where you go when you dream. Shouldn't it be a lovely and peaceful place where you could sit back, relax, and enjoy the show? No. Instead it was creepy, dark, musty, and downright unusual. It was also the last place in the world, dream or not, she wanted to be. She knew that she had gotten one element and needed to get the others, which in turn required the new location, which required her to meet the White Witch, which required her to be here. She did not mind the Witch as much as she did the meeting place. When she thought of the Witch, gloomy and depressing were not the first things to come to her mind. The White Witch was the exact opposite of the room which made her seem out of place. Then again everything in this world seemed out of place, at least to Rosey it did.

She repositioned herself on the bed and played with the lace end of the comforter to pass the time. She had been waiting for what seemed like forever for the Witch and needed something to keep her occupied. As the seconds dragged on she couldn't help but think about how much was depending on her completing this journey to ultimately save this world. Nothing like an evil menace to help motivate a teenager, Rosey thought with a smile. *I wonder if I will finally end this nightmare for these people. I hope I can.* Andraste hummed against her back as if it disliked her thinking in such ways. Rosey was unsure about Andraste, she hadn't bothered to worry about how it vibrated, shook, and seemed almost alive, reacting to whatever she reacted to. Rosey simply assumed it was the power of Andraste. The long sword hung on her back comfortably as if it had always been there, Rosey liked the feel of its long edge against her back. Was this how her mother had felt? What about her father, had he carried any weapons? With all the focus on her mother she'd forgotten to inquire about her father. She bent her head, ashamed that she would forget him so easily. She reached behind her and grabbed a hold of Andraste's hilt. She ran her fingers over the designs etched in the hilt, memorizing each line and crack as if some message or imprint of her mother's hands would be left behind. This was the very sword her mother had held and gone into battle with. Rosey wondered if her mother had looked as magnificent as she had in her fiery form, or had she looked even better? Rosey didn't care either way. It was the simple act of knowing that she wanted. This small, simple bit of information would have meant so much to Rosey, some way for her to visualize her mother. A strong winged warrior with long black hair like her own and blue eyes to match surrounded by flames with an orange crystal glowing at her chest. Rosey felt herself wondering what her mother smelled like, how she had walked, talked, dressed, and more. Her mind flew through every spec of memory trying to dredge up something real and tangible for her mind to grasp, but there was nothing. The same thing happened for her father. The only image she had of her parents was the picture that her Uncle John had given her. She's been separated from them as soon as she'd been born so it made sense that she would remember nothing. She wished now, more than ever, that she had decided to bring that picture with her, but there was no way that she could have ever left her uncle there without an image of Esperanza. Thinking back on it, if she had had a second chance she would have made the same decision to leave it behind with John, it had been the right thing to do.

Suddenly she felt the familiar jumble of wind and song that she had heard before when the Witch came. Sweet and spicy smells drifted all around her, there was no doubt the Witch was coming. She looked up sharply and straightened up, listening. The sounds had hardly been noticeable when Rosey first met the Witch but now she heard the notes clear and strong. They were more in her head than out loud. This place worked in a strange way that made you think every sound was an echo through your mind. It was like talking through your mind but your lips were moving. Like one of those Japanese movies.

Casting her gaze at the door she turned just in time to see the Witch standing proud and tall. She seemed happier than usual. Her eyes were brighter, more alive, and her smile was genuine and had an almost calming effect. Rosey was a little confused by the smiles that the Witch was giving her. Before, the Witch had been very collected and stolid looking with a luminescent layer of shimmer surrounding her, making it look like a light was shining behind her. That same light effect was still there but the broad smile on her lips made her look almost like a person who had just been embalmed. Her face was too perfect and her skin was too white. Rosey gulped but after a few moments she finally began to understand. She had just collected her first element so it only made sense that the element's messenger would be proud of her. Despite herself, Rosey felt a grin twitch at the corners of her mouth.

"So...what now?" She put her hands on her hips and stared at the Witch expectantly.

"First I would like to congratulate you on winning your first element. How does it feel?" She tilted her head toward Rosey, curiously. Suddenly forgetting how old she was and how much of a child she would sound like, Rosey almost squealed with delight, proudly proclaiming in broken sentences, "It's amazing...I can't even begin to describe it. The rush, the power, the heat, the strength, the wings....oh the wings, no one ever told me I'd have wings!" At this Rosey swore she saw the Witch's brows furrow in surprise, but the look was gone as soon as she saw it and Rosey was too excited to care. She continued on, "I was so happy, so complete, I felt so...so...perfect. I guess it feels...hot? Yeah, hot. Umm...?" They stared at each other in silence for a few seconds, and then they both started laughing. It was the first time Rosey had heard the Witch laugh and it reminded her of honeysuckle for some reason; the sound seemed to match the sweet taste. Briefly she wondered how her laughter sounded to others, was it like her mother's...her father's? And just like that, Rosey's sudden jubilation crashed like waves against the shore, as the idea entered her head and she stopped laughing. The Witch noticed and politely followed suit, though she looked as if she could have continued. Noticing the Witch staring at her, Rosey smiled and pushed the thoughts away.

"I'm sorry," Rosey said, quickly composing herself, "I'm not sure I understand what you meant before when you asked, how does it feel?" Growing serious and hard-faced all of a sudden, the Witch spoke, "In the past the elements have been known to affect the Keeper's emotions or cause a reaction to them in a way. I just wanted to know if you felt any difference in emotions since receiving the element." "No, not at all," Rosey said, feeling a prickle of apprehension at the woman's words, "well...I feel a little braver because I no longer feel as helpless, but besides that, no." She lifted her left arm and flexed what Rosey had to admit was a pretty wussy looking bicep, but she showed it off with a big smile. The Witch regarded her amused, "It may get worse as time goes on, just keep an eye out for it. It is nothing to be too concerned about, just if you do start to feel a little different, then experiment with it and try to control it. If worse comes to worse you can always talk to Ysandir about it." Rosey nodded but she still didn't like the sound of it, "So...why would the elements do that?" She wasn't sure how the Witch knew about her friends, but this was a Dream World so what Rosey knew the crystal probably knew. The Witch took a turn about the room, speaking as she went as if lecturing Rosey. Rosey followed her with her gaze. "No one really knows, not even me. Some say it is because there are so many elements to choose from when a normal person usually only has access to one, in your case, none. Even though they are in the crystal your body has to understand each element and be able to use it when the time comes, allowing your body to be subject to the elements' influence. Others say it is because the elements simply become restless, but it is controllable and not at all dangerous. The worst that would happen is that you would become angry or sad and the elements that are more closely related to those emotions would change you into that Elemental State without your conscious effort." "Elemental State?"

"The new outfit, the wings, and eye and hair color change." The Witch numbered them off with a wave of her hand. "Your transformation is what is called the Elemental State." She turned to Rosey swiftly, her whole body seeming to turn all at once. "Because the elements you hold are so powerful they affect you physically when you use them. You may have noticed that you grow larger and your musculature becomes more pronounced, the element will often combine your body with its own strength to make you into the element's perfect warrior. Thus it can also affect your emotions and react to them, causing you to spontaneously change your Elemental Form without your will to do so. That is about as bad as it can get, simply changing your Elemental State. It won't make you go on a rampage or anything. However, if you're in a battle, the changing of one element to another because of your emotions could be disastrous. So watch for it and practice on controlling it if you have any problems. " Rosey gave a determined nod of her head, "I'll make sure to do that. Thanks for the heads up." She could only imagine how dangerous a situation that could be and Rosey didn't intend for it to happen any time soon. She'd have to be very careful.

"It's my job," the Witch said matter of factly as if it was of no concern. "Now, your next destination is in the Seventh Sea, Broken Castle Island." She paused and her smile disappeared. She stared at Rosey with her strange eyes, and Rosey had the sudden thought that they were probing into her soul.

"Now listen carefully." She fixed Rosey with her gaze. They held an intensity that she had never seen before. Rosey felt her blood freeze. What now? It was scary how quickly the White Witch could change emotions. The tall woman continued, "You must understand that after you receive the second element things will become much harder for you on your quest.

You will be expected to fight with all that you have, you'll have to rise and be a warrior like the Keepers before you. You'll have to become a leader, not a follower. You must be prepared to take on that responsibility because once it comes, there'll be no turning back." Rosey looked down and nodded, "I know." She clenched her fists and said, "Don't worry, I will be ready." The words seemed so empty to Rosey and yet they held such a powerful promise. The truth was she had no idea how well she'd handle things when the time came for her to act. Would she really be ready? She'd have to be.

The fire inside her erupted in agreement and Rosey could have sworn she felt the air get a little warmer around them. Andraste hummed against her back sending slight vibrations throughout Rosey's body. The White Witch seemed to notice this and nodded, pleased by what she saw. Bowing slightly to Rosey and without another word she turned around and disappeared. Rosey stood and stared at the musty room for another few minutes before letting her mind yank her back into the living world.

She woke to find the camp already alive with action. The fire was being coaxed back to life for the morning meal by Ysandir and the horses were being fed by Rochell. Alex was just waking and Eglen and Wolvereen were pulling in a stag they had killed for breakfast. When she saw it she almost gagged. She hated seeing animals killed but they had to eat something. She pulled herself up and watched as Rochell left the saddled horses and skillfully began to skin one of the stag's legs. Then she rolled it up over the muscle and cut out a large chuck off of it. Nodding to Wolvereen and Eglen she left to cut the piece of meat into strips for dried meat. Rosey has seen both her and Alex make dried meat before. Rochell used her air element to smoke it and Alex could do it with a simple flick of his wand. Rosey felt a small stab of uselessness, but the presence of the burning fire within her reminded her otherwise. Her eyes followed Rochell as she left three larger pieces of the meat to begin sizzling on the fire for her, Alex, and Rosey's breakfast. A rustling nearby drew her attention. She turned to see Wolvereen and Eglen dragging the rest of the stag away, including the leg Rochell had partly skinned, for their own meal. Near the fire, Hazel was finishing up a mouse and Noly was chomping down on what looked to be the last of the dried meat which would explain why Rochell was making more. You would think that Noly and Hazel, being used to cat and dog food, would not be good hunters or meat lovers, but the two of them had practiced while at the Golden Goddess's castle. Hazel had learned how to catch a mouse and other small animals but Noly wasn't too happy about the bloody mess of hunting and preferred the dried or raw meat from one of Eglen's or Wolvereen's kills. After learning about the Rules of the Hunter from Alex Rosey had quickly gone to Noly and Hazel to be sure they were aware. They had been informed at the palace by other animals about the rules. Curious, Rosey had asked them what they did to honor their prey when hunting. Noly didn't hunt, but she said that if she ever did she would lie down next to the dying animal and lick its face in farewell. Hazel said that she preferred to find the food that her prey ate and then present it before their dead body in homage to them and then burry it with the animal's bones, or whatever she didn't eat. Hearing this made Rosey wonder at what she would ever do if she had to hunt, but she preferred not to think about it and hoped the day would never come when she had to. Her eyes inevitably wondered to the bow that she had agreed to practice with. Rosey had had little time to do so and was, regrettably, happy about that. It meant that she didn't have to face the horrible embarrassment of not being able to hit a target with a long skinny stick. Rosey eyed the bow and arrows nervously and tried not to think about using them, but she knew she'd have to at some point.

She gazed around her, content. It was strange to see all her friends doing things that she had only seen on television, and she knew that if she was going to succeed she would probably need to learn these things too. Alex and Rochell had been teaching her and she had learned a lot in Jasira's library. She had even, one night, practiced making camp with everyone and sleeping in their bedrolls while in the castle so Rosey would be able to get used to it. But there was one thing she still had a problem with: hunting and skinning. It was hard for her to skin and prepare meat being such an avid animal lover. Still, her friends commended her on her perseverance and willingness to learn.

Turning she surveyed the large volcano towering above them. Despite the warmth and protection it offered she'd be happy to be heading towards the second element. Now that the elemental power within the volcano was gone it seemed oddly lifeless and dead. It reminded her of how it might have been her fault for its current condition. It scared Rosey to think that she might be that powerful, and this had only been one element. What would the others be like? Rosey hated to think about things in such a way but she couldn't help how she felt.

Wishing she could catch a few more winks she stretched in her leather/cotton-like outfit enjoying the smell of the sizzling meat on the fire. She had been surprised to find that the outfit, even after a few days of wearing, remained just as clean and fresh smelling as it had before. She'd been told that everything was spelled to remain clean and well-tended. Still Rosey wouldn't mind having a bath soon, she liked the feeling of being clean and though camping was fun it was hard to forget the modern accommodations provided by Earth.

Knowing that she couldn't stay in her bed roll all day she tucked her parent's locket away, scrambled to her feet, and started packing the sleep wear. Once she had finished packing her saddlebags she groomed the horses while the last preparations for breakfast where being completed. Rochell finally called everyone over and Rosey sat down with her friends. Alex had scrambled the eggs while Rochell had cooked the meat to perfection. Rosey savored the sweet tender meat and the fluffy eggs turning the juices around in her mouth while her tongue tried to figure the best way to break the news to everyone about their next destination. The atmosphere

The Mystics

around her told her it wasn't the right time. Everyone was relaxed and at ease, still celebrating the successful collection of the first element.

They chatted for a few moments. Most of it was small talk concerning the weather, recent events, festivals and such. One event in particular caught Rosey's attention. Eglen, as usual, had everyone's eyes on him, talking about the upcoming Yuletide celebrations.

Rosey looked up surprised, "What is Yuletide? I've heard something similar on Earth but what does it mean here?"

Eglen tossed his mane happily, "Yuletide is a lot like Christmas, decorations are put up and gifts are every now and then exchanged on the 25th of December. The gifts can range from services, to special items, to favors, and so on. Gifts aren't required, they are given from the kindness of one's heart. We kinda stole the idea from Earth, when the researchers returning from there would tell people about the amazing celebrations that Earth hosted each year. Other holidays like Easter and Thanksgiving have also been adopted but they are given different names and are changed to fit our own traditions. The upcoming Yuletide will last for several weeks before the twenty fifth. During that time there's a huge party where games like baking contests, races, various dances, concerts, and prizes are drawn throughout the Yuletide celebration. They can last each day from sun up until sun down! I, myself, am personally looking forward to it as I always perform each year an amazing new array of Yuletide poems."

Wolvereen huffed and shook out his fluffy fur, "Oh no! No more poems, last year one got stuck in my head and it took me forever to look at a Yuletide mantel differently!"

Eglen chuckled, "You just don't recognize art when you hear it."

"Yeah, right, art my fluffy butt..." Wolvereen mumbled under his breath.

The two started bickering and Rosey lost track of it as they resorted to a strange form of growling and yipping.

Watching them made Rosey grow nostalgic all of a sudden. She had been so busy lately that celebrating Christmas had completely escaped her mind. Christmas was a little over a month away but it was her favorite time of the year and she loved decorating the tree and putting up decorations. She had always unpacked everything and decorated and then at the end of the season, her Uncle would clean it all up and repack it away. She had hated repacking everything because it felt as if she was storing all her memories away and all the Christmas cheer and that was something Rosey believed could never be stored. Her uncle didn't mind this about her, in fact it was the only time when he had ever told her that she reminded him of Esperanza, her mother. She, like Rosey, had hated putting away the decorations too each Christmas and so he had always put them away for her. He had cried the first time that Rosey had told him that she didn't want to put the decorations away. It was one of her uncle's cherished memories of his sister. Rosey felt tears welling up at the corners of her eyes and she quickly wiped them away pretending that she had something in her eye. She fiddled with her eyelashes to seal the white lie but Rosey's heart ached deep within. Sudden realization hit her like a cold bucket of water: this would be the first year she wouldn't be celebrating Christmas with her uncle. It startled her for a few moments and she felt herself grow stiff with sadness but she pushed it away quickly. *That's okay*, a little voice in her head said, *I can celebrate it here, in the world that my mother loved and died for, surrounded by people who care for me*. Rosey smiled feeling the crystal against her chest flare with warmth and Andraste vibrate slightly in its sheath.

As the talking died down Alex solved the problem of telling everyone about the next destination for her. He was finishing up a small story he had been telling Rochell about a strange dream he had had the night before about some creature called a Fogor and a Griffon when he turned to her expectantly.

"So, I hope I wasn't the only one dreaming?"

The Mystics

At first Rosey was unsure of what he was talking about. She had become so lost in Eglen's storytelling and her own inner thoughts that she had completely forgotten about the next destination. Smiling, she proudly proclaimed teasingly, "Well, mister smarty pants, it just so happens that I did dream last night."

Hearing this everyone immediately became still and quiet listening closely to Rosey. What had once been a campfire filled with voices, conversation, and good natured companionship was suddenly a serious meeting. Rosey was almost taken aback by how quickly they transitioned but this wasn't something to be taken lightly, after all. She cleared her throat and straightened in her seat, suddenly self-conscious with everyone's eyes on her.

"The next location is the Broken Castle Island."

Everyone stared at Rosey with a mixture of looks ranging from surprised to worrisome. Rosey gulped. Upon arriving in The World Within A World Rosey had realized that using her ability to observe things around her would help her often on her journey. It offered her a better insight into the inner knowledge of the people that were so alien to her, more so than talking ever would. Right now the words, 'why do we get the most unusual places on this planet to go to' seemed to pop into Rosey's mind. Were these locations that strange? The Volcano was strange because it was infused with magic, both inside and out. What was so strange about an island?

"What?" she said after a few moments. As usual, with most of her questions, Alex answered.

"It's nothing really; it's just that….well, Broken Castle Island is another one of those mystery spots. It's pretty complicated to explain and I'm afraid that many of us don't know that much about it, not even I. All we know is that it is forbidden for anyone to go there because it is too dangerous. Of course, you'll be allowed, but…it's just better to talk about it later, after we've boarded the ship. The ship's captain will be better suited to explain it. He'll know more about the island than any of us."

Rosey gritted her teeth at the word later, it had been a while since she had heard that vile world but now it was back to haunt her. Like a giant wall blocking her view it was the only thing keeping her from continuing her education and learning what she needed to know. Feeling a sudden heat rise within her she had to force herself to calm down. The crystal absorbed the powerful heat and glowed orange against her chest for a few seconds. No one seemed to notice and Rosey was grateful for that. The Witch was right. She would need to be careful with the elements. Evidently they did flare up depending on her emotions and fire seemed to be reacting towards her anger, which made sense. She'd definitely have to keep an eye on her powers in the future.

They talked a while longer then Rosey and Alex helped clean up. They had decided that they were going to stay by the volcano until word was brought to them about when the ship that the Goddess had promised them docked. There was no reason to leave the safety of the volcano until they knew when the ship was at port. They would be putting themselves in danger of attack if they left before they were sure they had a shelter to go to. They had to have a ship; that much was certain for there was no other way to reach the island.

Suddenly she heard the flapping of large wings and a sharp thud as a creature landed behind them. Startled she turned, unsheathed Andraste and had it expertly hovering a few inches from the creature's neck. To her surprise it was only Argno. He gasped and stepped back, gazing down the long blade of the sword. She almost laughed out loud with relief. She knew that Raptors found it impossible to enter the area surrounding the volcano but Rosey wasn't going to let her guard down just because she was in supposed protection. Looking around everyone else seemed to have been just as startled as she had been. Only Ysandir didn't seem alarmed, she was as calm and carefree as ever. Despite knowing that Argno was a very quiet flyer, Rosey had to admit that she didn't feel too good about how easy it had been for Argno to sneak up on them. She took solace in the fact that Raptors could not fly and that Blood Goron's were not silent flyers and never worked in a group smaller than ten making them easy to spot.

Turning back to Argo she saw his startled and fearful face. She then realized that she still had the sword close to his neck. She quickly apologized and sheathed her sword. Walking forward she said as friendly as possible in an attempt to quiet his fear, "Hey Argno, how are you? Sorry about Andraste, you just startled me, that's all."

He smiled at her, understanding crossing his face, "Oh no problem, just wonderful and don't apologize, it's nice to see my Keeper can handle herself." He then leaned towards her as if telling her a secret. "The Golden Goddess still does that every now and then when she is practicing her moves, so I'm used to it. How are you doing by the way?"

"I'm doing really well, I collected the first element of fire yesterday!" she said proudly, "Wanna see?"

"Oh do I ever!" Argno exclaimed excitedly.

Rosey searched deep within herself and found the Fire power, taking a deep breath she pulled it to the surface and her whole body ignited into flame. Rosey's giant wings stretched out wide and encircled her body. Her eyes, long hair, and new outfit were tinted a bright orange shade. Her crystal glowed brightly against her chest and Andraste hummed to life in its sheath seeming to crackle and pop along with the flames of her wings. She stood before Argno, now taller than him and did a complete 360 degree turn to show off her Elemental Form. Argno pawed the ground with excitement and oohed and awed at her fiery display. His eyes burned bright with pride and possibly something else…hope.

No matter how many times she had heard it, Rosey had never really understood the reality of what it was she was doing…until now. Argno's eyes shone with happiness, as if he was seeing something for the first time. He seemed to be gasping for breath though his breathing was normal.

Looking around Rosey saw the same thing in the faces of the others watching. In sudden, unsettling clarity Rosey realized that she was, to them, a savior. To see her showing off her fiery outfit was a blessing and a promise. It was something more than just an interesting display it was meant to save lives and rescue a whole world from destruction. Watching Argno, Rosey made a promise to never, no matter what, forget what it was she was here to do and why.

She smiled at him, showing no signs of her inner declaration. Studying Argno she suddenly noticed something different about him. Looking closely she gasped in surprised when she saw a long scar running from in-between his legs to the top of his shoulder blade. She quickly inquired after the wound, sudden anger flaring within her, making her burn brighter.

"Argno, who did that to you?!"

"Oh this?" he said pointing his head at the scar running along his shoulder. "I had a little run in with one of the Evil One's Minions the other day. Nothing to worry about, it's just a long scratch. I was ready to get back to work after a good night's rest."

Rosey nodded but eyed the wound with anger. How could someone attack him like that? Argo was a kind Dragnagor, who valued life and the world. Why would anyone want to hurt him!? She hadn't known Argno for long, but she'd developed a kindness for him in the short time she had known him. Suddenly, her anger grew in intensity and the burning fire insider her threatened to erupt all of a sudden. The pure sensation of hate raced up her arms and legs and charged through her veins. She could feel the heat soaking out of her and making any hydration in the air evaporate. The idea that someone would attack Argno was so infuriating that Rosey felt the heat boil up within her, threatening to overflow. Realizing that the element was heightening her senses and her emotions, she quickly calmed herself, taking deep breaths through her nose. The fiery hatred died down, but it was lying there in wait. She shook her head and clenched down hard on the power within her, as if she was putting out a fire, which, basically, she was. She sighed with relief as the element finally disappeared deep within the crystal. Her regular outfit reappeared, her hair was black and her eyes were blue. Argno didn't seem to have noticed Rosey's inner struggle because it had taken place while she had been in her Elemental Form. She was thankful for that. At least her sudden flares of anger weren't being noticed, for the time being. Rosey had expected that if Fire was to feed off of any emotion it would be anger but she never expected just how immediate that reaction would be. She'd hate to see how far she would go if her entire being was consumed by it, she would need to be careful.

"Are you sure you're all right?" Rosey said, gingerly touching the scar after Argno nodded for her to do so.

"Don't worry; I'm fine, nothing a warrior like me can't handle," he said comically, but upon seeing her worried face he said more gently, "Rosey don't worry, I can take care of myself."

Rosey nodded though she remained angry and unsure. She smiled, not wanting to upset him by making him think she was fretting over him. Trying to get the conversation back on track she said, "So what brings you here to the volcano on this fine day?"

"I came to tell you about the ship that was promised you."

At this Rosey brightened, "Wonderful, let's hear it." "The ship will be waiting for your arrival at dock thirteen at the Felbor Docks. The Goddess sends her apologies for how long it took to prepare the ship; apparently the Captain was away on Earth visiting a friend. The messenger bird just arrived yesterday morning from the commander of the Goddess's Navy units telling us that your ship is ready to sail when you are," said Argno.

"Sounds good. Thank you, Argno. Give the Goddess my thanks. Dock Thirteen was it; at Felbor Docks…is that near here?" She asked running the name of the place around in her head, trying to remember if she'd read about it.

He nodded, sending the long feather on his head flapping. "It's not too far away, about a two hour ride. Wolvereen will take you there; he's been there many times, haven't you?" Argno asked, turning to the armored wolf.

Wolvereen nodded, looking annoyed as if being asked to admit to something that he knew was insulting, but said nothing.

Argno smiled at the sour wolf then said, "Oh, and one more thing, because you'll be heading out to sea, it might not be me that delivers you messages from now on. I mostly work within this continent, Hondan, working close to the Goddesses. While you're on the water and off Hondan, someone else may be coming to you in my place."

Rosey remembered studying maps of The World Within A World, mostly she had studied Hondan, because it was the continent she was on at the moment. It was one of the larger continents and its capital was Neran because it was where the Goddess lived. Rosey had been surprised to see that there were only 1,312 cities here on this continent. On Earth there could be 1,000 cities in one state. It amazed her that there were so few people living here but then another fact she had dug up gave her the answer. Despite the fact that this planet lived side by side with Earth in a dimensional pocket, it was at least three times bigger than Earth was, which meant that it could fit the same amount of people on it as Earth had with more room to spare. Rosey had asked Jasira how the Earth could be smaller than The World Within A World yet be living with it and inside it? Jasira had told her that no one really understood how it worked either but according to the researchers that had been sent to Earth to study it, it was much smaller than their world was. Knowing what she knew, it made sense that Argno's operations wouldn't travel outside Hondan. The land was vast, and the planet was huge. There was no reason why he should fly to her when she was all the way around the world.

Looking back at Argno she said, "So, who can I expect to see?"

"Mostly you'll see Eyasha; she's a superfast Capricosi that is known for her flying skill and speed. She's a good friend of mine and trustworthy. If

The Mystics

she doesn't come to you someone else will. Don't worry, the Golden Goddess will let you know one way or another. More than likely, she'll scry you unless the information is too sensitive for that. Anyway I need to be on my way, I have a lot of stops to be at." He shifted his weight nervously, fidgeting where he stood. He was in a rush, that much was for certain. Rosey quickly nodded, she didn't want to hold him up.

"All right then, be careful and take care of yourself. See ya…and safe flying!"

He bowed to Rosey and nodded deeply to her fellowship in the customary bow. He extended his large dragon wings and began to softly flap them. He fanned them outward, flexing the large muscle at each shoulder. Being careful of the boulders and various rocks, he lifted off with two giant flaps of his long wings.

"Goodbye Rosey, I hope to see you all again and good luck!" With that he turned and flew back in the direction of the castle.

Rosey and the others shouted out their farewells, waving at him as he vanished in the distance. Rosey watched his flight for a few moments before sitting down on a midsize boulder near the fire. *A Capricosi, I don't think I remember studying that particular creature,* she thought, running through her studies in her head. Turning in her seat, she faced the gathered group of friends. They stared at her expectantly. Rosey gazed at them unsure of what to do; then she realized that they were waiting for orders. Taking a deep breath she addressed them.

"All right everyone, you heard what Argno said. We need to get to Felbor Docks. Wolvereen, you'll lead the way, we leave in thirty minutes."

The large wolf nodded, and walked over to his pile of carefully laid out armor, he must have removed it to polish it. Expertly he slipped the armor back on. Rosey watched him, amazed by how easily he adjusted everything. Sighing, she quickly began helping them to tidy up the campsite, still finding herself a stranger in a very familiar world.

About thirty minutes later Rosey's fellowship was walking single file through the various boulders and volcanic rock that littered the ground following Wolvereen's trail. Rosey reined Sarabie into formation enjoying the ease to which the new bridle led Sarabie so gently. The horse obeyed willingly without too much direction from Rosey herself. She patted Sarabie's head happily. She had gotten used to the horses' silent but powerful support. It seemed to be a common thing amongst the equines: silence and quiet. The beautiful animals were very reserved, barely talking or asking questions although she was certain that they were listening. Certainly, Sarabie had spoken to her on many occasions, but they had never really been big contributors to their conversations. Maybe they had been quieter for her, not to frighten her too much with the change, yet Hazel and Noly had no problem yapping a mile a minute when it suited them. Though the horses had never spoken to her in length she had seen Sarabie entertaining the other horses some nights and seen Bronzo and Phana talk as well, but mostly amongst themselves. Rosey did recall overhearing a conversation between Ysandir and Wolvereen about the fact that horses tended to be a little more silent around others, especially when there was a unicorn around. Rosey could only assume it was because a creature like a unicorn was so well respected by them that they were content to stay on the sidelines. Despite this, Rosey didn't doubt Sarabie's power or courage. The gentle giant was strong, brave, and powerful enough to challenge even someone as big and scary as Wolvereen. It mattered not why Sarabie and the others horses preferred to be quiet, it was simply a part of what made them individuals; besides, there was something wonderful about an animal that was purely content to just share a moment with you in silence rather than conversation.

Rosey found Sarabie's slow, gentle gait to be very soothing as they drew close to the border. Wolvereen told them to wait as he plunged into the snowy world beyond. For a good fifteen minutes they waited, silently, looking on into the snow laden ground beyond. To Rosey it felt like hours.

The Mystics

Finally, he returned, a slight dusting of snow littered his back. He nodded to them that it was safe to proceed. While the others had been packing up camp earlier he had checked their path and reported it to be safe but Wolvereen was cautious and Rosey couldn't blame him. She was precious cargo and her destination was a long way off.

They drew close to the edge of the volcano's two mile radius and its protection. Beyond she could see the world transform into a white wonderland and she tensed up, prepared to be hit with the chill of winter. As soon as they stepped over the barrier the raging cold, winter weather would steal every bit of warmth from them. She gritted her teeth and pulled her hood up. They had all dressed themselves and the horses in their winter gear before leaving the camp. It might have made the trek to the border a little uncomfortable but they would appreciate it when they left its barrier. Slowly they made their way forward and Rosey gasped as she went from the sudden comforting warmth to the harsh cold stealing the warmth from her body. Hazel, who was perched on her shoulders underneath her hood and surrounded by Rosey's hair that she had braided earlier, shivered against Rosey's shoulders as she too felt the cold hit her. Wolvereen didn't seem fazed. His thick fluffy coat was easily able to contain his heat. In fact during their stay at the volcano, Wolvereen had found it hard to sleep because the volcano's warmth made him hot with all his fur, so the cold must be a blessing to him. She quickly urged Sarabie after him as he plunged his way along a small path only wide enough for one at a time on horseback. If they kept moving then they would stay warmer. All she could do now was to keep her eyes sharp for any potential danger.

About two hours later the air started warming until it was a more comfortable forty one degrees and the path had widened making enough room for two horses to walk side by side. Now that they were past the volcano and getting closer to the seas the land had started to become more temperate and snow was less common. She remembered that on the maps she had studied, Hondan was closer to the equator, not close enough to provide an all year round temperate climate, but enough so that the sea breezes kept the coastal lands facing the north a little warmer all year around. She was about to ask Alex about the different biomes of the planet when he rode up next to her, touched her arm gently, and gave her the 'Alex' look. It was a look he gave her whenever he needed to speak to her about something important. Seeing this she glanced at Wolvereen who got the message. He lifted his snout to the air and breathed deeply, then ordered a temporary stop. They waited as he plunged ahead and took a good look around. He returned shortly and nodded that it was safe. Rosey turned to Alex as the wolf dropped behind with the others while they pulled forward to talk. Rosey could tell by the smell in the air that she was nearing the sea, and Wolvereen hadn't veered off the path since taking it which meant that they were going to follow this same trail all the way to the docks, so having Wolvereen's guidance wasn't necessary at the moment. She could talk with Alex without worrying about losing her way.

She looked at him with a worried expression and he quickly consoled her. "Don't worry it's nothing bad. I just need to tell you something."

Immediately she relaxed, whatever it was, it wasn't anything severe. "What is it?"

"Last night my mentor, Thera told me something that I think you'll want to hear."

Rosey had almost forgotten about Thera. Alex had told Rosey when they had been with the Goddess about his strict mentor. The only thing Rosey knew about her specifically was that she was a Leron, however, there was one thing Rosey knew that Alex had made sure to tell her: when Thera talked, you listened. According to Alex, she was the hardest mentor and the toughest magikin, second only to the Goddesses. So if Thera had told Alex something, Rosey wanted to make sure she didn't miss one word.   "I had almost forgotten about what she told me with all the excitement of Argno's arrival and your meeting with the White Witch, but that move you performed with your sword reminded me," he continued.

The Mystics

At this she perked up and gave him a curious look, "What do you mean? What move?"

"The one where you had Argno almost peeing on himself, his throat inches away from being sliced," he said incredulously, as if it was a crime that she didn't remember.

"Oh, well, what was so interesting about that?" She said confused, finding herself suddenly defensive.

"The Goddess, nor Rochell and I, ever taught you that move."

His words hit her in the face. He was right! He and Rochell had watched most of all her sparring with the Goddess and had even sparred with her on occasion themselves. She had never learned anything like that from the Goddess or her friends and she didn't remember learning it in her Kendo and Iaido classes. You would think it would be a simple move but, it wasn't. Not only did she not know where Argno was when he landed and still had had the sword positioned perfectly beside his neck she had also predicted where his body would be in relation to her own and adjusted the length so that she would be able to more easily move the blade. Rosey stared at the saddle horn suddenly feeling sick to her stomach. How had she known how to do that? At the moment it had felt so natural, so right. If Alex hadn't have pointed it out to her she never would have noticed it. She glanced back up at him. Alex wouldn't be telling her this if it wasn't important, but what did her sword maneuvers have to do with it?

"Go on," she said, finding her throat suddenly dry. "What else did Thera tell you?"

"It was about her former apprentice. Apparently…he was your Uncle."

Alex allowed it to sink in and Rosey was happy that he let her sit and think for a moment. She knew her Uncle was a God level Magikin but she hadn't known who his mentor had been and hadn't expected to find out so soon.

Gathering herself she said, "He was her apprentice? Talk about coincidence."

"I know! I was her next apprentice after your uncle. He was one of her best students," he said this last a little jealously. "She said that he often spoke to her about your mother, his sister Esperanza. Thera was, essentially, with Esperanza on her journey since she was in your uncle at the time, like she is now with me. She just told me this last night, I promise you I would have told you if I'd known sooner," he said, apologetically. Rosey smiled, she had no doubt that he would have. He continued, "Though she never did interact with Esperanza, she believed in her like I believe in you. She looked up to her…"

Alex was quiet for a few moments thinking. Rosey watched him out of the corner of her eye, sensing that he needed time to phrase his next words carefully. After a few more moments he spoke.

"Thera remembered your uncle telling her that as soon as Esperanza found out that she was pregnant she began working on something with the crystal. She was trying to mold herself with it or connect to it or something like that. Whatever it was, your uncle was worried about it. He was concerned for his sister. From what I hear, when Esperanza got pregnant with you she started doing a lot of weird things, well not weird," he quickly corrected seeing Rosey's concerned expression, "but…it was like she was preparing for something. I don't know. Thera was unsure herself, so much so that she hadn't wanted to say anything, but she believes that you should know as much about your mother as possible."

Rosey's hand flew to the crystal. Was it possible, could the crystal have a little of her mother within it? She had no idea. Was that why the Witch had been so silent about her mother? Was it because of this? Her mind was racing suddenly and she wanted to back out of this conversation. At the same time she wanted to know. She was frightened at what he would say, but she had to know. Seeing her grab the crystal, Alex stopped and respectfully let her ponder for a moment. When she nodded, lowering her hand from the crystal's warm, comforting surface, he continued.   "He said that it was almost like she knew that she would not be around to raise

The Mystics

you. She wanted to leave you something. She didn't want you to be alone. But it was like she knew she wouldn't…get that chance." Alex's voice was steady, but Rosey could tell it weighed heavily on him.

Alex's words struck her like a thousand blows to the heart. She felt wobbly in her seat and lightheaded as if she was riding on a cloud not a horse. Her hands tightened on the reins as she desperately fought to hold back tears. On her back, Andraste let loose a slow whistling sound, like air escaping a balloon. Rosey knew she was the only one that could hear it. Was Andraste crying?

Alex continued on gently, unaware of her thoughts.

"Thera said it was the most pathetic thing she had ever heard ..." he smiled and laughed a little at his mentor that lived within him. Rosey glanced at him with annoyance and he quickly continued, " ... she did respect your mother's feelings though. She said that even though she was skeptical, she was happy with what your Uncle said next. He told her that Esperanza had been successful. Somehow she had made it so that the crystal would remember certain things about its previous Keeper, enough to subconsciously pass them on. Thera said that it was amazing that Esperanza could figure that all out. She never really believed that Esperanza would not live to teach her child how to be a Keeper. It wouldn't be the first time she was wrong."   Rosey felt a sudden sadness overwhelm her, crushing her. She felt as if a boulder was pressing down on her chest and she found it hard to breathe, yet air was flowing freely in and out of her lungs. She gripped the crystal and its warmth flooded through her washing away her sadness. Inside it she felt a stirring heat that was the element of Fire; its strength held Rosey together and dried her hidden tears. Alex was aware of none of this, Rosey was good at making sure no one did.

"Do you think that explains how I did that move back there a minute ago with Argno?" She almost choked out the worlds. "The crystal remembers it from my…mother." She said the last word with difficulty, suddenly feeling her mouth go dry. Her hand sought the locket in her pocket, tracing an arch over the simple oval shape.

"That's exactly what I think it means." He watched her, seeing an inner turmoil that she would never admit to having. Carefully he said, "She might not be here physically, Rosey, but she will always be with you, in your memories…and your crystal. She was always planning on being here with you even if she couldn't be here physically. She wanted to train you, to prepare you. She never got that chance." He was silent for a while looking at the sky and then he said, "I bet she's out there somewhere watching over you, watching over all of us. Don't ever doubt that crystal, Rosey. It has power no other could understand. We are all in this together and if there is something you need to talk about, then talk. We will listen to our Keep … no … our friend." She smiled. Alex was always able to make her feel better. But before she could thank him Rochell came up from behind and raced past them.

"Hey you two, race ya to the beach!" she shouted behind her. Noly yipped at Phana's heels in excitement, looking much like a rocket.

The two of them had been so caught up in their conversation that they had barely noticed when the path had begun to widen and sand had started to replace dirt and stone.

Rosey and Alex exchanged glances before tapping their horses lightly into a full gallop. Alex, grinning from one ear to the next, urged Bronzo after Sarabie as the big horse lurched forward, swinging her head back and forth. Rosey yanked her hood back and let the wind whip her braid into a dance behind her back as Sarabie pounded toward the docks on the sandy ground, her hard conversation with Alex seemed light years away.. Rosey's heart was once again filled with joy as she and Hazel lifted their voices and laughed out loud. No matter what happened, she knew she could be a good Keeper because, even though her mother wasn't there to teach her, her friends were and they loved her just as much as her mother had.

Rosey glanced behind her and laughed when she saw the look on Wolvereen's face. Even Eglen had joined the race, leaving a flabbergasted Wolvereen behind to gawk at them. Ysandir joined in and caught up to Rosey, shooting past her quickly on her long legs. Wolvereen could be heard swearing under his breath as he took off in hot pursuit of his rambunctious Keeper.

Chapter Eighteen: The Silent Marine

Rosey never got seasick, something her Uncle had always been envious about, but she didn't love the sea. She was one who loved to watch it, not sail on it for days. Unfortunately she had no choice. Most of the Elements were spread throughout the world and she would need a ship to travel to some of their locations. Portals were too dispersed and they limited her on where she could go so the sea was the fastest and most effective way for her to travel. Looking at the water lapping against the sandy shore, she wasn't sure if she liked the idea of being surrounded by nothing but water for days, maybe months, on end. There was no going back though. She needed to do this, whether it was by boat or land.

Urging Sarabie forward she joined Rochell and Alex who were waiting for her a few yards off. She had stopped for a few minutes to admire the view of the ocean and breathe in the salty fragrance of warm winds and quite, calm waters. Ysandir had won their little race and had woven in and out of the group to celebrate her win, throwing her mane and tail around with confidence. She and Rosey had been neck and neck, racing for the waves straight ahead. Ysandir was so huge compared to Sarabie that Rosey had felt like a small car next to a giant semi on the interstate, both racing for first place. In the end, Ysandir's long legs had won out, carrying her ahead of Sarabie by a few seconds. Rosey suspected that Sarabie may have not put her whole effort into beating Ysandir because she was a unicorn but Rosey knew that Sarabie had the pride to match any unicorn's and would not show favoritism in a friendly competition, so it was unlikely that she lost on purpose. Even though Sarabie had barely spoken throughout her time here Rosey had known the horse long enough that even though she could now talk, words were unnecessary and the one thing she knew about Sarabie was that she was a proud Friesian. Despite the fact that they lost, the race had been a breath of fresh air, a reminder of the races she had often had with her friends back home, races she had always won. It was nice to lose for a change, as if it was some confirmation that despite her status as the Keeper she was still equal to everyone around her.

Though everyone had been pretty close to winning, Wolvereen, on the other hand, had been the last, trotting up behind them all the while grumbling under his breath about childish nonsense. Just to poke fun at him Noly ran around him calling out small but friendly taunts, one in particular made Wolvereen mad enough to actually start chasing the dog around, inevitably joining him in on their little race.

"What's wrong Wolvereen, armor slowing you down?" Noly had said, teasingly.

"What! How dare you, I can carry this armor going any speed I wish you bag o' bones you!" Wolvereen had said nipping at Noly with obvious frustration.

Noly had easily sidestepped him then, giggling rather childishly, had launched into a series of jumps and runs to out maneuver Wolvereen. Amazingly, Noly managed to stay away from him the entire time. Hazel had rolled her eyes upon seeing them and muttered something about canines and their lack of dignity. Rosey only smiled.

After they had all settled down Rosey took the lead and proceeded towards the docks which were slightly down the beach front. They rode the horses close to the waves, enjoying the sound of the water as it moved over the sand and the crash of waves against stone as the large tides hit occasional rocks. The docks were only a few yards away when Ysandir pulled up beside Rosey, her giant body almost blocking out the sun over Rosey. The ever moving patterning across Ysandir's skin made it hard to look at her for more than a few seconds. Rosey found herself oddly calmed by the images.

Rosey looked at her expectantly, "Let me guess, you need to go attend to something important?"

Ysandir lowered her ears in a sideways position and lowered her head solemnly, as if she had been a bad unicorn and deserved to be scolded. To Rosey she looked like Noly did whenever she did something wrong.

"Unfortunately yes, now that I know you are safely at the docks there is something I need to get to, also there's this whole 'unicorn walking amongst the people' business."

"Don't worry about it." Rosey shook it off trying not to laugh at Ysandir's apologetic expression. "Will you be able to get to us once we're out at sea?" She said this last worriedly, she didn't like the idea of not having Ysandir around, she was a unicorn and a great ally.

"Oh, yes indeed. Do not fear, there is no place on this planet I cannot find you."

Rosey nodded, remembering how the unicorn had appeared during the cave collapse to help, but she felt a little apprehensive by Ysandir's words. She knew that the unicorn hadn't meant it to sound threatening in any way but it was hard not to feel strange especially when she was, essentially, on the run from the enemy. She shook it off and said, "Okay, I'll see ya later then."

With that Ysandir tossed her head and took off at a full gallop. A large whirlpool of air opened up before her and she plunged into it, her horn slightly aglow as she disappeared within the vortex. Rosey sighed and rested her arm on Silver Knight's hilt; this was going to be a long day.

As they neared Rosey saw a long line of evenly spaced, golden armored guards surrounding the docks. There was no wall in sight. If this were an official dock where food, supplies, and other miscellaneous items were exported and imported Rosey could understand it being well-guarded, but this was just supposed to be a low level fishing dock. From what she remembered from Wolvereen, small time fisher men and women docked their ships here and only occasionally was it ever used for big business associated with the Goddesses, so it was only lightly protected. In fact, it may have been its very history as a small fishing dock that made it ideal for the location of Rosey's own ship. Such an unprotected place, though the guards looked fierce enough, would be the last place Raptors would be expecting Rosey to set sail. It was a gamble, but one that seemed to have paid off. Wolvereen had proudly told them that his scouting had revealed no evidence of Raptors near the ports or along the beaches. They were safe for now.

With this in mind, she made sure her crystal was out for all to see. One part of her wanted to be inconspicuous, but she was tired of hiding like a scaredy-cat. She wanted to be seen. She wanted them to know she was there. Letting her be seen every so often would be an inspiration to the people. It would help to spread much needed hope and give people a chance to see their savior. She didn't want them to think they were alone. Rosey straightened in her seat, her head raised proudly.

The guards were well armored with a variety of weapons. They stood at attention, their eyes focused on the forest just beyond the beach. They were a variety of species, some Rosey remembered from her reading and some she had never heard of. Many were human and one looked to even be one of the Five Species of Elemental Humans that the Goddess had told her about. As she passed through a break in their guarded ring around the docks beyond, a tall blonde woman with bright blue eyes nodded up at her but said nothing. She nodded back. Was it possible that she was an Altantian? The woman was very tall, almost as tall as Wolvereen, clearly over six feet, so it was very possible. She definitely matched the physical description. Rosey swayed in her seat, suddenly overcome with surprise. She barely had time to think more on the subject as they drew near to the people surrounding the docks.

Now amongst the sailors, Rosey felt herself relax and take in her surroundings. People began to look up in awe as she passed them. She couldn't exactly blame the people and the various animals and Leron that littered the docks for staring at her but it made her feel rather awkward but she was determined not to falter.

The docks weren't anything special; they were like any other normal docks that Rosey had seen on a beach front. Large stone blocks anchored wooden docks to the land and the shallow sea beaches. The larger ships were docked further out in the waters while the smaller vessels were docked closer. The smell of fish and seaweed along with crisp, clean salty air lingered on every tiny plank of the carefully built structure. The ocean breeze swirled around her in the strange way that ocean breezes can. It made her feel like she was weightless, as if she could float away at any second but being anchored to a horse would make that difficult. The wood that made up the docks was a lighter color, probably very strong and durable and, Rosey would guess, spelled somehow to never rot or deteriorate from the precious salty water. If only Earth was so innovative.

As they entered the docks Rosey and the others dismounted, leaving the reins hanging on the saddle horns. Rosey walked onto the docks without much trouble. She had been expecting it to be one of those floating docks but no, it was sound and solid, apparently anchored all the way out until the water became too deep for stone blocks. Rochell and Alex, as usual, took their places on either side of her, their horses following behind them. Noly skipped ahead, yipping out 'hellos' and 'how ya doins' to the people on the docks. They responded in kind with bright smiles on their faces. Rosey absently stroked Hazel who purred with delight from within Rosey's hood and broad shoulders. Looking over the edge she saw that the water was like normal sea water, a mixture of green and blue. Waves of white foam pulled at the sandy beach revealing the vegetation that was just visible below the surface. The only thing that was different was the clearness of the water. There was not a sign of pollution anywhere, in fact, the water was so clear that Rosey could see a good 100 yards out into the sea until light began to fade at the unimaginable depths. Hazel peeked out of her hood in curiosity. The tiny cat took one look at the rolling waves and quickly ducked back into the protective black of the

The Mystics

hood, mewing with embarrassment. Rosey chuckled to herself and continued along.

The people that worked along the docks were normal, everyday people. They resembled closely the people she had seen in Neran, which made sense since most of them were Neran citizens. According to Alex this particular dock was used for seasonal shipping vessels not importing and exporting. Most of the vessels were captained by people who went out to sea for their particular season. When they were done sailing they would return home to Neran.

The same strange arrangement of society took place here as it did in Neran. Animals and Leron ran around with humans in harmony, helping to lead, fix, hitch, or prepare vessels for the winter season while some were preparing to ship. Some were helping to haul in their catch for the day or packing it away for shipment to Neran. Other vessels were family owned and were for recreational use only. Most of the boats were small enough for the family to drag back home with them or leave on the beach instead of tying them up. Rosey enjoyed watching the numerous busy tasks that the people did. She also loved the various designs of the boats and ships themselves. Some looked to be out of the olden days from Earth while others were of a complex strange design Rosey had never seen before. The colors of the boats were also eye catching. Most boats Rosey had seen were white, blue, or green, but these boats were all colors of the rainbow with ornate designs, rinky-dink drawings, and hand done artistry, probably applied by a family or organization. Rosey could have stared at it for hours, the beach was clean, the water was clear, and the smell wasn't at all what she thought it would be.

Taking a deep breath she assumed the role of Keeper as was expected of her. Many individuals turned and waved at her, shouts of blessings, prayers, and wishes for good luck reached her ears from all sides. The docks were big enough so that Rochell and Alex with their horses could walk on either side of Rosey acting as a buffer zone, but just as before in

Neran, people did not rush her or crowd her, they simply admired her from afar. Rosey even saw some of them in tears. She tried hard not to look too closely at them, fearing that she would start crying herself. As with Argno before, she was afraid she'd see that same desperation and confirmation that she was their last and only hope. If she couldn't win for them than what did they have left? Rosey couldn't look into their eyes; she just couldn't bear to see their hopes and fears. She feared that if she did she would carry all the weight of their emotions on her shoulders if she should fail. Andraste hummed soothingly at her back. She reached up and fingered the sword's hilt, gently. Andraste seemed to feel her and grew warm at her touch. The crystal glowed slightly, illuminating her face under her hood. She imagined she looked something like a ghost to these people, a stranger behind a saviors mask. In time she hoped that would change. Straightening she threw back the hood of her cloak and let the crystal's light shine against her chest, she wasn't ashamed of what she was nor was she going to hide it. She squared her shoulders and Hazel purred happily on her neck kneading her shoulder with sheathed claws. Everyone in the fellowship seemed to sense the change in Rosey, they all straightened and smiled and waved to the people as they passed, but Rosey stared straight ahead, still unable to meet them.

When she saw the ship tethered further out along the docks she was surprised at how large it was. It was about one fifth the size of a cruise liner. It was beautiful with dark woodwork that looked like black paint had been inlaid within it giving it a rustic, majestic feel; like an old log cabin. Along the sides ornate golden vines spiraled and looped into a synchronized pattern that formed a mermaid whose outstretched left arm reached up and clung around the bow of the ship with her slender fingers. The hair of the mermaid flowed smoothly over the surface of the ship forming the words *Silent Marine* behind her. *That must be its name*, Rosey thought, tracing the lettering with her eyes. There were two decks and a small, half-deck above that. A small building sat at the top where the half-deck was, it must be were the Captain's steering room was. The decks were protected by fine golden railings and even the hull of the ship was covered in a golden colored casing. There was one thing Rosey did not see: sails. The ship had no sails whatsoever; it looked a lot like a ship from Earth. Despite the missing sails, Rosey had to admit, it was a masterpiece of a ship. It was so good that she felt a little embarrassed, after seeing all the smaller more nostalgic looking vessels, to actually know it was her vessel from this day on, or at least in her services until all the elements were collected.

Standing on the second deck, which looked the largest and the most widely used, was a young man, that couldn't have been much older than she was, peering over the edge of the boat wearing a Captains' uniform; at least what she thought would be counted as a Captain's uniform. Strangely he had the same startlingly blue eyes and black hair that Rosey had, though his was cut short with a stray piece falling lazily across his forehead. He stared at them expectantly, sizing them up. When his eyes rested on her she could tell he recognized her as the Keeper immediately. His brows lifted and his eyes grew large upon seeing her. For a few moments he seemed unsettled where he stood looking down at them from the deck. Rosey noticed his eyes wandering away from her eyes to her chest where the crystal glowed, a look of wonder crossing his face as if he was seeing a fairytale come true. Despite his wonder his voice was perfectly calm and his stance betrayed nothing out of the ordinary. He looked the perfect captain with straight back and squared shoulders. In a powerful voice, that reminded Rosey of the cello, he called down to them.   "Hello, Keeper! Welcome to the Felbor docks. The Silent Marine is at your command!" He bowed in the customary bow and Rosey returned with her slight head bow.

"Yes, thank you Captain ..." she lingered, waiting for him to introduce himself. He complied.

"Marine, Captain Marine. Please come aboard. It will be a pleasure and an honor to have you sailing with us." His smile was genuine and his words greeted her warmly.

"Thank you, Captain, I'm sure it will be a pleasure."

A large wooden plank made of the same material as the rest of the ship's wood was lowered and the team boarded the giant vessel. Rosey looked at the plank of wood for a few minutes like it was some snake coiling to strike. This was it; she was leaving the land that held her only way out of this world. She glanced behind her and spied some of the people working on the docks. Men and women cast glances at her, their eyes hopeful but unsure. Their posture was that of a person who is fearful for their future but is only capable of sitting back and waiting for something to happen, going about their daily lives as if nothing was wrong.

Rosey was afraid of what was to come, she had admitted as much to Nagura, but she had stepped past that threshold when she took the power of Fire in her hands. She could not sit back and wait for things to happen. She had to step up and take on the challenge no matter what it was. Turning to face the crowd, she reached deep within herself and pulled at the power that lay there. Her friends stopped to look at her, their faces a mask of confusion. Alex paid close attention, his eyes unfocused like he was trying to see something that wasn't there. Rochell noticed and laid her hand on his shoulder. Rosey breathed deeply feeling the fiery power start to course through her veins. At her chest, the crystal hummed. Her body exploded in a wave of heat as crisp wisps of fire began boiling up along her skin. Her hair and eyes turned orange and her leather outfit was replaced. She stretched out her wings and sent an explosion of power outward from her body making the air immediately warmer and the nearby water sizzle slightly, throwing up steam. By now everyone on the docks had stopped what they were doing to stare at her. Their mouths hung open, agape, at the young woman who stood before them, brows furrowed and fists clenched. Rosey's transformation complete, she stood before them, fiery heat rolling off of her in waves. Hazel purred by her head, not in the least affected by the fire surrounding her. The flames were colored a shade of blue wherever the cat's body touched hers just as they had been around

The Mystics

Alex when Rosey had hugged him before in the Volcano. Evidently the fire would harm only creatures of evil. Rosey did nothing and said nothing; she simply stood there before them. Slowly everyone began to clap and cheer. Their eyes filled with tears and large smiles stretched across their faces. Rosey continued to stand there, smiling slightly. Her fellowship looked at her, smiles creasing their lips as pride in their Keeper glowed deeply in their chest. After a few minutes Rosey transformed back to herself, bowed to the still cheering crowd, and then boarded the ship.

On what was the second deck a number of stewardesses, stewards, and deckhands immediately appeared with welcoming smiles and bows of respect. After her little show, the entire crew seemed to be infused with excitement to be meeting Rosey Mystic. They all parted respectfully and watched as Captain Marine approached Rosey.

He bowed slightly at the waist and said, "Welcome, Keeper. I hope you will find this vessel to your liking. The Goddesses use it all the time. It's one of their favorites, and I hope you will feel the same. If you have any questions feel free to ask me or any of my staff. We will be taking great care of you and your fellowship, so do not worry."

Captain Marine was as dignified as could be. He wore a red uniform with a purple sash and golden armor instead of silver. Rosey noticed that he didn't wear any kind of hat. She was used to seeing, in movies and in real life, ship captains wearing a Captain's hat, but apparently such was not a part of the appeal in this world. Nevertheless, he resembled a Captain with medals and ribbons plastered on his vest and different colored tassels hanging from the sash at his waist. Also attached to his sash was a sword that looked to be a Katana, a Japanese style sword with a slightly curved blade and a particular grip. It had a bronze hilt in a decorative, red scabbard.

Turning he indicated a tall woman who stood next to him. She came forward and bowed. Rosey returned the bow with her head bow as was customary. She was an older woman of about forty. The woman gave her a warm smile as she bowed. Her shoulder length, red hair was curly and well kept, tied loosely at the back of her neck. Her amber eyes almost looked like tiger eye jewels; they were so amber in color. Her outfit was the same as the Captain's, except that it was in white and she didn't have as many medals or tassels hanging from her chest and belt. At her side hung a long sword that Rosey noticed was also a katana. The katana had a red handle with a golden hilt and rested in a white scabbard to match her outfit. It was an impressive sword, one Rosey would have been proud to show off. On Margaret's other hip she sported a long skinny scabbard that Rosey recognized as a wand scabbard. *Is she a magician?* Rosey thought, eyeing the skinny scabbard. It was a simple white scabbard like the skinny Katana's except it had silver designs and etchings along it. Margaret seemed to embody the image of what Rosey thought a young enthusiastic mother would look like and not at all what Rosey was expecting to see on a ship.

"My dear friend and first mate, Margaret, is going to introduce you to the crew while I finish up some last minute details. Afterwards, she will give you a tour then show you to your rooms. Is that to your liking, my Keeper?" Marine said, motioning to her.

Rose stood shocked. Since Captain Marine looked to be a teenager no older than herself, she was surprised to find his first mate, a woman in her forties to be so much older than him. It seemed that rank wasn't given by your age but your ability to complete the job. Rosey smiled, impressed by the simplicity of the system and the maturity of the younger population in this world. She didn't know of too many teenagers from Earth that could handle so much responsibility.

"That sounds wonderful, thank you," said Rosey genuinely excited. She had been on tours of older ships on Earth and found she enjoyed the seafaring technology and the craft that went into it. It would be interesting to see how a ship from this world operated. She was especially interested in how it worked without sails. It had to be powered somehow.

The Mystics

"Splendid, but before I turn you over to Margaret I must ask where it is we are heading."

"Oh, yes, of course, the Broken Castle Island," she said, feeling a little embarrassed that she hadn't mentioned it already. For a few moments he stared at her, as if she had said something completely out of the ordinary. Rosey wasn't too surprised; her friends had given her the same expression when she had first told them and they had told her that a Captain would be better suited to explain to her what exactly was going to take place. Rosey had half a mind to ask him right there and then but she had a feeling that right now was not the appropriate time. To save herself from another conversation ending with the word 'later' she decided not to ask.

He finally nodded. Though he looked a little unsure, he only said, "Good, I'll chart a course immediately."

Rosey watched him go, vaguely wondering what it would be like to be a Captain on the great seas, with all the knowledge of the waters in her little noggin. If it were up to her, Rosey would not be traveling by sea. She knew that a life on the ocean wasn't for her, but she needed to get around in the shortest amount of time so she could collect the other elements. Ultimately, going by sea was the fastest and safest option available so she would just have to adapt.

Once Captain Marine left Margaret took over and began the introductions.

Rosey took each name into her mind and held it there, trying to attach it to a face. This was going to be her crew for a while after all, she might as well know as many as possible. Wolvereen seemed to be enjoying himself the most, which surprised Rosey, it was her first time seeing him show affection to anyone besides Nagura. He was weaving amongst the people talking to them and accepting their various 'welcome backs' and 'how ya beens' that the people were calling out to him. He even allowed some to shake his head and hug him! Rosey was truly flabbergasted but found herself warmed at the image, unable to deny that it was sweet to see him so popular. As she had noticed many times, humans weren't the only ones on board. There were also animals and Leron. Rosey even spotted a Dominant grey wolf like Wolvereen and Nagura amongst the crowd. When the time came to introduce himself she learned his name was simply Grey. He had been honorably disbanded from the Golden Goddess's guards to work on the Silent Marine in the animal quarters after a terrible wound in his left shoulder had left him with a permanent limp. He was an older wolf, with a graying muzzle and kind green eyes. He was also Nagura's father, which was why Wolvereen seemed to be giving him a lot of attention.

Though Rosey paid close attention to their names she also observed their outfits. They all wore fine black shirts and pants with purple sashes. Metal strips of silver armor were worn on their hands, boots, and chests. They looked grand and professional and not at all like deckhands. Their pants looked to be loose and made up of the same cotton/leather like material that she and her friends wore except their shirts had hoods on them that made them resemble sweatshirts. The animals wore much the same thing; although, theirs were in the form of vests with various armor styles, though they were not as extensive as Wolvereen's ensemble.

Another thing that stood out to Rosey was their weapons. Most everyone was wearing a sword or another type of weapon, even the animals were wearing them. These swords weren't like the sabers that the Goddesses wore or the knight's sword that she wore but they were more like katanas, just like the swords that the Captain and Margaret wore. Even Grey wore one on his back. It had a black grip with a mahogany hilt resting in a dark green scabbard. The stewards, stewardesses, and deckhands all wore katanas strapped to their backs or sides or behind them in various angles. Some had one, others had two, but they all wore one of some kind. The ones that did not wear a sword wore a dagger instead or another weapon like a staff, or a bow and arrow. Either way they all wore a weapon of some kind. Rosey reached up and touched Andraste's hilt wondering what it was about the swords and other weapons that were so important here. People on Earth didn't carry weapons around without a permit and weren't allowed to show them off when they did. Of course, weapons on Earth were guns. They would laugh if someone carried a sword. But here the swords and other weapons meant more than a means of protection to these people. Like Andraste, the weapons were alive in some way and as normal to everyday life like sleeping and breathing were. With Raptors around it made sense to carry a weapon, but they were going to be at sea which meant that the Raptors would be nowhere in sight. Maybe the sea had more dangers to offer than the Raptors. Rosey gulped and tried not to think about it, there was no sense in worrying.

Once all the staff had made their introductions and shaken Rosey's hand to the point that it almost felt numb, everyone left to finish whatever it was they needed to take care of. Margaret walked up to one of the stewards, a young boy with wild brunette hair and kind green eyes and spoke with him briefly. The boy nodded and left the First Mate to talk with Eglen and the horses, "I am Nuwell, and I will be in charge of your care. If the Keeper does not mind, I would like to show you to your rooms." He turned to Rosey for approval.

When Rosey nodded, a little taken aback by how formal he was, he gestured for the Horses and Eglen to follow him, "Right this way, please. Our Animal Quarters have been recently updated." The horses and Eglen nodded. Rosey and her friends said goodbye to their horses and Rosey nodded to Eglen. He smiled at her and then led the way as he and the horses accompanied Nuwell to their quarters somewhere below deck. Hazel and Noly stuck with Rosey determined not to move from her side. Nuwell, who looked to be no older than fourteen smiled knowingly as he was leaving. It must be common here as it is on Earth for smaller animals like cats and dogs to remain with their human companions. Noly sat behind her and put her head under Rosey's hand, peeking out, daring anyone to try and lead her away from Rosey. She smiled and began itching Noly's favorite spot to assure her she wasn't going anywhere.

Just then Wolvereen moved in front of Rosey, a clear 'I need to speak with you' was written across his face. Rosey looked up at him in amazement. Now that she was no longer mounted on Sarabie she was no longer at an equal height with the large wolf. He stood before her, a giant, larger than she could ever hope to be. His searing red eyes stared at her, bearing deeply into her own blue orbs, but this time they weren't challenging. Wolvereen knew who was in charge despite how small she might be compared to him. She was surprised by how much he intimidated her. Rosey had stood beside Nagura many times comfortably and she was bigger than Wolvereen. It had to be his big black body and fluffy fur that made him seem even bigger and had a habit of startling her. Either that or it was his piercing red eyes. Rosey wasn't sure. However, even if he was imposing and impressive, she knew that he was in no way, shape, or form unworthy of being on her team. She had no doubt that he would gladly give his life to protect her. She had nothing to fear from him, so raising her chin high and looking him square in the eyes, without flinching, she stood before the fanged and armored wolf with confidence.

"Something wrong, Wolvereen?"

Wolvereen's eyes grew large for a moment, as if he was seeing her for the first time. A small grin twitched his lips as he saw her confidence glowing in her eyes. "I just wanted to let you know that, having been on this ship many times, there are things that I must attend to. I will mostly be with the Captain, other times I'll be somewhere else. I hope that is not inconvenient for you?"

Rosey spied Grey standing not too far away, obviously waiting for his son-in-law. He was bigger than Wolvereen, and looked much more like his daughter. He was skinny, but well-muscled and big boned. There were no marks on him, except for the large scar running down his left shoulder from the wound that caused him to limp.

Rosey shook her head, "You go on ahead Wolvereen, I know you'll come if I need you."

The Mystics

The big wolf flashed his teeth at her briefly, it was all his face seemed capable of doing for her in way of a smile. Her acknowledgment of the faith she had in him seemed to please him. Nodding his head he turned and joined Grey.

Before Rosey could think of anything else Margaret appeared by her side, she looked flustered and a bit annoyed, "I'm so sorry Rosey, could you wait here for a bit. There's a problem I have to take care of before I take you on that tour."

Rosey nodded, waving her away kindly, "No problem, I'm sure my friends and I can entertain ourselves for a bit."

"Good, I'll be right back."

Rosey watched the tall woman walk away and take a stairway down to the first deck, the lowest on the ship. Noly and Hazel parted from her and went sniffing and inspecting the deck while she turned and looked out over the distant expanse of blue. She inhaled deeply enjoying the gentle breeze across her face and the scent of sea water. As she looked out over the ocean she thought she heard her name whispered on the wind. She shook her head and turned to look around but no one was close by for her to have heard. Sighing, she ignored it and looked about examining the rest of the ship. There were stairs that led up to a higher deck that she was sure held the Captain's quarters, and stairs leading down to a lower deck, the first deck. Next to the stairs was a ramp descending into the ship where the servants had taken Eglen, and the horses. A few other staircases lead down to other rooms and decks, all of them accompanied by a ramp on the opposite side.

"The ramps for the animals are unique," said Alex, having noticed what she was examining. He came over and stood next to her, motioning towards the ramps. "Each one has a special material over it that allows for plenty of traction. According to Thera, my master, the material is made from the skin of giant anoles mixed with a mineral that gives it traction."

"Why an anole?" she asked, curiously. "Have you seen what happens when most anoles get wet? The water runs right off their skin leaving them dry. It has the same effect here. It's useful on ships during storms and when moving baggage around. It's also good for animals who find stairs difficult to walk down like horses and Eglagors. The stairs are also covered in the material; after all, it's not just animals that can find stairs difficult. Humans' slip often enough on stairs as well, especially when they're wet." She smiled her thanks to him and together they moved away to talk to Rochell who was examining the design of the railing.

After a few minutes passed by Margaret returned, an embarrassed smile on her face, "Sorry about that, we're all a little dazzled. The Captain was away visiting a friend on Earth. We just made it here a few hours ago." Rosey nodded and said a little shamed faced, "No problem, I'm sorry that he had to leave his friend for me."

"Don't worry about it, it was about time he came back and sailed the seas again. In the meantime, I am here to give you that promised tour of the ship."

"Thank you," Rosey said as her friends gathered around her. "We'd be happy to follow you."

Her friends nodded their agreement. Noly came up to stand beside Rosey, panting happily, while Hazel jumped onto Noly's back and then into Rosey's arms where she climbed up and settled around Rosey's shoulders as she normally did.

Seeing that they were all together, Margaret gestured towards the stairs and said, "My pleasure, right this way please." She took them down a series of stairs that descended onto the first deck or lower deck. Suddenly there was a slight jerk of the ship forcing Rosey, Alex, and Rochell to grab the walls in surprise. A voice came over the intercom saying that they were moving out. No turning back now, Rosey thought. *Wait, they have an intercom!* She glanced around her trying to pinpoint where she had heard it come from, but the sound was already behind her so she ignored it. Well, they certainly are more advanced than she'd thought.

Walking along the first deck they passed carefully arranged tables and chairs that were bolted to the deck. They passed by many doors that Rosey could only guess as to what was behind them but they didn't stop for any of them. The doors were all made from the same reddish-brown wood and decorated with the same golden lettering and vine designs. As they continued along they came to a small garden that was situated in a small greenhouse-like structure that covered the whole side of the ship. You had to walk through the garden to get to the other side. A flap had been rolled up at either entrance which was probably lowered when stormy weather was about. Despite the winter weather the garden was flourishing and beautiful, the greenhouse helping to keep it warm and humid. Once they passed through the garden they encountered nothing else except for a few decorative benches and lawn chairs. Rosey took note of their location. It would be a great area to rest and watch the sea go by. Finally they came to a door like the others they had passed labeled in gold-vines: Engine Room.

"Here is the engine room," Margaret said indicating the label. "This is where the Jigaronto Quartz crystals are put into the sun sphere that runs the ship. Most electronic devices and such are run in this way." They all entered the room. Rosey's interest peaked as she heard Margaret's words. Standing at the center of the room surrounded by wires and other mechanical devices was a silver cylindrical pedestal with a domed container filled with bright green quartz crystals. The dome gave off a soft humming sound like a machine running smoothly. Its interior was glowing green from the quartz. Rosey eyed the thing in wonder. "Margaret, what exactly is this thing?" said Rosey, still eyeing the device. "The Jigaronto Quartz Crystals are created by the Energy Flows in the planet. Many times the rocks and minerals will capture some of the energy from the Energy Flows that can then be harnessed by sun spheres like these," she said pointing to the dome. Rosey thought that it sounded a lot like how the Emerald Jewel had been formed, when the Energy Flows scrapped information into its surface. "The sun spheres are simple devices carved from Tagoa Mirrors, which capture the sunlight. The mirror is bent into a sphere shape and the quartz crystals are placed inside. The quartz grows hot from the heat of the sun releasing the energy trapped inside them. The ceiling hatch above..." she gestured above the dome and everyone followed her gaze, "is opened every morning for two hours, in those hours we have enough energy to run the ship all day and night." "Wow, that would solve the energy crisis on Earth," said Rosey amazed. "True, but these special quartz are only made here. Since they get their trapped energy from our Energy Flows we have no idea how they would respond on Earth, besides we have always done our best to keep things from Earth and our world strictly apart. It's a shame."

Rosey nodded in understanding.

After the tour Margaret showed them to their rooms. She led them to the second deck and walked all the way around to the right side of the ship. There were several large doors on this side of the ship, even more elegant and decorative than the rest. Margaret opened the third door for them and they hurried inside. A wide staircase descended down to a long hallway that ran in either direction. The rooms were on both sides of the hallway. The ones on the left, facing towards the bow, had balconies and they each had one. Rochell and Alex were shown to their rooms first and Rosey bid them a good rest until lunch was served which Margaret said would be around one o'clock. When they got to Rosey's room she could barely hold her excitement. Rochell and Alex's rooms had been amazing: fine embroidery, decorative bathrooms and various appliances, even a small personal fridge. She couldn't wait to see her own room. Margaret opened the door and she stepped inside her room to see ... nothing. There was absolutely nothing in the room except a large stone table illuminated by a large beam of light. The rest of the room was bare wooden walls. It vaguely reminded her of the Dream World she went to and she was, at first, annoyed but then thought better of it. There must be something she was missing. She was the Keeper. They wouldn't just dump her anywhere. She began looking around the door for a switch or button, something. She giggled as she imagined a button that opened a fold-out room; then stopped when she realized they probably did. It didn't help any that Margaret was just standing there, not saying anything, motioning for her to enter the room with one arm extended and a bright smile on her face. Rosey looked from her to the room. She reluctantly, but curiously, walked in with Noly at her heels. If there was something magical, and for their sake there better be, then she didn't want to miss it. Once inside Margaret closed the door behind them and said, "This is known as the Room of Desires ..." she began. *How ironic,* Rosey thought, looking around. "The Goddesses use rooms like these when they come here to stay. They require a lot of magic so most ships only have three Rooms of Desires: one for the Captain and the other two reserved for the First Mate and an influential guest. This ship, however, is different. Captain Marine's father never liked having a Room of Desires and Marine shared his ideals on that so the Captain's Quarters are a regularly crafted room. Two of the Rooms of Desires are usually used by the Goddesses when they are aboard, the other one is then occupied by me. This time, we decided, so as not to show favoritism within your fellowship, to give you a room of desires while the other ones are being used by myself and our healer, Moano. We thought that the Keeper deserved to have one of these after all that she would be going through and Wolvereen has checked with Rochell and Alex ahead of time to see if they would be angry that you were getting one and not themselves. They, of course, didn't mind."

"No offense or anything, but how exactly is this a 'Room of Desires'? There's nothing in here I'd desire," asked Rosey gently so as not to sound snobbish. Margaret smiled with a hint of sly optimism and said, "Yes, I thought you might think that. This room is magical, you lie down on the table and it will form the room into the room of your most cherished dreams. The table basically reads your thoughts and builds the room according to your inner most likes." Before she could stop herself her old school girl talk came right back to her, "No way dude! That's awesome!"

Realizing what she had said Rosey quickly reached her hand behind her head to scratch an imaginary itch and said, "I mean, interesting." As soon as the words left Rosey's mouth, Noly quietly began giggling. Hazel mewed sharply and the collie fell silent.

Margaret just smiled and beckoned to the table, "Lie down and give it a try, it is your room for as long as you stay here. I will step out into the hall while the transformation takes place. Go on, it's okay," she said, seeing Rosey's skeptical expression. Rosey watched uncertainly as Margaret left the room. She then turned back to the table and stared at it. She finally walked up to the stone and waited as Hazel quickly jumped off of her shoulders onto the table and then onto Noly's back as she walked by. Rosey gently removed Andraste and the standard bow from her back and laid them against the table. She then plopped herself rather unceremoniously onto its stone surface. When her skin touched it she flinched, instinctively expecting it to be cold but it was warm. She happily lay down, enjoying the warmth on her back and pulled her long hair onto her chest. For a few minutes she waited. Nothing big happened, she felt an itch here, a breeze there, but besides that everything remained as it was. Soon she began to feel drowsy and after another three minutes of lying there with nothing happening Rosey almost got up to get Margaret and ask if it was broken or something. Turned out she still had a lot to learn. Right as she started to sit up a powerful blast of energy escaped from the table and the whole room began to hum. Rosey panicked and jumped off the table. The room seemed to be spinning. She cowered close to the table covering her head. Noly whimpered and cowered close to Rosey burying her face in Rosey's arms. Hazel, who was still riding Noly, let out a startled yowl and climbed onto Rosey's shoulders, pushing her shivering body up against Rosey's neck. A kaleidoscope of colors twirled around her vision making her lose focus and become nauseated. She threw back her head and closed her eyes, willing it to stop and just like that it did.

The Mystics

Rosey opened her eyes slowly and was completely taken aback. The room was truly something from a dream. It was bathed in blue and silver giving the place an unnatural shimmer. Ornate cushions decorated the furniture and unique mosaics painted the ceiling (in what she thought very much resembled the Sistine Chapel). The light was cast around by a brilliant chandelier, illuminating the fine wood finish and gas fireplace. The room was perfect and even included a large bed for Noly to lie on and a smaller one for Hazel. A small fridge rested against one wall, Rosey opened it to discover it was packed with cherry coke and grape soda. She quickly grabbed a coke and drank in its sweet caffeine, enjoying the feeling the carbon made as it washed down her throat. She had missed coke. Sipping her coke with relish Rosey started exploring her wonder room. There was yogurt, fruits and vegetables, and various cold snacks she hadn't had since leaving her house. Toaster Strudel, Eggos, and frozen vegetables lined the freezer like an art gallery. Looking to the left of the fridge she saw a small kitchen area with a microwave, toaster, sink, and a two burner stove with a teapot on it. To the left of the small kitchen was a door leading into a small pantry stacked with chips, popcorn, candy, tea, hot chocolate, and more. Rosey gazed at it all in wonder. Beyond the kitchen was a large bathroom, complete with a jet tub and separate shower. Her closet was just her size, she didn't wear a huge variety of clothes and she was happy to find it packed with earth like clothes as well as some of the styles she had seen while here. She flung her pack on the bed, still dazed; it was draped in a blue comforter that smelled like lilacs. Looking directly across from the bed she saw a huge big screen T.V. with PlayStation, X-Box, and Wii gaming systems, as well as a Blu-ray DVD player complete with as many games and movies she could ever play and watch in her lifetime. Against the wall that the door was on Rosey saw a large desk with a double screened computer system and all the P.C. games she had ever wanted. Rosey rushed over to it and checked it for internet service, and there it was, like a dream. On the desk was her iPod with all her songs on it. Rosey grabbed it, believing for a minute that it might disappear. She put it back, and walked backwards slowly. She sank onto the small bench at the foot of her bed and sat there starring at everything. For a while, she seriously thought that she could hear the halleluiah song being sung behind her. It was a teenager's Dream World complete with sea view balcony.

Noly stood frozen, looking around. Hazel slowly slid down off Rosey's shoulders and onto her bed, sniffing at it cautiously. With excited yips and meows the two of them suddenly started running around the room inspecting everything. Rosey laughed as the two fuzz balls bounced upon their new beds sending up mews and barks of utter excitement.

Suddenly an idea crossed Rosey's mind and she turned as Margaret entered the room, staring about at all the strange electronics and devices. To her this room was like entering an alien space craft. With worry written across her face Rosey said, "Are you sure this is okay, I thought you guys didn't mix things from Earth with this world!"

"It doesn't matter. These things are magically sustained and created, once you are done with this room they will disappear as if they never were here. So, technically, we aren't really mixing the two worlds," Margaret said, turning reluctantly away from all the strange sights that surrounded her.

"But…how do I have all this…internet…games…how?"

"Magic, Rosey, magic can do anything."

"But…this has to be using up a lot of magic, right?" Rosey said, still unconvinced. She didn't want to be a burden and she'd hate to know that she had zapped their magic supply for some fun items.

Margaret shrugged her shoulders, amused, "Yes and no. The stone table you sat on before contains a lot of stored magic inside of it. It was carefully collected for years into the stone table and then crafted by other spells to allow it to create a room such as this. As you can imagine, they take a long time to create. So there's not that many of them out there. Sometimes magikins make them for themselves as a luxury item. Like any regular table, they can be moved and relocated to any place at any time.

This one was made by a friend of Captain Marine's family long ago. Cool huh?"

Rosey smiled and decided that that was the best answer she could ever receive. At that moment she really didn't care, she was just happy everything she had ever wanted was there. She hopped up from the bench and bounded onto what used to be the table but was now her heavenly soft bed and began to feel herself drifting off. Rosey had never realized just how tired she actually was. Now that she was lying down she felt the waves of exhaustion wash over her and her body began to sink into the folds of the bed beneath her.

She was hardly conscious of anything as Margaret removed her heavy cape and boots. She felt more comfortable afterward and was vaguely aware of being covered in a downy soft blanket and the lights dimming as Margaret whispered "Get some much needed rest, Keeper," as she shut the door and left.

Chapter Nineteen: Dreams on the Water

Rochell screamed as the fire ball raced over her head. Rosey laughed and yelled, "Yes!" into the sky. She had been practicing almost all afternoon on that technique and she was thrilled she had finally mastered it, though she felt bad for Rochell, who had agreed to be her target, holding a wooden box above her head on wobbly arms. Turned out that calling up the power of fire from deep within was the easy part, learning how to manipulate the element and make it obey your will was the hard part. Nevertheless Rosey was surprised by how quickly she had mastered almost all the moves Rochell had shown her: Fire swords, fire scythe, fire rockets, and now the fire ball. She had learned a lot for the day and Andraste had been a big help. Rochell and Alex did not carry swords so Rochell had crafted herself some Wind Swords and used them against Rosey's fiery Andraste as well as some of Rosey's own fire swords. Rosey had asked them if Andraste's reaction to the element was normal but they had both said they had no idea since not much was known about the sword or where it had been made. Rosey wondered about the sword every day and her mother who had had it made. She knew by now from observation alone, that some swords in this world had a mind of their own depending on how powerful they were, but how far did that extend? It was another mystery that Rosey wanted to solve. It was another clue, in a long list of unknowns, to understanding her very powerful mother. Staring at Rochell, who had thrown herself to the ground as the fire ball passed over her head, Rosey felt the power within her flicker and Andraste vibrate in her hands. Was the sword trying to tell her something? Rosey was never sure. Just then Alex ran up behind her and threw his arms up in the air, "Perfect, well done!" he said happily.

The Mystics

"Thanks," she said quickly, hoping not to draw his attention to her inner conflict, "Although, I think I still need to keep practicing. Practice makes perfect, right?"

"Of course it does. The first time I got the hang of my element I went floating off into the wind. Took my parents two hours to find me," said Rochell stifling a giggle as she reminisced. She was bending over and gathering the pieces of what used to be the box she had been holding that was now a pile of burnt wood, compliments of Rosey's skill. Rochell's job during the practice was to try and divert Rosey's attacks away from the box she had held above her head. She had failed, hence the burnt wood. Alex's job was to make sure none of them got hurt, which was why Rochell had not been flambéed and the box had, when the fireballs hit their mark. Rosey had to admit she was a little jealous that Rochell was able to do wind techniques powerful enough to divert fire attacks with both her hands occupied, but she knew that with practice she too would become strong enough to do the same thing. She just had to keep at it.

"All right, I think that's enough for today. If we don't stop I think next time you really will cook me to a crisp because I'm too beat to keep deflecting your attacks," said Rochell as she tossed the last of the burnt wood into a pile and came over to stand beside Rosey, massaging her neck all the while.

"You, tired? No, can't be," said Rosey teasingly while sheathing Andraste effortlessly.

"Oh, believe it, it can be."

"Okay then, let's take a rest. I'll lower the protective shield," said Alex taking out his wand. He quickly waved it around chanting a small, quick saying. The tip of his wand lighted and the yellow protective shield around them vanished. Rosey had seen him perform magic before while training at the Golden Goddess's palace but it always amazed her to see the magic he used. She thought it had something to do with the fact that she couldn't do magic and, as the Keeper, she never would.

As the shield lowered she noticed the bow and arrows waiting on a nearby bench. She had started their practice session with a few sword maneuvers with Rochell and Alex to warm up. When she had successfully beat her friends at every move they could muster they then moved on to the bow, hoping, Rosey secretly thought, to get a little revenge in for her aggressive sword play. To her delight, she had actually hit the target a few times. She had been nowhere near the bull's eye but that alone was a start. At least she wasn't completely missing any more. *That bow might just survive after all if this keeps up,* Rosey thought, knowing perfectly well that her fire element could make cinders out of the wooden thing at any moment. After her grueling but successful archery lesson her friends had moved her onto the real awesome part of her job: her element. She had to admit, it had been a great practice and one she intended to continue.

Rosey had awoken that day to the late afternoon sun, groggy eyed but feeling well rested from the unexpected nap she had taken. She realized that she had slept through lunch time but had been too tired to really care; besides, her room carried enough junk food to make her uncle mad and to keep her stomach full. Strangely enough she hadn't been hungry and had settled on a bottle of water instead. Her two fluff balls had followed her example and taken a nap also. They had remained asleep when she woke so she decided to explore the ship and not disturb them. She had made her way down to the first deck and with the help of a passing stewardess found the Animal Quarters. It really didn't look any different than the hallway where she and her friends were sleeping except that the rooms were designed with the same blue floor keypads so that the animals could step on them to open their doors, just like the pads at the Golden Goddess's castle. After she had checked in with Eglen, Phana, and Bronzo to be sure that they were well taken care of, Rosey visited Sarabie's room. The large horse had been happy to see her and had gladly reported that she was being treated like royalty. Sarabie's room resembled a royal barn stall, with crisp fresh hay covering her floor, decorative grooming kits, and a large pillow

The Mystics

area where she could go and lay down to sleep. There was even an official bathroom, made especially for horses and other hooved animals. Rosey had to admit it was a beautiful place and very comfortable.

After spending an hour with Sarabie she had gone back up on deck to check on things and had run into Rochell and Alex. Her two friends had also taken naps of their own and were just as relieved as she was to be sleeping in a bed instead of on the ground. Rosey partially thought that was why they had fallen asleep in the first place. Alex suggested they practice some more with her element and she gladly agreed, unable to contain her excitement. It would be nice to apply all the techniques that she had learned at the Golden Palace to the actual element. They had decided to practice for the rest of the time until dinner, taking occasional breaks.

Now, enjoying each other's company, the three friends watched the sun as it was just starting to go down; resting from what Rosey hoped was the first of many well spent practice sessions. While they had been practicing, Noly and Hazel had awakened to find her gone and had dashed off to find her. It wasn't too hard, seeing as how all they had to do was follow the sounds of exploding boxes and the flashes of fire. She watched them as they played together, enjoying the moment. It reminded her of her afternoons back home when she would sit on the sofa, doing her homework, watching her self-proclaimed kids roll around on the floor. During their practice sessions, Noly and Hazel weren't the only ones to find them. Before they began their practice session a steward had brought them some cool refreshments and small snacks to hold them over until dinner was ready. Probably compliments of Margaret who knew that they had slept through lunch. Rosey smiled as she remembered how they had eaten them up ravenously. Now, after their strenuous practice, Rosey couldn't wait until the dinner bell would sound. Margaret had assured them that dinner was at six and Rosey was going to hold her to it.

A large wave crashed against the side of the ship making it rock some. Rosey walked forward and rested her hands on the wood railing. The smell of the sea itched at her nose and the ocean's sweet scents felt like soft caresses to her senses. She watched as the swirling water moved around the ship, gently touching its sides with its wet hands. The swirling white, blue, and green, rapid waves that formed around them as the ship cut its path through the water began making Rosey's head dizzy. Her eyes did that strange thing where her vision seemed to be crossing itself and all she'd have to do was refocus in order to get it to normal, but she didn't. She liked the way the ocean played tricks on her eyes and awakened her senses. A slight sensation tickled the back of her head as she gazed at the water, as if something was trying to get her attention. She rubbed her neck and ignored it, too absorbed by the sea to care.

She shook her head and straightened up as Alex and Rochell joined her. Looking out over the water she imagined it was like living on an oil rig in the middle of the sea except for the oil. She lifted her head and let the fresh cool air push her long black hair into a soft dance. She had let it loose from its braid after practice, loving the way it bounced against her back and swayed in the wind off the sea. There was something about the feeling of air as it passed through one's hair that was invigorating. It made you feel free, almost like you were transforming. Rosey had felt it many times, when she climbed a mountain and rested to let the wind try and blow her back down, or with her uncle when she went skiing and scuba diving, but there was something different about this time. Was it because she had always known deep inside that her uncle had been preparing her for something, toughening her up so she could face the rising storm? Maybe or maybe not, she didn't know. Cool sea water sprayed upward and bathed her fingers in wet droplets, yanking her out of her thoughts. Naturally, she licked them and tasted a bunch of salty sweet goodness. She had always liked the taste of salt water. It had a certain tang that was sour but not too sour. It reminded her of her empty stomach.   As if in response, the bell went off signaling dinner. Alex smiled as she lifted her left arm giving him the invitation to walk with her to the dining hall. He smiled and slipped his arm through hers. Rochell came up behind them and took Rosey's other arm in hers. Noly and Hazel barked and mewed with excitement as they hurried to the dining hall walking together like they always had many times before.

As they entered the dining room Rosey almost lost her footing. Having eaten in the Golden Goddess's palace and the Silver Goddess's Caverns she was used to eating like royalty but here on the sea she had expected something a little less grand. She should have known better. Ever since she got here they had done everything they could to pamper her to death, not that she was complaining, but it was getting a bit old. The table was huge. It was draped in an elegant white cloth with ornate decorations so well patterned that if she tried to follow them with her eyes she would lose her place. All sorts and sizes of cutlery and silverware, matched with what looked to be fine china, gave the dining table a welcoming almost surreal look like having tea with the Mad Hatter. A purple and gold table cloth matched the china under the shorter white cloth and the seats had fine gold and woolen embroidery. Rows upon rows of delicious entrees filled the table down to the last square inch. Rosey was blown away and apparently so were her friends. They stared on in wonder at the assortments laid before them, apparently as surprised as she was to find the ship so well decorated. Rosey was just about to sit down when she caught a glint of silver in the corner of her eye and glanced up. Standing there was Captain Marine and Margaret wearing their formal silver uniform for the dinner with their Katanas close at hand, Margaret's snapped to her waist and Marine's to his back. Rosey felt a little embarrassed for she had worn nothing but her new leather outfit, recently washed, and Andraste and Silver Knight, but so had Alex with his wand and Rochell with her...fists, so what the heck? Giving Marine a small smile she sat down and waited for her friends to do the same. Both of them took the same places they had sat with Rosey all her school days with Alex on the right and Rochell on her left.

Noly and Hazel took their seats last. Meat dishes were brought in for them. The meals they received were always conducive to their diets and made especially for their particular species. Rosey could only imagine the complexity of the dishes that every cook in the world had to know. Since animals were a part of everything and were treated just as humans would be on Earth, cooks would have to have a wider range of knowledge on what foods were okay for a particular species' diet and what wasn't. The wrong recipe could spell disaster. Just thinking about how many different dishes would have to be completed for the people on the Silent Marine was enough to make Rosey's head spin.   Once they were all seated, Captain Marine lifted his goblet. Rosey saw that it was filled with a strange grape looking juice that slightly resembled the drink that Rochell had brought to celebrate Rosey's first element collection, but this was a darker color and looked richer like wine. Tentatively she lifted hers too and so did her friends. "I propose a toast to the Keeper, may she complete her journey and may we reach our every destination," he said, with a smile, to her before drinking. She smiled back but felt a little awkward and so was the last to take a sip. What she got was not grape juice but a type of non-alcoholic juice with a texture that she had never tasted before. It was like clear soup but with a pleasant after taste that left her hungry for more. It left a tangy yet delicious taste in her mouth. She licked her lips, hungrily sipping up every last drop. Seeing her reaction, Margaret kindly explained, for once beating Alex to the finish line.

"The drink is called Wineswallow; it is made with a special mixture of spices and juices that are from a lot of rare and spicy fruits. Do you like it?" Rosey nodded, unable to speak, she was so taken aback by its delicious flavor. Margaret smiled and drank the rest of hers. Rosey then realized that the word rare had been used which meant that to get it must of cost a lot, maybe not in money but in something else. When she asked Margaret she simply said that it was no problem. Rosey rolled her eyes, but drank it nonetheless, she wasn't going to waste it no matter what it had cost. At

The Mystics

least that was what she was telling herself. She hated the fact that they were pampering her so much but she knew that she was not here to play and that she should enjoy the comfort while she could. Perhaps this was the *only* way they could help her. They could travel with her, laugh with her, sing with her, and protect her but they would never be able to do what she was doing: saving their planet. They were helpless. All they could do was offer her every service they could to give her thanks for what she was doing.

She cast her gaze around the table. Her mind suddenly wandered back to the docks. All the people who had stood there watching her, a stranger, walk off to save their world, when they, the citizens, could do nothing but wait and hope. Rosey shook her head. She had to succeed. Somehow she had to win this. She had been given a large responsibility and was expected to accomplish a great deal more than any seventeen-year-old would agree to. But she had agreed, and for her friend's sake and her planet's sake she had to succeed. She took a bite of her mashed potatoes before someone noticed that she was staring off into space, mainly Alex, who seemed to be watching her like a hawk since she got back from the volcano. Thank God that the meal had distracted him, that and a conversation with Grey who had joined them a little late following Wolvereen.

Usually she would talk with Rochell, Alex, Noly, or Hazel but Noly was busy bothering Wolvereen, Grey had Alex's full attention, Hazel was talking with Margaret, while Marine was telling Rochell about the design of the ship. For a few moments Rosey found herself comfortably alone. Though she was surrounded by people, her thoughts were free to herself. It would have been easy for her to join into a conversation but chance had given her this moment to reflect and think about things. Almost unintentionally the next element popped into her head: Water. Its location, the Broken Castle Island, also came to mind, as well as the fact that she had been waiting for the right moment to ask about it, now seemed as good a time as any.

"Captain Marine," she said as soon as he finished his tale about the ship to Rochell. He gave her his full attention and for some reason so did everyone else. Not losing a beat, despite all the eyes that were on her, she said, "I am not familiar with the Broken Castle Island. What is its history?" Silence settled over the table as Captain Marine wiped his chin and cleared his throat. They were all interested. According to Alex, no one really knew much about the Island and no one had been willing to talk to her about it, even Alex. It was time they all knew and no one wanted to deny the Keeper some very valuable information.   Captain Marine began, "The Island was owned by one of the influential families under the Leaders of the World. They lived about a hundred years ago or so. Despite this relatively small moment of time, no one seems to remember who lived there and who they were. They were very secretive and only know by their association with others as 'the family that lives on the island'. We don't even have pictures or family names...it's almost as if they never existed." He took a sip from his water then went on, "We do know they were powerful. They were more known for their works and discoveries, but, because of their insistence on secrecy and their often...unkind and unorthodox ways of doing things, they became the unfortunate recipients of the rumor that they cursed the whole ocean," he said, watching her features unfurl to one of pure shock. Her friends around her seemed to react the same way, even Wolvereen had his eyes trained on Marine.

Rosey didn't know much about curses and hadn't thought about something like that being included in the magical and elemental fairytale she was living through. It was the whole reasoning behind a curse that had made Rosey think this way. Curses were things that someone put on another person usually for the purpose of revenge. In a world that was very utopian, such an idea was almost preposterous. She stared at him for a few minutes intrigued and eager for him to continue. In a manner, much like a teenager, Marine folded his arms in front of him and leaned forward onto the table. He looked mad, as if he was offended by the usage of magic in such a horrid way. It now struck Rosey that she had no idea if he was a magikin or an elemental, but that wouldn't necessarily affect the way he felt. He could be either one and be just as annoyed by the misuse of magic. *Maybe he's potential and doesn't have a talent for magic,* she thought suddenly, remembering what the Goddess had told her about potential users. Despite Rosey's curiosity, it was none of her business. He carried a Katana but so did everyone else and based on what Wolvereen had told her, many sea faring creatures chose the katana for a sword, though there didn't seem to be a particular reason why. She shook her head, there was no sense in trying to figure it out.

"Did they?" Rosey said, bewildered.

Marine shrugged. "There's no official evidence, but when the curse did happen there was no one else to blame. No one came forward and Adina was never able to find anyone that might have done it. All the energy Adina could trace lead to the epicenter being the Broken Castle Island...but even then that was no evidence that the family was directly responsible. But there was nothing else to go off of."

"But..why did they curse the ocean?" she said prompting him to continue the tale. Marine went on, "No one knows, we're not sure if it was truly intentional or if it was a mistake but they never came forward and confessed anything which leaves us at a loss to know the truth. That being said, one hundred years ago the oceans became cursed and the evidence points to its origins being the Broken Castle Island. The curse also made it virtually impossible to reach their island, which didn't help their cause any. There were seven different 'curses' on the world's ocean that caused us to split it up into seven different areas or what we are now calling seas. It's like hell to try and travel through them," he said annoyed.

Margaret rubbed her head, her eyes suddenly tired. "A curse like that is a big one. For it to cause seven different individual affects on one body of water is an astounding feat. The amount of power it must have taken...I can't even imagine."

Marine went on. "Then, afterwards, the family just disappeared and nobody knows what happened to them, which is further evidence to support that they were the ones that cursed the seas or accidentally did so." His brows furrowed and his expression softened." I suppose something may have gone wrong; perhaps the curse backfired, taking the whole family with it. They may have been trying to make it impossible for people to find them, since they were so secretive, and something went wrong? The curse could have even been made by the island itself for all we know...but normally curses are made intentionally not naturally. No one really knows. There's hardly anyone who remembers them."

"Can't you just remove the curse?" Hazel asked, across from Rosey.

This time Alex answered, taking his spot as the magic wiz once again. "There's only two ways a curse can be removed. It can be removed by the one that made the curse and it can be removed if the thing that is cursed no longer applies to the curse. If that cursed thing or person is changed somehow to become something different than what they once were, then the curse can no longer apply to it. A curse can stay intact forever or at least as long as it is supposed to stay. In a few years' time the curse of the seas may just vanish from the ocean, the duration is unknown because we don't know the full scale of the curse or curses that were used. We don't even know if it was through one curse or two that the seas were cursed." He sighed in exasperation. "So far they've lasted for over one hundred years, which tells us that they are pretty much permanent, at least for now. Unfortunately, in this case, the way to remove the curses died with their creators..and there's certainly no way we could safely change the entire ocean so the curse no longer applied. We're stuck," Alex finished bitterly. "Yeah, whatever they did, they did it well. Not even the great Master Healer, Cascade, could find a way to remove them," said Margaret from her seat next to Captain Marine.   At the sound of the name Cascade, Rosey turned her head abruptly towards Margaret, "Who is she exactly?" Rosey had heard the name many times now and was beginning to be curious.

Based on what she had heard, this woman was a healer and a powerful one at that. Margaret looked up suddenly from her soup, "What, Keeper? They haven't told you who Cascade is!?" Margaret said incredulously, mentioning no one in particular, though anyone in Rosey's fellowship could have been at fault except for her dog, cat, and the horses.

"A lot of people have mentioned her, but they didn't go into any details and I didn't think about asking until now. They said she was a healer, though, a Master Healer," said Rosey hoping to take the blame off of anyone who felt responsible for not informing her correctly.

Margaret smiled and nodded, "Well, I'd be happy to oblige. Cascade is the first healer in all of existence. We know she is hundreds of years old, possibly as old as the universe, but that is something we will never know. She keeps everything to herself and is very secretive. She is very wise and powerful, some think more so than Adina."

Rosey gawked at her, "As old as the universe, that's a long life," she said, trying hard to keep her mouth from hanging open. "But, wait, what do you mean no one really knows how old she is?" "She is…another very interesting case. You see, she travels from planet to planet somehow, giving her healing advice along the way. She came to our world right after our original planet was destroyed and we were reborn from the asteroid in Earth. She's kind of like Valley Elathos and Sheorie, always appearing and disappearing. She travels everywhere. We heard rumors about her and were surprised to see her here on our planet. " Rosey scratched her head trying to keep up with the story. Her mind buzzed comfortably as if the Winsewallow really was alcoholic, even though she knew it wasn't. "I know you said that she's the first Healer in the entire universe but does that also pertain to your planet or was there some other physician like Dr. Leron? "Well, when our planet was destroyed in the supernova we lost everything, not just most of the population. Books, records, medical practices, and so much more were gone in a flash. Our first priority upon exiting the asteroid was to start building shelters, getting good water, adequate food, and so on.

Even if we did have a father or mother of modern medicine we wouldn't remember them. When things started getting bad, that's when Cascade arrived and helped us with our various health problems. She taught all the other healers here everything they know. She's the reason we even have advanced healers. It's a shame she couldn't figure out the animal reproductive issues before Dr. Leron got involved." Rosey thought it sounded a lot like Sheorie, the librarian. She had also come to this world to provide it with the help it needed after losing everything. Sheorie came to provide knowledge while Cascade came to teach medicine. It made perfect sense, and Rosey found herself grateful that such beings existed who would be so willing to assist others and would…could travel the universe to do so.

"Are they like doctors and vets?" she finally asked, taking a drink of her Wineswallow. "They are both," said Captain Marine taking over the conversation. "They have all the medical experience they need. They can reverse curses and cure the most gruesome of ills and wounds." "Wow, I wish Earth had people like that. They only have people with certain expertise in one form of medicine, not all of them. Do they even do psychiatrist work?" "Psychiatrist?" said Marine and Margaret together. That answered Rosey's question. Alex, knowing what a psychiatrist was, turned to Rosey and said, "There are two different kinds of Healers, mental and physical. The two practices require entirely different strategies and so are separate areas of expertise. Nornell, the younger sister to Cascade and just as equally traveled through the universe, is the first and only mental healer. She, like her older sister, is an unknown age, not from this planet, and is usually never seen unless she wants to be. She is the most elusive person you'll ever meet, and tends to keep to herself. Some say it's because she is hiding from her sister and others say that she makes personal calls as a mental healer and so is not usually seen outside. No one knows for sure." "Why would she be hiding from her sister?" Rosey asked, startled.

The Mystics

"Well, apparently Cascade has over 300 lifetimes worth of apprentices all throughout the universe on different planets, her sister, however, has none."

"None! Why not?"

"No one knows, maybe it's just because there's no one who is good enough to be a mental healer, maybe she just doesn't want to take on an apprentice. Whatever the reason, her sister is always nagging her about finding an apprentice."

Rosey sighed, magical and elemental beings were becoming a hassle to understand. "So, how did this Broken Castle become, well, broken?" Rosey asked considering the title of the place, hoping to turn her attention to something else.

"According to legend, Blood Gorons attacked it and destroyed it way before Maharen started her journey. We believe it is this attack that caused the family's disappearance," said Marine. "But, like everything else, that could also be a theory. The Island is too complicated to understand." He put his hand to his head and rubbed his temples in annoyance as if talking about the island was giving him a headache. "That means," said Rosey, leaning forward, "that these...curses are pretty new to this world, right?"

Marine nodded, but said nothing. If the Blood Gorons had attacked the Castle then it must have been for something very important. Whatever the family had been doing or had in their possession was important enough to protect, to the extent that they cursed the oceans. Rosey couldn't help but think that the family was being rather selfish but, depending on what it was, she might have done the same thing if she had been in their shoes. But what could have been so important that it justified cursing the entire world's oceans? Rosey wasn't sure she wanted to know. What would the Evil One want with an island? It couldn't have been in response to the Keepers because the attack happened before Maharen was anything more than a citizen. Even if it did have something to do with it, Rosey didn't suspect that the locations would be the same for each Keeper. If that were true then all the Evil One would have to do was lie in wait at each site hoping to get her. No, there had to be another reason why the Blood Gorons attacked and destroyed the castle. A reason that didn't involve the Keepers.

"Anyway, we are going to need to prepare for tonight, Keeper. The curse of the Second Sea is storms; however, they can only be triggered by dreams and nightmares. Once you start dreaming, you can't wake up either unless someone else wakes you. We have a special device created by Cascade to destroy the effect of this curse," said Captain Marine pulling Rosey away from her rampant thoughts.

Rosey looked up, "We're already getting to the Second Sea?!"

"Yes, the First Sea is the smallest of them all, a day or so of travel and you're onto the Second Sea."

"So…what is the First Sea's power?" asked Rosey.   "The First Sea's power causes disorientation, a simple spell on the ship keeps it at bay and Margaret is a great Magikin," said Captain Marine patting Margaret's shoulder proudly.

"Margaret, you're a Magikin?" Rosey asked, incredulously. She had had her suspicions when she had seen the small scabbard that Margaret wore that resembled the Goddess's but she had been unsure till now.

Margaret nodded, a small smile crossing her lips at Rosey's surprise. "Yeah, I would have told you sooner but there was so much to do and you were all so tired," she said giving her a kind look that reminded Rosey of a mother consoling her children. Margaret had a very protective air about her. It hadn't taken Rosey long to sense how protective she was over Captain Marine, and the rest of the crew. She was the kind of person that would throw themselves in front of a bus to save another person and Rosey found it very likable in the tall red head.

"So what then is this 'special device' you were talking about?" Rosey said.

"Well, Cascade may have not been able to lift the curses but she was able to create devices powerful enough to destroy their effects, bless her," said Margaret moving her hands to her head and casting a glance upward as if Cascade were dead and she was an angel in heaven.

"These devices are called Cleansing Songs", Marine said. "It's an ingenious device that you place in your ears before bed and do not take out until you wake. It sings a sweet lullaby in your ears the entire time you sleep making you fall into such a deep sleep that you do not remember your dreams. It is very effective. It starts working at midnight and goes on until noon the next day, unless you get up earlier and remove it. The storms are only able to happen from twelve at night to twelve in the morning, thank the Almighty One. If you don't dream: no storms. The Cleansing Songs make sure of that, during that time, you are dreamless." Captain Marine signaled to a timid waitress waiting by the door. Rosey had seen her refilling their water and Wineswallow glasses throughout the night and had tried to give her a smile whenever she caught her eye. It was hard to do since the small woman had her head down almost the entire time. Rosey didn't know why she was so nervous but she thought it had something to do with the fact that she was serving the Keeper, although it could have been many other things. She looked young, younger than Rosey, at least fourteen years old, with straight black hair cut short to her shoulders and darting green eyes. The shaky woman moved from her spot by the door and nodded when Marine told her to bring the Cleansing Songs. While she was gone waiters and waitresses began to clean up and remove plates.

A few moments later, the shaky waitress, as Rosey thought of her, appeared again holding a small package. Inside were tiny, round balls. The first thing that Rosey thought of was that they looked like candy or pearls. She leaned forward to get a better view of them. They were white and had a marble-like texture to them. Captain Marine signaled for them to be passed around and they each took two. They were soft enough to form to your earlobe, just like the gels they used on Earth to keep the water out of your ears while swimming. When she pushed down on one, the indent grew back to make a perfect sphere once again. They were like foam but they did not feel like it. They were harder and smoother but very soft. When they were in the ear they didn't feel uncomfortable. In fact it didn't feel like she was wearing anything at all and she could still hear perfectly well. Even though it wasn't blocking any sounds, she could still tell that something was in her ear. It wasn't an uncomfortable feeling like when a fly flies by your ear, it was a soothing feeling like when you go underwater and your ears are filled with water but you can't really tell the difference. Marine gestured his head downward and said, "Your companions below in the Animal Quarters have already been informed while they ate their own dinner. At night before you retire make sure to put the Cleansing Songs in your own ears, their music won't start until twelve at night which is why you don't hear them now. A steward will come around and make sure that you put them in, they will insure us a safe storm-less passage."

Rosey held the tiny device to the light. "What about regular storms? Are these storms that much different?"

Marine nodded with solemn authority, "Yes, my Keeper, they are very different. The storms the curse makes are far more powerful than normal ones. Our ships have advanced to the point that most normal storms are nothing...but these storms. They are hell on water."

Rosey trusted every word he said. She knew nothing about seafaring, and wasn't about to try. Rosey also knew from her studies that the magikins and elementals never tried to redirect the weather patterns of the planet because it was far too dangerous to mess with the balance of nature. If they did anything at all, they could stabilize structures against an earthquake's tremors, or shield themselves from a raging tornado, but they'd never alter the very path of weather itself. To do so was far too dangerous, they could curse the planet without meaning to or cause a natural disaster somewhere else. It was better to leave things untouched and that also meant allowing a natural storm to blow through. However, these storms weren't natural.

The Mystics

They were the product of a curse, so they were okay to mess with. In fact, preventing them was better than allowing them to happen.

"Normally it would be a bad thing to affect nature in such a way," Alex said, mirroring Rosey's thoughts. "But not allowing these storms to develop is very important."

"Did they cause a lot of problems before the Cleansing Songs were made?" Hazel asked.

Marine's eyes glistened with unseen memories. "Indeed. My parents used to tell me stories from their parent's days...of how there were tsunamis on coasts that never had them before...and lightning storms that split the sky. For the longest time, no one was allowed to travel the Second Sea, not just for their safety, but the safety of others."

Rosey gulped, and a somber mood settled over them all. Rosey looked at the Cleansing Songs in her hands and could only hope that the night would bring nothing but calm and serenity.

A loud bang, like an explosion, drew Rosey from her deep sleep. She awoke with a start. Something had fallen, though she couldn't tell what. Obviously, it was big; big enough to break her away from the soothing lullaby of the Cleansing Songs in her ears. As she groggily rubbed her eyes she became fully aware of the violent rocking of the ship. Scrambling out of bed, Rosey groped at the Cleansing Songs, pulling them out in a hurry. Once they were free, she was hit by the full ruckus of a storm at sea. Loud winds whistled between the smallest cracks, bone-jarring slaps of what must have been ten foot walls of water flung themselves against wood. Turning swiftly in the dark, Rosey's eyes settled on the large windows leading to her balcony. The brightest lightning display that she had ever seen lit the sky, followed almost immediately by explosions of thunder that painted the atmosphere a malevolent grey, sending blasts of light into her room. She held her ears for a moment, completely overwhelmed after hearing the soothing melody for so long. Mustering her courage, she straightened and headed for her clothes that she had thrown over her comfy loveseat before going to bed. An intense rocking sent her tumbling back and forth as she half-stumbled, half-crawled to the red loveseat. Groping in the dark she grabbed her leather clothing and slipped them on.

Something was drastically wrong. A storm raged outside and there was only one explanation for it: someone was having a nightmare. All of the passengers had received the Cleansing Songs and a steward had come around to remind everyone to wear them as Marine had promised, so who could it be? They were designed not to fall out so…why the storm? Could there be a stowaway on board? If only she had the water element… this would be so much easier! She could calm the storm or at least stop the waves. She had to get to Captain Marine to see if he was okay and find out what she needed to do to help! Rosey was vaguely aware of Hazel and Noly scrambling to her side, their Cleansing Songs making tiny tinkling noises, as the frightened two scratched them out of their ears. They appeared as fast-moving black shadows against the pitch black floor. Compared to their expert night vision, Rosey couldn't see a thing. The only light came from the balcony windows. The startled dog and cat pushed against her legs worriedly, making her unsteady on the already moving floor. Giving up on walking, she bent down and crawled. With her left hand outstretched in front of her and Noly helping to steady her, she searched her surroundings trying to get her bearings. It was so dark and the light from the balcony wasn't reaching very far. Suddenly it gave her an idea; she could use the balcony as a reference point. The door to her room and the light switch should be right behind her. But the door wasn't her main goal; she needed to find Wolvereen. He had insisted upon staying in her room that night just in case something went wrong and a storm did start up, so where was he? It now seemed kind of stupid because, even if he was in the room, he too would be unaware of any danger with the Cleansing Song's singing him to sleep. There was no time to think of that now, she had to find him. It was hard to miss a six-foot-tall-wolf. *He wouldn't have left without waking me,* she determined, still unable to make out a shape where she

The Mystics

remembered him laying down for the night. Turning to where she thought the door was, she said, "Hazel, get the lights if you can!" Hazel gave a determined "mew" in response, leaving Rosey's side and sliding across the floor, as another collision of waves smashed against the ship. Hazel slid and hit something. She mewed a coarse 'oomph' as if the air had been knocked out of her. Rosey felt herself grow numb at the sound. Rosey fell against Noly and the strong collie braced herself against the wood to keep from falling back, her claws scoring scratch marks in the fine wood. Rosey couldn't tell if Hazel was all right. She called out to her and gave a sigh of relief when the cat let out a small meow, signaling she was unharmed.

A few moments' later Hazel succeeded and light exploded all around the room, illuminating the scene. Rosey gasped. Wolvereen was pinned against the wall with a desk on top of him! That had been the loud bang she had heard. Wolvereen howled and struggled a little against the heavy desk when he saw her. He looked smaller now without his heavy armor, which lay not too far away. It was so heavy that it had barely moved during the storm. Looking at Wolvereen, Rosey noticed that he seemed out of breath and weak from struggling. She lunged toward him, forgetting about the rocking ship. She grabbed the desk leg and heaved herself to Wolvereen's side, hanging on as another wave hit. The desk moved slightly but did not budge very far. It seemed to have hit the wall so hard that the top part of it was plunged into the wall and stuck on something. Glancing at the balcony as she grabbed the desk, she saw the withdrawal of the water as it grew into another wave. Time seemed to slow down and Rosey could feel each heart beat that echoed through her ears. She braced herself but was unable to draw her eyes away from the approaching wave as it bore down on them. Then it came: the huge wave hit the ship and the desk came flying forward. Rosey tried to jump out of the way in time, but the sharp decoration at the top which had been responsible for getting the desk caught in the wall, cut a large gash in her left shoulder. Wolvereen slumped to the ground, all six feet of him. The giant wolf seemed unconscious or a little stunned; she wasn't sure which. He laid there, eyes closed, taking large gasps of air.

Rosey had no time to worry about the wolf for she was in danger of bleeding to death. She fell to her knees, sharp pain slicing through her nerves. Noly and Hazel gazed at her, speechless with fear. She gripped her shoulder in a desperate attempt to stanch the gushing, rich, red liquid. Through the piercing pain, she cleared her head and knew what she had to do. She called upon the element of fire and immediately felt the fiery essence running throughout her body. Her veins exploded with fiery power and she felt the core of her body begin to burn, the heat so intense that her skin started smoking. She felt the red and gold armor seeping from her flesh and the two tuffs of fire growing from her shoulders. Tendons and ligaments stretched her skin as it connected giant wings to her back with a crack of heat down her spine. Slowly, two, large, burning wings unfolded from her back. A good twenty four foot long wingspan stretched around her, the sharp red and yellow feathers encompassed most of the room's interior bathing the entire place in light. Her body was engulfed in a flaming radiance, so hot that Hazel and Noly had to move away. Her left shoulder stung horribly but the wound was burnt clean and partially healed. She probed the area with her hand and felt a long scar burned into the flesh. She closed her eyes…her first scar. How many more would she get before her journey was over? Then she remembered Wolvereen. Moving to his side, she examined him, checking for any wounds or breaks, trying to remember the basic medical training she had been given at the Goddess's palace. The giant wolf was still slumped against the wall. His breathing had slowed to normal and his red eyes were open and alert. The desk must have deprived him of air. He lifted himself up gently and swayed, as another wave hit. He stared at her transformed self and gave a small smile. She smiled back and got up; she had to find the others. "Are you all right, Wolvereen?" she asked, gently handing him his armor. Wolvereen growled a "thanks," and expertly slipped it on as she hauled it over, almost losing her grip on the heavy golden substance. Even with Rosey's enhanced strength from her fire element, the armor's weight still tugged at her biceps; but the large wolf gripped it in his teeth without the slightest trouble. "I'm fine my Keeper. I was just getting up to warn you when the desk flipped on top of me. Do forgive me for causing you to get that wound," Wolvereen hastily apologized, speaking around the armor in his mouth. His massive head nodded toward Rosey's shoulder and she laughed. "Don't worry about it. I think it's fitting for a first time Keeper to have her fair share of scars, like you do..." She paused, unsure if she should have mentioned them, but Wolvereen said nothing. It was true: on small areas of Wolvereen's body, there were scars. She had no idea where they had come from but she figured they were acquired in the protection of the Goddesses and the townspeople of Neran. She shook her head; she had to stay focused. Using her wings, Rosey easily brushed aside the large desk which had banged against the wall causing another large crack with its deadly decorative top. Another wave hit and the desk toppled down onto the bed, cracking it in two. Rosey folded herself, Wolvereen, Noly, and Hazel into the protective shelter of her wings when the desk fell, hoping to protect them from any debris. The bed along with the desk had slid more into the middle of the room blocking her way. She moved them effortlessly to the side revealing the door ahead. Looking back at the ruined bed, she vowed to never imagine furniture with sharp decorative tops ever again and next time it would all be bolted firmly down to the floor.

Rosey looked down at Hazel and Noly, she saw determination in Hazel's eyes but fear in Noly's. She smiled and said, "Do you want to stay here, or are you going to help me?" She felt Wolvereen, now fully armored-up, give a low annoyed growl at the dog's cowardice. Noly heard this and, mustering whatever courage was left in her, leapt forward landing next to Wolvereen. Noly bent her head and smiled at him, then at Rosey. Wolvereen snorted but did not say anything. Rosey turned to Hazel and stretched out her left arm. Being careful of the scar, Hazel jumped onto

Rosey's outstretched arm, ran its length, and then settled herself expertly around Rosey's shoulders. The flames flared slightly blue when touched by something that was not to be torched making Rosey's head seem like it was bathed in a blue halo. Rosey smiled, comforted by the presence of her brave little cat and her courageous dog. She turned her head to the door and grabbed the handle, "Search for someone who is having a nightmare. Find my friends and tell them I'm all right. Hurry now. I wonder where they are."

As Rosey opened the door, the boat rocked again and the door went sailing forward, hitting Alex right in the nose. "There's one," said Wolvereen, snickering a little. Rosey looked back and gave him a scowl. He put back his ears and shrugged his massive shoulders, the armor clinking to life.

"Alex, are you okay? I'm so sorry about that!" She flung herself at him helping him up. With her extra strength from the element she lifted him to his feet with one arm. He stumbled and fell against her, holding his head. She easily steadied him, aware of just how much taller she was to him in her Elemental Form.

Once he was balanced, he righted himself and said, "I was just coming to see if you were okay before I began searching."

"Thanks. Where's Rochell?" "Up on deck helping the wind and water elementals to soothe the storm as best they can till the dreamer can be found."

"Where have they not searched?"

"I'm not sure; could be anywhere." His voice sounded strained, he was exhausted. Alex pitched forward as another wave hit. It carried them out into the hallway where they frantically tried to steady themselves. Rosey caught Alex while Noly and Wolvereen steadied them against their weight. Alex thanked her and righted himself again, this time holding onto Wolvereen's armor as the wave passed. Wolvereen stood there now, his behind pressed up against the opposite wall to steady himself. Rosey

The Mystics

grabbed the door and closed it behind her, they didn't want to find themselves back inside if another wave hit, she then grasped the handle for support. Noly held her legs as steady as possible.

Alex then noticed her scar. His eyes grew wide when he saw how big it was. "What...what happened?" he asked worriedly. He had known her long enough to know she didn't have any scars, at least none that big. "Nothing to worry about. Can..." Rosey stopped suddenly and slammed against Wolvereen and Noly as another wave hit. Suddenly the walls groaned and creaked with the strain of the storm showering splinters down upon them. The wind howled through the newly cut holes and made the weakened walls shudder. She grabbed Alex and Noly and encircled everyone in her giant wings. Splinters turned to ash when they neared her fiery wings, raining ash down harmlessly onto the group. When they had righted again, she unfurled her wings. The group stayed there, startled. Wolvereen spoke first, his voice commanding but kind, "Let's get moving, before the boat is ripped apart! I'll take the back of the ship. Rosey, you and Hazel take the front. Alex and doggy here can continue checking the rooms, understood?!"

Noly was too scared to snap at Wolvereen's remark so she simply nodded her head, her eyes wide but focused. Rosey set her lips determinedly and said, "Good luck, guys, and be careful."

"You too, Rosey," said Alex.

They stared at each other for a brief moment, friend to friend, as if their will, alone, could keep them safe. Then they broke away, Wolvereen moved his massive body down the hallway with a determined growl. Noly and Alex took off side-by-side down the other hallway, helping to keep each other balanced. Hazel gripped Rosey's shoulders determinedly, and the duo followed Wolvereen. Halfway down, they broke off from the main hallway and raced up the main flight of stairs leading to the deck. Wolvereen was at the top, just exiting. He turned right and headed towards the back of the ship. She used her mighty wings to stay balanced, as the boat pitched from side to side, once again, throwing her off balance. Her wings flared blue, as they touched the walls, leaving the wood unscathed. Orange feathers burnt out in a flash of blue smoke, as they fell to the cool wooden floor. Finally, it settled and she reached the door Wolvereen had left through. Bracing herself, she opened it. She was almost blown away by the power of the fierce winds. They tore at her fiery wings, adding their sizzling popping to its deafening roar. She fought against it, shielding herself from the hard freezing rain with her massive wings. Unfortunately that meant she couldn't see. *Great, I've stepped out of the kettle and into the frying pan,* she thought acidly. Movement by her shoulder made Rosey laugh a little as her frisky dilute tortoiseshell Hazel peeked out from between her long black hair.

"Rosey, stretch out your arm for a moment," she said.

Not knowing what else to do Rosy obeyed, stretching out her left arm. The clever cat raced forward perfectly balanced and peeked out between the wing's feathers just enough to see. Using one wing for protection and the next for balance, Rosey navigated along the path using Hazel's perfect eagle-eye night vision to spot anything out of the ordinary. She stumbled into a couple of rooms finding nothing. The two momentarily rested then went back out again.

Rosey pulled her wings up high casting fiery light everywhere, their length was long enough to cover her entire body from head to toe. There was one last room to check before moving on to a new level. Hurrying, Rosey pushed forward and rested against the door. Using one hand she opened the handle and fell into the dark room. Turning on the lights she lowered her sore wings and folded them neatly behind her back, the feathers just skimmed the ground. Hazel jumped off her shoulders to allow Rosey's neck muscles a rest and began sniffing around. Rosey could see they were in a large storage area. In the back Hazel suddenly began scratching against a wall were a small door had been covered over by a toppled, shelving unit. Like most everything else the shelves had been buckled down to the wall but the pitching of the ship had released the shelf so that it covered the small door. Pieces of ripped wood were still attached to the bolts that had held it, attesting to the power of the storm. Breathing heavily from exhaustion, Rosey went over to the shelving unit. Grabbing it she easily lifted it up and placed it behind them without any difficulty. She tried to open the door but it was locked. Rosey concentrated her power to her right hand and watched as it glowed a beet red. Reaching down she gripped the door handle and it melted away. The door creaked open slowly. Rosey peered through the black abyss beyond to see a strange looking dog. It was huddled in a corner, whimpering in its sleep, obviously dreaming. Rosey lurched forward and quickly shook the dog awake. It bolted upright out of its sleep and their eyes met in a dead stare. Rosey knew from what Marine had told her that the one who created the storm by dreaming could not be awoken by the storm, only by outside forces. Not the shelf falling or the ship breaking apart would have done so, only her powerful intervention had caused the dog to become aware.

Rosey gazed at the dog, her head tilted in amazement. This dog wasn't just any dog, it had three large blades on it, one on its forehead and the other two on its shoulders. She lifted her head and got up rather clumsily. She stared at Rosey, fear in her eyes at being discovered. Cautiously the dog creature took a step back, pressing it's body up against the wall. She looked pathetic, cowering and hiding her face. She had deep blue eyes and a red and brown tinged body that was shaking like a leaf in autumn. There was nowhere to run and the dog knew it.

Rosey was about to demand what the dog was doing sneaking onto the ship when she was suddenly blinded by a blast of light filling the room from a small window. She blinked several times as her eyes adjusted to the sudden light illuminating her face. Curious, she looked out to see that the clouds had cleared, the rain had stopped, the water had smoothed out, and the winds had died down. It was morning. How close were they to noon? She must have been searching longer than she had expected. She shielded her eyes from the light and found that the dog was gone; typical. She ran to the outside door, her fire powers still aglow. She bunched her muscles readying for a fight and almost ran into Rochell. The brown eyed air apparition was smiling like always, looking as calm as ever amongst the dying winds. A movement caught Rosey's attention. She looked down to see Rochell's index finger pointing upward twirling.

Ignoring her friend's odd behavior she said, "Rochell, did you see it? It was a dog…thing," she sputtered, not really sure what to call it, "…and it was the one having the dream. I followed it out this door." She gestured to the open doorway behind her.

"Oh, you mean this dog," said Rochell pointing with her other hand to a spinning figure in the air. Rosey looked up to see that it was the weird dog she had seen before. Rochell was twirling it around in a circle with her air powers. The wind caught in her hair making it twist in uncontrollable patterns. All around them the ocean was quieting, the waves coming in smaller proportions and the air clearing of angry grey clouds.

Rosey laughed, "We can always count on you, can't we Rochell."

"I try," she said with a broad smile.

Chapter Twenty: Interrogation and Inner Knowing

Captain Marine was not happy about the strange creature that he had identified as a Blade Dog taking a ride on his ship and was even more upset when he heard what she had to say. They were all crowded around the cowering creature on the lowest deck, in the room where the storage was kept back, behind the animal quarters. Alex leaned against the left wall of the room eyeing the small dog with suspicion. Rosey stood not too far away with Rochell by her side, her hands folded across her chest making her look like some prim and proper business woman. Marine stood facing the dog in the middle of the room with a hard set jaw. His eyes bore down on the creature with annoyance. He paced slightly, his fists clenching and unclenching as if they were trying to grab at something that wasn't there. Rosey believed his anger to be more directed at himself than the little dog. He was probably ashamed and embarrassed that a stowaway had managed to come aboard the Goddess's ship while the Keeper was aboard. It was a direct hit to the young Captain's pride in his ability to protect his passengers.

Noly and the giant Wolvereen, who looked none the worse for wear after his incident with the desk, were protecting the closed door. Wolvereen didn't seem too focused on the dog, as if he knew that the little thing posed no threat and was more of an annoyance than a possible security measure. He sat on his haunches leaning against the wall, the most dog-like thing Rosey had seen him do since meeting him. Noly simply stared at the dog with a twinkle in her eye and Rosey knew that the only thing she was thinking about was just how fun it would be to play with the Blade Dog. Rosey smiled and rolled her eyes. *It would be a great way to practice avoiding sharp objects*, she thought, eyeing the large blades on the dog's shoulders and forehead. Hazel, as usual, hung around Rosey's shoulders playing the evil cat Minion that walked around on the evil mastermind's shoulder while they plotted their revenge, except neither of them was evil and Rosey, having transformed to her normal form, now looked anything but threatening. Margaret and Grey had stayed on the upper decks with the stewards and stewardesses, directing the damage assessments and the repairs of the ship.

The storage room they were in was, in full, nothing more than a giant closet. The place was just as clean as the rest of the ship but nowhere near as inviting. It was dimly lit by small lights casting eerie shadows within the nooks and crannies of the dark knotted wood making the room seem like it was slowly rotating. Rosey was glad that the ship was anchored at the moment to evaluate the damage or she might have become dizzy from all the tricks the shadows were playing on her eyes. It was hard to be in here for very long and that's why Rosey figured it was the perfect place for an interrogation.

Rosey shivered, the place was freezing because it was also used to house a giant freezer at the back of the room that held meats and liquids. The door leading into the freezer was nothing more than a regular wooden door like all the others. She had no idea how the cold was kept inside or why the ice never melted. *Probably with the use of a magic spell, Margaret could have cast it*, Rosey thought. Hanging on shelves about the room were tools, ladders for emergencies, and cleaning equipment. A large area of the wall was nothing but a cage with extra wood in it. It smelled like old things, meat, and wood with the tang of salt and seawater. Mixed together it made an unusual smell, somewhere between a forest and a cave. Apparently this was where they kept their emergency equipment for repairs as well as the giant freezer. Rows upon rows of strapped down repair equipment lined the walls. Nuts and bolts, tweezers, lines of pipe, and so on, took up the wall space from the ceiling to the floor. Large boxes sat at one end, strapped to the floor. What was in them, Rosey didn't know. Once Margaret had made her assessment of the damage she would probably be down here organizing the equipment needed to make repairs.

Rosey squared her shoulders and tried to be tough looking, though her heart broke when she saw the terror in the dog's eyes. Marine had wanted her to stay in her Fire Elemental Form to impose fear in the small helpless dog, however, Rosey didn't want to be thought of as an object of fear in her Elemental Form. She wanted it to be a sign of hope, after all, it wasn't out of fear that the people on the docks had clapped and cheered for her when she transformed and she wasn't about to do that now so, despite his urging, she declined. Rosey didn't approve of the Blade Dog sneaking around, but she wasn't going to condemn her for it either. Rosey would make no moves to judge until the dog had had time to explain herself. Looking at her now, Rosey couldn't help but feel sorry for her. In a way the dog reminded her of how she had first felt upon coming to this world: helpless and scared. Now Rosey was strong, powerful, and capable. In comparison, the dog looked so cowardly and pathetic that it was making Rosey uncomfortable to stand before her so high and mighty. Though the dog touched her heart, she was unsure of whether it was friend or foe. For now, she would leave it up to Marine. He was the Captain and this was his ship. Marine started without waste, his hands grasped tightly behind his back, "So blade dog, what are you doing on my ship. Understand that I am not too fond of stowaways!"

The dog quivered at the anger in his voice. She looked up and said, "I just wanted to see my old home again." "Old home, where?" Rosey asked in spite of herself. She had wanted to let Marine handle this, but she just couldn't ignore how hurt the blade dog looked. Marine didn't seem angry at her interruption; he went along with it smoothly as if he had planned on her getting involved in the conversation all along.

"T-The Broken Castle on Broken Castle Island," the dog stammered, seeming to shrink into herself as if it would give her some protection from Rosey. She looked pale, almost ghostly. Rosey wasn't sure if an animal could look pale but the little dog was playing the part well if they could. Being spoken to by the Keeper must have been a thousand times scarier than being addressed by the Captain. Unfortunately Rosey had no time to consider the dog's feelings.

As soon as the dog spoke those words everyone tensed up. The Broken Castle had been destroyed ages ago and had been abandoned ever since. This dog was an actual survivor?! It seemed impossible, yet here she was. Rosey didn't know anything about blade dogs. They were a species that wasn't mentioned in the books she had read in Jasira's library. She had no idea if she was able to live for hundreds of years, thousands, or regular dog years. They needed to know more, the dog could always be lying.

Rosey turned to Alex, "Is it possible?"

"Yeah, blade dogs can live for over 100 years," Alex said seemingly aware of exactly what Rosey had wanted to know.

Upon hearing this, Noly now looked at the little dog with something like envy on her face.

Rosey continued with her own interrogation, "What is your name?"

"Nora," she said tentatively, not daring to look Rosey in the eye. "Do you know who I am, Nora?"

The dog shook her head at first, stopped and thought for a moment then nodded, "I think I do...my Keeper."

"And you were not here to cause me or my friends harm?"

The dog quickly shook her head, and then her body; the blades sparkled in the small light hanging from the ceiling, "Oh no, Keeper, never. I am loyal to you just like any other citizen of The World Within A World, I just...didn't know any other way to get to my homeland." "How did you know we would be going to the Broken Castle Island?" Rosey asked as suspicion blossomed in the pit of her stomach.

"I d-d-didn't, Keeper. I've been hopping military ships for the longest time in the hopes that one of them would be going to the island, only now have I gotten lucky," she said with almost a chuckle in her voice, as if she was proud of herself and her luck. Rosey saw Marine's eyes grow hard within upon hearing this, as if the dog was mocking him, though he remained in control and outwardly calm. "My keeper, Captain, please...I didn't actually sneak on board this ship. Let me explain. I tried many times to seek a ship to take me to the island...but time and time again they would refuse. It's forbidden, and hopping ships wasn't getting me anywhere, so, this time around I asked a magikin to make me a Say and Go spell..."

At this, Alex gasped and then groaned with exasperation. Rosey gave him a strange look and he said, "It all makes sense now. A Say and Go spell acts like a miniature transportation scrying pool. Transportation scrying pools work like scrying, only they transport things to places instead of acting as a means of communication. It's like communicating by transporting. Anyway, a Say and Go spell allows someone who's not a magikin to transport something one time only. It is only supposed to be used to transport items...not living things." He fixed the dog with a hard stare, "you transported yourself didn't you?"

The dog tentatively nodded. Alex shook his head and said, "And instead of dropping you on the island, it landed you here on this ship. You are one crazy dog...no island is worth that! You could have ended up in limbo...or another dimension...or planet! Only portals and vortexes can transport living things."

Rosey looked back at Nora, stunned. "Was it really worth that?"

Nora nodded, looking sad and embarrassed. "I have wanted to see it for so long now...I have nothing else to live for, so...why not?" She gave them a deep bow, "I apologize. The Say and Go spell dropped me off here and well...I was unconscious when it did."

Rosey looked at Alex and he nodded, "It's not surprising, given that she attempted something that could have killed her or worse."

Rosey wasn't sure what else could be worse than death, so she left it at that. Obviously the dog's actions had not been intended to hurt them and she hadn't even been awake to seek the crew's help. To think that the spell delivered her somewhere so secluded on the ship was also baffling, though no one was looking for a lost blade dog at the time, and the closet she'd been in was just used for storage.

Rosey squinted, looking at Nora skeptically. "You said you also hopped ships, right?" The dog nodded, half-heartedly and Rosey went on, "How could you have avoided the curses for all this time? Obviously this time around you were unconscious. What about the other times?"

Nora looked away a little embarrassed, "Usually I stole what I needed...and most of the curses are taken care of by automatic systems so...I didn't have to worry too much...I never got to the Seventh Sea nor the Third..." she trailed off, not taking any pride in her words.

Rosey turned to Marine and he confirmed Nora's claim, "Only the Second, Third, Fifth, and Seventh Seas require specific individual intervention. The rest are automatically accounted for by the ship or the people on the ship. The items needed could, theoretically be stolen... I suppose." His eyes hardened on Nora and she whimpered.

Rosey remembered about how the First Sea's curse was counteracted by a spell placed on the ship and hadn't required her to do anything in particular like wearing the Cleansing Songs. If given the chance the dog wouldn't have put them in danger by falling asleep while they were in the Second Sea. Not only that, but if she had arrived as suddenly as Alex claimed she did through that spell then Nora wouldn't have had any idea what sea they were in to begin with. More and more, this looked to be the desperate attempts of a nostalgic person, more so than a hard-wired enemy.

"I'll make you a deal," said Rosey moving closer to the cowering dog. Nora almost flattened herself to the floor as Rosey faced her, bending gracefully in front of her. With a soothing yet authoritative voice Rosey said, "We have reason to believe that the next element, Water, is located on your island."

"Rosey!" said Marine startled, staring at Nora suspiciously. Rosey raised her hand signaling Marine to stay silent, a small token, reassuring everyone that she knew what she was doing. "When we get there your little stunt here will be forgiven if and only if you take me to a spot on the island that you think may hold the element of Water. Seeing as you have lived at the Castle before, I would think you would know some unusual or magical places worthy of such attention. Am I right?" She asked, her gaze was hard but gentle. Nora nodded smiling, seeming to sense that the tides had changed for her, "Oh yes, I have a few places in mind." She was no longer cowering, she stood happy and tall, it was amazing how well she adjusted.

"Also," said Rosey, "I would like you to share all that you know about the Broken Castle and its residents."

"I'm sorry keeper, but that I cannot do," at this Rosey frowned and the dog quickly continued, "all workers at the Castle were put under a spelled oath not to talk about the place besides the fact that it existed...ever, so, though I'd love to, I can't."

Rosey glanced at Alex and he nodded knowingly, confirming her words. If people who'd worked at the castle originally had been allowed to talk about it than more would have been known about the family and its secrets than what was known now. She turned to the dog.

"I see, well then you can serve as our guide, okay?"

Nora smiled and nodded vigorously, relief highlighting her face.

Rosey turned to Marine, "Captain Marine, do you agree with the terms?" Rosey turned and stared at the Captain. Nora whimpered a little and looked at him hopefully. After a few minutes of staring at the dog he smiled and nodded.   "Great," said Rosey, "Nora, since you're part of the crew now, we all have to pitch in to help fix up the ship and that includes you. Are you ready?"   "Definitely, I know that I am the cause of the damage and I want to help fix it. I promise you Keeper, I'll be the best team member and guide on the Broken Castle Island you will ever have!" Nora whipped around and around in excitement. Now that the danger was over, Noly came bouncing up to her and the two touched noses then exchanged pleasantries. Hazel jumped down to join them settling on

Noly's back. Wolvereen rolled his eyes and opened the door with the blue floor pad, ready to leave. Before he could take one step, the three rambunctious fluff balls ran between his legs and out onto the deck. Nora was courteous enough to jump over him instead of going under in case her blades got him. Rosey couldn't help but laugh and then had to stop herself from weeping when she realized her terrible two had just turned into her terrible three.

As they left the storage room Captain Marine gently grabbed her arm and pulled her aside to talk. Rosey waved her friends on when they stopped to look at her. Whatever it was, the Captain wanted to talk to her alone. As soon as they walked off, Captain Marine looked at her with strained eyes. She could tell he was trying to stay calm though he looked very shaky.

"Keeper, are you sure this is such a good idea? We can't trust this dog, what if she is a spy or something?"

Rosey held up her hand, "Please Captain, the only enemies I know of so far are the Minions, the Raptors, and the Blood Gorons. Unless there is a recent discovery to make me think otherwise, those are the only enemies I need to watch out for. She's definitely not a Blood Goron or a Raptor and I didn't see a black stone on her chest, which, if I remember correctly, according to reports, is located on the chests of all the Minions encountered so far. Thus she cannot be a Minion. Also, Alex has confirmed that she is not spelled in any way, so really I have no solid proof that she is an enemy."

Marine nodded, seeing her argument. He seemed much more relaxed now that she had presented him with evidence to support her claim but he still fidgeted, moving his weight from foot to foot. It must be hard for him, he was the Captain but she was the Keeper. It wouldn't have surprised Rosey to know that he was highly skilled by now at voicing his opinions without undermining the authority of the one he was speaking to, especially considering the fact that he was used to transporting the Goddesses. He trusted Rosey, that much she could tell, just like everyone else. However, as any good Captain would, he had his doubts and his suspicions. Rosey needed to make it clear that she had no proof to condemn this creature and neither did he.

"Look," she said, drawing his attention, "The fact that she was going to the island just as we are seems more than coincidental...we're going to need a guide. This might have been meant to happen or something. I can't ignore that. Plus, she's not going to be on her own, she will be watched closely by myself, Noly, and Hazel throughout this whole trip. If anything happens, we'll know about it."

Marine nodded, though his eyes held uncertainty.

"There is one thing I don't understand though," she said, hoping to get his mind on something else. "I know that it's forbidden to go to the island...but why couldn't she just get her own ship? How do people usually travel by sea? Is it that restricted?"

Marine took the bait, his features evening out to calm acceptance, "Well, usually when a citizen wants to go somewhere by sea they will board a Community Ship, a large ship, much like this one, that has trained elementals and magikins on board. Unfortunately with all the Blood Gorons, Raptors, and Minions about, many people are staying within the safety of their city walls and magically spelled barriers. No one goes out to sea anymore and most all the Community Ships have stopped running. It's just too dangerous these days," he said sadly. For a few moments he no longer looked like a proud Captain but a hurt boy who had been backed into a corner with no other options but to hope for the best. She had been seeing that look in the eyes of people everywhere she'd been since arriving here. The loss of hope, the act of knowing that what you had was your reality and there was nothing you could do about it. Rosey could feel his pain rolling off of him in waves. It must be hard for a person of the sea to realize that sailing is now a danger instead of a thrill like it was before. She listened as he continued, "The only ships that are out and about now are the army and Resistance ships transporting warriors all over the place as well as goods and supplies. Of course there are the occasional fishing vessels, but most are family owned, not passenger ships..." He paused shaking his head. "I guess…it's not so unusual that the blade dog would resort to such measures. An army ship nor regular citizen's ship wouldn't carry around a civilian nor transport them to the island. It's just too dangerous since a lot of times those ships are targeted by the Blood Gorons and the Minions."

Rosey nodded, understanding now why the dog has been so desperate. "Then you can understand why she did this," she said voicing her thoughts. She hoped to boost the Captain's understanding of the dog, at least so that he wouldn't feel so hurt by her stowaway activity.

Captain Marine looked at her abruptly then cast his gaze back to the floor as if he was being scolded for something he did wrong. Rosey had to stop herself from laughing. Thinking for a moment, though she wasn't sure she should say it the temptation was just too ripe for the picking. She smiled and said teasingly, "I hope that your lack of trust in her isn't coming from the fact that she may have hurt your pride by managing to get aboard your ship?"

Marine looked suddenly annoyed at the idea. He clenched his mouth shut, and a small twitch started at the corner of one eye. Rosey noticed that he was slightly shorter than her and it made her feel like a teacher giving a calm lecture. It was time for the moral of the story.

"You know, Captain, you shouldn't feel insulted. You should take it as a compliment. If she has been hopping military ships, then you're probably the first Captain to find her after all these years. If you weren't then there would be reports of the notorious blade dog ship-hopper all over the place. She may have hopped many ships, but you were the only Captain to have ever found her." She said this last with her head held high.

Rosey smiled at him then turned and walked away to find out what she needed to do to assist Margaret in the repairs. Marine watched her go, a smile spreading across his face. He was beginning to like this clever Keeper.

The ocean breeze was fabulous this morning, small sprays of cool ocean water touched her face sprinkling it with little refreshing kisses. The sea acted like it had never caused any trouble in the first place. It was as calm and collected as ever it could be on a fine morning. Thankfully Marine and Margaret reported that they had stopped the storm in time before it could cause damage to existing weather patterns in the area. Besides an unusually hide tide, everything was normal. A quick check in with the Golden Goddess from the ship's scrying pools confirmed that. That was one less thing to worry about. Rosey smiled, happy to be working out in the open, fresh, sea air. The water was tinted with different shades of greens and blues and was so clear she could see the dark shadows of a far off world of exotic life down below. Alex came up from behind her and smiled at her as he passed, then, taking out his wand, he ran toward the stairs to the upper deck areas to help clean. Rochell flew to the top deck with a stack of wood suspended in midair following behind her. Rosey breathed deeply, feeling her tired, aching muscles relax. They had been working all day and the sun cast its loving warm arms around them, soothing their thirst for light after the storm's darkness. They were just now finishing up and most of everything else from here on out was simply tidying up the equipment and repair systems. She, Alex, Rochell, and her now three fluff balls were not skilled in the art of The World Within A World's particular repair equipment and so had been told not to worry about tidying up except for if it simply concerned transporting something. Rosey would have thought that the repairs would have taken longer but, as the Goddess had said, things were done faster here because of their elemental and magikin abilities. What Earth did with machines The World Within A World did with their powers. All in all the repairs had only taken five hours, and that was five hours of running around, lending strength where needed.

With the repairs done, Rosey leaned against the railing, letting her head fall back and her long black hair dance down towards the ocean waves that lapped against the side of the ship. It danced in a sudden cool breeze and she smiled feeling the tingling of life spread throughout her body as goose bumps appeared up and down her arms. It felt like someone was reenergizing her nerves. She loved the feel of the wind through her hair. The tingling wasn't completely on account of the goose bumps, however. Though Rosey hadn't yet collected the Water element, she was beginning to feel that same nagging in the back of her head the closer they got to the island. She could feel something trying to touch her and reach out to her. It had happened at the volcano, a nagging that she couldn't ignore. She knew that Mercury had told her that something like this happened when you were close to the element, but Rosey was nowhere near it. Why was it happening when they were still so far away? The first nagging had been caused by the presence of the fire element that was then taken by the Mother herself and amplified to intense levels to make Rosey find her way to the Mother. This time, the element was nowhere near her, yet Rosey could still feel it. They weren't near the island yet, they still had days of travel to go. Could this Mother be sending out signals over long distances? Maybe she was trying to draw Rosey to her by using the nagging feeling in the same way that the first Mother, Mercury, had used it. Rosey knew where she was going though, so why? So many possibilities swam through her head that she thought she'd give herself a headache. Was it because they were sailing? Was the reach of whatever was calling to her strengthened by the water itself? It was reaching across the world to contact her, to find her, and it was using the water to help it do so. The volcano hadn't had anything, but water…water had everything.

    She was unsure, she knew it was the element but she wasn't sure why it was calling to her so strongly, almost longingly. She could feel it there in the back of her consciousness, a slight touch. It wasn't as strong as it had been with the volcano, but, of course, Mercury had been amplifying it then.

The Mystics

This was normal, this was right. This was more along the lines of what she had felt before Mercury had tampered with it. It wasn't overly magnified or intense, it was easy and flowing, like water. It was manageable and easily ignored.

A sharp bark broke into her thoughts. She turned her head quickly to see Noly chasing after Nora with Hazel running behind. The two had been given the responsibility, by Rosey, to watch the eager blade dog, although she hardly needed to ask them, since the three had formed a small pack being the smallest members of the fellowship. She laughed as the trio raced around the corner with what looked like wood in their jaws.

She shook her head in amusement and then entered her Elemental Form effortlessly, feeling the fiery richness spread through her chest into her arms and through her legs till the energy exited the tips of her toes and fingers. Her hair seemed to fizzle and pop with fiery splendor and her wings cast an illuminated glow, even in the bright light of the sun. The fire trailing from her body seemed to be pulled toward the sun just as a moth is lured by a flame. She flew to the top deck where Marine was busy mapping out their course on a small table sat outside. He was bent over his work, perfectly distracted by what he was doing but, in that authoritative way, still very much aware that she was there. Why did everyone with power always seem to have eyes in the back of their heads? He was fiddling with a strange looking instrument that was probably being used to calculate distance or something. It resembled those things she saw on the History Channel that old time explores used to navigate. She landed perfectly and folded her wings neatly behind her. "Anything new, Captain?" she asked when she saw his detailed maps. He looked up from his work as if he had always intended on stopping at that precise moment to talk to her. "No more than the usual. I am just calculating the distance from where we are to the Third Sea," he said confidently. "Oh, what curse does that one possess?" She asked, not sure she really wanted to know.

"Illusions." He glanced up at her, a light entering his eyes. "Have you ever worn Real Deal Goggles, my Keeper?" He asked it in that way someone does when they already know the answer.

She smiled and played along, "I don't believe I have." "Well these little babies...," he said quickly turning and rummaging around in a small box he had resting on the seat of one of the table's chairs. Finally finding the goggles he pulled them out and held them up, "...are perfect. They make you see what is really there instead of the illusion."

"And when do you think we will need these goggles?" "By my calculations...," he said looking down at the map again. A few seconds passed by as he scribbled some notes hurriedly on a small pad. Looking up sharply with the confidence of a skilled mathematician he said, "...in about six days starting now, somewhere around 7: 00 a.m."

She nodded taking the goggles he handed her. At first she thought they were the kind of goggles you go snorkeling with but no, these goggles were more like high grade sunglasses. They had a small golden outline around the eyes and the lenses were elliptical and tinted a light blue. The material felt something like the Cleansing Songs, soft, but harder than foam. Long flexible strings were attached to the sides of the lenses and a small, harder string connected the two lenses in the middle, holding them tight against the head. With more scrutiny she determined that they were adjustable to different sizes. She slipped them on to find that the world was no different than what she had seen a minute ago. It was like wearing glasses without any lenses just for the heck of it. Obviously, they wouldn't work their magic until they were in the Third Sea. She laughed and thanked Marine, handing the glasses back to him.

Opening her wings once more and giving Marine a farewell she flew to the second deck where their rooms were. Alighting down, she transformed back into her regular leather outfit and walked to her room, feeling the weight of all the work she had done that day falling over her shoulders like she was lugging around water. On her way she wondered just how many of the stewards and stewardesses knew the majority of alien things in her room. Based on their hurried and strange expressions the few times she saw them leaving her room after cleaning it she was certain they knew little. She also considered the fact that their being in the room belonging to the Keeper might be what made them hurry and worry. She noticed that some of the staff still stiffened up when they saw her. Many of them were very joyous to see her but seemed awkward around her as if they didn't know how to respond to their savior. She still saw the hope and longing in their eyes that she had seen in the citizens on the docks and in the city Neran but these people were more professional about it. They were used to being around large figures of authority since they ferried the Goddesses around all the time. Was she really on par with those great women? She was still herself. She still found joy in eating popcorn while watching a movie on her stomach from her bed. She still loved plopping down outside and reading, letting the stillness of the day settle around her like rain falling on water. She still loved smelling the air after it rained, how it reminded her of crisp honeysuckle and she still enjoyed the sound of lightning as it broke over the sky sounding like crackling rock candy on her tongue. She still wanted to feel the clear flowing essence as the wind blew around her and through her hair. Most of all, Rosey still had her dreams from before she had come here. She had had plans to go to college to be a veterinarian. She loved animals so much, especially horses. She had hoped to possibly one day become an equine veterinarian or maybe even open her own horse training ranch or a breeding organization. She had never intended to leave her little house in Montana, where the mountains ran rampant through the long stretches of wild terrain that gave refuge to wildlife so diverse she could never hope to learn it all.

So many things she had wanted now seemed gone. It was much the same way for the people here. They had wants and dreams. They, too, had plans and then the Evil One had come and snatched them away. When the citizens looked into her eyes did they see everything that had been taken from her by having to come here just as she saw their hopes and dreams lost to the cruel hand of fate? Maybe that's why she always tried to avoid their eyes, so they wouldn't see her loss.

There was one thing she knew for sure, she would never tell these people who had all their hopes riding on her shoulders that she had doubts. Not about being the Keeper, she was well aware that she was the Keeper. The fire burning inside of her and the tugging pull of the water's call was enough to convince her of that, but she had doubts that she could be the Keeper she needed to be. Would she have the courage to be a warrior, after dreaming her whole life of being nothing more than a rancher or vet? Could she be more than what she was in such a short time? Rosey didn't fear the powers in her hands, for some reason, they felt natural to her like they had always been a part of her. What she feared the most was failing all those people. Failing this world that she was a citizen of, even if she had no memories of it, she was one with it. She knew what it was like; she knew how it felt to have everything you wanted taken from you. The people here had had their want for happiness and safety destroyed while she had been yanked from her planet and thrust into a whole new world. She was the same as they were and even though she might never return to Earth she didn't mind. Coming here had been the craziest and scariest thing she had ever done, but… she didn't care. This was an adventure right out of a book. It was her adventure, a far off world, a new place to discover and explore, and a new her to become. Here she was a blank slate, still the same Rosey, but with a whole new purpose: the chance to be a hero and save the world. And that was something she was willing to die for. There was no way she could turn her back on this world, whether or not the people saw her lost hopes in her eyes or not. She had to stay and fix this. Maybe one day she'd return to Earth but Rosey had the gut feeling that she never would and that was okay.

Reaching her room Rosey went in, flipped off her boots, and flung her coat on the rack. She felt the ship begin to move, they were back in action heading towards the island. Smiling she sank into the bed and closed her eyes, wishing that it was all a dream. Noly and Nora's barking brought her out of that dream. She lifted her head and smiled as the three of them came trudging into her room. Every door on the ship was equipped with a blue pad that an animal could step down on to open a door since they did not have hands like humans. They were the same pads she had seen down in the animal quarters where she and her friends visited the horses and Eglen daily. Noly and Hazel had had their fun with it when they first discovered it. The two of them had stepped on the pad for almost ten minutes delighting in the simplicity of opening a door and thoroughly making Rosey annoyed. One of them would step on the pad while the other would then run through the open door. Rosey knew better than to scold them, they wouldn't be captivated by such a device for long. She, of course, was correct. The two of them had gotten bored and gone to do something else not twenty minutes later. Still, it was reassuring to know they could enter Rosey's room whenever they needed to. She wouldn't have to constantly be getting up to let them in or out like on Earth. However, both the pad and the door could be locked to keep any unwanted persons out if the necessity ever arose.

Rosey had, at first, been worried about the damage in the Room of Desires but, as she suspected, all she had had to do was reset the table, lay back down on it and presto, a new room exactly the way it had been before all beautiful and junk food stacked had appeared except that, this time, there were no sharp edges and everything was securely bolted down. After hearing what had happened to her, Marine had suggested that while creating her new room she could simply add this touch to be sure that she wouldn't be attacked again by loose furniture. She had only been too happy to do so. Margaret had explained that, normally they didn't need to strap things down because the ships were very good at maneuvering the seas, but the recent upheaval had caused them to rethink that. The other repairs outside her room hadn't been so easy, mostly they concerned replacing wood and missing parts torn off by the strength of the waves, but the rooms were pretty fixable even if they weren't a Room of Desires. Apparently, every single room had a re-due switch that fixed everything including holes and destroyed furniture. These switches didn't extend everywhere but accounted for some of the smaller furnishings. Rosey had been very impressed and even more so because it had meant that the shelving unit she had torn off to get to Nora had easily been fixed.

She cast her attention to her rambunctious duo that was now a trio, with a smile on her face. When Nora saw her she whimpered and backed out of the doorway, looking at Rosey with her head bent and her ears cocked sideways. Rosey waved her in with a kind smile, too tired to talk. Nora yipped in pleasure and raced in after Noly who had taken up a playful position at the corner of her bed. The two tussled and Rosey listened amused as Hazel played referee. Once the three of them had settled down she told them how long it would be before they reached the next sea. They groaned, a little disappointed by how long they'd have to wait but Rosey had no worries. She was looking forward to those next few days. It would fly by for her and would also give her some much needed practice time with her element and the dreaded bow and arrow. She smiled as the trio went racing off and then stretched comfortably.

She got up intending to take a shower, but then decided to soak in a warm, soapy bath, smelling of lavender, instead to help her aching muscles. After about an hour of soaking with Hazel and Noly licking at her fingers and toes that she put over the side to tease them with and watching Nora nip at the small bubbles that rose from the water occasionally, she lifted herself out of the tub. Once she had dried off she wrapped herself in a fluffy robe and sat outside on her balcony, holding her parent's locket and gazing at their pictures. She'd long ago told her friends about it. She'd done it all nonchalantly, as if she didn't care. She knew they'd seen right through her.

The Mystics

She let the ocean breeze cool her warm skin. She sat there in perfect bliss with Noly's head on her lap, Hazel hanging around her shoulders, and Nora curled up on the chair opposite hers. She let her mouth hang open to catch any small ocean spray that wafted up from the seas rough calculated currents and watched as the sun sank below the horizon. She had talked with Marine after dinner at 7:00 p.m. The dinner had been small, enough to replenish their strength from all the hard work to get the ship up and running again but not as elegant as the formal meals they had been having. That had been two hours ago, it was 9:00 p.m. now. The colors swirled in the sky: reds, oranges, the last tiny bits of midnight blues, and then the bright yellow shine of golden fire. After about an hour she fell asleep on the very comfortable, blue, cotton seat.

Chapter Twenty-One: Captain Marine

After Rosey left him Captain Marine spent another half hour checking his work then, sighing heavily, he gathered his tools from the old wooden table that sat outside his quarters on the top deck. He stopped for a moment and ran his hands over the old wood, memory flooding through him. That old table was the same one that his great grandmother had used when she sailed the oceans in the Silent Catapult, the first ship in the family. His great grandmother had been the first to bring Marine's family into shipping. At first she was just a simple fisherwoman who read the waves and breathed the ocean air for almost the whole year.

"She could never pull herself away from those waves," his father had told him about the famous woman who started their love of sailing.

Fishing hadn't been enough for her though, after a while, she left home completely to journey across the world in nothing but her small boat. She traveled everywhere but wrote home every chance she got. Her parents worried over her, all alone at sea, but she was a fearless sea-goer and they trusted her. During her journey she took the chance to study all the different ways of sailing. She learned, modified, and studied hundreds of methods, trying to find a way to make a ship sail so smoothly that it hardly rocked. She had been a genius engineer and sailor. She was someone who could sail the oceans so well that some said that she had seawater in her veins instead of blood. Others said it was because she was a potential water element and that her connection with the sea was just the potential power of her water element showing itself to her in the only way it could. Kind of like when a blind person's other senses compensate for the missing sense. Whatever the reason, for she never truly said whether or not she was a potential or elemental, she was still a genius sailor.

The Mystics

After years of traveling she finally developed a system that worked. She renamed her small little boat from The Catapult to the Silent Catapult. She shared her idea with the world and eventually all ships carried the Silent System developed by her. Ever since then each of Marine's family members had given the name silent to their ships. Out of respect for the great woman, no other ships carried that name but Marine's family line.

Marine closed his eyes fondly at the memories. The Silent System that Salem had created wasn't actually responsible for making a ship silent. It was called the Silent System because it made a ship sail smoothly, so much so that it stopped a person from getting seasick and it even made sailing through storms a synch. The ship still rocked but it was nowhere near as violent and it certainly never tipped over. According to what his father had told him, Salem's father had always described the movement of a ship not in words of motion but in words of sound. So when he said silent he really meant smooth. Despite the fact that it wasn't making anything silent, Salem stayed true to her father's belief and called her invention the Silent System in honor of him. Marine's father believed in the Silent System as everyone did but he knew that the storms created by the Second Sea were spelled and strong enough to go against their Silent System.

Marine remembered the stories well about his great grandmother, Salem the Silent, the title she had received after making the Silent System. Until Salem's mother had come along Marine's family had just been farmers, Salem's mother had fallen in love with a man of the sea. Marine's father had always told him that that was the way that the love of sailing had come into the family, through that pairing. The two lover's daughter, Marines great grandmother Salem, had left home as soon as she could, having been taken on many trips out to the ocean by her father, and never looked back. Her father had given her her own boat on her twentieth birthday and she sailed it like sailing had been written in her DNA. At that time the seas had not been cursed and so had been safe for people to enjoy and explore. Marine wondered if Salem's parents could ever have imagined what their daughter would discover. He wondered if they had been proud of her. Marine gave thanks to his great grandmother who bore within her the love of sailing and the taste for the ocean's power and strength, without it he'd have grown up on a farm planting seeds and preparing for the harvest. Yes, he was very thankful.

He rubbed the old table that each member of his family had saved in order to remember her: Salem, the red haired explorer of the ocean. He ran his hand slowly over the old cracked wood that he had taken care of, trying to keep it in working order as his father had showed him, and his mother before him. The wood was slightly different from the wood of The Silent Marine; after all, it had been transferred from ship to ship all these years. It was a lighter wood, not the rich mahogany with the red hints as the rest of the ship sported. It had dark brown blotches with knots that twisted and turned in fantastic patterns and light brown bark traveled down the legs. According to his father, his great grandmother had loved the feel of bark on a tree and wanted to have some with her, at least on the legs of the table. Salem had made the table with her father; it was the one thing she never changed about her little ship. She had spent a good deal of her travels modifying and changing the ship in order to discover how to make it a silent sailor, everything, except that little table, which she kept exactly the way it was. Salem and her father had even had the table spelled to guard against all sorts of damage, basically acting as a shield. It was practically indestructible. Marine swallowed hard. There was so much pride and love written in the wood of that table. Marine could feel it, it was soft and smooth and perfect, but it carried within its rings a history that was carved into the memories of everyone who had sat at it and known what it had seen.

A powerful gust of cold air settled around his shoulders. He cast a glance at the falling sun. The last light of day was fading fast, soon it would be dark. He could continue if he wanted to but Marine hated to keep any light source near the table that wasn't the natural sun. He quickly gathered the rest of his things and went into his quarters. He passed the ships wheel and opened the door to his room at the back of the Steering Deck. The Captain's Quarters were always located behind the Steering Deck, which was always located on the Top Deck. He switched on the lights and began stacking his things away within the large desk that had belonged to his father. It was made of the same wood as the rest of the ship and like all of the furniture on the ship it was built into the actual architecture. The furniture in the Room of Desires was the only furnishings that were not built into the ship, which was why Rosey had been wounded.

At this Marine halted and rubbed his temples, feeling ashamed. He was happy that after talking with her after their interrogation of Nora that she had gotten it looked at by a nurse in the infirmary. She had given her a cream to help soothe the scar and keep the muscles from bruising but said that it looked like Rosey's powers had cleaned it up pretty well. Marine had never liked the Room of Desires because he didn't like opulence it could give someone. As the Captain, he wanted to live as all his crew members did: in normal rooms. It was an idea that had been shared by his father and the reason that the Captain's Quarters wasn't a Room of Desires. Marine hadn't liked that Rosey was put in one of the rooms but after seeing everything that she was going to have to go through everyone agreed that Rosey deserved a room that would hold her every wish and dream to make her stay as comfortable as possible. Despite that, he still should have thought sooner to ask her to imagine the room with everything tied down. It had been his lack of duty and responsibility that had gotten her hurt. He knew that he'd been distracted and kept busy with his ship but that was no excuse. He rubbed his hands together, annoyed and paced unhappily. At least she hadn't been more seriously wounded.

Marine shook his head, he had trusted the Silent System to keep them safe, and most of the time no one was ever without the Cleansing Songs for fear of destroying their ships or killing themselves. It had been years since anyone had actually been afflicted by the Second Sea and he felt ashamed that something had gone awry on his ship with the Keeper on board. He should have known better, he shouldn't have been so careless. He could have kicked himself for his stupidity. He laughed under his breath, if his parents could see him now they'd scold him for being too harsh on himself, but he deserved it. The Keeper's life was his responsibility on this ship. He must not mess up again.

He sat back in his chair, the only thing not bolted to the floor but that could be folded and put away when not in use. *Maybe it wasn't such a good idea to put the Keeper in the Room of Desires,* he thought shaking his head. What would his father and mother think of him? Rosey could have been killed, but nobody was supposed to be sleeping without the Cleansing Songs. His father had never trusted the Rooms of Desires on ships. They were too dangerous he had always said. The Magikins were working on a way to make it so that the furniture attached to the architecture of a ship automatically when the rooms were used on ships but they were having a hard time figuring it out. Marine didn't even like that the Goddesses used the rooms, but they preferred the luxury that the rooms provided. It was ever said that the Goddess were the ones that made the two tables in the first place for the ship, though they had never owned up to it. Could they have been the 'old family friends' that had made them? Marine's guess was as good as any. This once he had allowed the Keeper to use one and look what happened. He shook his head; there was no reason worrying about it now. It was done, they wouldn't face anymore storms and after they left the Second Sea the normal storms wouldn't be strong enough to affect the Silent System on their ship. Rosey had assured him that she'd imagined the new room with everything bolted down and that was all that could be done. He'd just wished he'd thought to mention it sooner so none of this would have happened.

A knock sounded at his door. He knew without thinking who it was.

"Come on in," he said.

The Mystics

As expected Margaret walked in. Marine studied her for a few minutes. He saw that the lines on her face had deepened since they had become Captain and First Mate two years ago. Her red hair had become a little frizzier after all her years on the sea and her lips seemed whiter as if the salt from the sea had painted them a crisp, clean color. He noticed the veins in her hands beginning to show and the wrinkles gathering at her brow. They had both gotten older, but he was just nineteen and she was forty five.

Margaret had been good friends with Marine's mother. They had grown up together and shared everything together even the same dream: to work on or become Captain of a ship. They loved sailing and had dreamed of it. Their families had been pretty normal. Margaret's family had been a clothes designing company while Marine's mother Casi had come from a regular elemental family with a diverse range of talents and dreams. Casi Michaels and Margaret Elion had become infatuated with the sea and, as soon as they were old enough, had enlisted in the Sailing Academy. It had been a few years before Maharen, the first Keeper, had been chosen and they were looking forward to serving the planet and sailing at the same time. They quickly graduated at the top of their class and began going to interviews to be placed on a ship.

Marine's father, Carl Turbine had given his services to the Goddesses as a favor to their father, Roderick. The Goddesses had been in their early twenties then, their power and influence blossoming while the war with the Evil One was at its height. The Keepers weren't even a thought in anyone's mind yet. Maharen was just a normal sailor like the others, the best builder of the legendary War Ships. Like Casi and Margaret, Carl and Roderick had grown up together as very close friends. In exchange for dedicating his ship to the Goddess's private use, Roderick promised to build Carl a brand new ship of whatever design he favored. Carl had agreed and began making plans for his new ship.

Margaret and Casi wanted to stay together and signed onto the same ship which, because of their high honors from the academy, had been

Carl's ship. Carl and Casi were drawn to each other immediately, and even though Carl knew it was unprofessional to ask out one of his crew members, he could not stop himself from falling in love with her. They got married not too long after. Margaret had been thrilled. Casi took the name Turbine from Carl because it was a family name from the great Salem Turbine, the Silent. She thought it was an honor to have that name, though Carl insisted that she keep her last name, Michaels, as her middle name. Two years before Rosey was born, Marine came into the world, and in honor of his son, Carl called the new Ship the Silent Marine. It turned out to be a perfect match because Marine was a very quiet baby, hardly ever crying. It had made his mother worry but a healer had assured her that Marine was as healthy as could be. As the healer said he would, he grew up well and thrived when on the ocean. Carl had wanted his wife to be a captain with him but she refused saying that it was his ship. He continued to insist and so finally she settled for being his First Mate and her friend, Margaret, became Second Mate.

Margaret loved Marine. She had watched over him, babysat him and was like a second mother to him. His mother had insisted on him calling her Aunt Margaret, though she wasn't Casi's sister. She might as well have been. Marine missed his mother and father. Like so many others, they had died during the war. While Rosey was safely growing on Earth, The World Within A World had fought on and attacks had continued. Marine had lived through all of them but his parents hadn't been so lucky. They never brought him with them when they went out to sea with the Goddesses for fear of attack. It was on such a day that Marine had lost them. He was just a boy of eight when he received word that a group of Blood Gorons had ambushed the Silent Marine intending to get at the Goddesses. They killed almost everyone on board. His parent's had been among the casualties. Margaret was one of the few lucky survivors. If it hadn't been for her, everyone would have died. She told him, when she returned, how his parents had ordered her to save as many as she could and get off the ship.

The Mystics

Margaret had led the retreat as the Goddesses, Casi, and Carl held back the tides till they were safely on board the backup war ships coming to the rescue. The Goddesses tried all they could but Carl and Casi died in the chaos. The Goddesses managed to obliterate the hordes of Blood Gorons, the remaining few fled. The Goddesses had given him their deepest regrets when they accompanied Margaret back to his house. He could tell that they felt very guilty for what had happened.

A few months later, Margaret became Captain and took over the ship. The ship had been patched up and the remaining crew members had come back to sail her. Marine was one of them. He had asked special permission to travel full time on the ship to let Margaret finish his training to become a Captain. The Goddesses gladly agreed and when he became old enough at seventeen Margaret gave the title to him. He took it willingly but was unsure if he could be a good Captain at so young an age. So far, however, he had proven to be up to any challenge.

Margaret was his only family now. He had no one left. The war had taken them all. He was the last of the Turbines, the last of Salem Turbine's great line and he didn't want to mess things up.

Glancing at Margaret again he noticed just how much she was still the same despite her age. She still had a light in her eyes that he could not ever find the bottom to. It was a light brought about by happiness and a good outlook on life no matter how bleak things might get. Many a time she had made him laugh when he had felt like crying and other times she had held him close like a mother would a child when the pain became too much.

Marine had been so young when his parents had died that his memories of them where small and in between. He often times thought that the reason why this was so was mostly to try and stop him from being so sad about their deaths, with no memories it was hard to remember why you were crying. He still missed them. He held tight to the memories he had of them: memories of cold mornings walking through fog covered banks with his mother as they waited for the sun to rise over their little cottage house by the sea, of riding on horseback with his father, of long afternoons playing cards with Margaret and his parents when they were on holiday and of telling stories as the fire died down. His father had always told the best ghost stories. He brushed a stray strand of hair out of the way. He had to stop remembering these things before he made himself depressed. To distract himself he got up and began making tea for him and Margaret, her favorite was Sew Con tea made from the Sew Con plant and his was Orange Spice. As he waited for the water to boil he turned his attention to her.

"So what brings you here," he said almost teasingly. He knew why, she always came to give him a daily report.

"Well nice to see you too, Captain," she said following up on his teasing, "If I'm not wanted I'll just leave then."

"Who would drink this awful Sew Con Tea then?" He said smiling as she mockingly went to the door as if to sourly storm out. He wondered if she did this to make him laugh or because she still thought of him as a child, probably both. Either way, Marine was grateful for it.

She smiled and turned back around, "Well all right then, I guess I'll help you drink it. Honestly though, it's delicious. I don't understand why you insist on hating the stuff?"

She plopped down on his perfectly made bed exasperated and watched as he moved the tea pot off the burner as it began to whistle. He poured the tea and handed her hers then took his seat at his desk swinging it around to face her. His bed was freshly made each morning by himself. He couldn't stand his bed being untidy. He couldn't stand anything being untidy really, while Margaret didn't seem to mind at all which blew his mind and she loved teasing him about it. He blew on his tea then sipped from it carefully, enjoying the spicy orange zest that went down his throat. He considered Margaret's question.

"I'm entitled to my own taste buds, right?"

Margaret gave him a skeptical look but said nothing.

The Mystics

"So, really? What's the report?"

In a split second she became serious, all manner of jests left behind. "Surprisingly there wasn't a lot of damage. We got it all repaired pretty quickly. We can continue on now if you like," she said this last quickly, as if she had rehearsed it.

"Thanks Margaret, I'll get her moving to the Third Sea."

Before he could reach the door, Margaret asked another question as she rose to follow him out, "What do you think of Rosey?"

It was a simple question. Marine considered for a moment then smiled and said, "I think she is going to be an amazing Keeper."

Chapter Twenty-Two: Lie of the Sea

A sharp prod in her right arm drew her from a lovely dream. Rosey looked to her right groggily and stared up into the hard, scarred face of Wolvereen. He was so big she was surprised he could even make it into her room. He gave her a smile, so small she almost missed it. She groggily lifted herself from her bed, rubbing her eyes softly. Looking to her left she yelped in surprise. Beyond the door of Rosey's balcony was a wide expanse of boiling lava with occasional large rocks poking out of the ground. The image was so real that there was light from the lava cast all about her room and heat was pouring in from the outside. Rosey could almost see it shoving itself against the glass of the window doors of her balcony. The sky was black with soot and raining down from the sky were hot embers and grey ashes. Rosey gasped as a bright light exploded amongst the clouds, a large rock fell from the sky and hit the lava sending up a wave of frizzing superheated molten rock. She shuddered and felt herself go numb. What was happening? In pure panic she turned to Wolvereen and saw...the goggles. He was wearing them! Rosey immediately collapsed into the pillows of her super soft bed in relief. It was an illusion cast by the Third Sea. Memory came rushing back. It had been six days since repairs had been made and they had discovered Nora in their storage rooms. Marine, the night before over dinner, had told them that they would be entering the Third Sea in the middle of the night and should not panic if they woke up the next morning and saw something horrific, it was just an illusion. Rosey sighed happily. After six days of uneventful travel and dreamless sleep they had finally entered the Third Sea. They were getting closer to their goal. Marine's earlier calculations were a bit off but he had assured them that they'd be passing into the Third Sea by around 6:00 a.m. the next morning. They had all gone to bed with their Cleansing Songs on for even though

The Mystics

they were entering another sea that didn't make the Second Sea's power any less real. Now she hurriedly pried them out of her ears and placed them on her bed stand.

Rosey breathed deeply, feeling each breath move in and out of her lungs as if it were her last. The illusions could be different according to the person. Why would Rosey see fire and brimstone? Was it a possible sign that she was going to fail her mission or was it because she had just collected the Fire element and fire was on her mind? Rosey shook her head. There was no reason worrying about that. Turning she lifted herself up in the bed and grabbed her Real Deal Goggles that she had laid on her nightstand before she went to bed. Captain Marine had given them to everyone over dinner last night.

By now Noly and Nora were awake and talking away uncontrollably as they had been for the last six days. Rosey was happy for the two but they were really starting to get on her nerves. They were so fussy that even Hazel had become distant towards them, meowing something about how dogs had no dignity every time the two of them went running by. Both of them, upon looking outside yelped in surprise and stuck their heads under the covers of Rosey's bed, whimpering silently. Thankfully, Nora was careful of her blades and the sheets. Rosey wasn't sure what it was the two dogs had seen but she was sure it wasn't good. Hazel stretched and yawned from a pillow beside Rosey, awakened by all the commotion. She looked out the window, then looked back at Rosey and seeing the goggles in her hands, smiled at her, then promptly went back to sleep. Rosey smiled, she could always count on Hazel.

Rosey turned and surveyed Wolvereen. He stood next to her bed, towering over her as he always did. When he saw the dogs he cringed and growled deep in his throat. His rough voice came out as a powerful bark, "Get a hold of yourselves you flea brains. It's just the illusion of the Third Sea, it's not real!"

Suddenly the two dogs stopped quivering and raised themselves from the sheets looking as if nothing had happened.

"We knew that," said Noly happily, letting her tongue loll out the side of her mouth.

Nora said nothing but nodded all the same, though she continued to cast glances back at the outdoors as if she was now more intrigued by what she saw then frightened, like Rosey had been after her initial shock had died down. Rosey stared at the blade dog for a few minutes wondering what it was she was seeing in that illusion. Rosey looked once more at the fire and molten lava swirling around in an eternal dance of motion, then placed her goggles over her head and looked once more. The ocean was back to its normal splendor and the heat and rocks were gone. Reaching over she grabbed the other Real Deal Goggles on her bed stand and put them on Noly and Nora. Looking at them, she had to stop herself from laughing at the comical sight they made. She left another pair of goggles by Hazel and figured the little cat would put them on when she awoke. Shaking his head in disbelief at the two dogs, Wolvereen turned to her.

"Good Morning Keeper, I came to make sure you wouldn't get panicked in case you forgot what the Captain told us last night. Also, the Captain wishes to speak with everyone at breakfast about something important. I'll wait for you in the hallway."

Rosey nodded and said, "Thank you Wolvereen."

He bowed his head slightly then turned and exited her room. Noly and Nora looked at her expectantly when they saw the open door. Rosey laughed.

"Go on, I'll see you in a bit."

They barked happily and leapt off the bed. Laughing evilly, they zigzagged past Wolvereen's legs and up the stairs for breakfast. Wolvereen puffed irritably, blowing out air in small but strong hot breaths then growled out some choice words Rosey was really glad that she didn't understand.

The Mystics

Hazel yawned next to Rosey then rolled over on her back and stuck her four paws up in the air sighing as she stretched her back legs. She then rolled back over and sat up stretching her back up till it arched. Then, in that cute cat way, she walked slowly forward lifting her back legs up and stretching them outward as she walked.

"Did we finally decide to get up?" said Rosey teasingly, petting her soothingly and scratching her behind the ear, her favorite spot.

"Oh I would have…eventually, but if it's something important I better be there," she said referring to what Wolvereen had said about Captain Marine's impending announcement at breakfast. Rosey grabbed the little set of Real Deal Goggles by the cat and put them on her. It was pretty hilarious to see a cat wearing goggles but Rosey managed to quiet any giggling she might have made. Many things on this planet were made for both animals and humans so everything came in multiple shapes, varieties, and sizes to fit any need. The goggles, in this case, were cat sized and the ones on Noly and Nora had been dog sized. They were all made according to their species; however that didn't stop it from looking any less funny.

"Admit it," she said as she adjusted the straps to Hazel's liking. "You just didn't want to be seen wearing these goggles."

Hazel looked up at her after she had securely strapped them onto her little cat head, "Would that have been such a bad thing? You don't look any better."

Laughing Rosey rolled out of bed and grabbed her freshly washed leather clothing and headed into the bathroom. She dressed then brushed her hair and teeth. Lastly she put her hair into an intricate braid that Margaret had shown her. It was very useful for keeping her long black hair tied up and out of her way. As she did this her mind raced through the last week.

Six days at sea had made Rosey pretty comfortable with everything sailing related. She had gotten to know the crew very well and she'd advanced farther than she'd ever thought she would in her elemental studies. She'd learned much with Alex's wisdom and Rochell's ever powerful guidance. She'd especially started practicing on controlling the way the element of fire affected her emotions. She'd intentionally get herself angry and then focus on recognizing and controlling it. She'd gotten pretty good at it. She'd even managed to improve in her archery, something she thought would never happen. Everything seemed so surreal in those past few days. The need to reach the island was high but they couldn't go any faster than was permitted. Rosey had been impressed by how fast they had managed to cross this section of sea; of course, they weren't using sails and rigging to move the ship. It moved just as fast, if not faster, through the oceans waves just as most modern ships on Earth did. Rosey knew all about the Silent System from Grey. He had, like Nagura, attracted Rosey to him with his kind words and gentle spirit. He had told her many stories while they traveled, especially about Captain Marine and Margaret. He'd told her their backgrounds, their tragedies and their worries. She had listened intently wanting to catch every whiff. It was because of Grey and his affinity for storytelling, very close to that of Eglen's, that Rosey had learned about the woman known as Salem the Silent. She had been overjoyed to hear this because Salem was one of the people she had learned about in Jasira's library. She had never thought that she'd meet her surviving heir. As Grey had described Salem, Rosey could only find herself impressed. This device she'd created was beyond any science known to their world. It was a mixture of magic and scientific ingenuity, a gift from Earth, no doubt. It was obvious how good it worked. They had sailed through the oceans like a rocket ship, moving over water faster than they ever could over land. It was an impressive feat, and with its speed, Rosey had been shocked that it had taken only six days to cross just one portion of the sea, especially given that this world was much bigger than Earth. She was grateful for the advanced technology, or, maybe she should say the magical technology. It had insured that she wouldn't have to be at sea for a month and had also provided her with the pleasure of knowing that she'd get to the element sooner.

The Mystics

Rosey had enjoyed learning about Marine's past but the only thing Grey hadn't told her was anything about Marine's powers and Rosey was starting to think that he had none and was simply a regular man with a Katana and the title of Captain. Still, she respected him and his capabilities. One did not become Captain unless they were well qualified.

A story about the Captain and his First Mate was not all she'd gleaned from Grey. She'd also discovered that most people with power were always referred to by their title, followed by their first name. Usually the title would come first followed by the last name, but, in an effort to be more informal and friendly, calling each other by first names after being introduced was seen as a sign of camaraderie. Captain Marine's name was actually Marine Turbine, but his title was Captain Marine, not Captain Turbine. Rosey liked their insistence on family, friends, and common courtesy. It was such a relief from Earth's apparent survival-of-the-fittest-excuse that many had begun to use to wipe away their sins. It was hard to miss it now, and, days later, she could barely remember what it was like to live there.

This last thought made her pause and examine her features in the mirror. She still looked like herself. There was the same smile, the same white teeth, the same coal black hair, the same bright blue eyes, the same eyebrows, the same…everything, yet, Rosey felt a difference inside her that hadn't been there before. It was so strange but so true, and she couldn't exactly say why, but she liked the new her. She had been transformed, reborn, and she wasn't going back.

She grabbed her parent's locket on the sink and attached it to her belt as always. As she did this, she saw the newspaper article she'd been reading the other night. The World Within A World's local newspaper was a lot like Earth's in that it did everything a newspaper was supposed to do: keep you informed. Rosey hadn't even considered a newspaper, and happened upon it by chance one day when making her way to the dining hall. The daily delivery had just been dropped off and a group of deckhands had been gathered around with the pages thrown open reading away. She promptly started reading up on what was taking place, grabbing a new issue each morning or afternoon while usually on her way to the dining hall. Many times she would read it out loud with Rochell or Alex while they were taking a break from practicing. She liked to have them there to ask about anything she was unfamiliar with, but by now she was starting to get the hang of it.

Being the Keeper made Rosey feel like what she imagined the president of the United States might feel. She had an obligation to stay informed and alert for trouble and, unfortunately, as with Earth, the news seemed to only bear trouble. The newspaper would report about deaths, births, various celebrations and festivals, and weather reports like most newspapers but it would also report on Raptor attacks and movements, local devastations, and the latest army and Resistance movements. Rosey had paid extra attention to the reports on Raptors, even going so far as to map out their movements on a map for herself. As each day passed Rosey could feel herself growing into the role of the Keeper more and more. Her friends could feel the change in her and had adapted themselves along with her. She wasn't a school girl anymore. She was a warrior and a hero, and she needed to act like one. Taking a deep breath, she left the bathroom and squared her shoulders, after six days of waiting and preparing it was time to get down to business.

"I am never coming to wake them up again," Wolvereen was mumbling to himself as Rosey met with him in the hallway, Hazel draped around her shoulders. The giant six foot tall black wolf had his head hung low in boredom and his red eyes were proud slits. She came up beside him and had to stifle a sudden giggle. Hazel wasn't the only one who looked funny. In the room she had been so shocked that she hadn't really noticed the way the goggles fit on Wolvereen. He looked exactly like a big dog wearing sunglasses. It seemed even someone as cool as Wolvereen wasn't able to escape the humor of an animal wearing what was considered a human

The Mystics

decoration. She brought her voice under control before saying, "Thank you for waking me, I admit I might have been pretty panicked if you hadn't reminded me."

The wolf nodded and grunted as he leapt forward. She followed him to the dining hall and took her seat. Alex, Rochell, Captain Marine and Margaret, were already there eating and talking away, she sat down and immediately started piling her plate high. Rosey had come to understand that Marine didn't do things in small proportions. When he did something, he did it big and meals were no exception. Every meal that Rosey and her friends had feasted upon since boarding the ship had been a large expanse of delectable, rich foods covered in various sauces, vegetables, and fruits. It never failed to trump the seemingly amazing prepackaged foods from Earth that the Room of Desires had for her in her small kitchen pantry, though it was hard to replace candy bars and Hostess cupcakes.

They weren't the only ones to enjoy such fine foods. Rosey had visited the cafeteria in the last six days where the crew members ate and ran in and out on a regular basis in between their various chores. They were provided with the same luxury foods with rich flavor and powerful aromas. Rank and title meant little when it came to people's treatment. Everyone got what they needed and weren't served disgusting, half-par dishes because they were just crew members, no; they were treated with compassion and given the same attention as others. It had warmed Rosey's heart and made her feel a little less guilty about enjoying all her fabulous meals. This wasn't luxury, this was just the way people were treated.

For a few moments they enjoyed each other's company, making small talk and filling each other in on the latest news from the closest continent. Rosey wondered if Eglen would have been able to heighten the mood with one of his stories. She wished he and the horses could eat with them but Rosey new that a ship was a very unforgiving place for animals with horse-like legs like Eglen and the horses. With such unpredictable weather and cursed seas to contend with, they could easily get hurt so it was required that they stay in the specially designed Animal Quarters to be sure of their safety. Creatures like Wolvereen and Noly did not face as much risk of being unbalanced or hurt from an accident so they were allowed to move around, still Rosey felt bad that they couldn't be with them. She, Rochell, and Alex had made sure to visit them every day to make up for their apparent ship arrest. They had also continued to groom and look after their horses, feeding, watering, and exercising them. Though the deckhands were willing to do that for them, Rosey knew of the importance of taking care of one's own horse and spending time with them. Even though the horses were now intelligent, they still appreciated that special relationship between horse and rider. It wasn't all bad and secluded, they too had a dining hall that was made specifically for their delicately legged species and often Rosey and the others had gone down to eat a snack with them and talk. They were also provided with the same amazing variety of gourmet meals, all designed according to their specific species. Rosey had gotten to know Sarabie, Phana, and Bronzo much more than she had before and cherished her time with them.

 Rosey noticed after a while that everyone seemed to be having trouble eating and then realized it was because they were trying hard not to laugh. The goggles weren't exactly stunning. They were just normal red and blue goggles. It was almost like looking at a bunch of people wearing tanning-bed glasses while they all tried to be civilized. She herself had to stop from bursting out in laughter at how funny everyone looked. Despite how rambunctious they always were, Rosey was happy to see that Noly and Nora were managing to control themselves, though she could tell it was killing them not to tease Wolvereen.

 After everyone had eaten and settled down it was time to talk. The hushed, quick way everyone had eaten, despite the constant threat of laughter, told her something was up. This was going to be an interesting conversation.

The Mystics

"In about four days we will make it out of the Third Sea, but that is where the tricky part begins," Marine said. He leaned forward and took something from his back pocket. He slid it over to Rosey. It was a map of the ocean with the seas marked plainly. "Remember how I explained that the family living on Broken Castle Island was very obsessed with keeping the place secret. Look at this map. See the continent in the middle of the sea?"

Rosey looked and indeed there was a long skinny continent in the next sea.

"The family living on the island released the information that the Fourth Sea was on the northern side of that continent and the Fifth was on the southern side. The far eastern tip of that continent was then, supposedly, inside of the Sixth Sea; when in actuality, that is not true." "How so?" Rosey asked curiously.

"The southernmost side of that continent is actually the Seventh Sea, not the Fifth. Many have died going into the Fourth Sea thinking that the Fifth Sea was south of the continent and expecting the Sixth when they passed the tip of the continent. Remember, the family told everyone that the Fifth Sea was the southernmost sea even though the southernmost sea is actually the Seventh. So , if they are passing through the northernmost sea which is indeed the Fourth Sea," his hand moved over the map from the Third Sea into the Fourth Sea that hovered over top of a small, skinny continuant. "If you followed this, thinking that below that continent was the Fifth Sea and it wasn't'...."

"You'd be expecting the Sixth Sea at the end of the continent, but it's actually the Fifth," Rosey finished for him. The map was marked correctly with the Fifth Sea beyond the tip of the continent and the Seventh Sea marked below the continent, the southernmost part.

Marine nodded, "Thankfully, they were telling the truth about the Fourth Sea, it is the northernmost sea. This means that at the end of the continent it is not the Sixth Sea people should be expecting but the Fifth

Sea as it is marked on the map. Each sea has its own protection put on it and thus if you're expecting one sea and get another, you can become very confused. If they survived that then they'd spend days and sometimes weeks looking for the Island which was in the elusive Seventh Sea. Because of this trick many people were lost and or killed. You're lucky the people discovered the family's trick before you came here, Rosey. Then, when the castle was destroyed, Adina forbade everyone from trying to find the island. No one has been there since." Rosey grimaced in horror, "Why would they do that! I don't care what you are protecting it's not worth the life of another."

"We don't know why the Blood Gorons attacked it or why the family lied about the arrangement of the seas to hide their location, all we know is that the island hasn't been inhabited for years and no one goes near it anymore since Adina made it forbidden to do so. The only reason we know what we know now is because of the few individuals that ever actually found their way to the island, before it was forbidden to do so, and made it back alive. These few told us about the horrible rubble that was once the castle and the family that was oddly missing. For all we know they were attacked by the Blood Gorons and so abandoned their castle, but that seems odd seeing how far they were willing to go to hide the place. They could be alive right now, living amongst us and we'd never know. There's really no way to be sure. The family must have done what they did for a reason."

Rosey felt the fire element clawing at her consciousness, a rage that was so strong that Rosey could swear she could feel heat starting to flow from her skin. She clenched her firsts and calmed herself, gently pushing the flowing energy back into the crystal that hung from her neck as she'd practiced. Breathing deeply she said, "For whatever reason, that still does not make it justified to put all of those people at risk. Not everyone would have been looking for the island. If it was just a regular passenger ship, this little lie could have killed innocent people," said Rosey angrily. "Were there any repercussions for what they did? I assume they were around at that time if they lied about it?"

Marine shook his head, "When Adina went to see them personally to confront them about it, she found the castle destroyed by the Gorons..that was when it became forbidden to go there."

"She felt it was too dangerous since the Evil One was obviously involved." Margaret added.

Marine nodded, " You'll be happy to know that we weren't fooled for too long. It only took about two months before people understood they had been deceived and began to recognize the Fifth Sea as the Seventh. Word traveled fast and we all adjusted our maps accordingly. The people who'd managed to make it there before Adina, confirmed the castle's destruction. Like you, Rosey, there were some that weren't too happy about the family's little lie, so they went to the island to get to the bottom of things and found rubble, just as Adina did when she went there."

Alex scratched his head, "Wait a second...so when did they become suspected of cursing the oceans? I don't think the people would have asked the suspected cursers to document the ocean they cursed?"

Marine, looking flustered, said, "Of course, I can see how that might be confusing. Let me explain. When the seas were first cursed, no one ever pointed any fingers at the family. It was a complete mystery who did it. The problem came when the family was asked to document the ocean's new powers when the curse was enacted. Tracking the epicenter of a curse as large and as powerful as this one was taking some time, so Adina hadn't yet tracked down the culprit. Because of that, she had had no reason to suspect it was the family's' fault or that they were involved. She had personally made them responsible for mapping the oceans. You can imagine her distress when she discovered the epicenter was *their* island. When it was discovered that they also lied about the seas, well, only then did people start to spread ugly rumors that they were responsible for the curse in the first place. There really is no proof that they were the ones who did it, but their lie has always been against them ever since."

Rosey folded her arms with disgust, "For good reason, too."

Marine smiled at her bravado. "That coupled with their sudden disappearance and Adina finally tracing the epicenter of the curse to their island eventually lead to them being the accused, but, by then they were already gone."

Rosey scoffed but felt a little better. "Hold on, Adina made them responsible for the documentation? Then did she know them?"

Marine bobbed his head with uncertainty, "Yes and no, Adina knows a lot of people but even she dealt with the family on a limited basis. Adina has also refused to release any information she has about them to the public because...as we've said, there is no explicit evidence."

Seeing Rosey become flustered by his words, Margaret took up the discussion. "You see, the fact that the Blood Gorons attacked it has always made Adina believe that the family may have been acting with desperation. Possibly they were being harassed or something. Because of this one small doubt, she's determined not to add to the rumors."

Rosey frowned, she supposed it was possible. What if a Blood Goron had abducted a loved one and was threatening them with that person's death if the family didn't cooperate? Still, they could have sought help...couldn't they? What would she have done if it had been her uncle or her friends being held against their will? Rosey's eyes quickly regarded her friends before they noticed her staring and she shivered. She could never imagine what it would be like to have the ones she loved held as hostages against her. Rosey's position as the Keeper might one day mean she'd have to face such a situation. Could she really judge the family knowing this? She felt her fire die down all of a sudden as understanding took over.

Marine continued, drawing Rosey back to the conversation, "Despite all the rumors and speculation, the seas remain cursed. As you know, with each passing sea the challenges get worse, and many were not expecting the level of cruel enchantment placed on the Seventh Sea. So far all the other seas had been manageable, even kind compared to this." Rosey tensed up feeling her throat go dry, what could be worse than a rampaging storm and misleading illusions?

"Are you familiar with the theory that if you believe something with all of your heart, your mind will make it happen to your body?" asked Marine. Rosey's brow furrowed, "How do you mean?" "Let's say that there is an illusion, and it takes up a knife and impales you. Even though it was just an illusion, your mind thinks that it is real, so much so, that your body makes a knife wound appear and you bleed out as if you actually were impaled. You would kill yourself, in essence."

Rosey shivered. Everyone around her had their eyes trained on Marine. They all seemed entranced as if they were under some spell. Rosey heard Andraste, which she had hung on the back of her chair, rattle in its sheath. She couldn't tell if it was worried or just reacting to the moment, but she got the feeling it wasn't because the sword was happy. No one else seemed to notice the swords odd behavior, no one ever did, only Rosey noticed. She eyed Marine, afraid of what he would say next.

"Now, imagine if that illusion was the person you most held dear," said Marine. "You would die believing that the person you loved had killed you." Rosey took a sip of water and swallowed slowly, feeling the coolness trickle down her throat. The sea's power was a lot like the illusions of the Third Sea, but those illusions would cause you to lose control of yourself by causing you to see things that weren't actually there. These illusions could kill you and in a very personal way, created by your own ideas, family members, and feelings. "So, what do we do?" she said, sitting up straight and trying not to think about it.

"We've found that the safest thing is to put you all to sleep," Marine said. "A special drug created by Cascade, of course, puts you in a very deep sleep that you will not awaken from until we get to the Island and administer the antidote. There are different variations of the drug depending on species, so not everyone will get the same thing."

"What about you, Captain? And Margaret and the servants, what will happen to them?" Alex asked. "They will all be put to sleep as well, except for Margaret and I. Nornell, the mental healer, gave us a potion that we will drink before we enter the sea. It gets rid of our emotions towards our loved ones and leaves only what we need to know, like operating the ship and an understanding of who our allies are. It removes all emotional attachments, leaving us basically like robots with a duty or command to follow but no emotional pull towards it. It's very effective. Once we get to the island Margaret and I will take the anti-potion and be as good as new." "Wait, how will that protect you? Won't the curse pick some other form?" asked Noly cocking her head to one side in curiosity. "Possibly, but the curse does not have much power, it draws energy from the memories of your family and friends and your emotional attachments to them, people you trust. If you have no emotions attached to the memories then, it is highly unlikely that the curse would have enough persuasiveness to deliver a solid figure."

"Can you attack these things?" asked Rosey.

"In a way, yes. They are little more than illusions. All you would do is break up the figure into smoke, like a vanishing ghost. It would probably just reform though. The curse is very good, if it finds the slightest evidence of a connection it'll feed on it and kill you with it so don't think you don't need the drug," said Marine giving Wolvereen a knowing smile. The wolf rolled his eyes but didn't respond. He'd probably tried to get out of using the drug before on a previous voyage in service to the Golden Goddess. Rosey chuckled allowing her mood to brighten, but only for a moment. "I see," Rosey said. She had heard many tales about people who had been given a drug and woke up from it early during surgery or it kept them trapped in a dream state forever. For a split moment she was filled with fear. What if she never woke up? What if she was trapped like that and then died? She knew they wouldn't let her use it if they weren't sure she'd be okay. She was the Keeper, the last thing they wanted to do was kill her. Tentatively she asked, "Why can't we use the same potion you'll be using from Nornell?"

Margaret answered. "The potion is hard to make and there's not enough for everyone. Though the potion is not dangerous, Nornell prefers that such a powerful drug only be used when absolutely necessary and on as little people as possible. It's also easier to deal with two people who are emotionless than an entire ship full."

Upon hearing this, Rosey felt a lot better about the situation, but she knew it would still be gnawing at the back of her mind, like an old regret that you couldn't shake.

"One more thing," Marine said. "As you know Margaret is also staying awake; so she will be keeping an eye on all of you and will be there in case I need help. The night before we enter the Seventh Sea, in four days' time, you will not be having dinner. This is so you can empty out your digestive system of foods. Without foods your body may be hungry but it allows for the full effect of the drug. Though we won't be able to eat anything, liquids, however, are fine, preferably water. Is that understood?" "Yes, Sir," everyone replied at once though Noly lowered her head, obviously saddened by the prospect of no food "Good, I'll of course remind you of this in four days' time but, remember, keep your goggles on till then. I don't want any panic stricken people running throughout my ship screaming that we're being chased by a giant alligator," said Marine fixing his gaze on the more eccentric of their group. Noly avoided that gaze like the plague. "These are comfortable to wear to bed or you can try removing them but the illusions are very real so I wouldn't advise it," he said tapping the glasses he wore. "That's all for now, enjoy these next four days, because after that, its sleep time." He rose to leave signaling the end of their meeting. Everyone followed his lead and dispersed from the room, gathering in various groups to talk.

Walking back to her room with Hazel once again draped over her shoulder, Rosey watched as Noly and Nora ran along beside her, supposedly beating her to her room, though she was not racing them. She smiled at them as she grabbed a hair clip on the desk and pinned back some loose pieces of hair from her braid. She slipped off her long leather jacket and hung it up on the coat rack. She grabbed her water bottle and raced up the stairs with Noly and Hazel close behind. As they ran on, Hazel jumped in and out of Rosey's legs. Nora and Noly watched amused but too respectful of Rosey to join in, plus with Nora's blades and Noly's height, it would turn the game into something dangerous. Rosey had experienced this little game many times before and after years the tiny cat had perfected it so that Rosey never tripped. It was the one thing Hazel loved to show off whenever she had the chance.

When Rosey turned a corner, Alex and Rochell were already waiting for her. Alex smiled and motioned to a pile of boxes ready to be charcoaled. He quickly placed a protective barrier around them, and then nodded to her. She smiled back and felt the fiery heat of power rising within her. It raced along her arms and legs, sending shockwaves of power along her spine. Andraste hummed in her sheath, happy to feel the power of fire racing along her blade. Large wings broke free from between Rosey's back bones while tendrils of flame licked at her face. Her long black hair and deep blue eyes turned a fiery red. Yellow and orange embers swirled everywhere when she beat her massive wings, sending sparks flying. Her leather outfit melted away covering her body in hot convulsions as her muscles grew stronger and a glowing orange outfit replaced the one she had been wearing. Two large, fiery torrents leaked from her shoulders like jet streams of heat. It was getting easier to change, she noticed. Looking at her chest she found the Shanobie Crystal beating along with her heart, a florescent orange poured from its interior. Beating her wings she lifted into the air. Her friends covered their faces as she gathered fire into the palm of her hand and shaped it into a white hot, burning sphere. Aiming, she sent the fire ball at the boxes and watched as they exploded into flame. Within seconds the boxes were reduced to a mere pile of ashes. Alex turned, gazing at her with a triumphant sparkle in his eyes. Rosey crossed her arms and smiled at them, "Better watch out guys, I'm on fire today," she said laughing.

Chapter Twenty-Three: Behind the Fog and Mist

When she awoke the world was not as it used to be. Rosey swallowed hard and slowly sat up in her bed. Her throat felt tight and clenched as if all the water had been sucked from it. She licked her lips, happy to find moisture there despite her dry throat. She slowly sat up; her muscles ached as if she had been asleep for a long time. She rubbed her eyes sleepily as if the action alone would help to wake her up. The drug they had given everyone worked all right. She groggily got to her feet, yawning and stretching cramped muscles. Carefully she found her woolen robe and wrapped it snuggly about her. After making a quick trip to the bathroom she made her way slowly to the balcony to check on their progress. She opened the sliding glass door clumsily. Her fingers seemed incapable of doing what she commanded them to. Finally she stepped out onto the dark brown wood of the deck tracing the mahogany etched lines in the deep wood as she went, unable to completely support her head. Taking a deep breath she gasped in surprise as she was immediately hit with a wave of freezing misty air. Completely startled, all her muscles suddenly responded and she half fell, half flew back into the room slamming the door closed in her wake. She stood there, quivering slightly, as her body adjusted to suddenly being so active. Rosey glanced down at her hand and watched it shake slightly. It was the same hand that she wrapped her parent's locket around every night before going to bed. She stared at it a while mystified and scared at the same time by such a reaction. She grasped the locket, determined not to let go. She leaned against the glass doors, feeling the warmth return to her limbs. Slowly she stopped shaking. She looked through the chilled glass into the world beyond, her breath making abnormal circles in the windows. It was night. That much she could tell. The

The Mystics

clouds and heavy mist would part every once in a while showing off a wide expanse of clear water and the reflection of tiny stars. Plus, the small lights on board were lit, something only done at night. She wrapped her arms around herself as if she could still feel the chilly cold wind. It made gooseflesh rise on her arms.

The four days in the Third Sea seemed far behind Rosey now. They had been filled with endless practice, relaxing, and learning. She could have filled a book with all that she'd learned but she would never have had the patience to write it. She'd been given the drug two days ago when the Seventh Sea loomed ahead of them, and now it must be time for them to awaken. Otherwise, why else would she be awake?

She quickly changed into her leather clothes, carefully fastening the locket to its secure location on her belt. She pulled an extra heavy coat out of her closet and slipped it on over top of her leather jacket. She grabbed Andraste and fastened its buckles over the thick coat but left Silver Knight and her bow where they were. Her shaky body was so unstable, she had been lucky to get Andraste in place.

The air was much chillier as it often was at night and tonight was no exception. That she was used to. What made her so edgy wasn't the mist and fog drifting about since weather patterns were always changing. What really worried Rosey was the pitch black abyss that surrounded her. According to what Marine had told her it would be daytime outside when they would be awakened. There wasn't even a hint of light on the horizon. Something was going on. It was then that she realized that the ship wasn't moving. She had been so focused on her own shaking, half asleep body that she had barely noticed that the ship was still. Oh yes, something was definitely wrong to make Marine stop the ship. What if something happened with the drink they'd given them, she thought suddenly. *I've got to check things out.*

By the time she finished dressing she felt much steadier on her feet though her muscles still ached a little. Her eyes scanned the area where

Noly and Hazel usually slept. Because of the particulars concerning the Seventh Sea, Captain Marine had asked that Hazel, Noly, and Nora be temporarily moved to the Animal Quarters where they would be placed in a cushioned room according to their size so if things got rough sea-wise they would be safe. She had had to talk her two fluff balls into agreeing. Now she wished they were here with her. She may have been able to judge what was going on with their help. There was no sense worrying about that now, she had to find out if something was wrong. She left her room and hurried through the hallway to the stairs that led to the second deck. Bursting through the door, she was immediately hit with a strong cold wind. She pulled the gloves from the pockets of her heavy coat and put them on. Looking around she scanned the decks.

The others should be up by now, where are they? she thought. The lack of people only confirmed her fears that something had gone wrong, but she had to stay calm and cautious.

She walked up to the top deck and up a flight of open stairs to the Captain's Deck. There in the Steering Room she found Captain Marine. He was there as usual. Rosey breathed a sigh of relief, everything was all right. He was hunched over a map, deep in concentration. He was so absorbed that he hadn't noticed her entering. "Hello, Captain," she said to get his attention.

He jumped and stared at her, then glided over to her softly and cautiously. His eyes seemed unfocused and dark rims had formed under his eyes as if he hadn't gotten enough sleep. He considered her, looking her up and down. She watched as slowly his hand crept towards his Katana strapped to his back. Seeing this Rosey did the same. She grasped Andraste's hilt, apprehension clawing at the back of her mind. Marine seemed to tense when she did this, fear seemed to leak from him in all directions. Andraste suddenly sent a shiver of power through her arm. Deep warmth spread throughout her body igniting the ends of her nerves and calming her aching muscles. Rosey relaxed and released her grip, he was not an enemy. Seeing her relax, Marine seemed to relax himself. He took his hand from his Katana. Rosey was almost disappointed. She would have liked to see how good he was. He still studied her, unsure.

Why is he doing that? His face was not as it usually was: controlled and calm, displaying the utmost pride as a Captain. Now, it was questioning and untrusting. Rosey stepped back. "Is there something wrong Captain Marine?" she asked, her voice quivering slightly, it was so cold. Andraste's heat seemed to have been zapped from her.

Marine seemed to relax a little more at the sound of her voice, "Rosey, it is you, right?" he said, tentatively. Rosey almost flinched away from him. His voice sounded very unemotional, as if someone had reached their hand inside him and flipped the emotion switch to off. He seemed…bored almost, though the fear in his eyes was genuine. It must be that potion they took. Marine did say it would rid them of their emotions too or affect them somehow, she thought eyeing him. His question came to mind and she shook her head impatiently.

"Well, of course it's me, who else could it be?" "I only ask because we…had to wake you up early." "What!" Rosey said, startled. When she had walked out her door, she had suspected that something was wrong but it had never occurred to her that she would be woken earlier than she should.

She stared at him hard, "Why?! I can fall victim to the sea's powers just as anyone else can!" she said worriedly, looking around as if she was expecting an enemy to jump out at any time. No wonder he had been unsure, he hadn't been sure she wasn't a horrible illusion cast by the sea. *And going for my sword must not have helped, but in all fairness he went for his first,* she thought irritably. "I know, but only four more hours or so and we are out of danger. The Island is not too far away."

"What's going on? Did the stuff not work? Do I need that potion you and Margaret took?"

"No, no, no, don't worry," he waved her worries away, "that stuff did work. We were the ones who woke you up early. As for the potion, there is no need for you to have it. Since we are only four hours away it would be a waste to have you use it. That stuff doesn't just grow on trees. Cascade has to make it herself" He shook his head as if to clear it of some unusual idea then said, "Margaret is going to let you use a special drink that should take care of any problems you might have. This drink is only for emergencies but it doesn't mess with your emotions like the potion does. Don't worry, Margaret will be with you the entire time, she will know if anything is wrong."

He was talking with that same lack of emotion. It was strange hearing him talk in a monotone way, each syllable pronounced slowly, as if they were being swept away on waves and carried out to sea. He moved sluggishly as well. Every now and then he would shake his head, as if something was stuck in his ear and he couldn't get it out. His whole body seemed tense but well relaxed. He seemed like a drunken person would be without the alcohol.

She regarded him quizzically, unsure. Still, Marine wasn't arrogant, he was simply dedicated to the waves that had been bred into him and the expectations set for him by his family. Rosey had come to trust him in the short time she'd known him, and she wasn't about to go back on that belief now. If he woke her up, it was for a good reason.

Sighing she said, "All right if you are sure, but what was so important that you needed me?" "I did not predict the weather well, my Keeper. I did not see all this fog and mist coming in. It seems rather odd, but we are getting closer to the Castle, so it could be some sort of protection thing. Margaret's been trying to figure it out but can't sense any magic. Anyway, I can tell what direction I need to go to get there but the real problem will be the large rocks just off the shore of the island. I can't see them in this and neither can Margaret. I stopped the boat an hour ago and had you wakened. Rosey, I need you to clear my path of the fog. The closer we get to the coast the larger and more unpredictable the rocks become." "All right," she said nodding briskly, "I'll get right to it." She turned to leave but stopped, "Are you sure it is safe out there, those ghosts still can't trick me can they?" she asked turning to face him. She felt a twinge of fear at the back of her head. Why was it that an unseen enemy always seemed scarier? "They still can, but since we are closer to the island their effects are weaker. It would be unlikely that they would be able to make you kill yourself." He considered for a moment, and then said, "Margaret went to prepare the special drink after she gave you the antidote, you have woken much faster than we expected. She'll come straight here when she sees you're not in your room." Reassured, she nodded and made her way out onto the Captain's Deck, calling on her fire element as she walked. She felt her back bones shift and her skin split as new bones grew from her back to form two giant wings. Hot embers floated around her and when they touched her leather outfit it was replaced by a shining orange wardrobe with gleaming armor. Her hair and eyes turned orange and her crystal shone brightly. Heat pulsated through her body like a heartbeat and Rosey got the idea that if seen from afar she might resemble the beacon of a lighthouse. Her breath became hot against her skin, sending smoke spiraling in the chilled air. It was getting easier to change now. She didn't have to reach for the element as she did before. It was there waiting for her, bubbling over with excitement to be used.

 She stood a few feet away from the old, lighter colored, wooden table that sat at the front of the Captain's Deck and raised her giant wings high. Gathering power within the core of her stomach and rising it up to the palms of her hands, she slowly sent out waves of fiery energy, crashing around her like a strong gust of wind. Andraste hummed against her back as if humming to the beat. The heat spread like wildfire, burning blue when it touched the wood of the ship. The mist around her was not so fortunate. It began to sizzle and pop as her wings red inferno of heat met the cool moist air. Suddenly dry mist surrounded her then slowly it dissipated. Rosey raised her wings and lifted off the ground sending waves of red hot heat flying through the air. The mist slowly, but surely, evaporated making a long wide path through the mist and fog. After about five minutes the fog and mist were completely gone. Rosey alighted back down on deck then turned to see Margaret watching from the second deck.

"Oh, Rosey, there you are. I was wondering where you'd gone. I went by your room and found you gone. I'm sorry, I should have stayed there. Well done, Keeper."

She sounded just as unemotional as Marine had, though her sentences suggested otherwise. Her eyes seemed glassy and untouched as if she was very bored. Rosey felt awkward talking to her because, with the lack of emotion from Margaret, it made what Rosey say sound like she was explaining something to a child and Margaret was definitely no child.

"Thanks Margaret, and don't worry about it, when I wake up I stay up."

"Good because you'll need to stay awake in case the fog comes back."

"No problem," she said watching as Margaret joined her at the Captain's Deck. Now that the fog was clear, the boat started up full speed and the waves crashed against the sides as the boat lurched forward. Rosey was still a little suspicious of the world around her, expecting one of her friends or loved ones to come out of nowhere brandishing a pitchfork. She giggled under her breath visualizing Rochell in a full out devil costume with horns on her head and a forked tail twitching back and forth, waving a pitchfork around like she was signaling a plane for landing.

Looking ahead Rosey gasped as a large rock came into view. Marine hadn't been joking; these rocks would have caused the ship a lot more damage than the storm had. Marine adjusted the ship expertly and they glided by unharmed. Rosey, for some reason, had the sudden urge to wave to it, but she sat down instead at the little table. Margaret joined her, her face a mask of unknown.

Rosey examined the water for a few moments, unsure of what to do. Upon seeing the water Rosey's head suddenly burst in pain. She grabbed her forehead, and leaned forward in her seat. The force of the pain was unlike anything she had felt before. No, it wasn't pain, it was pressure. An enormous amount of pressure was bearing down on, not just her head, but her whole body, spreading like wildfire. Rosey knew this pressure, it was the element. Before they had even reached the Third Sea she had begun to feel the touch of the element of water pulling at her. Before she had been put to sleep, she had begun to feel its power growing and the pressure that was, before, a simple annoyance had become a real distraction. Because of this she had been very happy about being put to sleep because it would mean that the ever growing influence of the water element would be quieted. Upon waking up, she had, once again, felt it nagging at the back of her mind like a child pulling on its mother's clothes and saying mom over and over again. Now, for some reason, it was screaming at her, as if it was trying to break free of something and get to her or was trying to communicate with her. She shook her head trying to clear it, but that only made her head ache more. She breathed deeply and tried to focus, but despite everything, the power kept jabbing at her. She quickly made it look like she was tying her shoe so that Margaret would not get suspicious. She leaned down over her knees and tried to mimic the motion but she was losing the battle. Thankfully, Margaret didn't seem to notice. She was staring off into the distance as if she had seen something. Her eyes seemed glassy and blank, though her body looked relaxed in its stillness.

Rosey was unsure of what these feelings were or whether or not they were normal for a Keeper, the Mother, Mercury had said as much. But what if they weren't? The thought echoed in her mind, a solid doubt. Rosey couldn't even begin to answer something like that. A burst of pain shot through her and she gritted her teeth, breathing deeply. She had to stop this or she would be useless to help Marine, then what would she do? The White Witch had said that she could control the effects that the elements had over her. Maybe she could lessen the strength of the power. She focused all her concentration and formed a mental barrier. Putting it into place she sent out a burst of fiery energy from within the crystal. Abruptly, everything stopped and the intense pressure was gone. It reverted back in on itself. She had successfully diverted and suppressed its power. There was still a slight hum in the back of her head, but it was weak and manageable. Breathing deeply she straightened and sighed with exasperation as if she had been dealing with a stubborn shoe lace.

Margaret was a still, solid figure against the growing mist and vapor. Rosey studied her for a few minutes, worried that there might be something wrong with her. It was so strange to see the happy woman so solemn looking with little to no emotion decorating her beautiful face. She then noticed that Margaret held a vile in her hands. The older woman looked away from whatever it was she was staring at and said rather out of the blue, "This drink will help ward off any hallucinations. I'm sorry I didn't get it to you before you left your room. I thought I would be back in time, but you woke up quicker than I expected. Make sure to keep your fire from burning out the effects." Without another word she held the bottle out to Rosey. Rosey took it and fingered the bottle in her hands for a few moments. It was like any other small, brown bottle she had seen before. It had an odd symbol on its front and a cork as a lid like a wine bottle. She stared at it for a moment then glanced at Margaret, awaiting instructions but she received none. Margaret was, once again, staring out into nothingness.

Rosey felt like she was the one sober person at a drunken party. Everyone else was indulging except for her. Looking at the bottle she shrugged; they wouldn't give her something that would hurt her. She tipped it back and slugged it down easily, enjoying the rich flavor that washed over her tongue. It was almost like sparkling grape juice, it had that richness but with an almost carbonated feel to it. It bubbled and popped all the way down her esophagus as if someone was doing a tap dance in her throat. Rosey's eyes watered slightly as the fizzing strength slid down to her

The Mystics

stomach. She almost choked on it, it was so strong. Looking at the bottle again Rosey leaned forward towards Margaret and asked her what was in the drink and how it would work. It took a good two minutes before Margaret even began to answer her. She seemed distracted and captivated by something that Rosey couldn't see. Rosey wondered if it was an illusion but she knew not to underestimate Margaret and Marine's abilities to protect themselves. Nevertheless she kept a close eye on Margaret.

When Margaret did answer it was so quick and garbled that Rosey had a hard time understanding it, but she got the gist of it. Margaret told her it was nothing but an alcoholic beverage mixed with an anti-damage drug that would protect her system from the alcohol but still allow the giddy effects, that way if a ghost tried to kill her she would probably laugh at it instead. Rosey wasn't sure how much of this was accurate, seeing as how strange Margaret was acting, but Rosey was willing to trust her. She wasn't too sure how she felt about drinking alcohol at her age but at least she knew she would receive no damage from it. After learning this, Margaret's comment about not letting the fire burn it out made a lot more sense. Rosey knew her fire Elemental State could be used to 'burn out' different types of poisons and drugs in her system, but only if she ordered it to, though it would act on its own if her life was in danger. She'd have to make sure not to let it do it this time.

Rosey settled at the old table and stared out at the sea, waiting for the fog to try and build up again. In the small amount of time it had taken for her to stop and drink the potion a thick layer was already settling. She waved her arm and sent out a burst of fiery energy. The gathering fog dissipated and returned to normal.

Looking back at Margaret Rosey wondered what it was she was seeing. Together they kept an eye on the returning fog. Even though Margaret seemed strange she was still alert and focused on their goal. Rosey realized that perhaps she was acting that way because she was putting all her energy and focus into watching for large rocks and returning fog. The effects of the drugs were unusual and probably affected people in different ways.

Oh, what would my uncle think if he heard I was doing drugs? she thought giddily. *I bet he'd want me to come back then...* Rosey's thoughts hit her in the face. Was she still that homesick? Or maybe... she just wanted to know what it was that was keeping him away from her. He was the only father she'd ever known, the only person besides her friends who'd stayed with her through it all and now, when she needed him the most, he couldn't be there with her! Rosey felt her body relaxing as the drug began taking effect. There was no sense in thinking about it. His reason for staying behind had to be vitally important or she knew he would not have sent her on without him. What could have been more important than her quest as the third Keeper? Rosey decided that she didn't want to know, one crisis was enough to deal with. She just prayed that, whatever it was, it wouldn't lead him towards harm.

Before the drink took full effect she wondered why they hadn't used this drink in the first place. Then Rosey realized that though there was an anti-damage drug mixed with it, the alcoholic properties probably did a fabulous job of making you woozy and woozy people could fall off boats easily without supervision. It was most likely for this very reason that Margaret was staying with Rosey until the drink wore off, which would be around the time that everyone else was ready to be awakened. Rosey folded her arms behind her head and gazed out into the sea, waiting for the fog to try and roll back in.

Once the drink had taken effect Rosey slipped into a happy state, still aware of her surroundings and responsibilities, but fizzy with joy. During her three hours of grogginess she only vaguely remembered some things that took place. She partially remembered getting up five or six times to clear away the fog again and she could have sworn that she'd told Margaret about how she could make a fortune on earth selling the alcohol vials. Margaret, from what she could garner from her fractured memories, had sat and listened quietly, looking ahead as always, not paying her any mind which had suited the harmlessly intoxicated Rosey quite nicely. Rosey even believed she had waved her hand in front of Margaret's eyes once to try and catch her attention but it didn't.

Rosey wasn't sure of all that happened but she remembered one thing in particular. Despite her wooziness her abilities were well in control. Rosey had jumped up whenever the fog rolled in and would blast it away in a burst of hot steam. She noticed that her fiery power had been hesitant as if it was aware of her giddy state and was being extra careful when carrying out one of her commands. Rosey had to admit, she was happy it did so. She could just see herself setting something on deck ablaze, then they wouldn't need her around, the whole bonfire on the front of the ship would be sufficient enough to destroy the fog instead of scattering it.

Once the three hours were up Rosey's mind started clearing and her giddiness began to dissipate. The drink left her system rather quickly and she soon no longer felt giddy, instead her body was calm and comfortably relaxed like lying in a hot bath. It was then that she noticed how tired Margaret looked. Her eyes had bags under them and her curly red hair was messy and tied back loosely with a red ribbon. She knew that Margaret and Marine had taken turns during their time in the Seventh Sea operating the ship. While one piloted and planned the other slept, cooked, and cared for the other. One slept mostly during the day while the other attended the ship, then, at night, the other took over. It was a system of teamwork that seemed to have worked since the ship hadn't crashed, yet it must have still faced its effects. Rosey felt sorry for them, having to adjust must have been hard on their already strained systems. Seeing Margaret made her wonder what *she* looked like.

As soon as Rosey's mind began to clear Margaret left her and went to retrieve her kit, it was about time to wake everyone up. She also confirmed that she'd be taking the anti-drug with Marine to bring back their emotions. She said this all with the same unemotional response that Rosey had heard before with a blank face and straight mouth. Rosey had long learned since joining them to look at their eyes for emotion instead of their expressions. For some reason their eyes still carried emotion even if their nerves refused to shift their faces into place. Margaret's eyes, however, had been very hard to read. She had spent most of the time staring out into the distance, looking at nothing and not bothering with any small talk. But every once in a while Margaret's eyes would flash with emotions and Rosey would be reminded of the passion behind those beautiful orbs.

Margaret returned about twenty minutes later carrying a container holding what looked like syringes and bottles full of liquids. Rosey watched as Margaret sat down and allowed the anti-drug she had taken to slowly bring back her emotions. After a few moments she was back to her old self, a beaming, motherly smile on her lips and a bright light in her eyes. She stayed sitting at the table and gave Rosey a stern but kind expression. Rosey vaguely wondered if she was making up for all that time her face was left emotionless? Seeing her serious face, Rosey believed it was an appropriate time to allow her fire element to burn the rest of her grogginess away. Once it did, she listened closely as Margaret began to explain how to wake everyone on board. Only when Rosey was able to repeat it back to her twice did they set out to wake everyone. Rosey reverted back to her normal form as she followed Margaret.

"What if the fog returns?" Rosey asked as they made their way to the living quarters of the crew. "We'll check every now and then, if the fog returns then you can stop briefly to burn it away then continue where you left off." "Are you sure we are out of danger of the illusions now?" She said, still a little jumpy. Her eyes seemed to think that every little shadow was a potential killer.

During the whole ordeal, Rosey had never even heard a strange whisper in her ear or a creak in the floorboards suggesting there might be something there that wasn't. No illusions ever approached her. According to what Margaret had told her, the drink she has taken was supposed to make her drunk-like to make the effects of the ghosts' useless, not prevent her

The Mystics

from seeing them. So why hadn't she seen anything? She was sure no one else had seen anything either. Marine hadn't said anything and neither had Margaret, but their potions could have been muddling their thoughts. Rosey was unsure, maybe she was just lucky or maybe she did have something approach her and not remember it. Whatever it was she was grateful for it.

"Don't worry Rosey, dear. We're very close to the island now, so the fog will be clearing up and we'll be safe from the effects of the curse."

About a four mile radius existed around the coastline of every body of land that was a Safe Zone. In this zone the effects of the curses did not apply and they were nearing the Island quickly.

Before Rosey was given the all clear to start, Margaret showed her what to do on the first crew member they came to. All it required was a quick poke in the thigh or the upper arm and that was that. The drug would do the rest. Rosey, at first, was unsure, but Margaret helped to guide her and by the third time Rosey had it down pat, although she seriously doubted she was qualified to be a nurse. Margaret told her that if she had any doubts or questions just to come and ask.

About an hour passed by as Rosey worked to wake everyone up. The Fog remained thick and powerful enough to require her attention every so often, but she could tell that it was starting to thin out. Finally, after another hour, she finished administering the last of the antidote. Margaret had been busy in the Animal Quarters taking care of the more delicate patients. Rosey was glad she didn't have to prick anyone else. She didn't have a strong hatred for needles but it still bothered her that she was pricking someone who was asleep.

She quickly disposed of the needles as Margaret had told her to and returned to the Captain's Deck to check on the fog. Even though the sun was coming over the horizon the fog still lingered, dimming the light. The good news was it wasn't as thick as before, but it could still cause some problems. Rosey had to admit that it was a little eerie feeling. She had spent so much time in it that she could almost feel it lingering on her skin, like it was trying to invade her. Dew drops scattered all over the place, sparkling in the dim morning light. It wasn't cold but the fog held a chill in it that Rosey felt lingering on her clothes. While administering the drug to the crew she had given the fire power a break and returned it to the crystal. Now, standing there in her leather and cotton outfit she could feel the slight cold biting at her where before the heat of her flames had kept her and probably Margaret warm. Despite her heavy coat over her leather jacket, the cold was seeping through. The small chill settled on everything and Rosey wished she could have some hot cocoa. Seeing that the fog was nowhere near blocking Marine's sight she quickly went to make her some. On her way she had the pleasure of seeing people coming out of their cabins as they recovered from their deep slumbers. They all groggily stumbled around each other in the hallways like some nighttime ballet. Rosey giggled, imagining them like human bumper cars. Hazel, Noly, and Nora were the first to emerge from the Animal Quarters since they were the smallest and it took less time for the drug to move around their bodies. They came barreling up from the first deck almost knocked Rosey over when they saw her mixing the hot chocolate with a spoon in her room. They had definitely missed her. Rosey laughed and wrestled with Noly for a bit, then kissed Nora and Hazel's foreheads being careful of Nora's blades. She marveled at their energy and their ability to walk without stumbling. Hazel then took her place on Rosey's shoulders, purring loudly as if she missed her favorite spot more than she did Rosey. Rosey sat down for a few moments enjoying the hot chocolate running down her throat. It took the edge off the cold and gave her some much needed sugar for energy. Once she finished she hopped back up to go check on the fog.

After Rosey's three trouble makers awoke pretty much everyone else was back on their feet and recovering. Rosey and Margaret ran in between the waking crew, getting them water, watching to make sure they didn't leave their rooms or the hallways until they were totally in control of their movements. As time went by others took their place and helped to make sure everyone was well watched and accounted for. Not only did Rosey spend time helping everyone to recover but she also ran back to the Captain's deck every so often to check on the fog. Happily, it seemed to be clearing as the sun came up, making her job easier. All this took a total of two hours.

When they finally were awake enough the cooks prepared a small meal for the ravaged crew and passengers. A large meal was out of the question, it was dangerous to feed someone who hadn't eaten for so long a large amount of food all at once. Rosey couldn't help but agree, although she was hungry enough to eat anything. What excited Rosey the most was that for the first time she was eating with the whole crew and not just the Captain and her friends. Since the crew had numerous schedules and different jobs it was unrealistic that they all ate together, this was one of the rare moments that they did, though the animals were still restricted to the Animals Quarters for their safety. Rosey was amazed at the level of fun and boisterous activity amongst the meal. Everyone was laughing and joking, it was much louder than it usually was when Rosey ate but the cafeteria was completely full this time, so not a seat was empty. She rather enjoyed it, she talked with a few crew members asking after them and if they were feeling all right after their long sleep. They accepted her words in kind and inquired after her as well. The meal passed by in much that way, filled with smiles and stories.

The island was now in sight. The fog and mist had cleared almost completely as the sun came up higher in the sky. The worst of the monster rocks were far behind them and dawn was rising quickly.

Rosey went back up to the Captain's Deck after the meal one last time to view everything and make sure that the fog was gone for good. She stood there staring out at the sea for a few seconds. She gazed at the smooth blue water and closed her eyes as a cool ocean breeze washed over her. Alone there, Rosey felt free, as if she was on a cruise and not some journey to save the world. Her body relaxed. She let the warmth of the sun warm her face, tilting it back as if she was going to start catching snowflakes on her tongue. Then it hit Rosey like an explosion. The pain shot through her head and tore through her consciousness. It took Rosey all but two seconds to recognize it. It was the water element. It was back, banging at her head and forcing its way into her without the slightest bit of a fight on her part. The ferocity of its attack was so strong that Rosey could almost imagine little fists inside her skull banging against its sides. She clenched her teeth and closed her eyes. Her whole body seemed to shake. Electric shockwaves forced themselves up and down her skin. She felt cold, so cold that it burned. She stumbled where she stood, her whole balance thrown off. Something wasn't right. Before, the water element had simply been happy to see her, greeting her like it was greeting a lost friend. Its influence had been an annoyance, a small problem that bounded at the back of her mind like an excited child. This wasn't just a result of her being closer to the island, this was something else. It was in full out panic. Yes, panic. That was the best way to describe it. The water element was acting panicky. She could almost see it in her mind racing over large rapids destroying everything in its path, unable to stop. This wasn't a simple annoyance, it was painful and it was strong. Rosey felt the pain as sharp as knives cut through her thoughts slicing them into little pieces, leaving her exhausted and strained. She breathed deeply, gulping down the air believing that if she took in enough that the pressure would overpower the strength of the water's power.

 This wasn't a greeting, Rosey could tell that much. This was something else. She tried to focus, tried to calm her racing heart and focus on what the element was doing. She had never felt so helpless. After a few seconds that felt like hours Rosey began to see something in the waves of water that seemed to crash around her. Small torrents and furrows in the water seemed to copy a pattern of speech like the way some radios had five or so bars that would stretch and lower according to the sounds on its screen.

The water was trying to talk, trying to tell her something. She could only guess it was something bad. But no matter how hard she tried she couldn't understand what it was trying to say.

At the corner of her eye she caught a flash of movement near the stairs. She was vaguely aware of Alex and Rochell coming to join her. When they saw her, bent over and out of balance Rosey heard their steps quicken and, though she could not see them, she imagined they would have worried faces. Rosey could barely hear them as they asked her if she was okay, their voices sounded muffled and out of focus. Rosey shook her head. Rochell ran her hand up and down Rosey's back soothingly while Alex held her steady and helped her to her knees before she fell over. Rosey felt helpless, completely at the mercy of the element but it wasn't showing her any mercy. Couldn't it tell that it was hurting her? Rosey wasn't so sure, but in its panicked state it might be just as confused and scared as she was.

Then an idea struck Rosey so hard she imagined it would have knocked her down if she wasn't already kneeling. Carefully, she steadied herself, then reached deeply within and pulled out the fire element. Her hand wrapped around the crystal and the warmth of fire flooded her body immediately. Happily, it encircled her body racing through her arms and legs. Fire seemed to flow from her fingertips and set her hair aflame. Rochell and Alex jumped away in surprise, though the fire would have never harmed them. Her back split open and the bones of her wings formed, attaching to her sinew and skeleton. The cold power of the water element was suddenly melted away, though the pain and the panicky strength remained. It seemed to shrink in the presence of the fire element, as if Rosey's connection to it scared it. The fire power blasted through her body and warmed her from head to toe. Her body grew in height and her muscles doubled in size. Rosey felt heat coursing through her every pore as she always did when she transformed. Her breath rolled from her lungs in hot bursts and embers began to fall all around her as dew began to sizzle and drip onto her giant wings. The heat was so strong that Rosey felt as if lava, instead of blood, was pumping through her veins and a sun was beating in her chest, slowly rotating the molten heat around her body.

Her senses seemed to be kicked into overdrive as soon as the fire element recognized another element's presence. The two elements seemed to regard each other. They swirled around each other in a mix of blue and red, so fast that the color purple could be seen in Rosey's vision. One had already been accepted into Rosey's embrace, the other was causing her pain. The fire inside her seemed to grow hotter, but Rosey soothed it and slowly relayed her instructions. *If I can't understand it, then maybe another element can,* Rosey thought. The fire power seemed to growl at the water and it in turn backed away. It sent vibrations and ripples through its surface, like it had been doing before. This time what the ripples said was clear, so clear that Rosey wondered why she hadn't been able to understand it before. The realization of what it was saying rang across her thoughts. Her whole body seemed frozen in place, where before it had been wobbly and unbalanced. Her two friends, who had stood by helplessly unable to assist her, regarded her uncertainly. Rosey could barely see them she was still staring at the words that blared like neon signs across her consciousness. They were so clear, so powerful that Rosey was almost knocked to the ground by it. Two words flashed through her mind, repeating over and over again: Blood Gorons.

Chapter Twenty-Four: Attack

Rosey was still frozen when the realization sunk in. Another word sounded out behind the first ones, it said 'coming'. Suddenly, like a bucket of cold water being thrown in her face, she leapt up high sending embers raining in all directions as she gracefully settled on the ceiling of the Captain's Quarters. She extended her wings out to their full length. The sun shone through them casting fiery shadows on everyone milling about on the decks. All eyes turned to her. The Shanobie Crystal gave off a faint hum of power as Rosey took a deep breath and yelled out to them in the loudest voice that she could muster, "BLOOD GORONS ARE COMING! EVERYONE GET READY!"

Marine suddenly burst out of the room and looked up at her. His face filled with fear. Everywhere there was sudden chaos as people immediately started running in all directions. Margaret appeared and began barking out orders while Grey and Wolvereen took over on the other decks. Everywhere Rosey could hear people drawing their weapons and readying themselves. Rosey's mind flew back to the first time she'd experienced a battle, the battle in the woods outside the cave systems. Rosey felt her heart suddenly drop at the idea but no one was running to pin her to ground, not this time. This time, she was the Keeper and she was here to fight! She clenched her fists and felt the fire element flare up inside of her. It was time to make her stand.

"Rosey, my Keeper, are you sure of this?" said Marine as she lighted down back onto the Captain's Deck. He didn't look panicky, just unsure and almost pale, as if he had seen something he didn't want to see. Grey had told her about what had happened to Marine's family. They had been killed at sea by Blood Gorons. She could only imagine what was going through his head right now. She could almost see his past unfolding in his eyes and the memories of his parents flash across his face.

"Yes, the water element told me so," she answered back not bothering to worry about his state of mind. He was a Captain, he would handle it.

He stared after her, confused. He studied her for a bit, a little surprised, but composed himself. Rosey could understand, she had not collected the water element yet, so, how then could it have told her anything? Rosey was glad that he said nothing and did not question the validity of her claim. Margaret appeared by his side her weapon drawn in one hand and her wand held in the other.

Seeing her, Marine wasted no time, "Margaret, guard the Animal Quarters. Tell Grey he is to take the port decks and Wolvereen is to take the starboard decks. I will relay orders as time goes on from my position here. Go."

"Yes sir!" she said turning briskly and running off.

"What about the ship, aren't we getting close to the shore?" said Alex coming up from behind Rosey, his wand drawn.

"I'll stop the ship. Don't worry, we're at an advantage. Blood Gorons fight better on land then in water." He sounded confident and not in the least bit worried, but still, Gorons were nothing to laugh at and Rosey knew it. This was going to be some battle.

Out loud she said, "I'll leave it to you Captain." She made sure to put every strain of trust into her voice to boost Marine's morale, but the story of what happened to his parents and their crew came rushing at her all of a sudden. Blood Gorons may fight better on land but their numbers were what concerned her, hopefully there wouldn't be that many. This would be nothing like the forest battle, those had been Raptors these were smart, devious, Blood Gorons.

Snapping into action he plunged back into the Steering Room and slowed their speed. They went from full throttle to a slow crawl, simply to steady the battlefield. Slowly they began to turn and run along the shore of

The Mystics

the island. After a few moments they came to a steady stop. The shore was about 500 yards away, plenty of distance in case anything went wrong. They were inside the Safe Zone of the island so they did not need to fear the Seventh Sea's affects. They would be ready for battle when it came. Rosey studied the island. Now that the sun was out, it looked like any normal forested island. She searched for a castle but was unable to see one this far away. Focusing she turned her attention to her two friends.

She called to them, "Hey, guys!"

Both of them turned to her at once. Wind seemed to swirl around Rochell in waves and Alex was already busy making a shield around the ship with the other Magikins, one of them was probably Margaret. Rosey sent up a small prayer hoping that Margaret would look after Sarabie and the other horses while she was down there. Staring at her friends, she took their hands in hers. Her body tensed, this would be the first fight she would be in. Surprisingly she wasn't afraid, only apprehensive. Looking at them she said, "Watch my back."

The two of them glanced at each other and smiled. They nodded and said in unison, "Always."

Those were the only words she needed to hear. Rosey opened her fiery wings further and stood back to back with her friends. With the last large waves hitting the boat from their quick decrease in speed the world suddenly went silent. Everywhere Rosey looked she saw people and animals crowding the decks, their various weapons raised. Looking at her friends, Rosey saw Alex bowing his head, chanting something under his breath while his wand was out and at the ready as it had been before. His eyes were closed and he was focused on something. His lips moving in balanced rhythm and motion. Rochell had large wads of air swirling around her hands, at the ready for an attack. Reaching behind her, Rosey took a hold of Andraste's hilt. The sword hummed to life in her hands. She glanced at Alex in surprise. Where was the shield!? It should have been cast by now.

Alex's face looked drawn and a confused expression spread across it. What was going on. She wanted to ask, but feared disturbing him.

Rosey looked about her and saw that most everyone had a weapon drawn and were poised at the ready. The crew that was usually so busy was suddenly still. The silence was so thick Rosey could hear white noise echoing around them, causing a cold chill to run down her spine. Her body ached for some action. Suddenly doubts started to flare through Rosey's head. What if the element had been wrong? What if it had been lying? She doubted that, it wouldn't play around with her like that, would it? She extended her reach and opened up her consciousness to the water element. It hovered there looking scared and unsure of itself. Rosey imagined it as the image of a small child crouching in fear. She let the fire element talk with it. The two elements mingled for a few moments before the fire power returned to Rosey. But the fire had nothing to say; apparently the Water element was confused. It knew there were Blood Gorons nearby but it couldn't pin point where...something about them was unusual? She shook her head, she had to stay focused, she couldn't be caught off guard because she was trying to get information.

Then it happened, all around them heads began popping up out of the water! Rosey yelled it out as loud as she could that they were under water but it was too late. Their surprise worked, all around her Rosey saw people being dragged into the water by dragon-like creatures. Blood was spattered everywhere in just a short amount of time. Rosey felt herself go weak kneed as she stared at it, blood. Rochell and Alex jumped into action. Alex sent swathes of concentrated energy at the Blood Gorons saving a warrior who was about to be grabbed by one. Now that the initial surprise was over, they backed away from the edge of the decks and made the beasts come to them. They wasted no time in doing so. All along the decks the monstrous beasts came out of the water, almost slithering like snakes. Suddenly, as one, the beasts let out a blood curdling scream. What had once been silence was now a deafening, high pitched concoction of caterwauling. Soon the screams of the crew joined the Blood Gorons' screams melding into one horrid symphony. Their screams were not only being used to cause a loud noise, they were also creating a distraction. It was working. People couldn't handle it and slowly their ranks began thinning. Rosey couldn't see Grey and Wolvereen furiously barking out orders along the decks, trying to rally their warriors. All she could see was the blood spattered against the side of the ship running down it like the rivers on a map.

The Blood Gorons, though distracted by the fighting crew members, where after one thing and one thing only: her. Rosey shone like a beacon with her fiery wings and outfit against the dark wood of the ship. A large group of Gorons took to the skies and plummeted down to get at her. Rosey stared at them frozen, then she saw something different. She saw the people on the decks, the people in the city, all staring at her wanting her to succeed, knowing she was their last hope. It was just what she needed. Clutching Andraste tightly she watched in satisfaction as the red hot blade severed the legs off the approaching Gorons. They screamed in pain and crashed over Rosey's head and onto the deck. Rosey turned and launched herself at them. Quickly she cut off their heads with three quick strikes of Andraste, ending their misery. They may be evil but torture was torture. Turning she eyed the sky, where Gorons were beginning to perform aerial maneuvers. One particular group was forming above to watch the action from below.

She turned to her friends, "You guys okay without me?"

"Sure," said Rochell as she twisted the air around one flying Goron making it fly into another approaching Goron. The two tangled into one another then hit the side of the ship sliding into the water.

"Don't worry about us, you go on ahead. Show them that the Keeper is back." said Alex. He blasted a spell at an approaching Goron then whipped his wand in an arch that sent a stray box flying at it. The box hit it dead on shattering into a million splinters which all then jammed themselves into the Goron's body. She had no idea why the shield had failed, but had no time to ask or distract Alex with it. She assumed there was a reason.

"Okay, she said, awed and amazed at her friends abilities. Turning to stare at the flying Gorons she thrust up her chin and said cockily, "Who's next?"

They stared down at her, their red eyes narrowed in concentration. They seemed to be studying her and strategizing the best way to attack. Some seemed confused by her look, as if they had never seen it before and that made them hesitant but Rosey didn't care, all that mattered was how she was going to kill them. A group broke off from the thirty or so Gorons that had taken to the skies, a good twenty where coming her way. Rosey smiled. It seemed animalistic in a way, but it made her feel strong. Immediately, she felt the heat rise within her. Her wings fanned out, casting fiery shadows. She gathered the fire powers within her chest and felt the heat rising, it boiled and surged against every organ and every blood vessel. It felt as if blisters had suddenly sprung up inside her, searing her body from the inside out. Her heart ached and Rosey could almost imagine the muscle melting away into molten rock, the blood heating to a boil and slipping though her veins, scorching its way into the deepest crevices of her body. In a few seconds she was ignited in flame. Suddenly her whole body temperature rose and the energy scorched its way to the surface of her skin. Alex and Rochell, who were fighting close enough to feel the sudden change, backed away, taken aback by the sudden intense heat. They turned to her surprised, and so too did everything and everyone else. So hot was the heat that it spread from Rosey like a wildfire, making the temperature rise several degrees, but that heat was nothing compared to what was building within Rosey. It scorched the sides of her throat and made steam roll out from her skin. Her breath burst out in a haze of smoke and embers, speeding around her in a fog of ash and soot. Andraste hummed with excitement, its blade so hot that it glowed white. The engraved woman on the hilt seemed to be screaming and the image of Adina seemed to be flapping her wings in triumph. Focusing Rosey filtered as much heat as she could into her chest. The energy grew there until it was as powerful as a sun, twirling and flinging its energy at her ribs in desperation to be let loose. Rosey intended to do just that. With as much momentum as she could she thrust her head back and let loose an inferno of fire from her mouth. It was so hot that Rosey herself could feel the heat tearing at her skin and making her lips crack like the desert ground after it had been parched for way too long. Rosey's chest began to glow like the rising sun. It beat there pulsating forth a rhythm of synchronized fiery power. The rhythm turned into shock waves that traveled from her throat and across the fire bomb she was releasing above the ship. Wherever the shock waves hit, destruction followed, but they weren't needed. The fire had been so hot that before it had even reached them all, the Gorons, including the ones that had held back, were incinerated in a matter of seconds. Not a drop remained of them, but, nevertheless, Rosey spewed forth her volcanic dance. Beneath her feet the wood of the ship cracked and splintered as a magnitude of pure power flowed from Rosey's body. The whole ship shook violently, like a volcano erupting. Magma began to leak from Rosey's mouth and drip to the ground, staining the wood at her feet.

Suddenly, as quickly as it had started, it stopped. Rosey closed her mouth and the inferno crept back within. Rochell and Alex watched her, completely filled with fear. They were blown away, unable to speak, or move. Everywhere there was silence, not a fight was still going on. Everyone seemed completely frozen in utter terror and amazement. Rosey turned to them and her friends gasped. She was as white as could be from head to toe, outlined in a faint red and yellow hue that made her seem like the sun. Her outfit was still there, but it seemed to move and swirl about her of its own accord, as if resting on a lake of lava. Her long orange hair was no longer hair, but fire. Nothing could hold a torch to her eyes though. The pupils were missing entirely and all that was left was clear, unblemished white, rimmed in red and yellow. For lack of a better term, she resembled more of an alien then a human.

Rochell took a step forward, carefully examining her friend.

"Rosey," she said tentatively.

"Yeah," Rosey said, not exactly sure what was going on. She almost jumped at the sound of her voice. It was not just her own. There was another voice overlaying hers, it was deep and rough like the voice that the fire had at the volcano. It surprised her but she was completely unaware of how different she looked so she paid it no heed.

"Rosey, you're….you're….," Rochell said, searching for the right word. Then smiling she said, "…you're radioactive."

Rosey stared at her for a few moments before she burst out laughing. As always, Rochell was the first to recover, and recover with style. Looking at Alex, Rosey's heart fell. Despite Rochell's joke, he hadn't laughed. He continued to stare at her with fear on his face. Rosey stepped toward him and he stepped back. They stared at each other for the longest time, and then he seemed to come to his senses. He jumped forward and hugged her, completely unafraid of the heat pouring off of her. When his body touched hers, it turned blue and did not hurt him. Rosey pulled away and looked around. Everyone was still frozen, but things couldn't stay that way forever. Soon a crew member took a stab at a Goron while it was turned. And just like that, the fighting started up again. However, it was not fear that brightened their faces, it was hope. This wasn't the lost hope that Rosey had seen before at the docks and in Neran, this was better than that. This was pure, joyful, harmonious, and determined hope. In a few short seconds Rosey had given them something they hadn't seen for a long time: their Keeper. She was their chance to be at peace once again.

Feeling that responsibility surge up in her chest, she beat her wings powerfully and launched herself into the air. She looped around the ship, chopping at Blood Gorons as she went. Some strikes were fatal, some just proved enough to give a good distraction, and some saved the lives of crew members. No matter which, Rosey kept it up. Around and around she flew, blasting Gorons with fire, slicing off heads with Andraste, or punching snouts back into the ocean, but Rosey could tell something was wrong. Blood Gorons kept coming. No matter how many she cut down, more came. The black and red tide of blood thirsty monstrosities kept pulling themselves from the dark blue depths of the ocean, from afar they looked like a black wave banging against the ship. Rosey was aware of the limited amount of crew members here, there were way too many Blood Gorons for it to be a simple ambush by chance. This was a planned assault. These Blood Gorons knew she would be here. But how? Did they really know or was it something else? All too quickly, Rosey got her answer.

From behind a whistling sound grew until it became so loud it was like white noise. Rosey held her ears tightly, and flapped her wings irregularly, thrown off by the sudden noise. Her muscles grew weak with the unusual flying, she was about to light down on the deck for fear of falling when a blast of strong wind knocked her in the back and sent her reeling. She was caught by a strong gust of wind that flipped her over and over again, as if she was on a wheel going round and round. Her body then smashed into the top of the ship and rolled to the Captain's Deck. The splintered wood creaked with her weight, but held. Rosey was so dizzy she felt as if the world would never stop spinning, but more than that she was embarrassed. Before, she had been powerful and strong, now, with one gust of wind she had been knocked to the ground rather unceremoniously.

After a few moments the world stopped spinning and Rosey looked up into the hooded face of a floating figure. Rosey was unsure if it was a man or a woman for all but its eyes were covered in thick brown rags. It stared at Rosey with blank black eyes, dead and unfeeling. Rosey felt all the feeling drain from her face when she looked into them. They were like black holes, sucking in her energy. Rosey then realized that her energy wasn't the only thing that was being sucked in but so was all the air. She started to choke and could no longer breathe. Her fire flickered in and out as her fire encased form, which had frightened everyone and excited them only moments before, started to die out. Now it melted away, revealing Rosey's regular Elemental Form. This person was not deterred by her Elemental Form, as the Gorons had been, no, this person was only interested in one thing: how they could kill her. Rosey had no time to ponder the irony of this situation that had left a good thirty or so Blood Goron's incinerated a moment before, for the air was forever being ripped from her lungs and her fire. She gasped and collapsed to the floor, her breath viciously ripped away every time she tried to inhale. Her mind seemed to slow down and her body became numb as if her feeling was being sucked away as well. Her lungs seemed to shrivel in her chest, collapsing with nothing to fill them.

Just as Rosey's consciousness was beginning to peel away from her air came rushing into her lungs again as the floating figure was blasted in the side and sent reeling off the ship. Rosey gasped, taking in great gulps of air. Rochell ran past her firing two larger gusts of wind at the recovering figure. While the cloaked attacker was distracted by them, Rochell jumped off the railing into the air, hurling herself at the cloaked figure in a solid body slam. She then flipped them upside down, still gripping the person in her arms. Using the momentum of their flip she let go then swinging her outstretched arms inward she created a vacuum, sucking the person down fast, right into the water. The attacker hit the water at a high speed creating a resounding smack that could be heard echoing off the island that waited not too far away. Rosey was too busy greedily sucking in air to congratulate Rochell on one hell of a rescue when her friend floated down next to her. Rochell placed her hand on Rosey's chest and with small motions of her wrist helped the airflow in and out of her lungs. Even at a molecular level, elementals were very powerful.

"You okay Rosey!" said Rochell worriedly.

Rosey coughed, and found her throat to be parched and dry. She coughed again and felt blood slip down her throat. She tried to steady her breathing, but Rochell had that covered. She thrust a flask at Rosey. Rosey took it without hesitation and drank down a long swig. She was surprised to find that it was Winsewallow and not water. Rosey looked at her questioningly.

Seeing her face Rochell explained, "It's better for stuff like this."

Rosey wasn't sure what the 'stuff' was in this situation, but she trusted Rochell's know how when it came to all things air related.

"What..." she said, staggering over her words, "was that? Who...was that?"

She took another swig from the flask and felt her throat relax slightly. It felt good against her parched lips.

"That was an air elemental, and a powerful one too. Not even my dad can do what she just did. That was some wicked stuff," said Rochell, almost jealously. She licked her lips nervously, as if she wasn't too sure of the situation.

Rosey looked at her surprised, "She?"

"Oh, yeah, when I grabbed her I felt boobs. Whoops," she said, putting her hand to her mouth, "did that sound inappropriate."

Rosey laughed, "For you, not at all."

Rochell smiled. Rosey then saw just how beat up Rochell was. She had a long scratch on her side that drenched her clothes in blood but, from the look of it, it had already stopped bleeding. A claw mark on her forehead was also already dried and crusted over, other than that she was okay. Rosey wondered how Alex looked; he was mostly a long range fighter. She hoped he was okay.

Rochell glanced at her, "You let me handle her, she'll only suck your air away if you come near her again. I know how to combat that, but you don't. You take care of the Blood Gorons."

Without waiting for a confirmation Rochell leapt off the ship again. Rosey watched then gasped as the confirmed woman, still draped in brown rags, lifted herself out of the water to meet Rochell. Rosey felt her heart beat rise in fear for her friend but knew she had to trust Rochell's strength.

She wasn't so sure she liked all this. Who was the woman! There was no one on The World Within A World that would fight Rosey or go against her, and they'd especially not try to kill her, so who was she!? The answer was clear to Rosey, she had to be one of the rumored Minions she'd heard about. If a Minion had been sent then the Evil One must have known she'd be here! Or, maybe not, the cloaked woman could just be a sentry or a look out! She might have happened upon them by chance. Rosey was unconvinced, she had no answers right now. The woman could be anyone, they just had to fight back and hope for the best.

She watched helplessly, still trying to catch her breath. She weakly crawled over and propped herself against the wall of the Captain's Quarters. She still held the flask in her hand. She capped it and put it in her back pocket. Then Rosey realized that she was no longer fiery. Her wings were there but they were only half formed as if they were caught between growing from her back and being sucked back in. Her long hair was black with red patches here and there. She wore the top half of her fiery outfit while she wore the leather pants and boots of her normal outfit. Gone were the fire armor and the tendrils of smoke. This woman, whoever she was, had almost blown Rosey's element out. She was only half transformed.

Focusing, she searched deep within her for the fire element. She found it, but when she inspected it her heart grew cold. The element was small and shrunken, as if its life had been stripped from it. It was a small flame, with a faint blue glowing haze. It flickered and sputtered weakly against the corners of Rosey's consciousness, like a weak candle ready to go out. Rosey felt its sadness and its fear. It had almost died with Rosey. Rosey's brows furrowed. Died? How would her death have caused it to die? She studied the small flame. What had, only a few moments before, been a raging proud inferno was now a small flickering flame. Rosey reached out her consciousness and touched it, gently. It stirred at her touch and seemed to grow warmer by her presence. She knew, without words, that it would be a while before her fire power would come back to her. How long that would be she wasn't sure. Rosey laid her head back against the wall, her head pounding as she pulled away from her vision. She slowly let what was left of the power slide away back inside her, hoping that it would replenish itself faster that way.

Dead ahead, she watched in awe as Rochell and the woman became locked in an air battle demonstrating the skills of two obvious masters. For a few moments Rosey was mesmerized by the sheer silence of their attacks. Not a sound could be heard as pure gusts of wind were turned into deadly punches or stray sharpened wheels of air. Frustratingly, Rosey was utterly helpless to aid her friend, she couldn't stand doing nothing. Without her power what could she do? Then the sun caught the reflection of something shiny. Staring, Rosey saw Andraste, embedded in the wood not too far away where she had dropped it when the air had smashed her into the ship. She wasn't helpless. Quickly she launched herself at it and felt it vibrate in her hands. It could feel her adrenaline pumping, for that was the only thing keeping her going now.

Rosey swung herself over the railing and dropped to the second deck then jumped again to the first deck this time landing on the back of a Blood Goron. It buckled under her sudden weight. There in front of it was Alex. He had made his way down to the bottom deck where the Gorons were most prominent. He stopped mid spell, his wand raised and ready to fling the magic her way. Rosey ducked out of the way, just as another Blood Goron took her place. Alex released the spell upon seeing it and it went flying backward, shrinking to the size of a mouse before falling into the water. Rosey raced forward and chopped off the head of the Blood Goron she had ridden a few moments ago and then patted Alex on the back.

"We make a great team."

"What happened?" he asked, looking her up and down, a look of concern spread across his face.

She quickly explained, helping to defend him as three other Goron's reached up out of the water. Alex kicked the head of one to disorient it, and then sent a spell at it. Its body crumpled in on itself as if it was surrounded by a vacuum. What was once a Blood Goron was now a ball. He then flung that ball at a flying Blood Goron coming in from above. Rosey sliced Andraste through the remaining two then cut the head off another as it pinned a crew member against the wall next to them. He thanked her then dived back in, swinging his katana relentlessly.

Rosey licked her lips, tasting salty sweat. With the fire element, she did not have to worry about sweat but right now she was just another warrior with a sword, the fire element safety tucked away and hopefully recovering. Rosey slashed and diced next to Alex for a good few minutes hoping that as each minute passed by the element was growing stronger within her. Time seemed to fly by in a whirl of slashes and cuts. Hot black blood spattered everywhere and drenched everything. There were so many bodies that Rosey and Alex had to lift them and dump them into the water. Other warriors up and down the deck were doing the same, though the tide of Gorons never ceased. For the first time since coming here, Rosey was battered, bruised and covered in small scratches. The Blood Gorons were powerful but small enough to easily kill and overpower, however they knew how to scratch you up good. Rosey received scratch after scratch but gritted her teeth and moved on, remembering every blow that her friends and the Goddess had taught her. Rosey knew the wounds would plague her later, but for now adrenaline was keeping the pain at bay.

She glanced over at Alex, "What happened to that shield you were making before?"

He seemed annoyed by her question and a bit ashamed as if he'd done something wrong, "Not sure, it was all going well but then it sputtered out as soon as they started attacking. I don't know why it would do that." He paused as he sent a bolt of lightning through the middle of a Goron,

The Mystics

leaving it sizzling in the water. "It's never done that before…none of my spells have ever done that before. I…don't understand."

Rosey could see him struggling with not knowing why. He probably wanted to get to his books or ask Thera, his mentor, what he could have done wrong. Perhaps the Gorons were only serving to annoy him since they were keeping him from knowing the truth. Rosey smiled, it must be something else to be so smart and capable.

"Perhaps there is not enough magic around to support such a shield?" she ventured, trying to get him from blaming himself. She sliced through a Goron then kicked one's head that appeared over the side of the railing. It lost balance and fell back into the water.

"No, not at all. I checked the levels before I attempted such a spell, just to be sure there was enough. There's plenty. It doesn't make any sense." He tipped his wand upward and sent two Gorons flying backwards into two other flying ones, dead on. Vines appeared from nowhere and entangled them. They fell to the water and sank. "I mean, there was enough right before the Gorons appeared…maybe something has zapped the area of magic…I just don't know!" He yelled out as he aimed a conjured sword at a Goron. It diced it into three, then puttered out of existence. "I can use small spells, but large ones seem to be evading my ability…"

Rosey nodded but had no advice for him. He was the magic expert, if anyone could figure it out he could. She did not have time to try and work through things that even a master at the craft couldn't figure out, but it did sound to her as if the area had been quite suddenly drained of a lot of magic. She knew that there were some natural occurrences that could drain areas of magic, but they were rare. Still, with the island being so close and its history being so unpredictable she wouldn't put it past it to be the source of the problem. She frowned, she just hoped whatever magic was left over was good enough for the magikins they had on board with them to continue the fight.

Rosey kept on fighting, her vision blurring with nothing but the death of her next victim in her eyes. Only a sudden shout of orders from a commanding officer made her look away from her onslaught. A large group of warriors were holding off the Blood Gorons that had left the water and were attacking from the second deck, trying to get down to the crew on the first deck from behind. Rosey realized quickly that this was a losing battle. The only thing stopping the Gorons was the line of warriors battling them from the railings and each time one fell that meant more Blood Gorons would have to be killed by others.

Desperately Rosey tapped Alex on the shoulder, though they fought on, she could tell he was listening.

"Is there any way we can get a shield up, we have to stop them and re-group or we'll lose! She shouted over the turmoil.

Alex nodded vigorously, swinging his hand wildly at three Gorons he made them swing around each other than, dropping his arm abruptly, he sent them crashing into the ocean. Salty spray mixed with the blood at their feet and a growing reek was beginning to fester in the mixture. Rosey wrinkled her nose but fought on.

"Margaret, myself, and the rest of the magikins could...possibly create a shield if we combined all the magic stored in our wands...but I have no idea how much they have stored...and on such a large ship! No, a shield is out of the question." He talked in broken sentences as he thought, fighting the whole time. He held his wand in one hand and his dagger in another. "Rochell, however, can widen a Ward Spell. Wards act in the same way as shields, but..." he paused to take care of an attacking Goron, then jumped right back into his tale, "...but they act more like deterrents and traps then impenetrable barriers. They can be stretched like rubber around the ship. That might hold them off for a while. I'm afraid that without Rochell I can't establish a barrier effectively since the amount of magic seems to have faded. We need her back in order to make it work."

"She's a little busy right now. I'll see what I can do."

The Mystics

With that Rosey leapt away and left Alex to continue on his own. She hoped he'd be all right. She flung herself around a bend and then found a small niche. There she rested and focused on the fire element within her. It was no longer a candle flame but instead a small bonfire. It was still weak but strong enough. Rosey thanked the heavens then quickly transformed. Bursting forth she sent two hot jets of energy at the Blood Gorons. They fell back, screaming as their bodies were badly burned.

Rosey kept at it, fighting against the unending mob of Gorons all the while trying to think of a way to help Rochell and possibly get a shield up when suddenly she saw something no friend should ever have to see. Hovering above the water was the brown hooded woman and in her arms was Rochell. The woman had her hanging there by the arm, her body limp and unmoving. Rochell had a long bloodied scratch running from the top of her left shoulder to her opposite hip. Blood drenched the entire front of her body. Rosey feared… prayed… anything, that Rochell wasn't dead. The woman's eyes glowered evilly and Rosey noticed with some satisfaction that she wasn't completely without injury. Her right shoulder was scratched leaving the brown rags covering her drenched with a mixture of blood and sea water and her feet looked as if she had walked through a briar thicket. The woman's eyes caught a hold of Rosey's and didn't let them go. Rosey held her ground trying to force every bit of hatred into them as possible. Rosey gasped as a wicked gleam flashed in the woman's eyes as she dropped Rochell, letting her fall tumbling towards the ship.

As she watched Rochell fall, Rosey felt an unimaginable anger rise within her. Fiery power burst forth from her body sending out a sudden shock wave of heat. Everywhere Blood Goron's fell to the ocean dead, half their bodies incinerated. Rosey beat her massive wings, sending embers and licking flames in all directions. She shot forward like a rocket straight toward the woman. Hatred burned through her, her emotions fueled her element on, giving it the energy it needed to burn brightly. She felt an animalistic flush of heat burn through her. Suddenly her mind snapped to attention. *Stop Rosey, think! If you get too close, she may use that vacuum again and you'll die. Calm down and think!* She had to distract her or she'd just prevent her from getting to Rochell, she told herself sharply stopping in midair.

To Rosey the moments lasted like hours as Rochell was falling in slow motion. She eyed the woman, searching for a weakness, wishing she had the air element. The woman couldn't suck away her air because she was too far away, Rosey remembered Rochell saying that air elementals can have trouble with distance. Rosey knew what she had to do. Taking Andraste she pumped a large amount of energy into the blade. It hummed to life and turned a deep orange, its hilt glowing slightly. The woman's eyes widened, suspicion furrowing her brow. With a powerful swipe Rosey flung the sword around in front of her in an arch sending a crescent moon shaped energy blast right at the woman. She gasped but had no time to block. It hit her right in the stomach flinging her back a good 100 yards.

As soon as Rosey had released the blast she had folded her wings and plummeted down to Rochell. She grabbed her in midair then swung around abruptly and angled back to the ship. Her fire powers searched Rochell frantically and Rosey cried with delight when she discovered a heartbeat. Rochell was still alive. Rosey quickly burned Rochell's wounds to stop the bleeding, though it was little. It seemed that Rochell was only exhausted, not mortally wounded. Rochell didn't stir when Rosey cauterized her wounds, it either meant she was too tired to awaken or she was hurt in another way. There was nothing that could be done now. Rosey was going to have to face the evil woman alone, whoever she was, but first she needed to do something for Rochell. Rosey wasn't sure where a healer was so she flew down to Alex with Rochell gripped in her arms. There, Blood Gorons were greedily trying to get over the railing and Alex was faltering. He too was now covered in scratches. Angling her wings outward Rosey twisted her body in a circle. The hard, sharpened tips of her wings sliced through the Blood Gorons and sent them falling back into the ocean or onto the deck in a bloodied mass of bodies. Alex fell back as she landed, taken aback by her sudden change and her brilliance. Rosey encased them in her fiery wings, letting their inferno protect them from any Blood Gorons.

"Here," she said, handing him Rochell's limp body. "Look after her. I'm going to stop this!"

Alex nodded and took Rochell placing her behind him, he cast a small barrier around her. It looked blue and revolved around Rochell's body in rings instead of the pinkish shield Rosey was used to seeing. It must be a ward instead of a shield. Rosey had little time to question it. With Rochell out for the count, Alex's idea was as well. The only thing Rosey could do was find another air elemental. Her mind rushed through all the names of the crew members and their powers but Rosey's mind went back to the woman instead. If she didn't handle her, they'd be dead anyway. Alex watched as Rosey pulled away, her bright large wings vibrant against the ocean background.

Rosey turned her attention to the woman again. By now she had regained herself and was heading back. Rosey readied Andraste for another blast of fire when the air in front of Rosey began to swirl into the shape of a vortex. Rosey stared at it confused, then realization hit her as the figure of a horse burst out of the portal and sent a blast of searing lightning right at the woman. The woman veered wildly allowing the lightning bolt to just barely miss her, her eyes darted with fear as Ysandir stepped out into the open from the vortex. The lightning bolt crashed against the sky, sending a resounding bomb over the waters. Its yellow hue had been tinged with blue and seemed very strange but like all lightning bolts, it was too quick for Rosey to adequately examine. Rosey blinked seeing the residual light create a temporary image across her eyes, like when you looked at the sun accidentally. *Well thanks for coming Ysandir, but now I'm blind!* she thought, irritably, rubbing her eyes frantically.

Ysandir turned toward Rosey abruptly. Her words came out in rushed tones. It was obvious she was feeling very guilty, "Oh Rosey, I'm so sorry it took me so long. We just discovered what…when…oh please forgive me. I should have come to you a long time ago, but I didn't…oh…I…"

"Ysandir!"

Ysandir stopped mid speech, taken aback.

"Less talking, more fighting. You can explain things later. I'm going to try and figure out what I can do about these Blood Gorons. You take care of her," said Rosey pointing a menacing finger at the woman who was floating about 200 yards away, watching the unicorn with weary eyes.

The unicorn looked happy to have something to do and threw herself after the woman without a moment's hesitation. Rosey watched, mildly pleased to see the woman dodge clumsily and focus all her energy on staying away and defending herself rather than attacking. After seeing Ysandir's attacks, Rosey wasn't so sure she could smile at the woman's misfortune. Ysandir would gather energy in her neck where it formed into a massive ball at the back of her throat that would bulge outward, then it quickly traveled up her neck until it reached her mouth which she opened wide. She gathered the energy outside her nostrils then the energy would fling itself at the woman so fast that Rosey wondered how she was able to dodge it. Ysandir could fire these relentlessly. Rosey watched her fling thirty of them at the woman one right after the other without breaking a sweat. The woman was clearly tiring. She, in a last attempt, sent a few pockets of air at the unicorn only to have two lightning bolts capture them in a lightning ball and swing them back at the woman, this time supercharged. The woman frantically swung them away with two whirlwinds, the effort throwing her off balance. She righted herself then floated there, panting hard, obviously outmatched by the unicorn. Rosey nodded and turned her attention to the boat. The people needed Ysandir's help more than they needed her fighting the woman, but, at that moment, Ysandir was probably the only one powerful enough to face the woman. She hoped that the unicorn would finish her off quickly.

Rosey sped through the air, beating her massive wings in perfect rhythm as she soared around the ship. She surveyed the damage from above and cast her attention on the group of people holding off the Blood Gorons trying to attack from the second deck down onto the people holding off the Blood Gorons on the first deck. One group was failing, their people being killed one by one. Rosey quickly dived toward them. As she neared them she came in from behind the Gorons then pulled up sharply and flapped her large wings with all her might. That one flap of the massive inflamed wings sent long billows of fiery energy straight at the backs of the Gorons. They screamed in pain, their bodies half burned, half intact. Rosey then fell on them with Andraste, the blade red hot and pulsating with each slash. It was holding true to its name: unconquerable. With Rosey there the group was easily able to dispel the twenty or so Gorons and then direct their attention to the first deck where their numbers were steadily falling. Some crew members stayed behind to watch and make sure that the Gorons did not try again, so Rosey left them to it and flew off to see who else needed her. Suddenly she was hit from behind as a Goron rammed itself into her. It dug its claws into her back and wings holding on for dear life as Rosey frantically tried to loosen its grip. She beat her wings with a massive effort as she was thrown off balance. She used that momentum to slam her back into the side of the ship. The creature let out a puff of air as the wind was knocked from it, but to Rosey's dismay, it hung on. The creature then roared in her ear, a blood-wrenching scream that seemed to vibrate its way down Rosey's body. Then, while she was distracted, it bit down hard into her shoulder. Rosey screamed in pain as the monsters teeth ground their way through muscle and touched the bone of her collarbone. She did the only thing she could, she stopped in midair. As soon as she did the beast went flying from her back and crashed into the deck. A few crew members disposed of it then looked up at Rosey worriedly. She alighted down and held her shoulder, bending under the pain. A giant fluffy head caught her as she stumbled. Shaking off her blurry vision she spied Grey, the father of Nagura. He helped her to her knees, the short sword he carried on his back grasped in his jaws and drenched with Goron blood. Twisting his head around, he expertly slid the blade back into its sheath then took a look at the wound. He sniffed it then licked it gingerly. Rosey squeezed her eyes shut at the excruciating pain. Then slowly, the wound began to grow numb. Rosey gathered fire energy in her hand then reached around and seared the wound closed. She held back a scream at the intense pain, like white hot liquid flowing down her back. The numbness helped. Whatever Grey had done, she was thankful for it. Straightening, she glanced at him.

"Hi Grey, how we do'in," she said in a slurred voice, the pain still lacing down her spine. Her wings didn't feel that good either.

Grey's eyes seemed to be unfocused, as if he was seeing something that wasn't there. His whole frame seemed to be shaking. His giant body belittled hers as they sat next to each other. His fluffy, yet skinny body, angular and muscular as it was, was covered in scratches. A giant bloody wound had been carved into his right shoulder, mixing with the soft grey pelt. She hoped it wouldn't cause him another limp like the one on his left shoulder did. When he looked at her his kind green eyes seemed lost and dulled with age. Rosey's heart fell when she heard his words.

"Rosey, we're losing this. I just came up from the Animal Quarters to find you. The Gorons are punching holes in the hull. We're sinking. There is not enough extra wood and magikins to help put them into place to fix the hull. The loss of magic isn't helping either...we just can't keep up! As soon as one hole is fixed, it is reopened as a Goron forces its way through. We have to evacuate. If we don't then..." he didn't have to finish.

Rosey let her weight fall against the ship. She hated this. She could do nothing. She was so strong before, now she was weak, battered, and bruised. Flashes of light burst against the sky as Ysandir and the woman fought on. Rosey couldn't see them to know who was winning. If the woman didn't have a few tricks up her sleeve then Ysandir would have

The Mystics

been here, helping her to figure things out. How would they evacuate now? The Gorons wouldn't let them and the island was too far away. Rosey let her head fall against the ship, her thoughts running wild. Then she looked at Grey. He was watching her with wide eyes, looking to her for hope. Hope. Rosey saw it there, deep in his eyes. He needed hope; he needed to believe in something, in someone. She had to be that person. Setting her jaw and clenching her fists she stood up tall. She lifted her chin and said,

"Get Marine to move the ship to the island, we'll transfer who we can from there. Do you know of anyone who is a decent air…"

She stopped mid-sentence as something caught her eye. A Goron was suddenly pulled back into the ocean by a bluish-green, scaled hand. Rosey crept forward and Grey followed her eyes, a strange expression crossing his face. At least she wasn't the only one to see it. Suddenly a Goron sprung out of the water and attacked a crew member. She leapt at it expertly wielding her katana but again, a clawed hand, this time painted shades of red and orange, thrust out of the water and grabbed the Goron dragging it back into the water. Air bubbles floated to the surface of the bloodied water, where the Goron had once been. Grey's ears pricked forward in astonishment, and then he dashed off towards the Animal Quarters. Rosey watched him go, and then took to the skies. She flew around the ship and watched as Goron after Goron was grabbed and dragged into the water. Rosey didn't know what to make of it, just that it was a miracle. Suddenly a large woman burst from the water wrestling with a Goron. The woman had long bluish black hair and red eyes. She had a heavily muscled torso and long extended arms with webbed hands. They were colored yellow and green with vibrant shiny scales running over the smooth lustrous skin. On her fine fingers there were sharp curved nails almost like claws. As the large woman twisted in the water she plunged the struggling Goron back into the ocean depths. Propelling her into the water was a long scaled tail. It hit Rosey then that these were mermaids.

Everywhere mermaids were reaching up with giant hands and bodies and pulling the monstrous Gorons back into the water and drowning them. Pools of bloodied water began to become more apparent around the ship as Gorons were stopped before reaching the surface. What the mermaids were doing to them to leave such bloodied pools was a thought Rosey didn't want to entertain for long. She was just thankful that the tides had turned.

Rosey quickly banked and rolled to the side sliding effortlessly onto the first deck in time to see a giant woman hoist herself gracefully over the railing and fling her large tail into the interior of the ship. She was the largest of the mermaids that Rosey had seen so far. To Rosey she looked to be a good twelve feet long, and that was including her long tail. She had long red hair and bright glowing green eyes. Her long hair was held back with a golden crown and all along her body was golden armor. Her arms, tail, and midsection were all covered in shimmering scales. They were a deep neon turquoise, so bright that Rosey almost had to look away. The turquoise on her arms darkened through different shades of blue as they neared her finger tips, painting the fingers a deep black color and then ending in crimson red nails. The same patterning continued on her tail, ending in a red tipped fin. Her face was long and perfectly angled with high cheekbones and soft curved lips outlined in a thin line of turquoise. The turquoise, once again, like on the tail and arms grew darker towards the inside of her lips till it was black. A slight yellow hue painted her skin in barely visible ornate patterns around her eyes and down her neck. Her skin was so pale that Rosey thought that the sun had burned away all imperfections leaving it flawlessly beautiful. Her long tail was much like any tail you would expect to see on a whale or dolphin except that the two halves of the tail were more curved and angled downward. In between the two halves were long feathery tendrils of thin fins whose tips were fringed in red. The ends of her long hair, which Rosey could barely see because the hair was so long, transformed at the ends into the image of colored seaweed and seemed to move of its own accord. Under her eyes were turquoise scales, some of which were tinted red. Above her eyes, black highlights gave them an intense animalistic feel. At first she thought that maybe the woman was wearing make-up but Rosey knew better than that. The colors were natural and applied themselves to her skin. Make-up couldn't come close to her beauty. Small perfectly rounded breasts were covered by a golden armor breast plate, but Rosey could tell that the scales covered her breasts as well.

None of the old fairy tales or legends told on Earth had given adequate descriptions of this beautiful creature. However, as in some stories, this mermaid indeed held an almost scary air of power. The clawed hands and the glowing eyes added to her captivating look and sent chills down Rosey's spine. She couldn't help but stare. Then the mermaid's tail began to change, slowly the two fins became feet and the long muscular tail split in two creating long muscular thighs and calves. There was no way to tell if the woman was naked she seemed to be wearing a skin tight bodysuit. She walked towards Rosey, her head barely lower than the floor of the second deck above them. She moved gracefully, her body fluid and strong, each muscle pronounced and tight under the smooth flesh. With a tilt of her head she addressed Rosey in a voice like silk.

"Hello Rosey, I am Queen Ashti, leader of the mermaids and a member of the Resistance. Sorry we are late, it is difficult to swim so far and there are not many portals underwater."

Rosey was unable to speak for a few moments, Queen Ashti waited patiently an amused smile crossing her lips. Rosey felt much like she did when facing the Golden and Silver Goddesses. She felt awkward and humbled before such obvious power. Rosey gathered her wits about her then bowed her head as was custom when bowing to a Leader of the World.

"Queen Ashti, it is good to meet you. Thank you for coming. We would have easily lost this fight without you."

The beautiful queen bowed her head as was custom for a Leader of the World. As the Keeper, Rosey had the same status as a Leader of the World and so she always bowed her head no matter who it was. Others who did not carry such a ranking would bow at the waist to show respect. This was the only form of etiquette Rosey had learned while at the palace and it seemed to be the only one The World Within A World followed. It existed solely as a physical way of showing respect and courtesy.

"Do not fear, young one," the Queen said with dignity, raising her head. "We are fierce in the water and easily stronger than these monstrosities. However, there is something that we cannot destroy." She fixed Rosey with her shining emerald gaze. "It lies beneath the water and is multiplying the Gorons. As long as it exists, the Goron's numbers will not falter."

At this Rosey could almost scream with joy and sadness. On the one side of things it was something that could be destroyed. She, at least, now knew that she had an answer to her dilemma instead of some large, hidden army numbering in the thousands. On the other side, it also meant that something was causing an army sized problem to rise up from the waters and attack her crew. Maybe it is what caused the magic to be zapped from the area, Rosey thought, suspiciously. Looking at the Queen determinedly she said, "How do we destroy it?"

"Not we, you. Only you have that power..."

"...But the wrong element," Rosey finished for her.

The Queen nodded, impressed. What was Rosey going to do? She didn't even know where to find the Water Element. She needed to speak with it.

She gave the Queen her most powerful gaze yet, not willing to let her see her fears. "I will try and contact the water element. In the meantime, the Gorons are putting holes in the bottom of the ship. Is there anything you can do to at least keep us floating?"

The large woman laughed knowingly, it sounded like rain falling on water, "Oh indeed, my Keeper, indeed."

With that she thrust herself back into the water with one giant leap. As soon as her skin hit the salty water her legs formed themselves back together and became, once again, the smooth long tail. Crew members who had stopped to stare at the large woman hurriedly went back to helping the large mermaids to attack the Gorons, though they hardly had to do much. The mermaids seemed to number in the hundreds. They sprang up out of the water with lightning fast skills, killing so many Gorons that their bodies began to create quite a dense array of floating carcasses. Still and lifeless in the water, some were only pieces of their whole, others had gaping wounds. Whatever it was that had seen the beasts to their end, the mermaids were viciously turning the tides. Many of the warriors, that had fought for so long, where given a break and were able to stand by and let the mermaids take control. The Resistance had sent a good army to help divert the Gorons, but, from what Queen Ashti had told her, the Gorons were a numberless group of creatures fighting their way to the surface. If she didn't destroy whatever it was that was multiplying the Gorons soon, the Queen's own army would tire and lose their ability to fight on, or worse, would be overrun and killed like the crew members had been but moments ago. They'd be slaughtered slowly but surely. She had to make her way to this thing that was copying them and destroy it, but first, she needed the water element.

Chapter Twenty-Five: The Water Element

Deep in the thralls of the Animal Quarters Hazel and Noly fought side by side against the Blood Gorons breaking large holes in the bottom of the ship. They bared their teeth, scratched with claws, and bit with sharp canines against the relentless tide. Hazel breathed deeply, trying to stay calm. When the battle had first started they had wanted to find Rosey to help protect her but Wolvereen had asked them to help defend the bottom of the ship where Gorons were forcing their way through trying to sink it. The horses and Eglen had, of course, been the first to witness the blood thirsty monsters and had quickly reported the ferocious beasts and what they were doing to the hull of the ship. Noly and Hazel agreed to help only because they were not in a position to argue and figured they could watch after Sarabie for Rosey instead. Nora, the newest member of their little group, was busy slashing and dicing the Goron's expertly with her long bladed shoulders and head. She might have been dangerous to play with but she made one hell of a fighter. Goron after Goron fell to her onslaught and she seemed to fight on with no regard to how much energy was being used up or how many times a stray Goron tail flipped her across the room. Every time she would lift herself back up and charge them with renewed strength. Hazel found herself growing jealous. She was the smallest member of this fellowship and so far had only managed to irritate the Gorons while Noly bit into their necks or their underbellies. Despite that, she intended to be as much use as possible and had to admit her diversions were working well with Noly's strike plans. She had to hand it to the dog, she might not be the smartest canine but she knew how to fight.

All around them water had started to rise as the Gorons dug out more and more holes. Margaret, the commander of the small army they had, was trying her best with magic to plug up the holes, but the Gorons were never-ending. Flashes of multicolored light zoomed across the room casting wildly colored shadows across the dancing water from Margaret's unbroken barrage. She was a whirlwind of red hair and flailing arms. Spell after spell hit their targets perfectly and yet the Gorons never ceased. The holes weren't staying filled and the water kept growing ever deeper. Hazel had never been a scaredy-cat of water but she didn't like it either, and being so little didn't help any. If they didn't do something, this was going to get hairy.

The horses and Eglen had joined them to help fight. They hadn't liked the notion of being protected when their sharpened hooves and claws could cause some damage, especially since Eglen was a part of the Resistance. Margaret was only too happy to let them join the fight. All three horses protected numerous holes, kicking the life out of any Goron that came up. They were vicious little creatures, but they were much smaller than any horse, especially Rosey's Sarabie. All across the interior of the ship the horses' whinnies of battle trumpeted out, echoing off the walls and the slowly rising water. The water was now up to Hazel's belly fur and it lapped there, a slow rhythmic reminder that she was going to be the first one to have to find higher ground.

A Blood Goron burst through the floor a few feet away, its small head creating another hole to add to their demise. Hazel hissed a warning then launched herself at the creature's head. It screamed in fury as she racked her claws down its face and into its eyes, bloodying them. It swung its head, its lower body, including its sharp claws, were still trapped by the wood of the hole, preventing it from scratching at her. Noly leapt at the creatures exposed throat, sinking her teeth in tightly but the creature rammed its head into Noly throwing her off of it and dunking Hazel into the water. Hazel resurfaced, spitting out the salty taste of the seawater, and swearing because some had gotten up her nose. She sneezed weakly then watched as the Goron, with bloodied eyes, pulled itself from the floor. Behind them the other Goron they had just killed was moved out of the way of the hole they had been defending and another Goron stuck its head up. It squeezed out and came at Hazel, scratching her side with black claws. Hazel hissed and turned in frustration, launching herself at its clawed hand. The creature screamed as she tore at it with tooth and claw, her bloodied side stinging as the salty water mixed into it. She hung on with sheer determination; there was no way she was going down without a fight. But the Goron was smart. It stopped trying to fling her off and instead tried to bite down on her. Hazel saw an opportunity and jumped off right before its jaws clamped over her. Its eyes grew large in surprise as it bit its own clawed hand. It staggered backward and rammed into another Goron behind it that was coming from the hole. The two plummeted into the rising waters.

Hazel was about to attack again but Wolvereen appeared, plucked them from the water in his massive jaws and bit down hard, easily breaking their necks. He dropped the lifeless bodies into the water where they floated. Behind her, Hazel could hear Noly grappling with the Gorons from the new hole. Wolvereen's huge bulk made Hazel feel inadequate, more than Nora ever had. He was there before her in his dazzling armored splendor, his fluffy muscled body rippling, though scratched and bloodied. At least he too was wounded. One large wound in particular made Hazel stop and stare. It looked as if a Goron had ripped off a chunk of Wolvereen's skin above his right leg. Hesitantly she spoke to him. His red eyes stared down at her neither happy nor annoyed by the little cat's presence.

"You look like hell. How ya hold'en up?" she asked, clawing the leg of an approaching Goron making it stumble. With a lightning quick flash of his teeth Wolvereen picked it up in his jaws and flung it into another group of Gorons a few feet away.

"I'm doing just fine, cat. You're the one that needs to watch out," Wolvereen said deep in his throat. Even now he was cranky. His voice sounded annoyed, as if this battle was just another practice exercise and their lives weren't really in danger. *Is this just a game to him?* she thought. *No, he's just used to fighting that's all.*

The Mystics

She said nothing else and, for once, Noly said nothing as well. She did not try to harass, annoy, or enrage the giant beast. She was completely focused on her enemy. She only gave the wolf a slight nod of her head to acknowledge that he was there and thank him for it, beyond that she did nothing. Hazel was impressed and purred in her chest, despite herself.

Wolvereen continued to help them fight the Gorons from the two holes and as time went by Hazel realized that he might have come over to them with the sole intention of helping them. Hazel didn't know how she felt about being looked after, but she was glad for it nonetheless. She had promised to serve Rosey and love her before she was ever the Keeper. She was not going to give up on that now. If she died, it would only make Rosey sad.

Finally the inevitable happened. Hazel could no longer stand in the water. She had to climb onto Noly's back. Noly didn't mind, it made it easier for them to attack as a team. Noly would submerge herself, leaving Hazel visible above water. Hazel would launch an attack and draw them in, and then Noly would burst up and attack them herself causing them to panic and back away. As the battle raged on, Wolvereen focused his attention on the old hole they had been protecting, allowing them to take care of the new hole. After a while he was suddenly joined by Grey. The other giant wolf was battered and bloodied as Wolvereen was but looked none the worse for it. Wolvereen whispered a few words to him then Grey went galloping unnaturally, because of his limp, up to the main floor in a hurry taking out a Goron as he went with a swing of his short sword. Where he was going, Hazel could only guess.

Hazel turned back and eyed her surroundings. The horses were still alive and well, though they had all received scratches and bite wounds. Eglen was proving to be very helpful taking out multiple Gorons with the skills he'd developed over years of training in the Resistance. She and Noly were doing all right, despite her side wound and Noly's numerous cuts while Wolvereen was doing more than fine with his large bulk ever present amongst the rising tides. Nora was still going strong, slicing through the Gorons and trying to find ways to block the holes with large furniture and such. It was only the crew members that seemed to be faltering. Some were floating in the water dead, while others were trying to stay out of the fighting, holding a horrid wound or a broken appendage. Whatever it was, the humans weren't faring so well.

The salty water stung her eyes and made her nose itch. Her fur was wet and dried in some places with a thin layer of salt. It stuck to her pads and made her already wrenched claws sting with pain. Hazel gritted her teeth, they were all suffering. She shook her head to clear her pain and prepared for Noly to submerge herself as another Goron began to surface. Just then she heard something that stopped both her and Noly in their tracks. It was Nora. She was screaming so loudly that everyone, including the Gorons, was looking at her in bewilderment. She was jerking herself around in strange movements as if something was on her body that she wanted off. She swung her head from side to side and howled in pain. Hazel desperately searched her for a wound, but she had none that looked to be life threatening or a cause for such extreme pain. What was Nora doing? The small dog continued to whip herself around. She was so out of control that she accidentally scratched a crew member with one of her long blades. Everyone fell away from her as she continued to twist and turn in apparent agony. Then, just as quickly as it began, it stopped. Nora stood there, her head bowed, her body shaking. The water reached to her belly, lapping at her sides where long scratches were visible. Her gasps of breath bulged at her ribs, showing the thin skin moving over them. She seemed to be hyperventilating, though she looked normal and calm. No one moved, even the Gorons were silently watching through narrowed eyes, curious as to what would happen next. With a speed that Hazel wasn't aware was possible on such a small dog, Nora turned tail and ran up to the top deck. She turned and ran so fast that she left a jet of water spray behind her, it foamed over the water before evening out again. Anyone who was in the way stood aside as the blade dog zipped by. Hazel watched after her, shocked. Wolvereen, however, was not. He turned to her quickly.

"Follow her!" he barked sharply. "She must not be allowed to wander around freely. What she just did was not normal. I want to make sure it's not something bad."

Hazel did not argue and neither did Noly, instead they took off after Nora. Hazel held onto Noly's back as she plunged through the water to the stairs. She stayed there as Noly climbed to the upper decks. As soon as they reached the stairs, the fighting started back up again. What was it that had caused Nora to go crazy? Hazel could only guess. Hazel willed that they'd catch up to the crazed blade dog. After a few moments they did. Nora came into sight and Hazel jumped off Noly's back. Being smaller and much faster she caught up to Nora first and pulled up alongside her, being careful of her blades. Noly did the same on the opposite side.

"Nora!" Hazel screamed over the clang of swords and the screams of pain that erupted all around them as they got to the first deck. "What's wrong, what are you doing?!"

Nora did not answer. Instead she sped up, her destination unknown. Hazel could only follow and hope everything would be all right.

Rosey stopped and opened up her senses to the water element. She was hit with a barrage of want and pain. The water element was scrambling, trying to reach her. It was filled with rage, almost screaming. It could sense her wounds and pain and was angered by it. It wanted to protect her, to be with her. Rosey fell against the ship, her senses blurred. The water element was so strong it overpowered the fire element and almost caused Rosey to revert back to her normal form. Exerting her own will she pushed back and forced herself to close her senses to the water element. She slumped against the wall, taking deep breaths. The water element was stronger than she had expected and close by, but where? It was too irrational at the moment for her to get it to calm down and talk to her. She was on her own. What was she going to do? Glancing at the far distant island, no more than a floating hazy landmass, the answer came to her. She had to get to the island. The element was somewhere on that Island, maybe she could find it there if she could reach it.

She was about to take off when she heard her name screamed over the chaos of thrashing Gorons and the clang of weapons. Looking up abruptly Rosey saw Nora running her way. The little blade dog was accompanied on either side by Noly and Hazel. The two of them seemed concerned and not too sure about Nora. Rosey was horrified to see that all three of them were injured. Noly was scrapped and clawed and Hazel had a long scratch on her side, while Nora sported a chip in one of her shoulder blades and three long scratches on her right shoulder. Nora was in the lead, running fast. She seemed out of control. As she drew closer Rosey saw her eyes were full of tears. She seemed to be tripping over herself and running wildly. There was one thing for sure though. She was running straight at Rosey. Rosey watched her coming, worry filling her from head to toe. She looked around but saw nothing chasing them and no Blood Goron coming after them from the sky; there seemed to be nothing wrong.

As Nora drew closer, Rosey realized that she wasn't going to stop but she had no time to react. Nora jumped up and slammed Rosey right in the chest with all four paws. Rosey was surprised by the strength behind the attack and how easily it had unbalanced her, but, after all, she hadn't been expecting to be body slammed by the little dog. The air was knocked out of Rosey and she dropped Andraste. The sword clattered on the deck. Rosey and Nora both fell over the railing and right into the blood red water. As soon as her body hit the water, the fire element, which was weak and had only been sustained by Rosey's will power, snuffed out almost instantly. It scorched the water and sent up a billow of steam all around her and onto the deck of the ship. People backed away and Noly and Hazel scrambled back as the hot steam poured over the side and onto the deck.

Rosey's form returned to normal as the fire element faded away. For a few seconds she was unaware of what was going on, she fought hard for breath only to find there was none. Salty water filled her mouth instead. As memory returned, she sputtered and kicked her legs with as much strength as she could muster. She broke the water's surface and took in huge gulps of air. *That's twice I've almost been suffocated,* she thought in annoyance. At first she was fearful of any Blood Gorons but the Mermaids had done a great job of taking care of all the sea bound ones. The main threat now was from the ones flying above the water that had managed to escape the mermaid's deadly attack and the few that were still making holes in the hull. She looked up to see if any were coming for her but the steam from her transformation was doing well at hiding her. With the threat of those beasts out of the way, she then turned to look for Nora. To her surprise she wasn't around.

Sudden fear filled her heart for the little dog. No matter what had just happened she wasn't going to pass judgment until she questioned Nora. The memory of her mother's friend who had been forced to kill her by the Evil One came to Rosey's mind. No, she would not get angry until she knew why Nora had done it. Rosey began to dive down to see if Nora was drowning when all of a sudden she was yanked under the water. She was just barely able to gasp some air before her head went under. She looked down at her feet, where she felt the pressure pulling on her, expecting to see a Blood Goron but instead she saw nothing except a line of white mist that rolled around underneath her, pulling her down. Her eyes blurred as the salty water got to them and stung them violently. Right now she wouldn't mind some Real Deal Goggles.

She was utterly helpless. When Nora had hit her she had dropped her sword on the deck, Andraste was not there and neither was her element. She wished she had remembered to grab Silver Knight or even her bow and arrows when she had gone to make herself some hot chocolate before the attack, but the dagger and especially the bow had been of little consequence to Rosey at that time. There was nothing she could do about it now. She was unable to defend herself from whatever it was and her air was running out fast. Suddenly, Rosey's body slammed into something solid and, like glass breaking, she broke through and dropped onto a hard surface. She gasped in large breaths of air and sat up as best she could. She wiped the water from her eyes and closed them shut as the sting of the salt continued to torture her. Her own salty tears flowed down her face and she desperately tried to clear them so she could see. She had no idea where she was and could not defend herself. It was an utterly helpless feeling that made her angry and annoyed, yet no one had touched her or come near her yet. She was alone, or at least, whatever had dragged her down was waiting for her to clear her vision. She wasn't sure.

Finally her vision began to clear, and Rosey opened her red rimmed eyes taking it all in. If she didn't know any better she would have said that she was sitting on glass. She could see right through the floor to the deep sandy bottom below covered in rocks that were plastered with corals and seaweed. Small fish were swimming around lazily, just as any group of fish would. Schools shot by heading up to the surface, causing Rosey to lean back in surprise as they zoomed past. All around her the walls were like glass, allowing her to look out at the watery world. It was just like when her uncle took her to an aquarium. Rosey was filled with awe, as she had always been, by the sea. It was the one place she could watch over and over again and never become bored.

She peered at the surface of the apparent glass and frowned. Glass didn't describe the walls adequately, they resembled white ice. Pure, flawless, ice with its own natural air bubbles and designs etched into its surface. To her surprise, it was not freezing cold as she would expect but warm and smooth. She bent down, examining the wall and ground more closely, then gasped, it was ice! But how could that be? It's warm and yet it wasn't melting! Memory of the Silver Goddess's Crystal Caverns came back to Rosey. This was much like how they had been but it was ice instead of crystal that greeted her, still the effect was the same. The room itself was actually pretty humid, the air was thick with moisture but not uncomfortably so. It almost felt like she was being misted by a light spray of water that cooled her flesh and soothed her sore muscles and wounds. Wherever she was, it was beautiful.

"Rosey! Hurry and follow me!"

The sudden voice jolted Rosey and made her turn abruptly. There, standing not too far away was Nora. Her small face was still covered in tears and she moved around restlessly as if she was in a hurry and could not stay long. Tears looked strange on an animal and reminded Rosey of when her cat had gotten sick once and one of her symptoms had been watery eyes. Still, the tears were tears, there was no doubt about that. Why then did she cry? So many other questions clouded Rosey's mind that she felt jostled by them. Rosey wasn't sure what she should do. Why was Nora here? How did she get here? Did this have something to do with the water element? Then a strange thought crossed her mind. Was Nora the one that had dragged Rosey down into the water? Rosey wanted to ask this but her mouth seemed frozen in shock. How could it have possibly been Nora, she had seen a white mist, not a bladed dog?! Still, the evidence seemed to speak for itself. Nora had rammed her into the water and now she was here, seemingly having appeared from nowhere. Maybe it was a part of Nora's powers or something, perhaps she was a water element or a magikin of some sort? The blade dog had never mentioned anything like that to Rosey, but Marine had never spoken of his powers either. It was just something that some people didn't talk about. She opened her mouth, finally finding the courage to speak but wasn't able to get out a single word. Nora took off, away from Rosey at a breakneck speed. It was so sudden that Rosey was left shocked. After a few seconds though, she started up after her, running as fast as she could.

As Rosey ran forward the small room she had been in extended and became a tunnel, closing off as she left and opening up as she ran forward, like she was moving through some expandable tunnel. The effect was disorienting and put Rosey off balance, making her head spin. Focusing on

Nora's running figure she found that the effect was lessened so she quickly took her gaze from anything but the blade dog. As she ran Rosey found her voice and said, "What's going on Nora? Why did you do that up there? Where are we?"

Nora yipped and said in broken phrases as if the effort of talking was wearing her down, "Not now…no time…must hurry…forward…please."

This last word was spoken gently, pleadingly. Rosey couldn't deny that voice and she couldn't turn Nora down, besides, if she remembered correctly, they were running in the direction of the island. Nora had to be leading her to the Water Element. At least, she hoped that was what she was doing. She's doing what she promised to do, guiding her there. *But why is she so frantic, does she know we can't win without the element?* she thought, surging ahead with what energy she had left. Her body was weak and tired, battered and bruised, she was running on adrenaline, but that could only last for so long. Sooner or later Rosey was going to have to stop and rest. She could already feel the strain on her stretched muscles. Still she pushed on, hoping that Nora was leading her to the element.

As time passed, Rosey tentatively opened her senses to the water element. It was still just as strong but less chaotic and wild. It seemed to have calmed down now that she was drawing closer. As she withdrew her senses, Rosey began to feel that same sensation she had had when approaching the volcano. It was a nagging sensation that traveled down her back and into her consciousness. The nagging was getting stronger the closer she got. It wasn't like Rosey's usual senses for she couldn't turn this off as easily, especially with the Fire element out of commission. When they had been miles away, it had been easier to ignore it and to tune it out, but now it was growing in strength. During the battle, the threat from the Gorons had provided Rosey with the perfect distraction from the nagging sound, now she was safe and calmed by the knowledge that the mermaids were there to help, while she couldn't. There was nothing to hold it back now, in fact,

The Mystics

Rosey didn't want to. She let it roll over her, hoping it would help her to track it down.

Thinking of the fire Element, Rosey became worried. She hadn't had the chance to check on it since its power was snuffed out. Now she gently prodded it and it weakly responded. As long as she didn't die, it would live, but the water was fire's natural enemy and the fire element was just unable to sustain itself when it was already so weakened surrounded by water. However, now that she was out of the water and drying off, the fire element was starting to recover with each passing second. It drew its energy from Rosey, but it could not sustain itself in its natural enemy, at least, not yet. She retreated and hoped that it would replenish itself in time and be as strong as it was before. For now all she could do was run on, her wet, salty, leather clothes sticking to her body, Nora just ahead of her. As she ran her skin and hair began to dry, leaving a salty crust all over her and her clothes. She tried to wipe it off, but it seemed to be everywhere. Like sand from the beach, it rolled into places it shouldn't, making Rosey's skin itch. She decided not to bother with it and just imagined how wonderful it would be when she next got a shower and hot bath, if there was a ship to return to by then.

After a few moments they appeared before a passageway cloaked in darkness. Rosey stopped abruptly for she was not too happy about jumping into dark spaces. She looked above her and saw a black expanse of nothingness stretching overhead. Behind her stretched the ocean and the blue sky, which, from underwater, resembled an expanse of blue dotted with white. The black space ahead and above her must be the island, looming above them. The tunnel was continuing underneath it. Rosey could see nothing beyond. Nora pulled to a stop when she realized that Rosey was no longer following. She yipped worriedly and jumped around awkwardly. Rosey checked the fire element once more, she didn't want to go anywhere without making sure she could defend herself. With Andraste gone, the fire element was all she had. She gently touched it and found it to be strong and powerful. Rosey was amazed at how quickly it had recovered, but, as she was told, the elements strength depended on her and nothing else. As long as she was safe, it was safe and strong. Feeling better, now that she knew she could easily transform, she had no problem following. However, she stayed as she was, instinct told her not to transform. If she was right, Nora was leading her to the mother and the water element.

"Come on Rosey! She's not too far away now!" Nora said hastily, turning in a circle. When she completed that circle she took off into the darkness and Rosey followed.

Something Nora had said alerted her. She? Who's she? Could it be the Mother? Rosey had no time to comprehend that for they suddenly burst into light. They hadn't been running for very long, and now they were surrounded by a bluish light. Rosey's eyes quickly adjusted and she gasped at the view. The clear ice covered tunnel they were in expanded widely to encompass a huge room as big as a baseball field. All around them pillars of white crystal-clear ice and light billowed down around them casting blue and purple shadows. Rosey was amazed. There, in the middle of the room was a blue unicorn. Her coat was a dark navy blue and her mane and tail were made up of creamy white ocean waves. Watery greens and blues rippled across them as she moved, making it look like the waves were rolling out from her neck and hindquarters, crashing into the open air and then receding back into the unicorn's body. The same kind of waves came from her forelegs and her shoulders except they had a deeper blue tint than the mane and tail and her eyes where the brightest sky blue Rosey had ever seen. They burrowed deep into her soul gazing at her from under green eyelashes. Silver hooves made lovely metallic sounds on the icy floor and a bright, navy blue, crystalline horn shone strong upon her forehead.

Rosey took this all in as she approached but her fascination turned to one of horror as she stared at the blue creature. What horrified Rosey was not the beautiful unicorn but the element that was ripping itself away from her. The unicorn was tottering on her feet, her head lowered like she was

The Mystics

some defeated soldier. Her body started releasing a thin layer of dark blue fog. With a shocked whinny she fell on her side, her chest heaving with great gasps of air. Suddenly, tendrils of what looked like water in some goo like form started detaching themselves from her body, stripping her of her beautiful colors and the watery additions that made her body shimmer. Color started stripping away from her flank, leaving it white and bloodied in some areas. Her tail, which was as watery as her mane, transformed into a regular horse's white tail with strips of hair missing. The back hooves turned black, no longer the silver they had been and the watery patches were gone from the back forelegs. The tendrils of water looking goo converged just ahead of the unicorn and at their center was a glowing blue orb. It was pulsating a deep blue color that cast brilliant blue light everywhere. The orb was pulling itself, almost yanking itself, away from the mother and reaching out to Rosey. A unicorn's body, if Ysandir was anything to go by, was never white. Rosey knew that from Ysandir herself, it always had some sort of color, but whatever was happening was strong enough to not only strip away the Elemental Form surrounding the unicorn but also what natural color was in the unicorn's own body.

Rosey's hand flew to her mouth in horror. She was flabbergasted and shocked beyond anything she could ever know. Her body shivered with apprehension. This was something that wasn't supposed to be happening and worse yet, she had no idea what to do about it. This had not been in any of the Goddesses stories or in any of the books she had read. If the crystal had any knowledge of it, it had not shared it with Rosey and neither had the White Witch. She didn't know what to do, she felt utterly helpless. The very idea made Rosey cringe with anger. She was supposed to be the hero, she was supposed to be the one to help these people and their world…no her world. Yet, she stood here unable to do anything. She was unable to take her eyes off the writhing Mother. She felt angry tears sting the corners of her eyes in frustration at her own uselessness.

She took a step closer. The orb twitched to life as she did so. Confused, Rosey stopped, and then cautiously began forward once again. As soon as Rosey drew near, the orb began pulling harder and the unicorn whinnied in pain. The orb pulled so hard that the tendrils attached to it and the unicorn yanked her forward. It was now so strong it was almost dragging her with it. The mother cried out in pain, her whole body shook and her eyes squeezed shut. Nora zoomed past Rosey and came to the unicorn's side screaming and crying.

"Rosey! Help her!" She cast her pained expression at the writhing Mother, clearly upset by what she was seeing. Rosey could only agree with her.

Rosey held her head in despair. Then a sudden shocking revelation barreled into Rosey making her gasp. There *was* something she could do. The water element was ripping itself away from the Mother in desperation to get to her! No words were needed. With the knowledge of what she needed to do now revealed, she leapt forward and ran straight to the orb. Extending her arms she grasped it and pulled it towards her chest. Immediately, as if they had never been tied to the Mother in the first place, the tendrils released their grip on the orb and Rosey held it against her chest triumphantly where it then quickly absorbed into her body. Rosey stood there frozen for a few moments in utter surprise, unsure of what to do. She stared down at her chest where the orb had disappeared into it as if there was some unusual substance growing on her skin. Suddenly, she felt the air knocked out of her as if someone had violently punched her in the gut. A huge explosion of energy encircled her and the whole of the cavern began to collapse. As soon as the orb had been absorbed, the tendrils snapped backwards encircling the Mother. They healed what little wounds she had as well as repainted her rump and back legs once again in their blue hue. As with Mercury, the unicorn no longer had the watery mane and tail but the colors had been restored and refreshed. Now that the element had left her, her job as the Mother was complete. Nora sat there crying as the unicorn lifted herself to a sitting position then got up on wobbly legs. She resembled a beautiful, proud unicorn once again.

Rosey barely had time to see the unicorn's recovery before water encircled her and her whole being was ripped away from the large room. The water element's joy at being united with Rosey was so strong that the structure of the room began to crack and shake apart. Rosey vaguely glimpsed Nora and the unicorn vanish in a shower of droplets before the ceiling collapsed and water came rushing in. Rosey was flung upward and she felt her body begin to shake. It felt as if liquid were pouring into her and trying to merge with her. Apprehension filled her whole being then she realized that her body was eighty percent water. Her mind cleared and in a flash of understanding she realized that the water element wasn't ripping her apart, it was combining with the water inside her. It rushed through her body, surrounding her heart and filling her stomach with its clear crisp contents. Rosey gasped as it rushed through her veins pushing the blood aside and exploring the inner workings of her body. Though none of it was painful, it felt tremendously weird. She was ticklish all over and her body felt part solid, part liquid.

The water element surged around her, as happy as could be. It skipped and danced and raced around her in all its magnificent glory. Giant waves of water crashed down around her, as if she was standing on a hill overlooking the waves bombarding the coast of Maine's rocky cliffs back on Earth. Their blue power filled Rosey's mind and began transforming her. The fire element, present already within the crystal, welcomed its counterelement in blasts of smoke and ripples of cackling laughter. It seemed to roll its eyes at the enthusiasm and silliness that the water element was displaying, even though it had done much the same thing when it had first come to Rosey.

As with the fire element a figure seemed to condense in front of her where she floated, mixed in the water's presence. This time the image before her was clear. The water formed the figure of a giant moray eel, blue from the top of its head to the tip of its tail with brilliant green flashes of light shimmering along its watery body. Its liquid lips parted and a sweet female, whispering voice came from within. It reminded Rosey of a gentle stream falling over smooth rocks. Once again the voice was as much around her as it was in her mind, soothing and strong.

"Oh, Rosey! How I have missed you and longed for you after such an interminable separation. I will serve you forever more, use me as you will!"

Rosey frowned, but not in anger. Once again, the voice of the element had spoken to her as if it had already known her and been with her. *What does it mean?* Rosey thought, remembering her first encounter with the fire element. Then, she had pushed it aside, but now it caught her attention. Was there more to her than met the eye? She barely had time to ponder this for the element wasn't finished with her yet and Rosey couldn't help but give herself over to it enthusiastically. Like the element, Rosey too, felt an unbelievable love at being united with the element as if she really had been separated from it at one point. Her thoughts jumbled as the water rose about her in gigantic waves.

The watery image broke into a million watery fishes and rushed at Rosey, encircling her body. She gasped as their individual fins touched her skin and goose bumps broke out along her arms and legs. Rosey could feel the power of water changing her, molding her, and filling her to the brim with its strength, transforming her into its Elemental Form. Slowly she pushed her body forward. A massive form of water that much resembled a moray eel encircled her. Together they plunged towards the surface, the eels jaws gaping wide and ready for battle.

Chapter Twenty-Six: Water's Fury

Rosey's back split open and bones began to grow forth extending outward to become the skeleton of two large dragon wings. They were longer and bigger than her feathered fire wings, stretching to at least three times the length of her body. The wings had four finger-like appendages at the end. Thin, vein filled membrane stretched out between the four individual appendages. Covering the thin membrane was a thick sheet of closely knit blue scales to act as armor for the vulnerable material. The long second-arms were blue and the membrane in between was a lighter sky blue color. Rosey knew from her studies that dragon wings could either be like bat wings, which had joints in the fingers, or they could be joint-less wings, where the finger-like appendages were simply straight and unable to bend or grasp onto things. Rosey's wings were the latter kind for they had no individual joints in the wings. They were long, slightly curved, and sharp at the ends like sharpened pieces of steel. The membrane in between the long thin fingers, as they were called, didn't extend all the way down to the tips, instead it ended at about two inches from the tips and Rosey could tell that they were as sharp as knives. She looked at them in wonder and then beat them slowly, feeling how the new muscles worked under her fine skin. She sucked in her breath sharply when she realized just how different they were from her feathered wings, the muscles felt much bigger and the membrane stretched further down her back, almost to her buttocks. Rosey smiled and breathed deeply moving her wings in different directions to get a feel for them. She could only imagine how it would feel to fly with them.

Touching her face, Rosey almost gasped with surprise. Small blue and white scales ringed the edges of Rosey's eyes making glittering patterns across her face. Her whole body extended and elongated, her muscles bulged and her wounds disappeared replaced by smooth scaled skin the color of flesh. Her leather outfit burst into dew droplets and was replaced with a thigh-length blue shirt, split at the sides up to her waist and held in place with a navy blue belt. The belt was nothing more than a long tendril of fabric tied loosely at the side. The shirt dropped down in the back just above her buttocks and looped upward towards the front over her breasts, converging into a small hoop of fabric fastened around her neck was a dark blue button holding it in place at the back under her hair. Long thin pants extended down her elongated legs. Navy blue embroidery outlined the ends of her pants and the edges of her shirt with images of fish, dolphins, and other marine wildlife and plant life. Long dark blue gloves covered her scaled arms up to her enlarged biceps. They formed a V shape on the back of her hand and slanted downward to the wrist in an oval. More navy blue embroidery outlined their ends. Rosey's skin tingled as two long waves of water crashed in and out from her shoulders, just like the waves that had been on the blue unicorn. Blue and green water flowed out two feet away from her body to foam up white against the air then recede back into her shoulders to come out again. Two large opals in the shape of an oval were attached to special silver loops around her wrists and a smaller opal sat on her forehead in its own V shaped, silver crown that disappeared behind her long hair. Her jet black hair was now a glossy dark blue and her eyes that had always been blue seemed to be intensified into a deeper blue color, more sky blue then her usual sapphire. Below her left eye was the image of a blue tear drop and sky blue painted her eyelids with its natural makeup. On her feet were navy blue, embroidered, light blue slippers and running along her arms, attached to the long sleeves, there was silver armor. Embedded in the armor were thin layers of shimmering opals. The silver armor was also attached to her chest by an intricate breast plate and more of it looped around her midsection and fell down the sides of her legs.

   The Shanobie Crystal at her chest grew bright with blue light at the water's presence. It was no longer white but a deep sapphire blue, so beautiful and pure that it made Rosey shiver. She grasped a hold of it and felt the warmth of its power surge through her. She had collected another element, finally. Looking down at herself she was amazed. Her scaled skin was very alien to her, she ran her hand over it, feeling the strange texture rough but also smooth against her fingers. The salty layer that had covered her body before was no longer a nuisance. Instead it mingled with her skin comfortably and slid over her scales in rhythmic strokes. She shook her long hair from side to side, enjoying how it twisted and turned about her as if she were underwater, and, in a way, she was. Her body was wrapped around a great pillar of water, long and slender. The top of the pillar was in the shape of a great moray eel, its mouth agape with sharp teeth and large white eyes.

Rosey's whole body felt tingly, the new musculature was simply marvelous. She could feel the strength and the power returning to her limbs as the power of water raced through her, injecting her with renewed vigor. Her body seemed to hum with life and her heart beat with pure joy to be one with another element. The element raced through her body and made her feel ticklish wherever it lingered. It relayed pristine images of information to Rosey's senses on watery waves of whispered voices. She could feel the temperature of the water, she could feel the salt content, and she could even taste the different minerals of the water and its sandy bottom, but that wasn't all it told her. As soon as the water element had merged with her Rosey's range of senses could be extended out to every corner of the world where water touched. Every stream, every valley was home to her senses. She breathed in the sweet smell as it tingled her nostrils. She felt as if she was running as her new awareness zoomed across the planet, touching every expanse of wetness and all the creatures in it. Rosey's eyes widened as images burst into her head, of lakes, rivers, streams, and clouds that held dew, and even the cracks in the vast icy planes where crevices reached so deep it would be an eternity before you reached the bottom. There was so much life in the oceans and the seas. All of it was so colorful, vast and vibrant, covering great distances over endless expanses of blue and green. Down in the deepest oceans there was darkness and the creatures that swam there were strange and alien. Many of them Rosey recognized from her studies and some she did not. They were just as white and ill formed as the deep ocean beasts of Earth. They blinked with fluorescents and shimmered as they turned and twisted in the endless darkness.

Rosey's senses moved on to the great lakes of the south, covered in long ranges of wetlands and marshes. Small villages claimed their most stable ground, where fishing was plenty and the giant crocs were scarce. There were huge flamingos, with ostrich feathers and fish so small that Rosey wondered how they survived with so many predators. She followed the waters further until they poured down the magnificent hole of a giant cave, straight down into a dark abyss so much more silent and lifeless than the oceans. Here, life was scarce. Bats the size of houses occupied them, with long snouts like horses and lizard like bodies and tails. They were much larger and more beautiful than the bats of Earth. They scurried around the vast caverns, inspecting the waters for eyeless fish and snakes.

All these images flashed through Rosey's mind in an instant. She would have loved to continue exploring but she had to save her friends. Time to explore and savor this new world of water would have to come later when she had time to sit and relax. Mixed in with all the other motions and whispers of the great waters was also the chaos of the battle that her friends were desperately fighting. It yanked her back to the present and the dangers at hand. Quickly Rosey shut off the input of information and limited it to only the area surrounding the ship. The water element obeyed and lowered its reach to the desired area, laughing in tiny gargled giggles as it did. Her senses returned to the present and she sucked in her breath when she beheld the horror before her. The waters were tinged with blood and bodies floated everywhere, the perfect food for the scrounging fish that waited at the bottom or the large sharks that knew better than to draw close to a battle but would come later to feast. The stench of the bloody water and the salt of the sea made Rosey want to retch. It filled Rosey with anger and with a renewed strength she forged on ahead, the water element charging around her in the constant shape of a moray eel.

Finally, after what felt like hours to Rosey, they broke through to the surface in a blast of salty water. Spray rained down on any that were present above the crashing wave that had become turbulent with her surge of power. The waves buffeted the slowly sinking ship. Rosey's heart skipped a beat, she had to get the ship to safety. The mermaids were still doing a fabulous job though she saw some mermaid bodies mixed with the Gorons and closed her eyes to the sight. She extended her wings out on both sides to their maximum length. Everyone on the decks, including her cat and dog, were staring at her wide eyed. Rosey had no idea how amazing or frightening she looked, but it didn't matter. All that mattered was getting them to safety.

Rosey started for a moment. What was she supposed to do? She had never had any training with the water element and its powers felt very alien to her. An idea struck her and she pulled forth the water element from the crystal. It surged forth and whispered in her ear, so fast that she was surprised she was able to catch it all, some tactics and techniques that she could use. The information was transferred so quickly that she was nearly overwhelmed. As soon as it came, it stopped, leaving Rosey with an overpowering source of information. The water element quickly receded back into the crystal. What had felt strange and alien before was now seemingly an easy task to complete, her mind opened up with all sorts of possibilities. Thanks to that small moment she now had everything she needed.

In a rage she lifted her arms and felt the water power flow over her arms and out towards the water surrounding the ship. With a silent command it pushed itself violently away from the ship's side, sending any Gorons that managed to surface back away from the ship's railings. Everyone saw that Rosey was handling the attack from the water and so turned their attention to the Goron's on board or in the sky. Rosey flicked her wrist and twirled it in small circles. Slowly the waves lapping the ship's side reversed and began pulling away from the ship. Now the waves looked as if they were originating from the ship, as if it had been dropped from high up in the air to splash down into the water. It was impossible for any sea bound Gorons to get to the ship, but there were still a good number of them in the air attacking the battered crew.

Rosey's anger swept over her like a wave. Extending her arms she sent the large moray eel made of water that had accompanied her toward the ship. It swam around the vessel in great circles. Suddenly its giant watery head leapt out of the water grabbing a mouth full of Gorons that were in the air. It then dived into the water, releasing the grip on its eel form and reverting back to plain water. The Gorons struggled in the water but were quickly dragged down by clawed hands from the mermaids. The moray eel resurfaced, its watery form fed by the limitless supply of endless seawater. It reached back its head and blew a super pressured water spray at a few Gorons flying overhead. They crashed down into the water to be dragged under, while others scattered and began bombarding the eel from the sky. Their attack was futile for the eel was not a creature of flesh and blood. It was made of water and sustained by water. As long as water was around, nothing could kill it. Seeing how useless their attack was, the Gorons stopped attacking the eel and instead focused their attention on Rosey. Roaring with frustration a large group of them flew towards Rosey quickly. Smirking, Rosey lifted a wall of water in front of her to block them. It lifted from the sea obediently in a great towering behemoth of thousands of gallons of water. Some rammed into it before they realized what was happening. Before they could rescue themselves, the water captured them in its torrent then dragged them to the sea where the mermaids waited. The remainder of the Gorons broke apart and started attacking Rosey from multiple sides. Thinking fast, she surrounded herself in a water shield, folding her wings around her body as she did. Gorons rammed the shield to no avail. The sound of their bodies hitting the shield was loud and deafening like bombs going off all around her, but Rosey held her ground. The Gorons then tried covering it with their weight. The image of the water disappeared to be replaced with a mass of twisting and snapping Goron bodies. Their anger and hatred was apparent in their eyes as they bombarded her shield. Rosey had been expecting that. She quickly extended her wings and arms outward and the water bubble exploded away from her, scattering the Gorons in every direction. Quickly she reformed the scattered water droplets and sent them hurtling toward the Gorons at full speed. Some of the water droplets blasted large gaping holes through the Gorons bodies spraying blood everywhere. Rosey tried not to look at them as they dropped from the sky and plummeted to the water, which ran red with blood. Other water drops broke bones and smashed skulls but some only bruised the monster's black bodies, a painful attack but not enough to kill them. All around her screams of pain erupted, but their recovery was swift. The ones that were still alive shot at her again with anger burning in their eyes.

Rosey battered one Goron after another away from her easily enough with the sweep of her large wings. Without Andraste, her wings and the element were all she had. Rosey noticed as she bombarded Gorons with spurts of water and long tubes of water whips that, unlike the fire element, that derived its power source from her internal heat source, the water element was solely derived from outside water sources. If she wasn't around water, the water element would be useless. Rosey wondered if she could take the water from her body, knowing that humans were made up of eighty percent water, but that could cause serious health issues, after all the water was in their bodies for a reason. Rosey didn't have time to ponder this, but it was something she would need to ask about for future battles.

Rosey found that fighting the Gorons was much easier with the water element then it had been with the fire. Mostly because there was so much water around for her to use and her wings were scaled and sharp at the ends making the perfect weapons for tearing the bloodthirsty monsters to shreds. Despite her success, they kept coming. Looking down, Rosey saw that they had turned their attention away from the ship completely. The mermaids were having so much success destroying their underwater numbers that trying to do damage to it was too costly to them and the giant water moray eel she had on standby to protect the air was a bothersome enemy the Gorons could not kill. Their main focus was to destroy her, so instead they came at her, angry and determined. *Good, now my friends can focus on saving the ship. Marine…Margaret…Alex…Rochell… and everyone else…you all better survive!*

The Gorons were leaving behind the ship and flying straight for her. Doing so was making it harder for the mermaids to latch onto them. They would go straight for the surface instead of trying to fight on the sides of the ship and trying to make holes in its bottom. Large groups were bursting out of the water quickly, faster than they had before with their new purpose in sight. Where were they all coming from?!

Vaguely, Rosey remembered what Queen Ashti had said about something under the water multiplying the Gorons and that they couldn't destroy it without her power. Quickly she sent two waves of water crashing against the Gorons around her creating a hole. She then plunged straight down into the water. The water grabbed a hold of her gently like a mother cradling her child. However, in all her haste to help her friends and defeat the Gorons she had forgot one crucial thing: she couldn't breathe underwater. Or could she? She relaxed her body and breathed it in deeply. The water rushed in but filled her lungs comfortably with oxygen. Rosey's mind almost screamed with happiness. *This is so cool, I can breathe under water!* she thought happily, but she had no time to celebrate, she had to find whatever it was that was producing the Gorons and destroy it.

Twisting in the currents smoothly, she used her long wings to navigate through the bloodied water. She circled the ship searching for something. She had noticed before that most of the attack had been focused on the starboard side of the ship. She sent the water speeding past her as she swam there, the water's icy tendrils whipped her hair up in crazy patterns behind her and smoothed over her face as if she were a fish in water. She glided effortlessly and felt as if she were flying. She dived deeper and saw a mass of mermaids. All around her they swam effortlessly through the salty water. They changed directions quickly and attacked any Gorons approaching Rosey with precision and skill. They were painted an array of colors from orange to yellow to purple to blue to red to green and so on. They were even decorated in colors that Rosey didn't recognize and wouldn't be able to name. There were so many of them that Rosey was amazed that the Gorons were managing to outmaneuver them. They swam so fast that they shot by Rosey, their eyes only on the target they were pursuing. It was so chaotic and the water was so murky with blood and guts that Rosey couldn't identify Queen Ashti amongst the swarming ranks. Rosey hoped the queen was helping to turn the tides and not dead somewhere amongst the small collection of mermaid bodies. She doubted a Queen would die so easily. The Gorons were there as well, twisting through the water with amazing speed. Rosey watched, hypnotized for a few moments by the deadly dance taking place in front of her, then memory struck her and she surged forward being careful not to run into any mermaids or Gorons and attract attention. She had an idea, manipulating the water around her she shifted the images that the water gave off to make it seem like she was nothing but a stray group of floating bubbles, churned up by the fighting. How she wished she had Andraste now, it would make it easier for her to kill any Gorons but using a weapon underwater might be more cumbersome than helpful so she shrugged it off. Wherever Andraste was, she hoped it was being looked after.

 Carefully she swam, keeping her eyes peeled for anything out of the ordinary. Then she saw it. Rosey could only describe it as a giant, oval mirror with a thick black back and outline. A dusty cloud of red and black particles zoomed around the mirror making it look like the mirror was above a black hole. Rosey remembered Alex's words earlier about the area suddenly being stripped of its magic. If it was magical, the mirror certainly looked as if it could have been responsible for zapping the magic but she couldn't be certain. She examined it closer. Near it the water was undisturbed, but the mermaids around it kept a good distance just in case. The Gorons were swarming out of it in large ranks and then quickly and mercilessly attacking whatever was in sight, oblivious to anything but their need to kill. The mermaids that were not engaged at the moment were waiting patiently for Gorons to emerge, and then attacking them. The mermaids' numbers heavily outweighed the Gorons' so they could spare the mermaids to wait by the mirror. Rosey waited nearby and watched, observing and taking everything in. She hated not doing anything but, when it came time for her to make her move she didn't want to get it wrong. Happily, Rosey saw that the mermaids were much stronger than the smaller Gorons but the evil creatures had numbers on their side. At least twenty Gorons were ejected every three minutes, making it very difficult to keep the numbers low, many slipped past the mermaids and made it to the surface.

Being careful of the mermaids and the swarming Gorons Rosey waited until no Gorons were coming out then positioned herself above the mirror. Frozen inside the glass was a single Blood Goron. A light would run over the creature, like a copier machine and then blast out the copies. Rosey, still hidden as an image of bubbles, banked out of the way as twenty new Gorons swam out towards her, not knowing she was there. Slowly she twirled around herself and circled the edge of the black hole-like dust cloud. Carefully she floated in behind it. Closing her eyes she concentrated on pulling in the membrane in between her long finger-like appendages as the water element had told her she could do. She felt the skin break and twist, sinking into the flesh of the second arms themselves like it was dissolving away. The four finger appendages on each second arm molded together to form two large, sharpened scythes. Rosey opened her eyes and admired her work, the scythes were very intimidating. They were Death's most popular tool after all and this was a fitting use for them. Drawing them back she slammed the two long scythes into the black back of the mirror with all the force she could muster. If she had been floating over top of the mirror she would have seen her long scythes pierce through the mirror and cut the frozen Goron contained within in two. It did not cry out or move at all, it simply died. The glass from the mirror shattered and the mermaids scattered wildly. They watched as the black material surrounding the mirror broke apart and disappeared.

Rosey yanked her second arms out of the mirror then allowed the membrane to grow back between the returning fingers of her second arm. They were scythes no more, they were back to their normal dragon winged selves. She dropped the image around her and the mermaids jumped back in surprise to see her. When they recognized her they smiled wickedly then watched the giant mirror break apart. The edges of it suddenly lit on fire and touched the mirror, making it disintegrate as it neared the center. The mirror was gone in a matter of seconds and the Gorons, that had once been a massive flow, were now no more. Rosey smiled, proud of her work, the mermaids nodded to her and smiled as well, their faces happy and victorious. Then an ear splitting crack rang out over the water. Rosey flinched away from it. The mermaids recoiled and swam away, covering their ears. Rosey cast her eyes to the ship in horror. Massive cracks were starting to appear at the bottom of the ship. The last of the Gorons were killed and thrust out of the way but they had created too many holes in the bottom. The weight of the ship would soon collapse onto the Animal Quarters. The mermaids realized this as well and their whole group, hundreds strong, surged against the bottom trying to support its weight and stop the cracking. Rosey could see flashes of light from the various holes. Margaret must be trying desperately to fix them. She wondered if Alex had joined her. The power of the surging water was too much, Rosey could attest to that.

Taking a deep breath Rosey knew what she had to do. She flung herself upward and blasted through the surface of the water. Spray followed her and the salty water ran off her body and clothes leaving them dry, after all a fish doesn't get wet. The moray eel was still there, waiting for any Goron to try and attack. Quickly she redirected the eel. The watery creature obeyed and began wrapping itself around and around the base of the ship. Slowly the ship was lifted out of the water, supported by the eel's constantly circling body. It became a long spring of coils that continued up and up until the water leaked from the ships bottom in huge gallons cascading over the eel's water body adding to its size. The people on deck had long since stopped fighting to hold on for dear life as the ship was carried by the massive eel towards the island. Rosey kept up with it, the strain pulling against her every muscle. *Boy am I going to be sore after this!* she thought, gritting her teeth. Slowly but surely they drew closer to the island. Rosey pushed on, relieved to see the mermaids keeping up, watching for any problems, either that or just watching out of amazement. Their bodies bobbed in and out of the water as they followed, reminding her of dolphins and penguins when they swam.

After what felt like hours to Rosey they made it to the island. To her surprise, as they neared the island, large planks of wood began to spring forth from the tree line forming a dry dock on the island's sandy beach. It didn't take Rosey long to realize that the Earth Elementals on board the ship were hard at work forming the docks for her. It took them hardly any time at all to form the structure. Rosey was reminded of the time when the Golden Goddess had told her that building structures that took people on Earth years to make only took the people of The World Within A World hours or minutes. The proof was happening right before her eyes. By the time they neared the beach the dry dock was completed. Rosey gently sat the ship down on the dock. It was built in such a way so that the hull of the ship wasn't touching the ground. The ship was supported from the midsection leaving the holes exposed so they would no longer be bearing any weight.

Rosey relaxed her muscles and stared down in wonder. A ramp was extended and people began jumping off and screaming her name with joy. Over and over again they celebrated her success and her great power that had not only saved them but their ship as well. Mermaids transformed their long tails into long legs and joined them excitedly on the beach, their much larger bodies shadowing the smaller humans and animals. They hugged each other and cheered up at her, happiness surging through them like a wave. It was over, finally.

Suddenly, Rosey was thrown off balance by a blast of air. It hit her back with such force that she was unable to right herself. She plummeted fast to the tree filled ground of the small island. Jerking her large dragon-like wings she managed to whip herself around and face whatever had just hit her. To Rosey's utter astonishment and surprise it was the woman who Ysandir had been fighting, flying towards her with hatred in her eyes.

Chapter Twenty-Seven: The Eye of the Enemy

Rosey was confused to no end. What in the world happened to Ysandir? When Rosey had left her to fight the woman, she had been easily outmatching the air elemental blow for blow. A sudden fear gripped Rosey's heart, had this woman been strong enough to kill Ysandir? Rosey had no time to entertain that idea for she was still falling fast. Hurriedly she flapped her wings hoping to slow her descent. It worked. Instead of crashing into the sandy ground she landed softly, but still with enough force to make her legs buckle underneath her. She sank to her knees, exhausted from the strain of lifting the ship and now faced with fighting this mad woman. Rosey couldn't believe that she had managed to kill Ysandir, it just couldn't be true, but then what had happened to her? Whatever the woman had done to the powerful unicorn, Rosey could only pray it hadn't been life threatening.

Rosey had landed a good 300 yards away from where the ship rested on the newly formed dry docks on the beach. Sand mixed with earth crunched under her feet and stuck to her sweating body. Her large dragon wings rested gently on the ground, exhausted from carrying Rosey's weight and flying through water. Rosey knew she was on her last bit of stamina, but she had to keep going. She wouldn't stop until everyone was safe. About 200 yards away from where she was crouching down, resting as long as she could before she would have to fight, the wooded trees of the island stood proud and tall. Some resembled palm trees while others looked to be normal evergreens and deciduous. Unlike near the town of Nera, the trees here weren't preparing for winter. They still had all their leaves and unusual colors, however cold winds and patches of frost hung in the air. Rosey would have to ponder the island's beauty later for the woman was drawing ever closer and would soon require all her attention.

Rosey gritted her teeth in annoyance tasting some grains of sand, disgustedly she spit them out. That was the second time the woman had attacked her from behind. *Coward*, she thought bitterly. Rosey prepared to meet the woman but then saw something hidden in the folds of the many brown rags. It was long and curved and glowed whenever the light touched it. The woman held it tightly, her arms bent to the left of her body trying to hide it from sight. Swearing Rosey realized it was a sword. Clenching her fists she raised her voice to the heavens.

"Andraste!"

The sword, which had been safely guarded by Hazel and Noly where it had fallen from Rosey's hand, went flying to her faster than any bird. It careened over the sand, whipping up a cloud of dust in its wake, snaking its way through the people on the beach, never harming any of them. Rosey kept her eyes firmly on the approaching woman. Without looking she reached out and Andraste gently slid into her hand perfectly, defying gravity and the speed at which it had been traveling. The woman was drawing closer, her rage apparent on her blood stained face. As she came, Rosey got an idea. Using the momentum created when the sword returned to her, Rosey whipped around to gain speed. As she did so she spat out with vengeance, "WILL YOU STOP HITTING ME FROM BEHIND!"

The woman came up before her and brought her sword up to strike Rosey's perfectly as Rosey completed the circle. Rosey's circle, however, carried more power behind it than the woman's had. With more force than Rosey believed she had left, she slammed the woman backwards and into the sandy earth with Andraste. The woman carved out a long trough in the sand as her body was dug into the ground, sending a large wave of sand in her wake. She came to a stop about 100 yards away. Panting heavily and obviously just as tired and beaten as Rosey was, she lifted herself up on one arm. The left side of her face and left arm were rubbed raw by the sand where they had been dragged through the earth. A few places along her body began to bleed from the impact with the earth and large bruising began to show. The brown rags she wore to hide herself were falling away bit by bit, but still Rosey could not be certain of her identity. She was already badly wounded from Rochell's and Ysandir's fights. Rosey marveled at how the woman was still able to stay conscious.

Rosey came forward, walking slowly towards the woman, hoping she would surrender but she wasn't ready to give up yet. She stared at Rosey hard, her black eyes boring into her soul. Rosey eyed her back, undeterred. Suddenly a roar of voices could be heard over the breaking waves on the sand and the wind from the south blowing in over the crashing waves. Rosey looked to her right and saw the whole of the ship's crew members and the mermaids from the sea running towards them, brandishing their weapons. They were coming to help her.

Seeing them the woman furrowed her brows in annoyance and got up to run toward them. Fearing the worst, Rosey leapt after her but she was too late. The woman pulled up and twisted around and around creating a whirlwind around herself. Slowly the whirlwind stretched up toward the sky. The clouds began to darken and swirl into a sickly greenish tint. A huge wind came forth from the skies and blew itself around them, toppling some of the large palm trees and other trees whose roots weren't deep enough. The intense winds stirred the already agitated waters and beat sand against the ship making a harsh whistling noise as it passed over the ship's broken underside. Mermaids grabbed the crew members and tackled them to the ground before the wind could snatch them away. A mermaid shielded each crew member, being careful that nothing would fly into them and making sure they firmly stayed rooted to the ground. Rosey was amazed at their size and strength compared to the humans. When she had meet Queen Ashti she had thought that the woman was huge, but Rosey's Elemental Form was very large itself so she had not truly grasped just how big the mermaids were till now. Most of the crew members, however, were regular sized and they were dwarfed by the mermaids, even the animals and Lerons of their crew. *Is that what it's like when I stand next to my friends?* she thought, remembering the fear that their eyes showed sometimes when looking upon her transformed body. She searched among the crew and mermaids with her eyes but could not see her friends amongst them. She hoped they were all right. Rosey bent her head, she would have to talk to them about all that later, right now, she had to stop the Minion before she did any more damage.

Rosey watched as the wind formed a massive tornado headed right for the ship. The huge vessel shook violently and pieces of wood were snatched from the railing and sides. Rosey screamed in frustration as she saw mermaids pulling crew members towards the forests to grasp a hold of trees to anchor themselves in the deadly winds. Once again, Rosey was stuck and utterly helpless. She could do nothing to stop the violent storm. She had not the element to do so. Rosey stared ahead, angered by her helplessness. The water element would be useless against this, or would it? Hurricanes gained energy when they passed over warm water, taking in the heated air to add to the storm and tornados depended on conflicting warm and cool air flows that mashed into each other. If she put enough super-cooled water in the atmosphere it might mess up the energy of the tornado. It might work. Stepping forward she began to do just that but was rammed in the side by a blast of wind. She staggered and fell a few feet away. She cursed herself for forgetting that her enemy was still there. The tornado was on its own now and its creator had no intention of letting her interfere.

Rosey staggered to her feet quickly, just in time to block a blow from the woman's deadly sword as she came at Rosey with a wicked ferocity. The woman held her sword in her right hand, the left one seemed to be too painful to lift so the woman fought one handedly. *That's good news for me, but I don't know how good she is with a sword.* Rosey would just have to keep fighting and hope to wear the woman out. Their swords clanged against each other over and over and it was only now that Rosey got a good look at the long sword. It was ivory white, with black markings. It looked, for all its strangeness, to be made of ivory instead of…whatever it was that made up her sword. Its hilt was curved at the ends like talons and a blue stone rested in the middle of the hilt. Rosey thought the blade was quite beautiful, too beautiful to be in the hands of the enemy. She seared the image of the sword into her mind, hoping that it would help solve the mystery as to who this woman was.

It didn't take Rosey long to realize that the woman was easily and definitely weakening under each of Rosey's attacks. Each time the woman went in for a strike, Rosey would easily block then counter. The woman would only just manage to block the attack then stagger backwards drawing Rosey onward. Each of Rosey's blows was heavy with power and she could have sworn that the ground shook whenever she slammed her sword against the woman's ivory one. Rosey marveled at how the woman was still standing after blocking so many of her attacks. Nevertheless the woman continued to parry and block each attacks rather awkwardly, but still managing to do so. Rosey kept at her. She was relentless, even though she could tell the woman was losing the fight, she still put as much power behind her blows as if she was fighting a fully prepared opponent. This woman had hurt Rochell and possibly killed Ysandir, oh no, she was not going easy on her.

As they danced around each other Rosey watched the tornado out of the corner of her eye. It was drawing closer to the ship. Rosey had to finish this if she wanted to save them but the woman was surprisingly good on her feet despite her injury and was using that to her advantage. She kept Rosey away from her, drawing her away and making her come after her. It was tiresome and annoying for Rosey knew that she was trying to keep her distracted long enough for the Tornado to do its dirty work. Rosey had to continue fighting her, for if she didn't than the Minion would resort to her wind powers again and that was something that Rosey would have a far worse time fighting off. She had to knock the woman out and quickly.

The crystal glowed at Rosey's chest and she briefly wondered if she was using any of her mother's sword tricks stored in the crystal's memory. If she did than she didn't know. She doubted it though for the fight Rosey was engaged in now was anything less than life threatening. The woman was in no position to push Rosey away nor hurt her, avoid her maybe, but not hurt her.

Finally Rosey huffed in annoyance and lunged forward quickly, determined to end this. She touched blades with the woman's and spiraled it around her own then yanked the sword from the woman's hands with a violent movement of her wrist. It went flying a few yards away. The woman eyed her angrily, but Rosey didn't care. Before she could dance away from her again she lifted her leg and slammed it into the woman's gut, throwing her off balance. The woman sank to the sandy ground, clutching her stomach, the wind knocked out of her. Rosey had no time to ponder this irony, she was far too angry.

Rosey was about to use the opportunity to help her friends, but she didn't need to. A sudden burst of blue and yellow light exploded around the ship. The tornado slammed against a wall of dust and particles making a high pitched squealing noise. It veered sharply over the shield-like ward then continued on towards the water as if it had bounced off and was repelled. Once it hit the water it sucked up the water into its long black tube. Before Rosey could do anything, two figures stepped onto the beach from the side of the ship. One of them brought in their arms toward their chest in the shape of an X like a mummy for burial, then quickly, extended their arms. Rosey watched in amazement as the tornado disappeared in seconds. She stared in awe identifying the figure as Rochell leaning heavily on Alex, his wand held in one hand. Margaret stood not too far away with Captain Marine by her side. Alex, Margaret, and Rochell had put up a magical ward and then Rochell had worked on the tornado. *The ward reflected the tornado, bounced it, like a trick,* Rosey thought, remembering Alex's words.

Rosey was so happy to see Rochell alive and walking, even barely, that she almost ran to them, but then memory came back to her and she turned to face the woman, her sword held high and ready. With the threat of the tornado gone, it was time to finish this. The woman had reclaimed her sword but she stood frozen, looking at where the tornado had been. Her brow furrowed in fury, her gaze turned on Rosey and she could feel the intensity of the woman's eyes slice into her with loathing. Staggering slightly, she ran at Rosey crying out a vast war cry. Rosey had had enough. Raising her large wings she transformed them into the large scythes once again, feeling the membrane fold back into the skin of her second arms. The opals on her body shimmered as daylight poured back through the breaking clouds of black and grey. The woman came at Rosey in a mad run, her eyes blazing and unfocused. It was clearly the desperate attempt of a downed enemy. As she came close enough, Rosey extended the second arms in front of her and pierced the shoulders of the woman, slamming her into the side of a nearby boulder, weathered smooth by years of sand, rain, and wind. The woman was pinned there, unable to move. Her body was torn and ragged, the brown rags she wore easily revealing the female body underneath. She wore a black shirt and pants with a plain, white sword sheath hanging from her side. As soon as Rosey pinned her she dropped her sword to the ground, where it buried its long blade into the sand, then tilted at an angle. It stood there, as if it was aware of its defeat.

Rosey watched the woman's eyes, burrow into hers. She had not screamed at the pain when the blades pierced her shoulders, nor as she hung there, the blood slowly dripping down Rosey's second arms. Her Scythes hadn't burrowed very deep into the woman's shoulders, just enough to support her weight against the rock. Still the pain must be excruciating. Rosey eyed her, her whole body shaking with rage. She raised Andraste slowly towards the woman, and kept it hovering at her neck. It was then that she noticed how different Andraste looked. Like with the fire element, it had changed according to Rosey's current element: water. The blade was a bright blue with two pillars of water twisting in alternating patterns about the blade and ending in points. The blade shimmered as if it was made of water droplets. Rosey wasn't sure if it was normal for Andraste to change with the elements. Next time she talked to her friends she would have to ask. She looked back at the woman sharply, Andraste still at her neck. It would be so easy to kill her, just a flick of the wrist and she'd cut that precious jugular. But that was not what Andraste was for. She sheathed the blue sword carefully. The woman looked surprised.

"Why so surprised, I'm not a heartless killer like you," said Rosey bitterly, thinking of Rochell and Ysandir.

The woman laughed a dry laugh showing her exhaustion as well as her need for water. Rosey had very little sympathy for her. The woman glared at her with a crazy twitch in her left eye, as if something was bugging her. Rosey couldn't tell if it was from the nasty scratches along the left side of her face or just her lunatic way of doing things. For the first time, the woman spoke. Her voice was clear, despite its dryness but tinged with pain and as sharp as the sting of a hornet.

"You don't kill, ha! What about the Gorons pretty girl," she said mockingly.

"They are mindless creatures, created by evil for evil. You, on the other hand are a Minion, or perhaps a captured innocent. I will not kill you unless I am certain there is no way to save you. Besides, I'm sure the Resistance would love having someone to interrogate."

"Hum, good thinking..." she laughed again, more of a gurgle this time. "And...what about me, I'm sure this is no way to treat an...innocent." She cast her gaze at the scythes buried in her shoulders with an evil look.

"Don't make me explain something you already know," Rosey said haughtily, "You're an air elemental, and your arms are your best weapons. I don't want you trying to suck anyone's air from them again, nor can I allow you to move freely. This...is kind." Rosey buried her scythe a little deeper into the woman's shoulders making her writhe in pain.

The woman chuckled as if the pain was a good thing and fulfilled some inner love or need. Rosey narrowed her eyes in thought. This woman was not in her right mind. She was just acting, not really thinking. She had the skills but she didn't seem to have the mental awareness. It could be proof that she wasn't acting of her own accord. *Whoever she is, I will help her or kill her trying.* Rosey was about to say something more when she was suddenly joined by a group of people. Alex arrived, supporting Rochell, her right arm hung over his shoulder with her left arm bandaged with white cloth up to her neck where the cut had been. Rochell had been changed into a light green shirt and pants that much resembled the medical clothes worn in hospitals on earth by the patients. She could see that the bandages continued all the way down her chest. Rosey hoped it was okay for her to be out and about. Eglen came with the horses beside him, they were all bloodied and cut but the wounds looked to be minor and not life threatening. Wolvereen pulled up around the boulder with Hazel and Noly in tow, his armor gleaming where the sun touched its bloodied and scratched surface. Margaret and Captain Marine came too, a group of crew members and mermaids joined them. Rosey could just see Grey amongst them. He pushed his way through the crowd to stand by Wolvereen, and then, turning his head, he grasped the hilt of his sword quickly unsheathing it. His teeth clenched down on the hilt ready for a fight. Rosey smiled, this was her crew, her friends, and her fellowship. They were all here to support her and to offer her assistance. All but one was there: Ysandir. Rosey hoped she was all right.

With vehemence Rosey addressed the woman. "What happened to the unicorn you were fighting?"

The woman laughed once again, but did not have time to answer.

"She trapped me in a vortex and sent me somewhere that was really hard to get out of, crazy bitch," said the tall unicorn as she materialized through her own vortex.

Rosey turned to her happily, "Ysandir, it's good to see you. I thought something bad had happened."

Ysandir snorted, and tossed her head, the blue twisting patterns on her body shimmered strangely in the sunlight. People made way for her giant frame as she passed through to stand beside Rosey. "Don't insult me," she

The Mystics

said teasingly, "this woman is no threat to me, but I have to hand it to her, she knows how to keep someone…occupied." She said this last word slowly and hatefully giving the woman her best horse scowl. "She did real well at dodging everything I threw at her and launching little to no attacks herself. She kept me busy to give the Gorons time to do their work, but was smart enough to know she stood no chance against me if she tried to attack so she kept on the defensive while keeping me engaged. When she saw the ship was rising out of the water, I guess she realized that taking you down was more important than dancing with me, so she sent me somewhere else."

"How exactly did she do that, by the way?" said Rosey, looking at Ysandir out of the corner of her eye.

"Not with her own powers, a wind elemental can't create vortex's…"

"…but the Evil One can…right," Rosey said, finishing Ysandir's thought.

The unicorn didn't say anything, only snorted in agreement. Her warm breath washed over Rosey's scaled face. The water element in her flared cold with apprehension. This woman had to be a Minion.

"So she's definitely a Minion then," said Rosey, voicing her thoughts.

"Only one way to be sure," Ysandir said. Turning she eyed the crowd, her piercing blue eyes penetrating into each one, "Who wants to check?"

"No one go near her, I'll blow the rags off her chest. We'll see if she has a black stone," said Rochell weakly.

Rosey's heart fell when she heard her friend's voice. It was muffled and low, with obvious pain laced through it. Rosey admired her friend for her strength and bravery. She nodded, "Go ahead, but don't strain yourself."

"Don't worry about me Rosey, the air and I are good friends."

Rochell lifted her left, bandaged hand slightly then pulled it back sharply. The cloth covering the woman's chest flared forward and up as the wind unwound the tight rags concealing her figure. Rosey gasped as the black stone embedded in the woman's chest, came into view. Rosey stared at it and felt something strange start to prickle at the back of her mind. Her vision began to blur and she felt as if something had hooked a claw in her chest and was yanking her forward into something or somewhere. She couldn't move, scream, or do anything, she was stuck in…whatever this was. Fear rose in her throat but she was paralyzed by whatever was pulling her in. Suddenly, a dark shadow obscured Rosey's vision. She was plunged into a world of darkness. Screams and cries of hatred resonated around her. Rosey saw twisting columns of black mist and purple shades of blood running all around her. She could not recognize a structure, just a solid mass of darkness stretching for as far as she could see with no recognizable ground or ceiling. She felt claustrophobic as if everything would come crashing down onto her if she didn't get some space. She looked down at herself, the water element was gone. She searched for it and then for the fire element, but they were unresponsive. Looking at her chest, she saw that the Shanobie Crystal was not there to offer her its warmth. She was just little old Rosey, with only her leather outfit to protect her. Not even Andraste was there, strapped to her back as always and neither were Silver Knight or her bow. She was helpless. Filled with annoyance, rage, and frustration that she was without her powers she put her fists up in front of her, ready to fight. If she didn't have a weapon or an element, she would at least have her body.

Suddenly a light presented itself before her. It grew and grew in a long line stretching above her, or what she thought was above her, her sense of direction was thrown off here. It was almost like she was moving toward the horizon, as if walking around a very small planet and coming upon the portion that was lighted by the sun. Rosey's equilibrium was thrown off and she teetered on her feet, but held her ground, fiercely determined not to be caught off guard. The line then lifted and fire seemed to explode from within it. Rosey looked on in horror as the line turned out to be the lid of a giant eye. It stared down at her with a cat's pupil, narrowed to a fine line with scratch marks all over the sclera. The iris was missing, it was just

The Mystics

that diamond shaped pupil, burning brightly against the searing white sclera. The pupil was a purple color with black marks around the edge leading away from it in thick black veins. The veins pulsated as if black liquid were rushing through them. The eye undulated, its shape barely contained, sometimes it was an eye the next moment it was something else, but Rosey couldn't tell what. Black fire seemed to fringe the whole eye in spirals and loops like the loops on the surface of the sun. Black ooze leaked down from the eye and ran past Rosey's feet making her shudder where she stood. Grey fog banked around them, and it reached towards her in long tentacles of black and purple vines. She backed away, sickened, but none of them came near her. They were like a three dimensional effect, they seemed to be getting closer but in reality never moved near. They retracted back into the eye and then came back out, pulsating and investigating all around them. Some switched places with others, while some split into two or divided down the middle, making bulges. Some burst, spraying liquid everywhere, but none of it ever seemed to touch Rosey. Of that she was grateful.

Rosey backed away, her mouth agape in fear. She almost fell back, her whole body frozen. She was terrified from head to toe, her heart beat soared and her breath caught in her throat. Then like a whisper from death itself she heard a voice in her head. It was like wails and screams were tearing apart her conscience. Rosey slumped to the ground, holding her head, the blood pounding in her ears. The voice rose and became recognizable as words.

"Roseyyyyyy...." It said, drawing out the last letter of the word, "Welcome homeeeee...." It slowly began laughing evilly, the sound resounded into an earsplitting scream that made Rosey's ears want to bleed. Rosey knew that the last thing the voice was doing was actually welcoming her. To Rosey it sounded like an obituary welcoming her into death. Hot breath rolled over her and seemed to scorch her small body, though she had no idea from what mouth it had come. The eye continued to stare down at her, changing its figure every now and then to resemble some kind of floating creature. Rosey could only sit and squeeze her eyes shut, praying it would stop. Suddenly a bright light enveloped Rosey. It glowed brightly and spread like wildfire. The eye screamed in rage as the light poured over it. Rosey could barely make out the image of a black haired woman standing between her and the eye before she was pushed out of wherever it was she had been trapped and thrust back into her own body back on the beach.

Chapter Twenty-Eight: Explanations and Preparations

Rosey jumped away in fear as her consciousness slammed back into her body. She fell to the ground and the scythes embedded in the woman's shoulders were released. Ysandir and a few others flew forward to stop her, but the woman was too fast. She swept her arms outward and then brought them down to her sides quickly. A gust of air pushed her upward and into a black and purple vortex that swallowed her whole. In the blink of an eye she was gone.

Alex bent beside Rosey, Rochell steadying herself next to him.

"Rosey are you okay!? What happened?" They said almost at the same time.

Rosey could barely see them, her vision was blurred. After a few minutes it began to clear like a slow haze lifting from her vision. She shook her head and steadied herself. She had fallen to the ground disoriented. The sand was rough against her scaled skin. *Scaled skin!* she thought happily. It was good to know she was still in her water form. What she saw must have been only an illusion and not something real. She quickly raised herself to a sitting position, holding her head.

"It's...okay," she said hesitantly, "I think I saw a vision when I looked at her stone."

"What did you see?" Alex asked, leaning forward with apprehension laced through his voice.

"I believe...I met the Evil One."

Quickly she explained what happened. Everyone tensed up when they heard the Evil One's name and the eye that it had been seeing through, they were all amazed and fearful of the news more so than Rosey had been to experience it. When she got to the part about the woman, it only seemed to heighten everyone's suspicions even more. Some suggested that it was the White Witch but she had white hair not black. Other's said it was a new foe or maybe a new ally since she had saved Rosey.

Rosey didn't add to the speculation for fear it would only raise more questions, but deep inside she had a small glimmer of hope that the woman had been her mother. Rosey had no evidence of this and did not present the idea for she did not want to make anyone feel sorry for her or pity her, besides, if it was her mother, than she wanted to keep the idea to herself locked away in the deep recesses of her heart. Years of answering questions about her family and the loss of her parents had made Rosey an expert at hiding her feelings. To distract everyone from the woman Rosey moved on to the stone. "Has this ever happened before upon looking into the stones?" she asked, turning to Ysandir, remembering how the Minions were only recognizable through their stones. If they didn't have a black stone then they weren't a Minion. She wasn't the first person to have seen one.

Once again the large unicorn only shook her head sadly, confirming Rosey's suspicions that it had been her status as the Keeper that had pulled her into the stone. Rosey looked at the spot where she had pinned the woman. There were two bloody spots against the stone where the woman's blood had drenched it. She had let the woman get away. She pounded her fist on the ground in frustration. She had no idea if the Evil One had deliberately distracted her to get her to release its subject from capture or if it was just by chance that the stone drew her in, whatever it was she was not going to let it happen again. Looking to the right, she realized that though the woman had escaped, she had left her ivory sword behind. Getting up carefully Rosey walked up to it and gently took a hold of the hilt. Alex helped Rochell up, still supporting her weight as they watched Rosey carefully. Rosey lifted the fine blade and balanced it in her hands. She looked it up and down then turned to everyone around her. They had some work to do but first things first: they needed to know why a group of Blood Gorons had discovered them.

Taking a deep breath Rosey turned to Ysandir.

"Before we do anything else, Ysandir, do you have any idea why there were Blood Gorons here?"

Ysandir bowed her head ashamed. It was a strange sight to see in a horse. The large unicorn bent her graceful neck, blowing out a puff of air that sounded to Rosey like a sad sigh. The blue designs moving over her body seemed to shimmer and dull as if Ysandir's emotions were coming through the color of her skin. She cast her eyes away then said, "Do you remember the night you spent with the Silver Goddess?"

"Of course," Rosey said, crossing her arms curiously.

"That night there was a disturbance. Remember, the Silver Goddess told you it was a Resistance matter and would not tell you anything else?" Rosey nodded and she continued, "It seems that Argno, the messenger was attacked by a Minion, most likely the one that attacked today. She was able to steal some information from him, mainly that you were traveling on the Silent Marine."

Rosey remembered that Argno had a large cut on his shoulder when he came to tell them where to find the ship after she had collected the fire element. *Did that woman do that to him?* she thought angrily. If the woman did take something from Argno, it made perfect sense. She was obviously an air elemental and Rosey knew from Rochell's lessons that air elementals could get some information from you by touching your thoughts with their wind, at least that was how Rochell had described it. It only made Rosey hate the woman more for her trickery. Her fists clenched tightly and the water element seemed to swirl around her in waves of water vapor. A cold crisp sensation ran up and down her arms, the coolness dropped her temperature and a slight mist began to accumulate. Realizing this, Rosey breathed deeply, getting the water element under control. If anyone noticed they did not say anything, possibly because they were too tired or were too enthralled by Ysandir to say anything.

"By the time he realized that the woman had taken information from him, it was too late to warn you, you were already being attacked. We had no idea that the Evil One had instituted a plan like this one. I am sorry I was not here to warn you." Ysandir lifted her head, her eyes sad and thoughtful as she looked at Rosey.

Everyone was silent listening intently. Seeing that sadness and despair in Ysandir's eyes Rosey came forward and gently stroked the large animal's long face.

"Don't worry Ysandir, you did your best to warn us and you came to help us even the odds. I doubt that a warning ahead of time would have made much of a difference."

The unicorn lifted her eyes to Rosey's and smiled, "Thank you, Keeper."

"Tell me, though, how did Argno find out that she had taken info from him? And did it have anything to do with that attack at the caves where we were almost crushed?"

Rosey still remembered the caves, how she and her team had almost been crushed together by the collapsing rock and how they'd been ushered out into a battlefield of Raptors and Silver and Golden Guards. It had been the first fight Rosey had witnessed and the last one where she'd even been useless. If the Evil One had learned of their ship from Argno then it might have also learned of the caves from him as well.

The unicorn lifted her head, pride and power seeming to have been returned to her. "After what happened with your mother, it is now required that whenever someone is touched by a Minion they must then be checked over by a mental healer or someone with those…capabilities," she said this last tentatively. Rosey had a feeling that it was yet another Resistance secret but she didn't care, now was not the time. "We had Nornell check him out before sending him on his way. And no, the Minion didn't learn about the caves that way. The Evil One must have assumed the Silver Goddess would use the caves to hide you and so decided to get rid of them."

"I see," said Rosey, trying not to let the mention of her mother get to her. She remembered Nornell from what the others had told her on the ship. She was the younger sister to the Master Healer Cascade and the only known Master Mental Healer. She wondered how they had managed to get a hold of her or how they kept her in one spot long enough to make her be of service. From what she had learned, these healers traveled the universe and went where they wanted, not where others wanted. She shook her head, there was no sense worrying about that right now. "Do you know of how the Gorons knew where we would be going?"

"That we don't know," she said regretfully, "but we're doing everything we can to find out."

Rosey nodded. Everyone was silent, considering what they had heard. It was a shock to hear that their ship was discovered to be Rosey's and would now make them a target, but what everyone was truly worried about was the unknown attack that came under their ship. How had the Evil One learned where they were going? Who would have known besides the people on board? Not even Argno or the Goddess had known that they were heading towards the Broken Castle. A while ago, Rosey would have suspected Nora, but she was obviously in league with the Mothers. Rosey was at a loss as to what to think, the obvious answer was that they were being tracked and that once the Evil One realized their destination a plan of attack had been set up. Anything was possible, but it was over now and there was no sense in dwelling on it when there were other things to do.

"Thank you Ysandir, and please do not blame yourself or anyone else. We fought bravely today, and gave them a little taste of what the crew of the Silent Marine and the mermaids of the Resistance can do," she said turning and extending her arms out to everyone around her.

They all beamed at her praise and raised their voices in a loud cheer. Rosey was glad to see that a vast amount of the crew still possessed such energy because they were going to need it. After all they had been through, she hated to ask anything else of them but it was going to take a lot of work to get things moving again. She waited until everyone had quieted down before speaking again. Realizing that they might suspect Nora as the traitor Rosey hastened to assure everyone that it couldn't have been her.

"Now listen everyone, the nature of what took place with the Mother of Water was…unusual. Nora helped me to get there, wherever she may be, she is a friend and trustworthy, despite her strange behavior before. Do not go looking for her. I am unaware of where she is, but she is not anywhere we can reach so do not waste time looking for someone you will not be able to find. Now, I need everyone to stay strong and pull through."

Her eyes skimmed over everyone around her, meeting their tired yet spirited eyes one by one. Her gaze rested on Marine. "Captain?" she said stepping toward him, her large wings folded neatly behind her.

"Yes, my Keeper," he said stepping forward beside Margaret. His face was pale and spattered with blood just like the rest of him. A long four clawed scratch ran across his chest. The blood was dried and caked there; the wounds hadn't gone very deep. A few other scratches were visible on his arms and legs but he looked okay despite them. She could see how tired and worn out he was, but his eyes were bright and alert. He wasn't out yet.

"How do you usually contact the Golden Goddess?"

"Through the Scrying Unit on the ship, but it's down at the moment. It was damaged in the battle."

"Alex, can you scry her from here using something else?"

Alex nodded, a smile crossing his face as he eyed the sword she still held in her hand.

"Eglen," she said, directing her attention to the Eglagor. "I need you to go with Alex and report to the Goddess what has happened here and tell her we have something the Resistance would be interested in seeing. Have her send more medical supplies, please."

He nodded swiftly, "Yes ma'am."

The Mystics

She then walked forward and handed Alex the sword. He gently transferred Rochell to Margaret and then he and Eglen turned to head towards the water, his wand in hand. Rosey watched them go, weary of her role as leader but prepared to lead nonetheless.

Turning, she faced Queen Ashti who had joined them silently, her large frame standing well over everyone else, including the other mermaids. Rosey met her powerful green eyes, almost overcome with their depth.

"Queen Ashti, I am very thankful for your help, we would not have lasted as long as we did without you. Thank you."

"No problem young Keeper, it was our pleasure as members of the Resistance. The Golden Goddess contacted us to find your ship as soon as they found out that the Minion had stolen the information from Argno. I'm just thankful we arrived in time to help."

"Do you have any pressing matters to attend to?"

"No I am at your disposal, the Golden Goddess was adamant in her request that we stay until we were no longer needed."

Rosey nodded, aware that the Goddess probably felt as ashamed and angered by what happened today as Ysandir did. They had vowed to protect her and had still allowed an ambush attack to take place. Rosey, however, did not care, they had done their best and in the end she was still alive and so was most of the crew. Looking the giant woman in the eye she said, "Good, I would much appreciate it if you and your mermaids would assist the Captain and the crew."

The Queen bowed her head respectfully, her bright green eyes flashing with pride, "It would be an honor."

"Captain Marine," she said turning back to him. "I leave everything up to you."

Everything passed by in a blur after that. Immediately Marine marched away followed closely by Margaret with Rochell in her arms. The red haired First Mate immediately made her way down to the medical team leaving Marine to organize the rest of the battered crew. Marine wasted no time and started barking out orders to everyone in sight. They all ran off and did whatever it was that he said. After careful consideration, Marine decided to take everyone remaining, including the mermaids, past the ship and down the beach to where a group of people were gathered. Rosey flew above them and saw that the group of people was actually the medical team attending to the injured. Marine organized the non-elemental and magical of the crew to help start collecting wood for fires and then gathered earth elementals around to discuss building shelters. The first thing to happen was the construction of a temporary infirmary. The head of the medical unit on the ship had already begun to see to the most wounded of their team, including Rochell, whom Margaret had gently laid down to rest amongst the other injured.

To Rosey's surprise the head of the medical team was a small mongoose-looking animal. His ears were bigger and more pointed like a serval's and he had three tails instead of one. He was a purple color with bright pink eyes and black markings. Looking closely Rosey thought she could see what looked like scales on his legs and head. He scampered through the most injured checking their pulses and directing the nurses that he had at his command. When the ship had still been on the water the little mongoose had been flitting about the ship to the wounded with his nurses scattered everywhere helping whoever they could while the fighting was still taking place. It was much easier to tend to them where they were then to try and move them. All of the nurses held small stones enchanted to create a shield around themselves and their patients when rubbed to protect them from attack. Moving the patient was more dangerous than just attending to them where they were. The stones fascinated Rosey. They were small, round, blue pebbles with a single sign on them in the shape of a crystal, much like the one around her neck though she didn't think they were connected.

After the ship had been placed on the dry dock each nurse, with the help of the magikins among them, had moved their patients to a secure location away from the fighting in a meadow surrounded by trees farther down the beach. Most patients had been levitated safely down, it was better than handling them for fear of injuring them further. They had laid their injured on long pieces of wood, taken from the trees by earth elementals. Rosey gazed at the long line of injured people, animals, and Leron lying on the wooden boards. She was amazed and awed by what they had accomplished in such a short time.

Quickly she asked a passing nurse what she could do to help. He looked flabbergasted to be talked to by the Keeper but quickly told her they needed hot non-salty water and that the fires needed to be lit. They had already found a small spring to get water from but Rosey knew she could get them water faster. She thanked him and quickly pulled in large buckets of water from the sea with the water element then separated the salt from it easily. The people at the streams, a mixture of nurses and regular crew members, were called in to stop their work and to start building the infirmary or attend to patients where they were needed more, leaving the water work up to Rosey. Rosey took the water and lowered it into large cauldrons. She gently pushed the water element back into the crystal and summoned the fire element. She was happy to find its fire power teeming with strength and happy to be of use again. She quickly set ablaze the fires that were prepared under the cauldrons then intensified the heat to boil the water inside them in less than a second, super-heated and ready to go.

Rosey spent the rest of the day helping wherever she could by purifying and heating water plus lighting fires where needed. She did anything and everything she could do to make the injured more comfortable. She worked tirelessly, a continuous image of power and strength amongst the people surrounding her. The mermaids spoke of her kindly and regarded her strength with awe and pride, honored to be working by her side. They helped in much of the building, their large muscular bodies and strength well received. They worked fast without stopping to help make large temporary structures along the beach for shelter from the cold of night, swiftly approaching. The infirmary was finished quickly, just as dusk was setting in. The earth elementals among them had easily manipulated large trees into growing up around them to form a long house. Afterwards they had formed tables, chairs, and anything else needed from branches sprouting from the wood. Others brought in pads from the ship or packed down thick soft leaves from the greenery to make beds. Once everything was done, Margaret led the magikins in helping to levitate the injured into the infirmary, gently placing them on the modified tables. Rosey and Marine watched them, unable to help except to make sure that none of the injured rolled off the beds. Rosey's eyes spotted Rochell amongst them. Marine saw this and gently touched her arm to comfort her. She nodded her thanks.

Alex joined them just as the last of the injured were moved inside. He came up abruptly with Eglen in tow. It had taken longer than they expected to explain everything. The Goddess had had numerous questions, but she was sending more medics and medical supplies along with other crew members to replace the ones lost. When he mentioned this Rosey turned her attention to a long line of bluish tinted bodies that were laid out upon the beach. A small group of mermaids, led by Queen Ashti, had been dragging them in all afternoon along with their own small number of lost mermaids from the sea before the fish and the other sea animals could feast on them. Rosey turned away from them saddened. The Goddess was sending someone to retrieve the bodies and ship them home. Margaret had already placed a spell on them to stop them from decaying. The Goddess would also alert the families of the ones that had perished. Upon hearing this, Marine had said it was his responsibility but given the circumstances he decided to write individual letters to the families explaining the bravery displayed by their honored sons and daughters and send them with the ship ferrying the bodies home.

The Mystics

Just then, as he watched the bodies mournfully, Marine was called away by a crew member. He stepped aside a few yards to look at what looked like blueprints for the ship. Alex gave Rosey's arm a reassuring squeeze then left to help with anything that required magic. Eglen went to find Wolvereen, murmuring about hunting as he went. Glancing at the bodies, Rosey thought that she too should do something. She walked up to the bodies and tried not to cry at the sight. They were people who had, only days ago, introduced themselves to her with smiles and friendly handshakes. Now they were silent and still, motionless watchers to the endless night above. Their bodies were scored with long scratches that had become bloated from the water. Their bluish skin was soggy looking with wrinkles. The wounds that caused their deaths were evident. A tail that had gouged a hole through their abdomen, a scratch through their neck, a missing section of their side, the wounds were endless. The only bodies that weren't bloated were the mermaids. Being born in water, bloating was something that did not happen to them. Instead they had turned a strange shade of red. Rosey saw a large wound and realized that the blood was blue, like a horseshoe crab. *Huh, humans turn blue and mermaids turn red*, she thought. For some reason the irony did not humor her as it normally would. Rosey felt numb as she gazed down at them: twenty seven humans, Leron, and animals with ten mermaids. The crew member's weapons were laid out next to them, honored blades that had fought with them till the end. Rosey felt Andraste hum against her back, it was weeping silent tears of rage and sadness.

Staring at their faces, Rosey found that she didn't even remember most of their names. She had hardly had time to get to know any of them. Taking a deep breath she felt tears slide down her face against her will. Then an idea came to her. When she had paused in her work with Marine while the magikins brought in the injured to the newly built infirmary she had given the elements a break and had returned to her usual form in her brown leather outfit. Now, sensing the water element, she tapped into it and hurriedly caught her tears. Quickly she split them into thirty seven different tear drops and hardened them. Walking forward she placed each tear drop on the forehead of each fallen comrade. The tear drop soaked into their skin and branded them with a bright blue tear drop that shimmered in the night sky. It would remain and never fade, even after the body had perished, branding the soul where the body rested. As she placed each one she thanked them for their loyalty and bravery. Next she transformed into the fire element and took up each of their weapons. Carefully she sent a long strand of molten rock into the weapons. Like the tear drop the molten rock would never dull and would keep the blade from rusting or decaying. The weapons, along with the bodies, were to be sent back home to the families, the mermaids would ferry their own home. The families usually kept the weapons of their fallen warriors. This embedded molten rock would be a reminder of their bravery. All of the mermaids had carried small daggers with them, though their clawed hands and pointed teeth were weapons enough. She put molten rock into their blades as well and whispered words of thanks. When she was done Queen Ashti approached her, Rosey had reverted back to her human form so the giant woman was a monolith compared to Rosey's size. Taking a step forward the queen bowed at the knee before her. Rosey was shocked and not sure of what to do. Even on her knees Queen Ashti's body came up to Rosey's chest.

"Rosey, you have honored my warriors tonight. Thanks be to you," said the giant woman.

Rosey was amazed at the queen's humility, as she bowed to such a little human as herself. But she was not just any human, she was the Keeper.

"No, no, Queen Ashti, it was an honor to fight beside your warriors."

The Queen raised herself, towering over Rosey's human form once again. Rosey breathed deeply, the queen smelled of seaweed and saltwater, a not altogether unpleasant smell.

"Rosey!" said Captain Marine, coming up behind them. He quickly bowed to Queen Ashti, who bowed her head in return. The man he had

The Mystics

been talking to walked away towards the ship with a small group of people. Rosey guessed they were mechanics of some kind or maybe they were scouring the ship for what they did and didn't have. Whatever it was Rosey wished them well for the ship didn't look all that safe to be on at the moment. She turned her attention to Marine as he continued, knowing that the crew members wouldn't do anything that they couldn't handle. "I hate to interrupt but the medics need more water, please." He gave her a pleading look as if she'd actually decline. Rosey smiled despite herself.

She nodded, "No problem, Queen Ashti," she turned to the woman, "would you excuse me?"

"Of course, I think I'll accompany you to see how my warriors are faring."

With longer legs, Queen Ashti pulled ahead quickly. Marine hung back. As they walked Marine touched her arm gently and said, "I saw what you did. Thank you, I will be sure to tell the families how you have honored them in my letters."

"I just had to do something, you know. I couldn't just…"

"I understand…thanks."

They stared at each other for a few moments. His handsome features outlined by the fires from the torches she had lit earlier as dusk had fallen. Rosey looked away first, she could feel the blossoming of true friendship and trust coming between them. Marine walked beside her, confident, a solider following his Keeper.

As the day passed into night, Rosey continued her relentless fetching and heating of water and setting fires to the various torches. Between breaks in her dedicated work she would revert back to her normal form and walk among the injured and talk to them, asking how they were doing and thanking them for their bravery and service to the Keeper. The people she met received her with open arms and smiles. They looked genuinely happy to see her and even more overjoyed at her kind words. For the ones that were unconscious, Rosey took their hands and sent a prayer to the heavens asking that they heal quickly, and making note to visit them when they woke. She paused the longest at Rochell's bed. The brunette was deeply asleep but looked content and calm. A nurse assured her that she would heal in time.

When there were no more patients to talk to she approached the little mongoose doctor. It had finally quieted down in the infirmary as the nurses had brought everyone into stable conditions and they were all either resting or sleeping soundly. The little mongoose creature was worn out, his little body was shaking but his eyes were bright and focused, ready to jump to action the moment something went wrong. He was perched on a wooden stool of dark wood that came up to Rosey's waist. If Rosey hadn't seen him move every now and then she would have sworn he was stuffed. She felt a little ashamed that she had yet to meet him after being on the ship for so long, but she had little reason to see a healer till now.

"Hello there Healer. I am--"

"Rosey Mystic, the Keeper. Yes I know," he said, interrupting her in a gruff voice as if a squeaky mouse's voice had been altered to somehow resonate a bass tone. Rosey was shocked by the indifference he had. He didn't even look up at her as he surveyed everyone around him. Shocked by his manners she prepared a lengthy comeback, but then stopped herself. He was probably worn out. Maybe he was just grumpy from all the work.

Carefully she spoke, hoping her voice didn't betray her annoyance. "I just thought I should meet you. I don't recall seeing you when I first boarded the ship so…"

"That's because I like my privacy," he said quickly, not in a mean way but in a matter of fact way. She stared at him hard. He still had not met her gaze. His eyes flitted about the room, searching the nurses and the patients alike. It then occurred to her that maybe he was using some sort of magic or something but she did not see a stone hanging around his chest. Being an animal, he would have to use a stone as Alex had told her animals do to use magic. All she saw was the same small stone with the crystal image on it that all the other nurses used to create a barrier around them. Rosey shook her head. Maybe he was just paying attention to his patients. Still, it was rude of him not to, at least, look at her and if he interrupted her again, she thought she would punch the little weasel. Before she could say anything he spoke first

"Name's Moano. Been the healer on this ship ever since it was built. I was the healer on his parent's ship when Marine was a baby in his mama's arms. I was a friend of hers, Marine's mother. Stayed on after their deaths," he said in broken sentences. His voice was calm and unemotional. It reminded Rosey of when Margaret had talked to her when they were on mist watch.

Before she could say anything his ears twitched and pricked forward. He seemed to notice something but to Rosey everything looked okay. He then jumped down from the stool he was perched on and went running through the beds at top speed off to some patient. Rosey watched after him and lost sight as he weaved through the fifty or so patients.

"That was…interesting," she said into the cool night air. The earth elementals who had built the infirmary had left a few pockets open in the shape of windows, though they were not all square.

"Don't hold it against him, my Keeper," said a young woman. She joined Rosey on her left, so silently that Rosey flinched away. The woman didn't seem to notice. "The death of Marine's mother affected him more than he lets on. He acts all tough, but he's not."

Rosey looked at her, not sure of what to say. The woman had pale, almost white skin giving off an ethereal feel. She had a flower tattoo on the left side of her face. It was a pretty blue color and looked to Rosey to be an iris, though she wasn't sure. The woman's long brunette hair had green stalks entwined in it, with small purple buds and flowers poking out between the strands. A crown of oak leaves decorated her forehead. She wore a simple light blue slip with dark blue long pants underneath. On her arms above her biceps were two golden rings. The same green stalks entwined her ankles and wrists, making intricate patterns up her arms and legs. She wore simple, light blue, slippers on her feet and stood a foot taller than Rosey. What startled Rosey the most about her was her bright yellow eyes. They were so yellow that Rosey could barely make them out from the sclera. The iris was not black as usual but was white. Around her eyes was a light dusting of midnight blue and small silver dots. The dots swirled down from the corner of her left eye to join the flower tattoo image. The other silver dots and blue coloring swirled down her right eye and formed an arch under her eye. Her lips were a pale pink and it looked to Rosey like liquid was present on them. Rosey had never seen a woman more beautiful in her life. Her beauty even rivaled Rosey's, which many a boy had congratulated her on, including Alex. The woman turned to her kindly.

"I am Loraine, a Dryad, and Moano is a Three Tailed Mongoose. I am his apprentice and very close to graduating, I might add," she said with a kind smile. It was apparent that she wasn't boasting, but she was definitely proud of her position of which Rosey could understand.

Rosey smiled back, enchanted to be meeting a dryad, a creature she had only heard about in legend, once again, the legends of Earth held no comparison to the real thing. Another nurse at the end of the building signaled to Loraine. She saw and nodded, waving back.

"Please excuse me Keeper. It was nice to meet you."

"Of course, likewise," Rosey said, not knowing what else to say.

There is just no end to the mysteries of this world, she thought as she watched Loraine hurry away to attend to a patient.

Turning, she exited the infirmary and took a look around, ready to get to work once again. Not too far away, the earth elementals and magikins were back to work making temporary tents and buildings. There was one thing for sure, the ship might not take long to repair, but the crew members would. Looking around she spotted Marine nearby giving orders. She walked up to him.

"Captain, how are things going."

"Pretty well," he said turning to her. "The repairs to the ship have been estimated to take only a few days at most. The injured crew can be moved to it easily enough once the repairs have been made. The people I sent earlier to scout the ship have reported that everything is accounted for and the ship suffered no more damage. We will begin the repairs tomorrow." He beamed happily, much more relaxed now than he had been before. It put Rosey's mind at ease.

She nodded, remembering the group of people he had talked with when she had given her blessing over the deceased crew members. They had definitely been scouts then, gone to check the ship.

"What about food supplies, do we have enough?"

He glanced down a clip board he had under his arm and read down the list checking off a few things here and there. After a few moments he answered, still looking at it.

"Most of our supplies were kept in the Animal Quarters in a giant freezer and closet. As you know, that part flooded so we lost a good amount of meat and vegetables. I've had Wolvereen, Grey and Eglen hunting, along with a small group of gatherers to restock. We can always stop off at another port once we're back on the water. As it stands we have about four days of food for everyone, with Wolvereen's haul that he'll bring in, we should have at least five days. Queen Ashti, however, has agreed to help catch us some seafood and gather various sea plants. It should be plenty to hold us over until we can dock somewhere to restock."

Rosey turned to him with a quizzical look on her face, "I'm a little surprised that our supplies could have gone bad. Aren't they spelled against something like that?"

Marine nodded, his eyes darted about with embarrassment, "Yeah…we think that maybe the Blood Gorons were carrying a spoiling potion but we're not sure since all traces of it would be washed away when the water receded and it leaves no evidence on the foods it spoils." He quickly moved his gaze to the clipboard.

Seeing that Marine was more than irritated that his ship's food supply had been so easily destroyed Rosey nodded and moved on to something else.

"What about the Golden Goddess's supply ships? How long do you think it'll be before they get here?"

He looked up, "Knowing her, she's probably not sending ships. They should be here within two days tops."

Rosey's brow furrowed in confusion, "If not ships, then what?"

"We'll know when they get here," he said smiling up at her. He surveyed the work and then called out to an earth elemental. He excused himself then ran to the woman to talk to her. Rosey watched after him, confused but content by his report.

After hours of work, everyone was settled down and eating the newly cooked stew that the cook had prepared for everyone after Wolvereen and his team had returned with fresh meats and luscious fruits. Rosey had been a little worried about them hunting on the island. It was, after all, a forbidden island and steeped in mystery and ruin but upon Wolvereen's return he had huffed confidently, reporting that the only thing bad about the woods was the lack of large game animals to hunt. She had shrugged and left him to deliver the meat, trusting his judgment.

Now she sat around the fire, hungrily taking in the stew. It was only now, after she stopped moving that the pain and stretch of her muscles became evident. She was covered in bruises and the place on her back where the Goron had bit her and she had healed, ached. It wasn't just her. Everyone was feeling the pain. With the adrenaline rush gone, there was nothing to keep the aches away.

Rosey waited until everyone around her had quieted down and finished eating. She had been sure to tell her whole fellowship, excluding Rochell, to meet her for a final discussion. There was something Rosey needed to tell them. Also joining them was Marine, Margaret, Ysandir, and Queen Ashti. She surveyed the group, just now seeing them after hours of work. She had been so busy that she had lost track of where they had all gone, but they were all there now, ready to listen and to talk. There was not one of them that wasn't bandaged. Even Rosey had a few scratches she hadn't known about and a few bruised ribs she wished she didn't have. The little mongoose, Moano, had hated that she refused to be looked at until everyone else had been looked over first. He had scowled at her when she turned him down, muttering something about her stupid views on honor and being noble. Rosey had only smiled.

Taking a deep breath she told everyone about what had happened to her and Nora. How Nora had dragged her down to the water element. What she saw when she got there and last but not least, how the Blood Gorons were nothing more than copies made by the use of the elaborate device she had seen.

Ysandir shook her head sadly, "We knew that the Evil One had learned of what ship you were on but we had no idea that they had such a strange weapon at their disposal."

"Which leads me to question," Rosey finished, casting her glance around the circle of friends. "Are we safe here? Now that we know that the Evil One hasn't wasted its whole Blood Goron army, won't it just send more to attack us while we're down?"

Marine answered, "No, since the battle started I have been wondering as to how it was possible for Blood Gorons to get here. Your explanation answered that. You see, while sea creatures are not affected by the curse on the seas, flying creatures can be affected. Not all the sea's powers affect them, but the seventh sea's powers, definitely can. So you can imagine my surprise when a group of flying animals of that magnitude attacked, from underwater no less."

"If they had flown to the ship then they would have died before they got anywhere near us, falling to their watery graves," said Margaret, rather coldly and there was nobody there that didn't know why.

"Couldn't they just take that potion that you and Marine took?" Hazel asked from Rosey's lap where she was curled up tightly.

"That potion is only made by Cascade and she only gives it to the most powerful people that patrol the seas. If the Evil One wanted some, it would have to attack a number of ships inhabiting the oceans with its precious supply of Gorons, traveling over cursed seas. Not to mention that she only makes enough of a supply for two people on a ship at a time and unless it has a lot of these mirrors at its disposal it's very unlikely," said Marine, taking a bite from his stew.

"So, there's no chance of them coming here now then?"

Marine shook his head, "Here no, but other places yes," Rosey sighed, she had wondered about this before but things were happening so fast that she hardly had the time to ask when there was so much that needed seeing to. A sudden thought jumped to Rosey's mind.

With worry she said, "What about the Goddess's supplies? Marine, you said that they might not be coming by ship?"

Marine smiled, his voice was kind, "Don't worry Rosey, the Goddess will make sure everything gets here."

Rosey nodded, chiding herself about worrying when the Goddess was one of the most powerful beings on this world. She'd know better than to send something that couldn't make it; that would be foolish. Looking up at the night sky another possibility screamed at Rosey nearly making her jump with fear. She quickly turned to Marine.

"I know there are no Raptors here on this island; however, in the case of a Minion couldn't it be possible that another one might attack?"

Marine glanced at Margaret, a sense of fear passing between them, "That is possible," Marine said hesitantly, "but I guess that all depends on the particular circumstances behind the control of a Minion. This is the only time we have been able to successfully identify a Minion. We still have no idea if this is the only Minion that the Evil One has at its disposal or if there are more. If there are more, then how many can the Evil One use at a time? It may be limited to one at a time, we don't know. However, we have had magikins and elementals on the lookout this whole time and nothing has happened. Let's say it this way, if the Evil One had the ability to send something to finish you off this would be the perfect time yet nothing has happened since we landed and that last Minion disappeared into the vortex. This is proof to me that the Evil One, at the moment, is not capable of doing something against us. Margaret, a few magikins and Alex have all set up non-lethal wards, traps and detection spells within a five mile radius of the camp in every direction. If anything tries to get near, we'll know about it."

Margaret nodded encouragingly and Alex squeezed her arm. "Good," Rosey said thankfully, but still unnerved, these Minions were going to be a problem. She was happy to hear that magic levels hadn't been affected on the island and were still high enough to support such spells. The mirror had zapped a lot of magic but it hadn't gotten all of it. Thinking of the mirror, Rosey said, "As for the giant mirror I saw, have any of you heard of such magic? We know for sure that it was responsible for the drain on the magic from the area, possibly when it was activated by our coming, but still…has anyone ever seen such a thing? Ysandir, have you?"

The large unicorn shook her long head solemnly, "I have heard nothing about such a creation. It is a mystery to me."

"As it is to me as well, Keeper," said Margaret shrugging her shoulders apologetically.

Rosey turned to Alex, "Sorry, but at least it explains why it was impossible for me to make a shield, the damn thing took all the magic from the area when it activated," he said bowing his head, the shadows cast by the fire making his already tired face even more strained. He cast a glance at the infirmary where Rochell was, Rosey could tell he was stricken by her condition, "I know nothing and…" he paused for a moment as if something had hit him in the face. He touched his forehead as if thinking really hard about something. After a few moments he said, "…but Thera, my mentor, does."

Rosey had almost forgotten about Alex's internal mentor. One day she would like to meet this Leron that Alex talked about, but she was not to leave Alex's body until his final training was complete. Rosey wondered how long it would take him before that time came. When Ysandir heard this she cocked her head and a look of disgust and shame crossed her face as of the idea that any other creature that was not a unicorn knew something about magic that she did not was a horrid idea. Rosey tried not to laugh.

"She says," Alex said drawing her attention, "that such a device as the one you described is called a Copy Mirror. It is actually a form of Forbidden Magic that even the new generations of unicorns do not know of," hearing this, Ysandir no longer looked so ashamed. Now, she looked interested, "Apparently, Adina made it forbidden due to the particular process behind a Copy Mirror's creation. It requires a living person to become trapped inside of it while the mirror makes copies. Often times the person doesn't survive the process afterwards or are altered beyond help to the point where they die anyway. It's forbidden…for a reason."

Rosey shuddered remembering the Goron she had seen inside the mirror. She had thought it had been dead, but she had been wrong. To think that it had been trapped alive was horrifying, even if it was an evil creation. No wonder Adina made the mirrors forbidden!

"The only reason that Thera knows of it is because she was alive before it was forbidden. It takes a huge amount of time, effort, and energy to create. Most of them can take up to six years to complete or longer. Creating something that can put out that much magical power is very hard to form and create from scratch especially if the area you're placing it in doesn't have the magic to sustain it. You'd have to gather and capture magic within it over time so that it would have enough, even then it could still zap the area of its magic, which it did. This island is powerful but it's not a hot spot of magic so most likely the Evil One had to gather magic into the mirror ahead of time, which could up the creation time to easily over fifteen years. Elements are easy to control because they are naturally a part of this world, magic is not. It is its own energy and form. Unless the Evil One had help, it's safe to say that that was probably the only one it made."

"Well that's some of the best news we've had all day," said Eglen. He and Wolvereen were chewing on a bloody haunch from some water buffalo-looking animal. Rosey had yet to ask what species it was but found it hard to when she was looking at its carcass. The mermaids had hunted for themselves, pulling in a huge fish and eating it raw. The Queen had eaten with her warriors, without using plates or silverware. They had dug into the scaled body with their sharp claws and had ripped out large chunks with their sharp teeth. They had eaten the whole fish, even the bones before the stew the cook made had even been completed. Now that things had slowed down enough for Rosey to relax, she then realized that she hadn't seen a single male mermaid amongst them. She asked Alex about it and he told her that there were only female mermaids on The World Within A World. They apparently reproduced whenever they wanted by spontaneously becoming pregnant through an evolved form of asexual reproduction. That information had been enough to make Rosey view the giant women with even more amazement than before, despite their wild eating style. The horses nibbled quietly as always whenever Ysandir was around and enjoyed a greener dinner. The cook had made them a blend of grasses with apple and carrot slices. Rosey winced whenever she looked at their scratched bodies, bandaged as they were, they must be hurting. They were all hurting. This had been their first battle together after all. She didn't count that scare they'd all had outside the Silver Goddess's caves when the Raptor had dropped a bomb on them as their first time because Rosey had been completely useless then, this was the first time she had fought as their Keeper.

"It's good to know that that device is not going to become a daily part of our journey, however, what I really want to know," Rosey said. "is how did they know where we were at? I know that they discovered what ship I was on from Argno, but that doesn't explain how they found out where exactly we would be and I know they didn't use scrying. Scrying would only show them an image of the ship, not its location."

Everyone was silent, all of them turning the possibilities over in their heads. Rosey could see the strain on their faces and realized that they had no good answers. Finally Alex spoke, "I think it's safe to say we don't know how the Evil One figured it out. However, this wouldn't be the first time that Blood Gorons have been associated with this Island. Maybe when they last attacked it they put something on the island, like a sensor. I don't know. I've scanned the area we were at with magic and I didn't find anything that could have given away our position, nothing magical at least. I even checked the oceans and land surrounding it, nothing. The elementals and mermaids checked things out too, they came up empty."

"So, that means that we're missing something. Either someone betrayed our location, and I have a very, very hard time believing that, or the Evil One, by some means, was able to discover my location," Rosey said, staring at her bowl. No one said anything. What could they say? It was true, they had no idea how the Evil one had discovered where she was. After a few moments Rosey's brow furrowed in confusion, looking up she said, "One more thing, is it normal to be able to call a sword to you?"

"Like what you did with Andraste?" Eglen asked, casting a knowing glance in her direction.

Rosey was worried about her strange display of swordsmanship. Calling a sword to you and having it fly through the air as if it had sprouted wings was more than a little strange, but the look on Eglen's face assured her that she had nothing to fear.

"It is a common thing amongst sword masters, my Keeper, though not all of them learn how to do it as quickly as you did." He squared his shoulders, the muscles rippling beneath his skin, "This can't be the first time you've noticed something strange about Andraste."

Rosey shook her head no.

"The weapons of this world have the capability to, almost, combine with their master's power. They can shape themselves and basically gain a mind of their own over time. Andraste was the second Keeper's sword and now belongs to you, her daughter. Though it is already mightily powerful from its first owner, it may begin to change over time to suit your needs…or not," he said shrugging his shoulders.

"What about my grandmother, did she have a weapon, or my father?"

"Oh yes, your father wielded a long spear that was buried with him and remains there today. Your grandmother had twin blades, and oooweee she was good with them," he said as if the scenes of one of her battles raged on before his very eyes. "My father used to tell me stories about how Maharen would swing those blades as hard as she could. They were so attached to her that when she died, they died with her."

Rosey started and stared at him in disbelief, "What?"

"Yeah, apparently they withered away as if time sped past them in a blur making them rust and crumble into dust. At least that is what the Golden Goddess said Adina saw happen."

"But," said Rosey, "If that is true then why didn't Andraste do the same when my mother died?"

Eglen shrugged, "I don't know, maybe it knew its job wasn't done yet."

Rosey nodded, unable to speak. Though Eglen's meaning had been ambiguous Rosey had the feeling she knew what he was talking about. Andraste may have stayed on because of her, Rosey. Perhaps she had done it for her former master, Esperanza. She reached her hand up and felt the hilt of the sword lying against her back. She smiled. It didn't matter why Andraste had stayed. Rosey was just happy to have something of her mother's to use in battle. Thinking of her parents, Rosey's hand sought out the locket. It was still there, safely attached to her belt. With all that had happened, she was happy to know it hadn't gotten knocked away or lost.

There was one thing they all agreed upon though. Rosey's encounter with the Mother of Water had been very unusual and somewhat disturbing. Ysandir didn't have anything to say about it but, nonetheless, she seemed as unbalanced as the others did. Rosey had the feeling she wasn't telling them everything but she didn't have the energy to confront her about it and right now was not the right time. Rosey knew that what happened was not normal and it worried her, not only about her powers as the Keeper but also about the power of the elements and their connection to her. She still did not tell them about the water's or the fire's recognition of her, as if they had met before. Something told her that maybe she should, but until she was sure it wasn't just some coincidence she would keep it to herself.

Her true fear was for Nora, what had become of the little blade dog? The unanswered questions wavered in her mind, like something hanging over her head. She felt responsible somehow, as if Nora's disappearance was her fault and maybe it was. She didn't know but she had hoped that the Mother would come and talk with her or Nora would return. She needed something, some way to know that Nora was all right. Don't leave me hanging, she thought sending her prayer up into the night sky twinkling with stars.

After they talked for a while longer, laughing and joking as they normally did, they all retired to their individual sleeping areas. A temporary barn-like structure had been erected for the animal-like of their crew, including the horses and Eglen, while Rosey and the rest of the human-like of the crew slept in a long wooden house that looked much like the infirmary. Once again Hazel and Noly, all bandaged in white, opted to stick with Rosey following her devotedly to her sleeping area after she had cooed and petted Sarabie lovingly. Ysandir, however, with a toss of her head, said that she did not like the idea of sleeping in a structure and disappeared to

The Mystics

who knew where. Rosey shrugged, knowing that the unicorn would be perfectly fine wherever she went.

She followed Marine and Margaret inside the large building feeling her eyelids grow heavy as the prospect of sleep became a reality. Everyone slept huddled together for warmth with blankets to cover them and soft sand and leaves to cushion them. It wasn't the most comfortable bed but Rosey didn't really care, she was just happy to finally be resting. She took the locket from her belt and wrapped it around her right hand as she always did before bed. She glanced at the images within. She had survived her first battle. Would she survive the rest? She felt a stroke of determination shoot through her body, of course she would. *Are you proud of me...Mom...Dad?* Rosey thought, her heart aching. With the knowledge that guards were on watch and the special traps placed by the magikins were in place she fell to sleep with Hazel's soft purring in her ears and Noly's silky head under her hand.

Chapter Twenty-Nine: We Go One

Rosey breathed in the warm scent of fresh ocean air. The waters lapped the beach lazily. She walked along them in the early morning, enjoying her time alone before anyone woke up. For once Noly and Hazel stayed asleep when she arose, so she quietly left them to greet the sun. It shone bright and the clouds floating high above shimmered over the landscape with their strange shadows. With the guards posted and the magical traps ready Rosey knew she would be safe as long as she stayed within a five mile radius of the camp. She had spotted Ysandir that morning as she made her way to the beach. Though the unicorn had nodded a greeting to her she had made no attempt to follow, still, Rosey had a feeling that the unicorn wasn't too far away.

Though it was winter the island was warmer than normal and covered with sparse vegetation. It was still colder than normal but not so cold that it was uncomfortable. Rosey had been so busy before that she had barely noticed the climate of the small island. There was certainly no snow and most of the deciduous trees still had their leaves plus the evergreens, if any, were still lusciously green. The place looked like it was locked in between fall and winter with a little bit of spring thrown in just for fun. It was a strange island but she figured that this world's biology most certainly did not have to follow Earth's. Anything was possible.

Rosey watched the approaching waves, their white waters held her gaze. It was hard for her not to follow the currents throughout the world, connecting everywhere and anywhere. The water was pulling her out to sea, beckoning her. She felt her skin ripple and her muscles twitch with excitement. A cooling sensation traveled down her arms, legs, and back, bathing her in great torrents of feelings. She could almost feel the water pulsing within her. Carefully she pushed the water element away. It joined the fire element reluctantly. The two of them sparked away from each other, complete opposites but one within her.

She sighed and listened to the waves, relaxing as best she could. Her body was still bruised and battered like everyone else's but it was slowly healing and already she could feel the effects of the exercises. Her muscles were harder and her stamina higher. The one thing that Rosey did not like, or, at least, what she feared was the lack of fear she had had when facing the Gorons. It was like a whole other person had taken over. She had left Rosey Mystic behind and leapt into battle like some hardened warrior unafraid because of years of battle and experience. Yet Rosey had no experience, only training to guide her, and she had fought like a maniac. She had hacked, and diced, and sliced with Andraste killing mercilessly as if she had been doing it her whole life. Suddenly the image of Lyesal, the wolf that had died when she'd been on her way to the Golden Goddess's palace, burst into her mind, and Rosey felt sick. Had she, like the Raptor that had killed Lyesal, only been thinking about killing the enemy no matter how she did it? Had she sliced and diced mercilessly because it was the thing to do, the need was strong so it didn't matter how it happened!? The question hung in her mind unanswered. The wolf's death seemed so numb to Rosey now. She had really changed hadn't she if even that image had become normal to her. Was it normal? Rosey shook her head, she still felt tears sting her face when she thought of it, so no, it couldn't be normal, it just wasn't as startling as it used to be.

At the time, during the battle, Rosey had been a wild rush of adrenaline and emotions, a surging wave of power doing whatever she could to protect everyone around her. It was just like the forest battle at the caves, she had felt that same surge of anger and the need to jump in to protect her horse Sarabie. At that time, she hadn't had the power to do much of anything and against a Raptor she would have been all but helpless, still, her instincts to protect had almost overwhelmed her concern for her own safety. Maybe that was it! During this fight she had never been fearful for herself, only for her friends. She could only image that the same thing may have been happening to Lyesal, she wasn't concerned about herself, only the safety of others. Like her, Rosey had battled on for them, vowing to save them and guard them. *Was that really so bad?* she asked herself. No, she had done what she had to do to keep people safe but that did not make the blood that was still soaked into her leather clothing any less real. The water element may have healed most of her wounds but the scars were still there. A large bite wound, three scratches on her shoulder and one on her arm were still there and always would be. Then, of course, there was the one left by the falling desk in her room when the storm had hit. It was not technically a battle scar, but it still touched the skin of her shoulder. She'd been on this world less than a month and she'd already been scarred far more times than she liked. She had a feeling she'd get more in the future. They would be a constant reminder of the battles she had fought and the lives, however evil and mindless, she had taken.

Rosey hung her head, but not out of shame, only out of acceptance. This was who she was now. She was the Keeper. She was expected to fight, and kill, and destroy in order to bring peace. But she was not evil. She killed to protect and that's the way it would always be. Besides, it wasn't all true that she hadn't been afraid. There were moments when she had been filled with fear, for herself as well as her friends. The most vulnerable she had felt was standing before that cursed eye. It had seemed to suck the life out of her, suffocating her. She never wanted to feel that way again. Her hand gripped the crystal and it warmed in her palm. It's comforting warmth fueled by the fire element covered her, mixing with the cooling sensation of the water element. *It's my own Icy Hot patch!* She laughed at herself, and knew without a twinkle of a doubt that the happy and calm Rosey Mystic was still there, she just had a little more power than usual.

Rosey looked out over the ocean then reached down and took off her boots. She waded ankle deep into the frothy waves and smiled as the cool salt water splashed over her legs with the tide. She lifted her head and let the cool ocean breeze blow against her skin. The water was crystal clear blue and shimmered like a dream across her vision. She leaned her head back and closed her eyes, letting the warmth of the sun and coolness of the ocean wash over her. She dug her toes in the wet sand beneath the water, the only time where sand between the toes was enjoyable. She stood there for the longest moment, just like that, listening to the world around her. Being still never felt so good.

A slight patter of paws on the wet sand drew her attention. She lazily looked down to her right and saw Nora standing beside her. Her own eyes were closed, her thick fur rustled in the breeze, her head slightly lifted. Rosey wasn't at all surprised. She knew that at some point Nora would return or the Mother would come to her, or, at least, she had hoped that they would.

She stayed there for a while with Nora by her side simply enjoying her companionship. Time swept by lazily but Rosey didn't mind, she was having too much fun right where she was, simply being still.

After a few moments she said, "It's good to see you Nora, I was afraid something had happened to you."

Nora's closed eyes opened and she gazed at the horizon as if seeing something for the first time. Rosey could see her body shaking slightly, her whole frame seemed transparent. Rosey thought it was a trick of the eye, but it wasn't. Nora looked like a ghost and for a few moments Rosey was afraid that she was. Rosey had no time to ask, for before her, rising out of the water, was the blue Mother. Her body simply materialized from the water, like the moray eel that had fought for them before, except this time it was a real creature not some conjured water form. She was as large as Ysandir was, if not bigger, and her horn was just as long, like a lance. She stood on the water, defying gravity, her silver hooves shining in the light. Any evidence of her once watery form was gone. As soon as she had 'given' the water element to Rosey she had reverted back to her normal unicorn form, just as Mercury had done at the Molt Volcano. The giant creature stared down at Rosey with big sky blue eyes. She looked healthy and powerful with her large muscular body and silky smooth skin. She looked as if nothing had befallen her. She was perfection in a bottle.

Rosey gaped at her, surprised but happy to see her. She quickly closed her mouth then smiled and bowed her head. The unicorn did the same.

"It is nice to meet you Rosey, My name is Antalanta,"

In that instant, Rosey froze. *That was in my head!* she thought, with shock.

"Indeed it was." Antalanta snorted and raised her knee, prodding the water she gently sent ripples through its surface. *"I speak only through telepathy. It's not a trait that is required by us unicorns, but it does appear in some instances. I am one of them."*

Her voice was silky smooth, like water flowing over silk. She had a calming voice, like a mother singing a lullaby. Rosey gawked at her, amazed, then smiled from ear tip to ear tip, *"That is so cool,"* she thought. Rosey quickly regained her composure. *"Anyway…what happened to you? Are you all right?"*

"Very much so, now that I have had time to recover. What happened to me was," she paused for a moment, *"…unusual. The simple explanation is that the element sensed that you were in danger and so desperately wanted to get to you. That was not the first time it had gone amok. It sensed your presence the moment you touched the water and had been tracking you ever since then."* She bowed her head knowingly. Her blue eyes shimmered with uncertainty. *"Water's influence travels all over the world, its senses stretch far and wide, thus it was easy for it to know you were coming. I had been fighting against its wishes the entire time, but your arrival here set it off."*

Rosey bowed her head, *"I'm sorry, I was afraid that I was the reason for your pain."*

"Don't be sorry for your powers, Rosey. Look at this in a good way. You have a very strong connection to the elements. Mercury told me that I am not the only one to have had the element be more than persistent about joining with you," Her thoughts were like clear water running through Rosey's mind.

Rosey looked at Antalanta in surprise. She remembered Mercury, the large horse covered in fiery flame and surrounded by molten rock. Rosey had not been aware that what happened to Antalanta had also, in a way, happened to Mercury, though not on the same scale. According to Antalanta the water element had been sensing her for weeks now, since Rosey boarded the Silent Marine, which meant that the element had more time to oppose the Mother and pull against her will, more so than with Mercury. *Could I have caused that to happen to Mercury too?* she thought, this time making sure to keep the thought to herself. Mercury had used the connection Rosey had with the elements to attract Rosey to her, but she had never had any problems with it acting against her or trying to pull away from her, at least, the Mother had not mentioned any. In this case, however, Rosey's life had been in danger. Could that have really set the element off so much that it would risk the Mother's life to get to her? It scared Rosey. Was her connection to the elements that strong? If so, why? What was different about her?

Antalanta did not hear Rosey's thought, but seemed to understand what she was going through. "*Rosey be joyous, you have two elements now. You are stronger than you were before and this powerful connection that you have may, indeed, be the thing that has been missing from the other Keepers. You may indeed be the one that will save us all. I have faith in you. Now you must have faith in yourself.*"

Rosey looked away unsure, her eyes settled on Nora. The little blade dog had said nothing throughout the conversation. Whether it was because she did not hear them or because she was being patient and respectful, Rosey did not know. The transparency was still there, a silent reminder that Nora was not what she seemed to be. Rosey was afraid to ask but she did anyway.

"*What about Nora, what is she?*"

Antalanta looked down at her. Nora met her gaze and something passed between them. Sighing, Antalanta began.

"Originally, I gave Nora the task of leading you to me once you arrived on the island. But that plan changed once the water element began getting aggressive and the Goron's attacked. As soon as the water element attacked me I contacted Nora and told her to bring you to me right away. She did as instructed, though I admit, it wasn't the most elegant way to do so."

Rosey nodded knowingly, remembering all too well the body slam the little dog had given her. Her chest was still sore, but Rosey held no grudge, she knew Nora had been trying to help.

"When I contacted her she sensed my pain, it hurt her too. She acted a little rashly, but all turned out well," Antalanta continued. Nora squirmed, embarrassed.

That must have been the moment that Hazel and Noly told her about when Nora freaked out, Rosey thought, remembering what her dog and cat had told her. This time she made sure to hide her thoughts. She did not want to remind Nora of that moment; it would only embarrass her more.

"Nora is a remnant," Antalanta explained, casting her gaze down on the blade dog. Nora wagged her tail happily when Antalanta smiled at her. "She's a ghost who's been allowed back into life for a brief moment of time. Adina herself issued the command."

Rosey's thoughts stretched to Antalanta's, "Why Nora?"

"She used to work here," she said simply. "No one knows this place better than her. Also, I was worried about the condition of the water element and its acting up. If something were to go wrong, which it did, she could still get you to me."

At least that part of what the blade dog had told them was true. Nora had originally worked at the Castle, but the part about her hopping ships and using the Say and Go spell was obviously just a part of the story to avoid suspicion. Rosey grimaced, remembering how she had told Marine about his success at being the first Captain to catch the little stowaway. He wasn't going to be happy. Hearing this also confirmed Rosey's suspicions that Nora was the white substance that had dragged her down through the water during the battle. After all, it had been Nora that had knocked her into the water. If Nora was a remnant, a ghost, then it made sense that she could transform into a white substance.

"Why a remnant?" Rosey asked, rolling the word around in her head. *"You mean, why was a remnant required and not someone living, well… there is no one living who could have guided you to me, at least, none that were accessible at the moment. All the people who shared time in the Castle have passed away, so a remnant was the only choice."*

"What do you mean by 'not accessible'?"

"I'm afraid I cannot tell you." *"Fine."* Rosey didn't feel like arguing, it wasn't worth the effort. *"What about the Castle? Who was the family that built it? What's the story behind it? Who lived here?"*

Antalanta shook her head solidly, *"That is not important. You may, in time, discover the truth, but for now simply know that the Castle is here."* Rosey nodded, unable to respond. She was annoyed at the lack of information but wasn't going to pester the Unicorn any more than she had to. Especially, when it was apparent she wasn't getting any more answers on the subject. At least she didn't use the word later. Seemed the mystery of the Broken Castle Island would continue to remain.

Rosey fixed the blade dog with a look, and then frowned at Antalanta. "Did you know that you were sending Nora to us while we were in the Second Sea? She almost sunk our ship!"

Antalanta looked embarrassed, *"That was my fault and now, along with the battle, I am considering it your official test. Originally, Nora's 'dreaming' had been planned to be only the first part of your test. To see how well you handled a weather crisis that your current element was not exactly…appropriate for. You did splendidly. Do not be too angry, I was watching the storm the entire time. If you didn't find Nora in time before the storm got too bad, I would have intervened and woken her for you. Finding Nora was not important, handling the crisis was."*

Hearing the Mother's words made Rosey feel a little better, but it amazed her that, even from that distance, the Mother had been aware of where she was and what she was doing. Rosey's brows furrowed. *"You didn't sense or find the Copy Mirror?"*

The Mother shook her head, looking ashamed, *"My attention was focused on you, not the surrounding waters. After all, if I were to be focused on ever strange object in the ocean, I'd be alerted every time my senses found a rock. Once the mirror activated and you were in danger, the element started pulling away from me and I was helpless to assist you."*

Rosey nodded. Now it was her turn to feel ashamed. Why did she have such a powerful effect on the elements? She had never heard of her mother or grandmother causing such a reaction? Was there something different about her?

"As for the second part of your test...well, I believe the battle was enough of a test to prove your worth. Once again, you managed to use the fire element in an effective way even though the battleground was covered in water. Well done."

Rosey bowed her head in thanks. At least she had excelled in that. Knowing that the battle counted toward her test made Rosey feel as if she had earned the element rather than what had actually happened. It was true, Rosey had fought her heart out before being 'pushed' into the water and accepting a very anxious element. It then made sense that Rosey had, in a way, earned the element's trust and acceptance...even if it was a little unconventional.

"Do you have any other questions?" Antalanta gazed at Rosey with a calm expression.

Rosey relaxed and shook her head, *"No. Thanks for coming back. I would have been confused if you hadn't...and worried."*

The horse bent her head in a small bow, *"It would have been wrong to leave without telling you the truth."*

Knowing that the unicorn was leaving and Nora was going with her, Rosey bent down and, being careful of the blades, hugged the blade dog. Her body was very transparent now, proof that she was a remnant. She pulled away from the dog to see Nora smiling kindly. Her eyes looked

The Mystics

watery but controlled and full of the light of life. This time she spoke out loud.

"*Good bye Nora, it was great having you aboard.*"

"*It was my pleasure Rosey. My past home is yours,*" she said tossing her head toward the island. "*Stay as long as you like.*"

Rosey nodded and stood up. She turned to Antalanta slowly, feeling a great weight in her shoulders. It seemed strange to be parting ways like this, yet, it was the way things had to be.

"*Goodbye Keeper,*" The giant unicorn's voice was like smooth water. "*I'll be taking Nora home, so do not worry about her.*"

The beautiful unicorn backed away, walking out to the ocean on the water as if she had always had the power to do so. Rosey realized that she probably always had. After all, Ysandir had basically walked on air during her fight with the Minion woman. It must be a unicorn thing. She watched the blue unicorn before her. Antalanta's horn pulsed navy blue and energy gathered at its tip. Throwing back her head a white light appeared in the sky matching Ysandir's vortexes. She was opening one of her own. Nora looked up at Rosey happily then strode forward, walking on water as Antalanta did. She stopped and looked back at Rosey with her long tongue rolling out in a dog-like grin. Nora winked and smiled at her then sat up and jumped, turning around. Antalanta leaned her head down and touched her horn to the dog. In an instant, Nora burst into water, the sparkling silver droplets rolling into Antalanta's mane and tail, the strands of hair rippling with pleasure. The blade dog had been a ghost and a reminder of what was left of the Broken Castle. Rosey was honored to have met the loyal soul.

Antalanta smiled and jumped around in a circle, throwing her mane and tail out in a dance of pure energy. The blue unicorn lifted into the air giving off a powerful whinny. She bucked and dived into the white light, disappearing in a brilliant flash of multicolored lights. Just before the light faded it spread out around Rosey filling her with a calm delight. "Goodbye Rosey," the powerful winds whispered through her hair.

"Good bye," she answered back, this time out loud for all to hear.

When Rosey returned to camp that day, everyone was up and busy. The cooks were preparing breakfast and Wolvereen was leading the carnivores of their group on a hunting party into the woods. The earth elementals and many magikins were busy repairing the ship. They worked tirelessly, determined to have it finished. Rosey was amazed at how quickly they worked and how easily everything was repaired. She and a few other water elements spent a good amount of time washing the ship, getting rid of the dried blood and the guts that were strewn across most of the first deck. Rosey had to stop herself from gagging from the stench but a spell from Alex dissipated the smell making it easier for them to clean.

As the end of the day drew near, Marine proudly proclaimed that the ship would be ready to sail tomorrow. Rosey was overjoyed to be getting back on the water again, though, so far, none of her dreams had been visited by the White Witch telling her where to go. Rosey hoped that the reason the White Witch hadn't shown up yet was because they weren't, presently, able to go anywhere and not for some other reason. If it was the latter…she didn't want to even imagine what it could be. Throughout the rest of the day she occupied herself with whatever tasks where needed, mostly to take her mind off the Witch.

Marine filled her in on the best place for them to go while they were waiting for her next location. They would head south through the Seventh Sea again and to a place called Feldor. It was the perfect destination to quietly get some rest while they waited. Rosey agreed, it made sense and she certainly didn't have a better idea.

To Rosey's annoyance Moano, the little Three Tailed Mongoose and the ship's healer, managed to corner her. Reluctantly she agreed to be looked over thoroughly and he even scolded her for not letting him look her over sooner. She took it all with her ears closed, but smiled nonetheless. He was amazed to find that she wasn't harmed anywhere on her body. She was slightly bruised and even a little bit sore, but not harmed. When he asked her about this she explained how both her water elemental and fire elemental forms seemed to cure her cuts. They either burned them clean and healed them up or cleaned them out with saltiness and then glazed them over to heal quickly. Moano had given her a skeptical look. He'd then dismissed her, giving her a clean bill of health. He walked away whispering under his breath about how the Keepers were weird and never seemed to obey the laws of nature. When Rosey had overheard this she had asked him about it. He'd turned to her and said, "Even the best elementals find it hard to heal themselves and usually they can't do it in a day's time, nevertheless in a split second. The healing power you just described is abnormal, Keeper." He had turned away as if he didn't want to talk anymore, but Rosey wasn't having any of that.

She had pursued him saying, "What do you mean it's not normal, have any other Keepers been able to do it?"

Moano hadn't stopped walking but he'd answered her nonetheless, "None have."

It had been so simple, but Rosey had been left completely shocked. She'd then shaken her head. There was no use in getting worked up over it; right now she needed to do what she could to help. Of course she wasn't going to be like the other Keepers. Each Keeper was different. So she shouldn't worry. That's what Rosey had told herself and that had been enough.

To Rosey's surprise the supplies sent by the Goddess arrived late that night. Adding even more to her surprise was the way they arrived: strapped to the backs of two blue and green whales. The whales were a part of the Resistance, as were the twenty crew members that the Goddess sent with them. The whales had lightweight coral armor on their thick bodies, stitched with golden designs to shine in the watery light. The crew members were inside a dome container filled with air strapped to the backs of

635

the whales. A water elemental and an air elemental would replace the air inside every few hours, filtering the oxygen from the water outside their dome. It was very rare for people to ever be transported this way because it could be dangerous if things were to go wrong, but this was an emergency. The new crew introduced themselves readily to Rosey and Marine, pledging their allegiance to his ship and crew. Marine later told her that they were some of the people he had interviewed for his possible crew members a while ago. They had not received the vote but were qualified for the position.

Queen Ashti and her mermaids helped to unload the heavy equipment then she informed Rosey that the Goddess had asked her in a letter to bring the Ivory sword to the Resistance herself. She showed the letter to Rosey, given to Queen Ashti by one of the replacement crew members. Being underwater was the safest way to travel with the cursed seas and the fastest, plus it would be harder for a Minion to attack them. Rosey nodded, approving of this idea. It was safe for water creatures, but they'd yet to make something that could travel underwater effectively and carry passengers like the Keeper and her crew to their destinations. Their need for oxygen, food, and more made travel under the oceans difficult if it was longer than a day. Even the extra crew members had been spelled into a deep sleep to allow for continuous passage without stopping.

Once the supplies and crew members were unloaded, the magikins then levitated the deceased crew members, except for the mermaids, into the whale dome along with their weapons, glowing red from Rosey's blessing. Sadly, this time there would not have to be anyone to filter in new air. Marine then placed a sealed plastic bag containing the letters he had written to each family inside. Alex put a spell on them to guard against any further damage in case something happened. The whales then left, wishing them luck in deep bass voices. Rosey waved them farewell as they dived into the deep depths. The water was now black against the night sky. She couldn't make out the horizon from the sky it was so black and beautiful.

The next day Rosey and her friends watched as the magikins carefully loaded the injured onboard. Moano and the nurses watched anxiously as Loraine directed them inside the ship. Once the injured were on board and strapped down and all was accounted for, everyone got to work. Crew members ran through the ship following orders barked by Marine and Margaret. The ship had been finished early that morning and was set to sail at noon. The engines had been checked, the supplies loaded and accounted for and the passengers settled back into their rooms.

The earth elementals had fashioned a large gangway, making it easier for the horses and other animals to get on board as well as for the loading of the massive boxes holding their supplies. Rosey stood in awe of the brilliant dry dock the earth elementals had made to keep the ship suspended above ground while they worked. Rosey wondered if she would be able to do that when she received the earth element.

Before they left, the earth elementals returned to deconstruct their temporary infirmary, house, and barn. The fires were thoroughly doused then buried and the grounds were cleaned to be sure nothing was left behind. The last thing they did was to remove the various wards, traps, and detection spells they had set up. There would be no use for them once they left.

Rosey then said goodbye to Queen Ashti and thanked her again for her assistance. The Queen bowed before her happily then turned and signaled to her warriors, the ivory sword in hand. The warriors turned and picked up their fallen, making sure that the small daggers Rosey had blessed were still there. Rosey and the others waved farewell as they splashed into the water.

Rosey had, at first, thought she was going to have to lift the ship up and back into the water but, once again the earth elementals proved to be very resourceful. They had made a huge ramp leading out into the sea that gradually sloped down into the water. A large plank of wood was all that was keeping the ship from sliding down a very slight incline into the water.

As soon as everything was aboard and ready, the order was given and the plank was thrown aside by the earth elementals. Rosey hung on as, slowly, the ship slid gently into the water. As soon as they hit the water, the ship began moving out to sea, it would be another six or so hours before the effects of the curse would activate so they had some time. They would travel around the island and then head out straight towards the Legarru continent. Unfortunately that meant they would have to travel through the Seventh Sea again for another two days, but even that notion couldn't dampen Rosey's spirits.

Rosey watched the sea happily, both Alex and Rochell by her side. Rochell was well enough now to be walking around but she was still banned from any strenuous activity so today, after agreeing to sit quietly, she was allowed to play as referee while Rosey got in a little practice before hitting the Seventh Sea and having to enter the world of sleep once again. Rosey turned expectantly. Alex had moved and was standing a few feet away ready, with his wand out. It was time for some good old practice and Rosey was more than ready to show them what she was made of. Hazel watched from Rochell's lap and Noly came around the corner leading Wolvereen. When he saw what they were doing, he shrugged and settled down to watch with Rochell. Ysandir was, for once, staying on board as she promised to protect them. She stood behind Wolvereen, easily keeping her balance, having no regard for the unstable ground of the ship. Being a unicorn had its advantages and Rosey knew that no one was going to ask the unicorn to do something she wasn't certain she could handle.

As Rosey walked towards Alex she changed shape into the element they had agreed upon. Giant, membrane filled wings stretched out from her back while her leather outfit, newly cleaned and washed, disappeared and was replaced with her new aquatic one. Waves rolled from her shoulders, opals shined on her forehead and wrists. Long pants and shirt encircled her legs while long gloves enclosed her muscled arms and small slippers protected her feet. Her crystal exploded in a haze of blue light, turning a deep sapphire blue. Moving a strand of long blue hair out of her face she faced her friends with fire in her heart and water at her fingertips.

Epilogue

The evening was slowly coming in off the horizon, coloring the waters a sunny red. Rosey's practice had been long over with. Everyone had retired early in order to prepare for when Margaret would come around and give them their dosage. The Seventh Sea was almost upon them and with it, another two days of sleep but not for her. She was beyond such nonsense and such curses. She was too powerful for them. She was one of the few species that found them…annoying instead of deadly.

Ysandir made her way silently to the Captain's Deck. She stood there, looking out at the sea and its glittering water. Only a sparse amount of crew still ran about doing this and that. Ysandir paid them no mind, they wouldn't see her here and if they did they wouldn't dare interrupt her.

She bobbed her head and breathed deeply. Gathering magic at the tip of her horn she connected with Adina's own horn in Valley Elathos. In the connection Ysandir saw nothing, heard nothing, and felt nothing except for the sound of Adina's voice in her head. The whole world became silent. The magic needed for this connection did not cast a shining light or require much energy. A quiet, undisturbed space was sufficient to sustain the connection and what better place to find peace and quiet than nearing night when Rosey wouldn't be practicing her battle moves, Rochell wouldn't be whizzing around the boat though she probably couldn't anyway with her wounds, and Wolvereen wouldn't be chasing after Noly and Hazel. Yes, evening was perfect, but the news from Adina was not.

"Antalanta told me what happened, and it only confirms what Mercury told me about the Molt Volcano," said Adina with a quiet sigh of apprehension, her voice clear in Ysandir's head.

"What does this mean, my lady?" Ysandir responded in thought, holding her breath.

There was a long pause before Adina responded.

"It means that Rosey Mystic is much more powerful than we could have ever imagined," was the final response.

Ysandir breathed in deep and steadied herself despite her racing heart.

"And is this good or bad?" she asked tentatively.

"We shall see, my friend, we shall see."

With that the connection ended. Ysandir stared out to sea with troubled eyes as the ship plowed through the quiet waters.

About the Author

Leyna Barill attends Bellamine University and has always loved creating stories and characters. She strives to include animals in her writing as well as a sense of science as the road to enlightenment. A strident feminist and environmentalist, Leyna incorporates both her love of nature and strong women characters in her plots. Her early writing influence was anime and uses the concept to take fantasy to the next level.

"For me," Leyna says of her writing, "writing is about so much more than creating a story; it's about making a difference through words. My hope is to simply inspire and to teach. Though my dream is large, my ambition is small. I only seek to entertain. If I can put a smile on someone's face, then I'm happy. I hope that you will enjoy reading my stories as much as I have enjoyed writing them."

If you liked *The Mystics*, please leave feedback.

You can email Leyna with your questions and comments at leynaberill@wordbranchbooks.com.

For a limited time, you can get 10% off your entire book order from Word Branch Publishing. Enter the code CD10 at checkout. https://www.wordbranch.com/book-shop.html

We recommend these books:

Forsaking Magic by Julian Norwood:
https://www.wordbranch.com/forsaking-magic.html

Ursa Kane by Stacy Bender:
https://www.wordbranch.com/ursa-kane.html

Dark Dreams by Christina Gray:
https://www.wordbranch.com/dark-dreams.html

Word Branch is an independent publishing company located in the heart of Appalachia. We represent talented new and emerging authors who need a venue to make their voices heard. Visit our online book shop and discover a world of imagination, facts, stories, and entertainment. Written by some of the finest rising stars in the book world, Word Branch Publishing offers a diverse selection of drama, science fiction, personal growth, young adult, indigenous titles, and more. https://www.wordbranch.com/

Word Branch Publishing:
Independent Publishing
For Independent Readers